ILLUMINATE

AIMEE AGRESTI

HARCOURT
Houghton Mifflin Harcourt
Boston   New York   2012

Harcourt is an imprint of Houghton Mifflin Harcourt Publishing Company.

www.hmhbooks.com

Text set in MrsEaves.

Library of Congress Cataloging-in-Publication Data
Agresti, Aimee.
Illuminate / by Aimee Agresti.
p. cm.
Summary: A brainy, shy high school outcast interning at a Chicago hotel discovers
that the hotel staff has an evil agenda planned for her classmates on prom night.
[1. Supernatural—Fiction. 2. Internship programs—Fiction.] I. Title.
PZ7.A26875411 2012
[Fic]—dc23
2011027326

Manufactured in the United States of America
DOC 10 9 8 7 6 5 4 3 2 1
4500340716

FOR BRIAN

The soul is a terrible reality.
It can be bought and sold or bartered away.
It can be poisoned or made more perfect.
There is a soul in each one of us. I know it.

—Oscar Wilde, The Picture of Dorian Gray

Part One

1

A Rare Opportunity

Up until that point, English class had been unremarkable. We were halfway through *The Picture of Dorian Gray*. Mrs. Harris, with her voluminous behind precariously perched on the front of her strained wooden desk, scanned the room searching for flickers of comprehension—or, at the very least, consciousness—in a sea of clueless faces. I slid down in my seat, letting my long wispy hair, still damp from my morning encounter with winter's sloppy-wet sleet, fall around the sides of my face: trying to hide. I've never much been one for participation. I generally know the answers—I just don't appreciate the attention that comes from knowing them. Answer correctly and you have further cemented your reputation as a brainy, hopeless outcast. Answer incorrectly, and not only are you considered a bookish nerd, but now you're even bad at that. It was a lose/lose situation. So I read ahead in the book, tuning her out, glancing up every now and then to the clock above the chalkboard or to the windows where blustery, chalk-white skies hung over another frigid January day. Evanston, Illinois. The tundra that was the greater Chicago area would likely look this way until April, but it never bothered me so much. I liked the way that braving its wind-whipping wrath could make a person, even someone as easily tossed around as me, feel stronger.

"So let's talk about the nature of good, evil, and hedonism," the teacher droned on.

At the mention of hedonism, on reflex, my eyes darted two rows in front of me. Buzz-cropped Jason Abington, wearing his basketball jersey, number 9, to advertise the big game this weekend, nibbled on the cap of a blue ballpoint pen—*my* blue ballpoint pen. Somewhere inside my stomach, swarms of butterflies fluttered from their cocoons. It was for this very reason that the front outside pocket of my backpack bulged at all times with scores of these pens, which I had, optimistically, bought in bulk. Jason never seemed to have his own, and he had asked to borrow one from me weeks ago and then again and again and now this is what I had become to him: a purveyor of pens. At the desk beside him, a blond creature—*his* blond creature—named Courtney twirled her artfully hot-rollered, bodacious curls. This is what boys like him were conditioned to expect. This wasn't me, and I couldn't imagine it ever would be, regardless of what magical metamorphosis one was expected to undergo during high school. I was a work in progress, but I had no reason to believe the finished product would ever be quite like that.

I had stopped paying the least bit of attention to Harris's lecture when she called, "Ms. Terra? Haven. Did you hear me?"

To be honest, no. Scrambling, I shuffled through the shards I had caught of her lecture, searching for the most likely line of questioning and then shooting out an answer that ought to fit. "Um, Dorian and Lord Henry believe in following the senses, pursuing whatever pleases them, uh, no matter the consequences, and, um, not worrying about right and wrong?" I proposed, sweat dampening my temples. Jason angled his head back just a touch in my direction. I felt other eyes on me too.

"Thank you, that's lovely." She was holding a slip of paper she had just taken from a senior girl, bored, chewing gum, who now left the room. "But your presence is requested in the principal's office."

A weak chorus of "Oooooh" broke out as I gathered my books and boulder of a backpack. As I squeezed through the aisle, passing Jason's desk, he looked up for only a moment, expressionless and still chewing on my pen.

In my two and a half years of high school, I had yet to set foot inside Principal Tollman's office—I'm just not that kind of girl. So I couldn't imagine what this could be about. On the walk there, footsteps echoing on the linoleum, faded voices muffling out from passing classrooms, I tried to think what it could be: Was it Joan? Was something wrong with her? This is how it is with me, always expecting the worst.

But in our case, this sort of overreaction was justified.

This is just what happens when you are discovered, as I was, at roughly age five, in a muddy ditch somewhere off Lake Shore Drive in the dead of winter. A little Jane Doe, barely breathing, no memories of anything that came before that night, no one to ever come looking for you. And you get raised by the kind nurse who eventually takes you in, names you, feeds you, clothes you. After a thing like that, worry becomes more than a reflex; it becomes an umbrella shading daily life, hovering closer every time someone gets home late or doesn't call when they say they will.

"Ms. Terra, have a seat," Principal Tollman said over the top of the rimless reading glasses perched on her nose when she saw me standing in the doorway of her office. She squared up in her chair. "So it looks like congratulations are in order." I felt my eyes involuntarily bulge. "We've just been notified that you and two of your fellow eleventh-graders have been accepted into the Department of Education's Vocational Illinois Leaders internship program."

It took me half a second too long to process.

"Oh, wow. That's great, thanks," I said, more reserved than she probably expected, but I was preoccupied. In my mind I was sorting and sifting through everything I'd applied for in the past year. There was just so much. Anything that could earn me extra cash for college or would sound good enough to help me clinch a scholarship to one of my dream schools. Internships, fellowships, essay contests—my mailbox flooded with the constant stream of applications and deadlines and hopes. And yet, somehow, this didn't even ring a bell.

The principal took off her glasses and stared at me with a faint smile, a director waiting for the reaction shot she wanted. "This sounds fantastic," I said. "I really am honored. But forgive me, I can't seem to recall actually applying for this." A nervous grin propped up the corners of my mouth.

She laughed, a small, charmed chuckle. "Yes, well, that's because you didn't. That's the beauty of this particular internship. They just pluck the best and the brightest and place those students with a thriving Illinois enterprise for the semester. It's a new pilot program the state is trying out. You will each be paired up with someone at this business who will act as a sort of advanced independent-study tutor and a mentor. And—" Glasses back on, she read from a paper. "It appears you're going to be placed at the Lexington Hotel in Chicago. Why, that's really remarkable, you know. They're about to reopen, and the woman who owns it has become the toast of Chicago's business world practically overnight. You may have seen her in the *Tribune* and on the news.

This is a tremendous privilege. It says here that room and board are provided, and there's a considerable stipend in exchange for good old-fashioned hard work."

Her words rushed at me too fast to make sense of. So I would be living at this place? Living at a hotel? Working full-time? No actual classes? "Considerable stipend"? It was a lot to wrap my head around. Do things like this just fall from the sky? Perhaps the near-perfect grades I worked so hard for, the afterschool job I had held for pretty much a decade, the Saturday nights spent at home studying, were finally paying off in something that could give me a shot at the pricey and prestigious schools on my college wish list.

"I know we've started our semester—the timing is a bit odd; I suppose the state board is still ironing out the kinks—however, we'll make it work since this is a rare opportunity." She said this with a hands-clasped, tilted-head gravity that suggested she would like some gratitude and gushing in return.

"Thank you, Ms. Tollman. I appreciate it. This is really great." My mind was already five steps ahead, wondering what Joan would say. *Would she even let me go? What would I bring? How would I tell them at the hospital?*

"You start next week. Everything you need to know should be in here." She stood and thrust a slim manila envelope at me, then surprised me by grabbing my limp, unsuspecting hand for a firm shake. "Do us proud, Haven."

I had never seen so many people crowd the half-moon of the pediatric nurses' station when there *wasn't* an emergency. There must've been at least three dozen of them pulled from even the farthest corners of Evanston General Hospital's compound and representing the full color spectrum of scrubs—pinks, blues, greens, Disney characters—all buzzing around me, nibbling on heaping slices of red velvet cake (my favorite).

Joan had, of course, orchestrated the whole thing. Now she bent over the sheet cake bearing the message HAPPY BIRTHDAY AND CONGRATULATIONS, HAVEN! WE'LL MISS YOU!, dishing out precisely sliced pieces as fast as she could and, naturally, with a smile.

She had just turned fifty a few months earlier, but besides her gray hair, which she hadn't bothered to dye, you would never have guessed her age: her social calendar, from her book clubs to her bridge nights, put mine to shame. I wished that she tried to date more—of the two of us, she seemed to have a better shot at it—but she could be stubborn about that. It was the only thing she got touchy about. Joan had divorced a year or so before she found me, after discovering she couldn't have kids of her own. She didn't talk about it much, but the other nurses had over the years, so I'd gotten the whole story in bits and pieces. They thought she was too scared now, and they tried to push her into dating and set her up to little avail. But at least she had plenty of friends. She was always either going to a party or throwing one. I wished to one day be such a good hostess. At the moment, though, I was doing my best as the center of attention, another tricky role for me. As problems went, this was a fine one: surrounded by so many well-wishers I had managed only one bite of my celebratory confection before being pleasantly besieged by a tug at the arm of my salmon-hued scrubs here, an ambush hug or a jolly pat on the back there.

"Y'know, I just don't know how I'm going to tell some of my patients about this. They'll be devastated!" said blond-bee-hived Nurse Calloway from cardiac. She stabbed at her cake as Dr. Michelle from pediatrics—the youngest resident in the entire hospital, and my idol—and white-haired Nurse Sanders, with glistening eyes behind her thick glasses, nodded in agreement. This was my little sorority. "You'll break all their hearts," Calloway went on.

"And those are hearts that are already in pretty bad shape to begin with!" Dr. Michelle chimed in with the punch line. We all laughed. This is what passed for humor in these parts. Indeed, a few patients liked to call me a "heartbreaker," which was certainly something I never heard from anyone who wasn't an octogenarian with failing vision. Dr. Michelle smiled. "We'll miss you, Haven." She could almost pass as a patient in her department, being so energetic, young, and, like me, only a couple inches over five feet.

Sanders sniffled. "Could you still come on weekends? Or evenings?"

"Now I'm starting to feel bad," I said. "Maybe I should stay."

At the other end of the nurses' station a good fifteen feet away, Joan perked her head up, waving her cake knife in the air. "I know you're not guilt-tripping my girl, are you, ladies?" she called over to us, cutting a piece of cake for herself at last. Propped up on the table behind her was a framed photo of me, about ten years old wearing a mini—candy striper's uniform. Images of me were all over this place: I was everyone's surrogate child smiling from their desktops and cabinets and computer wallpaper. The hospital had pretty much been my daycare center for as long as I could remember; I came to work with Joan and was babysat by anyone and everyone until I was old enough that they could start giving me something useful to do. Joan wandered over, plate in hand, mouth full of cake, and put her arm around me. "We have to let this one spread her wings. She'll fly back." She winked.

"I'll be back at the end of June. You'll barely have time to miss me," I said, a crater deepening in my heart. "I'll do a goodbye tour before I go today."

And tour I did, making the rounds to see all my favorites and ending the day with the toughest stop of all, pediatrics. I cut a pied piper's path through the ward, collecting pajama-clad followers as I went room to room dispensing hugs and kisses and promising to be back soon. We landed back at the playroom and gathered at the bulletin board we had assembled together: a collage of photos of each child in the ward, running the length of the wall, with a border in a riot of colors. It looked like a massive yearbook page, and we updated it with new photos of everyone on a regular basis. It had started as nothing really, just a little project for photography class last year. I had asked a few kids if they would be willing to let me photograph them and they agreed, and then somehow everyone wanted in on it. Jenny, a bandana-clad fourteen-year-old, had explained once, "we look better in your pictures than we do in the mirror." I assured her no Photoshop was involved—this was them.

The strangest thing of all though was the reaction back at school. Most of the kids in that photography class were in there either for easy As or were really tortured artist types who dressed all in black. Then there were people like me, who could appreciate the arts, even if we didn't quite have the skills to participate, and figured we couldn't be that bad at pointing and shooting. When I put together that project though, something clicked. You looked at the pictures and jumped into the eyes of those kids and felt like you knew everything there was to know about them. Each semester the class voted on someone's work to be displayed in the glass case in the school's front hallway, and somehow they chose me. Every time I walked by it, I would see a handful of people stopping to stare, kids who never seemed to notice anything. Even Jason Abington had looked—a few times in fact—and once when I happened to be walking by (because I walked by a lot) he saw me and elbowed me, nodding at the case, and said, "This is yours? It's really cool." That meant more to me than I'd like to admit. But it was true; the sweet faces of my subjects did all seem to glow in those pictures, like the camera cut down to their core.

I addressed my little posse now. "I'm officially putting you guys in charge of the Wall of Fame." I knocked a knuckle against the bulletin board. "Dr. Michelle has kindly promised to take the photos so you can keep rotating in the new ones. Don't let her slack off. I'll be back soon and it better be in good shape." I smiled.

"Ooooh, um, she's not such a good photographer," Jenny whispered. "Remember the one of me with just one eye open when you were out that one day? It took, like, an hour to get something even that good."

"Good point. We'll just hope that she's improved since then. Or else, you can be camerawoman." I winked. "I'll miss you guys. Okay, high-fives, everyone." I raced around slapping each soft palm.

Night had fallen by the time we left the hospital. The lights of Chicago were a dull glimmer in the distance as Joan drove through the windswept suburban streets of cozy, quiet Evanston. The city felt much farther away than it actually was from home and the comfortable routine of my life. The car heater blasted, and beneath my puffy parka I could feel cold bands of sweat trickling down my skin. I sighed.

"You okay?" Joan asked, peeking at me from the corner of her eye.

"Sorry, yeah." I kept my gaze straight ahead into the ice-encrusted, velvety night. "That was a lot tougher than I expected."

"Of course, honey, they're all like family. Besides, going-away parties are designed to make you sorry you're leaving—they're sneaky that way." She smiled, and I did too. "But you know what? We're all right here. We're not that far away. It'll be fine."

"I know, I'm just sort of, I don't know, nervous." A twinge of guilt nipped at me. I didn't want Joan to worry, and I certainly didn't want to remind her that just about twenty-four hours ago she was completely vetoing this whole plan. She had sounded all the expected alarms: *Why do you need to stay there? How hard are they going to be working you that they need you on the premises 24-7 when you only live an hour away on the L? Don't they know there are child labor laws?* Sure, I had told her, the whole thing is organized by the state Department of Education so obviously they're not shipping us off to some sweatshop. But, in the end, there was no denying the honor that seemed to come with this, and that stipend (Joan's eyes had positively bulged). I had pulled out the packet from Principal Tollman, with all the particulars about the hotel, glossy photos of its grandeur, and a host of clippings from every newspaper and magazine in the city about the glamorous woman—Aurelia Brown, blond, stunning, unbelievably young, and powerful—who would be my new boss. Joan had to say yes.

But now, as Friday night closed in on me, ushering in what I knew would be an intense weekend of preparation for this sudden new chapter, nerves were getting the best of me.

"I just don't know what this will be like," I continued. "I don't know if they'll like me or if I'll do a good job. And it's just weird. I mean, I've never even been to camp and now I'm going to be living somewhere else. And I know I want to go away to school, but

I would have a whole extra year to get ready for that, you know? I just feel really . . . off." That was the only way to put it. I felt that I was playing the role of me—and doing it badly—in what would be a spinoff of my life. The glow cast by the streetlamps transformed the bare trees lining our path into spindly, tentacled beasts. I shivered and took a deep breath.

"Don't worry. They picked you, remember? They know you're special," she offered, in soothing tones. "And, besides, Dante will be there. You kids will have each other."

"I know. That's the only reason I'm not totally freaking out. Imagine what a basket case I'd be if I had to go it alone."

"No kidding."

Dante Dennis had been my security blanket, and best friend, for about ten years now. That he was one of the other two kids going to the Lexington with me might have otherwise seemed pure, dumb luck, except that he and I were always neck and neck, vying for the top of the class (politely, of course). So it made sense when he hedged at lunch, sheepishly peeking out from behind his chin-length dreadlocks and grabbing a french fry from my tray.

"You wouldn't happen to have any news, would you?" He had eased into it, then bulldozed on. "Because I do. And I will die if you *don't* have news. Please tell me you're ditching this town and breezing into the Windy City for a certain fabulous internship." He raised his eyebrows at me—up/down, up/down—conspiratorially. Instantly a wave of relief washed over me.

"You wouldn't be checking into the Lexington Hotel, would you?" I answered.

"Yesss!" He was practically jumping in his seat now. "Oh my god, we're going to have so much fun. I mean, who lives in a hotel? Only, like, rock stars and celebrities and maybe those messed-up starlets who, like, divorce their parents. Get me out of this horrid high school and into Chicago society!"

"Yes, please." I smiled. We looked around at the tables full of people who would elect us president of things like French Honor Society, but yet not talk to us ever. "Are you a little . . ."

"Nervous?"

"Yeah."

"Hello?! Yes. Totally nervous. I mean, the whole thing seems like kind of a big deal—Tollman was, like, weirdly excited, and I sure don't want to mess up. We could get total kickass college recommendations out of this. And these people could probably get us into any school in Chicago without even trying: Northwestern, U. Chicago, they probably know everyone. We'd be idiots *not* to be nervous. But we're smart and seriously, we work hard. It's all good." He swatted his hand at me, no sweat.

And I exhaled. This was Dante's rare talent—far more impressive than his tenure on the honor roll or his landslide reelection to student government, or the absurdly gourmet bake sale he organized for charity each year, full of the most precious confections you've ever seen (he was no less than an artist whose chosen medium just happened to be frosting). No, his greatest accomplishment, as far as I was concerned, was his ability to act as a human tranquilizer for me. He could keep me operating at a sane and steady level no matter how twisted up I felt inside. He had proven his aptitude for it from that very first day I met him at the hospital so many years ago.

Back then, I was a five-year-old roaming the pediatric ward halls waiting to find out who I was and where I would be shipped off to. He had been rushed to the emergency room by his frantic mom after he had fallen climbing a tree. He had landed on a mess of sticks and rocks he had collected to build a fort and ended up scraping up his back something fierce and mangling his arm. Tendon damage forced him to stay overnight, and he wandered into my room with his broken arm plastercasted in a sling. We were up till nearly daybreak telling ghost stories. He went home the next afternoon, but became a regular visitor for the month I was there. Every few days he would appear, running down the hall, pulling his mom Ruthie with him, his little arms always full of coloring books or stuffed animals or pictures he'd drawn for me.

Joan pulled into the driveway of our town house. Home never looked so good as when you knew you were going to leave it. Ours was tall and narrow, a faded royal blue out front, with brown shutters and a slim covered porch. The place was plenty big for just the two of us and mere blocks from Lake Michigan, which was still and icy now, but would be our favorite escape for afternoon sunbathing and picnicking when the weather was warm.

"Go on in, I've gotta get some things out of the trunk." Joan shooed me away.

"Need help?"

"Nah," she insisted. "I'll be just a sec."

With that, I ran up the front steps and to the porch as fast as I could, the icy air chilling me to my bones as the wind howled and whooped around me. My gloved fingers fumbled with the keys and finally the door opened and a blast of heat warmed my skin.

I flipped on the light. Through the living room, back in the kitchen, a shimmering silver balloon shaped in the number 16 danced above the table. A homemade cake and a palm-size box, wrapped in glittering silver paper with a matching bow, waited for me.

I dropped my backpack on the floor and beelined straight to my birthday shrine, unzipping my coat as I went and disposing of it on a living room chair on my way. Joan was already at the door by the time I dug my finger into the fluffy icing and licked it off.

"Part two of the birthday extravaganza!"

"Delicious. And amazing. But it's not until Monday." That, at least, was the date we had always celebrated since we didn't really know for sure when I was born. It was the anniversary of the day when I had been found and taken to the hospital where Joan was the first to tend to me, patching up my gashes and scrapes, checking for broken bones, and slowly getting me to talk to her, though I had nothing to say, nothing that was helpful at least.

"I thought since we were already in such a festive spirit, we would just continue the party. Let the good times roll!" She set down her purse and shimmied off her coat, hanging it on the rack by the door. I took the glittering box in my hands and shook it.

"So can I open it?"

"You'd better!" she said, joining me at the table and sampling a finger's worth of icing herself. "Go on!"

I tore at the paper and opened a white velvet box. Its contents sparkled.

"I know you're not into jewelry, my precious little tomboy," she said. "But sixteen is a biggie and I thought you should have something pretty."

I pulled out a necklace, webbing its gold chain around my fingers. It's true: I didn't wear jewelry, and what few pieces I'd ever gotten had always sat in their boxes untouched. But this one already felt different. For one, it wasn't a heart or a dangling birthstone or any of the typical kinds of things I was used to seeing on the girls at school. Instead, this pendant, almost harp-shaped and running the length of my fingertip, was something entirely new: a single gold wing, its texture softly rippled to give the illusion of feathers.

"I found this at that antique shop I always drag you to with me," Joan said.

"Right, the one next to that bookstore that I always sneak into when you take too long."

"Exactly." She smiled. "I just thought it looked special, like you, and unique." She kissed the top of my head. "I liked the wing, because you're really going places, you know that? You're soaring, Haven. You have so much ahead of you."

"Thanks, Joan, I love it, I really do." I gave her a hug and held her a few seconds longer than I normally might.

"Maybe you'll actually wear this one, you think?" she asked, smoothing my hair.

"I'll prove it." I dangled the necklace from my finger and lifted up my hair. "Would you?"

"I'd be honored." She fastened it on, then turned me around by my shoulders and straightened it in place so it hit just at that little indented spot at my throat. "Perfect, go see."

I studied myself in the bathroom mirror. My eyes went directly to the pendant. Generally, everything about my appearance seemed either imperfect or, at best, plain Jane. My nose always looked to me like a blob of uncooked cookie dough. My hair, skin, and eyes were just one shade off from one another in the color spectrum: caramel skin, bone-straight honey brown hair, dark amber eyes. The pink scrubs hanging as they did on my boyish frame did nothing to improve upon all this.

And I had worn entirely the wrong long-sleeved thermal shirt underneath the V-neck top today. My favorites were in the hamper and poor planning had left me with only this old one, with a V-neck just a touch too deep. I looked at the mirror now and wondered if that corner of my scar—the three nasty stripes angled like accent marks and pebbled in texture like burns, located in the space above my heart—had been peeking out like this all afternoon. It was only two inches long but, when coupled with the pair of scars on my shoulder blades, collectively signaled one big, marred canvas. The necklace clearly should have looked glaringly out of place having me as its unworthy mannequin. But somehow this new piece seemed at home. The intense shine of the gold caught the light and cast a soft glow upon my face. I did like it actually. Perhaps I was growing up at last. Maybe this was the first sign of the sophistication to come. *Sixteen.* It felt weighty, substantial, important.

"I love it," I called out, still admiring it in the mirror. "Thank you so much."

2

Good Things Come in Threes

Monday came entirely too fast, as it always does. But this time the new week landed with a greater thud in the pit of my stomach. The weekend was a blur of packing. I felt as though I were going as far as the South Pole, not as near as the South Side of Chicago's Loop. Finally, with two large, overstuffed duffel bags in tow, I found myself outside the imposing fortress of the Lexington Hotel.

My new abode was set on the block's corner plot where South Michigan Avenue and Twenty-second Street crossed. The brick behemoth reached ten stories into the sky and was belted a third of the way up and again near the top by bands of ornate terra cotta in a pattern of curlicue designs. The bloated vertical seam along the corner of the building bulged where half-moons of bay windows jutted out on each floor. Those were probably some of the best rooms. I had always wanted a bay window—it seemed that girls in old movies were endlessly curling up by them to read or daydream. At the very top, where the sides of the building came to a point, a triangular flag stood proudly, like a college pennant, but rigid, not waving an inch and likely made of steel. It was strung with lights that glowed to read LEXINGTON.

"Not a bad second home, honey," Joan said.

"Yeah." The awe in my voice was evident as I peeked up through the car window. "Wow. It'll do."

Joan had pulled the car up to the grand entranceway, which glittered with the promise of romance and style within. Lined by a pair of pillars on each side, the doorway was shaded by a crimson awning and framed in a stone border dotted with golden disks bearing the hotel emblem: the letters L and H entwined nearly one on top of the other. The revolving door, set above a handful of red-carpeted steps with a ramp beside them, beckoned me now. The ground-level exterior, unlike the rest of the hotel, was modern, with swaths of opaque black glass in place of picture windows set in the brick, making it impossible to see in but leaving you to wonder what might be looking out at you.

"Let's get you moved in, shall we?" Joan said, climbing out to unpack the trunk. I nodded and pushed open the car door to follow.

Overnight, that aggressive winter chill had mellowed into a curious, unseasonable balminess. I pulled off my parka, rolled up my sleeves. I had done my best to look as professional as possible, in a button-down shirt, black pants, and flats, but I still felt too plain for this place. I had spent enough time Googling my new employer and the goings-on of the hotel itself to know that there would be a level of style here that reached far beyond what I was capable of. This Aurelia Brown, from the pictures I'd seen, was perfect—brilliant and beautiful, all things every girl wants to be—and yet somehow looked like she wasn't even old enough to have graduated from college. I suspected I would have much to learn here.

I lifted the body bag–size duffel onto my shoulder, stumbling under its weight.

"Oh dear, give me that," Joan said, lifting the other bag onto her shoulder and taking mine from me so she was equally weighted. "Do you want me to go in with you? What time is Dante coming?"

"Five minutes ago." I studied the building's entrance. My heartbeat sped up.

"That's our Dante," she said.

I shook my head and smiled. He was always late, but it was part of his charm. You couldn't be mad at him, because when he finally did arrive, it was always with such fanfare, you got swept up by it. I checked my watch: 8:52 a.m. Our start time had been called for 9:00.

"I think I'll wait another minute. At least it's weirdly warm out," I said. "But you go, I'll be fine. Really." I stuffed my parka under my arm and took the straps of the bags from her hands.

"You sure?"

No. I nodded anyway.

"Isn't there at least a bellhop or something?"

"The place hasn't opened yet. And besides, I'm not a guest. I'm probably going to end up *being* the bellhop."

"I hope not. How would you lift all those heavy things all day?"

"I don't know, but it would be fun if I got to wear one of those jaunty little caps, you know the ones?"

Joan wasn't listening.

"Don't let them have you doing anything dangerous." She pointed her finger at me, in that way of hers.

"I'll be fine, Joan. Promise."

"Don't be nervous." She pulled me into a bear hug and rocked me back and forth, then kissed my forehead.

"Joan, I'm fine!"

"I know, I know, no PDA, got it." She pulled away smirking. "You're gonna do great. And home is just an L ride away. Call me later, okay?"

"Will do." I bit my lip, looking over her shoulder at the street behind her. None of the cars matched Dante's mom's old station wagon.

"Happy birthday, Haven." She climbed into the car with a wave. I touched the necklace and waved back, watching as she inched out into the light traffic and disappeared down the street. I was on my own. A chill shivered through me even though it was so warm. On a day like today, Dante was the best and most necessary crutch imaginable. But he wasn't here yet and now it was nine o'clock. Bells chimed in the distance, a church somewhere scoffing that I was about to be late. Not the ideal first impression. I had no choice.

I heaved my bags one on each shoulder and trudged up the red-carpeted ramp and through the revolving door. I had made it only a few steps inside when I let the bags slide to the floor with a thump and dropped my coat on top of them, involuntarily abandoning them to explore. The lobby of the Lexington sparkled; unreal and untouched, pristine and glorious. And empty, too. It felt magically hollow, a place you had stumbled upon that you shouldn't have, somewhere that was supposed to be locked up and then unveiled with all the pomp and circumstance it deserved.

A carpet of red and gold, with that L and H insignia, sprawled out in all directions and up a grand staircase. Hallways to my right and left held the promise of beautiful gathering places, rooms still to be discovered. Straight ahead, a plush golden ottoman—raised to a point in its center so it looked like a giant spinning top—stood ready to seat at least a dozen or more. But the real show played out directly above: a crystal chandelier shimmered, casting prisms in its countless dangling facets. Beyond that, ten stories up, sunlight streamed down from a skylight so immense it seemed to illuminate the whole place without electricity at all. A portion of each floor of the hotel featured waist-high barriers allowing guests to peer over at the lobby below or at the skylight above. I sat on that ottoman and gazed above, past the magnificent chandelier, and had the sense of being in a giant Gothic church, a place so airy that you felt immediately uplifted. I had never been somewhere so vast and splendid all by myself. Majestic spaces like this were made to be full of people, bustling with bodies. But now it was all mine. It thrilled me, this freedom fluttering inside me, my fingers tingling. Free, for a moment at least, from anyone's rules or expectations. I wouldn't have thought I would have liked this feeling, because it came with uncertainty too. But I did.

However, I knew that someone, somewhere in this opulent new home of mine, was waiting for me, ready to show me the ropes. And I had to find them. I hadn't necessarily expected a welcoming committee, but it did seem odd that there wasn't a single soul around. There was no one manning the imposing marble front desk opposite the sweeping staircase. No one at the narrow oak bellhop stand near the doors. No one filing out from the bank of elevators. Was it possible that everyone was already corralled in some conference room?

"Hello?" I called out, but my voice was so meek in this grand setting. "Hello?" I wandered to the front desk, letting my fingertips run along the length of the cool, smooth marble. It was set a step or two above me and I stood on my toes to try to see beyond it. Then I heard it: the faintest of whispers. Behind the desk there was an archway, and a corridor in near darkness. A quick blade of light sliced into the dim hallway—a door opening—as an hourglass figure stepped out, silhouetted. A man's silky voice followed her, wrapping around the air. "You forgot something." A hand grabbed her bare upper arm and a tall, lean suited-up man stepped into the light, pulling her close and breathing, "This." He planted a kiss just below her ear and combed his fingers through her shoulder-length waves, kissing her once more.

The woman lifted his chin with her delicate fingers, looking into his eyes. I was so mesmerized I didn't register the swoosh of the revolving door.

"There she is!" a voice rang out, yanking me out of my haze. On reflex, I jumped away from the desk, jittery as if I'd been caught shoplifting, and stumbled while running toward the front door. There stood Dante with his three matching leopard print suitcases and the quiet guy from our AP European History class. My best friend stretched out both arms: "Happy birthday, sweetie!"

"Aww, thanks." My heart was still racing. I tried to settle down.

Dante gave me a hug and kissed me on the cheek. "Sorry I'm late. Did we miss anything?"

I shook my head. "No one has come out to meet me yet."

"Hey, you remember Lance," Dante said, gesturing to the kid beside him.

"Of course, hi." I recognized him but I didn't know if we'd ever actually spoken to each other in so many years of school.

"Hey," Lance offered, barely audible, nodding once in my direction. Reed-thin in baggy jeans and a Cubs T-shirt beneath his hooded zip-up, he towered over both Dante and me, but seemed to compensate for this with a concave posture. He leaned forward as though forming a cage shielding the center of his chest. His hands were plunged deep in his jean pockets. "And, um, happy birthday, I guess." He pushed his horn-rimmed glasses up farther on his nose.

"Thanks." I quickly smiled, awkward. Our eyes danced around each other, then his gaze dropped.

"He's the third intern, so the gang's all here," Dante said. "Don't they say good things come in threes?"

"Except for three on a match," I clarified. "You know, if you light three flames off one match someone dies? Something like that."

"What?" Dante asked, his voice tinged with annoyance, as it was whenever one of my trivial facts got in the way of an otherwise pleasant conversation (which was often).

"Yeah, that's bad luck," Lance agreed, glancing sideways from behind his glasses, his eyes grabbing at mine for another flash. The overbearing frames dwarfed his face. They were all I could focus on when I looked at him.

"Well, then you're lucky I didn't have time to find a candle." Dante held out a plastic container and gave it a gentle, celebratory shake. "Ta-dahhh! For you, my friend," he said, handing it to me. Inside the small, clear dome was a single, perfect cupcake—pink icing dusted with round confetti-like pastel sprinkles and 16 in candy numbers perched on top.

"Dan, you shouldn't have."

"Please! It's nothing."

"Thanks, you're the best," I said but he was already walking away, transfixed.

His eyes rose upward toward the skylight. "Whoa."

Lance, equally entranced, kneeled on the ottoman staring up at the hundreds of tiny lights along the cords suspending the chandelier. His lips were moving like he was counting: "That's

1,482—no . . . 83, 1,483 lights. How 'bout that?" he mused. "How do you think they change those when they burn out?" He then wandered toward the front desk. Above it, a screen flashed through a series of the stories that had run in the *Tribune* and some of the other local papers and magazines.

"This place is outta control," Dante gushed.

"Yeah, I know, right?" I answered.

"I'm so glad you like it." From somewhere behind me, another voice, a woman's low and sweet rasp like a crackling fire, shattered my thoughts. This was the voice I'd heard in whispers earlier. She floated down the grand staircase from the second floor, long and lean with a model's proportions. She wore a fitted black suit jacket over a knee-length black dress, a frill of lace peeking out above the front buttons. She held a clipboard in her hands and now had her light locks pinned up in a French twist, soft tendrils escaping to frame the sharp, unreal angles of her face. We watched her without a word. Lance shuffled over to stand near Dante and me, the three of us side by side like soldiers.

"Hello, I'm Aurelia Brown, owner of the Lexington Hotel. It's a pleasure to meet you." She came up to each of us to shake our hands. I had never seen anyone this stunning up close. Her sapphire eyes were clear and welcoming, sparkling even. Her skin was bone china, smooth and firm, without a single line etched upon it.

"Nice to meet you," I said finally. Her fingers felt like twigs, so slim, but then they tightened around mine, nearly crushing them.

"And this . . ." She gestured behind her. I hadn't even noticed that a man had appeared, seated, legs crossed, leaning back just enough on the mammoth ottoman to show he didn't have to try hard to look this way. He wore a slim gray suit and a satin tie of

pink and purple checks, all so precisely tailored it took me a moment to realize he looked fresh out of high school. His features
were impeccably carved—an almost-too-delicate nose, chiseled
cheekbones, full lips. He had slicked back his hair in a way that
made him look like he had stepped out of an old movie. It had
never, until this point, occurred to me to describe a guy as being
beautiful, but he was. "This is my second in command, Lucian
Grove." He stood now, buttoning his suit jacket and adjusting his
cuffs. When he stepped forward to greet each of us as Aurelia had,
the thrill of those impending few seconds of attention wracked
my body.

"A pleasure," he said to Lance, shaking his hand. They were
nearly the same height. Everyone here was impossibly tall. I felt so
small, so insignificant.

Dante was unflappable, offering his effortless "So nice to
meet you, great to be here." But my fingers trembled even before
Lucian took my hand. When he did, a sharp jolt charged through
me, a hot tremor hitting every nerve in my body. I hoped his fiery
grip wasn't reading my pulse. His eyes, gray woven with threads of
crystal blue, burned into mine, and then he arched one eyebrow
at me—playful, knowing—and smirked. My heart stopped. What
did that mean? He hadn't seen me watching him and Aurelia earlier, had he? I mean, it had only been a flash, a few seconds. And
yet, from his look, I felt like he had found me out.

Dante read some of this from the corner of his eye. "I hope
there are more like him around here," he whispered into my
ear, after Lucian had turned his back to us to resume his place at
Aurelia's side. "I want one." I took a deep breath and felt my feet
return to solid ground and my pulse begin to slow. Aurelia was
speaking, so, with some effort, I refocused my attention on her.

"You'll be working closely with a group we've already

assembled as part of our social outreach cadre: we call them the Outfit." At that, as though choreographed, a group of people flowed and floated in from rooms on our right and left. Though there were many of them, collectively they sounded as hushed as fluttering butterfly wings. Ten men and ten women all the caliber of Aurelia and Lucian, perfectly attired and all wearing black suits and dresses. All, I guessed, to be in their late teens or their early twenties at the most, yet they seemed worlds older than me. It was something about the way they carried themselves: regal, with proud, straight backs, and their heads tilted just a touch upward. They swarmed around the three of us, creating a cocoon with their bodies. They didn't say a word and didn't look at us, but kept their eyes glued to Aurelia, their faces still, a serene air surrounding them. So we did too, after exchanging a few confused glances with one another.

"Play your cards right, and you three just might be the youngest inductees into this exclusive society," Aurelia said. "Everyone in Chicago wants in. People would give their souls to be part of it. You're very lucky, you know. Come, we've much to discuss."

3

Your New Surroundings

"So, welcome," Aurelia announced as we began the official tour, the low pitch of her voice melodic and calming. The Outfit, still surrounding Dante, Lance, and me, swept us along as we followed our leader past the front desk and the grand staircase and straight down the center of the lobby. In our hands now were gift bags brimming with swag: pens, mugs, notepads, postcards, T-shirts, and candies all bearing the hotel's gold-on-black LH logo. "Today we'll walk you through what you'll be doing, show you your accommodations, and get you situated and feeling at home." She paused, turning to look at each of our faces. Inside the open doorway to our right, I caught a glimpse of walls lined with floord-to-ceiling bookcases and one of those ladders attached to a gold-plated track running along the top near the high ceiling. Stacks of books lined the floor near a fireplace and an emerald-hued velvet sofa.

"We're almost in place for our grand opening, but there are still projects to be conquered and we will be depending on you and on the Outfit." Aurelia gestured to them with a delicate hand. "You will have a privileged look at how this establishment will be run. What will be expected of you? Anything and everything. That's why you were recruited—we know you're among the best and brightest. We are proud to have you and hope you will be just as proud to be aiding us." The register of her voice had hypnotic powers, an ebb and flow that had the effect of a lullaby. Beside her, Lucian watched us, hands in his pockets. His eyes met mine for a second and seared me. I pushed up the sleeves of my shirt and hoped I didn't look like I was sweating. "Keep in mind we wouldn't be providing room and board for you if we didn't expect to be able to call on you occasionally at odd hours, but it will be worth your while. You'll find that a job well done here will translate into enrichment and success elsewhere. We can open doors."

At that last promise, I straightened my back, standing as tall as possible. Now she really had my attention. She seemed to know it too. She held my gaze. I had the feeling she could tell by looking at a person whether or not they would disappoint her.

She spun back around, heels clicking, off again. We scurried to keep up. "A few things you may or may not know, but that you will need to know. We are a reincarnation of the original Lexington Hotel, and are as respectful and mindful of that history as possible. The legendary Chicago gangster Al Capone once lived here, and we allude to this infamy often, while also trying to brand ourselves as an arbiter of cutting-edge taste and a vanguard in the art, culinary, and nightlife worlds. We intend to be a celebration of both the dangerous and the beautiful, because these are the things that everyone most craves. We are going to be a destination for Chicago natives and visitors alike. We open to the public in mere weeks, on February 14, in honor of the

St. Valentine's Day massacre. I'm sure you know what that was, correct?"

I knew roughly that it had to do with Capone's gang killing a bunch of members of a rival gang, but I was too scared to give any detailed answer. I could not bear to be wrong in front of this group. My stomach knotted up. I glanced at my compatriots. We all wore the same in-over-our-head expression. Silence. Aurelia stopped short and turned to us again, shaking her head. "Oh dear," she chided. "You're going to need to brush up on your Chicago history, my lambs. You're representing us now." Her voice was icy.

"I thought it was rhetorical, that question," Dante piped up. I almost gasped but caught myself. I shot him a look. Aurelia studied him, a faint smile on her lips.

"You'll find that very little of what I ask is rhetorical. I don't like to waste time. I either give orders or I ask questions with the intention of receiving answers." Somehow, these words didn't sound so hostile as they trickled out sweetly and slowly, only lightly laced with bite. Through all of this, the Outfit remained quiet and still, encircling us like a chain of paper dolls. Aurelia set off again.

"You will each be assigned a mentor, from whom you will receive your assignments. Whenever possible, you will be given projects commensurate with your interests and talents. Lance"— his whole body jolted at the sound of his name—"you'll be shadowing Lucian, handling day-to-day operations, a good deal of management responsibilities, and various projects with our amenities: the nightclub, the gallery, the library."

"Thank you," Lance said shyly to the back of her head. Lucian looked over his shoulder and gave him a nod in acknowledgment.

"Dante, your mentor is our head chef, Etan. He has some innovative plans for the menu in our restaurant and lounge. He is currently away on business, but he'll be here in another day or so. In the meantime, he asks that you familiarize yourself with the kitchens—you can start with the one adjacent to the Parlor, which is our more casual restaurant."

"Of course. Looking forward to it," he answered, his voice bright.

"And, lastly, Haven, you will be with me." We had reached the far end of the ground floor and stopped before a glass-enclosed elevator.

"Great, thank you so much." I waited to hear more. I wanted to know exactly what Aurelia expected from me, so I would then know how to surpass it and impress her. But that was it.

"Now let's have a look at our nightclub, the Vault." She pressed the elevator call button. "It opened last month to great fanfare and we're doing a tremendous business." That seemed to be true, according to what I'd read about the club. Everyone had filtered through there: celebrities in town shooting movies; every remotely important athlete the city had; musicians on tour. "We realize that you three aren't of age . . ." She paused, perhaps finding a way to let us down gently that this wasn't a place for high school kids. "However—"

At that, we all looked at her with renewed attention. The elevator opened and she stepped in, Lucian behind her. We followed, tentative, Dante first.

"—you will be permitted into the club as long as you're responsible."

What? I wasn't sure I heard right. Beside me, I felt light beams shooting out of Dante's eyes, ears, fingertips. The Outfit turned and walked down a side hallway, single file, like one long, chic snake, and finally disappeared.

"Members of the Outfit have specific duties there, and you may, in fact, be asked to work there at times as well."

"All right!" Dante, I knew, couldn't help it. The outburst just escaped his lips, no hope of being held back.

Aurelia's eyes zipped in his direction. Lucian leaned in toward Dante, almost conspiratorially, and said, "It's a pretty fantastic place. You won't be disappointed."

"Onward," she said. The elevator doors closed and we plummeted to the hotel's depths.

Once downstairs though, we were permitted to see only the sealed door of the nightclub—a black-painted slab of steel like the kind you'd find on a bank vault—leaving us to imagine what lay beyond it.

The rest of the tour felt endless, a blur of elegantly appointed rooms and an onslaught of facts and figures. The Outfit mysteriously met up with us again later when we reached the upper floors, fencing us in, which continued to make me nervous. I wished I could drum up some intelligent questions to ask, something to show how serious I was—something also that would force Lucian to look at me. His gaze remained firmly set on Aurelia, his eyes traveling over her face like ocean waves lapping at rock, painting her with devoted attention as she spoke. And who could blame him? She had such presence. You could feel the control in her voice, in her sharp movements and the forthright, steady pace of her walk. She was so unlike the women I knew, the no-nonsense, practical, get-the-job-done women at the hospital, like Joan. There was a polish to Aurelia. Could that be learned? Or was it just something you either had or you didn't, the way that seemingly overnight some of the girls at school had become these creatures who could lure and lasso even the most elusive boys?

As we wandered, so did my mind, more than I would have liked. But I was tired. We all were. I caught Lance stifling a yawn at one point. The place was mammoth and we covered a lot of ground.

I scoped out so many intriguing spots I hoped to inspect more closely. On the main floor, in addition to the library, there would be a restaurant called Capone and a lounge called the Parlor—these were located to the right and left of the main entrance. Back near the elevator to the Vault, tucked behind the thick folds of a gold and burgundy velvet curtain, was a glass door leading into what would be the hotel's own art gallery, which would be a museum of macabre artifacts from Chicago's sordid past with plenty of original works of art and photography by local artists mixed in. For now it was no more than an empty expanse of blank white walls and glass cases, just waiting for beautiful and special things to display. Another elevator led down to a posh and tranquil spa.

On the second floor at the top of the grand staircase, behind ivory-paneled doors, was the ballroom, complete with a painted ceiling that was the hotel's answer to the Sistine Chapel. However, instead of the heavenly creatures depicted there, this length of ceiling was a stormy sky festooned with heavy and foreboding clouds, lightning bolts so vivid you could almost hear the crackling thunder that would accompany them, ravens and crows flying in formation, and other dark-winged, part-human characters slinging arrows, gorgeous but deadly.

By the time Aurelia led us all back down these stairs, my feet were aching—unaccustomed as they were to doing this much walking in anything other than sneakers.

At last, she dismissed us. "I'd like you to take the rest of the day to acquaint yourselves with the rich charms of your new surroundings, find your rooms, and so forth. Should we need you for anything, we'll find you." We thanked her in unison, as the Outfit slithered away without a sound. Lucian slipped back into that infamous darkened hallway behind the front desk and Aurelia pranced toward the library. Lance, Dante, and I were all fishing in our gift bags for the keycards to our rooms, when the sharp footsteps stopped and I heard that low rasp again.

"Haven, a moment," Aurelia called from the middle of the sprawling lobby, gesturing for me.

"Yes, Ms. Brown," I answered in my brightest, most respectful tone. I waved Dante and Lance on without me, as my nerves began their steady, ominous climb to the top of a roller coaster.

"Aurelia, please," she corrected as she started walking again, not waiting for me. I was jogging now, racing to get to her faster.

"Of course. Aurelia." I tried, but it sounded funny. I couldn't quite call her that, even though, if we had met under different circumstances and she was dressed more like me, I might have mistaken her for a peer. Panting, I caught up with her.

"I have a project for you to begin, if you please."

"I can't wait!" I nodded, too much, too eager, my head bobbing around. My feet couldn't match the rhythm of her steps. I bumbled along.

"The gallery is to be a focal point of the Lexington, a cultural cornerstone, and I have something I'd like you to work on over the next several days. I understand you're a photographer."

"Oh, well, yes, I mean—" I stammered, caught off-guard that she knew this about me. But she cut me off.

"Are you or aren't you?" she asked, her words firm. "I was under the impression I had hired talented students."

Man up, Haven, I told myself, *and don't be modest.* "Yes," I said, matching her strong tone as best I could. "I'm good. I won first place in a countywide competition at school for a series I did on—"

She cut me off again. "Excellent. Do you know why our group is called the Outfit?"

I didn't. If I had time, I would unearth every last scrap of trivia there was to know about this place, I just needed more time. "I don't, but I'm anxious to learn."

"That was the name of Al Capone's gang. And, like his, our Outfit is about exclusivity and it's also somewhat underground." She walked at a quick clip down the hall, the material of her dress and jacket swishing as she went, and her heels clicking staccato against the marble floor. We reached the velvet curtain shrouding the door to the gallery. She gathered it, pushed it aside, and pulled out a keycard.

"But just without the, uh, Tommy guns and things?" My joke flew by, unnoticed, like a blackbird in the night sky. She sliced the card in the vertical pad.

"Instead of a rogues' gallery, ours is more a royal court. It adds a patina to the hotel. They are beautiful for a reason, our members, they are our ambassadors. We have all of Chicago looking at us and talking about us. But, unlike with Capone, it's socially acceptable for people to want to be part of us. And they do."

Lights twinkled in the keypad and a lock popped. She held open the glass door for me and I stepped inside the bare space. She swooshed past me, into the darkness, and a light mushroomed out from a room we hadn't seen on our tour. I walked toward it, into an area staged for a photo shoot. A white screen curved toward the floor, creating a seamless background. Spotlights, covered with umbrellas to direct their glow, shone onto the set, trained on a single wooden stool awaiting its subject. A camera sat atop a tripod, prepared to snap. Extra lenses, like a wardrobe of long and short noses, were lined up on a tabletop.

"We are our best advertisement. We embody the youth and vitality that people want a piece of. We are that touch of wild and unpredictable and untamable that they crave. So we're going to celebrate that, and anoint ourselves more powerful in the process." Aurelia shed her blazer and slung it over a freestanding light not being used, then took a seat on the stool facing toward me. "Over the course of the next couple days you're going to photograph each member of the Outfit, Lucian and myself to be included on a wall of our gallery." She folded her hands in her lap, hooked one heel onto a rung of the stool, and twisted toward me.

"Thank you, I appreciate that you would entrust that to me."

"So, let's go."

"Oh?"

"You'll start with me today. Then we'll unleash you on the masses tomorrow." Her eyes were flinty with a burning efficiency, as if to say, *Get on with it already.* "Everything you need is here. I trust you're well versed in how to work it all."

I nodded, just once—not the most resounding show of confidence, but I figured I would rather underpromise and overdeliver. I set down my Lexington Hotel tote bag and took a place behind the camera. A quick scan of the bells and whistles told me this equipment was worlds more advanced than anything I had ever used. My own digital camera was a secondhand number I'd had for years. It didn't do much and could be a bit slow (sometimes I felt it would be faster to chisel someone's likeness out of marble), but it took decent shots, and that was enough for me. Now that I got to investigate close-up, I realized I had seen this model before, but only inside a glass display case at the camera shop I always went to. It was professional quality, single lens reflex, and the guy at the shop always said it could make up for any multitude of lighting sins—from too dark to too blinding—which was a relief because I didn't know the first thing about adjusting these monster lights and didn't want to embarrass myself by touching them.

"This is quite a camera," I said mostly to myself, but she overheard me anyway.

"I'm glad you like it. You'll be spending a good deal of time with it." She smoothed her dress and patted her hair, barely touching it. I don't think she even noticed when I snapped a shot—this camera was silent, stealthy. Looking through the viewfinder, with that barrier of a lens between us, gave me just enough distance to feel my stomach untying its knots, probably for the first time all day. Aurelia seemed less intimidating from here. She was under my control now. Or at least we were collaborators. I made a few quick adjustments, framing her, deciding just how much to get in the shot, setting the shutter speed.

"Ready when you are," I said, doing my best in-charge voice.

"Then fire away."

I snapped rapidly, capturing a million shots a second it seemed. This camera had such power, I couldn't keep up with it. Aurelia made subtle tweaks to her pose. Never allowing a full grin, she would vacillate between a soft smile and a wistful look. The hollows of her cheeks and sleek line of her delicate nose, the tiniest of clefts in her chin, all caught the light and danced with it, coloring her expression—sometimes she looked solid and strong, other times, thoughtful to the point of melancholy. Within the first minute alone, I was sure I'd gotten the shot I needed, maybe more than I needed.

She unpinned her hair from its twisted prison and shook the waves over her shoulders. I continued snapping a few minutes more until, at last, she declared, "We're finished. Let's see your work. Come." In a burst, she was up from the stool and had disappeared behind the backdrop.

My hands shaking, I flipped through the last couple of shots, confirming what I already knew—they looked beautiful. I freed the camera from the tripod, cradling it in my arms like a baby.

The room in the back was a whitewashed cubbyhole of an office, no more than a desk, a computer, with a slim screen the size of a TV, and another flat screen twice that size mounted on the wall. Aurelia, blazer back on and buttoned, sat before the computer, waiting to be impressed. I hooked up the camera and hundreds of postage-stamp-size photos littered the monitors. Aurelia clicked on the first shot: she was touching her hair at the beginning, before she knew I was paying attention. She looked at me, a hint of admiration flickering in her eyes, then returned to the screen. She shuffled quickly through dozens of shots, all uniformly stunning. She was one of those people blessedly immune to bad photos. I, on the other hand, hardly ever found a picture I could tolerate of myself. In fact, I had been systematically destroying all photographic evidence of me at twelve and thirteen years old—those were particularly gruesome.

"Lovely. You're done for today. Tomorrow you'll begin shooting the others."

Aurelia clicked away the photos and the computer faded to black.

"Great, thank you."

She switched off the monitor on the wall, shut the lights, and held the door for me to exit. I scurried to get my gift bag, still beside the tripod, then met her at the gallery doors.

She bid me farewell with "Tomorrow, eight o'clock in the lobby," then clomped away, escaping back through that curious doorway behind the front desk.

I found my legs carrying me to the library, a lighthouse bringing me in from the storm. The soft tap of books being placed onto shelves echoed from the room. I peeked my head in and saw Lance standing on one of the ladders, clutching several volumes in his arms and sliding them one by one into empty gaps on a high shelf. He looked over when he heard me enter.

"Hi, sorry, didn't mean to interrupt. You're actually working in here." I started to leave.

"Hey, no," he said, looking away quickly. "No problem." He fidgeted with the books in his hand. One fell. I stepped back into the room, picked up what had dropped, and handed it to him. "Thanks. Lucian put me to work shelving and alphabetizing."

"Wow."

"Yeah, it's going to take me forever. The Harold Washington Library has got nothing on this place. And they say that people don't read anymore."

"Do you want some help?" I wandered in farther and sifted through a stack left on the long wooden table near the door. Shakespeare, Marlowe, Oscar Wilde.

"Nah, I'll save you. I bet you've got your hands full anyway." He snuck a conspiratorial glance at me.

"I'm on a photo project."

"How did that go?"

"Okay so far, I think. Check back with me tomorrow. I'm off the rest of the day, I guess. Which feels weird."

"Yeah. Right now we would be in AP Euro."

I checked my watch; he was right. That reminded me.

"I think I'd better do a little reading up on Chicago history, you know? After this morning . . ." I didn't need to elaborate.

"I know what you mean." He pushed his glasses up on his face and shook his head, recalling our collective embarrassment earlier. "I've been trying to pull some books out as I go. I put a couple good ones over there. Great history ones and some really good Chicago architecture coffee-table books too, but I've got first dibs on those." He pointed to a stack on a delicate wooden secretary's desk.

"Mind if I take a look?"

"Help yourself," he said, and returned to his shelving. I took a seat and began leafing through a book called *Chicago During Prohibition*, with a grainy sepia-toned cover shot of men in 1920s-style suits and hats lined up against a bar.

"I almost forgot." Lance swung around again, climbing down the ladder. It creaked and moaned as he hit each rung. "I found something for you."

"For me?" I twisted around in my chair, resting my chin on its back.

He tapped the tops of the stacks on the long table, searching. Finally he grabbed a slim black hardcover sitting on its own in the corner. He pulled at a slip of paper on the cover.

"Yeah, I mean, I guess. I was going through one of the boxes and I found this one with your name on it." He held out a leather-bound tome, old and worn, with gold-etched lines bordering the spine and front cover. Sure enough, on a black-and-white postcard of Michigan Avenue from a bygone era taped to the front, someone had written "For Haven Terra" in a script I didn't recognize.

"Huh. Thanks." I took it in my hands and leafed through. The wispy pages, all edged in gold, were entirely blank. Lance nodded and creaked back up to his place at the top of the ladder. "You sure this is for me?"

"It had your name. That's all I know."

"I just mean, it's totally empty."

"Yeah, I noticed that too." He scratched his head, shrugging. "Maybe it's a birthday gift or something."

"Maybe," I said, looking at the postcard again as he got back to work. I opened the book again, this time going through slowly page by tissue-like page. They crinkled and crackled under my gentle fingers and seemed almost too delicate to write upon.

Suddenly, a bell pealed, ringing out *Ding-dong-ding.*

Lance and I looked at each other, eyebrows twisted in puzzlement, then we looked toward the hallway where the sound was getting louder.

Dante appeared in the doorway, apron on, dreads tied back in a bandana under a cylindrical marshmallow of a chef's hat. In his fingertips, he swung a piercing golden bell. We stared, speechless.

"Check this out. Cool, right?" He grinned, thrilled with himself.

"I dig the hat," Lance offered.

"Yeah, but it's the bell that really makes the outfit," I declared.

"Thank you, I'm flattered. Now, ahem." He cleared his throat and made a grand bowing gesture, over-annunciating. "Lunch! Is served." He walked away.

"Really?" I called after him.

Lance scurried back down the ladder, and we followed Dante to the Parlor, where he had set a table with three silver-dome-covered plates and unveiled our precious meals all at once. There was something royal about having the run of this place, lunching on immaculate white cloth-covered tables while curled up in cushy armchairs amid armies of potted palms. Naturally we took the best table, beside the long, tinted picture window looking out on the street.

"I think from now on 'familiarize yourself with the kitchen' will be code for 'make us lunch,'" I joked, biting into my sandwich. "This is amazing, D."

"Be nice and I'll keep cooking—that kitchen is stocked. This is nothing." He gestured to our three matching plates of grilled chicken and gruyère sandwiches on brioche, with skinny, crispy french fries. To wash it down, sparkling water bubbled in our crystal wineglasses. And just for me, a chocolate milk shake with mountains of whipped cream. "I made myself a caviar appetizer."

"Dan! You'll get us all into trouble."

"Please, I just had a little spoonful. Good stuff, fish eggs."

"Ew." I made a face. "But I like these!" I held up a blue-corn tortilla chip in the shape of the hotel insignia. I dunked it into a dish of salsa and popped it in my mouth.

"I know. I found these great cookie cutters."

"Apparently," I said, lifting from another communal plate a sugar cookie in the same exact shape but larger, and then a brownie too.

"It's possible that I got carried away."

"We're glad you did. This is amazing."

"Thanks, man, I was starved," said Lance, already nearly done with his sandwich.

"Gladly," Dante said, regally. "The pleasure is mine."

We chatted about the day's events, munching on the food until we finished it off. "Anyone else ravenous and weirdly exhausted today?" Lance polled us as he sat back in his chair to digest.

Dante and I both raised our hands. Now that I was finally

sitting down and not under Aurelia's watchful eye, my body could acknowledge how worn-out it was. In our defense, it was after three o'clock by now.

"Glad it's not just me," Lance said, rubbing at his eye under his glasses.

"But nothing like a little gossip to get the blood flowing." Dante turned to me. "So, back to the important stuff—Aurelia and Lucian. They were, like, all over each other?" Dante said with his mouth full, something he only did when he was really excited.

"They weren't exactly 'all over each other'; it was just a kiss," I clarified. Dante stopped chewing and looked disappointed by this. "But still interesting, no?"

"Only *mildly* interesting at best, Hav. Please. I mean, look at this place. Of course they're all gonna hook up. It's like a reality show: toss a bunch of gorgeous people in one place, make sure there's a club nearby, booze, the whole thing. It would go against human nature if they didn't all go after each other. You're so precious, Hav."

Lance shrugged and nodded in silent agreement.

"Okay, okay, so my gossip isn't that juicy," I said in a flat tone. "So, what are the rooms like?"

4

Not a Bad Place to Visit

Dante and Lance, as it turned out, were sharing a room. I wasn't sure what this might mean for me. I made my way down in the moaning elevator to the basement level: home sweet home.

"Your rooms are part of our staff quarters and are not as luxe as the rest of the hotel's accommodations," Aurelia had explained to us. "However, I'm sure you'll find them to your liking." She had also mentioned that some members of the Outfit stayed in rooms on this level so it seemed logical to think that I might be paired with one of them. I didn't completely love that idea. On one hand, it could be a quick way to make friends; but on the other, none of them had been especially warm so far, and I got the impression that those barriers might not be broken down no matter how much time we spent together. I hoped I was wrong about that, but my instincts were generally pretty good, even when I didn't want them to be.

The door to my room was located at the very end of the wide, dim hallway. Along the wall to the left was Dante and Lance's room. I was glad to have them so close. I swiped my keycard, quick and sharp, in the lock. Just in case, I knocked softly as I pushed open the door. Nothing. I peeked inside to find my duffel bags and coat sitting on a twin bed—the only bed in the room. Relief washed over me and I exhaled: I would be bunking alone. I plopped down on the bed, which was pushed lengthways against the near wall, and slipped my battered feet out of the torture traps of my shoes, wiggling my toes to regain feeling.

My back against the wall, I surveyed my kingdom. I certainly hadn't expected anything palatial like the guest rooms we had viewed on our tour, so this place seemed just fine. Joan liked to say that much of finding joy in life lay in keeping expectations in check. I didn't always believe that—because I do have a tendency to dream—but in this case she was right. Mine was a slim shoebox of a room, long, narrow, and windowless, but in addition to the bed there was enough space for a desk like those that studded the library (though this one was slightly nicked around the edges), a delicate lavender velvet-cushioned chair, and a wooden four-drawer dresser with those animal-like feet you sometimes see on old furniture. At the far end of the room was a closet the size of a phone booth, and at the opposite end, a bathroom not much larger than the closet.

The color scheme mimicked that of the larger suites we had seen: lavender and green, from the wallpaper and the worn carpet—which also bore the hotel insignia—to the floral comforter and the curtains covering a blank, windowless spot on the wall. (I couldn't imagine why anyone would have gone to such trouble.) Aurelia had informed us this was the original color scheme of the Lexington, but that now only one room per floor retained this pairing—the rest were done in the more opulent burgundy, black, and gold. It was nice to feel a bit of history in my room, even if it wasn't as posh as the renovated rooms in the rest of the place. The basement itself wasn't as bad as it sounded either. It had those same colors in the carpeting and in the faded striped wallpaper on the top half of the wall; the bottom half was a mahogany wood paneling. Very speakeasy.

I looped the duffel bag strap around my leg and dragged it across the bed to me. It seemed as good a time as any to start unpacking. I had just begun taking out sweaters, jeans, rolled-up socks, when a few quick knocks made me jump and then the door burst open. Dante breezed in and plopped down next to me.

"I can't believe you've got your own bachelorette pad and Lance and I have to share," he said with an exaggerated pout.

"Sorry . . . but not that sorry." I smiled.

"You know that dude got almost twenty-four hundred on his SATs?"

"Why is that always the first question you ask people? If you weren't so cute, people would really hate you."

"Let it go, fifteen hundred."

"I don't test well. You're mean."

"Please, you love me. Just saw a bunch of the glamazons in the hall. Can we please revisit our discussion about how everyone is, like, drop-dead gorgeous around here?"

"Must be something in the water."

"Let's hope. Drink up, sister."

"You said it. Seriously though, what's the deal with them?"

"Got me. Sexy, but a total snooze. I feel like there's no personality under their perfect shells."

"I guess personality is overrated: note to self." I shook my head and emptied the last of the duffel, then started in on the second one, stacking everything on the bed surrounding Dante. He just lay there not particularly bothered by the mounding, teetering piles of clothing. I took an armful and kneeled on the floor, sorting them into drawers.

"Who needs personality when you look like *that?*" he said. "Didn't know they even made them that way in the Midwest. At least there's some good eye candy for me. And you, depending on how they swing."

I had to laugh to myself; this was what I loved about Dante. He had declared himself out freshman year—he liked to joke to me that he knew that if he didn't like me in that way then clearly there had to be a reason. It was just flattery but I didn't mind. Of course, being open about his sexuality didn't do much for his popularity. There weren't really any other guys so sure of themselves in our school. But it only made us closer—we threw ourselves into our schoolwork and friendship and bonded over our lack of social lives.

My mind flashed to Lucian. Then I tried to snuff it out. I had no business even thinking of him. He looked high school aged, yet he had this awesome responsibility, this real job. I got the impression he was a sort of wunderkind or something. He had the air of someone who had breezed through school early or else he was doing a gap year before college, like they do in Europe. Or maybe his dad was someone important who'd ushered him into this place. Either way, he was obviously out of the realm of sensible crush objects for me, but I couldn't help it.

Dante read my silence. "Uh-huh. I noticed someone got a look from the superhot sort-of boss."

He knew me too well. "Please." I looked him square in the eye, but my blush gave me away. "You're crazy. And besides, I'm sure I

wouldn't know what to do with him or any of these Outfit characters. As you might have noticed, everyone here is just a little out
of my league."

"Ugh!" he groaned, stomping a foot on the bed. "Enough with
you and your inferiority complex." He threw a pair of balled-up
socks at me, hitting me on the head.

"Hey!"

But he kept the hits coming, pelting me like a batting machine. I swatted and yelped, throwing my hands up to block, until
finally every pair of socks—and I had a lot of them—lay on the
floor around me and the tumult ceased.

"You deserved that."

"Very mature." I laughed, lobbing one back at him .

"Haven, girl, you are no fun. You think *everyone's* out of your
league. You're sixteen now. Own it, baby!"

"Um, sure." I threw myself on the bed, yawning. It was just
after seven in the evening but I was worn-out. I felt more drained
than I ever did after a full afternoon on my feet at the hospital.

"So how are we celebrating anyway?" Dante asked. We both
studied the cracked eggshell surface of the ceiling.

"Oh, I don't know, we really don't—"

"Oh yes we do. We *are* celebrating your birthday, so get over
it." He sat straight up and snapped his fingers. "I've got an idea.
We're going out."

"Define 'out.'"

He sized me up. "If I were a tomboy turning sixteen with limited sartorial resources, what would I wear?"

"I guess not this?" I rolled onto my side, propped my head up
on my arm, and gestured to the business casual attire I had worn
all day.

"Dear god, no. I'm sure we can find something." He sprang up, now on a mission, and began rummaging through the dresser I'd just loaded so neatly. He didn't look thrilled with the selection, but he couldn't have been surprised. I had never been much of a shopper, which he knew. Shopping for me consisted of following him around and scurrying back and forth to the fitting room when he requested new sizes and colors of whatever he was trying on. He had a gift for that type of thing, a style and signature. I was a little more utilitarian in dress. "Tell me you brought some good jeans and not just those beat-up ones you wear all the time—anything but those. Where's your white V-neck T-shirt?"

"In there somewhere." My hand flitted at the dresser he was hunched over. I made no attempt to help. "Tomorrow's our first full day here—I already have an assignment—don't you think we should get our rest?"

He wasn't listening to a word of it though—or else he would have surely mocked me. With his back to me, he opened the top drawer, scanning quickly, then closed it. He tried the middle one—pulling out a pair of jeans and throwing them on his shoulder—and then dug into the bottom drawer, rummaging some more, locating a shirt. He tossed it and the jeans at me, and the shirt landed on my head like I was a coat rack.

"Put that on. I'll give you a belt. It'll be sort of a rocker chick kind of look."

"You're serious?"

He gave me that exasperated look I knew so well, the one with the scrunched-up nose and mouth that said I was trying his patience, then pointed toward the closet, snapping his fingers.

"Okay, okay, okay," I said. I tucked myself behind the closet door, yanking a chain to turn on the bare light bulb above.

"Thank you. You know I live for these rare occasions when you let me play stylist. And someone has always been very pleased with my work."

"I know, I know. So where are we going anyway?" I called to him, slipping out of my pants and button-down, and tugging on the jeans—of course he would've chosen my tightest pair. I pulled on the T-shirt, tucking it in. "Won't I be cold in this? I'm sure it's chilly outside now that it's dark. I think I need—"

"We're not going outside," he replied, cutting me off. "We're going to . . . the Vault."

I burst out of the closet. Dante was curled up on the bed, tossing around a pair of socks I'd missed, but paused to give me a once-over. "Cute," he said, clearly trying to distract me. But I was wearing the look I gave him when I was on the verge of vetoing one of his brilliant ideas—my signal that I was a flight risk.

"I'm sixteen, not twenty-one," I said.

He waved his hands at me to halt my protest. "Please, so am I, get over it already. You know that secretly you totally wanna go. All the cool kids are doing it," he teased. We said this all the time, usually when we weren't about to do anything even remotely close to what the cool kids were doing. "C'mon, seriously, they said we're allowed in, so let's test it." He leaned over and untucked my shirt all around except a bit right in front. "Sloppy chic, I like it."

I barely noticed. Arms folded across my chest, I weighed this possibility, knowing that it wasn't something that should even require convincing. And then I surprised myself.

"Okay," I started carefully. "Suppose, hypothetically, that I did possibly want to see what this Vault business was all about—"

"Really?! Wow, I was expecting I'd have to do a way bigger sales pitch. This is fabulo—"

I held up a hand to hush him.

"Hang on. Just suppose I said yes. You have to promise not to run off and leave me alone there when you get your groove on." On the few occasions we had actually made it to a party, Dante usually inadvertently abandoned me at some point, his ADD kicking in, and I'd be forced to search for him, often finding him dancing—in his own world, not necessarily with anyone—or, more likely, he would have rounded up a group of poor, unsuspecting partygoers for a poker game and he'd be cleaning out every penny they had on them of their parents' money. Being a mathlete did have its advantages, he used to say. Either way, I was left to fend for myself.

He thought about it for less than a second.

"Deal."

I studied myself in the full-length mirror on the back of the closet door.

"So, is this really okay, do you think?"

"Yeah, we've totally made lemonade outta lemons. I've got a belt that'll be perfect. Seriously though, if we start hanging at the Vault every night we're gonna have to get you some new threads."

"We'll see." I took a seat beside him.

"Speaking of . . . ooooh, what's this?" He reached out, taking the pendant of my necklace in his hands, examining it from every angle. "I like it. It's so not you and yet so you." He leaned back to get the full effect.

"I know, right? It's from Joan. Birthday gift." My fingers ran over the smooth ridges of the wing. I could only imagine what Joan would say if she knew I was even entertaining the idea of going to a club.

We waited until a respectable hour—which according to Dante was about eleven o'clock—to launch ourselves into the revelry of the Vault, killing time in my room, while Lance took a nap in theirs. Dante had crept in earlier, while Lance was sprawled fast asleep—his glasses still on—on the bottom of their bunk beds, and procured his promised belt. It was a thick and worn chocolate-brown leather piece adorned with a clunky buckle bearing DANTE in rhinestones.

"Really?" I said as he suited me up, looping it into my jeans.

"It's fierce," he assured me.

On him, yes, but on me, it didn't quite pack the same fashionable ferocity. "I feel like this is one of those tags: 'If lost please return to . . .'"

"Well, you told me not to abandon you, didn't you?" He laughed back, taking great pleasure that this wasn't quite my style. "Love it."

When the time came to get Lance, I hovered while Dante poked him in the arm, getting in a few good jabs before he woke with a start, arms flailing, and rolled right out of bed landing at our feet. We tried to stifle our giggles, but couldn't.

"Rise and shine, time to party," Dante said.

Lance sat up and rubbed his eyes then his elbow; it looked like he had landed on his funny bone. He laughed too.

"Thanks. Kind of. Ow," he said, bending and extending his arm.

Much more low-maintenance than Dante or me, Lance was ready in a flash—he literally rolled out of bed and was set to go. Dante had decked himself out in a pink plaid button-down and his best jeans, the slim dark indigo pair he saved for special occasions. The three of us found our way to that elevator just beyond the lobby, descending in silence, imagining what we might find.

Even before the elevator doors opened, the music hit us,

traveling up the elevator cables and into our car, pulsing. When the jaws did finally part, we were deposited before that imposing steel door. Coming in as we had from the hotel, we had the advantage of no line—most club-goers were forced to queue up in the alleyway outside (among Dumpsters and the occasional rat—not a pretty place; we had seen it that afternoon and were told the line could snake all the way down the side of the building) and then were led inside to another elevator taking them to this point.

This second elevator opened now, disgorging a handful of revelers—three high-heeled, short-skirted women and a pair of blazer-bedecked, open-collared men, all flirting with one another, whispering in one another's ears, complimenting one another's clothes for the sake of giving that guy an excuse to touch the sequins on her dress, or that girl a reason to run her hand along his lapel or undo another button on his shirt. Dante, Lance, and I all traded glances. We got a few looks ourselves, but no one bothered to say anything. The group was granted passage through the checkpoint and into the main event—music crashing out at us as the doors opened and the club swiftly swallowed them.

I could feel the music regulating my heartbeat, forcing it to settle on a new rhythm, something syncopated that my body had trouble keeping up with. My lungs seemed to forget how to take in air, remembering too late and then scrambling for it with a gasp. A blond woman, who had handed us our tote bags earlier today, stood at the door, clipboard in hand, along with another perfect male Outfit specimen by her side. Before today, I hadn't known that people like this existed outside of movie screens and magazine pages. It took so much less to be special at school. I now felt that if I were forced back into a room with the classmates who had seemed so perfect, I would no longer be nearly as intimidated. These people here were absolutely otherworldly.

"Hi there. Dante, and my fellow interns," he started to introduce us. The woman's smoky, black-smudged eyes showed no trace of understanding. But she and the man—as chiseled as Lucian, but a hollow brunette version—just nodded at us, looking not quite at us but rather *through* us. Dante was unconcerned; his eyes bulged at something else: "Wow, man, nice kicks!" He pointed to the man's shoes, a shiny black patent leather—looking sneaker, which looked completely unremarkable to me. "Those are totally the limited edition Palindromes, right? Only fifty in existence?!" He crouched down to get a closer look. "Whoa." The man nodded again, but said nothing. Dante pointed toward the door. "So it's cool if we check the place out?" The woman didn't say a word but the man grabbed hold of a steering-wheel-size dial at the center of the black-painted steel door and pulled it open for us. "Thanks, man," Dante said. We all exchanged jubilant looks, quietly shocked that this was so easy. We were in! I smiled shyly at the man as I passed.

Absorbed into a narrow tube-like corridor of more black-painted steel, we walked slowly toward the riot of flashing lights ahead. Bodies gyrated in the distance. Music wrapped itself around us, flowing into our pores.

"Wow, so many people out on a school night," I said, but my voice came out wispy soft. My companions, whether they heard me or not, were both too captivated to form a response anyway. As we neared the arched end of the walkway, the curved mouth that would lead us out into the club itself, a black light spun, sending its beam speeding around the whole hallway, lighting up scribbles on the walls. Finally, it landed on a patch of the wall to our right. In a luscious script that looked like cake icing, this four-foot-long swatch had been painted with the word *Lust*, which glowed iridescent and alive.

"Nice," Dante said, pointing at it.

Aurelia had explained on our tour that the seven deadly sins were on a shuffle here, and each night a different one would be celebrated. She said it was about branding—a gimmick people would go for, an excuse to serve expensive, signature drinks.

"That's definitely the best of the seven," I said. What did I know, really? But lust is surely more fun to think about than sloth or gluttony. I bet it was lust night often here. Lust was probably good for business.

The light went out as fast as it had flared up and within a few steps we emptied out into the expanse of the club. It was like landing on another planet. For a moment, we were rooted in place, taking it all in as the action swam and spun around us in all directions. The place was easily the same sprawling size of the ballroom but without any of the stuffy formality. Down here, it looked like a cavern and gave the impression of something wildly, alluringly primitive, carved out by nature, yet all with the surface of shiny black licorice. Everything, floor to ceiling, was bathed in this oozing black, but given an infusion of shimmer by the undulating lights in a palette of reds and oranges that danced off everyone's skin and reflected a distinctly devilish, sinister glow. The walls bulged out, lumpy as though riddled with rock formations. A smoky dance area, packed tight with bodies, was cordoned off toward the back. Behind it, a flame roared, running floor to ceiling like a waterfall. From here it looked to be a screen projecting this giant fire, but who could tell?

Horseshoed around the dance floor were layers of seating

and places for cozying up and carousing. Oil-black stalagmites reached up in huge, menacing cones from the floor. Some were carved hollow, with crushed-velvet-cushioned benches inside for couples to rest their weary feet after dancing or to find other ways to set pulses racing. Stalactites in an array of lengths and widths and girths dangled like giant daggers and slim-fingered claws from the ceiling. Tables and banquettes along the outer periphery were recessed back into the walls and aglow in ruby-hued light.

But all of this was nothing compared to the detonated dynamite at the center of the room. A circular platform, raised at least ten feet up with a waist-high wall, had been perched atop another of these rock formation—like structures, and was large enough to seat nearly two dozen with its own nook of a bar and room in the center for dancing. The area teemed with Outfit members. You could just watch them for hours, dancing, drinking, draping themselves on each other. And if that wasn't enough to capture the crowd's collective attention, there was this, which I saw only *after* noticing the Outfit members: a low flame burned around the entire circumference.

"This is probably what hell looks like. Like, in a good way," Dante said finally, when we had been silent for longer than I realized. The three of us were standing there like we were waiting to get picked for teams in gym.

"Yeah, not a bad place to visit," I said.

"But would you want to live there?" Lance offered.

"Depends on how the night goes," I said.

Dante elbowed me. "This from the girl who didn't want to go out at all."

"I know, I know." I shook my head. I was all talk.

"So . . . what now?" Lance said, hands plunged in his pockets, like this was just another day at work.

"I know," Dante said, a hint of trouble ringing his voice. I peeled my eyes from the whirlwind swirling around us and looked at him, following his line of vision.

"No, Dan, you've got to be kidding me."

He was staring straight at the platform with the Outfit.

5

Welcome to the Ring of Fire

"Let's just try to go up there," Dante said. Not waiting for an answer, he took off, a bullet straight to the heart of the room. Lance had taken off his glasses, wiping the lenses on his Cubs shirt, and could only squint in the direction of Dante's destination.

"Shall we?" I asked him.

Lance shrugged and smiled.

Waves of revelers, drinks in their hands, coursed around me as I darted between them, in and out, almost jogging to catch up to Dante. I looked over my shoulder and caught sight of Lance, glasses back on now, his head peeking out over most everyone else's. He kept his own easy pace, looking around, taking it all in. Dante was already halfway up a spiral staircase hidden amid the rocky mass leading to the platform.

"Hey!" I called up from the bottom.

"What're you waiting for? Get up here!" he called back, his grin wide and his perfect white teeth gleaming pink in the light.

I climbed the coiled steps and grabbed for his arm when I got close enough, halting his ascent. He looked back at me with impatient eyes.

"I know you think I'm no fun, but seriously, do you think we're allowed up there?"

"Only one way to tell." He beamed. "C'mon, where's your sense of adventure? Honestly, Haven, the worst thing that happens, they say no." He continued upward and I let go of him.

He was right; I was making too big a deal of this. We had already gotten into the club, after all, so it didn't seem anyone was too concerned about our presence here. I followed him twisting up and up and up. I spotted Lance just below; he hooked my eye with a quick smile.

Steps away from the top, I saw Dante already seated on the black crushed-velvet bench that ran along the rim of the circle. The Outfit members we'd seen earlier danced in the center and gazed out onto the dance floor, making eye contact with some of the partygoers. Dante waved me over, patting at the sliver of an empty seat between him and a table stocked with all manner of partially drained bottles.

"Looks like we're in," I said.

"Nerds' night out!" He thrust both arms in the air, cheering. Then stopped abruptly, resuming his party pose, slouching back on the cushy bench.

"Right, because the important thing now is to play it cool and look like we belong," I joked.

"It goes without saying."

"So how'd you get us in?"

"I asked and they just gave me that look." He did it now, the vacant stare over my shoulder. I let a quick laugh escape and glanced around to be sure no one noticed. No one was looking at us at all.

Lance appeared at the top of the steps. Since we were hemmed in by the table beside me and a gaggle of the long-limbed Outfit girls beside Dante, he found a seat across the circle from us.

"We need some props," Dante said. "Switch with me, I'm going to familiarize myself with the bar." He got up and I shifted over to his seat.

"Um, I don't think we should—"

"Relax, I'll keep the cocktails strictly virgin for you. Hey, Lance!" he called out through the sea of milling Outfit members. Dante made a motion with his empty hand, like he was drinking something, then pointed back at Lance. "Anything?"

I shielded my face behind my hand, on reflex, as though this small action could hide me. I thought the idea was to not draw too much attention to ourselves. I had the feeling that Aurelia would find out about anything that happened tonight. Drinking was probably not the best idea.

"Sure, thanks. Surprise me," Lance called back. He leaned back into his seat, content to watch the electric current travel between all of these figures around us.

Dante, bobbing his head to the music, looked like he was doing an experiment in AP Chemistry—holding up his glass as he poured in each new liquid, touching his fingers to his lips, deep in thought, deciding what to add next. I had to laugh watching him: he didn't really know what he was doing. This just wasn't something we ever did. We had decided early on that we didn't want to be those kids who got wasted and sloppy on weekends, and then we had really sealed our fate by getting elected co-presidents of the Students Against Destructive Decisions chapter at school. So that was that. I had had no more than a few sips of alcohol in my entire life.

Recipe complete, Dante weaved between the beautiful people

to deliver to Lance his concoction, a tall glass brimming with an amber liquid. He nodded in appreciation and Dante crossed back toward me. "You're next!" He pointed, making pistols out of his hands.

Across the way, I spied Lance's taste test. He tossed back his head, taking his first gulp, then spit it right back in the glass. He made a face and wiped his mouth on the back of his hand. He caught me looking and shook his head at me. I chuckled to myself. Dante, who missed the response to his bartending skills, parked himself on the other side of the table and began mixing some more. Another amber-colored libation took form, and he allowed himself a healthy guzzle. He looked at me, rolling his eyes.

"I know what you're thinking. When in Rome, okay? Let's have some fun for a change. No one here knows us, it's amazing! Reinvention, baby!"

I put my hands up, surrendering. "I didn't say anything."

A song with a throbbing Tommy-gun beat cranked up and everyone who was standing in our area began swaying, moving. Dante hopped up from his seat, drink in hand, and took to the dance floor, in his own world now. I was on my own. I watched the bodies around him. Some of the men had rolled up their sleeves, while those in jackets had taken them off, revealing muscles that were perfectly formed and rock solid. The girls looked so at ease, dancing in the highest heels I'd ever seen. I studied everything: the cut of their dresses, the way they parted their hair, the length of their eyelashes. A girl twirled, finishing her move with her back to me. She wore a one-shoulder plum dress that came to a screeching halt midway down her thigh. She swung her glossy auburn locks and I caught a glimpse of her bare shoulder: it seemed to be looking back at me. Branded there was a tattoo of an open eye so vivid I thought it might blink. The iris was black with a white pupil and a pentagram inside it, and it was fringed with lashes of orange and red, resembling a burning flame. It looked oddly familiar. And then, a glance at the crowd before me showed me why: I spotted another tattoo on the bicep of one of the guys, peeking out just below his sleeve; and one on the ankle of a blond woman with miles of wavy hair.

The girl with the ankle tattoo and all the hair drifted off from the group, appearing at the table beside me. I tried not to stare as she lifted an open bottle of champagne from an ice bucket and pulled a crystal champagne flute from the neat rows of glasses lining the back of the table. Bubbles frothed as she poured. I recognized her from my Googling: Raphaella. She was a model and socialite, always going to the best parties and photographed with important people. I had seen a few of these faces show up in my search, now that I thought about it. The one with the shoulder tattoo, Calliope, had been written about in an art magazine or something like it.

With delicate fingers, Raphaella held the glass out to me. "Cheers," she said. "This is liquid gold. Aurelia's favorite. The best you'll ever taste." The gesture was warm but her tone wasn't so much; it felt a little like she was doing a job. I caught myself before getting too hung up on it: *Haven, try to be a little less sensitive for a change, please?* I took the glass from Raphaella's hand.

"Oh, wow, thanks." Her chilliness aside, I was still oddly touched. It was kind of nice to feel included, even if I didn't plan to drink it. I looked over at Lance. He hadn't touched his drink. He sat there, almost invisible, taking everything in from behind those glasses, his hair still messy from his nap. He and I were like bookends, fencing in this party that raged between us.

Raphaella poured a glass of champagne for herself and took

a seat next to me, crossing her endless spider's legs. She took a dainty sip from her slender glass. I decided I should try to be friendly.

"You're Raphaella, right?" She nodded and smiled softly, her kohl-rimmed eyes two beautiful blank buttons. "I've seen you in magazines and things. You must have such an exciting life modeling and all. Do you hang out here a lot? I just started this internship. I'm really excited to be here." I was rambling now. There was a long, painful pause.

"I would be nowhere without Aurelia and the Outfit," she said, as if it were the most obvious and mundane of facts repeated emotionlessly millions of times, such as Chicago is cold in the winter.

"Aurelia said that being here can open doors. I guess she really meant it."

"She did. I promise you." This she said sternly, as though making sure I was paying attention. Then she smiled again, taking another sip.

"That's good to know. Do you have any exciting upcoming jobs?"

"Yes, there's the cover of the *Chicago Tribune*'s Sunday magazine next month, *Chicago* magazine's special spring fashion edition, and spreads in *Glamour* and *Seventeen*." She said it all much more flatly than I would have if it had been me with that news to tell. "I'm sorry," she said before turning away to whisper something to the girl seated beside her with the pin-straight jet-black hair and almond-shaped eyes.

I pretended to be fascinated watching the fizz of my champagne. The flames behind me breathed heat onto my neck. They were a tough group, these people, tough in a different way than the kids at school. There, they were just rude and hostile with no manners whatsoever, but here there was something else, an iciness I couldn't understand. I wanted to know where all these beautiful people had come from that they were so oddly alike. Dante was dancing in the middle of the group, but by himself. I looked through the mob to Lance. He gave a sympathetic shrug—he had seen me literally get the cold shoulder. I answered him back with a shake of the head and felt the embarrassment dissipate, newly calmed. Raphaella looked over her shoulder, canvassing the grounds below. The thought of sitting any longer in silence seemed worse than having to try again. So I did. No one knew us here, as Dante said. I could be brave.

"I, um, like your necklace," I said, sounding like a child. But it *was* pretty impressive: a stiff black-velvet ribbon choker holding what looked like an amethyst the size of a walnut. I glanced quickly again at that girl on the dance floor, Calliope—yes, she had one too. And I spotted one on another delicate swan-like neck or two on the other side of the platform. I pictured these women all shopping together, roaming the mall at Water Tower Place or perhaps ducking into some of those precious boutiques in Wicker Park that Joan always tried to get me into. I could imagine them walking down the street, shopping bags in hand, talking and laughing at inside jokes, and not even noticing the stares they got as they passed. Raphaella touched the stone with raisin-painted nails and smiled once more.

"Thank you."

Calliope, finished dancing for the moment, appeared with a drink in her hand and Raphaella slid over to make room for her between us.

"I'm Calliope," she said, holding out her hand for me to

shake. Her periwinkle eyes seemed somehow slightly more alive than Raphaella's. I shook her firm grip.

"Hi, I'm—"

"Haven, of course," she said, surprising me. "Are they recruiting you?" She said it with a seriousness I couldn't make sense of, leaning in closer to me. I didn't quite understand the question.

"Oh, well, we were just—"

"There's a lot to learn here," Calliope said sincerely. Raphaella set her hand on Calliope's forearm, and they exchanged a look that seemed to tell Calliope she was done talking to me, because she didn't say another word. She simply nodded blankly at Raphaella and then they gazed over the low flames to scan the scene below us. I followed Calliope's eyes until I saw her lock in on him. He wasn't one of the Outfit; just another guy out for an evening with his buddies. And he saw her.

Calliope simply smiled, perfect and gleaming. She flicked her head and that was it. The man wandered over toward our platform, staring up at her. She beckoned him with her slim fingers. Then she and Raphaella looked knowingly at each other. I imagined Raphaella was equally skilled in this sort of mating call. I had always wished to be the kind of girl who could rely on simply a smile to ensnare anyone. Win anyone over. They knew they had an advantage: that they were desired, and that was half the battle, more than half, toward getting anything *they* desired. Instant confidence lay behind smiles like that. Others of us shared the burden of having to develop some personality, which actually took time and cultivation; it's a much slower process wrought by trial and error.

"Have a good night, Haven. If you'll excuse me," said Calliope, as she rose gently from her seat and glided over to the top of the spiral staircase. In no time, he was there, looking nervous and thrilled.

I felt the champagne glass being pried from my fingers and I whipped my head around. Lucian.

It took me a moment to realize he was talking to me. What did he say? I think it was "Hello, Haven." But I might have been wrong. Was it possible he remembered my name? He sat down beside me, in the space left blissfully vacant by Calliope. There wasn't much room and his arm touched my shoulder as he settled into place. A wave of his musk and cedar scent enveloped me and made me lightheaded. He wore a black suit, white button-down shirt, and a skinny black tie. Everyone here was so dressed up all the time. His hair, which had been so smoothly slicked back earlier, was looser now, a blond forelock draping his left eye.

"Welcome to the ring of fire."

"Hi. Um, thanks." I struggled to get the words out. I felt my lips trembling and pursed them together to hold them still.

"And happy birthday," he said, slowly, in that voice that could lull me to a deep and warm sleep.

"Thanks. How did you know?" I could only look at him in short bursts. I would look for a second or two and then fix my eyes quickly somewhere else, letting them refocus, before locking on him again. He made me too nervous. A heat rose to my face.

"We know everything." His gray eyes beaming at me with a hint of that mischief I'd seen earlier today. "And, I'm afraid, Haven—" I was unable to mask my amazement that, yes, he had in fact remembered my name. "Champagne"—he held up the glass he had taken from me—"is too ordinary for a day like this. Here." He handed me a goblet with a blue flame dancing on top of the liquid inside. This drink en flambé had apparently been in his hands the whole time and I just hadn't noticed it; that's how distracted I was by him.

"Wow, thanks." I took it in both hands and watched the flame lick at the air, flickering between shades of blue and orange. What was I supposed to do with this? I worried I might somehow set fire to myself—I was clearly a little shaky. His arm brushed against mine again. "Um, I'm sixteen actually," I blurted out. I don't know why. I could not have been less cool. It was a struggle to keep my face from twisting into some kind of freakish, distorted cringe. My biggest problem, I scolded myself, was getting in my own way, derailing anything remotely exciting that might possibly happen.

"I know. Cheers." He took a swig from my old champagne glass. "I won't tell if you won't." There was no way he was twenty-one either. No. Way.

"What exactly is this anyway?" I tried to make my tone as light and carefree as possible in an effort to redeem myself. *This? Oh, sure, it's nothing. I drink fiery cocktails every day.*

"A house specialty. You'll love it."

"I guess you don't worry much about fire codes around here, huh?"

"Obviously not." He laughed and took another sip of champagne. "So, go on, make a wish."

A wish. Well, where to begin? I watched it burn and glanced quickly at his face. My heart quivered when I found that he was still looking at me. "Umm . . ."

"Relax, you've got some time. Let it burn itself out. It'll burn off the alcohol." He raised his eyebrow at me again, as he had that morning.

"Ohhhh. Good to know."

"Don't worry, we play by the rules here. Most of the time." He drained his champagne glass and reached across me to set it on the table.

"Glad to hear it." Nothing more enticing than a girl who follows the rules.

"Now be careful with that," Lucian said in a light, almost mocking tone. With one quick motion, he flicked my long hair over my shoulder and tucked a strand behind my ear, out of the way from the drink's small flame. I had to focus to firm up my grip on the chalice. "Enjoy," he said, rising to his feet. He swooped down toward me and, with his hand set lightly on my chin, kissed my cheek. The shock of it, of his warm lips against my flushed skin, sent every bit of feeling rushing to my head. I was sure the blush was overtaking my face. I saw it and felt it all in slow motion, assigning a weight to the action, something important and special between us. But I was smart enough to know that his days were likely filled with millions of kisses like this. Weren't they? He slipped away as quickly as he had appeared, absorbed into the crowd on the platform and then down the stairs and gone. I stared after him, not really seeing anything.

It took me a while to realize the tapping at my shoulder was Dante. He had come to sit next to me. I turned my head toward him and tried to catch up on what he was saying. His lips were moving so fast but my brain was moving so slow. The music had gotten louder. My drink, in this ridiculously large glass in my hands, felt heavy again. I tried to pay attention.

" . . . could not stop watching, it was unbelievable . . . I look up and you're in the middle of this little tête-à-tête with the boss. He's absurdly hot, it's out of control. So?"

His skin was slick from so much dancing.

"So?" My thoughts were coming down the pipeline again, only very slowly.

"So, what was that about? I'm dying here!" He leaned forward, making sweeping gestures with his hands. "I have to hear everything."

"I think I like the ring of fire."

"I don't know what you're talking about, but I like what you're sayin'."

"That's where we are—this is the ring of fire; that's what he said."

"What else? Tell me more."

"He gave me this for my birthday. Did you see? It was on fire!" I was beginning to break a sweat. The flame was long gone, but I blew into the glass just to be safe, rippling the surface with my breath. I lifted it to take a sip then stopped. "He said the alcohol burned off. From a scientific point of view, that sounds correct, wouldn't you say?"

"Theoretically, yes," Dante concurred. "Want me to try?" He grabbed it from my hands and took a sip. "You're fine, drink up."

"Thanks." I took a tentative sip. It tasted like carbonated fruit punch. I hadn't realized how thirsty I was—I kept drinking like it was one of those sports drinks and I'd just run a marathon.

"What did he *say*?" Dante pressed on.

"Not much really. He said to make a wish."

"Smooth. He's smooth," he said, with cool admiration. "I'm not surprised."

"Yeah, I guess," I said, my voice losing some of its steam and wild optimism. I knew I was blowing things out of proportion. I tried to bring myself back down to earth. "I'm sure it was all no big deal."

Dante shrugged, thinking it over.

And I jumped back in: "But I mean that whole bit with my hair, did you see that?" He nodded. "Was that just a safety precaution or something else?" I asked. He took it seriously, hand to his chin, thinking, thinking.

Finally: "Now, I want to say it was possibly something else."

"You do . . ." I brightened.

He continued, "But prudence dictates that we monitor the situation before getting too excited."

"Can we get a little excited?"

"A little excitement is definitely permissible since it's your birthday."

I smiled in a big way and whispered, "Yay."

He laughed. I settled back into the soft confines of the bench. Peaceful waves crashed over me. I felt like rays of light were shooting from my pores, and my skin was hot but so awake. Yet my mind was so much the opposite. The music, throbbing as it was, wooed me to sleep; the sparkling flames and the tremble of activity around us all carried me off. My eyes may have drooped shut; either that or I just couldn't remember what I had been looking at for the past several minutes.

"That blonde sure has been talking to Lance for a while, even though he's just sitting there. I'll have to give you both lessons in flirting," Dante said.

"Sure," I said, now certain that my eyes were closed. But I just couldn't open them.

"Uh-oh, someone's crashing."

"Who?" I felt myself slur.

It was after two when I made it back to my room, with great assistance from Dante and Lance. I remembered little between my talk with Dante in the ring of fire and getting tucked into my bed. But I did notice as we crossed the lobby to the elevator bank to descend to our rooms that the chandelier in the center of that majestic entranceway looked even better at night than during the day. Those white lights that Lance had counted were reflected in the skylight, making the night sky appear even more star-studded. Of course, some of the stars may have been provided by my own jumbled and slippery consciousness. Everything around me had begun spinning before I left the club and bursts of light that I knew no one else was seeing twinkled in my periphery.

Dante had nestled me into my bed, still in my party clothes, and flipped off the light, saying something that I heard only muffled, but that seemed to be a promise to check on me in the morning. My head was a lead weight crushing the pillow. Now that I was in bed, my body completely dropped its defenses. Everything ached. I was sweating torrents. My muscles felt like they were contracting and tearing, twisting like wet rags being wrung out. My stomach swam and lurched, a toxic pool threatening to rise up. But I was too drained to get up again so I just tried to imagine away the nausea. With my eyes closed I could still feel the rush of the spinning—it felt like I was being whipped around on that ride they had at the summer fair every year, the Scrambler. I let myself drift into sleep knowing I had to feel better on the other side of this.

6

It'll Probably Be Just Hideous

Ididn't know where I was when I woke up. I scanned the room
and then slowly it came back to me: the Lexington. My body
tested out movement, shifting, rolling to my side. *Ow*, everywhere,
ow, but especially my head. I touched my fingers lightly to the spot
near my right temple—*ow* again—it felt a little mushy, like a rot-
ten banana. What was wrong with me? I retraced my steps: the
room spinning, the club, Lucian and that drink—that drink! Was
this my first hangover? Was it possible there was enough booze
left in that drink to have done this to me? All of yesterday flooded
back. I hadn't called Joan, had I? How had I let that slip? Was it
too early now?

The bedside lamp was still on and it seemed blinding. The
numbers of the clock looked my way, the hands pointing with
rigid urgency. It had to be wrong, didn't it? It was just 2:00 in
the morning a second ago. I pulled it closer to me: it was, in fact,
7:45 a.m.

I took the world's fastest shower and didn't even bother washing my hair. I threw on my nice gray pants and a sweater, ran to
the elevator, rode up to the lobby, and sprinted to the ottoman

that sat like a sundial below the skylight. My watch read 8:02. I was alone. I breathed a sigh.

My body slunk onto the ottoman, shoring up strength for the day to come. I felt like I had been hooked to the back of a truck and dragged along the road. If I weren't here, I would have stayed home from school—and I never did that. Sun streamed down from the skylight, all blue and cloudless above. I raised my face and closed my eyes, letting the sunlight warm me, and felt myself drifting for a moment. I really needed to call Joan. If I didn't watch it, she'd be down here to check on me. I could see it now, her pulling up out front in the old Camry, strolling in, claiming she just happened to be in the neighborhood. I laughed to myself, which hurt my ribs, but the smile was still on my lips.

As sick as I was last night, and unsettled as my footing was in this strange place, the past twenty-four hours were probably among the most exciting of my life. This is what I had needed—to spring from the comfortable and protective confines of home, even to stumble. And there would be more of that, I was pretty sure. A telltale swishing rustled in the distance, from the direction of the elevator bank. I opened my eyes. Aurelia in heels and an elegant sleeveless black wrap-dress sashayed toward me, arms strong and firm. I stood, hands folded behind my back, trying to look the part of the perfect employee.

"Good morning, Ms. . . . Aurelia." I caught myself.

"Why, yes it is a good morning, isn't it, Haven?" she said as she reached me, just a hint of a smile. Her light waves brushed at her shoulders and her sapphire eyes twinkled, in a way that suggested she was looking forward to putting me through the wringer. "We have so much to accomplish today. I trust you've eaten and you're ready to get started?"

The idea of food made my stomach wrench. I still didn't feel quite ready for solids. If I had been hungry and had had more time, I would have explored the kitchen near the Parlor. She had told us yesterday that we were welcome to take meals in there whenever we pleased, at a table back near the meat locker, where we could park ourselves away from the customers. We weren't supposed to frequent the other restaurant, Capone—the more upscale dining room—where the kitchen would be harried and hectic. Aurelia had given us the impression we would be getting in the way if we were ever anywhere near there.

"I'm, uh, just fine, thank you."

"Very well, come to my office. I have some materials for you." She had already started walking, so I hustled to catch up.

"Thanks," I said shyly, then remembered. "Oh, um, speaking of materials, you didn't by chance leave a notebook for me in the library?"

"Did you lose something already, my lamb?" She sounded both annoyed and confused.

"No, I just . . . sorry, never mind." It appeared that empty book hadn't been from Aurelia. She pushed open a door—the door I had seen her and Lucian step out of twenty-four hours ago.

At first glance, the room looked like it should be the office of a grizzled old man who smoked cigars and told tales of drinking his way through Prohibition. The walls were paneled in the same cherrywood of the library shelves, and the floor was dominated by a battleship of a desk, a thick, boxy piece that must have consumed a forest of trees. It looked antique, with etched vine-like designs creeping along the sides and bordering the top, but it had been shined and polished. Behind the desk on a TV screen old and new shots of the hotel alternated on a loop. The only feminine touches were a sleek red-velvet sofa with gold feet and goldenrod and tiger-striped pillows and two matching tiger-print armchairs.

Aurelia settled in behind the desk and I quickly took a seat in one of the chairs facing her.

"Today you will photograph the members of the Outfit, Lucian, and your fellow interns, just as you photographed me yesterday. I've made a schedule here." She handed me a print-out with an endless stream of poetic names—some I already recognized from last night and new ones like Genevieve and Celine, Sebastian and Finn—and times beginning at ten o'clock. "Everyone will be coming to you ready to go. I have your attire for today as well. I trust you'll be able to photograph yourself or will you need someone to do it for you?"

My questions bubbled up. We were going to be included in this project? And what did she mean by "attire"? But I answered, "Sure, there's a timer and I believe I saw a remote control too."

"Excellent. With the exception of our chef, everyone else is here and you should be able to complete the shoot today." She tucked a strand of hair behind her ear and leaned back in her chair. She was so certain, and she spoke in such a controlled, firm way. "We won't trouble ourselves with the process of select-ing photos until tomorrow. If there's nothing else, you're free to go." She slid a slim keycard across her desk leaving it on the edge for me.

"Thank you." As I rose to leave, she had already begun flip-ping through a stack of papers.

The photo studio had been left almost exactly as it had been yesterday. The only difference today: a white ribbed tank top had been folded and left neatly on the stool with a piece of paper pinned to it reading "Haven." I held it up, letting it unfold. It had a bit of a scooped neck, which made me nervous. I couldn't tell how it would lie on me. I set it aside and tried not to think about it.

Raphaella appeared at 10:00 on the nose, slinking in without a sound. I just turned around and there she was. "Hi," I said. "I guess this'll be a cakewalk for you, right? You're a pro."

"I'll do my best," she said. Somehow, she seemed even more reserved than last night. Maybe she just didn't like me. I'd hoped her casual dress would make her more laid-back, but I guess I was wrong. Today, she was in dark, slim jeans that clung to her with great affection, and a similar white tank top—which would look far different on me. On her, it was an event. That necklace, the amethyst, glinted in the light.

"Did you stay late last night?" I tried again. "I was pretty wiped out when I left."

"A little while," she said, perfectly polite, but something was still off. Maybe it was just that necessary divide between an intern and someone so much more established at a workplace. Maybe this was how it was in every office. I guess, now that I thought about it, some of the doctors at the hospital could be a little aloof. I tried not to take it personally. She took a seat on the stool, and I decided to focus on my job instead of my hypersensitive feelings. I snapped my shots. In no time I had what I needed, Raphaella was out the door, and my next subject had arrived.

They filed in all day long, impeccably punctual, unflappably silent—a parade of designer jeans, collectively representing the denim departments from the nicest shops on Michigan Avenue, with the men in immaculate white V-neck T-shirts and the women in tank tops. All but two or three had that same tattoo, the eye with the pentagram pupil and fiery lashes. A handful of girls wore that amethyst necklace, and a few of the guys had thick beat-up black leather cuffs on their wrists featuring a small skull and crossbones in silver, with tiny black stones in the skull's eye sockets. I'd have to find out where these people shopped. The tattoos I wasn't so sure about—one of those might look ridiculous on me. Besides, Joan, I was quite sure, would kill me.

I gave up trying to talk much when very few responded to me. Even Calliope, who had shown brief signs of warmth the night before, was a little more standoffish today. "I'd love to see some of your artwork sometime," I offered. "It would be amazing to be able to paint or draw, but I really never could."

She just smiled and said, "Maybe sometime." It was almost as if she wanted to say more but had to shut her lips tighter to keep from interacting with me. I just let it go. What can you do?

On the plus side, at least none of these people required any direction: they knew how to move and pose; it seemed second nature to them. If Aurelia wanted to turn this place into a modeling agency, she had all the natural resources she needed.

The Outfit members adhered so firmly to the schedule that by two o'clock I had finished the last session. It was Beckett, the doorman from last night with the shoes Dante had loved so much. I had never seen arms like that so close up—rippled and straining the short sleeves of his shirt. He had just left and I began flipping through a few of the photos on the camera to see what I got—so far, so good—when Dante burst through the door.

"I'm ready for my close-up, darling," he announced, bowing as he entered. "But you've got to get rid of this bad boy in retouching." He pointed to a minuscule zit on his chin. I just shook my head, laughing.

fterward, Dante, Lance, and I decided another leisurely lunch was in order and took our table in the Parlor for grilled cheese and fries, intended as a cure for my hangover. My appetite was finally returning.

"I hear my boss comes back tomorrow, so we'd better do this while we can," Dante told us, his voice tinged with a nervousness I wasn't used to hearing.

We finished up and Lance changed into his white T-shirt and met me back in the studio. He knocked, to be polite.

"Hey, all set?" I waved him in.

"I think so. Didn't realize we were going to be part of the decoration around here."

"Yeah, tell me about it. I'm as thrilled as you are."

"That's good to hear." A few seconds of silence passed. He didn't budge from the doorway. "So what do I do?"

I pointed at the setup in front of the camera. "You can sit or stand or anything and I'll just snap a few and we'll call it a day. Sound okay?"

"Sure. So, like, stand here?" He took his place beside the stool, moving as if his slim arms and legs didn't have any joints.

"Perfect."

He stood in that pose I'd seen him strike so often, with his hands plunged in his pockets, slouching. He smiled only slightly and he didn't move an inch. I snapped a few shots and then noticed a problem: not only did his glasses cast a shadow on his face, they also reflected the light in a way I knew I wasn't skilled enough to fix. Not that I wanted to let on.

"Great!" I coached. "We're almost done. I feel like I should get a couple without your glasses." He tensed up, his arms straightening as he took a step back. "It's just that," I spoke softly in case anyone was in earshot, "I sometimes have trouble with glare, and

Aurelia will kill me if this comes back with flashes of light where your eyes should be."

He eased. "That wouldn't be so bad; it would just be a little more in the vein of modern art, right?" he joked—I think.

"True . . . but I don't think we're going for avant-garde here."

"Well, in that case." He took them off, blinking a few times to adjust and then hooked his frames so they hung on the V of his shirt. He looked in my general direction but not quite at me. He put one hand in his pocket and awkwardly held that forearm with the other; he was ready for this to be over. I centered my shot and, for the first time, noticed a slim line the length of a stick of gum just under his right eye where the bottom of his glasses usually hit. After several minutes of snapping, I looked up from the camera and nodded.

"Good enough?" he asked.

"Yes, definitely."

He smiled shyly, putting his glasses back on. He looked at me and then away. "Thanks. I guess, I'll . . ." He pointed to the door, already walking away.

"Sure, see you later." I gave him a wave and he slipped out.

Alone for the first time all day, I couldn't stifle my yawns anymore. But there was still work to be done. I uploaded the photos in the office, then changed into that tank top. I found the fancy remote control for the camera and settled Indian-style in a spot on the hard white floor. If I didn't move much, I could keep my scar from peeking out of the scooping neckline. I held my smile, hit the button, and heard the faintest of clicks.

I didn't hear the soft knock at the unlocked door.

"Hello?" A voice called out to me before I saw where it was coming from.

I hit the button again as I fumbled in surprise and the shutter sounded its click-click, snapping a few last shots.

Lucian appeared in the space behind the camera.

"So sorry to interrupt," he said in that honeyed voice, rich and deep. "I can come back later, whenever you want me."

"No, hi, um, not at all. I was just finishing up." I lunged for my sweater, pulling it on, then smoothed out my staticky hair and scrambled to my feet. "So, yeah, let's, um, switch places. You should be over here, in the spotlight and everything." My thoughts weren't quite making it out in full sentences. "This'll be fast. I'm sure you're busy." I adjusted the camera, angling it to properly frame him.

He milled around near the stool, loosening his tie, and looked at me. "What do you think: is the tie too much for this? Too stuffy?" He crinkled his face, like a kid who didn't like what was being served for dinner.

I was so flattered to have my opinion sought, I just stared at first, but then I really looked, studying him piece by piece.

"Well, there's definitely no wrong answer," I reasoned aloud, perhaps too candidly. "It's all degrees of good. Maybe compromise—untie it but leave it sort of hanging there?" It came out like a question even though I had meant it as a statement. I took a step forward, thinking that this should be the part where I loosen his tie, right? Dante would say, "Of course, fool, what are you waiting for?" But I could only take that one step. Lucian waited for a moment, as though that convergence of time and space had been an invitation, and then finally he untied it himself. He took a seat on the stool, one foot on the ground, the other perched on one of the rungs. "Okay, um, smile," I said.

"Whatever you say." He grinned for a second and then his face settled, not on a pose, but rather he just sat there watching me. I snapped, letting the clicks and the shots accumulate. *Rat-tat-tat-tat-tat.*

"So will I see you at the Vault tonight?" he asked, as though forgetting entirely that he was supposed to be posing.

I glanced up. "Um, I don't really know." And then back at the camera again. *Rat-tat-tat-tat.*

"Ohhh, is that right?" He said it as if I was purposely being cagey and just wanted to be convinced.

"I'm still sort of recovering from last night," I admitted.

"That's the sign of a good birthday," he said, his eyes twinkling. I kept snapping even though I imagined nearly every single one of the photos I'd already taken would have been worthy of display.

"Well, then, I suppose I had a great one."

"True or false: I heard you needed an escort back to your room," he said, teasing me.

"I'm going to plead the fifth on that," I said shyly. He laughed again, which, for some reason, made me blush.

"Wouldn't want to make you incriminate yourself."

"Thanks," I said, then it occurred to me: "And if you wouldn't mind maybe not telling Aurelia . . ." No need for news of my tipsiness to go any further.

"Wouldn't dream of it," he said, in all seriousness.

"Thanks." I breathed a little sigh of relief. "I don't know what you people put in those drinks."

"For the record, everything should've burned off."

"Well, then I guess it was some kind of immaculate intoxication." I fiddled again with the camera.

"You're funny," he said sincerely.

"Thanks." I was pretty sure I was blushing again. It seemed I was flirting, unexpectedly, and doing a decent job of it. *Good work, Haven.*

"So what do you think?" He got up from the stool and walked toward me. I snapped one more picture before he got too close.

"Oh. Yeah, we're all set here, thanks."

"No, I mean, the Vault tonight? Or, okay, I sense you're somewhat reluctant to return to the scene of the crime." He was making fun of me, but sweetly enough that I didn't take offense. I smiled and shook my head. "So, if I were to stop by your room later, on my way to grab a different drink, like, say, a coffee, what are the odds you might be around?"

"I'd say . . . pretty good." Dante would love this.

"I'd say that's a pretty good answer." He started retying his tie. "Thanks for this. Look forward to seeing the picture. Hope it turns out okay."

"Yeah, you're a real tough subject. It'll probably be just hideous. Lots of retouching." He let out a little laugh. "See you later, then."

As soon as he stepped out the door, I realized I'd barely been breathing for the past several minutes. My chest fluttered inside, inflating to full capacity finally.

My work done for the day, I decided to catch up on some personal business: calling Joan at last. I couldn't get cell reception anywhere in my room or the entire lobby, so I found my way outside. The bitter cold chilled me instantly, blasting through the knit of my sweater to my skin. Once outside, my Calls Received box appeared: seven missed calls from Joan. Seven. That was actually fewer than I expected. I wrapped my sweater more tightly around my body, hugging it to me, dialed fast, and then pulled the sleeves over my hands.

Joan answered before the first ring was completed and wanted to hear everything. I told her an edited version of my birthday celebration and answered all the typical questions about whether I was eating enough (yes) or working too hard (no) or ready for her to come visit (not yet). Even though I rolled my eyes at each question, it was nice to be checked on. I missed her.

That task completed, I retreated to my room. My eyes were just fluttering shut, a catnap in my grasp, when three quick knocks rattled the door. I flipped the light on and shook the life back into my head, perking up. A peek through the peephole showed Lance there, hands dug into his pocket, something tucked under his arm. He pushed his glasses higher up on his nose and rocked back and forth on his feet. I glanced in the mirror quickly, smoothed out my knotted hair, and opened the door.

"Hey."

"Hey. Sorry to bother you," he said.

"No, not at all. I'm glad I'm not the only one who's off-duty for the day."

"Nope, I packed it in too. Hard to tell when the day is supposed to be over, right? Without, you know, a bell going off."

"Yeah. Maybe we can have Dante run around with his bell every day at a certain time."

"That's an idea. Or, you know, our bosses could tell us or something."

"Yeah, that would be helpful too." He laughed at this. I decided to ask what I'd been wondering: "So what's he like anyway? Lucian?" I felt my heart pick up its pace. What would I have done if I had been paired with him as my mentor? I probably would have been too nervous to focus on anything resembling work.

"I guess I don't really know," Lance said, after giving the question some thought. "He seems okay. So far, he just gives me stuff to do then disappears all day to do more important things and never comes back."

I nodded. "Aurelia is the same way."

We were quiet for a moment. And then Lance shook his head, remembering. "Oh, so I found this one today and it's a really good one; thought you'd like it too." He held out a tattered book, the title on its worn, dusty cover: *Secret Chicago*.

"Cool, thanks." I took it, flipping it over to read the back. "Are you sure you don't want to read it first?"

"I skimmed through a little. Get this, there used to be tons of secret tunnels running under all these buildings right around here. They would pass booze back and forth during Prohibition."

"Seriously?" I fanned through the pages.

"I know, crazy stuff. You'll see."

"Thanks a lot."

"Sure thing." He started backing away. We traded smiles and he waved. "Later."

I watched until he got swallowed up into his room. He was awkward but cute, which, I imagined, was probably something people said about me, if I was lucky. They also described me as awkward, undeniably, but hopefully cute too.

*D*ante came by as soon as he was finished for the day and, of course, he was thrilled with my coffee date news. He even rigged up a date-worthy ensemble for me, basically consisting of my photo shoot attire and one of his ties as a sort of belt. And then he gave me the necessary pep talk.

"So, what's your opening line?" he asked, as he tied his silky pink tie around my waist.

"Opening line?"

"Tonight, what's your line?" He paused, looking up at me, frustrated with my lack of preparation.

"Um. Do I need one?"

"Helloooo, yes."

"Well, I dunno. I thought just getting to, like, hang out was a good start. And then, you know, I'll just see what he says, and—"

"Girl, you gotta have some game. That's why we have to think about these things. We can't have you missing key opportunities to loosen his tie—"

"Right. Got it."

"Consider this tie"—he yanked on my makeshift belt—"a subliminal message to him, and also a reminder to you, to act!"

He put me in front of the mirror. I had been dubious at first, but he insisted the outfit would work and in the end, I had to admit, it didn't look half bad.

We plopped on the bed.

"So he didn't say when?" Dante asked, for the millionth time.

"No!"

"Okay, okay, sorry, just checking."

We spent the rest of the evening chatting and waiting . . . and waiting and waiting for a knock at the door. Finally, as we took turns yawning and dozing off, we decided to throw in the towel at eleven o'clock.

"Dan, I'm such a total cliché," I grumbled through a yawn. "I can't believe I'm *that* girl, sitting around waiting for a guy to show up. I hate myself. I'm a girl I would make fun of right now."

"Well, yeah. But this is a first-time offense. And look at the bright side—it's definitely a step in the right direction. If you're gonna be stuck waiting for some guy to show up, it might as well be a superhot one. I'm superjealous, if it's any consolation. I can't even get stood up these days. I need a crush object." His voice lost a bit of its luster, his eyes cast down.

"You'll get one, I promise. And in the meantime at least you don't have to feel like an idiot like I do."

"It happens. Your plans weren't exactly written in stone. Maybe there's an explanation. But next time it's gonna be him waiting for *you*."

"I love you, Dante, you big fat liar."

"I'm so not fat." He kissed me on the forehead. "Night, Hav. Promise no sulking, okay? His loss."

I sighed. "Thanks. Night. I owe you one."

"I'll cash in, don't worry."

I changed into the beat-up old aquamarine scrubs I used as pajamas and curled up in bed with the book Lance had loaned me, hoping to take my mind off the world's most anticlimactic night. I skimmed through the chapter titles until I found the one he had mentioned about the passageways snaking beneath the buildings around this part of the city. There was supposedly at one time a whole network of them under the hotel and somewhere among them Capone had had a vault thought to be stocked with cash and assorted treasures. But only a few pages in and I already felt my eyelids tugging downward. I fought it as best I could but I knew it was a battle I would lose and eventually gave in to sleep.

But not for long.

1

Everything Sinful Is Glamorous

I awakened in the night. A thud, shattering the quiet, breaking me out of my dizzy slumber. The sound felt like it hit me in the head, echoing at my temple. I shot up in bed, soaked in a cold sweat, and my hand fumbled for the bedside lamp. Panting, with my throbbing head—wet hair matted against it—in my hands and my chest pounding, I tried to regain control. My eyes worked to adjust to the dim light but failed, a smoky haze coating the room.

I had dreamt that I was in my bed and heard a thump, and then the slow scratch of friction as something was being dragged down the hallway. A thump and then the dragging again. Over and over. And then a *BANG-BANG-BANG* rattling my door. In my dream I had gone to the door and opened it—something I couldn't imagine doing in real life—but there had been nothing there, even though the thumps and the dragging sounds continued. Sitting up in bed, I thought I could still hear it. It had to be in my mind. My shoulders ached, and those two scars on my back felt like I had been branded with hot pokers. My cheek burned, like something had slashed at it. I felt something wet and sticky against my fingertips. Blood.

I ran into the bathroom and dabbed at the wound, cleaning it off. Underneath the ruddy smear, it wasn't bad; just a slim gash no more than an inch or two across the fleshy apple of my right cheek. Once I rinsed the blood away, there was barely anything there. From the shape of it, I couldn't tell exactly what had done it: maybe my nails? But they were so short. I pulled out the anti-septic and Band-Aids that Joan had packed in my first-aid kit—a nurse never lets her kid go anywhere without one. I pressed the bandage firmly over the injury and took in my full reflection. I was quite a sight: dirty, sweaty hair, ratty scrubs, the beautiful, wholly incongruous necklace, and now this ridiculous Band-Aid across my cheek.

I crawled back into bed and checked the clock—4:47 in the morning. I switched off the lamp and laid my wounded head on the pillow. My body curled into the fetal position, settling into a tight ball, when something hard and pointy jabbed into my rib cage. My hand flew for the light again, nearly knocking it off the nightstand in the process. I sprung up on my feet, then crouched in bed and pulled back the covers, as though expecting something to leap out at me.

The book lay there, open and upside down.

Not the book I'd been reading on Chicago history, but the other one, the empty black journal that Lance had found labeled with my name. I picked it up and fanned the pages again. They flew by like so many milky wings.

Except for a few pages. Full of black-inked squiggles.

I snapped the book shut and dropped it, as if it had bit me and I needed to fend it off. I crept to the corner of the bed, up against the wall, trying to keep as far away from it as I could. I had looked through every page of that thing before. There was no way I had missed all of this writing, it wasn't possible. With tentative fingers

I pinched at one sharp corner and slid the book toward me. I opened the cover slowly, leafing through the bare endpaper, and then found on the next page these words scrawled out:

Be strong, winged one. And beneath that: *And beware all beautiful things.*

My stomach dropped to the floor. But I had to keep going. I flipped past this perplexing inscription to a full page of the messy, curly script that looked nearly as unruly as my own. Marked across the upper right corner was today's date. I curled my legs up, my arms around my knees, and began to read:

Happy belated birthday. You are sixteen and your life is about to change. You cannot possibly know how special you are going to be. You will be a legend. As powerless as you feel now, you will soon be nearly drunk with influence and control, astounded by the sheer force you possess within. But you must heed my words, Haven—

It knocked the wind out of me to see my name written by this mysterious hand. But I forced my eyes back onto the page. My hand to my mouth, my pulse racing, I kept on:

There is much to learn. And quickly, for you are in danger.

I hugged my knees closer to my chest, trying to steady myself. This was obviously some strange joke—maybe Dante was up to something, maybe he was making fun of me for being so cautious all the time, for treating everything like it was a life-or-death situation. But the handwriting didn't look neat and clear enough to be his, it didn't have the same bubbly quality. Even so, I wanted to bang on his door right now, wake him, wake Lance, wake the whole floor, do whatever I needed to in order to set my mind at ease. But I couldn't stop reading.

You're a smart young woman, Haven. You are no doubt won-

dering what to make of this book, of this writing. You have to trust me. As an act of good faith, I will tell you things that no one else would know. To begin: You have three distinct scars. Each consists of three stripes. One of these scars is above your heart. Two are on your back.

I exhaled. Fine, I reassured myself. Telling details, indeed. It's true there weren't a ton of people who knew this about me, but there were some—Dante, Joan, everyone at the hospital, anyone who had bothered to watch me change for gym class. I read on:

Furthermore, when you get anxious or frightened, your scars begin to sting and burn.

No one knew this. My fingers began to tremble; I opened and closed my hands making fists and shaking them out. It was true though. It didn't happen that often but then how often did I really feel scared on a daily basis? When you have an overprotective parent, there just aren't that many opportunities to feel true fear. Fear of the future, of getting into a good college, of doing well on the SATs—these uncertainties were generally what passed as fear in my world, and they didn't count. That wasn't the kind of bone-chilling fear we were talking about here. True horror, the kind beginning to creep in now, was another beast entirely. It went on:

I also happen to know the genesis of these scars and the purpose they will serve in the future. I know many things that you don't know about yourself. But now is not the time for me to be telling too much. You must trust me. Your life depends on it. Do not breathe a word of this to a single soul.

That was all it said.

With a gasp, I snapped it shut and threw it across the room, a reflex. It hit the closet door with a thump and fell to the floor.

I needed sun. I needed light and daytime and morning and people and air, cold air that could snap me out of this strange world that book had sunk me into. I showered and dressed even faster than I had yesterday and sprinted down the hallway. How was it possible to sleep when I had just read these things? How could life be normal for anyone? Even if this was some joke . . . I don't know. I couldn't even finish the thought because it seemed too true. How could anyone know about the scars burning? I hadn't told a soul.

I ran through the empty lobby, day just beginning to break and shed its first bright slice through the skylight. I pushed through the revolving doors, the icy wind pummeling my chest. The sky was painted in strips of violet, periwinkle, and orange, the clouds outlined in pink. I could've stayed out there for hours if not for the temperature, which finally forced me back inside.

It was just after six. Alone in the vast lobby, I watched the giant flat screen on the wall near the doorway flash snapshots of Aurelia and Lucian photographed at events at the Vault as news stories about the hotel flipped through on a loop. I stood there long enough that I managed to read each one. Even so, my mind wandered.

Supposing, somehow, this ridiculous book was actually true and I was in some mortal danger here. I couldn't believe I was having thoughts like this. *You should not be taking this seriously,* I told myself. *There's obviously some explanation and you're going to sort it out as soon as —*

The swoosh of the elevator doors startled me; I spun around. Aurelia—in another perfect slim dress and blazer, hair down and sleek, teetering on stilettos—stepped out.

She read the shock on my face.

"Why, Haven, good morning," she said, nothing but calm in her husky voice. "I had no idea you were such an early riser. I'll have to remember that. I respect that. I'm one too."

I was relieved to see another human, and yet, this wasn't who I would've picked if given the choice.

"Good morning, Aurelia," I managed. As usual, I felt underdressed. I was a high school student, and I didn't have little dresses and suits and heels.

She studied me, judging every bit of what she saw. Finally: "Are you all right, my lamb?"

"Oh, yes, never better," I said, in a shaky tone. I tucked my unwashed hair behind my ear and my hand brushed against my cheek. The Band-Aid. I'd forgotten to yank it off. "Oh, um, this? I scratched myself in my sleep, I guess."

"Be careful, we need you at your best."

"Of course."

She glanced down at her watch, her manicured nails fiddling with the clasp of the platinum chain strap; I turned just slightly away and swiped the Band-Aid off, sharp and stinging quick and stuffed the bandage in my pocket. Aurelia looked up.

"Come," she said. As I followed her silently toward the Parlor, she spoke to the space straight ahead of her. "It's a delight to be able to start our workday this way. I could use a second set of eyes this morning anyway. It's never too early for sweets, I believe. Besides, we've barely had the chance to get to know each other."

She led us past the potted palms to a large round table set for two at the center of the lounge. She took a seat, whipping her napkin and covering her lap. I did the same, making a louder snap than intended. Without a word, a stunning brunette Outfit member—I searched my brain for her name, Celine—emerged from the kitchen carrying a tray with two teapots hand-painted in a design of entwined cherry blossoms. She wore a formfitting black short-sleeved dress that looked like a tight and tailored flight attendant's uniform, with the LH insignia embroidered in red on the right breast pocket and left sleeve, her hair an endless rope of a ponytail. She set the teapots before us, beside matching teacups. I mumbled, "Thank you," but Celine simply walked away without looking at me.

"That is the new uniform. Lovely, don't you think?"

I nodded. "Very pretty." There were a few painful seconds of silence. Aurelia set the silver sieve across the top of her cup, poured the sizzling liquid through it, and then, tea leaves collected, returned the small strainer to the porcelain half-moon shaped perfectly to hold it. As I copied her actions, it occurred to me that this was possibly the most concentrated time I would get with her. I had to try to push past my own rustling nerves and get to know her. I had to stop worrying that everything I said wouldn't be smart or perfect and I had to just talk and hope for the best. "So, will we interns be getting uniforms too?"

"You will, indeed. Everyone will, no matter how big or small their job. I'm of the belief that a person works more diligently when he or she is wearing a uniform."

"I can see how that would be true," I agreed. "So you'll have one too?"

"No. I don't need one." She lifted the teacup to her mouth, the steam curling around the features of her face, and took a long sip.

Trying not to feel I'd said something wrong, I too lifted the delicate porcelain cup in my hand—I hoped she didn't see that it was shaking ever so slightly. Though a sedative, warm bed, and nightmare-free rest were most what I needed, the caffeine, I was sure, could do me some good. The day had only begun and I was already starting to feel the effects of not having slept nearly enough. I pressed the hot cup to my lips and took a sip, setting my lips, tongue, and entire throat aflame as it went down. I imagined a trail of blisters rising up along my esophagus. Aurelia didn't seem to notice.

"So, tell me, how are you enjoying your time here so far?"

I smiled and cleared my throat as a test to see if my voice could push through my scorched lips.

"Very much." The sound scratched as it came out. "It's really a remarkable place. I had a great time working on the photos yesterday. I'm looking forward to doing a select today. How many shots would you like to see of each person? I have so many beautiful—"

"One. Choose well, but choose one each. Show me tomorrow morning."

"Certainly."

She looked at me closely, like I was an x-ray of a tiny, hairline fracture.

"Are you surprised that I trust you?"

It felt like a trick question; I wasn't sure how to answer. After a second or two: "I'm glad that you trust me. Thank you. I won't let you down." At that moment, Celine burst through the kitchen door holding aloft a pair of trays. She set one before each of us. Each had three tiers lined with precious confections: scones, teacakes, petits fours, cookies, finger sandwiches of thinly sliced cucumber or salmon or lobster salad, bite-size fruit tarts and cheesecake squares, all tiny works of art.

"You'll find that the more I like your work, the greater responsibility you'll have," Aurelia said. Her pinky sticking out like a radio antenna, she selected a scone from the top tier, placing it at the center of her tea plate. "I won't give you one of those 'you remind me of me' soliloquies. But I will say there is a reason I am mentoring you myself. I think you will go far."

I hadn't expected to hear anything like that. My wheels were turning for the perfect response, but she continued on, leaving me no opportunity. "See that balcony?" She pointed to a protruding bulge in the corner, up near the windows. It looked large enough for only two people. "I think we may want a harpist during teatime every afternoon. What do you think?"

"I think people would like that." I could imagine how it would sound when the hotel opened and well-dressed guests sipped here to the instrument's delicate sounds; it would feel more alive. Right now the place was just a shell of what it could potentially be.

"Perhaps jazz musicians at cocktail hour," she mused.

"That would be nice too."

"Tell me, Haven, why do you think we celebrate someone like Capone here?"

This was feeling like a quiz, and I suddenly wished I'd gotten further reading that book last night. I took a stab: "To capitalize on the part of history that you own here."

"There's so much more." She took another long, slow sip. I touched the cup and then backed my fingers away, not prepared to inflict that upon myself again. Instead, I simply waited for her to go on. She took her time. "Everything sinful is glamorous these days, isn't it?"

"I . . . I don't suppose I would know."

"No, I don't suppose you would," she said in a tone that bled with disappointment.

I couldn't form any words to respond. She went on. "From a

business standpoint, naturally, we're making the most of it. We're fortunate enough that what we have is something inherently fascinating to many people—Capone, the lore, the legends. But what they really come here for is to be close to danger. To flirt with it, to be nearer to it than they would be in their daily lives, to imagine themselves to be different people than who they actually are." She picked apart the scone, dolloped a spoonful of raspberry jam onto it, and took the smallest of bites. I did the same, my actions trailing hers by mere seconds. The scone was lemon flavored, studded with cranberries and so warm it dissolved like cotton candy in my mouth. I would have eaten it much faster if I had been alone.

"Like amusement parks, roller coasters. They scare people and that's why they love them. They get a rush," I said, wanting her to think that I understood.

"That's charming. Yes, perhaps a bit like roller coasters. But this is darker. You don't even like roller coasters, do you?"

"Of course I do." I didn't. At all. I had been on one when I was twelve, and that was enough. I thought I was going to fly out every time we took a turn or went upside down. It just didn't seem like something I needed to be fond of.

"There is something alluring about being in the presence of something dangerous or even macabre. It breaks down inhibitions. It can be electrifying."

I just nodded. But she saw through me.

"I can tell you're not sure you agree." She nibbled on her scone.

"I guess I've spent too many years working at a hospital. I've seen my share of daredevils, people who've taken too many chances, thought they could beat the odds and do anything—driving too fast and crashing, falling out of everything you could possibly fall out of, doing ungodly harm to each other. It's enough to make you very content to live a safe life."

She considered what I said. "I can see your point. But don't tell me you haven't had the occasional reckless feeling from time to time."

"I'm not sure what you mean."

"You're so sweetly young, Haven." She flashed a wide grin that she might give to a child, and a child might believe to be sincere. "Have you never been consumed with greed or passion or emotion enough that you felt you could do something unseemly to get what you wanted?"

I thought about it. I wasn't one for instant gratification. My life had been structured to postpone enjoyment in favor of working hard to get where I wanted to be. A good school, a good life, a good career—I wanted to be something important. I did, suddenly, feel very young. Aurelia would probably think these were naïve, pedestrian desires.

"Is there nothing you want in life? Are you really so happy all the time?" Her voice had an edge I couldn't place and one I didn't think I deserved. My blood coursed to a low simmer, even though I knew, intellectually, it wasn't appropriate to feel this angry this quickly toward my boss.

"Of course I want things. I want so much that I surrender entire parts of my existence to get there." If I cared less I wouldn't have been sitting in this empty hotel right now. I would be going to school, I would have friends there, I would go to the mall after school and football games, instead of having tunnel vision about the future.

"At some point, you'll find that your morals only get you so far and that it can be a good bit of fun to loosen them on occasion."

"I suppose that might be true." I felt it might be best now to say as little as possible. As Aurelia poured her second cup of tea, I tried again with my first. The second sip burned less, but I may just have been numb.

"I wouldn't be surprised if even you found within you the tiniest lust for danger. It's human. There's nothing wrong with flying too close to the sun on occasion. Wouldn't you like to try?"

I knew Greek mythology. I knew of Icarus and his waxen wings that melted when he soared too high and had left him dead in the sea. But I couldn't for the life of me understand what she wanted from me. "I. Um. I'm sorry, I'm not sure I understand."

"You will." Her lips curled in a smirk, knowingly.

Before I could find a way to ask again, the kitchen door pushed open once more, but it wasn't Celine this time. I saw the chef's hat and uniform and wished it could be Dante—because I needed him then—but instead found a man that I knew instantly, in that way that best friends know, would be Dante's *type*. He certainly looked young enough to be one of us, and had smooth, perfect skin, but he was taller and more filled out and buff than Dante, and from what I could tell, had a shaved head. With his stony expression and serious eyes, his features lacked warmth but he carried himself like he was much more accomplished than someone our age. He reached our table and didn't even look at me, but faced Aurelia, addressing her instead.

"Mademoiselle, I hope you've been enjoying the traditional tea selections from the menu you requested," he said in a reverential tone. He held his hands clasped together at his waist, his head cocked to the side waiting for her reviews. "Please let me know if you'd like more of anything." He was all polish and perfection, just like everyone else around here. A spark of color crept out at the wrist of his chef's coat, catching my eye. He reached to refill Aurelia's teacup and I got a full view. On his wrist, he had that same eye tattoo I had seen so many times. He must have felt me staring. As soon as he finished pouring, he turned around to face me. I saw that his coat read "Etan" in an embroidered red script.

"Hello, I'm not sure we've met. I'm Etan D'Amour." He pronounced it AY-tahn and stretched out his hand for me to shake. The tattoo pulsed in the process. His smile, now that he had chosen to turn it on, was full of mystery. "I'm the chef here. Pleasure to have you in the Parlor."

"Thank you," I said. "Nice to meet you. My friend Dante is going to be working with you." I almost couldn't suppress my glee. I couldn't wait to talk to him about this.

"That's right, he is. I'm looking forward to meeting him today. He left me some fresh cookies he baked."

"Yeah, that sounds like him."

"I like him already." Etan turned back to Aurelia. "Generally, our guests will be taking their tea service between the hours of two and five in the afternoon, but I know you have a busy day and wanted to sign off on it all this morning. It is to your liking, I hope?"

"Excellent." She nodded firmly. "And Haven, what did you think?" They both looked at me.

"Delicious and really beautiful too." My eyes darted quickly to both of our nearly undisturbed tiered trays.

"Thank you. Well, don't let me keep you any further. I'll let you finish. Bon appétit, mesdemoiselles." He bowed slightly and strode off to the kitchen.

Aurelia leaned back in her seat, folded her arms, and said, "He's just lovely and so talented."

"He seems it."

"But, now, where were we?"

I didn't say a word; I just poured more tea for myself, the leaves collecting in the mesh of the tea strainer. The pot was still so hot that the handle burned me. She leaned forward now, looking right into my eyes. I folded my hands in my lap and straightened my back, prepared to receive whatever she would tell me.

"If I were a person who read these," she said, pointing to the wet black leaves collected before me, "I fear they might say that you could very well be eaten alive here." I felt my heart drop. My jaw dropped too. "But it doesn't have to be that way. Not at all." She smiled, and with that she folded her napkin into a precise isosceles triangle and rose from the table. "Thank you so much for joining me. I'll be looking forward to seeing your work."

She breezed out. I watched her until she disappeared out of sight. And then I let my head fall over the back of the chair and my breath rush out of me. So much of what she said, those disorienting questions I couldn't sort out, echoed in my mind. I had the sense that my life would always be divided into the pre-Aurelia and post-Aurelia eras.

The only silver lining of the encounter this morning was that for the hour or so we were together, I had managed to forget the strange warnings of that mysterious book that lay in my room.

8

What's with the Book?

The gallery was a welcome hideaway for me, and I fired up the computer and my giant TV monitor prepared to get lost in work. The photos shuffled past me, no clunkers to speak of from the Outfit. I could probably let the thumbnails fill the screen, close my eyes and point randomly, and I'd get a stunning group of shots with which to impress Aurelia tomorrow (if she was capable of being impressed at all). It was too easy, and it didn't engross me the way I needed it to. I decided to camp out in the library instead, scanning the shelves for more history tomes until Lance appeared.

"Hey, morning, how's it going?" He sounded surprised to see me. "Did you get breakfast yet? I'm starved and thought I'd check out the kitchen in the—"

I wasn't listening. A thread hung loose at the bottom of my sweater and I pulled at it, twisting it around my finger. If I wasn't careful I would end up unraveling the whole thing. I couldn't hold back: "Hi. Yeah, so what's with the book?" It came out hostile to my ears, but he seemed to hear differently.

"Good stuff, right? Thought you'd like it. There's another one here too." He scanned the long table, littered with stacks of books. "Did you get to the part about the vault?"

"Yeah. No. Not that book. The other one," I whispered. I don't know why—it was as though if I said it too loud then it would definitely mean it was for real.

"Whaddya mean?"

"Just promise me you're not playing a joke on me."

"What? What are you talking about?" He looked at me like I was losing it. I searched his face for any flicker that he might be on the verge of fessing up to having written it, but there was nothing there.

"Forget it." I shook my head. "Maybe it was the Outfit or something weird."

"Huh?"

"Never mind." I thought for a moment. "This is crazy, but can you show me again where you found that book with my name on it?"

"Sure, yeah," he said, confused. He waved me over to the side of the table. "I've emptied almost all of the boxes, but it was toward the top of this one here. Knock yourself out."

"Thanks." I stood over it looking down, like it was a well that might just throw coins back up at me. Then I knelt down, shuffling through and finding only more history books, more old classics. I don't know what I expected.

Lance had resumed shelving books but must've heard me stop rustling. I realized he was watching me from behind those glasses.

"You okay?" he asked finally. "You're acting kinda weird."

"Yeah. I know," I said. "Sorry. Fine, thanks." It wasn't my most convincing performance. I actually would have liked to tell him, to get it out in the open, about these creepy threats. Maybe it would sound less scary if I said it out loud. But it seemed safest not to just yet. "Thanks again."

"Sure." He shrugged and went back to work.

So did I. Sequestering myself in the gallery, I tied my hair back in a tight ponytail—always a sign I'm getting down to business—and decided not to leave until I'd made some headway. In no time, I had the entire Outfit finished and had printed eight-by-tens on the glossy photo paper loaded into the printer. I had lingered longer than necessary on the pictures of Lucian. My favorite ended up being the one of him walking toward me at the end. Maybe I was reading too much into that one, but I liked the movement of it. And that undone tie, of course. I considered printing one for myself. But it would be mortifying if anyone were to find out I had this picture in my room, like something I'd clipped from a magazine and taped in my locker. I stopped myself, attempting to refocus.

It was midafternoon, and I was in the process of Photoshop-zapping Dante's barely there zit when a faint knock rattled the door. Gentle as it was, I still jumped up in my seat and yelped.

Lance appeared in the doorway with his hands up, surrendering. In one hand he held a white paper bag with the LH insignia.

"Sorry about that," he said.

"No, no, it's me." I tightened my ponytail, pulling a few loose strands back from my face, and took a deep breath. "Just a little skittish today. What's up?"

"Dante made us sandwiches." He handed me the bag.

"That's sweet of him." I peeked inside. "He's going to be a great mom one day. How's his day going with the boss?"

"I don't know. He just came by for a second. He wanted to come see you but he seemed anxious about getting back."

"Yeah, he makes fun of me, but he's capable of getting just as freaked out about everything. He usually just hides it a lot better than me."

Lance nodded, hands in his pockets, leaning against the doorframe. He looked away for a moment and then back at me, and away again. Finally, he said, "So, I kind of have a favor to ask too."

"Okay, try me." I swiveled my chair to face him. "What can I do?"

He exhaled, ready to lay it on me. "Not sure if you noticed yesterday, you know, with the pictures. But I have this gnarly scar here." He touched the spot just under his glasses, below his right eye.

"Oh. No, I mean, just a little, it's hardly noticeable."

He returned his hands to his pockets, looking away again. "I just wondered, if it's not too much trouble, do you think there's any chance you could . . . I mean, you have Photoshop and stuff, right?"

"I do." I completed his thought for him. "And I will. If that's what you want."

He ruffled the back of his hair, like he had earlier, his relief slipping out. "That would be great, actually, if you could just get rid of it. It kinda bugs me." He looked up. "Thanks."

"Anytime. I understand," I said, my voice solemn. I considered telling him about mine, but I just wasn't sure. Maybe sometime I would.

"Thanks. Really appreciate it," he said again. "I'll, um"—he pointed to the door—"let you get back to it."

Once he'd left, I pulled up his pictures. Just as I suspected, the ones without his glasses were the best by far. There were angles to his face you didn't see in daily life, sharp lines along his jaw. His awkwardness didn't come through in the photos. And the slight squint of his eyes—a deep, melting brown—as he tried his best to look where the camera was, where I was, made him appear concerned and serious, even protective. I decided I liked his clunky frames best when they hung on his shirt collar. They looked so much better there than shielding his face.

Photo chosen, I zeroed in on my target, enlarging his scar on my screen for a better look. I wondered how he had gotten it. Its texture was like mine, the quality of a burn, but his was much more faint and just one stripe, not an unsightly trio like mine. Don't we always think we have it worse than everyone else? But his was on his face, and even covered by glasses, surely he felt its presence always. I tapped at that cut on my cheek. He had been polite not to ask me about it. Now I understood why.

A few taps shook the door softly and I jerked again, but my heart didn't stop midbeat like it had minutes before. Progress.

"Someone's getting high-maintenance all of a sudden," I called out, my back to the door as my hand clicked at the mouse fast, fast, fast to minimize the picture on my screen—I didn't want him knowing I'd been looking at his scar so closely. "So what else needs fixing now?"

"Well, for one thing, my manners. They could use a complete overhaul."

It wasn't Lance's voice.

I whipped around in my seat. Lucian stood just inside the doorway. Suit-clad again, tie snugly knotted.

"Hi . . . hi," I stammered, unable to hide my surprise.

"Sorry to interrupt." He stepped farther inside. "But I think— no, I know—I owe you an apology." He kneeled at my feet. His musk and cedar scent whirled around me.

"Oh? I don't know what you mean." I tried to play it cool.

"Last night . . ." He paused, serious. "I'm afraid I had some business to take care of and it just dragged on. So I'm sorry." His gray eyes pulled me in, grabbing hold and refusing to let go.

"Oh, no big deal." I shrugged.

"Well, I believe I owe you."

I didn't see any reason to dispute this. "I'm not one to go challenging anybody's beliefs."

He smiled. "I'm glad to hear that." His eyes wandered to my desk, finding the stack of photos I'd already printed out. He stood back up, reached over me, and grabbed them.

"I'm not finished yet." I swatted to try to reclaim the stack but he just held them farther away.

"Have you gotten to mine yet? Don't I get approval rights?"

"I was under the impression I had complete creative control." I said it just jokingly enough.

"Is that right? Well, we'll just have to see." He leaned up against the desk, his body toward me. Dante's picture was on top. He held it up and examined it. "Nice."

"Thanks." I was embarrassed. And it was about to get worse: his picture was next in the stack.

"Here we go." He held it close, hand on his chin. I'm sure he was surprised I'd even taken a shot of him walking toward me. "Now, the dilemma," he started. My face fell. "How do I compliment the photographer without sounding horrifically vain?"

"I think you just did." I smiled and looked away involuntarily. "I'm glad you like it."

He flipped through the rest of the stack, one by one, looking at each shot of the Outfit and then placing it on the table. "You seem to know what you're doing."

"It's all an illusion. I just choose really good subjects who do all the real work."

Lucian sat a few feet away and yet I could feel his breath. "Well, your strategy is obviously working. Either that or, you know, you're actually talented or something."

"Thanks, yeah, tough call." I wasn't entirely sure what to do with compliments, so it seemed easiest to bat at them, to volley. He was watching me, studying my face—though hopefully not that awful scratch. I kept talking as a distraction, if nothing else. "I kind of like how people transform when I look at them through that lens, or later when I see a picture I've taken and it captures something more than the surface of this person."

"So you have x-ray vision then? I knew there was something about you."

I shook my head, embarrassed. "No, but I just mean—" I picked up the shot of Dante on the table and dissected it with my eyes. "I feel like sometimes you can see someone's soul in a photo. It seeps out if you catch them unguarded for just a second."

Lucian took his from the pile and held it up. "Did you get mine?"

I looked from the photo to the real flawless honey-skinned face, and back again. "I'm not sure yet." It was the truth. I didn't know anything about him yet, but I wanted to know everything. I wanted to spend every minute with him. I wanted him to feel the same way about me. And I wanted to feel this pulsing in my veins forever.

I see." He nodded, thinking. "Then that's it. I think it's going to have to be dinner now."

"Dinner?"

"I just don't see any way around it. Friday?" He gave me that look, the one I was getting so addicted to.

"Sure." I could barely hear myself over my beating heart.

"Friday, then." He rose to his feet.

"Friday," I repeated, though it still wasn't fully sinking in. He smiled.

"And be careful, would you?" He leaned in and his warm lips found that injured spot on my cheek. I felt the heat of his kiss on my skin even after he had pulled away and slipped out the door.

Shockingly, I worked with a new efficiency after my surprise visitor. It may have been the lingering effects of the adrenaline rush of having him near. I flew through my retouches on Lance's photo, and chose my own photo, settling on the one I'd snapped just as Lucian had interrupted me that day. With a little Photoshop work, my scars, which had edged out from my tank top, were gone.

It wasn't until I was back on the basement level that it occurred to me that I didn't want to be in my room. I changed course, knocking next door. Lance opened up.

"Hey, how's it going?"

"Hi. Just thought I'd see if Dante was back yet." My voice had a breathy tremble to it.

"'Fraid not," he said. "I think they've got him working pretty hard today." A book lay upside down and open on his bed, a black-and-white postcard of old-time Chicago beside it.

"Yeah." I was running out of things to say but I couldn't bear to leave and face that strange book of mine. "Hey, do you want to, like, hang out? I mean, I was just going to read; you could bring your book; it'll be like study hall . . . or whatever." I sounded weird, even for me, but I couldn't quite tell him that I was scared to be alone in my room.

"Sure," he said. "Your room is nicer than ours. Probably neater too." He kept the door propped open with his leg and reached back to the bed to grab his book. "I drastically bring down the neat quotient of our room."

"Well, I'm kind of messy too, so you'll feel at home," I said unlocking my door, then pausing. "And I didn't even make my bed today. That's awful. Sorry."

"I haven't made my bed in years."

"Well, even so—" I flung the covers back up, tucking them into the mattress, and fluffed the comforter and pillows. Lance scanned the room, probably comparing it to his own.

"You know what we need at this place?" he asked.

"Windows."

"Yeah. And a TV."

"No kidding."

"It's like we're on a reality show where we never get to watch TV because that would be so boring for everyone else to watch."

I assessed my housekeeping skills. "Better," I said to the newly made bed. I picked up the crumpled scrubs I'd thrown off getting dressed this morning and folded them, sticking them in the top drawer. It occurred to me I probably didn't want that book of mine lying out in the open, but a quick scan showed, oddly, it was nowhere to be found.

"Question: where did Capone work when he was in prison?" Lance asked.

"I know this—he did the laundry."

"Correct," he said. "Question: where are we supposed to do our laundry?"

"There I'm stumped. I know it's down here somewhere."

"Yeah, that's all I know. We'll have to go looking for it."

"Sounds good." I slipped off my shoes and sat down, curling up my legs. He did the same on the corner of the bed. Neither of us spoke for a while; we read quietly and that was just fine. It was just a relief to have him sitting there with me. After about an hour of this, two spirited knocks banged at the door.

"Room service!" Dante's voice rang out. Lance reached over and opened the door. A white-tablecloth-covered cart carrying silver-dome-topped plates and wineglasses filled with water wheeled into the room, Dante grinning behind it.

"He totally doesn't want to like you and doesn't know why he does, but he maybe sort of does," Dante offered as an analysis. Unable to hold back, I had just shared my Lucian encounter in painstaking detail. "No offense. I think he's falling for your mind, you know?"

"What every girl wants to hear," I joked back.

"I don't get the appeal," Lance said, shrugging. Girl talk wasn't quite his thing. When I thought about it, I couldn't believe I was talking about things like crushes with this guy I never really knew from my AP Euro class.

Dante bounced in his seat like a little kid. "Can I talk about me?" he asked, raising his eyebrows up/down, up/down. It had to be something good.

"As if you need to ask," I said.

"So, my boss—"

"Etan—" I drew it out, anxious to hear.

"Good guy?" Lance asked.

"Superhot guy!" Dante gushed.

"I totally knew he would be your type." I poked him with my fork. "I mean, he's everybody's type, but especially yours. You like mystery."

"So true."

"And muscles," I added.

"Indeed. Speaking of—" Dante checked his watch. "Oooh, gotta get going. We're testing out some eats at the Vault tonight. Etan has all these ideas to try. He's a visionary."

"Seriously, you're still on call?" I asked. He began stacking the plates on top of the cart.

"I think I'm going to be working as much overtime as possible, if you get what I'm sayin'." He winked. We all said our good nights, Dante kindly promising to keep an eye out for Raphaella for Lance and Lucian for me.

After Lance went back to his room, I changed into my scrubs and got ready for bed. I had grand plans that I might sleep a few hours without a nightmare. But as I tucked myself in, I started to wonder: where was that book anyway? It seemed somehow worse *not* knowing where it was. I pried my weary bones out of bed and began searching everywhere, even places I knew with certainty I hadn't left it. I checked inside the bureau, the desk drawer, the night table, my backpack, the hamper, and even, absurdly, the shower. Nothing. I collapsed back onto the bed and then looked straight ahead: the closet.

I pulled the cord for the overhead light. The string came off in my hands—great—not that I really needed it. The narrow space was nearly empty. I tossed the duffel bags out, and there it was on the floor: the black leather-bound book. I grabbed it and stuffed the duffel bags back into the corner.

Ouch.

My hand scraped against something hard and metal. I set the book down and patted the worn, nubby carpet. Flat, flat, flat—and then my palm hit it again, this thing. It was a metal seam, a hinge more than a foot long and raised up only a few centimeters high. I traced it to where it ended and felt around.

Running perpendicular to it was the slimmest of gaps, no thicker than a piece of cardboard. I picked at it and managed to get a nail under it, tugging. With a squeaky creak, the panel lifted up like a jaw. It was large enough for a person to fit through it. I didn't want to open it the whole way, I couldn't see down there anyway, and without the overhead light I couldn't begin to see how far it went.

I had had quite enough. I sealed it back up, put my duffel bags on top of it, closed the closet door, and backed away. I didn't like this at all. I wedged the desk chair under the doorknob. Primitive, yes, but this gave me at least some peace of mind.

But my peace of mind disappeared when I opened that book again.

There was more writing. Another full page. I took a deep breath and began to read.

I trust you have found the pathway. You will learn that it will do no good to cover things over and pretend they aren't there, just as this doesn't work for the markings on your body. (You call them scars, but that is only because you don't yet know the distinction that comes with them.)

You will learn to break rules: your life depends on it. You will learn the art of trespassing, finding your way into places others don't wish for you to find. You will learn inner strength — to a degree far greater than you have ever known — and physical strength. None of this will be easy; all of it will be necessary.

You are in training now. And you shall answer first and foremost to me, to these words. You will save your questions about where these directives are coming from. You will receive answers only when it is appropriate for you to receive them. You will see that your purpose here is greater than you could have imagined. *Trust in these words, trust in yourself, and you will not falter.*

I stopped myself for a moment. *Trust* was a difficult word to stomach, a manipulative word. This book, which seemed to want to exert so much authority over me, had introduced itself by telling me my life was in danger and to keep quiet—that was kind of a lot. We were on shaky ground, me and this book. How could I be sure of its intentions? How did I know it wasn't going to lead me straight into danger? The more I thought about it, the angrier it made me. The book had trapped me. I read on:

Naturally, you want to doubt this. Yours is an analytical mind. You wonder why you should follow these words. Take heart, winged one—

What was that supposed to mean?

There is so much you don't know, that you need to discover for yourself. There is considerable interpretation to be drawn from every thought in this book. Remember this much: never count yourself out, no matter what you are told.

So it had accounted for my skepticism, but it answered riddles with more riddles. It would have to do better than that. It would have to prove itself to me. But still, there was more:

Your assignments for tomorrow: In the morning, you must forgo any engagements and instead venture out to amass emergency supplies. These items may one day save your life. Think of items to nourish, protect, heal, strengthen your senses.

At night, look for your next set of instructions. Continue to keep this quiet. One never knows whom one can trust.

One last parting admonition: your necklace has deeper meaning. It defines you and is one of a kind. It is meant to be with you. Treasure it and let it remind you how strong you are.

I turned the next few pages, but that was all.

I dropped the book on the floor. My trembling hands flew to the night table, fumbling for the gold pendant, which I had taken off before bed. It took three tries to get the tiny clasp to fasten around my neck, but once it did, I vowed to leave it there. I pressed it hard against me and felt my heart racing underneath it.

I left the light on and reached for the Chicago history book and began reading until I started to doze off.

The hours passed without nightmares, without injuries, but I wouldn't call my slumber peaceful.

9

That's Not Quite How I Imagined Paradiso

The beeping of my alarm, boring into my brain, woke me at seven o'clock. I was shocked to have gotten any sleep. I would have thought last night would have set me on a path toward becoming a true insomniac. But it had seemed that the toll of emotional and physical exhaustion had knocked me out and even my terror couldn't keep me awake anymore.

Now that it was morning, I hoped that what I had read last night would feel less grave. I reached for the book on the floor. To my relief, no new writing had accumulated. I showered, washing my hair for the first time in days, and tied it back wet. The scratch on my cheek, I noticed, had dulled to no more than a thin pink blade of grass.

It didn't occur to me until I was already seated in Aurelia's office for our meeting that this may have been something the book had intended for me to skip as per its request to "forgo any engagements" this morning. But that seemed ridiculous, didn't it? I couldn't even imagine how I would have gracefully bowed out of anything involving Aurelia.

One by one, she looked through my stack of photo selections, pausing to consider each—especially the shot of her. I had chosen one of the only ones that had shown any bit of vulnerability at all. Instead of squarely staring down the camera, she was positioned with her chin coyly against one shoulder, her head tilted and her posture almost slouchy. Her gaze came from just left of center. It all gave the illusion of her having a little less control than usual. She lifted her eyes from the photo to me for just a moment, which I read as a positive sign. The only other time she registered any reaction was when she came across my own photo at the bottom of the pile and nodded just once. She handed them back to me.

"You'll find a contact in the gallery office for the agency that will be printing and framing these. They have their instructions already. Just e-mail the files and schedule the delivery and installation for no later than Monday."

"Certainly."

"After that, find Lucian. He needs you for a project."

My nerves fluttered and I wondered if she could tell. "Of course." I tried to say it in my most professional, steady voice. "I'll go right away." I stepped toward the door.

"And Haven?"

I turned around.

"Lovely work on these."

"Thank you." Her praise was unexpected.

"I'd like you to take the camera and begin photographing the Vault nightly." She pressed her lips into a knowing smile. "It seems you've already become familiar with the operations there."

I left her office, wondering what she'd heard of that first drunken evening. I supposed it didn't matter since she was giving me the honor of another assignment there.

I found Lance pacing outside the door to the gallery.

"Hey," he said when he saw me walking down the lobby hallway toward him.

"Hey, what are you doing out here?"

"I'm supposed to be waiting for Lucian. I guess you and I are working together today—"

"Yeah. Do you know what we're doing?"

"No, because"—he lowered his voice and looked around—"what's with that guy? He's so flaky. I've spent a total of ten minutes with him all week and then he tells me to meet here at eight o'clock, and, I mean"—he held out his watch—"it's nine now. I don't get it."

I shrugged. "Maybe he's just really busy."

"It's just frustrating when you don't know what you're supposed to be doing. Don't you get the idea they're kind of disorganized around here?"

"Yeah, but what do we know about hotel management, right?"

"Good point." He glanced over toward the restaurant. "Hey," he said, "you know Dante didn't get back till, like, four this morning?"

"Really?"

"Yeah, I couldn't believe it."

"I bet he wanted to talk."

"Yeah, he tried to. That guy has a lot of energy, but I just went back to sleep. He was totally knocked out cold when I got up this morning."

"No breakfast for us then, huh?"

"I know, I'm starved."

I checked my watch. "We've probably got time . . ."

We opened nearly every cabinet, scoured every shelf of the pantry, and did a thorough investigation of all of the fridges in the Parlor's kitchen before settling on the box of Lucky Charms Lance had pulled down from a shelf too high for me to reach.

"I'm never allowed to have this at home," he said.

"Me neither. Too sugary, right?"

"Yeah." He sounded disappointed. "Don't our parents know we're the only ones in school not drinking and smoking pot? Give us some friggin' Lucky Charms, man." He laughed at himself and I did too. I set out two bowls and he filled them both.

"Tell me about it. I like this wild side of you, Lance. Who knew there was such a rebel under there?" I poured from the tank of milk—everything was giant restaurant economy size—in both the bowls and returned it to the fridge. He took a seat on a stool at an island with a butcher-block top.

I took a spoonful. "Good stuff."

He dunked some of the marshmallows with his spoon, lost in thought. "So, did you ever figure out who gave you that book or whatever?" he prodded lightly, not looking at me.

"No," I said, hoping he didn't notice the quiver in my voice. "Just one of those things, not a big deal." I wanted to change the subject desperately.

He set his spoon down and folded his arms on the table, looking at me with steady eyes. He lowered his voice to a whisper, scanning the room in case anyone were to suddenly appear out of nowhere.

"There's just, I don't know, there's something . . . sort of . . . off about this place." He searched my face for confirmation. "Maybe it's just that it's so empty. Maybe in a couple weeks with people everywhere, it'll feel normal, but don't you just get a gut feeling that something isn't right?" He focused his gaze on his cereal, picked up his spoon again. "I'm probably just being ridiculous." I could see he wondered if he had gone too far giving voice to these feelings.

"No, you're not necessarily being ridiculous." I tried to hedge and be as noncommittal as possible, but what he had said had filled me with such hope. At least someone else had his eyes open here. Even though I couldn't tell him all I wanted to, I still felt less alone.

With still no idea what we were supposed to be doing, Lance went looking for Lucian while I finished up my assignment for Aurelia and checked my e-mail for the first time in days. I wanted to write to Joan. I clicked through my in box and scanned the latest from the college lists I'd signed up for—Northwestern, U. Chicago, Princeton, Harvard, Yale, on and on—and updates from the kids in the pediatric ward at the hospital, whom I wrote back to quickly.

I had so many messages from Joan, I didn't think I'd even have time to read them. Instead, I just opened a new message and wrote, *Hi Joan. Finally got a chance to check my e-mail and just wanted to tell you things are going great here.* I shook my head. Really swell. *They're keeping us busy but we're learning a lot. Dante says hi. It's great to have him here. And the other intern, Lance, is a nice guy. My boss is*—What to say? She's the most intimidating woman I've ever met and seems to not totally like me for some reason?—*a smart businesswoman and gorgeous too, in a soap opera kind of way.* Joan would like that; she loved her soaps. She would DVR them every day and we would watch at night—or, rather, she would watch and I would do my homework in the same room and occasionally *ooh* and *aah,* making a fuss over plot twists with her. *I hope things are going well at the hospital—say hi to everyone for me and tell them I miss them. Love you, Haven.* I hit Send. We had been here only a few days, but it felt like forever. The Lexington Hotel seemed strangely cut off from the rest of the world. Maybe that was just because it was such a different universe from what I was used to.

I was watching the minutes tick by, debating whether to try to sneak away to complete the book's strange task, when Lance returned with Lucian and the three of us convened in the gallery. The place was still nearly empty—just a few portraits and dreamy landscapes hung on the walls. Inside a glass cube atop a pedestal near the entrance a Tommy gun had appeared overnight.

"It was said to be Capone's," Lucian said when he caught me leaning in to look. It was the nearest I'd ever been to a gun, that was for sure.

"Is it loaded?" I asked.

"Depends who's asking," was his playful response, before leading us farther.

We stopped when we reached the gallery's back wall, which looked like an unfinished page in a coloring book—a very grim and macabre coloring book. A mural stretched across the space, partially painted but entirely sketched as some sort of triptych, three panels in progression. We had seen this area only days earlier and it had been blank except for pencil sketches and a sheet of paper mapping out what it would look like when it was finished. This had to have gone up literally almost overnight.

Lucian spoke from behind us, letting us study the mammoth artwork.

"Unfortunately, due to sudden extenuating circumstances, our artist was unable to complete this mural, which we commissioned specially. It's not an ideal situation, but given our relative time crunch and the fact that the detailed work is largely completed, we would like the two of you to finish it."

Both of our heads snapped toward him.

"I know it seems like a lot of blank canvas here, but if you look closely, you'll see it's really just background work you'll need to do." He pointed along the sides and signaled in between the figures. It was true: all of the people and key scenes had been painted, but the background landscape—which looked like it would require mostly shades of black and gray and some flourishes of red and orange—had only been started, leaving wide expanses of white to be shaded in. "All of the materials are located in the closet." He pointed. "I think you'll find it'll be easier than you expect. I promise, it's actually pretty tough to mess up." He smiled, reassuring us. "I'll leave you to it, but if there are any questions . . ." He trailed off. His eyes held mine for a second or two, heat rising to my skin, until, hands clasped behind his back, he walked back through the gallery with echoing footsteps and out the door.

"Well, this'll be interesting." Lance scanned the mural, taking it all in.

"How were you in art class?" I asked.

"I'm better at art history and theory than practice."

"Well, if we make a mess, we'll call it abstract."

We didn't say a word for a long time. Instead, our eyes skittered up and down across the mural, which took up nearly the entire wall, save a few feet above and below. By my estimate, it had to have been at least ten feet tall and twenty-five feet long. Each of the triptych's three distinct parts was labeled at the bottom where a scroll had a word painted upon it in an ancient-looking script. A sweeping glance showed a progression from left to right. The first section, labeled *Purgatorio* on the scroll, was littered with withered men and women in tattered remnants of what looked to be dress of the Middle Ages, all shackled in chains. Some lay, as though dying, on a decaying landscape of dead, brown grass, while others were hunched over about to fall, chained at the waist to bare spindly trees; still others crept on all fours on igneous rock. There was no sky to speak of. All three sections shared variations on the same backdrop consisting of whorls of black and gray—and swaths of white space intended to be completed with mostly more black and gray.

On the far right, the scene was labeled *Paradiso*. The figures featured here, robust, hearty ones, reveled in good times, engaging in all manner of lewd and amorous acts, parading around in various states of undress. Yet the backdrop was no idyllic Eden—instead, it was (or rather, it would be, once we finished painting) entirely black rock and black sky, with a body of water the color of dried blood, studded with a few lifeless, floating bodies. Near the top was a silhouette of the skyline of modern-day Chicago engulfed in flames.

"Purgatory, paradise—" I read.

"That's not quite how I imagined *paradiso*," Lance said.

"Yeah, I guess that must be the point." I shrugged. "But then what's going on here?" I pointed to the center section. The scroll below trumpeted it *Metamorfosi* and people shrouded in black capes stood tall, strong, powerful, a red and orange glow around their bodies. Some floated a foot or two off the ground surrounded by people bowing before them. In the center, one of these people stood reaching out to a caped, floating figure, their index fingers touching. In the partially painted black sky, a shadowy figure with sprawling obsidian wings hovered.

"Good question," was all Lance said.

"Metamorphosis? What's that about?"

"I'm not sure I want to know."

We finally tore our eyes away, without a word, taking to the closet to pull out the paint, brushes, trays, tarps, and ladders stashed inside. Everything we needed, except of course artistic ability.

When the supplies were at last assembled—tarp spread out to protect the floor, paint-splattered smocks thrown over our clothes, paint poured—we debated where to begin.

"Should we start at the top?" I pointed to the white sky that needed to be black. "And work our way down?"

Lance folded his arms, weighing the work that needed to be done. "Or we could go from the ground up," he suggested.

"Sort of a grass-roots campaign. I like that," I agreed. He looked relieved. "I didn't really want to go up on that ladder yet," I added.

"Me neither, to be honest," he said.

We had literally covered a good bit of ground, mimicking to the best of our ability the brushstrokes the artist had made before us, when we heard the sharp pistol-crack of heels echoing against marble. The sound drew closer and closer, until we turned around and there she was. Even her footsteps could make a person cower. We both paused for a moment, brushes poised above the wall.

Aurelia stood before us, scrutinizing what we had done. She shook her head and let her eyelids fall shut for just a second. When she opened them she looked only at me, a smile—the iciest one I had ever seen—on her lips.

"Art is the quickest way into the soul," she said, in my direction. "This is meant to evoke a feeling. You have the power to convey that but I don't see that you are. Why don't you have any passion?"

Up until this point, I thought we had been doing a pretty passable job.

"I'm sorry," I said as a reflex, regretting how weak I sounded. "I'm a better photographer than painter. I'm really not a painter at all, to be honest." I fidgeted with the brush in my hands, drops of paint falling softly on my sneakers.

"We're doing our best," Lance managed, mumbling and adjusting his glasses. He got a streak of gray paint on his cheek in the process.

"*Never* show fear or uncertainty. I'm more angry at that than I am with the lack of fire in your work."

She was still looking only at me. I had nothing to say. It seemed safer to keep quiet.

"You'll visit the Art Institute, both of you. Do you know who Hieronymus Bosch is?"

"German painter," Lance blurted out.

"Dutch painter," I corrected softly.

"Dutch painter. Born Jeroen Anthoniszoon van Aken," he said, more softly this time, trying to redeem himself. I looked at him from the corner of my eye.

"See his *Garden of Earthly Delights,* and *Seven Deadly Sins.* They're on loan from the Prado. I want his hell here." She pointed to the wall. It was more chilling because her voice was so steady, serious, and, if anything, laced with as much longing and disappointment as fury.

Another set of footfalls clacked toward us: Lucian.

"A word please?" he whispered to Aurelia, resting his fingertips lightly on her elbow. She nodded. Together they walked slowly away from us.

Lance and I exchanged rattled glances, then silently took action. He started pouring the paint from the trays back into the paint cans. I collected our brushes and stalked off to the closet, where there was a sink inside. I was about to turn the faucet on when I caught a low murmur. I held my breath. It came through the vent—the closet backed up against the office with the computer I used. It was Lucian, a hard edge to his honeyed voice, a thread being pulled just too tight.

"If you didn't want this to have to be done by other people then you should have made some sort of dispensation for Calliope."

My mind flashed to the loopy scrawl at the bottom of the mural. I would check it, but I was almost certain I was right: it had been signed by Calliope. She had started this mural. So why wasn't she completing it? I couldn't imagine getting that far along, doing all that hard work, and then not finishing it. It just seemed odd. But I silenced my racing mind and struggled to listen.

"I will not have you issuing judgments on me." A tremor ran through Aurelia's voice. "I do not need to defend myself to you. There is such a thing as protocol, which is what I adhered to."

"Which is fine, but this is where we are now. Yes, we're ramping up recruiting efforts, but this is where we are presently."

"I'm concerned this will impact our timeline."

"I'm working as quickly as I can, Aurelia."

"We will finish this later. You'll take care of her at least."

Lucian didn't say anything.

I turned the faucet on, running my fingers through the bristles but watching the vent. Sharp, spiked footsteps sliced out of the gallery. Ten seconds later, a slower gait followed. A few steps, then they stopped, as though he were contemplating a change in direction, and then they continued on, through the door, which clicked closed behind him.

Lance and I barely spoke the whole way to the L. The January deep freeze gave us a fine excuse to keep quiet; no use struggling through chattering teeth or straining over the roaring wind as it swirled around us.

The Art Institute was quiet, save for a school field trip or two, and once ensconced inside, a lightness settled over me, a clamp that had been pressed over my heart released, and I felt like myself again. Lance might have felt it too—his pace slowed, his shoulders fell from their tense, hunched-up place near his ears, and his signature slouch returned. We grabbed a map with the exhibit marked and headed up the sweeping staircases running through the center of the building. At last, we passed through the pillar-lined doorway to the expansive room we sought.

"How did you know Bosch's real name and not know he was Dutch?" I asked in a whisper. All the marble picked up and carried the sound, making my voice so much more powerful.

"I got nervous," he whispered back, watching the walls for the two works we most wanted to see.

"She makes me nervous too."

"Well, you were really playing it cool with Lucian." He couldn't suppress the smile breaking out on his face.

"Fine, guilty."

We found what we had come to see, both works so important they had each been given their own walls. *The Garden of Earthly Delights,* I was surprised to discover, actually looked a lot like the *Paradiso* panel of the mural at the hotel, except in a garden, not in a barren, ugly landscape with a lake of blood. Two-thirds of it really was a garden, and the other third was hellish—no one was frolicking there. *Seven Deadly Sins* was a wild circular affair segmented by sin, with four bubbles depicting death, judgment, and seminal experiences of that sort pulled out.

"I'm glad to see these," I whispered after we had gazed quietly at both for some time. "But it's not like I'll be able to duplicate any of this, even in terms of color."

"I know. I'm not sure what they want from us."

"It's kinda nice to get out of the hotel for a little while."

"I'm in no rush to get back if you're not."

And with that, we set off roaming to the next exhibit room and the others, slow and careful not to miss anything, separating in each room, but never going in entirely different directions.

We had just wandered into nineteenth-century French art when it caught me. On a far wall, staring out, I went straight for it, seeing nothing else along the way. The subject was lying in shallow inky water at night, floating with her wrists bound in rope and a halo above her head. She seemed to be glowing, angelic, in her white dress in an otherwise nearly all-black painting. Somewhere far in the distance a shadowy figure watched from atop a hill, just a silhouette, but a menacing one. She appeared to be my age. She didn't look like me necessarily—her hair was much lighter, her skin pale—but the image felt . . . familiar. In a way I couldn't make sense of, it felt like *me*.

What had I looked like when they found me when I was little? There hadn't been water, but there had been ice along that stretch of snow-matted grass down from the road. I had been back there only once. I made Joan take me a couple of years ago. I just thought I should see it, even though she didn't want me to. It looked something like this painting, I supposed. A girl nestled at the bottom of a hill, left for dead.

I don't know how long I had been standing in front of that piece, but it was long enough that Lance had gone ahead to see the rest of the exhibit, and then come back for me when he was ready to move on.

He stared at the painting for a few minutes, quietly by my side. And then finally: "I'm thinking of Italian Renaissance next. It's the next floor up," he whispered.

"Have you heard of this before?"

He leaned in to see the placard posted beside it and read aloud: "*La Jeune Martyre*."

"The young martyr," I translated absent-mindedly, not like he needed me to.

"'By Paul Delarouche, 1855. Oil on canvas. Musée du Louvre, Paris.'" He stepped back to consider it once more. "No, never seen it. Pretty haunting, huh?"

I nodded, a shudder running through me, and soaked in one last look before pulling myself away.

10

You Will Be Spending a Good Deal of Time There

By the time Lance and I left the Art Institute, dusk had fallen. We had walked every inch of that museum, even stopping to get a snack in the café and browsing in the gift shop. I had scanned the racks of postcards, through so many of the usual suspects, Van Goghs and Picassos and Monets, until I found it—a card of *La Jeune Martyre.* I bought it, a dollar well spent.

We had just turned the corner to the hotel, the brisk, sharp wind forcing me to burrow my face farther into the puffy collar of my parka, when it hit me. My mind had been preoccupied, bracing for what might await us inside (and constructing a defense to the question, "What took you so long?"), and an uneasiness began to set in—and with it, a tingle, the prelude to an all-out burn, in the scar above my heart. I tried to imagine an ice cube there, cooling away the fire. I stopped walking, dead in the middle of the sidewalk. Lance continued a few paces ahead and then, looking as if he'd lost something, stopped and glanced back.

"It's warmer if you keep walking. Standing still only invites frostbite. Scientific fact."

"No, I know." I shook my head. "I need to run to a drugstore. I forgot to pack a few things and I've been meaning to get out the past couple days, but you know how crazy it's been."

"I think there was a CVS a couple blocks back," he said.

"Yeah, thanks. Do you need anything or . . .?"

"Nah, I think I'm good, but do you want company? It's kind of dark out. I think I should go with you."

I sort of did want company—now that I thought about it, I wanted constant companionship from now until whenever that book stopped issuing threats—but I felt like it would require too much explanation, more than I was prepared to give right now. *This book has told me to create some combination of bunker/fallout shelter/panic room, so I've got some shopping to do, no big deal.* It was too tall an order to try to make that sound breezy.

"No, I'll be fine. It's so close by, I'll be back in no time."

"You sure?"

I tried especially hard to appear at ease. "Yeah, I'll catch up with you back there."

"Okay. I get the idea there's no telling you what to do." I had to smile when he said this. Before this job and this book, I liked to think that. "Let me know when you get in?"

"Sure."

We waved awkward goodbyes and Lance continued on.

Once at the drugstore, I decided it made the most sense to walk up and down every aisle keeping in mind the few tenets of emergency supply shopping the book had dictated. Before long I had accumulated so much that my basket could barely hold it all. I already had a first-aid kit so I was generally in good shape with those medical staples, but I went to town on everything else. Among my finds: six-packs of bottled water and Gatorade, boxes of protein bars, a mini fire extinguisher, a pocketknife, a lighter, mace, a flashlight, packs of batteries, trail mix, and a few candy bars. (I was hungry, so it probably was not the best time to shop.) It seemed sufficient. I was about to check out when I decided to grab extra gauze and burn ointment for my tingling scars.

There was hardly anyone else in the store, but I noticed a guy in a parka, and not just any winter weather deterrent, but a black one engulfing him all the way down to his ankles. He was enormous—he had to have been at least six foot five. I had noticed him first in the snack aisle and paid him no mind, but now he stood before the display of medical tape and scissors and I could tell from the angle of his head, he was peeking over at me. He had the hood up, so I couldn't see anything except his feet: black patent leather sneakers like the ones Dante had made such a fuss over. The ones we had seen on Beckett. That made me feel safe. It had to be him, right? Should I take a chance and try to say hello? But if for some reason it wasn't him, then I'd be so embarrassed, and I might be just as embarrassed if it was him and he wasn't particularly friendly. I had to at least stop staring.

I refocused my attention on the gauze bandages, debating what size roll to get, when I noticed a rustling at the end of the aisle, and then the crack of plastic being torn open. I looked from the corner of my eye, behind a curtain of my hair. Slowly inching away from him, I spotted the rack holding the medical scissors, the ones used for cutting bandages: the whole handful of them were swinging. His hands, shielded by his body, were moving, and the plastic and paper of the scissors packaging dropped to the floor.

And then he took off.

He blew past me, giving me one strong-armed shove as he

ran, knocking the wind out of me. My forehead crashed into the shelf, and a flash of light knocked out my vision for a moment. I fell to the ground in a heap, boxes of Band-Aids, tubes of burn ointment and antiseptic raining down on me, the contents of my basket scattered across the floor. I struggled to pry my right eye open; the space above my eyebrow felt like it had been severed in two and a tennis ball was wedged into it. I touched it and could feel a bump rising already.

Then I heard the scream. I'd never heard a scream like that. Chills ran straight down my spine, so sharp I ached.

It took me a few minutes to move. I heard a man's voice at the front of the store. " . . . yes, Twenty-second and State Street . . . the one at the corner . . . Yes, a woman on the ground . . . Please hurry . . . thank you."

I slowly eased myself into a sitting position. Sirens shattered the night outside. The aisle was a mess. I didn't know whether to move or to hide or to run. I figured the guy had left if the clerk called for help, but how did I know he wouldn't come back? I heard another voice at the front now, murmuring. I crept to the end of the aisle and peeked to the front of the store. The cashier was speaking to another customer, a woman.

"And then he just ran outta here with a knife or something in his hand, stabbed her, I guess. She went down, but she got in a good punch to the eye, and he disappeared." The cashier heaved; they were both looking outside the front windows of the store. "Never seen anything like it, all my years. Guess I've just been lucky."

"Where did he go?" I asked from my spot at the end of the aisle, scared to move forward. My voice came out sounding so meek even I could barely hear it. Outside, a woman lay sprawled on the ground, with another customer hovering over her. I figured she must still be alive because the person seemed to be speaking to her and getting some response. "Did they catch him?"

"Don't know, hon," the cashier said, elbows on the counter. "You okay?" I nodded. "Hope you don't mind, I locked us in till the cops get here. Thought it'd be safer."

I nodded again, letting my eyes drift to the scene unfolding outside the glass doors. Blinding lights swirled, more sirens blared as an ambulance approached. But before the EMTs could get out, the victim sprung to her feet. She steadied herself on her heeled boots, gathered her black coat around her, and then took off running, so fast I never saw her face, just the dark hair swinging in the wind. It occurred to me now that she had been at the ATM when I got to the store. The paramedic in the passenger side of the ambulance jumped out and started to run after her but then stopped and gazed into the night, seeming to have lost her.

"Now, why would she go runnin'?" the cashier said, shaking his head.

I kept watching, expecting her to come back. More sirens sounded and a police car pulled up, lights flashing.

I told the officer—a forty-something man with a paunch, a thick mustache, and a thick Chicago accent, which I found oddly comforting and strong—what little I had seen of the man, but I didn't mention that I thought I might know who he was. It couldn't possibly be Beckett, could it? I had my first trip in a police car (it probably felt a lot different in the front, where I sat, than in the back). He told me they hadn't caught the guy and that he didn't understand why the woman took off either. "Shock, coulda been," he reasoned. "But if she ran, she must be okay. Youz be careful, 'kay?" I nodded. He chalked it up to just another mugging, but when you don't see that kind of thing on a regular basis—or ever—it sticks with you. When you've been told that you're in danger by a book that's writing its pages just for you, scenes like this tend to want to cleave onto your memory and not let go.

All I knew was that I was grateful not to have had to walk those few blocks back to the hotel on my own.

$\mathcal{D}$ante was working late at the Vault again, but within fifteen minutes of my arriving back in my room, Lance was knocking on my door—loud, urgent knocks. I opened it and he started talking before I could say hello.

"You probably thought I was just making conversation when I said, Please let me know when you get back, but actually, just so you know, I was serious. So, anyway, glad you're home." He began to stalk away, offended, it seemed.

"I only just got back," I said to his back. He stopped and turned around. "I'm sorry. It's been a long night."

"Yeah, I know. I left you almost two hours ago. Where've you been?" I could tell he was sincerely worried, which I was touched and surprised by. It helped begin to settle my own rattled nerves.

"I'm sorry, but I—"

"What's going on here?" He cut me off and leaned in toward my face for a closer look.

"A souvenir from . . . some excitement at the drugstore." I sighed. His face fell. I went ahead and gave Lance the condensed version of what had happened. He stood there in the doorway, listening. "So, at least I got to ride back here in style." I tried to end on an upbeat note, but my attempt at humor did nothing to disguise the underlying tremor in my voice.

"Are you okay?"

"Yeah." I sighed again. "Just really worn out."

"I bet. Well, that's the last time I let you convince me you're fine to go on a solo expedition after dark." His voice was tinged with guilt.

"I guess you're entitled to one 'I told you so.'"

"Just be careful."

I nodded and then remembered: "So did our bosses even notice that we were gone so long?"

"Nope. When I got back, there was no sign of anyone anywhere."

"That's a relief."

"Yeah." We were both silent a few long seconds. The evening had sapped all my strength. I think he could tell. "Well, I guess I'll let you get some rest," he said, but lingered another second or two, as though deciding whether he wanted to say something that was on his mind. Instead, he just looked at the ground and shook his head and then looked back at me. "G' night."

"Night," I said, swinging the door shut.

I shoved all of my new purchases in the closet to get them out of the way, and then remembered: I had been instructed to read the book tonight. Queasiness set in, which was my involuntary response every time I picked up that black leather-bound tormentor. Before tackling it though, I ran cold water on a washcloth, rung it out and folded it, making a compress. I lay on my back, the washcloth over my eye, and held the book above me, slowly turning the fragile pages one by one. Sure enough, a new page had been filled in.

Perhaps today proved that it behooves you to follow closely what is asked of you in these pages, when it is asked. There is a reason behind every task you will be required to perform; you need to trust implicitly in this book. If you fail to adhere to each task, you will only hurt yourself. There are opportunities every day to be killed.

That line set me shuddering. I read it three times before I could go on. Who was writing this to me?

But if you do heed these words, you won't be. There is much you don't know. Be patient and it will be revealed to you in due time.

I had to stop for a moment to let it sink in: that man who pushed me could have killed me if he wanted to. Something had kept that from happening. And the book wanted me to know that this near miss had occurred because I hadn't carried out this most mundane-seeming shopping trip in the morning. Well, I had tested what happened when I didn't precisely follow what it said. Now I supposed it was worth seeing what might be different if I *did* go along with it.

Consider evening engagements canceled for tonight.

What was I supposed to be doing? I searched my mind and then fastened on it: Aurelia wanted me to take photos at the Vault. It twisted my stomach into knots imagining the scene in her office tomorrow morning, when I would have exactly zero photos to show her, but it didn't seem I had much choice. The Vault would be there tomorrow night too, and the next night, and the next . . .

Tonight, please explore what's beyond that opening you found in the closet floor. Descend until you hit solid ground. There will be one direction to go in for quite some time. When it opens up, pursue all paths until you begin to understand the layout. Get comfortable, for you will be spending a good deal of time there.

Before the end of the day tomorrow, repair the closet light. Then return here for further instruction.

I closed the book but didn't move. I didn't want to go. But finally I laced my sneakers back up and loaded batteries into the new flashlight. Then I dragged everything back out of the closet: my duffel bags and coat, my supplies from the drugstore. I found that seam on the floor again and, this time, wedged the pocket-knife in there and pulled up the door. Musty, stale air wafted out at me. I thought of Lance. He wouldn't like this at all—not that I planned to tell him—but just the idea of it made me laugh to myself. Scared as I was.

I couldn't believe I was actually going to do this.

I shined the light down into the narrow black pit, but it was to get swallowed by folds of darkness. All I could see were thick wooden slats nailed into one side of the passageway to be used as a ladder. But everything below a certain point disappeared into this murky abyss. It was impossible to tell how far down it went. I would just have to investigate on foot.

I looped the flashlight around my wrist and tucked the mace key chain into my pocket (hoping with every bone in my body that I wouldn't have a reason to use it) and lowered myself down into the pit's clutches, one foot then the other feeling around in the darkness until each united with one of the planks. With every slow step down, the thick, stagnant air got warmer, as though I were crawling deeper into the bottom of a sleeping bag. My nervous hands left the floor of the closet and searched for a secure spot on the first rung—it was mostly sanded and smooth, with just a few errant, jagged patches here and there. Hopefully I could avoid too many splinters. The wood was several inches thick, giving me a little room to hang on; I dug my short, stubby nails in as best I could. The flashlight hung straight down from my wrist illuminating to some degree the darkness below. I could feel the brick walls of the passage close in around me. I had about a foot of space on each side.

After what felt like years, I ran out of planks and my foot poked around and found, at last, the bottom. I looked back up, long-ingly, toward the door in my closet floor, but I couldn't see any trace of light from up top anymore.

I breathed in the heavy air, thick with decaying brick and mor-tar dust. I was at the end of some sort of hallway. I walked along, the flashlight beam shaking in front of me, until I reached an open doorway with a hazy light leaking out. I stepped through, into yet another corridor, this one at least ten feet wide, its con-crete walls and the ceiling lined with long snaking pipes. I felt swallowed up. The only sound came from the hushed crunch of my feet over decades of dirt and crumble. The silence echoed deep into my bones.

Finally the pathway opened up into a fork, both sides lit dimly, but lit nonetheless, with bare bulbs dotting the ceiling amid end-less wispy, cottony cobwebs. I stuck to the path on the right — re-membering that old trick from cornstalk mazes as a kid that if you're in a maze and you place your right hand on the right wall eventually you will always be led out, even if it takes eons — and followed it until it spilled into a space that looked like it had once been a room. Parts of the walls were stripped away, leaving wooden beams exposed behind sections of plaster. Some spots were pock-marked with gaping boulder-size holes running straight through them, while other sections remained nearly intact, even display-ing traces of peeling, faded wallpaper that matched my room. At the very back was a red-painted door, with a single steel security bar horizontally set across it.

Outside the room, I turned a sharp corner and found nothing but a few boarded-up spots where there used to be doorways. Now I was sweating too. It had to be over 85 degrees. I unbuttoned my cardigan so I was just in my T-shirt and was tying it around my waist when I hit what appeared to be a dead end with a boarded-up wall. Beyond it I could hear the faint twang and thump of muffled music, like something brought forth from a crackly record player.

I put my hands to the boards and one swung open a sliver, creaking as it did. I had to squeeze in between freestanding shelves to get in—it seemed as if the people who owned this place didn't know they had this passageway. Now the music poured out at me, horns and bass and drums and piano, and the murmur of voices and clink of glasses and bottles. The space was hardly bigger than the size of my room, and stacked floor to ceiling with boxes labeled with brands of alcohol and shelves full of more boxes marked from a food supply company, bulk quantities of chips and peanuts. A fridge stood in one corner. A rickety wooden staircase poked up toward the source of the music. I ascended only a few steps, enough to spot glasses stacked on low shelves behind a bar. A pair of sneakered feet walked near the mouth of the stairs and I clicked off my light and crept back down. Lance and I had passed a couple of ramshackle-looking bars on our walk to the L earlier. I wondered if this was one of those. I couldn't quite get myself oriented to where I might be in relation to the street above; it had been too much of a labyrinth getting here. I slithered back out of the storage room and pulled the board shut behind me.

Then I heard it: a soft shuffle, footsteps echoing, like muted gunshots to my heart. I couldn't even tell what direction they had come from. The acoustics sent each one bouncing off a different wall or spot on the floor or part of the ceiling.

Paralyzed, except for the quaking of my nerves, I gathered myself enough to head back the way I'd come. As I neared that room with the red door, the footsteps got louder. I crouched to the floor, keeping low, crawling to that wall with the chunks missing. My knees seemed to shatter against the heavy concrete. The temperature, coupled with my fear, made me lightheaded and more feverish by the minute. The footsteps stopped: this person had to be inside that crumbling room.

Huddled behind the partially destroyed wall, barely breathing, I peeked between rotted wooden beams. Inside, Beckett stood in profile, choosing the proper key from the jangling key ring in his hands. He turned his back, unlocking the steel bar first, then the door. Yanking it open with both hands, he unleashed from the doorway a roar, the rushing fury of wind or fire, and, along with it, a red glow. And heat, so much that it dried out my skin, instantly coating it. He too turned away from it for just a moment, twisting in my direction. I saw it, just a glimpse: his right eye was swollen, the lid a puffy pink pillow. On reflex, my eyes shot to his feet: yes, black, shiny, and familiar. My instant nausea told me that it couldn't be pure coincidence. Adjusting to the heat, he took a few steps into the doorway, one arm up to shield himself from the light and the blaze. In the other hand, I now noticed, a pendulum was swinging—it sparkled, catching the light. It looked like one of those amethyst necklaces. He wound up to pitch and threw it inside, then closed the door, needing all his strength, putting his body into it, and pulled the bar down across it, giving it a shake to be sure all was locked up.

He turned around.

I ducked. Just in time. He had a fifty-fifty shot of walking toward me, and if he did, I had no idea what I would possibly do or say. My heart sped so fast I thought I might pass out from the force of it beating against my chest, trying to crash through my rib cage. If he started this way and I had enough time, I could try to wedge myself through this hole in the wall, but the wooden beams would make it close. I wasn't sure I would quite fit and if I did, I didn't know if I could do it fast and quietly enough. So I just held my breath and prayed he wouldn't approach.

The footsteps reached the threshold of the room. I pushed my back against the wall, wishing to melt into it. And listened. He took a step or two and then, as though remembering where he was going or changing his mind, he walked away, down the hallway I hadn't explored yet. I waited until I couldn't hear his footsteps and then I waited some more. Finally I crept from my spot into that room, toward that door. A column ran through the center of the horizontal bar, accepting a cylindrical key that would have to be shaped like a pentagram. On the door itself was another larger lock in the same design. I touched it and my hand flew back involuntarily. The door was stovetop hot. I shook my hand to cool it, but this did little more than make my wrist ache too. I needed to get out of here.

But there was one more path to try. I headed back the way Beckett had gone, past a few locked doors and an open one. Inside the narrow hallway, the only light came from slim strips along the tops of the walls. I followed them, feeling blindly for extra guidance. I was too scared to put the flashlight on. He could be standing here, waiting for me. But another fear propelled me, fear of what might happen if I didn't pursue this path, if I didn't complete my assignment tonight sufficiently enough to satisfy what this awful book expected of me. The temperature cooled off as I walked along, and my jumbled head began to clear. *Just see this to the end and you can go back up to your room and your bed, back near where Dante and Lance slept just a few yards away.*

I felt the bass first, beating and thumping in my chest and then my head. The volume got louder, and I could almost name the song. Then the track lighting along the ceiling stopped and so did I. In the distance, a cascading flame flickered.

I had reached the Vault. I was on the other side of that fiery wall.

I ran. I flew out of there before anyone might find me, back the way I'd come, through the dark hall, and the door and the corridor to the planks up to my room. I fumbled on the first few planks, my palms so sweaty I couldn't grip them; my feet slipped and slid. But I had something going up that I didn't quite have on my way down: a rush of adrenaline. I couldn't bear another minute down there. My skin crawled, every ounce of me burned to get back up to my room, to close up this portal. I made it up a few of the planks and got into a groove. I went as fast as I could, finding that if I just kept in motion not trying to get perfect footing, I could keep ascending. Sweat slicked up every inch of my skin, making my T-shirt stick to me, and my hair stick against my face. Finally I saw the light from my room. I pulled myself up with the last bit of strength I had and crawled onto the floor of the closet, slamming the door down with my foot. I couldn't move. My chest heaved. I closed my eyes; everything ached. Muscles I didn't even know I had cried out in pain.

I fell asleep on the floor.

And of all the competing images and horrific scenes I'd witnessed that day, the one thing that flashed like a strobe light in my mind as I dozed was the last thing I would have expected: I kept seeing that painting, *La Jeune Martyre*.

11

Tell Me You Forgive Me
or I Won't Let You Go

I woke up on the floor—my first clue that last night had really happened. I had hoped it was a dream, another bad one, but no, I was on that worn, matted-down carpet in my T-shirt and jeans. The only pleasant surprise: the swelling above my eyebrow had miraculously managed to deflate. At least my face had returned to a relatively normal state, even if my mind was as scrambled as ever. I got myself showered and dressed and then, hand to my stomach to quiet the queasiness, I slunk toward Aurelia's office for our morning meeting, still constructing an adequate defense for why I had failed to take photos at the Vault. I was nervous, and also in pain. It took great effort to move my legs after all that climbing last night. Simply lifting my arm up to rap on the door of her office strained my weary muscles.

"Yes, come." I heard her beckon. I opened the door and found her seated at her desk, papers in her hand. She barely let me take one step before asking, "Are you finished painting that mural?"

"Um, definitely not."

"Good, don't come back until you are."

I nodded and pulled the door shut again. I had gotten lucky. As soon as I was alone in the darkened hallway, my stomach steadied and I discovered I was starving. Ravenous. I needed to eat immediately. The mural could surely wait a few minutes.

Lance, it appeared, had had the same idea. I found him already seated at the butcher-block island of the Parlor's kitchen, hunched over a bowl of cereal.

"Hey," he said.

"Morning," I said as he pushed a box of Lucky Charms toward me. "Thanks. We need our strength to channel Hieronymus Bosch." I pulled a bowl down from the cupboard, grabbed a spoon, and took the seat next to him, pouring my cereal.

"No kidding." After a moment, he asked, "So what were you up to last night?"

"I pretty much just passed out. I was so tired after, you know, everything." Not a lie necessarily, I just omitted a few details.

"I came by. I couldn't sleep. I thought I saw your light on under the door, but you didn't answer."

"I must've been asleep already."

"I guess." He wasn't satisfied. I could tell by the way he poked at his cereal with his spoon. He tried again: "Should I ask if you want to, you know, talk about last night?"

"Um—"

"Fine, no problem, we can change the subject."

"Thanks." I didn't mean to be so evasive. I wanted to talk, but I had no idea what I could get away with. After the drugstore, and Beckett, and everything that happened last night, I didn't want to go inviting any daily opportunities for death, as the book so kindly warned. So I said nothing.

Finally, Lance gave in and spoke. "So, changing the subject: Who's George Phillips?" He tried to lighten his voice, as though he knew I needed to be distracted.

I brightened too and made a fake gasp. "I didn't want you to find out this way. But we're in love! We're running away together." I fluttered my eyelashes.

"Hilarious." He rolled his eyes.

"Please. Al Capone's alias when he lived here."

"Did you get to the part about how he used to see ghosts here? His henchmen thought he was losing it."

"Yep. Haunted by folks he knew who got killed in the St. Valentine's Day massacre." Now that I thought about it, I felt a bit of an odd kinship with Capone. Poor guy had those scars, was tormented by these visions, and no one believed him. Although, he deserved it, didn't he? I offered my own piece of trivia. "Here's one: what floor did he live on?"

"Fifth. You're good."

"We have to start reading different books so we can actually stump each other."

"That's a good idea." He thought about it. "Then we can compare notes. Okay, we're officially a study group."

"Deal."

Lance and I painted all afternoon, mostly in silence, starting at opposite ends of the mural and working our way in. We decided starting at the top made the most sense. After last night I wasn't so scared of ladders anymore.

I yawned my way through the day, exhausted and sore, and caught Lance looking over from time to time, no doubt wondering if a person this sleepy should be balancing ten feet in the air and trying to paint. He probably also wondered what had me so tired if I really had gone to bed as early as I'd claimed. But the repetition of the work, painting the same color for hours, this inky black sky, could make anyone at least a little numb. I felt my mind wandering. When it roamed too far—back to that book, to the idea that I would at some point have to go back down the passage in the closet again—I would rein it back in and send it off running in a more pleasant direction, if I could find one. This is what I was doing when I thought I heard my name. I must've missed it the first few times he called because when Lucian's voice finally reached me, Lance just shook his head at me.

"Looking good, guys." Lucian strolled toward us, hair looser, the way it was at the Vault that first night. He wasn't in one of his trademark suits either, but wore jeans, a slim V-neck sweater with a button-down shirt underneath, collar unbuttoned and sleeves rolled up: effortless, all of it. Dressed like this, it reinforced how young he seemed. But any way you looked at it, he was out of my league. He stood in the space between our ladders, looking up at us. "Move over, Michelangelo."

"It's Bosch, actually," Lance said, not in a know-it-all way, just putting it out there.

"Back off, Bosch," Lucian corrected himself.

It took me this long to formulate a greeting. "Hi," I said at last.

"Hi." Lucian held on to the side of my ladder with one arm. Lance turned back to his work. "Didn't want to startle you up there, so—"

"No, not at all." I smiled down at him.

"Hey, could I . . . ?" He motioned for me.

"Oh . . . yeah, of course," I said, slowly processing and savoring that he had come in here wanting to talk to me. I focused on stepping down from the ladder as gracefully as possible. If ever there was a moment for poise, this was it. I was a few rungs from the bottom when he held a hand up toward me. I looked at it, smooth and perfect with elegant fingers. I was supposed to grab it and let him guide me down. Shifting, I took his hand and then took the last few steps much too fast, one-two-three, nearly sliding down them and landing with the slightest bounce. It may have just looked like I had a burst of energy and not like I bungled those last few steps, but really I had come painfully close to falling. Even so, Lucian grinned, his blue-laced gray eyes swimming into mine.

He flicked his head toward the doors of the gallery and I followed.

"You guys are doing a nice job," he said as we walked.

"Thanks." I could barely look at him. "I think it's going better than we thought. As long as it doesn't come out looking like Jackson Pollock it'll be better than I expected."

He laughed.

"We just got a couple great pieces in today. I'll have to show you," he said. "And supposedly we're getting one of Capone's old hats too." He held the gallery door open for me and I stepped through.

"Well . . . hats off to you." I smiled.

"Indeed," he said with that look, the playful one that drank me in. We were outside the gallery now and wandering toward the front of the lobby. We had it all to ourselves. "I heard Aurelia was happy with your photos of the Outfit."

"Oh? I'm glad."

"She would never tell you this but she loved the one you took of her. She even called the printer to have them blow it up bigger than she had originally planned." He paused and then lowered his voice. "But you didn't hear that from me."

"Hear what?" I said, playing along.

"Exactly," he whispered back.

He stopped walking and looked at me. "But I didn't come by to talk about Aurelia or photos."

He looked serious. "I feel awful about this, but is there any chance we could reschedule that dinner? Things are getting hectic with the opening so close. I know that's a terrible excuse but I'm hoping you'll let me make it up to you?" He looked like he was bracing for me to be upset. What alternate universe had I slipped into that *he* was trying to convince *me* to see him? These few minutes were the highlight of my year so far. Or at least, this came in second to my birthday. So, yes, a resounding yes, he was welcome to make it up to me anytime.

"Sure." I was a little nervous anyway and could use more prep time—this alleged dinner was going to be my first date. Ever. I didn't count the homecoming dance this past fall with Dante, for obvious reasons. "Totally understand."

"Thank you." He was serious, his expression stormy for just a flash. "There's just . . . a lot going on these days."

"I imagine. It sounds like the gala is going to be incredible."

"We hope."

"It'll be strange to see this place full of people."

"I know." He scanned the lobby, distracted.

"It must feel like you're about to open up your home and take on, like, three hundred boarders."

"Yeah, I guess it is like that."

"What's your favorite thing about this place?"

"I don't know, I never thought about it," he said, eyes away for a moment, as though he were finally giving it some consideration. "You?"

Me?" It came out before my reasoning faculties had kicked in.

I had skidded into some intersection of dream and reality. But, no, slow down—he hadn't meant *me*, specifically. "I mean, oh my favorite—hmmm—I like the chandelier." I pointed toward it. "The way it looks different depending on the time of day. It has personality."

"I suppose it sort of does, doesn't it?"

I shrugged, shy again. We had reached the gallery entrance, that curtain shrouding the glass door.

"Well, I guess I can't let Lance paint that whole thing . . ." My hands fidgeted.

"No, I guess you can't, can you?" he said. With an outstretched arm, Lucian pulled the velvet curtain back for me to pass, then in one sweeping movement, wrapped it around both of us so we were cocooned in it. His cedar scent made my head spin and my skin bake. I'm sure I couldn't hide the shock in my face.

"Tell me you forgive me for Friday or I won't let you go," he said.

"Now I'm not sure what the right answer is."

"Good." He kissed me quick on the cheek.

Then he spun us out of the curtain. I stumbled toward the gallery door.

"Dinner soon, I promise," he said.

I nodded, still lightheaded, in the most wonderful way.

He slipped out behind the curtain and was gone.

Lance was still up on the ladder when I glided back in. I had to collect myself before going up. My arms and legs felt like liquid, nothing the least bit sturdy about them. "Important business meeting, Ms. Terra?" he asked, eyes on me for only a second then returning to his work with a smirk.

We painted steadily, with only a short break to make sandwiches at lunchtime (not as good as Dante's but edible nonetheless), until we could feel the shift of day melting into dusk.

Lance checked his watch and announced, "Quittin' time. Six o'clock. I think that's fair, right?"

"Sounds good to me." I put the finishing touches on a milky gray patch of sky hovering over the bloody lake. Staring at this long enough wouldn't help with my nightmares.

As we packed everything up, my mind began its transition to my nighttime persona—the scared girl who was a slave to this curious book. My hands were still raw from clawing at those planks last night. My muscles had eased but they didn't feel ready to go through all of that again.

"So what are you up to tonight?" Lance asked. His hands were full with paint canisters, after reorganizing the shelves of the supply closet, while I rinsed our brushes in the sink.

I had almost forgotten: "I'm supposed to take pictures at the Vault."

"I'm sure you'll find plenty of willing subjects."

"No kidding." People there certainly didn't seem shy. Maybe I'd even get to see Dante. Our schedules were so different, I was starting to really miss him. "I do kinda wanna try some of the snacks and things Dante's been testing out in the club. It beats having to make our own dinner, right? You should come too."

"You had me at snacks."

"I figured that would clinch it. I guess maybe eleven again?"

"Works for me."

I finished with the brushes and then went to collect the camera. I thought I might try to sneak in a nap before my photography duties.

Lance had just finished up and was turning off the light in the storage room.

"I think we're all set here," he said. And something occurred to me.

"Question." I hesitated. "Do you think anyone would mind if I stole one of the ladders, real quick?"

He gave me a funny, what-are-you-up-to look.

"The string broke on that light at the top of my closet. Have you noticed the ceilings are freakishly high?" Probably not, since he's about six feet tall. "I mean, not for you, but—"

"If you wanted help, you just had to ask."

"No, I wasn't—"

"Sure, I know, you have your pride. Let's go."

Lance hauled the ladder down the elevator. It was kind of nice to have the help. It would've taken me twice as long and I probably wouldn't have been able to lift it in the first place and if I had then I probably would've knocked out a lighting fixture or something along the way. He also insisted on reattaching the string himself. I stood nearby shining the flashlight up at him as his nimble fingers worked.

"I'm impressed you have a flashlight," he said. "That's more of a guy thing, to bring something like that."

"Well, I brought stuffed animals too."

"Did you really?" He looked down at me.

"No."

"Oh." He sounded disappointed now in my lack of girlishness.

"Not that I don't appreciate this, but just so you know, I could totally do this." He wasn't listening.

"How many honors students does it take to change a light bulb—"

I cut him off: "It doesn't even need to be changed; it's just the string that—"

"Two. One to do it while the other one argues that she doesn't need help because she can do everything by herself."

"I don't need help," I said, smiling at my own expense.

"Exactly."

"But if you want to be macho, then who am I to stand in the way." I gesticulated with the flashlight.

"Light please. Up here."

I shined it right at him, blinding him for a moment. He shielded his face. "Yup, thanks."

I wasn't trying to be difficult. I just wanted this all wrapped up as quickly as possible. I couldn't decide whether the book would consider it some sort of violation that I hadn't repaired this myself. With a click and a twang, the light went on.

"You're in business," Lance said, giving the string a couple extra tugs to secure it.

"Thanks."

"Any other odd jobs?" he asked as he stepped down from the ladder.

"No." I laughed. "I think that's it for now, but I'll let you know. Thanks again."

"Sure thing." He breathed on his glasses and cleaned the lenses on his T-shirt. "Dusty up there." His eyes were bigger without them and a little spacey, since he couldn't see well. His scar wasn't so bad at all. Maybe it was selfish for me to think that I liked it because I had three sets of them, but he wore it well. It made my heart ache just a little to know how much it bothered him.

"Yeah, turns out there's no maid service for our rooms," I said, with just enough sarcasm.

"I'm still waiting for them to tell us that *we're* going to be the maid service."

"Funny," I said. "Or, I mean, I hope that ends up being a joke. Between you and me, we'd get fired."

"At least you started making your bed."

"Ha-ha."

"So, eleven."

"Eleven it is," I said.

He started to let himself out and then turned back around. "You good till then?" His protective streak setting in.

"I'm fine, just gonna do some reading, hang out." I thought of the book, thankful it hadn't been out. But then, it never seemed to be around when anyone was in there, like a shy kitten who hides when the doorbell rings.

He nodded, finding this answer acceptable. "See ya then."

I waved and thanked him again. He had left the ladder, but no one would need it between now and tomorrow morning, so I just pulled the string and closed the closet door.

It was sloth night at the Vault, which seemed ironic to me since I had been ordered there to work. The two Outfit members at the door—the same girl as always, but no Beckett—waved Lance and me right through, no problem. Since I was on the job, I decided that also meant I didn't have to go to any extra trouble to wear just the right thing. My jeans and thermal long-sleeved tee would have to do. Besides, without Dante's styling help, there wasn't much hope for me anyway. Lance, unsurprisingly, showed up in the same thing he'd had on all day—jeans and a T-shirt over a long-sleeved shirt—even sporting a splatter or two of black paint. He stuck by my side as I roamed the place, snapping shots of the raucous partygoers and randy dancers, and the couples who had retreated into those hollowed-out stalagmite-like structures.

We had managed to orbit the ring of fire a number of times without either one of us suggesting we go up there. Raphaella, I noticed during our second trip around the ring, had latched on to Lance, her eyes following him around the club. I saw him looking up at her from time to time but then he would just as easily turn his gaze elsewhere. I finally stopped in my tracks when I saw that cascade of blond zeroing in once more from her perch. I faced him like I had serious news to tell him.

"Raphaella is totally checking you out again."

"Really?" He glanced over. There she was.

"Like you didn't notice," I teased.

He looked shy.

"Go on." I flicked my head toward the ring. "Just because she barely talks to me doesn't mean she won't talk to you." I cringed at the thought of my thwarted attempt to befriend her that first night.

He glanced at the ring of fire, weighing it for just a second. I looked up there too—I'd had one eye on that platform all night long but still no sign of Lucian. The camera had been a good excuse to come around here looking like I had a greater purpose than just finding him. It was actually comforting that he hadn't shown up—maybe he really did have that much work to do.

"You cool down here?" Lance asked, decision made.

"Totally. I'm just gonna take a few more and then probably head back. Go!" I smiled. "See you tomorrow."

He nodded and wandered, hands in his pockets, over to that spiral staircase. I watched him bounce up the stairs. Bodies circulated all around me but I felt strangely solitary, a lone tree growing in a completely barren and deserted field. Lance's presence had become a comfortable and familiar one. We could talk or not, it didn't matter. It was just easy. I could certainly follow him up there onto that platform. Even if I sat there alone I would have the warmth of all those desirous eyes, all those other people in the room who longed for an invitation up there, knowing nothing of the icy chill or the hierarchy or that Lance and Dante and I didn't really, truly belong. If we were in the ring, anyone looking in wanted to be us as much as they wanted to be any of the others up there. When you're on the outside of anything and looking in, there is a tacit understanding that everything on the inside has more value.

I had been standing still, watching too closely for too long, when I felt a playful slap at my arm.

"I haven't seen you in years, girl!" Dante said, wide grin, when I turned around. He held a tray in the other hand, with a single perfectly fashioned morsel of something.

"Hey!" I squeezed his hand. "You're looking pretty at home. So this is where you've been spending your nights."

"It's crazy but I love it."

"I bet you do. How's it going?"

"Great! Exhausting, but great. Oooh, you've got to try one of these." He held the tray out to me.

"There's only one left."

"They're that good. Take it, it's all yours!"

"What is it?" I picked up the warm cloud of puffed pastry with some kind of sauce and spice dusted on top. The whole thing was barely bigger than a chocolate candy.

"A little bit of heaven."

I popped it in my mouth, in one bite. "Mmmm," I purred. It was very pretty and very tasty—melty with cheese inside, and sweet with the slightest kick. Whatever it was, I could've eaten ten more.

"Good, right? Better go, Etan's got me workin' like mad. Catch up tomorrow?" He kissed me on the cheek.

"Definitely. Have fun!"

He waved and hoisted the tray up on one hand, making his way through the crowd. He looked like this was his party, and he was the perfect host.

I watched as the revelry spun around me. I was part of this too. But still, I wasn't sure what it would take for me to feel included, to not be waiting for someone to discover I didn't belong.

As the night went on, I managed to sample more bits and bites from Dante and Etan's test kitchen on trays hoisted by gorgeous servers. I'd eaten enough that the night could've been gluttony instead of sloth, but through it all I had snapped my photos, so there would be plenty to show to Aurelia. I could safely call it a night. But first, one last shot. The last shot is always the boldest, because you know you're about to escape and have nothing to lose.

I crept up the stairs of the ring of fire, and just before reaching the top of the platform, I caught sight of Lance and Raphaella. He was talking to her and she was just staring at him, her fingers playing with that necklace, fluttering over it. He didn't see me take the picture. I was sure he would be glad to know I had, though.

I scanned quickly: no Lucian. But I did see Beckett. He had a drink in his hand and watched the floor of the club over the top of the flames, in a way that convinced me this was the first time he had been permitted to leave his post at the door to see the place from this privileged vantage point. He was in profile and then he turned: he had a patch over one eye.

12

Don't Get Too Comfortable

I skulked back down the stairs and scurried out of the club, my pace as brisk as possible without incurring notice or causing alarm. I just needed to go. I was probably overreacting, but I preferred to overreact from the comfort of my room, not in close proximity to someone who may have possibly roughed me up in the aisle of a drugstore and mugged a woman. I got to my room and felt achingly alone. So much so that I didn't know if I'd be able to sleep. Then it hit me: it wasn't exactly my decision whether or not I could sleep. That book was really starting to cramp my style. I snuggled back against the wall with it and began turning those familiar pages, turning, turning. And there it was, as expected, today's date and fresh writing.

You are tired from the exertions of last night. Rest, winged one. But don't get too comfortable. Shore up your strength for what's to come.

Your training must begin in earnest tomorrow. Tomorrow night, you will steal away down the passageway you discovered and run from the starting point at the bottom of the ladder to the farthest point you found —

I thought of that distance now, that bar with the music, the storage room—that would be the finish line, according to this.

And then you will run back. Go to your fullest potential for an hour, every other day until further notice. You will eventually need to make this distance lightning fast; this skill may one day save your life.

I didn't know exactly how fast I was capable of running, nor did I know the precise distance between these two points. I only knew that it was pretty far and that I was no track and field champion. I got the idea that the book was taunting me for being in relatively poor shape, which I didn't appreciate. It went on.

This will be your primary interest for the next week or so. Otherwise, simply do as others tell you. Do your best to not draw attention to yourself. Whatever discoveries you may make over the course of these next several days, tuck them away. You will be told when it's time to investigate them.

And steel yourself. You will soon be tested in a manner you have never known.

I flipped through a couple pages to see if there was anything else, but no. This brief missive, more vague than any I'd received so far, hit me harder than anything the book had told me since that dreaded first entry. There is nothing worse than knowing something life-shattering is headed your way and being powerless to stop it.

But nothing could be done tonight, so I tucked the book away in the night table and, noticing the closet light on, ducked in to pull the string. It came off in my hands with the twang of a busted guitar string. I took out my flashlight and climbed up the ladder. I shined the light up, threaded the string through a tiny eyelet on the fixture, and tied a quadruple knot, giving it a few good tugs. But the motion made me slip, and I threw my hand on the ceiling to steady myself. To my surprise, the panel groaned hollowly and lifted up. My stomach tightening, I slowly slid the whole flimsy panel to the side, peeking in. My light beam caught a flurry of dust, cobwebs, and a narrow passageway, large enough to crawl through. I couldn't begin to imagine where this might lead but I had a feeling I would be forced to find out. Tonight though, it seemed I would be off the hook. So I wedged that trusty desk chair under the doorknob again and crawled into bed.

As instructed, I kept a low profile and spent the following day painting after showing Aurelia the club photos. She was pleased and told me to have Lance upload them to add to the loop of shots flashing on the flat screen at the front desk, then ordered me to take more photos the night of the gala opening, a vote of confidence that made me proud. But, even so, I sleep-walked through much of the day, that dread setting in at the back of my mind and in the pit of my stomach, clouding my thoughts as each hour passed bringing me closer to evening when I would be forced to descend and run through the underground. I prayed that I would simply be running and not running *from* anyone. It had been a close call with Beckett and I didn't want to think about what might happen if I saw him again and wasn't so lucky in hiding. I didn't really want to come across any members of the Outfit down there, or anyone at all.

At the end of the day, Lance and I cleaned up and grabbed a sandwich in the Parlor kitchen. I needed to think of something else, anything else, so I pressed him about a certain matter that he hadn't breathed a word of all day.

"So . . . how'd it go last night with Raphaella? She's, like, freakishly beautiful. Like, underwear model beautiful."

He shrugged, taking a bite of his sandwich. "Yeah." He

chewed, and then he took another bite. And then he chewed some more. Another bite. I watched him, waiting for him to expand upon this. But nothing came, just his soft gnawing at his food. *Yeah?* That's all I was getting? I let it go and we finished our meals and returned to our respective rooms, bidding each other good night.

Tucked back in my room, I couldn't delay the inevitable any longer. I put on a pair of sweatpants and a T-shirt, took my flashlight and a deep breath, and opened the closet door.

The climb wasn't necessarily easier this time, but at least it was slightly familiar—I had braced myself for the ache and sting of my fingers as I clung to the planks and for that queasy feeling of descending into utter darkness. As soon as my feet hit the ground, I silently congratulated myself on a successful trip down.

The running could have gone better. I got winded a few minutes in—*minutes*—and had to walk about twenty feet, then picked up running again but at such a diminished speed that walking might have been faster. This is why my most rebellious act to date had been faking a sprained ankle when we were running the mile in gym class because I just couldn't bear to come in last as everyone else watched and heckled me.

When I reached that storage room door, I caught my breath and then ran right back. Once my prescribed hour of exertion was up, I returned to the ladder, anxious to crawl into my bed and rest my spent muscles. If only there were some way that the climb *up* could be at the beginning of this conditioning and the climb *down* at the end. But I pawed my way up the planks—resting midway, panting, holding on with every shred of my being and eventually making it to my closet and the relatively safe confines of my room.

The days began to pass quickly. Lance and I finished the mural—and it wasn't half bad—and kept busy with a series of odd jobs: straightening up rooms here and there; unpacking the gold-edged china for the Capone restaurant; fluffing LH-insignia-embroidered pillows and folding towels and all sorts of other not so glamorous tasks. I hadn't seen Lucian for days and had barely seen Aurelia more than a few minutes, when she would order me to do something.

Dante had been keeping vampire hours. He was up all afternoon and evening feeding the Vault and fine-tuning the gala menu with Etan, then sleeping much of the day. We really were two ships passing in the night—or more like the morning, when he would roll in post-club and I would be up early, heading to see Aurelia and get my marching orders. My nighttime sprinting had been wearing me out, but I stuck to it, reveling in the quiet victory of snipping a few seconds off my time, or waking up the morning after and feeling even a shade less in pain than I had after my previous training session.

On that Friday afternoon the day before the opening-night gala, we were all summoned to the library for a staff meeting, instructed to wear our new hotel-issued uniforms for a sort of dress rehearsal. We had been given seven each, so we could get through a week before doing laundry. I had tried mine on for the first time in my room an hour before the meeting. I slipped into the slim black dress I had seen on Celine weeks earlier and zipped up the side. It fit just fine, even if it wasn't a bit like anything I'd ever worn. Dante came by to show off his uniformed look: he had a chef's coat with his name stitched in, and his own hat too.

"You look totally hot. You clean up nice, girl!" He sprawled out on my bed, watching me try to figure out how to secure my hair in the back without making it look even worse than it did down.

"You don't think it's too short?" I asked, watching myself in the mirror and tugging on the hem of the dress, then checking his reflection for the verdict. He shook his head and rolled his eyes.

"Ugh. Please. It's not short at all, grandma. Could you be more prudish please?"

"Sorry, geez, I was just asking."

"When did your gams get so good anyway? Is that actual muscle tone?"

I couldn't help but smile. "Maybe."

"Check you out!"

"You're not so bad yourself. Love the hat."

"Thanks, I know. Sexy, right?" He mugged, making a face.

"Totally." I laughed. I twisted my hair and wrapped an elastic around it, but it didn't seem to want to stay in place. Aurelia had ordered me to wear it back in a chignon, but I had no idea how to accomplish that. It didn't escape Dante's notice.

"Okay, step aside and make room for someone who actually knows what he's doing." He got up and waved his hands for me to relinquish my elastic, bobby pins, and hairbrush. He pushed me into the desk chair, facing the mirror, and twisted and fluffed and tied back and pinned — and in no time, he had me looking exactly as I hoped Aurelia had had in mind.

"Voilà!" he said.

"Not bad," I said, looking at my reflection.

"Hope you were taking notes. I'm not doing that for you every day."

I stepped into the heels—also part of the uniform—black and strappy and at least four inches high. I had worn heels only a few times in my life, and never for very long periods of time. These pinched and rubbed at the back of my foot and smushed my toes together, actively injuring me with each step toward the mirror. *Ow.* But at the same time, now that I studied my reflection, this finished product, I had to admit it all conspired to be a polished look. I felt like a slightly more adult version of myself, someone more serious and accomplished. As Aurelia had said, uniforms really did change the way you felt about the work you were doing. I wanted to be even more perfect than ever now. I wanted to do the uniform proud.

Dante and I stopped by to get Lance, who answered the door buttoning his cuffs and without his tie. The men would be in black pants, button-down shirts, and insignia-bearing vests with red ties. He looked at us, sheepish, and held up the tie. "I've always had trouble with this."

He looked more filled out in the black uniform, still long and lean but more solid than he had in his usual jeans and T-shirts. Or maybe I just hadn't noticed how fit he was.

Dante stepped in to help, whipping the tie with sharp whooshes. "I don't know what you people would do without me. Who's gonna get you dressed in the morning? Not it!"

"Thanks," Lance said quietly.

"I'll be giving a tutorial in hair and tie origami later," Dante added.

"Sign us up," I said.

When we reached the library, the Outfit was already suited up and stretched out in a line side by side. I tried not to pay attention to how stunning the girls looked in the same ensemble I had on.

They also all had their hair tied back—some in sleek ponytails, some in twists, some in buns—and the men had theirs slicked back like Lucian's. Uniforms normally evened the playing field by stripping away armor and peacock plumage. But with these people, who would look unbelievable in anything, all I could do was give myself a tiny bit of credit for looking better in these clothes than I had expected.

Aurelia swanned in, Lucian beside her, and studied us all.

"Tomorrow at three in the afternoon, our home is going to open its doors," she began slowly, thoughtfully, as though about to impart something vital and serious. "New rules will be put into place. You are no longer to be seen anywhere out of uniform, except in the Vault, where you are to be attired in a manner befitting a representative of the hotel after hours. To get there, kindly use the stairwell behind the gallery rather than the elevator. Use the freight elevator to get to your rooms. Other communal areas—the library, Parlor, Capone, and the gallery—are off-limits unless you're on official business there. Meals can still be taken in the alcove of the Parlor kitchen, but not during peak hours. When it comes to interaction with the guests, do not speak unless spoken to but radiate an aura of general helpfulness, utmost professionalism, and effortlessness." Lucian, leaning against one of the desks, looked forward. His eyes caught mine and I looked away. I took a deep breath.

"Each of you will get instructions on what your job will be at the gala. Many of you will merely be ambiance, decoration, the equivalent of background music, which in itself is an important role at an event like this."

We all nodded in unison, standing firm and stiff. She stepped toward the door. "Until further notice . . ." She didn't finish; she just let that fragment linger as she and Lucian disappeared, trailed by the Outfit.

The next morning, Aurelia dispatched me to the gallery to "supervise"—and by "supervise" she meant mill around just to make sure disaster didn't strike as the newly framed photos were being hung. They looked even more stunning as a group—the whole even greater than the sum of its parts. Aurelia's photo was, naturally, the biggest, roughly four feet wide by six feet tall and occupying a space dead center on the wall nearest the gallery entrance. The next grandest was Lucian's, half the size of Aurelia's but far more dramatic to my eyes: even now I felt that he was watching me. The photos of the Outfit circled these, in orbit around them. And on this galaxy's outskirts: Lance, Dante, and me, tangential and tertiary to their core. Off to the side was a small printed placard that read "Photography by Haven Terra." I drew closer to it, thinking my eyes had fooled me. But, no, there I was. That I hadn't expected at all.

I left the gallery, everything perfectly in place, and stepped into the lobby. For a moment I felt truly part of it all—part of the hubbub and excitement that bubbled up, ready to burst forth tonight at this event, which would have to be something more electric than anything I'd ever witnessed. I could already feel an extra buzz and current in the air. The lobby seemed to hum in anticipation of all these strangers descending, all these people who would flock in search of something special. And I had never seen the place looking more worthy of adoration. Flower arrangements of only the most exotic, wildly shaped, boldly hued blooms dotted every table and surface, along with candles already lit and flickering even though it was just after noon. The chandelier gleamed and sparkled. Swinging jazz music swirled all around.

I had done a lap around the lobby, admiring it on my way to find the freight elevator and make my trial run, taking that rickety ride down to the basement level, when I saw Lucian. He was suited up and sprucing up a flower arrangement at the front desk. Behind him the flat screen shuffled through the photos I had taken at the Vault. Every single person who stayed here would see them when they checked in, just as everyone who set foot in the gallery would see my work, and my name, there. I had left a mark. Lucian's eyes found me and he smiled, beckoning me.

"Haven," he greeted me as I got near. "Did you see the gallery?"

"I was just there. It's amazing. I had no idea my name would be up there."

"You deserved it."

"Thanks." I felt myself blush and tried to stop it by looking away, changing the subject. "So, it's almost showtime."

"I know, hard to believe. Don't let her make you work too hard tonight. You should get to have fun too, you know."

"Well, if you insist, then . . ."

He leaned over, fussing with the flowers again—there were black and white bulbous orchid-looking things and ones that looked like ruffly black roses. He picked out one, pushed one side of my hair behind my ear, and then tucked the flower there. The bloom was so full I could feel it tickle my cheek.

"I do. I'll see you around tonight?"

"Of course," I said as he wandered off, a few steps backwards, still facing me.

"Good." He grinned again. "Happy Valentine's Day."

Back in my room, I made a home for my precious flower—the only flower I'd ever gotten from any boy—in a drinking glass and set it on my nightstand. I had just buried my nose in its petals, soaking in its spicy almost-lavender scent, when a knock rattled the door. Through the peephole, I saw Dante in his chef's coat holding a plant in his hands. I opened up.

"We're so formal today," I joked. He wasn't one to knock if the door was unlocked.

"HAP-py Valentine's Day!" he greeted me, holding out the potted plant and walking right in. He set it down on the desk, clearing a place among the handful of Chicago books I'd been hoarding. "Something gorgeous just like you! I found it in our garden and thought you might love it."

"It's beautiful, Dan, you're too sweet!" I leaned in to smell. The scent was like warm cookies. "There's a garden here?"

He looked surprised that I didn't know this. "Um, yeah."

"Who knew?" I touched the flower. The waxy crimson petals were warm against my fingertips. The bloom was easily the size of my palm, shaped like a star and a few inches deep. "I've never seen anything like it. Is it an orchid or what?"

"Close, it's a hybrid of . . ." He slowed down. "Of . . . something and something else."

"Ahhh, well that's what I would've guessed if it was a hybrid." I paused for reaction, but Dante only looked hurt by my poor joke. "Kidding, I'm kidding. It's amazing, thank you. Totally brightens up this place. And, gotta tell you: I'm getting so many flowers today, listen to this—"

He cut me off. "Oh, and don't water it. It's tough."

"Like, ever?"

"For a while," he said.

"Okay, like a cactus, I guess." I stroked it like it was a pet. "Does it matter that there's no sunlight to speak of down here? How's this bad boy going to photosynthesize?"

"It's resilient."

"Aren't we all," I joked. "So c'mon and sit down. What's going on today? Crazy, right? I haven't been up there since people started checking in—what's it like?"

"Yeah, no, I'd better run, tons to do with Etan, but enjoy. See you tonight!" He kissed my cheek and ran out the door before I could stop him. He must've been stressed out. I sniffed the plant's sweet scent again. It was unlike anything I'd seen.

I had just stepped out of the shower and was still mooning about my Valentine's Day flowers when suddenly my room was filled with a buzzing that would not stop. It was an old-fashioned rattling sort of buzz, very bee-like, but loud. Not so loud that it might be a fire alarm, but loud enough that I had to figure out how to make it stop or risk losing my mind. But in order to silence it, I had to first locate it. It was coming from the back of the room, near those curtains that covered the empty space where a window might have been if we weren't underground. Gripping both sides of the curtains, I threw them back in one swift motion. And, sure enough, there it was: a small silver box, looking like something from the 1950s, with a couple of buttons on the top and a dotted circular panel for a speaker. How was it possible I hadn't known this room had an intercom? I pressed the button marked Talk.

"Hello?"

"Haven, Haven, Haven," Lucian's liquid voice flowed out, filling my room, rising above the gravelly static that came with it and making me dreamy. I started playing with my necklace absent-mindedly and pulled my towel tighter around me, as though he were actually in the room.

"Hi . . . Lucian, um . . . how are you?"

"Excited for tonight and, of course, slightly manic." He said it perfectly calm, so much so that his voice could lull a person to sleep. "I'm just relaying a quick message. Aurelia"—he drew out her name, giving me time to get nervous—"would like to see you. She's in her penthouse—penthouse one."

"Oh, certainly, I'll be up in just a minute." I flashed through all I had to do in order to look presentable enough to see her. "Um, is everything—"

"Yes, promise, everything's fine." I could hear the smile in his voice. "She has something for you. For tonight. So don't worry about being dressed now. Whatever state you're in is perfectly ac-ceptable." I scanned the room, but, no, that was crazy. I mean, he couldn't *see* me. Sometimes, whenever I had a severe crush on someone, I had this sense that they were watching everything I did, that they could see me even when I was completely and entirely alone. I think that just happens when someone occupies so much space in your mind. You're thinking about them more than you're not; looking at them, looking for them, looking at yourself to see what they would think if they were looking at you at that moment. It's exhausting, but exhilarating. That electric current, the stir-ring in your veins, and flutter in your stomach and your heart, is what can get a person through the day.

"Um, okay, if you say so."

"I do."

"Then I'll be right there."

That was it. He and the static disappeared on the other end.

13

Beauty Is Genius

The flutter and fire I felt when I heard Lucian's voice quickly revved up, morphing into fear, leaving me harried and over-heated. Obviously I wasn't about to go up to Aurelia's penthouse looking this way. What did she have for me? I threw on my uniform and I dried my hair as fast as I could and wound it into the best bun—or, rather, chignon, thank you very much—that I could muster, trying to remember how Dante had done it.

In record time I was out the door and up the freight elevator to the penthouse level, which I had only seen that first day on the tour. It was like an entirely different hotel up there near the skylight, and now that night was setting in, I couldn't help but linger to look up. From here it was clear which were stars and which were reflections of the chandelier's many bulbs—how many had Lance said there were?—and they all twinkled, assuring you that there was magic in this place.

The carpet in the hallway was so soft and plush under my heels, it had a quicksand effect, slowing my trajectory to pent-house number one. But I arrived there eventually, and knocked and waited. The door creaked open.

"Hello, Haven," Aurelia breathed out at me in her rasp.

"Hello . . ." I had planned to say, "You look lovely," but she was wearing a black satin robe, so I vetoed that line and was too flustered to come up with anything else. From the neck up, she was entirely ready to go, though. Her hair had been pinned in a looser, wavier version of what I'd attempted to do with mine, but hers was secured at the side instead of straight back. It was sexy and perfect, with just the right pieces falling at her neck and around the delicate angles of her face. Her makeup was appropriately smoky: kohl-rimmed eyes, shaded all around with shimmery blacks and grays. Sultry and smoldering, a look worthy of a perfume ad. Finally, I spoke again. "I like your hair."

"Thank you. Soon I suspect you'll like yours too. Come."

She waved me in, looking me up and down, with the kind of blank expression that can be taken as polite criticism. I followed her, glancing quickly around the room: no Lucian. I didn't know whether I was glad or not—maybe relieved actually. If he were here and she had opened the door looking this way, then I would be forced to think of only one thing—them together—and I preferred not to think about that.

Now that I could push that thought out of my mind, I was free to appreciate the splendors of the penthouse. A wall of windows looked out onto the shining lights of Chicago with the pulse of cars zipping along Michigan Avenue below. It was a good thing I didn't have a room like this or I would spend all my time daydreaming. Aurelia led me to a mirrored vanity with a precious little chair and so many cosmetics and hair products and appliances spread out in neat little rows. I stood nearby as she rifled through her closet, taking out a garment bag and hanging it on a golden coat rack. She unzipped the bag but didn't unsheathe what was inside.

"Well, go ahead, sit down," she said, gesturing to the vanity seat. I did as I was told.

"This is a beautiful room," I said, trying not to be obvious as I peeked into the bedroom doorway past the entrance to the walk-in closet. A corner of the lavender and sage satin-covered bed poked out. The same colors as my room but so much more plush and luxurious here. You could only have good dreams in a place like this. And a pleasant reality too.

Aurelia ignored my attempt at small talk. "So you'll be playing the role of my right-hand woman tonight. You'll be at my side, doing what I ask, acting as a face for the hotel, meeting the city's various influentials." She paused. Enough time passed that I realized I needed to jump in before she would go on.

"Wow, thank you. That sounds fantastic." I couldn't help letting on that I was pleasantly stunned.

"You sound surprised."

"Oh, no, not at all—" In my attempt to sound confident, I was now starting to sound obnoxious and egotistical, so I shifted gears. "I'm thrilled . . . Absolutely . . . What can I do?"

"First, you can start looking the part." She stood behind me, her hands on my shoulders as she considered my reflection in the mirror. "If you're to be seen as something of my protégée tonight, then we'd better have you looking that way." In one swift motion, she unclipped my hair, letting my long mane fall and ruffling it up with her fingers. Just that motion made my hair more voluminous than it had ever looked when I tried to do anything with it. She looked me over with tense eyes and firm lips, as though proposing and rejecting in her mind a million different ways to transform this blank canvas. Finally: "There's a robe hanging behind the closet door. Put it on."

I nodded and disappeared into the walk-in closet. I had never seen so many clothes outside of a department store. Racks and shelves full of precisely folded or crisply hung garments, all in black, navy, or patterns with an anchor of black or navy, made of satins and silks, the most luxurious and slinky fabrics. I ran my fingers across a handful of dresses hanging innocently just waiting to be put on and instantly transformed into something that begged for attention and got it from so many eyes. Lined up on several of the shelves sat more shoes—towering, teetering heels—than it seemed possible for one woman to wear in her lifetime.

"Did you find it, Haven?" Aurelia called to me through the door. I quickly shimmied out of my uniform and threw it on the floor in a heap.

"Yes, got it right here," I called back, yanking the flimsy robe off the hook where it hung alone. It smelled like her, like those spicy florals of Lucian's flower. I tied it around me, the satin cool against my skin.

She already had a water spray bottle and comb in her hand when I emerged from the room. She pointed at the chair, I sat quietly, and then she made a motion for me to swivel toward her, away from the mirror.

"Beauty," she said as she took my chin in her hand and looked me over, "is a form of genius. Wouldn't you agree?"

"Sure," I said. I didn't really get it though. To me genius is genius—people like Nobel Prize winners and brain surgeons and artists. But beauty itself? The act of being beautiful? It wasn't even an action at all; it was purely passive. And genius is never passive. But I didn't think it was my place to say so. "I suppose."

"Beauty gets you what you want, every time," she went on. She spritzed my crown, took a glob of gel and coated my hair, then ran the comb through, slicing a side part on the right—I was generally a middle part kind of girl. She swiped the comb down smoothing my wet hair and then I felt her form what seemed to be ridges between her fingers and press them down against my head to set them. "It is the ultimate manipulation tool. It allows you to get away with certain things. People want to be near it, they want it to rub off on them. It's powerful, if you know how to use it." Finished with the ridges, she took a fat section of my hair, winding it around a thick curling iron.

"The greatest sin isn't taking advantage of it, but rather not knowing how to use it at all." She sprayed my hair and began curling another section. I wondered if this statement was directed toward me or if she was speaking in generalities. If this was about me then at least it would be flattering—it hadn't occurred to me that I possessed enough of this to possibly be used for manipulative powers. Now that I thought about it, that attitude was probably my first problem. "I shouldn't have to tell you that you could get away with an awful lot if you wanted to." My eyes shot to hers at this, on reflex. She only glanced at me as she set the curling iron down. Her fingers fluttered, twirling and tying back my hair low and to the side, like hers. Perhaps she was waiting for me to say something. I wanted to. I wanted to know more. If being at the Lexington had taught me anything, it was that I wasn't a thing like the people here. I studied them, dissected as best I could what made them *them*, but I didn't think I could duplicate their essence.

"I could?" I finally asked. Her hands paused in my hair for a moment and then resumed tucking in some final strands, pinning it all tightly against my head.

"Oh yes," she assured me. I liked this idea. I turned it over in my mind, looking at it from different angles. I pictured myself like these people, acting like them, carrying myself with that poise and radiating the alluring detachment that comes with knowing you're being watched and admired. She must've known I was thinking this. "You have to decide you want it," she continued. "You just have to commit to us, trust us." She looked straight in my eyes. Then, a compact in her hands, she swept a fluffy powdered brush across my face.

"Oh?" I thought I was already doing this. I had to try to defend myself a bit without being defensive, if that was possible. "Is there something that would show you how serious I am about doing a good job?" Her back was to me now as she selected her next beautification tool.

"We know you're a hard worker, Haven." With a sharp wand—liquid eyeliner—she leaned in. I closed my eyes and the wand licked at the edge of my upper lashes, warm. "You'll have a chance to prove yourself even more as we go forward. You're going to be key to our recruitment efforts."

"Recruitment?"

"You'll see." She lined the other eye, then she swept a series of other brushes across my lids, drawing and coloring me in. When she moved onto my cheeks, I opened my eyes. She dusted me with a blush from a rich pink compact then snapped it shut and scanned the perfectly aligned tubes of lipstick on the vanity. Deciding on one, she found the thinnest, most twig-like brush and coated it with a deep ruby color, dabbing at my lips.

"Youth is invincible, you know." She sighed. "The greatest tragedy is to be content with a boring youth." This felt like a knife to the heart. Was this how she thought of me?

"Sometimes I think you make sacrifices in the present, you play it safe, you keep your focus, so you can reap the rewards in the future," I proposed. But it came out hesitant, like I was trying to convince not just her but myself.

"There's no passion in that. A person has to live for the present."

That was exactly opposite everything I'd ever been told—to think of the future, lay the foundation now, know where you were headed. My life wasn't constructed in a way that offered any instant gratification, but I didn't quite feel like I was missing out. Not yet anyway.

She spun me around, facing the mirror at last. For the second time in as many days I didn't recognize myself. I loved it. Aurelia had given me an exact replica of her hairstyle: 1920s-era finger waves and a low, messy side chignon. My eyes were smoky and smudgy with so many layers of black and gray; my amber irises seemed sparkly slivers barely peeking through, glowing like a cat's gaze. My lips, painted a glossy lacquered red, looked fuller than I thought possible.

"Thank you. This is amazing," I said to my reflection.

She didn't seem to hear it, her mind obviously elsewhere. "Don't you ever get tired of being . . . perfectly good?" She seemed truly curious.

"Um, it's not something I ever thought about. It's not a conscious thing," I said, turning away from my reflection and toward her. "And I'm certainly nowhere near perfect."

"Don't you find it all exhausting?"

"I find it just . . . natural." I had that sinking feeling that I had done something wrong, something that was offensive to her.

"I think you may not realize there's much to learn from testing boundaries. There's much to be enjoyed from leaving your comfort zone. It has been said, in fact, that sinning takes courage."

She had this way of leading me down these paths in our talks from which I didn't know how to artfully escape. I didn't know where she was going, what she wanted, or expected from me. I was still attempting to formulate some sort of response when she abandoned it altogether.

"Go on and put that on." She flicked her head toward the garment bag hanging on the rack and began packing up her makeup supplies.

I took down the heavy garment bag and returned to the closet. Inside was a sparkly black flapper-style dress, complete with a long beaded fringe all over, with a tiny matching bag. It made a swishing sound as I pulled it off the hanger. I slipped it on and found it fit perfectly. If this had been Aurelia's, it didn't make any sense how it would fit me, since I had neither her curves nor her height, and yet it felt like it was the right size. I peeked at myself quickly in the full-length mirror in the closet. The dress was definitely quite short—the hem hit somewhere in the middle of my thigh—but it wasn't going anywhere. The V of the top, despite the thick straps, was cut in such a way that I'd have to be careful or a bit of those scars would peek out. It would be difficult to keep it in place, I could tell. I turned around, trying to check the back—my other scars were well concealed. I took a few tentative steps out of the closet, bracing myself for her critique. She nodded, as if to say, *Not bad at all.*

"This is really an amazing dress; thank you for letting me wear it." My hands smoothed it out, hoping the motion might elongate the fabric somehow. I tugged at the hem, not realizing it, and then caught a look from her—icy, like a lake freezing over—and stopped, straightening my back and standing tall.

She didn't speak; she just brushed past me into the closet to a narrow wooden armoire I'd seen there. She opened the double doors at the top and velvet racks of necklaces gleamed, gems of every hue so magnificent they looked like they should've been at the Field Museum. She opened another drawer and took out a ring, canary-colored and nearly the size of a golf ball, and slid it onto her finger, and then two matching drop earrings, lemon stones on a string of diamonds.

"I want it to be clear to our guests that you're one of us," she said as she closed up the case. "You do have pierced ears, I hope?"

"Yes, I do," I said, relieved to be able to answer that question correctly. Joan had made a big deal of taking me on my thirteenth birthday to get my ears pierced, but now I hardly ever bothered with earrings at all.

She fastened them onto my ears and then slipped the ring off her finger and onto mine. I looked in the mirror and sparkled back at myself. I couldn't see anything but the jewels. The earrings hung just below my hair, peeking out and swaying whenever I moved. I touched them with my ring-adorned hand. Now I definitely didn't recognize myself. Not in the slightest. It felt like I was playing a character—someone so much more interesting than the real me.

Aurelia looked less convinced though. She tilted her head, deliberating. "I think . . . no necklace," she said, delivering a verdict.

I looked down at my small, glinting angel wing, which seemed so insignificant beside the canary diamond earrings and ring. But I couldn't take it off. For whatever reason, according to the book, I was supposed to wear this always.

"I kind of like it. I think it all, um, works." I tried to sound fashion savvy, but didn't quite have the forthrightness to pull it off.

"No necklace," she said again, more firmly. I took it off and tucked it into the evening bag. "But I will make a trade: perhaps a bracelet, a quiet accent?" I stood still as she rummaged through that jewelry box again, returning with a thin gold bangle. "Now, this is very special and has been with me for years and years." She grabbed my hand and squeezed the narrow bangle on. It fit snug around my wrist and had the faintest heart-shaped etchings. "It's modeled after that famous, very expensive bracelet that you need a special screwdriver to get on and off, do you know the one?"

I shook my head. How would I know these things?

"Well, I desperately wanted one and so someone had this one made for me." She spoke so easily now, directly addressing this bracelet on my wrist, that it seemed she forgot she was talking and not just thinking this. I didn't want to break her trance so I remained quiet, hoping she would go on, and she did. "It was always my favorite. He was a nice man. I probably should have given it back to him when . . ." She trailed off. "But I just couldn't. It's not like he would have given it to anyone else, but still." She shook herself out of it. "He still has the screwdriver, unfortunately, so it's a good thing your hands are small like mine or we'd never get it on or off."

"Were you in love with him then?" I couldn't help asking. There was so much I wanted to know about her. But the window had closed.

"Of course. At that age you're in love all the time." She brushed it off, typically harsh, back to normal. I didn't understand what she meant. What age? This couldn't have been so long ago. "You probably fall in love a million times every day."

I wasn't sure how to respond to this; she sounded unsettled now, like she had been woken up in the middle of a strange dream.

"You're ready," she said without looking at me, straightening up the compacts open on the vanity. "I'll meet you in the lobby, beneath the chandelier."

As soon as I left her room, I took the necklace out again and looped it around my wrist beside the other bracelet. I could get it around three times and it didn't look half bad. Through the skylight the stars twinkled and the lights of the chandelier cast a heavenly glow on the lobby below, where '20s costumed guests mingled, sipping drinks. In the center, a jazz band roused passersby with the pep and spring of an old standard, something you could picture people doing the Charleston to. As I waited for the elevator, I turned the bangle around my wrist. When I did, I felt some etchings on the *inside* of it. I wiggled it off, too curious not to. Inside it was engraved "All my love, N." I jammed it back onto my wrist, feeling like I'd trespassed in some way, as the elevator opened.

It stopped at a few floors, picking up guests on the way down. A dolled-up couple got in on the seventh floor, hitting the button for the mezzanine—the woman, in a floor-length black evening gown, pawed through her bag in search of something, not giving me so much as a passing glance. But the tuxedoed man, in his mid- or maybe late forties, but handsome and distinguished, looked me up and down and gave me the slightest smile.

I looked away, but still, I followed them out on the mezzanine level, deciding a detour wouldn't hurt. I just had to see the ballroom. The pair peeled off, collecting their place card from a long flower-adorned table. I weaved through the crowd and poked my head into the room: round tables with towering black and white centerpieces had been set surrounding a dance floor with yet another band. The black tie dinner-dance was just getting under way. The lights were dim and the crowd already raucous, laughing and drinking. A few people were already dancing, while many of the others sat patiently as waiters flew out from a back door bearing trays with plates full of leafy salads. This room would house the most famous and well-heeled guests—the ones who weren't required to dress in period costume like the party-goers in the Parlor, Capone, the gallery, and the Vault. I could already recognize several faces from the newspapers and evening news. I had never been in such close proximity to so many promi-nent people. I couldn't resist feeling at least a tiny bit important by association.

True to her word, Aurelia introduced me to everyone: presi-dents of the city's best universities; Chicago's football, base-ball, and basketball stars; local artists and fashion designers and musicians; journalists and news anchors; endless city council members; the mayor. She referred to me as her "star assistant and greatest asset." I didn't quite know what I'd done to deserve the attention, but I soaked it in, letting it wash over me, feeling this power of hers by proxy. Everyone smiled at me because they smiled at her. They wanted to know me because I was squired around by her. It made my head spin. The night seemed orches-trated to make me feel at the center of the universe.

She had even dressed me to look like a darker-haired, shorter version of herself. Her dress was just a step up in degree of dazzle from mine: more low-cut and gold beads woven in with the black. Her heels were a bit strappier and higher, and she completed the look with a headband and a black feather poking up into the air, the plume making it easy to tell at all times where she was. I did my best not to ruin the effect of my look by tugging at the top of my dress too much, but I couldn't help it—I felt so conscious of its movement as I walked, so sure it would shift and these unsightly horrors would peek out for all of Chicago to see. It did, at least, have the effect of making me hold my posture and walk more slowly, looking directly in front of me, not at the ground as I often did.

We had met, it seemed, nearly every guest when we stepped into the gallery. It was filled with '20s attired revelers, all perusing at the work and chattering with one another about symbolism and style, heady conversations that I could have eavesdropped on all night. A silent thrill shot through me as I watched them all taking in the mural Lance and I had finished and studying my photos with such attention that suggested there was depth and value there.

Just inside the gallery, a man stood perched not far from the bar, sipping an amber drink and taking in the scene unfolding before him. Dashing in a way that made him seem like part of the artwork itself, he wore a tuxedo and did so exceedingly well. He seemed a bit like an older, taller version of Lucian. He had that same slicked-back hair and those sharply drawn features, but a stronger presence—he looked at the place like he owned it and had simply allowed everyone else to be there. You could feel his strength even in how he gripped his glass or the unwavering way he watched everyone move about him.

Aurelia's eyes met his instantly and she floated over to him, me trailing behind.

"So you made it after all," she said as he pulled her in, kissing her on the lips. I looked away for just a moment, but not before seeing enough to try to read into it: the kiss seemed familiar, in the way of a European greeting for him, but the tilt of her head suggested it might mean something deeper for her. I couldn't imagine ever greeting anyone who was anything less than a confirmed significant other with a kiss on the lips. I would love to be the kind of girl who could do this as if it was no big deal, because there was something so powerful about it, but I wasn't sure that would ever really be me.

"I promised. You know how I am when I give my word." His voice was impossibly deep and yet so soft, almost a whisper.

"This is true," she said.

"And who is this?" he asked, fixing his eyes—piercing, such a clear blue, it was like I could see straight through them—on me.

"This is the future of the Lexington Hotel, Haven Terra," she introduced me, so grandly I was unsure if she was kidding. The man's stare, like Lucian's, heated me to a boil. I felt myself flush. I held my hand out to shake his, so firm and smooth—so very hot.

"Hello, Haven."

"So nice to meet you," I managed.

"You look lovely."

"Thank you."

"Are you enjoying yourself?"

"Yes, very much. It's a beautiful night and a beautiful hotel. I've been learning so much here."

"I'm sure you have."

Aurelia looked at me now. "She's met everyone, so now I think I can set her free for the evening. She's still got to get to the Vault to take some photos."

"Oh . . ."

"Go on, enjoy. I'll see you tomorrow morning."

"Thank you," I said to her, almost bowing for some reason. "Nice to meet you," I said to the man again. Only after I drifted away did it occur to me that I hadn't gotten his name—I had been a little too overwhelmed to think of asking. He certainly looked like he might be some actor in from Hollywood to film something in town, but he wasn't anyone I completely recognized; he only seemed like someone I—or everyone—ought to know of.

I caught sight of a uniform-clad Lance through the crowd, standing off near the case shielding Capone's old fedora. He held a tray bearing two shot glasses of a flaming liquid: miniature versions of whatever I'd had on my birthday.

"Pretty good party, huh?" I said as I neared him.

"If you and I both take one of these," he said toward me while still looking at incoming traffic, hoping to give away his drinks, "I can be done for the night."

I picked both up. "Done and done. Go get rid of that thing."

"Thanks. Right back," he said scurrying off with his empty tray.

We meet again, I thought holding up one of the small glasses for a closer look. I stood there quietly pretending to look at the fedora, but really watching these two little flames burn. In no time Lance returned, pulling one of the shot glasses from my hands.

"Thanks," he said. He glanced at the drink. "Do we dare?"

"I don't know. I had a lot of trouble with this thing's big brother. Fool me once, shame on you but . . ."

"Ohhh, yeah." He remembered all too well. "So how'd you get outta wearing the uniform? No fair."

"Don't blame me, Aurelia did this."

"You look nice," he mumbled, eyes darting away.

"Thanks." I tugged at the top of my dress again, then caught myself and stopped. "You too."

"Right."

"No, really." It was true.

We watched as the well-dressed partygoers circulated around

us, tossing back their drinks and admiring the art and macabre artifacts. To my right, a glass cube on a pedestal displayed a blood-splattered shirt supposedly from the night of the St. Valentine's Day massacre.

"Oh, wishing you a heartfelt happy massacre day," he said, holding up his shot glass.

"To you too," I said, lifting my glass.

"It truly is a holiday of horrors, Valentine's Day, isn't it?"

"Cheers." I rolled my eyes.

"Seriously, its history is riddled with martyrs and deaths in equal measure."

"Bah humbug."

"I mean, dating back to, like, the fourth century."

"The third—but you've gotta let it go. So a priest was stoned to death for marrying people when it was outlawed. Get over it," I joked. This is what happens when you pay too much attention in AP Euro.

We wandered over to the photography exhibit, which, in addition to a host of old black and whites of the original Lexington, included the wall of my shots of the Outfit.

"I could go on: a holiday with a history of torture and injustices."

"And chocolate."

"And commercialism."

"Okay, okay, I got it."

We were silent for a moment, studying all the photos. So many perfect faces staring back at us. I thought if I looked close enough I might be able to see the reflection of my camera lens in Lucian's eye.

"What was I saying about injustice?"

"Hmm?" I was lost in the photos, trying to dissect them. *Beauty is genius, beauty is power.* I had never quite thought of it that way.

"You could've just told me if you didn't want to fix my picture." Lance's tone had dropped into the realm of muted, seething anger. It snapped me out of my reverie. I turned to him.

"What?"

"You didn't need to lie about it." His voice was flat as hurt stormed in his eyes, clouding them.

"What are you talking about?"

He knocked a knuckle against the wall near his picture and walked to the opposite end of the display, back near a picture of Raphaella. There, below his eye, the scar cut across his face, a puffy line underscoring a deep brown eye. It shot through my heart, draining it.

"I fixed this!" I called over to him, louder than I intended. He looked at me stone-faced, betrayed. "I swear, I saw this today—I saw it this morning. It was perfect." I shook my head. "This is a different photo, it's got to be. I don't know what—" I stopped myself. A few quick steps down the line, I stood before my own, focusing.

No!

There they were, the tops of my own scars, peeking out above the neckline of that dreaded white top, like thin, gnarled pink fingers reaching out. My stomach dropped. Every single person who had come through here all night had seen this. Those unmistakably ugly marks on me that I had so carefully erased, that I tugged at my dress even now to try to shield.

"Hey," I said to him again. He glared back at me, fuming under the surface but trying to hold his ire, I could tell. "Come 'ere."

He walked over—his face set in an expression that said, *You're lucky if I listen to a single word you say.*

"Look at this," I ordered. It came out terse, edging toward hostile. I slapped the spot below my picture. "And tell me if you think I wanted *this one* up there?"

He leaned in toward my picture and didn't see it at first—he didn't know what he was looking for—but then his face loosened, his eyes fastened on that strange burned-claw marking. He looked at me: the bottomless wells of his eyes behind those frames softened now, sympathy and confusion creeping in.

I glanced around us. Everyone seemed to be lost in their own witty banter and borderline inebriation, engrossed in different parts of the gallery. We were the only ones near this sweep of photos. So I moved closer to Lance, looked up at him, and, summoning my nerve, pulled aside the neckline of my dress an inch or so, showing just that spot, a hint of those disfigured marks. He looked down very quick, his eyes widening involuntarily, and then darting away just as fast as I patted my dress back in place. We both faced the photos again. We didn't say anything. But I needed him to know that I understood. And that I knew exactly how he felt, because that's how I felt too.

And I was scared.

14

You Might Have a Dark Side

I tried to retrace the past day: everyone who had been in the gallery since this morning, everyone who had access to my computer. Who would do something like this? Those pictures did not look that way earlier. What had happened in the space of those several hours? I had looked at each shot so closely and so proudly.

Lance and I stood facing the display, not a word for such a long time. I was still sorting through my loose, disjointed thoughts when he said into the space before him, softly, wounded: "I'm sorry."

"I'm sorry too—I don't know what—"

"I know you don't. It's okay." He looked at me, nodding once. "Let's maybe just not look at these anymore right now. I think that's the best thing."

I nodded back in agreement, even though I wasn't so patient. Lance started to walk away. I took a deep breath, shifted my dress into place, and took a few steps until I saw him get waylaid by Raphaella's tall, blond luminousness. I halted, frozen in my tracks. She swooped right in, sidling up to him looking like that uniform was made for her. Her hair coated her shoulders in flaxen sheets, and as she swung that silky mane, she seemed to hang on his every word. But he was doing a fine job playing hard to get—he almost didn't look interested at all. He wasn't fumbling or fidgeting in that way of his. He just looked like he could take it or leave it; take *her* or leave her. Well done, Lance. I supposed I could learn a thing or two from him.

Just as I thought this, *he* appeared: Lucian. Standing just off in the space behind Lance and Raphaella, back near that endless mural, with a drink in his hand. I looked away and my gaze flitted quickly to where I had last spotted Aurelia and that man. Both were gone. I could feel Lucian watching me. I waited as long as I could—mere seconds—and my eyes, unable to stay away, went to him again. The dim light glinted off his creamy skin and his slicked-back locks; he had on a tuxedo that he wore with perfect ease. He took a few steps forward. I slid into the dark corner near the Outfit photos, an internal alarm sounding in my quietly heaving chest as he got nearer.

"You did a lovely job on that mural after all," Lucian spoke into my ear. I felt the ground shift ever so slightly, and for a moment I was convinced I might melt into it but I steadied myself. "You've captured the spitting image of hell. I'm surprised, and it takes a lot to surprise me. If I didn't know better, I'd think you might have a dark side."

I struggled to find the words and still felt his breath lingering. I wondered if I should turn to face him, but I couldn't move. I just stared straight ahead at these pictures I'd already looked at for much too long. *Please don't let him see my marred photo,* I thought.

If there was anyone else in the room, any soul at all, I couldn't feel it. All had been drained from this scene save for the two of us and the strains of the music piped in from the lobby—slow, suggestive and seductive, with weeping horns. My pulse sped up.

"Well, thank you." I pursed my lips for just a beat to stop them from quivering. "But I think I was out of my element. I might have had better luck with his *Earthly Delights* than that."

Out of the corner of my eye, I could see his lips move. "I'm sure you'd be very successful in all matters of earthly delights if given the opportunity."

He stepped in front of me and then forward, a slow step or two, backing me farther into the corner.

I wasn't quite sure how to respond. "Thank you? And likewise." I was a little unsure of myself, which he seemed to read as coy—that was fine with me.

He smiled. Lightheaded, I took another step back; my free hand groped for the wall behind my back and found it. I let my body be supported by it. I wished I could have stashed this drink somewhere—I seemed destined to spill it on myself. Lucian leaned one shoulder against the wall, nearly touching mine so that we made a right angle. I felt trapped, in a pleasant way. He rattled what little ice was left in his glass, watching it swish in the remaining liquid, which seemed to match the color of my eyes. With the tip of my index finger I touched the spot where my scar flamed beneath my dress, wishing for some way to cool it, wondering if the fabric had somehow irritated it even though it was the smoothest silk. My body must have been mistaking my nerves for fear. Lucian caught my hand in his.

"Now, this is very nice." He pulled my hand toward him for a closer look at the ring. The giant diamond rivaled his eyes in sparkle and splendor, but lost out to them.

"I know. It's Aurelia's, of course. I feel like I should have my own security detail for all of this jewelry. It was very generous of her to let me wear her things."

"You wear it well," he said, smoldering.

"Thank you." He let my hand down. It didn't feel like it was attached to me anymore. I didn't know where to put it. It returned to its previous spot behind my back, against the wall. "She's been really wonderful to me tonight. She's introduced me to everyone."

"I hear she intends for you to take on even more responsibility as we move forward."

"She mentioned something like that. I would love that," I said, then decided to ask. "She introduced me to a gentleman tonight, in a tux. He was standing over there for a while—" I gestured toward the gallery entrance. "But I didn't get his name. I wondered if—"

"That's just the Prince," he cut in, a hint of annoyance curdling his milky voice. I briefly wondered if I got the luxury of Lucian's attention now only because Aurelia was caught up with this other man—but truthfully, I didn't care so much. I just wanted his eyes and his thoughts and his focus on me, any way I could get it. The more time I spent with him, the more I wanted.

"Just the Prince?"

"Yeah."

"From where?"

"Nowhere you've ever been. Not important. He's just a friend," he said, a little snide and cold for my taste. I was offended, but only for a moment. I shouldn't have brought any of it up, that's all. Why couldn't I just savor these times with him and not sabotage them?

"Well, it sounds like you have friends in high places." I glanced away, fingers fidgeting.

"Maybe so," he said, smirking as he sipped his drink. "Or maybe low ones." He sized me up. "You're different than the girls I'm used to." He said it with assurance, as a fact, a startling new discovery he'd just declared to be true. He was probably right. I was not a bit like the leggy glamazons of the Outfit. I wasn't sure that I should consider this a compliment. "You're sweet," he said now, seeming to have read my mind. "I love that."

I couldn't suppress my blushing or the soft smile that turned up the corners of my lips. I couldn't keep my eyes from darting to his and then away. I didn't say a thing. If I spoke it would only ruin it.

"What's it like to be you?" he asked, a touch of whimsy in his voice.

"Me?"

"What's it like to be sweet and kind?"

"I'm sure you know, you're—"

"I'm sure I don't."

"It's not very exciting, I'm afraid," I whispered playfully. "But I'm just wired this way, I guess." I shrugged. "But I'm no saint."

"Really, because I find that hard to believe."

"It's true."

"Tell me, though, do you think a person is predestined to be good or bad, or do you think someone could override that sort of thing?"

"I don't know. I guess it depends on the person and how badly they want to defeat it."

I could feel his eyes boring into me when I looked away, his focus unwavering. I couldn't quite look at him with the same intensity without going a little weak.

"You might be right," he said. He permitted himself one long sweeping look at the photos, taking them all in as one. If he noticed mine, then he was a gentleman because he didn't say anything at all about its imperfections.

"You know, some Native American tribes thought the camera could steal your soul," I said, just to get his eyes away from them. He looked toward me again. I felt a relief, and then a fluttering.

"These turned out beautifully. I know you said it's your subjects, but I have to disagree. Respectfully, of course."

"Of course."

"See, I think each photographer brings something of herself, or himself, to each photo. There's something of you reflected in these, whether you like it or not. You may indeed have to take some credit."

"If you insist."

"I do."

"Then thank you."

"You're welcome."

We were silent for a moment and it occurred to me: "Is this all a way of telling me it's time for me to get back to work?" I said. I caught sight of Lance, still talking to Raphaella. Or rather she was talking but he was staring at me with stern eyes and a furrowed brow. He didn't even look away or change his expression when he saw that I noticed him. Lucian was talking though, and I pushed Lance out of my mind and line of vision.

"What do you mean? Work?" Lucian asked.

"Oh, just . . . I'm supposed to take photos in the Vault tonight."

"Ahhhh, is that right?"

"Yeah."

"Well, then." He knocked back the last of his drink and placed his empty glass and my full one—brushing his fingers against mine as he did—on a passing tray. "What are we waiting for?"

I tilted my head at the *we*, wondering if I'd heard right.

"Hurry," he breathed. "Before someone comes along and I get stuck here."

Hurry? Hurry, he said. Gladly.

After I had grabbed the camera from the back office, Lucian led us down the staircase, wisely avoiding the long line that had formed at the elevator. As we walked down, our footsteps echoing in the stairwell, my feet almost didn't hurt. There was no one else for whom I could have braved all those steps in those heels. He had let me go in front of him and was guiding me with a protective hand on the small of my back. I was hyperaware of him there, attached to me, even with just these light, featherweight fingertips. We reached the door at the bottom and he pushed it open for me to step through. We could hear the music of the club now, beating fast as my heart.

"Do you know why we call it the Vault?"

I did actually. I'd done my reading. "Sure. When Capone lived here he was thought to have kept money and other treasures in a vault in the basement."

"You're good," he said. "You know they opened it up years ago and it turned out there was nothing there but empty bottles and a bunch of bullet holes." The music got louder as we walked down an empty hallway, coming at the club from the opposite direction I was used to.

"That's too bad."

"I know."

"So shouldn't this place look like the inside of a bank vault or something?"

"No." He laughed. "Who wants to hang out there? It needs to feel like another world, like somewhere where dangerous things are locked away and you don't know what you're getting yourself into." Music rushed out at us now, swirling.

"Ohhh. Well. Mission accomplished then." A dangerous feeling washed over me, as though I would do anything to spend more time with him. The magnetic pull was almost too much.

"The point is," he said, his hand on my back again, leading me through as the gatekeepers opened that giant door for us on cue, "you never know what people have hidden away. It can be so much more or less than it seems on the surface."

We were in the tunnel now, pitch-black save for the occasional flashing light. There were people ahead of us in the club and some behind us waiting to get in, but for a blissful, heady moment, Lucian and I were alone. He stopped and looked at me again. I felt for the wall for support.

"What do you have locked away, Haven Terra?" He leaned into me. Even in the near darkness, the blue lacing his gray eyes lit up.

I opened my mouth to speak but it took a few seconds for sound to actually come out. "I'm not sure I know what you mean." I felt like he was speaking to me in a language I desperately wished to be fluent in but wasn't.

"Everyone's hiding something. I know you are too."

"Oh, well, I mean . . ." What was he trying to say? Did he know something about that book of mine? He looked at me with fierce electricity, drinking me in, my whole life force spilling out into his piercing gray-blue pools. I wanted to say whatever the magic words might be to keep him looking at me this way.

And then, everything stopped.

The lights went out, complete blinding blackness enveloping us; the music hushed, quick and sharp. The shock of it all left the place encased in such pin-drop silence it made my ears tingle.

Suddenly, his lips were on mine—urgent, warm, hitting me so fast, so firm, that I lost my breath. He tasted like peppermint. The camera, in its case, dropped from my hand to the ground and I didn't care. One of his arms wound around my waist, squeezing me so tightly to him I gasped. His other hand shot up my neck gripping my hair. Everything went liquid. I melted into the wall behind me and into him. I wasn't sure if my feet were still on the ground. I didn't think they were—he was so tall, and he clutched me so close he lifted me up. He held me there in this perfect, wild, alive kiss. And somehow my lips knew what to do, like I'd been doing this all my life, having these mysterious sudden kisses in dark places. My hand, acting on its own, rose up finding his neck, and I pulled him closer to me, surprising myself. My skin, every single nerve, fluttered; my heart beat so loudly, throbbing inside my ears, I wondered if he could hear it too, as it galloped, unbridled.

He kissed my neck once, hard, my pulse rising to meet his lips. And then, just as fast as he had enveloped me, he was gone—extricating himself from me so swiftly that I stumbled, no strength left, finding the wall and leaning back against it. The volume suddenly came up on the rest of the world. I heard voices in the club, asking each other what had happened to the lights and the music and the power. I could see the flickering of the fire wall out through the end of the tunnel. I imagined the ring of fire continued to flame too. I didn't care to look more closely. Where had he gone? I was feeling greedy now. I wanted another kiss, an endless one, and I wanted the lights to never come back up. I just wanted to relive that again and again. Just thinking about it made my stomach flip and my head spin.

Around me, footsteps tapped closer; people muttered and

slapped against the wall feeling their way. Someone hit me in the arm as they walked by. "Sorry," came a woman's voice. I couldn't move yet—even if I got trampled, I couldn't move. People had begun to get restless. They wanted out and began to flow into the tunnel, smacking against one another and against the wall. Jostled, I took a couple steps and tripped over something. I ducked, feeling around, and found the camera bag. I picked it up, cradling it in my hands. Just then, the lights blazed on at full power. Collectively, everyone paused to adjust to the blinding light and then began to flee, flowing out of the club en masse. They all seemed to accept this as a signal that the party was over. I broke off from the crowd as soon as I could and stole away to that stairwell, walking up in my heels, which, now that I was on my own, had begun to terrorize my feet to such a degree, digging in so deep, that it felt like they had clawed themselves onto me and would need to be removed with pliers. But everything about this night was worth it.

It dawned on me that I hadn't taken a single picture. At this moment, I didn't quite care. I knew I would probably feel differently tomorrow in the harsh light of morning, seated in Aurelia's office trying to defend myself. But for the time being, it just didn't rank as a concern. I was too blissed out, navigating all of this in a dreamy state I wanted to live in forever.

As I slowly ascended, step by step, I replayed that scene in my mind on a loop over and over and over, only bringing myself back to the present as I neared the top of the steps, just before entering the lobby, to do a quick spot check. I could only imagine that, after all of that, I was something of a rumpled mess. I smoothed my dress, setting it in place where it had shifted when he grabbed me and held me so tight. My hair was now a loose nest, having come almost entirely out of its artfully secured style. Since I certainly didn't know how to restore it myself, I just pulled out the pins and shook it out, letting it fall around my shoulders.

I slipped into the gallery and found it empty—everyone must've flooded out of here, just as they had downstairs, when the lights went back on. The lobby was packed and the crowd all atwitter about what had happened. I returned the camera to the back room, locking it up in a drawer, then grabbed my evening bag, which I had stashed in the office. Since it was so peaceful in the gallery, I decided to stay a few minutes, catching my breath, collecting my thoughts, and trying to preserve this rapture that had swept me up so completely. I felt it would fade every minute away from him and that nothing would snuff it out more swiftly than a roomful of loud people.

I wandered, beginning at the back of the gallery. That mural, which I hadn't gotten a chance to look at yet tonight, had turned out so much better than had seemed imaginable. It looked more passionate, more expertly done than it had when Lance and I had finally retired our paintbrushes and declared it complete. There was such life—and, I suppose, death—in it. It didn't seem possible that our contributions had fit so seamlessly with Calliope's work. So I meandered through this space, enjoying my time alone with it, but as I did, my mind still flashed back to that interlude in the tunnel. Where had Lucian gone? And then I came upon that spot where he had leaned into me saying all those curious things and inviting himself downstairs with me. Had he known then that he would kiss me later?

I realized I had been staring into the blank air for a while now, pleasantly dazed. I could see a hint of my reflection in the glass of Aurelia's photo. I saw my features in the black dress of her picture, and from what I could tell my lipstick wasn't so bad. Another of the night's miracles. My vision readjusted to take in her image, bracing myself to be reminded of how much more beautiful she was than me. But something else caught my eye. There, on her cheek, was a darkened blotch. What was it? It looked almost like a splatter of sauce from one of Dante and Etan's precious canapés. I had been concerned when I heard they were going to allow food and drink in the gallery, but it wasn't really my place to say anything, was it? I leaned in for a closer look, my finger poised to brush away the offending mark—and then I froze.

It was worse than I imagined. This thing, this splotch, wasn't something on the surface to be wiped away: it was actually *on* her face. Roughly the size of a quarter, it had a depth to it and a spectrum of red and yellow shadings; it was some sort of festering lesion. I had never seen this on her face in real life—I certainly would have noticed—and I hadn't seen it on the picture either, but then again, I hadn't bothered looking at her photo all that closely since every one of her shots had been so perfect. But the picture was so large. Had Aurelia even failed to see this blight? It was ugly. I don't know how we all could have missed this. And now that I really studied it, the picture was far worse than I remembered. Her eyes were bloodshot and weighted with dark circles, with crow's-feet poking out around the corners.

Suddenly my picture didn't seem so bad. I checked it again. The scars didn't bother me so much now—maybe it had just been the element of surprise earlier. I had failed to notice that my skin had kind of a nice glow to it, as though light were shining through my pores. My expression was softer than I realized too. I looked comfortable. Not bad at all. Maybe this was just what it was like to have a little confidence; maybe this was all still that heady post-kiss afterglow.

I floated over to Lucian's image. Stunning, of course, but now that I looked more closely, his eyes looked maybe a little tired — or were they just heavy-lidded in a seductive way? My mind felt jumbled, but I didn't have much chance for internal debate on this matter.

A scream pierced the air, instantly shattering the dream-like feeling of the night, making my skin crawl. It wasn't so unlike the one I'd heard unleashed outside the drugstore that awful evening: a woman, screeching, her shrill cry pealing, an alert.

My legs took off before I could even tell them where to go or what to do. And instead of running *away* — as I would have guessed they would, a survivalist impulse taking over — they ran *toward* that painful wail, careening toward this unknown horror. I pushed my way through the jabbering crowd in the lobby and straight out the revolving door until I stood under the awning and at the front of the pack of gawkers, barely feeling the arctic chill on my exposed skin. On the red carpet outside the hotel was a body. If you could even call it that.

I knew it was a woman only by the mess of long dark hair and high-heeled boots. Even at the hospital, I had never seen someone so disfigured. She looked scarcely human. Her skin was gray, and every inch of it, from what I could tell, was riddled with bumps and festering sores and gashes. Parts of her looked charred and singed. The worst of it: a hole was burned straight through the right shoulder of her shirt, baring bone and raw flesh and tissue. It looked like something at the meat counter of the supermarket. I had to look away, suppressing the urge to faint.

No one seemed to be doing anything, myself included. In these few long minutes since that scream, everyone just stood back, huddling and silent and terrified. But then from the back of this mass of people came the sound of one person clapping.

Aurelia strode straight through the doors, a path clearing for her, her delicate hands clapping precisely, creating a wave of applause, everyone slowly joining in. She took a place directly under the heat lamp in front of the revolving door — the body crumpled behind her — and addressed the group with her smile.

"We hope you've enjoyed the night and the show," her voice rang out, and she gestured with an outstretched arm toward the figure on the ground. On cue, four men in hotel uniforms — members of the Outfit, Beckett among them — swirled through the revolving doors and fanned out around the body, lifting it up, each taking a brittle limb, and carrying it — her — off through the side doorway.

Aurelia continued, commanding the crowd: "Thank you for celebrating our opening with us. We look forward to serving you. Good night, all!" Wild cheers erupted from the group. She charged through the merry masses.

With that, everyone went their separate directions, either up to their posh rooms or out to claim their valet-parked cars or off to swoop into waiting cabs and limos. Smiles returned to faces, chatter resumed with snippets of conversation wafting here and there praising the night. "A shootout would've been more appropriate, but this is certainly bold and artistic," said one stuffy society type in an emerald evening gown.

"That looked so real!" gushed a flapper-costumed girl.

"Performance art: very edgy," concurred an older gentleman in incredibly baggy, suspendered plaid pants, which I recognized from one of my books as the clownish "Oxford bags" of the 1920s.

I just stood there as the crowd began to dissipate, trying to quietly wrest control of my wild emotions, which had shot from one extreme (bliss) to the other (fear) and back to somewhere in the middle (so everything's okay after all?) in such a short span of time that I felt wholly spent.

When the bristling cold became too much, I went back inside. Some people were still sipping nightcaps in the Parlor and taking midnight snacks at Capone. I waded through the sea of people, adrift, looking for signs of anyone I knew—Dante, Lance, Lucian—hoping to not have to be alone. But after a good half hour of searching, as men loosened their ties and women let their hair down and took their shoes off and more and more guests drifted wearily off to their rooms, I finally did the same.

Part Two

15

Be Cool, Please

The hotel felt different the next morning. Even though I was up much earlier than many of the guests, a current pulsed in the air, a sense that there were people everywhere, whether you saw them or not. I was putting on a show, playing the role of the perfect, helpful staffer. But the place would have felt different even if it wasn't our first full day open—because *I* felt different. I hadn't quite done my hair just right, and without Aurelia's supplies, my makeup regimen was back to being nonexistent, and I didn't fill out the uniform any more than I had the day before. What had changed was I felt *wanted*. Even if last night had been a fluke, even if that was the first and last kiss I would have with Lucian, for those minutes I had been desired, and there was a power in that. I just wanted any sign that last night had actually happened.

In accordance with our new post-opening set of rules, I avoided the main lobby and slipped into the back door of the Parlor's kitchen even though the restaurant had to be pretty empty now, at just after seven in the morning. The butcher-block island in the kitchen's back alcove was set for three, and a familiar figure stood at the stove in his chef's jacket, with a bandana tying back his hair. He picked up the omelette pan and gave it a shake and then a flip. As it is with a tree falling in the forest with no one there to hear it, I had always wondered if he bothered with that kind of cooking showmanship when he didn't know someone was watching. I loved that he did—that was so very Dante.

"Please tell me that's broccoli and cheddar and that I can have some," I said to his back. He turned around.

"Hey, you!" He smiled, pan still in his hand. "Yes and yes, of course."

"You're too good to me. I've gotta repay you one of these days."

"I know, I'm gonna start kicking this, quid pro quo style, and then you'll be in trouble. What can you offer me? You're definitely no cook," he joked.

"I know. I've got nothin'. But I did take a nice photo of you that everyone seemed to admire last night."

"True. I'll make you send that home to Mom."

"Consider it done."

"That's a start."

I propped myself up against the counter nearest him while he focused his attention on a second omelette, sprinkling in bits of ham, cheese, green pepper, and onion.

"And . . . I can offer you a little gossip, which I know you're always a fan of."

He looked at me, intrigued, folding his arms against his chest. "I'm listenin'."

"He kissed me," I whispered, bewildered. It was strange to say it out loud.

"Who?" He seemed to truly not know.

"Who?!"

Now he got it.

"Seriously?" He sounded skeptical and paused mid-omelette flip.

I nodded.

"How the heck did this happen?"

"I know, right?" I suddenly had to sit down. I took a seat on one of the stools at the butcher block.

"Oh! First kiss! My baby is growing up." He clapped and grabbed my shoulders, shaking me. "Better late than never, girl!" Now I was embarrassed. I rolled my eyes but secretly appreciated the fuss. "So, set the scene, what's the story?" He leaned over the island, neglecting our still-cooking breakfast. "I heard you looked a-maz-ing last night, by the way."

"You did?"

"Lance told me."

"Oh." I smiled to myself. That was sweet of him.

"But wait." Dante was shaking his head. "So, what? I mean, how?"

"Well, I saw Lucian in the gallery and he saw me . . ."

"Sorry, no, I need the CliffsNotes—just the action, not all the meaningful glances. Etan's got me on a short leash—not that I mind, LOVE him!—but I've got, like, five minutes." He made that twirling motion with his hand, telling me to wrap it up. So I obliged, giving him the most basic play-by-play as he soaked up every word. Until I began to smell smoke.

I poked him in the arm. "I think something's burning."

"Damn right something's burning. I mean, you've clearly got this smoldering thing with him and he kisses you but then—"

"No," I cut him off. "Something's burning." I pointed to the stove and rushed over to it. The broccoli and cheddar omelette was beginning to char.

"Oh please, like I would trust you to rescue this." Dante, unconcerned, nudged me out of the way, as he sauntered over to the stove and plated my omelette. "Do you want a new one? It's a little crispy."

"I like crispy."

"Then you'll love this." He slid it over to me, then set to work making another. I tucked into my breakfast—inside the cheese was perfectly gooey.

"This is amazing. You should patent this technique."

"It's called negligence."

"It's brilliant. Four stars."

"But back to you and Lucian."

"I like the sound of that."

"I'm sure you do."

"So? Your analysis, please—why do you think he disappeared right after we kissed?"

"Hmmm, I don't know," he said carefully. "I mean, it could be purely practical—maybe he needed to go flip some circuit breakers or something."

"I guess."

"Or it could be some sort of game, a hard-to-get thing."

"Mmm-hmm." I didn't like that possibility.

"Or maybe it was him being theatrical, like that bizarre scene out front with that, like, dummy or mannequin or woman with a horrific makeup job or whatever." He sprinkled peppers, cheese, and broccoli into his new omelette.

"Yeah, what was that about?"

"No idea. It was weird, right? I was standing way in the back, but it seemed pretty strange where I was."

"Yep, it was weird up front too."

"Huh." He slid the second omelette onto a plate and set it

down at the place beside me. "Guess maybe our sense of artistry isn't as developed as it should be."

"Guess so, because I was kind of freaked out by the whole thing." When I should've been dreaming of the more pleasant aspects of the evening, I had instead found that image searing into my mindscape again and again. Dante, however, steered us back to safer territory.

"So . . . Lucian. Have you seen him today?" He said it with a devious glint in his eye.

"Not yet." I breathed in, nervous.

"Be cool, please," he admonished me, flipping the final omelette.

"Of course. How else would I be?" I couldn't even say it with a straight face.

He slapped me gently on the arm with the spatula.

"Cool," I said. "Got it."

"And not to be a buzzkill—" he started, easing in. I had a feeling I knew what he was going to say. "But I thought he mighta, kinda, sorta had something going with Aurelia?"

I had managed to push this to the back of my mind and it had only begun creeping back; the kiss knocked all logic out of me. "Yeeeah, that's a good point. I don't really know. Tryin' not to think about that. I just know that he kissed me so I kissed him back." I shrugged.

"And for that, you're my hero. Proud of you, girl!" He patted me on the back and gave me a shake.

Lance appeared in the doorway, dapper in his uniform but yawning and scratching his head. "Morning," he said mid-yawn.

"Uh-oh, we have to stop talking about Lance now," Dante said in a loud voice.

"He's kidding," I said.

"That's for you, man. You seem like a western omelette type, am I right?" Dante said.

"Thanks, wow, looks great."

"Late night?" I asked, realizing I had last seen him with Raphaella.

"I guess so," he mumbled, digging into his meal.

"Do tell!" Dante perked up, taking the seat across from him, a plate with his own omelette in hand.

"Nothing to tell, just worn-out from everything yesterday."

"Haven's been regaling us with tales of her rendezvous with Lucian." Dante's eyebrows fluttered.

Now I got shy. "No, it's really no big deal. You looked like you were having fun with Raphaella."

"Yeah," he said. And that was it. He wasn't much of a sharer when it came to that stuff. I let it go. "So what's the story today? What are we supposed to do now that this place is actually open?"

Breakfast out of the way, I took a deep breath and knocked on Aurelia's office door. A faint, uninterested "Yes?" came from inside. I poked my head in. "Come, come, we have to make this quick," she said.

"Good morning, Aur—"

She cut me off, talking to me before I even reached her desk. I scurried in and took my usual seat, already feeling behind.

"We've gotten phenomenal press from last night."

"It was really an incredible night. And I can't thank you enough for—"

She cut me off again.

"I want you to amass our media clippings each morning and e-mail them to me."

"Certainly."

"Since we want to encourage this kind of notoriety, I'll be giving you a list like this one"—she held out a few sheets of paper for me to take—"of members of the press who've said nice things and you and/or Lucian's boy . . ."

"Lance."

"Yes, you and Lance will hand-deliver notes and small gifts. Consult with Etan's boy . . ."

"Dante."

"Yes, Dante, he'll have the gifts," she continued, waving another sheet of paper at me. "This is the note you'll be writing. On these." She handed over a stack of notecards bearing her name and envelopes with the Lexington as the return address. "Learn to do my signature."

"Got it."

"Now that we're open we need to be making news every day. We need these people coming back and we need to advance the story. Let's look for ways to do that."

"Okay." *Advance the story,* I liked that. That's what I needed—to figure out how to advance the story with Lucian. But first I had to refocus here.

"The office in the gallery is your official workspace. Keep an ear out when you're there. Everything is for sale for the right price and if someone comes in bidding on any of the art or memorabilia, I want to know."

"Okay."

"Any questions?"

I shook my head.

"Good." Her eyes returned to some paperwork on her desk, which I took as my cue to escape. And I had almost made it out when she said, "Am I wrong or are you supposed to have something for me?"

I halted and turned around slowly.

"No, you're not wrong." I wanted to say this without it sounding like a pathetic apology. "Due to some . . . technical difficulties and . . . lighting issues . . ." I started. She had to remember sending me off to the Vault just shortly before the blackout cleared the club. But still she watched me, smirking, finding this a fun game to see if I could get through this without squirming or groveling. " . . . I was unable to complete the task last night. But I fully intend to remedy this and have photos of the Vault for you tomorrow."

"I'm disappointed, as you can imagine," she said stiffly, sighing. "For now have Lucian's boy load the *Tribune* and *Sun-Times* stories to the monitor at the front desk. I'd like your photos tomorrow."

"Of course."

"Go."

That, it seemed to me, was as clean a getaway as I could've hoped to make. It certainly could've been worse.

It took me a while to find Lance—he had been wandering the premises, fruitlessly looking for Lucian, and he was relieved when I told him he could call off his search because I had his assignment.

"I'm a little annoyed that my deadbeat mentor seems intent on dumping me every day," he said as we made our way through the lobby, which was now bustling with early risers seeking breakfast at Capone.

"I think he's just really busy." I defended him. But truth was, I was disappointed that no one had heard from him today.

Somehow, in the hours since that kiss, I had gone from certainty that he was interested in me to trying to brace myself for the inevitable decline.

"Whatever. I get a weird vibe from that guy." He gave me a look, like the reproachful one of last night.

I ignored it and swiped my keycard to get us into the gallery. "So do we leave this open now so people can come in?" I asked him, changing the subject.

"It's strange having people everywhere. I feel like someone dropped an ant farm and all the ants are getting into everything."

"I know what you mean. I guess we're not the most natural hosts, are we?"

"Apparently not."

"Okay, let's be welcoming and leave it open," I decided. I propped the door wide open and pulled back the curtain.

We found those newspaper stories, and many more, online. So many pictures of Aurelia and Lucian and the Outfit; endless shots of partygoers drinking and dancing. We even spotted Dante's arm in one photo, holding out a tray of canapés (I could tell by the uniform and the watch). Lance ducked out to tend to the business of uploading the clips onto the screen, a fairly easy task but one I didn't envy since it involved commandeering a computer from one of the icy Outfit members working the front desk. They still weren't much for small talk, these people. If Raphaella was there, it would be a different story though, wouldn't it? I didn't know why he never wanted to talk about her. I would think most boys getting attention from a bombshell of that caliber would be all too pleased to brag about it at every opportunity.

At any rate, for a few minutes the little office was all mine.

I examined the note Aurelia had written in her elegant, long-looped script. It would take some doing to replicate. I studied the curve of her letters, the skinny loop of her *A,* the giraffe necks of her lowercase *l*'s, the precise slant of each word. I pulled a sheet of paper from the printer for a practice run and told myself what I always did: it's okay to take your time if it means you'll get it right. I liked being tucked away like this, having my own place to get things done, where I could feel free to go at my own pace. Somewhere that was considered mine, enough that others felt compelled to knock if they dropped by.

Like someone was doing right now.

I whipped around in my chair and found Lucian in the doorway, in another slim-cut suit, with my folded uniform in one hand, the one I'd last seen balled up on the floor of Aurelia's closet.

"I thought I'd find you here," he said, inviting himself in, leaning against the corner of the desk. So close. I bored into those gray eyes for any clue he might be looking at me differently today—like we'd crossed some threshold and entered a new zone in which it would be perfectly acceptable, for example, to seize another mind-blowing kiss for no reason and with no warning.

"Hey." I tried to imagine myself looking as I had the night before. Act like a girl who flirted—successfully—with this guy less than twenty-four hours ago. "I get it." I nodded toward the uniform, which I suspected he forgot was in his hand. "You're jealous you don't have a uniform of your own, am I right? You can have that one. I've got more, but I think the cut will be all wrong for you."

He smiled. "This," he said, handing it over, "is for you from Aurelia. She said you left it there." He set it down on the desk. "But I'm afraid I should have come bearing gifts." His eyes cast down for a moment, looking shamed. "I think I'll start by saying that's not how that was supposed to go at all. Last night."

I couldn't tell whether he regretted his disappearing act or kissing me in the first place. I didn't say anything, hoping instead for further enlightenment. Which he provided. "My abrupt exit."

"Oh, that." *Phew.* "No problem, I just figured the Vault had sort of a Bermuda Triangle effect. I knew you'd turn up again, and . . . here you are." It came out breezily, as I'd hoped. More than anything I felt relieved that his sense of regret was properly assigned.

"Bermuda Triangle, exactly." He laughed. "Needless to say, I got a little thrown off by the change in lighting."

"Totally understandable."

"So if you were a night at the Vault right now, you wouldn't be wrath?"

I returned the laugh. "No, definitely not." And it was true.

"Good, because I thought we'd give this another try—I feel like I'm always apologizing to you for something." He said this last part almost to himself; I loved it. "So, tonight." It was a statement and not a question.

"Tonight."

"I know that one"—he pointed in the direction out the door, toward Aurelia's office—"has you stuck playing paparazzo again, yes?"

"Yes." I let the disappointment creep in just a little.

"Well, let's be honest, that scene won't get going till nearly midnight; there's plenty of time before that. You're going to have to have dinner at some point tonight. Right?"

"Right again."

"So, dinner tonight. Pick you up at seven?"

"Pick me up?"

"I know where you live."

"Seven then."

The deal set, he took a few steps toward the doorway and craned his neck. "Yep, here he comes. I sent him to get the supplies."

"Supplies?"

"For your excursion. I had to give him something to do to get him outta the way," he said.

"Clever."

"I know. See you at seven."

With that—and one last playful parting grin to seal our flirty scene—he slipped out. I heard him pass Lance and thank him for something. Within seconds, my fellow intern appeared, his arms stacked with slim red boxes, at least twenty of them. Looped around both arms were small glossy gift bags to match and sheets of tissue paper poking up out of one of them.

"So, apparently," he started, setting them down on the desk in front of me, all four of our hands flying up to secure the two teetering towers, "we're delivering these."

"What are—" I pulled one box near me. The lid had an artist's watercolor rendering of the hotel, a painting we had on the gallery walls. All had gold ribbons tied around them except for one. I lifted that lid and almost a dozen perfectly formed cubes of chocolate, each with that ubiquitous Lexington insignia—in red on dark chocolate—stared back. "Ooooh."

"Chocolates."

"So we're like high-class candygrams today."

"For some reason it sounds seedy when you put it that way."

"Um, what happened here?" I tilted the box, with eleven candies and one conspicuous empty groove toward him.

"Guilty. That one's for us though. Dante hooked us up."

"Thank you, Dante." I picked out one of the bite-size morsels and popped it in my mouth. The filling was a chocolate ganache, soft and creamy and just a little bitter as the expensive stuff always is. Lance took another.

"They're really good," he said with his mouth full. "And I'm usually more a salty type but—"

"Yeah, you're very salty," I said.

"Yep, I get that all the time."

"I'm sure."

"No, but these are, like, incredible. I don't know what kind of magic they're doing in that kitchen." He took another. "So where are we going with these?"

16

You're That Girl

Lance and I divided the list ten each, but it didn't much matter. Most of the locations were pretty near each other, so we decided to roam together. It was such a novelty getting to be outside the hotel. Neither of us had left since that dreaded day of the drugstore scene. But this excursion more than made up for lost time: our travels took us all along the Chicago River, where the water was still and nearly frozen and the boats for the architectural tour were left docked and empty for another few months; along the Magnificent Mile, as bundled-up shoppers ducked in and out of posh stores undeterred by the bitter wind that ripped through us; and up into the offices of the John Hancock Center and the Sears Tower.

The recipients of our deliveries were universally happy to see us. Since we looked, of course, young and unthreatening and so proper in our uniforms, we managed to talk our way into the actual offices we sought, bypassing those impersonal messenger centers where someone sat scowling at a window and took whatever you had brought without even looking at you. Just before we left, Aurelia had instructed us with that stern tone and those pursed, glossy lips not to leave these gifts with anyone other than the person whose name was on the envelope: "I want the effect of you walking in with your uniforms and this gift, taking them out of their day for a moment and serving as a visual reminder of the enchanting evening they just had and the need to have another one like it again soon." After gaining entry into the offices, we were supposed to communicate all of this to the recipient with no more than a smile and our carefully scripted line: "Good afternoon. Compliments of the Lexington Hotel."

"Leave them wanting more," Aurelia had urged us. This, it seemed, was her general mantra. It was a good one, I had to admit. One it would probably do me well to employ, if I could figure out how.

So we clomped all over the city. My high heels were digging into my feet so sharply I thought for sure that they had sliced clean through my stockings. I kept looking down at my feet, perpetually shocked that everything was still in one piece. But Aurelia had been right again — infiltrating these offices, with unhappy people hunched over ugly desks, it struck me how spoiled I'd become. I worked in this beautiful palace, a fantasyland, with people who appeared so perfect, so much on top of the world, that their work didn't even look like work — or reality — at all. I wondered if Lance thought the same thing.

He and I barely spoke the whole day beginning to end, no running our mouths off meaninglessly to fill the dead air. But we didn't have to. That was the thing about us. Our silences were never awkward, like they usually are with most people. Maybe each of us was so generally awkward that we canceled each other out. It was oddly comforting.

Our next stop was the student magazine of the School of the Art Institute, which was located in the museum itself. They had given the gallery a ton of coverage online and apparently, according to the website, planned to devote several pages to it in their next issue. It was Lance's turn to deliver so I tagged along with him to the front desk to get our passes. As we bypassed that criss-crossing central staircase, heading to the elevators that would take us to the office, the memory of our last visit gnawed at me so much that I couldn't resist.

"Hey, would you mind — I mean, you've probably got this covered okay on your own, right? Would you mind if I caught up with you back at the entrance?"

"Uh, sure." He looked confused. The elevator arrived, and after a beat, he stepped in alone.

"Just wanted to see something real quick."

"Sure, see you out front," he said as the doors closed.

I couldn't resist. I went back for another look at *La Jeune Martyre*.

The whipping wind assaulted us, knocking the air from our lungs, as Lance and I made our way to the Monroe Street L station for our final delivery. We went through the turnstiles side by side, synchronized, our gloved hands fumbling to zap our fare cards, and took a place on the platform. Why did a city this cold build most of its public transit system elevated outside instead of underground? I had always wondered and would never understand.

Lance was still hung up on why I had needed to see that painting again.

"What is it with you and that thing?" he asked, leaning forward, staring into the tunnel as a burst of wind whooshed through, signaling the train nearing. The headlights grew closer and then with a deafening roar it pulled in. I waited until it stopped to begin talking again, since I couldn't possibly be heard over it. We found seats in the back and the doors closed.

"Don't you ever get that way about anything? Just obsessed and you can't get it out of your head?"

"Sure. I just give you a hard time to try to mask the fact that I'm obsessed with science and math and architecture and engineering, for god's sake, all way less cool than art. So, chill."

"Point taken. No, but it felt . . . this is going to sound crazy, but," I had to say it, "kind of . . . familiar."

"How do you mean?"

The train rattled through the tunnels, soaring and shaking. I thought about how much I wanted to say and decided: why not?

"Well, she had been left in this strange place, beat up . . . And that's kind of what happened to me, I guess, when I was little."

"Wait." He looked at me now, a flicker of fear. "You're that girl?"

I must've given him a look that said, *What do you mean by that?*

"No." He shook his head—it had come out wrong. "No, I mean, growing up we always heard that story of the girl who was our age and was found abandoned in the woods. But I never knew it was you."

"Yeah, I guess it was kind of a big deal at one point. But now not many people really know. Joan took me in and we sort of made a deal not to say anything about it. When I started school, they kept it quiet, and it eventually all died down."

His brown eyes raced side to side, taking me in, as though they were bubbling up with questions and couldn't sort out which line of interrogation to pursue first.

"Is that how you got—you know." He put his hand up to the place above his heart, where my scars were.

"I don't know. I had them when they found me, so, I guess." I pulled the zipper up farther on my coat without thinking, then a quick shudder shook my body. What had I been thinking showing him that last night? Wearing that dress and those jewels and all the makeup and having my hair done just right, I had been a bolder me. I was a different person within the walls of that hotel.

"Well," he continued, picking at something on the back of the seat in front of ours. "For the record . . . I think they're pretty badass."

"Thanks." I blushed. It was the strangest compliment I'd ever received and yet one of the best too. "Yours too." I gestured with my gloved hand toward his eye.

He just nodded, a flash of a tiny smile. We were quiet the rest of the ride.

Our last visit was a bit far-flung, a blogger in an office building over on Grand Avenue near Navy Pier, that strip of amusement park rides and shops and general touristy hubbub jutting out like a spear into Lake Michigan. After we dropped off the final package, our hands free at last and our load lightened, we allowed ourselves to wander a few blocks out of our way.

Being out of the hotel and suddenly reminded of the world that existed beyond that revolving door and red carpet and insignia-emblazoned awning, I could feel my mind start to clear. I wanted more time away, more time like this, set free in the city when everyone else I knew was trapped in a classroom within the fortress of a suburban school somewhere. Once I stepped back, took my head out of it for a moment and could set aside the parts of my new life that didn't make sense—or that terrified me at times—I could feel the thrill of this new world rising to my head. I could tell Lance felt this way too, because, despite the length of time we'd been gone and the bitterness of that cold, he certainly hadn't objected to taking the long route back to the L.

The rides of Navy Pier grew closer on the horizon now, the Ferris wheel creeping up into the white winter sky.

"I feel like we're playing hooky," I said.

"I know. Good for us, right?"

"No kidding." I still reveled in every slightly rebellious act, since we just weren't the kind to ever deviate from a rule.

"Hey, is that still going?" He pointed up to the Ferris wheel in the distance. "Even in this weather?"

"Sure, three hundred and sixty-three—I think—days a year. I'm pretty sure it's only closed on Thanksgiving and Christmas."

"Huh." He stared off, thinking, gloved hands plunged deep in his pockets.

"I haven't been on that thing in years." Though I didn't like roller coasters, I had no objections to the Ferris wheel at Navy Pier because you weren't just hanging out with your limbs wiggling in the air. It was a more civilized affair—you were tucked away in a nice little, nearly all-enclosed compartment, like old-fashioned train travel, or a carriage that could've been pulled by horses. It felt more insulated, safe. A contained pod, inching up into the heavens. And it moved incredibly slowly, which was about my speed.

"I've never been on it," he said, a little embarrassed.

"How is that possible? You grew up here, right?"

"Yeah, why?"

"That's unacceptable then. C'mon, it's, like, seven minutes."

"Seriously?"

"Sure, why not?"

He shrugged, which I took as a yes, and, sure enough, our bodies just kept walking along Grand Avenue, even though they should've made a U-turn and gone back. The pier wasn't quite as bustling in the middle of the winter as it would have been at the height of summer, but it was still surprisingly populated with people who seemed insistent upon pretending it wasn't below freezing, eating hot dogs and digging their faces into clouds of cotton candy. The Ferris wheel never stopped turning—which always struck me as a nice metaphor for something, maybe life in general? The idea that change or opportunity was always on the horizon because this thing kept going, an endless stream of people stepping on and off. I wondered if this was what others thought about as they waited for a little compartment to pull up. Other people were probably more in the moment, enjoying their day at the park. I was hardly ever fully in any moment, it seemed. My head always sped off in so many directions. *I* could be exhausting.

Finally the car that would be ours swooped toward us smoothly, becoming level with our platform. I stepped on first, settling into the wooden bench seat, then Lance, sitting opposite me. The doors swung closed and up we went, inching along, up and up and up, the icy breeze wafting in above the doorway. I watched outside the Plexiglas the ground and people and things shrinking down to dollhouse-size.

"So, seven minutes?" he asked.

"Yep, should we synchronize our watches?" I was kidding.

"And it's what, about a hundred and fifty feet up?"

"I think that's right."

"So." His eyes were focused off in the sky somewhere. This was his thinking face, I had come to realize. "Seven minutes for one revolution and a diameter of 150 feet, that would mean we're traveling at a speed of—"

"No," I said firmly. "No math allowed. You're missing the whole view. Go. Look." I pointed to the city outside our window. He did as he was told. We both watched quietly as the city passed by, so many of the sights we had visited today. This, all of it, was so much better than school. And there was a lot I liked about school.

"So how did you grow up here and avoid coming *here*?"

"I don't know. We came here but we went to, like, the Children's Museum." He pointed to it below, a sprawling complex adjacent to the pier. "There were always too many of us and the line for this thing would be too long for everyone to wait."

"Too many? So you have a big family?"

"Sort of. I grew up in that orphanage, you know, over on Lake Street?"

"Wow."

"Yeah, but the woman who ran the place liked me—I guess I just never cried, like even when I was a baby. I was quiet and stuff, you know. So she and her husband adopted me themselves."

"Wow. I never knew any of that."

"Yeah, I mean, why would you, right?"

"Did you ever go looking for your parents?" I wondered if he knew more about his than I did about mine.

"I thought about it but I haven't tried. I feel like the people who raised me are my real parents, you know? And where would I look anyway? They got me from some fire station, where I guess I'd been left."

"Really?"

He nodded.

"I had heard that people do that, but of all the places—I mean the sirens and alarms and all those guys—how would they know the first thing about what to do with a baby?"

He shrugged. "They were nice though. I go by there every once in a while ever since I was a kid. Now that I'm sixteen I could train to be a volunteer there, and I probably will. Maybe after this job."

"It sounds kinda scary."

"I know. It does. I was kinda glad when this internship came up, to buy me some time, you know?"

"Would your parents let you?"

"I don't think they're totally into the idea but they like the guys over there and I'll bet if they think it's important to me, they'll let me. We'll see, I guess." The air hung thick with worry and question, so I tried to steer us away.

"Well, I bet you'd learn how to cook. And maybe they would do one of those calendars that firefighters are always selling and they'd let you pose," I offered. "These are fireman stereotypes, I guess, but they're good ones at least."

"Maybe I can get them to hire you to shoot the calendar."

"I'm available!" We both laughed.

Our car pulled up to the very top now, and without meaning to, we both dropped out of our conversation and got lost in the scene: the lake stretching out endlessly; the jagged skyline of the city; dusk threatening to set in, dimming the cloud-covered sky from white to gray. It felt like we were floating so free, nothing holding us in. If I was a little lightheaded it was less from this apex we had hit, so high above the ground, and more just from the notion that up here we were so untouchable.

We spent the second half of the ride, the descent, in silence, staring out the window. But it wasn't quite like our typical spells of quietude. My eyes would occasionally drift over to see if Lance was still content staring outside and I would find him just as I expected. But then as I began to look away, I would feel him glancing over at me. We went back and forth like this a few times. I wondered if I should start talking again. Why did I feel this way? I never cared whether we talked or not. Was this going to start feeling difficult? What was going on?

At last we coasted into the platform. We descended the metal steps back to the ground, silent again.

When we got back, the hotel had come to life. Scores of suited-up types littered the bar at the Parlor, downing drinks over the din of jazz music, while a few pairs and foursomes crowded around tables at Capone for an early dinner. The lobby hummed with that overall vibration of activity and hustle-bustle: people checking in at the front desk and ascending to their rooms with luggage in hand; others spilling out of the elevators ready to begin their evenings out; people here and there walking fast in nice shoes with cell phones pinned against their ears. Lance went to look for Lucian or Aurelia in case we had any final assignments for the day, and I headed to the gallery.

Though it was still open and inviting, the gallery was nearly empty. There was just one man inside—the one I had shared the elevator with the night before, though it took me a moment to place him today since he had shed his tux in favor of dark pants and a sport coat. He stood before the photos of the Outfit, studying them so intently that when he heard my footsteps, he looked over for a second as though he'd been caught stealing something. But then he smiled.

"Good evening," I said in my most professional voice. I

sounded like I was trying too hard. "Everything here is for sale, if you're interested in anything. Just let me know if I can help."

"Thank you," he said softly.

I slipped out of sight, back to the office, to give him time alone. I could certainly understand the desire to be alone with something artistic. I thought again of that painting, *La Jeune Martyre,* and then Lance and his equally unusual childhood. I straightened up the desk, putting Aurelia's blank notecards and envelopes into neat piles and making a file for the list of contacts she'd given us for today. Then I unlocked the drawer with the camera, gathering the equipment for tonight's assignment. But I couldn't begin to think of that—first I had my dinner date with Lucian. I had managed to push it somehow, and with tremendous effort, to the back of my mind during the day in order to be even remotely productive. But now, it rushed back, all that fluttering anticipation. I had no idea what I was supposed to wear tonight or, for that matter, what I was supposed to say or do. A voice shook me out of my head space.

"Miss? Excuse me?" It was the man in the gallery. "Are you still here, miss?"

I hurried out of my office and found him just near the doorway, but far enough back that I could tell he was polite enough to not want to intrude.

"Hi, I'm here." I ran out. These shoes were really hurting, now that I'd had a few minutes to sit down. "Can I help you?"

"I'm interested in a photograph," he said. "Could I show you?"

"Of course, let's see," I said, following him. He led us to that wall with my photos of the Outfit. My heart sped up. He stopped in front of the giant shot of Aurelia.

"I would love to buy this one. I wondered, what you would like for it?"

"Wow, thank you," I said. I couldn't help it: "I actually took that photo, all of these." Now I was embarrassed, but it just leapt out of me.

"You're very talented," he said, the way a father might.

"Thank you so much." I bit my tongue to keep from saying any of my usual self-deprecating lines. If this man wanted to pay for one of my pictures I shouldn't go telling him I'm not that great. I looked at the picture of Aurelia: it just wasn't so good at all. Last night I had been so surprised to see those few wrinkles and the bit of red in her eyes, that strange mark on her cheek. And there all of it was again still, right here staring back at us. But this man, for whatever reason, seemed to like it, marred and inaccurate as it was. The customer is always right.

"So, how much would this one be?" he had to ask again.

"Oh, I'm sorry, that's right. Well—" I had absolutely no clue. And I didn't think it was within my right to invent a price. "The price list was finalized this morning." I hoped he couldn't tell I was making this up as I went along. "If you're able to wait just a moment, I can go grab it."

"Sure, thank you."

I nodded and hustled out the door of the gallery, cantering to the front desk, past the Outfit girls, and back into the darkened corridor. I knocked, loud and quick, rattling the door to Aurelia's office. Nothing. I pushed my ear against the door, but couldn't hear a thing inside. I sprinted back to the gallery. The man was still standing right where I left him, staring at that photo.

"I'm so sorry, sir, but I'm afraid our owner is, um, off-site."

Good one. "But if I could take down your information, I can have her contact you first thing tomorrow morning."

"That would be perfect." He took out his wallet and fished out a business card, which he handed to me: Neil Marlinson. He was a lawyer and lived in Boston. "I'll be here until Friday."

"Great. Thank you."

With one last look at the picture of Aurelia, he showed himself out.

17

An Evening in Alcatraz

The lighting in the basement hallway leading to our rooms was not particularly good—we didn't have the grand skylight running down the center like the rest of the hotel or the many ornate sconces punctuating the walls of each of the nine upper floors. There were just a few old fan-shaped fixtures casting a dim glow. But it was still bright enough that I could see that something had been left outside my door. It was a white box the size of a slim suitcase with a dark ribbon tied around it and an envelope slid in, as though belted in place.

I sped up, reaching my door in seconds—my feet, which had ached all day, suddenly not feeling quite so ravaged. I pulled the envelope out first. My name was written on the front in a neat, strong hand. On the crisp, creamy card inside, a note:

YOUR UNIFORM FOR TONIGHT. HOPE YOU LIKE IT . . .
LUCIAN

I zipped my keycard in the door, threw it open, and kicked it closed behind me all while unlooping the ribbon and tearing off the lid of the box. I couldn't tell if my room was the temperature of the center of the sun or if I was just overly excited, but I was burning up.

As I removed the contents of this package, with care and reverence, I let the bottom of the box fall without a thought.

This was a *dress*.

I held the crimson satin gown out before me, clipping my fingers on either side of the bodice. It was so shiny I swore I could almost see my reflection in it. It hit just above the knee, hanging straight and cinched in at the waist, making it a little gathered and ruched across the top. But what looked funny about it? I studied it and then shook myself from my dreamy haze back to reality: strapless. I didn't do strapless, for obvious reasons. Dress in my hands, I thumped onto my bed, aching and nervous now. Why did everything have to be so difficult? Couldn't I just be excited to wear this beautiful dress and look okay the way I was? My mind raced through the cardigans I had brought. Did I have any in colors that could go with this? My hand petted at the dress, as though apologizing to it. But as I ran my fingers across the top, some extra material bunched up. It looked like a flaw in the dress, but then I pulled it up and saw that it had one thick, slightly ruffled shoulder strap that had been tucked in when it was folded. The joy flooded back again just as quickly as it had drained. This dress was perfect for me. The strap was even on the left side. So did this mean Lucian had noticed my scars in that picture? I didn't even care if he had, I was just grateful for whatever had happened to make this a dress that I could wear tonight and actually feel good in.

I couldn't wait to put it on. I ditched my uniform, tugging to get it off—it still felt unusually warm in here. Sometime I would have to do an exhaustive search for a thermostat; there had to be one somewhere. I splashed some cold water on my face. The clock read 6:20—if I hustled I could jump in the shower.

When I slipped into that dress, I couldn't believe it was me in the mirror—this was becoming a common occurrence, seeing a costumed version of Haven staring back at myself from the closet door.

"Whoa," I said to myself. "That's really red."

I didn't own any red, now that I thought about it, but I could suddenly understand why girls do. There was no missing a person wearing this color. Brazen and relentless, it surged out, intensifying the more you stared at it. I wasn't the worst mannequin for it. It not only fit, zipping up without trouble, but also managed to cling just a bit in the way it was intended, and it looked goddess-like with that one-shoulder strap and that slight ruffle. Not terrible, I decided. Not terrible at all.

I was a bit at a loss when it came to hair and makeup though, without anyone to step in and play stylist—Dante was working as usual. I let my hair down and tried to fluff it up, shaking my hands through it. That seemed to work a little bit, giving it that messy, lively look that I'd seen on some of the Outfit girls. For my makeup, I worked with what I had: my brown eyeliner, which I wore occasionally, and my pink lip-gloss.

By 6:50 I was dressed, with Aurelia's evening bag in hand—how fortuitous that I'd completely neglected to return my getup from the night before. I would give it all back to her tomorrow. I sat on the bed to wait it out, my stomach tightening into knots now. The book, that book, lay beside me, so innocently on the pillow. I stared it down: no. I didn't want to look. I didn't want to think about what had happened to those photos and I didn't wish to be reminded of those nightly conditioning exercises I'd be forced to suffer through in the tunnels later. *Don't let anything ruin tonight,* I told myself. *Don't let it cloud how you're feeling.*

It might help if I weren't so hot. Six fifty-five. Five minutes. I put away my makeup, cleaned up the mess I'd made opening the gift box. I propped the chair back against the doorknob of the closet, a tremor quivering through me as I did, and tucked the journal back into the night table. Lucian's flower was still alive, even more vibrant than yesterday. I changed the water. Dante's plant looked hearty and thriving, so, recalling his advice, I just left it alone. One minute after seven. I sat back down on the bed, fidgeting with my hair and my nails and my dress, trying to cool myself down, in all aspects. Two minutes after seven.

I couldn't bear to wait. I grabbed my bag, burst up from the bed and out the door in one smooth motion.

I had gotten only as far as the gallery entrance when I spotted Lucian—in a sharply tailored black suit—on his way to me. A smile lit his face, like the sun breaking on the horizon.

We walked toward each other, through the lobby, not noticing the people milling around us. Watching him, I worried I couldn't even keep traveling along a straight trajectory. I had to pay attention to each step or I might topple over, swoon the way girls were always doing in those eighteenth-century novels I liked so much. But they all blamed the suffocating corsets—what was my excuse?

The lobby felt endless, our walk in slow motion, until finally we met halfway, in what seemed to be the exact mathematical center of the lobby—a fact Lance would have known. I would have to ask him.

"Hi." He spoke first, his eyes spearing mine as everything around us faded.

"Hi."

"I would've come down to get you. You're too punctual."

"Punctuality, it can be my worst trait, I guess."

"Then you're lucky."

I remembered my manners. "This is amazing, thank you so much." I smoothed out the skirt of the dress and tried to read his expression.

"You're very welcome." This was all he said, nothing of how I looked. I thought that's how dates were supposed to go: no matter what, the guy says *You look great* as soon as he sees you. Apparently I had been ruined by too many romantic comedies. After a pause, he went on: "So, we're gonna play a game. I hope you like games."

"Only if I win," I blurted out playfully before even thinking.

Lucian seemed entertained by this. "You'll win," he assured me.

"Then in that case . . ."

He led us toward the entrance to Capone and said, "It goes like this: Everyone is going to look at you as we walk by. Pay attention." His lips curled into a smile, like we were in on this wonderful joke together. Except I didn't quite get it.

"I'm sorry?"

"Just watch."

He burst into the packed dining room, slicing through the throngs of people buzzing around the bar. Every table was taken and many patient hopefuls lingered on the periphery staring down the lucky seated diners, willing a new spot to open up. He cut a diagonal trail right through and I followed. A few steps in, he reached his hand back and seized mine in his and we walked, like that, his grip so warm I felt the heat rise to the top of my head and down to the soles of my feet.

I wouldn't have believed it if I hadn't seen it happen, but he was right: people paused mid-conversation and watched us pass. They turned their heads. One woman pointed. I imagined the gesture was for Lucian, who had that effect in every room he entered, but then I saw the woman, well-dressed in her evening gown and pearls, nod at me in approval. Yes, when I dared to look right in these faces, I saw their eyes were on me. I wondered if they could read my shock. Through a cutout in the back wall offering a glimpse of the kitchen, I caught sight of Dante, shaking something around in a flaming skillet. He looked up, the blaze lighting his face with its fiery glow, and flashed me a look that said, *Not bad, Haven, and I want to hear about it later.* We turned a corner and Lucian and I were alone, side by side now. He linked my arm into his, making a place for my hand in the crook of his elbow.

"What did I tell you?" he asked.

"They were looking at *you.*" It came out shyly, or maybe coquettish. He shook his head. "Or else, I must just have something on my face that no one's telling me about." He studied me for a moment.

"I think you're right." He pushed my hair behind one ear and kissed my cheek, soft and warm. "Got it."

I had to consciously lock my knees to keep them from buckling. And now we were walking again.

"So where are we going?" I managed without sounding too breathless.

"Alcatraz, of course."

"Of course." I said it like I had some idea what he was talking about even though I didn't.

"You haven't seen it yet because it wasn't finished, but it is now, and you'll be the first there."

"Should I be wearing black and white stripes?"

"No, you're stunning as you are."

We reached the end of the shadow-shrouded hallway, stopping before a tucked-away elevator. He hit the down button and the doors opened. Inside it was entirely made of glass. He held out his hand to usher me in and then followed me.

"So, Alcatraz then?" I started as the doors closed. Outside the glass, the dark walls of the elevator shaft closed in as we shot down.

"Alcatraz." He let it hang there in the air, just to let the mystery sink in as the cables of the elevator creaked.

Nervous, I babbled, "Capone did some time there. Four and a half years, I think. The devil's island, right?"

"Indeed, they did used to call it that. Here, Alcatraz is a lot more pleasant than what Capone encountered. Ours is a private dining room," he explained. "He was there four years, but here people can stick around as long as it takes them to eat four courses. A meal in here costs more than you can believe, more than it should be legal to charge, but it's already booked solid for the next two months. We, however, get to be the first to try it tonight. Consider this a final quality-control test run before the unveiling."

The doors opened and we were met by a narrow metal gangplank, fenced in by ropes. From where we stood, it stretched out to a small caged-in island in the center surrounded by water. The whole expansive room, if you could call it that, didn't seem like a place that could be contained within the four walls of the hotel at all. A moat flowed on all sides of the island, and along its banks sweeping, lush nature flourished. If I hadn't known better, I would have sworn we had been transported outside to some sort of hidden pond, lined as it was with mossy trees and bulbous tropical plants in deep reds that looked akin to the one Dante had given me.

"Welcome to Alcatraz." Lucian stepped onto the walkway.

I took it all in, the visuals overloading my eyes, too much to process. "No one would ever try to escape this Alcatraz." As we walked, the panels beneath us lit up.

"That's the idea."

We made our way to that island in the center, a beacon at the confluence of romance and danger beckoning to us. My pulse raced at the idea of being suspended above this water, amid this strange indoor wildlife, alone with Lucian. The area we were headed toward was caged in by bars—a more literal interpretation of Alcatraz than I had expected. Inside that encasement, however, a perfect scene awaited us: a floating dining room and lounge. A table had been set for dinner with lavish damask linens and gleaming china, all glowing in candlelight, and two velvet chairs that resembled thrones. In the area behind the table, a matching cushy chaise longue and chair and a mirrored side table made for a cozy sitting room. Certainly the most beautiful jail cell anyone could hope for. The encircling metal bars ran a good twelve feet up but didn't come anywhere close to reaching the top. High above us, the ceiling sparkled like a night sky.

As we reached the lock in the bars, Lucian fished from his jacket pocket an old-fashioned key ring the size of a bracelet with one comically long key dangling from it, and twirled it around one finger. He rattled the key into the lock and swung open the cage-like door for me.

"Thank you."

He pulled it shut behind us and reached his arm through one

of the slats to lock us in, then looped it back around and returned the key to his pocket.

"Now we've officially locked away the rest of the world."

I liked the sound of that. The scar at my heart fluttered and burned. I touched the satin of my dress just above it.

"But what happens if you drop the key in the water or something?"

"Then we're in trouble. We'll be down here forever," he said matter-of-factly. I looked at him, just a flash of nerves. He grinned, lightening. "Don't worry. It's all for show. This is actually open. There's a switch so you can get locked out but never locked in." He brushed past me to the sitting area. "Come 'ere." He took a seat on the chair and opened a panel on the cylindrical side table, punching a few buttons. I sat down on the chaise, smoothing the dress over my lap. He flipped the panel down. "Watch this."

A low whoosh and rattle shook from inside the table. Within seconds, a glass dome shot up from the surface of the tabletop and split down the middle, opening like a jaw and then disappearing, leaving two wineglasses and a dark blue bottle.

"Wow!"

"Yeah, not bad, huh?" He poured from the label-less bottle and handed me the glass, now full with something effervescent and clear.

"You're not going to set fire to this or anything?" I wanted to find a nice way to ask what was in here.

"It's sparkling water." He poured a glass for himself.

"Oh." I felt like an idiot now. "Exotic."

"Thought you'd like it." He smirked and clinked my glass with his, then went on. "So generally people can order whatever they want in here. That's the idea at least." He stood from his chair and pulled me up, his hot hand gently tugging at mine, then slid back one of the chairs at the table for me to sit down. He pushed me in, scooting that huge chair and me effortlessly, then took his place across from me. "But I took the liberty of preparing a tasting menu of all the best dishes, because you shouldn't have to choose among the best—you should just have all of the best. And I mean that, not just in terms of what nourishes a body but a soul too. It's a way of life. But I'm getting away from my point. I hope you don't mind that I ordered dinner."

"Not at all. I suppose I'm okay with that," I said. *What nourishes a soul,* my mind turned that over.

"I thought so." He leaned down, clicking at something on his side of the table, and snapping something shut. Another *whoosh* swirled, this time from inside our dinner table. The silverware chimed together softly. Another dome shot up, erupting from the tabletop, encompassing the entire thing, save for an outer rim that included our place settings. The dome split away and retracted out of sight, and at least a dozen small plates the circumference of baseball caps now dotted the surface.

"Whoa."

"That's nothing. Check this out." He hit another button on the panel on his side of the table and the lights in the moat around us lit up brighter and bluer, a rippling glow encasing us as it spouted from beneath the water. The star-like pinpricks speckling the ceiling intensified so it looked like a replica of something you might see at the Adler Planetarium downtown. I gazed above, finding Orion's belt and Cassiopeia and Ursa Major. I noticed Lucian fiddling once more with that panel and music came on, something jaunty and swinging. "Are standards okay? Right now we only have Capone-era music."

"I guess that'll have to do." I smiled, dazzled by it all.

"So that's it for my tricks," he said finally, slouching back in his chair.

"That's pretty good."

"Hopefully you'll like this just as much . . ."

He took me on a culinary tour of our table, pointing out what each dish was—mini ostrich cheeseburgers, rattlesnake ravioli, alligator soup—so many things I'd never even dreamed of trying. I was overwhelmed by the array of odd delicacies. In an effort to appear adventurous, I planned to try everything, even if, in some cases, it would require blocking out what animal it was.

"This is like a trip to the zoo," I said when he had finished describing it all. "I mean, in a tragic sort of way."

"A very quiet and still zoo, I suppose." He laughed. "So, I guess, bon appétit?"

"Bon appétit," I confirmed.

He sliced a bit of the dish nearest him—the venison—and I speared a pair of the rattlesnake ravioli right in front of me, but as I did, the table jerked and began rotating away from me. "Omigod," I blurted out, as my ravioli and fork got whisked away clockwise toward Lucian. I looked over to see him suppressing a laugh.

"Okay, that's my last trick." He raised his hands up in surrender.

Hey!" The ravioli and fork had stopped in front of him. "Do I have any controls over here? You know, like a driver's ed car with the two sets of brakes and steering wheels and everything?" I lifted the tablecloth on my side but found only a solid cube that was some sort of elevator shooting the food up and out to us.

"No, I'm afraid I'm doing the driving." He smiled. "I suppose you'll be needing this back?" He waved my fork but instead of handing it over, he reached across the table for me to take a bite. "What's the verdict?" he asked.

"It's good," I said at last, as soon as I stopped chewing the tough meat. "Just like chicken."

"I think so too." He chuckled. "So tell me, Haven," he started, his eyes on me. "What do you most want?"

I paused for a moment. "Um, well, I guess maybe it would be a good experiment for me to try the escargot next?"

He smiled, a true, wide smile, rotating the table so the escargot landed in front of me, and continued: "Actually, I meant more in terms of, what do you want from life?"

"Wow." I set down my fork and looked at him and then away. "I definitely got that question wrong, didn't I?"

We both laughed in matching tones. I was still formulating an intelligent answer to redeem myself, when he jumped in.

"Remember when I told you to make a wish on your birthday?"

"Sure."

"So, what did you wish for?"

I wasn't sure whether I wanted to incriminate myself—that was, after all, the day I met him, and I had been pretty preoccupied calculating the odds of him ever being interested in me. So I answered simply, "I didn't get around to formally wishing for anything. I kind of got distracted. And, I guess, sorta sick."

"That's too bad."

"It's okay. It was worth it, you know?" I felt myself easing into that warm wooziness that I'd experienced that night, after that fiery drink. I had no idea why since I'd only had water. Maybe this was just my natural state around Lucian. It would take no prying at all and I'd be confessing that I was madly in love with him, going anywhere he wanted to take me. I felt addicted to him.

"What do you think of it here?" he asked. "Do you want to be in the Outfit?" He tossed it out, no big deal.

"Like, hypothetically speaking or . . ." I could feel my eyes twinkling at him. I played with my fork, turning it over and over, absent-mindedly.

"Hypothetically, for now."

"Well, everyone does, I suppose, don't they?"

"Yes. But do you?"

"I don't know. I mean, it never occurred to me it would be an option."

"Because I just joined pretty recently—"

"Really?"

"Yeah, that's the thing about this place. If you're doing a good job, you rise in the ranks. And suddenly you're at the center of the universe, you're running the city, you know everyone, you have everything you could want—success, attention, everything. You matter. Some people are never going to reach the highest level, of course, but some people—" His eyes dug into mine, holding on for a silent second. "Some people get on this track and they're unstoppable. And you're one of those, Haven. Everyone knows it."

"Um, that's good to hear."

"What would you give anything to have? What do you want most from your life? Right now? What would make you happy?"

"I am happy."

"I know. But what would make a difference to you, to your life? If you could have anything, everything you wanted? Today, tomorrow, forever. What do you dream about?"

I thought about it. Today and tomorrow were different than forever. Today, in this most immediate minute, I just wished for *him*. But I couldn't tell him that, and I liked that we were having this kind of heavy philosophical talk, so I decided to go ahead and give him my more serious answer. "Well, I guess I want to do something important. I want to go to med school eventually and be a doctor. I'm not sure what kind but I guess, if I'm being honest . . ."

"Yes?"

"I want to set the world on fire, you know? Cure cancer, save people, change people's lives on a grand scale. I kind of feel like there are a lot of people who changed my life. I've had to rely on people so much, and if they hadn't been good people I don't know where I'd be now."

He sat back in his seat, studying me, looking for something in my eyes or under my skin, something within. Finally, he spoke, choosing his words slowly and carefully: "What if I could tell you I could give you all of that?" The words swirled in my head, blowing in like a summer breeze, too sweet and perfect. I didn't understand. My skin felt fiery now. "And more. I could give you more."

"I'm not sure I—"

He leaned forward, like he was about to let me in on a secret, whispering in his honey-coated voice.

"Your life could be perfect and everything, everyone, you wanted could be yours." He didn't take his eyes from mine for even a second.

"I guess my only question would be—"

"Where do you sign?" He touched my hand.

"Or, maybe, what's the catch?" Nervous laughter slipped out.

"There's always a little fine print, I suppose. But aren't some things worth it?"

"I guess it depends."

"That's not the answer I expected," he said with a smile, as though he knew I would come around. "Think about it."

"Think about what?"

"Think about what it would feel like to get everything you ever wanted."

"Okay."

"And think about how that could be worth whatever price you had to pay to get there."

I nodded.

"You have no idea what could be ahead of you. What you're capable of." He said it with a reverence that surprised me, elevated me. "I don't think you know how remarkable you are."

That last bit I wanted so badly to believe.

"Thank you," I said.

"You're welcome," he said sincerely. "And Haven . . . it's true."

And with that, he leaned back in his chair again and surveyed what remained on the plates before us.

We finished eating and with the push of a few buttons, dinner was cleared and a dessert smorgasbord appeared in its place. We spoke easily about the hotel, the gala opening, the change in atmosphere now that our Lexington world was populated with guests, and then dissected the mechanics of how our food got onto our table.

"You really want to know?" he asked.

"Of course."

"Doesn't it ruin some of the magic?"

"I like to know how things work."

"It's basically an elevator, with someone monitoring everything I type in. Come 'ere, I'll show you." He let me over to his side and allowed me to punch in the directions to remove our dessert, returning our table to a clean, blank damask-covered canvas.

When it was time to go and I rose from my seat, I was light-headed and unsteady. He took my arm in his so we could walk through the gate and along the bridge together.

"Thanks. I think I must be in a food coma."

"Understandable."

"Maybe I should swim back." I gestured to the water. "Wake myself up a bit."

"You're welcome to, but it would be more wading than swimming. It's only a foot or so deep. You didn't hear it from me, though. It ruins the illusion."

"It's all about the illusion. Life is all smoke and mirrors, isn't it?"

"So true."

We made our way to the elevator, the walkway lighting our path with each step, until finally we reached it and he hit the up button. As woozy as I was, I still felt the butterflies rise, knowing we were closing in on the end of our date. The doors opened and we stepped inside.

"So obviously we have to do this again," he offered.

"Obviously." I nodded in return, with a shy, expectant smile. And then, his eyes reeled me in and he took a few steps toward me, until his soft, warm lips delicately found mine, his hand lightly feeling for my fingers.

But what was different? I couldn't make sense of it, except that I was aware of it happening, this kiss. I wasn't knocked out the way I had been the night before, when something else had taken over and I had cleaved to him involuntarily and he had grabbed me and there was frenzy, no thought, only pure feeling. This was more timid.

The elevator stopped and he slipped away. My eyes opened just before the doors did.

He led us out into the lobby through a back door behind the dining room.

"So I guess this is good night then," he said, leaning in and kissing me once more, quickly and too politely this time.

"Good night."

With a wave, he walked away, hands in his pocket. I watched him go, staring after him longer than I should have, then fetched the camera from the gallery. I had work to do.

18

We Mustn't Underestimate Her

The Vault was throbbing at its usual fever pitch by the time I got there. The lights emblazoned on the tunnel wall told me tonight was greed night. I wondered if that was a sign. Had I been greedy in my unfavorable analysis of that kiss? I had now received three kisses in two days. I was making up for lost time, to be sure, so maybe I should be less of a critic and more grateful to find my lips being put to good use at last.

I snapped shots without thinking and found more eyes connecting with the camera than I expected. It seemed these revelers, decked out in their designer clothes, painted with their makeup and perfectly coifed, were already looking in my direction when I trained my lens on them. I wasn't so much the fly on the wall tonight as I was a player thrust into the mix—not a role I was generally accustomed to. I guess it must've been the dress. It could be nice to be watched. The collective power of those eyes could swirl around you, bubble up inside you, and, if you let it, convince you that you were worthy of it and that you were something to see. I wasn't entirely sold yet, but I was getting there.

But what I really didn't expect was to find anyone going so far as to wave at me to get my attention. But as I circled the crowded dance floor, taking action shots of the sea of bodies swaying and spinning and shaking to the music, I spotted someone just on the outskirts, amid a handful of girls in black pants and an array of sparkly tops, signaling to me. I adjusted the camera's focus on my gesturing subject and zoomed in to find a smiling familiar face: Dr. Michelle. I looked again to be sure, but, yes, I was right. She put her hand up to her mouth and looked to be yelling my name, though I couldn't hear a thing over the ear-rattling beat of the music. I waved back. "Don't go anywhere!" I tried to yell, though I couldn't even begin to hear myself, and our view of each other kept getting blocked by dancers in the space between us.

Snaking through the crowd, jostled by flailing arms and sloshed by the occasional drink, I finally reached Michelle. It occurred to me I had never seen her outside the hospital. She had on an aqua sequined halter-top, black pants, and a brighter pink lip-gloss than usual, her dark hair still tied back, but in a lower ponytail than she wore at work.

"Hey, Haven!" She gave me a big hug. It was so comforting to see her that, for just a flash, I missed everyone, everything, even school. "This is the awesomest candy striper at the hospital," she announced to the pack of girls, who smiled and waved while still dancing. "I was thinking of you when Katie said she wanted to come here—"

"It's my birthday!" Katie, a blonde in a rhinestone tiara and pink feather boa, slurred, already tipsy. "Twenty-seven! Ugh! Sooooo olllld!"

Michelle shook her head. "But, anyway, I figured you had to

be twenty-one here so I didn't think I'd get to see you. But here you are and look at you! You look fantastic!" She stood back to look at me. "I bet you don't miss your scrubs!"

"There are definitely some perks here, I guess."

"I guess so! And don't worry, I won't tell Joan you've turned into a crazy club kid."

"Thanks, appreciate it. I'm on official business." I shook the camera. "Hey, let me get all you guys." I motioned for them to gather up and they squeezed together, arms around each other, posing. "Say, 'birthday'!" They did, and I snapped. A new song blasted and the girls all started jumping and cheering. Michelle shook her head again, like she was the sensible chaperone of the group. "Let me know if you guys need anything," I said, enjoying the thrill of playing hostess at a place like this, at having even the teeniest illusion of influence here. "And have fun and—oh yeah!—maybe just tell Joan we ran into each other in the hotel lobby or something?" I tacked on, just to be safe.

"You got it! So great to see you, Haven! We miss you at work!" She gave me another hug and I waved as I slunk back, swallowed into the surrounding crowds as I searched out my next target.

The ring of fire burned bright in the center of it all, and I decided to go ahead and make my way to it, weaving through clubgoers and snapping as I went. The sheer number of bodies on that platform tonight seemed almost too much to contain. I had never seen it crowded with so many people—so many unfamiliar faces, especially. I scanned all these figures looking for one in particular but I didn't see Lucian. A wave of peace washed over me. Emboldened by our date, by this night, I ventured up that spiral staircase on my own, joining ranks with all those beautiful creatures, dancing and flirting and drinking and locking eyes with the less vaunted partygoers down below.

Walk tall, Haven. For once, walk tall and belong. I snapped dozens of pictures. The Outfit members paid me no mind, and the others were only too happy to seek me out hoping to be shot. I squeezed through the clusters of boys and girls secretly sorting themselves in that silent dance to determine who would pair up with whom. After several minutes floating among them, I took one last look from the top of the staircase and returned to the main floor, that aura and glow still illuminating me.

I wound my way around the perimeter of the club making one full lap. I had stayed longer than I planned, but tonight, oddly, I had enjoyed myself. The heat and wooziness of dinner had worn off, leaving only the welcome sense of euphoria behind. I gave a parting glance to the ring but had to do a double take. Lucian was seated there now. He lounged nearest the bar, a drink in his hand, staring off into space. Something stopped me from trying to get his attention. He knew I was planning to be here, but he hadn't said a word about coming. Had he hoped to find me? Or had he neglected to look for me? I fought against the urge to let this snuff out the buzz I had. I couldn't read his expression at all. He stared off into the distance as everyone else swirled around him, existing in his own personal chamber it seemed.

I slunk away, back through the thick steel door, and onward to my room. All those unanswered questions flared up in me again. Still lost in thought, running through the night's odd twists and turns, it took me ages to fish my keycard out of my evening bag and swipe it in the lock of my room. The hallway was entirely silent, except for a crackling I couldn't place. It almost sounded like it was coming from inside my room, even though that didn't make any sense. It was along the lines of wind rustling, but there were no windows down here. The lock unlatched and I opened the door. A scream escaped my lips before my brain could even fully process the scene.

Fire! My room was on fire. Or at least a part of my room was on fire.

The blaze was consuming—and emanating from—the plant Dante had given me. A spitting column of fire shot up from the pot, reaching from my desk almost to the ceiling. A layer of dense, cottony-gray smoke clouded the top half of the room. I dropped my bag on the floor and ran to my closet, pulling out the mini fire extinguisher and yanking the locking pin out of the trigger. I pointed the nozzle at the dancing embers and unleashed a torrent of white spray. It coated the plant, snuffing out the danger until there was nothing left but a charred stem. The smoke and haze of misty residue hung in the air and in my lungs. I opened up my door wider, waving my hands to clear space to breathe, coughing fiercely. The room was a heat trap of burnt, bitter air.

I swept the potted plant off the desk and straight into the wastebasket and flew out the open door to Dante and Lance's room. As I banged on their door, my stomach muscles tensed and ached from the violent coughing and I doubled over against these tremors that shook my body. I just needed to be out of that room. I waited, trying to listen between my coughs, with my ear to the door to detect any movement inside. But when no one answered, I eventually gave up and walked away.

Back in my room, door still ajar, I collapsed onto my bed. The air had cleared a bit even in that short time and my coughing grew less frequent. I curled up, shielding myself. On the night-stand beside me, Lucian's flower, left entirely unscathed, seemed to have bloomed even more. Now it had opened up to the size of a grapefruit, splendid and glossy black. I could still smell its spicy flavor through the scent of smoke. It flooded over me, followed by a sudden wave of exhaustion. I could drift off to sleep now, in this dress, without even running through all the possibilities of how this might have happened in my innocent little room. I couldn't even begin to guess. Could the plant have done this on its own? What *was* that thing anyway? I rolled over and something jabbed into my rib. I pulled it out from under me: the book. I barely had the strength to open the cover, let alone do whatever it would inevitably tell me to do right now. But what choice did I have? Steeling myself, I paged through until I found the latest entry.

Your night is only just beginning, weary winged one. Proceed up the ladder. Yes, upward. Follow the corridor until you hear voices and walk toward them. Listen carefully. Pay attention.

Up. So now, just as I was beginning to learn how to navigate the plank-punctuated passageway down to the hotel's underground tunnels, I had to venture upward into this new unknown.

Well, I wouldn't be launching into this expedition in these clothes, that was for sure. I shed my heels and the dress in favor of my usual off-hours uniform of jeans and a thermal long-sleeve. Then I found the flashlight in the closet, pulled the string for the light and looked up, taking a deep breath—too deep. I coughed in the smoke-tinged air and steadied one hand on the ladder. Waiting would not make it any easier. I climbed rung by rung until I was near enough to the ceiling to slide that wooden panel away. I shined the flashlight up into this new expanse of murky darkness. Nothing but the beams holding up the walls and a wooden walkway. I felt around on all sides. It appeared just wide enough for me to fit if I crawled on hands and knees. I climbed up until I had been entirely swallowed into the stuffy tube-like passage.

Flashlight in one hand, I crept along, the wooden beams snagging at my shirt. I tried to ignore the cobwebs, the puffy bits of chewed-away insulation, and any reminder of wildlife that might be my companion. A musty scent hung in the claustrophobic passageway, but as I ventured deeper, I felt it dissipating. The four walls seemed to be expanding like blown glass in all directions. Slowly I pulled myself up, first hunching then finally upright, a relief for my aching knees and my hands. As I walked I could feel my path slanting upward, and new sounds filtered through, penetrating the otherwise eerie silence. Music with a familiar swing I recognized from the lobby, and voices I couldn't fully make out as I collectively took in the sense of activity and general hubbub.

Luckily, unlike the tunnels below, here there was still only one way to go, so I continued as the conversations faded back to silence and then eventually gave way to the murmur of more serene voices, ones not swept up by the excitement of the hotel. The path forked on my right side, and I spotted the faintest glimmer in the distance. A narrow beam of light pierced the suffocating darkness. I got closer and the light became two distinct pinpricks in the wall directly before me. As I continued on, the voices grew loud enough that I could almost make out the words: it was a man and a woman speaking. I could tell from the woman's low-pitched lilting tones that it was Aurelia.

A few more paces to the light, I found the wall straight ahead had been perforated with two peepholes. I squinted through and recoiled. The view, slightly muted and hazy, led right into Aurelia's office. She was seated on her love seat, the man's back to me, in one of the chairs. Her legs were crossed and she leaned back, her head propped up in her delicate ivory hand, dejected it seemed. He stood up and walked over to her, sat beside her, and took her chin in his hand as he looked in her eyes. It was that Prince, the man from the gala. "We're certain it is her," Aurelia said to him. "She has all the telltale markings, much as she works to hide them, but I assure you they're there. And we have our strategy in place. We will claim her before her full powers take hold."

"Well, we got to Lucian in time, and you too, now didn't we? So we have a fine track record."

"Indeed." Her smile was tainted by just a hint of melancholy.

"I don't think I need to remind you that your future depends upon your success in this matter," he said to her, firmly. "So you will succeed. It's that simple."

The peephole had to be on the wall with that flashing flat screen, but where? Could they make out my caramel eyes peeking in? The holes were fairly small, so hopefully not, but I'd have to study this tomorrow from the other side to gauge how visible I might be. For now, I simply listened.

"How is her suitor faring?" the Prince asked, in a voice that caressed the air.

"He is, perhaps, neither as powerful nor as ready as we hoped."

"Well, then he'll have to adapt quickly," he said in a sinister tone. "And the girl?"

"Infatuated, to be sure, but guarded. So unlike all the others. It's odd, I must say."

"We shouldn't really be so surprised, should we? After all, that's why we want her. But we mustn't underestimate her or the speed at which she will embrace her destiny," the man went on.

Aurelia wore an expression I'd never quite seen—deference, insecurity—in her knitted brows and downcast, lost gaze. "We cannot turn our backs but for a minute or we'll find ourselves suddenly powerless and bowing before *her*. Beware."

"I know this. I promise we're doing everything in our power here. This Haven is already more formidable than we anticipated."

For a moment, it all dulled—every sound, every word. I could only hear my heart beating faster and faster as my scars singed. How could they think this about *me*? What did they think I was going to do? What was this destiny business about? Could it be possible that I was strong enough to pose some sort of threat so impressive that they needed to stop me? Fear pumped through every vein. I wanted to run, away, out of this place, out of this hotel, anywhere, and never come back. But I knew that wasn't possible. I knew that all of this, whatever it was, would follow me. I willed myself back into the present. *Listen. You have to listen.*

"I won't tell you again how much hinges upon this. She *must* become one of us." His voice had changed now, full of dark corners and fire-and-ice edges.

"Of course, my liege."

"I trust you and your counterparts can resolve this on your own, in haste, and our recruitment efforts can be heartily increased."

"You have my word."

The lights blinked for a split second, a hiccup—I could've sworn I saw a flash of fiery light—and then it all went back on full force before anyone elsewhere in the hotel had a chance to notice. And he was gone. I didn't see or hear him go, I only knew that he had disappeared. Aurelia gathered herself, lifting a frail hand to her forehead as though she might be faint. I had never seen her look so concerned, so fragile. She rose from the couch and let herself out of the room, shutting off the lights and closing the door behind her.

I flipped the flashlight back on and walked as fast as I could, my pace evolving into a run, so brisk I worried I might go right through the wood panels beneath my feet, until my passageway became narrow and then I crawled on my beat-up, ravaged knees and scraped palms. Finally I spilled out onto that ladder and down to my bedroom closet rung by rung by rung, a descending xylophone, landing in a heap on the worn carpet. My entire body was covered in sweat, and yet I was shivering. *Wake up, Haven. Wake up*, I chided myself. *You've been letting yourself sleepwalk. You haven't wanted to see what's going on because you've wanted to believe that it could all be possible. But something is wrong here. That book of yours is right—danger is lurking here behind these beautiful faces and façades.* I felt my heart freeze over a bit, concrete poured over live earth.

But Aurelia and the Prince sounded afraid too . . . afraid of me. It didn't make any sense at all. I didn't know what they thought I was going to do, what kind of control I could possibly have over them or over this strange place. But it seemed that they had a strategy for dealing with me.

As my nervous pulse ticked up in terror, I felt the dread sink in the pit of my stomach. Lucian was part of this. He meant it when he said he wanted my soul. He had been instructed to seize this—me—whatever power I supposedly had. I had spent the entire evening with him and he had been putting on a show, and I fell for it so entirely, it made me boil now. I was such a fool. I scurried on wobbly legs to my bed, bone-tired but too terrified to sleep. Could I go next door at this hour—now well after three—and stay in Dante and Lance's room? How could I go on any longer not telling them about all of this? With furious fingers, I pawed through that offending book, looking for a new directive. But nothing had been added. I felt completely stripped of everything that could offer even the least bit of comfort to me. I was hanging off a ledge, nearly falling, and no one to catch me, no one to tell me I wouldn't hit the ground or that I'd survive at all.

I didn't fall asleep by choice, but finally my heavy lids lost their battle. When they did, I spun headlong into that hazy in-between. I couldn't be sure where my dream ended and bitter reality began. That familiar thump had sounded in the hallway, and in my dream, I had opened the door and this glowing apparition came toward me, dragging its lifeless limbs like unwieldy tree stumps. Its head was cast down but it was a woman, with long dark hair—when she looked up, her face, like the rest of her, was nearly all decayed, but also familiar. I had seen this woman before. This was the body from outside the hotel last night. But I knew with every bone in my body that she wasn't an actress or some prop, a mannequin or dummy. I didn't care what any of these people believed. It ate away at me, chilling me: that dead body had been real.

There was more though, now that I could study her with my fear momentarily suspended the way it can be only in dreams: this was also the same woman who had been attacked outside that drugstore. For some reason, in this dream I didn't slam the door shut. I watched long enough for the corpse's face to look up at me in all its ravaged glory. And when it did, for just an instant this whole figure was restored back to normal, to its human shape, and then I knew. It was Calliope.

My eyes flung open and my room was overtaken with a milky mist. I sat up in bed, trying to clear my vision, but instead the mist simply retreated, filtering out through the cracks around the door, leaving me alone, trying to regain control from the terror.

It's a strange thing to be so tired, with every bone in your body crying out for rest, and yet to be so incapable of achieving sleep. But there would be no muting those visions of my dream, because it wasn't just a dream. Something had happened to Calliope that no one wanted to talk about. I couldn't forget what I'd heard the Prince say to Aurelia. These dark characters whose mystery had crossed over into the realm of something more disturbing now seemed united against me. And then the fire in my room. I couldn't make sense of it; I only knew I was right to be afraid.

I showered, pulled on my uniform and heels, and grabbed the camera. I would throw myself into work. I had hundreds of photos to upload and I would print the best to show Aurelia. The thought of having to see her in our daily meeting, in that room I had spied on just a matter of hours ago, sent chills hitting each vertebra with icy precision.

The hotel slumbered as I emerged onto the lobby level. Light had only just begun to filter through the skylight and in through the revolving door. A relative quiet wrapped the whole place. Soft music piped in through the sound system, and a muffled clink chimed from the direction of Capone as tables were set with fresh silverware for the impending breakfast service. At the front desk, delicate fingertips clicked at a keyboard—a beautiful Outfit-caliber, uniformed redhead was on the early shift. I didn't recognize her and hadn't photographed her so I couldn't be sure if she was an official member.

I brushed through the velvet curtain outside the gallery and swiped my keycard. A red light flickered on, keeping me out. I sliced it through again, more slowly this time. The red light taunted me once more. I whipped it through another three times, getting more frustrated with each sharp swipe. I yanked on the knob, rattling the door and peered in. No one was in there. I was out of luck.

I marched past the redhead, straight to Aurelia's office, nerves fluttering the whole way. I knocked. No answer. I swore I could hear muted voices inside. I knocked once more. Nothing. The voices seemed to stop for just a second then they continued once more. I gave up, for now.

Inside the Parlor kitchen, a few members of the cooking staff, in their jackets and hats, silently cleaned and chopped vegetables, getting a jump on the day. We exchanged smiles before I assembled my usual cereal and milk and took a seat at the island. I wasn't hungry at all. Fatigue was starting to set in, and my lids began to fall.

Behind me, a pair of hands clamped down on my shoulders.

I jerked, screaming and jumping in my seat, and flung my head around.

"Sorry, geez," Dante said, patting me on the back.

"Morning," I gasped. I was certainly awake now. "Sorry, just had a rough night."

He swung onto the stool beside me, suited up in his chef gear, perky as always, the energy radiating out of him in waves. I hoped to catch some by osmosis. "A rough night? Does that mean your date went well or badly?"

"Funny."

"You looked superhot."

"Thanks."

"So." His brows fluttered searching for details.

"The date was fine. My night was . . . I don't know where to start." A sense of comfort blanketed me, relief at not being alone. Now everything could feel less upsetting and confusing. I could expel my fears into the air and he could catch them and defuse them.

"It was just fine?"

"Wait. Before I get to that, what's the story with that plant you gave me?"

"I know, gorgeous, right? Etan was like, 'These are so pretty, bring one to your friend.' And I was like, 'What a great idea!'" He was talking a mile a minute. I couldn't figure out a way to jump in. "Speaking of, I *have got* to tell you about my Valentine's Day! I'm soooo in love, Hav! I'm just like—"

Normally, I would've been all for girl talk, but I was too worn-out and confused. I just needed some answers first. "Dan, I totally want to hear all about it, but what was up with that plant?"

"Hmm? Keep up, honey, we're talking about love now. You look tired. I'm making you some coffee." He clapped his hands and rose from his seat, pouring the beans and firing up the machine. "I know you don't like coffee, but you'll thank me." The grinder buzzed and gnashed, but he spoke over it, pulling two mugs down from the cupboard. "Now let's talk Etan and, you too, let's talk Lucian! Can you bel—"

So, Etan told him to give it to me. "Dan! The plant somehow caught fire."

"Huh?" He looked at me with befuddlement, like the day during school spirit week when I showed up in pajamas only to find out it was actually hat day and pajama day was the next day. Like that.

"I think it, like, spontaneously combusted or something." I shook my head. "I know this sounds crazy, but last night it was on fire in my room. I mean, you didn't know it would do that, right?"

The grinding stopped and there was silence for a moment, then the coffee machine started to spit and percolate.

"Your room was on fire? Are you okay?"

"Yeah, yeah, I'm fine, it just freaked me out."

"I didn't hear a fire alarm."

"Yeah—" Now that I thought about it, shouldn't something have gone off with all that smoke? "It wasn't that bad. I took care of it. But you didn't—" I stopped midsentence; my mind had seized on something.

He went on, filling the void. "I promise, I didn't do anything. I still don't even know—"

"Etan." It just came out like a bullet, before I could soften it. I recalled the talk I had heard in Aurelia's office. I didn't think there would be any such thing as an accident here. "It had to be."

Dante shot me a look that sliced through my skin and my thoughts.

"What are you talking about? You think he *knew* that thing would set fire to your room? You're crazy. You probably put it right up against the radiator or something. You're always doing dumb stuff like that." He spat this out in a way that shook me up inside. We just didn't fight; we didn't talk to each other this way.

I tried to stay calm. "I'm just saying, it seems weird. There's a lot of stuff here that seems weird."

He looked enraged. "I'm not gonna have you talking shit about Etan!"

"Dan, I'm sorry, I didn't mean —"

"You don't get it. That guy, he's, like, the most amazing . . . He gets me. He knows that no one else gets me and he gets me."

"I get you," I said softly, hurt.

"You don't get how hard it is to be me."

"Dan, you know I'm always here for you."

"Are you?"

"Are you serious? Where's all this coming from? What's going on?"

"He knows what it's like to be me. I'm doing really well here and you just can't handle it."

"I promise you, that's not it at all." *I should tell him all the things I've been seeing here, I should tell him about that book,* I thought. But I was too thrown to even know how to respond. "I'm happy for you. You know that."

"He warned me about this," he said under his breath, shaking his head.

A light bulb went on. "I'm just, I'm getting kind of worried now. I feel like Etan's telling you these things that just aren't true. Talk to me. Can you trust him, Dan?"

"He said you'd say that. You're just jealous that I've been spending all my time with him. And that I'm in love."

This one, single point may have had a sliver of truth to it.

"Of course I miss you, but you know I'm happy for you."

"I don't know what happened to your room and I don't care. Don't go attacking my friends just because you don't have any yourself."

That stung. It felt like I'd been knifed in the heart. Nothing makes you feel more alone than when your best friend lashes out like that, turns his back and walks away without another word.

"Dan," I called after him, but my voice was too soft, buried under the weight of my despair. I ran out the door but was too late. He stalked off through the lobby, amid the guests who had begun filtering down from their posh rooms in search of breakfast and the excitement of a new day. The sun gleamed through the skylight. "Dan!" I called again. He didn't so much as look over his shoulder. Instead, he made the sharp turn down the corridor toward the kitchen entrance to Capone. I let him go. I had to, didn't I? I crept back to the Parlor kitchen, my heart bleeding out, deflating and leaving me weak and lost. Alone.

～ 19 ～

Please Give Me Your Soul

I tried Aurelia's office again. This time, she summoned me in on the first knock.

"Good morning, Aurelia," I said as I found my way to the chair that the Prince had sat in hours ago. I set the camera in my lap.

"Here's the list of gift recipients for today." She held out a piece of paper to me. Her hand trembled and her eyes left mine for a moment. Usually her gaze was that of a magnifying glass filtering the sun to fry an ant.

"Thank you." I took the list and noticed there were only a few names, nothing like the cavalcade of yesterday.

"You may order Lance to carry out this task if you wish."

"Thank you."

As she looked through the papers on her desk, my eyes searched the wall behind her desk. The flat screen was alive with the animated LH logo shimmering. Because of the height of the screen, I thought I might have been looking out from just above the center of it—there seemed to be a shadow there, a groove in the design of the panel surrounding the monitor. If that was the spot, the holes were small enough that I couldn't imagine anyone seeing a pair of eyes there. She didn't seem to find what she was looking for on her desk and stopped trying.

"I'll have more for you to do later. I need to locate some materials." Her voice had been drained of some of its life and power. She was jumpy in a way I'd never seen, a mood mutating out from that first crack in the veneer I'd viewed last night. "We have an outreach program you'll be working on. We're going to be hosting the proms for some area high schools. Including yours."

"Oh, wow." I said it with more shock than enthusiasm and wondered if she noticed. Part of the joy of this internship was that I thought I wouldn't have to worry about all of the hubbub of prom and the activities at the end of the year and wouldn't feel like a loser for missing them—or for not having much interest in going in the first place. But now, it would be coming to me. "I'll be, uh, looking forward to that."

"You don't need to look forward yet. It's in May. But I suppose you can wait and begin tackling that in the next day or so. I'll have that information for you shortly." She patted at her desk again and looked at me like it was time to leave. "Thank you."

I nodded and rose from my chair, remembering: "Oh, and, I, uh, think my keycard isn't working. I tried—"

"The gallery is closed today."

"Closed to the public?"

"Yes."

"But . . . closed to me too?"

"For now. Try back in an hour or so. We're doing some repairs and then you'll be free to return to your office, but the gallery itself will remain closed to the public indefinitely," she said with her usual glass-cutting sharp authority, giving the impression that I shouldn't bother with follow-up questions. But I couldn't help it. I allowed myself one. If last night's adventures had taught me anything, it was that I needed to start asking some questions around here.

"Is there any particular reason?"

She paused, looking at me like I was truly annoying her now. "Some of our photos have been . . . vandalized."

"Vandalized? But . . ."

"We're going to need to replace the photos of the Outfit."

"Oh, I can have the photo place print more, it's no—"

"Thank you. No." She snuffed it out so forcefully, I shuddered. "That won't be necessary. We'll be replacing them with something else entirely. Try back in an hour or so," she repeated. "In the meantime, if you need additional supplies for the deliveries, you'll find them in the closet in the gift shop. Thank you." She looked down at a paper on her desk. A sign, it seemed, that I should go. She was in such a hurry to get rid of me, but there was just one more thing.

"By the way." I fished into my pocket for the business card. "A gentleman stopped by there last night—you were gone from your office—and he was interested in buying the photo of you." I handed her the card. "I don't know if that one was damaged but—"

"No." She stared at the card, holding it so carefully as if it were made of crystal.

"Oh, good."

"No, I mean, no. It's not for sale. It was indeed compromised."

"Oh, well, if you wanted me to have another printed and framed, he seemed really interest—"

"No. Tell him those particular photos are not for sale. Give him a discount on anything else in the gallery."

"Sure. Did you happen to have the price list? I know you mentioned you would write one up so—"

"Just find out if he had seen anything else he liked, anything at all. I'll draw up the price list later." Her voice was clipped. She held the card out for me to take. "We're finished for now."

I nodded, leaving without another word, anxious to be out of that room.

I spotted Lance pacing around near the gallery entrance, arms folded across his vest-clad chest. He glanced at his watch now.

"I've gotta get a keycard for this place," he said to me when I was still several paces away.

"Doesn't matter, it wouldn't work—we're locked out for now. Something happened to the photos of the Outfit."

"Seriously? What's that about?"

"Got me. Aurelia called it 'vandalism.'"

"Weird. Did you hear we get to plan the friggin' prom?"

"I know." I felt better knowing that he was as thrilled as I was about this new assignment. "That'll be fun."

"Does that mean we have to go?"

"Probably. But technically, we're being paid to be there," I offered.

He pushed up his glasses. "I like your thinking."

"So, anyway, we have a few more of these deliveries to make. I guess we can do that now. Then I'll have some photos to put up on that screen, you know, at the front desk?"

"Sounds like a plan. Want me to grab the chocolates from Dante?"

"Yeah . . . thanks." I was relieved to not be the one to go. He and I probably needed some cooling-off time, even though it saddened me to think about our strange fight.

I collected what stationery and supplies we needed from the gift shop, passing by a few guests loading up on LH-logo-bearing souvenirs—and one of the Outfit, who was staffing the place. She stood behind the checkout counter, seemingly eight feet tall, swizzle-stick thin, with long blond waves cascading over her shoulders. She managed to look in my direction when I explained I was taking a few things from the closet on Aurelia's orders, but she gave me no sign of actual recognition. However, when the couple browsing the collection of tote bags finally checked out, their arms full of purchases, she smiled her most seductive smile. How nice for them.

I had made it only a few steps out of the shop, my arms full of supplies, when I heard my name in that sweet voice: "Haven . . ."

I stopped in my tracks, catching my breath and slowly pivoting to face him. He crept to me, slowly, cat-like, his eyes secured on mine.

"Lucian, hi, good morning," I said awkwardly. He kissed me on the cheek. My scars flared, and I paid attention to them this time.

"Where are we going with these?" He took one of the folded gift bags from my hands, opened it, and item by item, took everything else from my arms and placed it all inside.

"Wow, good idea. They didn't make you second in command around here for nothing." I wasn't prepared to process an encounter with him right now; I had too much to sort out. "Just going to the Parlor." I pointed, taking a few steps, and he began walking beside me. I kept my gaze fixed straight ahead.

"Busy day for you?"

"Just taking these to some writers and then we'll see. If you need anything then . . ."

"No, I wasn't testing to make sure you're earning your keep, I was just making conversation." He paused, then said, "Come 'ere." He gave the lightest tug, with his thumb and index finger, at the material at my waist and I followed him into that nook behind the Parlor kitchen.

"I had a nice time last night," he said in a way that any girl would find completely believable, but I had to wonder. I also had to go with it, for now.

"Me too."

He watched me, his eyes painting me, lingering. With a finger he traced the insignia on my sleeve, lightly going over the curves of the letters. Those three hatch marks hidden beneath my uniform sizzled like fresh wounds.

"That's funny," he said, a hint of dreaminess in his voice. "Ever notice how this could be our own personal logo? The L and the H."

"You're right, I hadn't thought of that." I was surprised I hadn't. It seemed the kind of thing I would have normally noticed and possibly, in my quieter moments, doodled in a notebook somewhere. But the cautious part of me knew that we were beyond that frivolity. *Remember what Aurelia and the Prince had said.* But I didn't want to believe them. I wanted to believe that Lucian really could like me, that this wasn't some strange game that I still didn't understand. He stopped tracing and his eyes fixed on mine again. When he stepped in closer to me, I could smell that cedar muskiness I'd grown so fond of. I looked away for a moment. He squared himself up, as though on the verge of imparting a vital bit of information.

"Now, did you give some thought to what we talked about last night?" he asked smoothly.

"I was mostly working—the photos, you know—and then I passed out, I was so tired."

"Think, Haven. There's so much you can do."

"I guess I'm not sure exactly what you want from me."

He leaned in and whispered in my ear, his hot breath sending chills sweeping across my skin, my scars alive and stinging. "Your soul," he said. "Please give me your soul."

He kissed me again, quick and soft, right there in that hallway. I was so stunned that I didn't kiss back. It sounded like something poets of another time might write to someone they loved. But then the romance lifted: there was another layer there, a hard-edged undertone to his voice, far different than last night. Or maybe it was me. Maybe I had changed a lot since then. I had to question everything now, even those things that only days earlier I would have given my life to hear coming from a mouth like his. He squeezed my hand.

"Tonight I want to see you." It was a command masquerading as sweet infatuation. Before I could say anything, he kissed my cheek once more, then placed the bag back in my hand, my fingers almost forgetting to grip. My mind raced. As he turned and walked away with his hands in his pockets, I let myself in through the back kitchen door and found Lance already seated at one of the tables, boxes of chocolates stacked up and a plate with two cupcakes.

"Waiting long? Sorry about that."

"No sweat," he said, slouched in his seat. I set down the bag with all the supplies and he began taking them out, organizing them into piles.

"What's this?" I pointed to the cupcakes, chocolate frosting with the logo in red script as a solid shiny slab of sugar.

"From Dante."

A peace offering? It gave me hope. "How'd he seem?"

"Not tired, that's for sure. I don't know how he does it—he hasn't been sleeping. He's running the kitchen over there, barking orders at people, no sign of Etan. I think there's a potential child labor law violation here."

"But he was . . . okay?"

He just nodded, looking confused by my questions, and I couldn't blame him. I let it go.

Lance and I made the deliveries together again even though there were only a handful this time. I liked the idea that as long as this business of being a messenger service continued, we would be guaranteed a field trip outside every day. For the first time in my life, I was beginning to understand what people meant when they said they needed to "clear their heads." It wasn't until I stepped outside the hotel that I felt every muscle de-tense. Once set free, my mind seized on entirely new concerns that had slipped through the cracks. It occurred to me I hadn't called Joan in ages. Though we had managed to e-mail a little bit, enough so she knew I was alive and well, I would have to phone her later.

We found our destinations more quickly than we had yesterday and with hardly any wrong turns. Progress. But we were mostly quiet in our travels today. Lance seemed perfectly himself, but I had too much fluttering around madly in my mind to be able to handle actual conversation. And in no time, we were back at the hotel, where it all faced me again.

Though a placard out front said the gallery was "Temporarily Closed," my keycard worked in the door now.

"I guess we're in," I said, opening up.

"What's this?" Lance crouched, grabbing a slip of hotel-logoed paper that had been slipped under the door. As I walked in, he followed me, reading aloud.

"'H & L: up for being guinea pigs? Shepherd's pie—with wild boar instead of lamb—for lunch, in the Parlor fridge. Bon appétit! Dante.' I'm starved, which must be the only reason that sounds remotely good."

We stopped walking.

"Whoa," I said, staring straight ahead at the wall that once displayed Outfit photos. It was entirely blank. Lance's eyes were still on the note.

"Wild boar could be gross, I guess," he said. "I don't know—" He looked up at last. "They don't mess around."

"It must've been pretty bad. I wonder what happened."

We stood there, staring at the empty expanse. I couldn't help but take it at least a little bit personally. I had been so proud of those pictures. And now . . . nothing. Why couldn't the vandals have gotten to something else? That was a pretty selfish thing to think, but still. Lance seemed to connect the dots leading to my silence.

"It's too bad. Maybe it just means they had really good taste in photography."

I laughed. "Thanks." Suddenly, I heard the tapping, soft and muted against the glass. I turned toward the door and saw that man Neil Marlinson standing there, peering in with his hands up for a clearer view. He waved and smiled at me. The show of familiarity didn't escape Lance's notice.

"Who's that? Your much-older secret boyfriend?"

"Yep, my sugar daddy. You know how it goes."

"I should've known. It's always the quiet ones."

"You would know."

"Funny. And true."

"No, he's just this guy who came by yesterday to buy the photo of Aurelia," I explained as we neared the door. "But I guess that's not gonna happen now."

"Shake him down, sell him something else."

"You sound like Aurelia."

"Really?" He looked impressed with himself.

"You're welcome."

Lance opened up the door and looked at the man, then walked past him and stood there, hovering for just a moment.

"Hi. Haven, right?"

"Hi, Mr. Marlinson." I looked over his shoulder to Lance. "I'll catch up with you, go on and get started without me." He gave a shy wave, walking toward the Parlor for lunch.

"Sorry to be pounding down the door," Neil said, polite and mannered, but real, not smooth the way so many of the people here could be.

"No, don't be silly," I said. "I had been meaning to check in with you, but it was sort of a strange morning." I gestured toward the CLOSED sign.

"I guess so, from what I've gathered."

"Yeah. And I'm afraid that photograph isn't for sale after all now, the one you wanted. I'm sorry."

"Oh." His voice fell and his eyes clouded over. "That's too bad."

"I'm really sorry." I paused. "It was somehow damaged or something so I'm afraid we're not selling it now. But was there anything else you'd seen and liked? The owner would love to give you an excellent deal on something else, anything else."

He was silent for what felt like a remarkably long time. Finally, he said, "No, no, that's all right. I really just wanted that one. It reminded me of someone . . ." He trailed off. "It looked just like her. Just, just like her. You know when you see something and it just sends the memories flooding back?" He said it like he was talking to himself, thinking aloud. I didn't say a word. Recovering, he shook his head and tried to smile. "I'm sorry, you must think I'm crazy. And old. And too nostalgic for my own good." He laughed to himself softly. "Thank you for trying."

"Sorry," I offered. I wished I could say something more comforting. "But if you change your mind, please come back."

"I will. Thank you." He walked away with his head hung low, brokenhearted, it seemed. I wasn't hungry so I returned to my little office and did a search for the clips talking up the hotel — the stories by the writers we'd just delivered gifts to, and got them set in case Aurelia wanted them flashing over the front desk today. Then I uploaded the pictures I'd taken at the Vault. There were even more than I imagined, and so many were good. All these beautiful people having the time of their lives. The ones from within the ring of fire were, of course, the best. That flame gave everyone a lovely pink glow, and through the natural selection at work within the club, they just ended up being the most perfect specimens.

I selected fifty shots and printed them and then I got to thinking: shouldn't I just print out a copy of that shot for Mr. Marlinson? It certainly wouldn't be such a giant, knock-you-out size like the other one or glossy or framed or any of that — but obviously it meant something to him, so maybe I could do that much. It would be a stand-in for the original, the way I had left the Art Institute with a postcard of *La Jeune Martyre*. Just as I pulled up that photo of Aurelia and hit Print, Lance shuffled back in, dragging his feet, and slunk down onto the chair in the corner.

"I don't feel good," he winced, clutching his stomach.

I turned around in my seat to face him.

"No offense, but you don't look so good. " His skin had taken on a sickly, sweaty sheen and he had gone ashen. He leaned his head against the wall and closed his eyes.

"I feel like I'm going to die."

"Was it the boar?"

"I don't know. Technically, food poisoning generally takes a bit longer to set in, so I'm not sure what's going on," he slurred, squirming in pain. "And it actually tasted really good." He paused. "I think I'm gonna puke."

With my foot, I pushed the small metal trash can over to him. "You should go lie down, I mean, if you can make it back to your room. Do you think you can? I can walk you down."

"No, I'll be fine." Slowly, he inched himself up. "But, are you sure? I know I have to do those photos and everything."

"Forget it, it's okay, really. Go. Please."

His eyes were barely open. They looked like mail slots in a front door.

"Thanks," he whispered and, hunched over, trudged out of the office. "First thing tomorrow, I'll do it, promise. If you want to leave it for me . . ." He kept talking even as he clomped away, his heavy footsteps getting fainter as he made it out the door. I kept watching in his direction even after he was long gone, wondering if I should've gone with him. It was probably how he'd felt that night when I went to the drugstore. I would be sure to check on him later.

Back in my office, I took my place at my desk and pulled out a blank sheet of printer paper—it was either this or Aurelia's stationery, which definitely didn't seem right. I began scribbling:

Dear Mr. Marlinson:
I know it's not quite the same, but I thought you might like this.
Yours,
Haven

I tucked the note and the printed photo into a manila envelope. I got his room number from the front desk and slid it under his door.

In search of comfort, I ducked into my room, plucked my cell phone from my bag, grabbed my coat and escaped outside, finding a spot along the cold brick of the side of the hotel. A hiding spot, a place to catch my breath even as the wind knocked it out of me.

Joan answered immediately, a torrent of excitement and gratitude at hearing my voice. It warmed me in the deep freeze and darkening sky of this late afternoon.

"Haven, honey! How are you? How was the big opening? I read all about it in the *Trib.* You're right in the thick of things there, aren't you? They covered it on the evening news too! The ladies at the hospital are so excited. So tell me, tell me, how was it?"

"Yeah, it was fine." I realized as soon as it came out that it wasn't nearly gushy enough for her. There was a pause; she was clearly waiting for more.

"Fine? That's all I get? C'mon, Hav, let me live vicariously, at least a little, for god's sake."

"No, yeah, I'm sorry. Of course, it was great. My mentor here gave me a pretty flapper dress to wear—"

"That Aurelia woman? I saw her on TV. She's gorgeous. These people are unreal, aren't they?"

"Yeah, a little bit."

"So she gave you a dress . . ." She dragged it out, waiting for me to expand.

"Yeah and she did my hair and makeup and all."

"Oh! I do hope you got pictures."

I thought about it and had to laugh: it hadn't even occurred to me to document that night for myself. "You know, I forgot actually. It was a busy night."

"Oh well, I'm sure there'll be other chances."

"Sure." Cars whizzed around the corner, careening past each other; one started honking, and then another answered with one long, loud relentless blare. A steady stream of cabs dropped off the afterwork cocktail crowd and early diners, and spirited away other guests waiting beneath the awning to take them to plays or concerts or elsewhere amid the city's bright lights. All so exciting. And then there was me—outside for the second time today and yet trapped by some unknown demons, by mysterious threats from a strange book, by the notion that I was some kind of odd entity that had to be controlled. Yet I couldn't quite permit myself to share any of this with one of the few people in the world who might be capable of making me feel better.

"Honey, you don't sound like you. Is everything okay? Is this because it was Valentine's Day? It's okay, you'll have so many years ahead of you filled with incredible Valentine's Days."

"No, that's not, I mean, I sort of . . ." It was impossible to reduce this to a digestible sound bite, it was all just too complicated. "Never mind."

"It's hard to never mind *now*."

"Try to never mind?" I pleaded.

"All right, I can tell you don't want to talk."

"Thanks."

"Say, do you think you might have time for a lunch one of these days? I could come down, take you out to Water Tower Place or the Cheesecake Factory or something? I miss you, honey."

"I know, me too. Maybe soon, okay? It's just been . . . busy." I knew if I saw her I would crumble.

"Okay then, I'll let it go this time, but I'm going to try again in another couple weeks and I'm not going to take no for an answer then."

"Fair enough." I laughed.

"I just worry. You sound awfully tired and overworked."

"I'm fine, promise. Love you, Joan."

"Love you too, dear."

On the way back to my room, I stopped into the Parlor kitchen. It was peak time there, cocktail hour. I offered a shy smile to the chefs chopping and sizzling and plating up their precious bits of classy bar food. What I would've given to reach over and steal a cone of those logo-shaped crispy french fries, or, rather, *frites,* as they called them here. But instead, I peeked into the fridge for a quick glimpse of the shepherd's pie I'd skipped out on earlier. I'd never had shepherd's pie before but it sure was a funny-looking thing: a layer of saucy meatiness topped with a cloud of mashed potato. Hmmm. Maybe not. I grabbed an apple and bottle of water and pulled down the half-full box of Lucky Charms, then slipped out the back door as quickly and quietly as I'd slipped in.

I went to Lance's door and knocked softly. A muffled voice came from within.

"Huh?"

"Hey, it's Haven," I called. "You okay?"

The door opened, but his eyes didn't. He looked like he was still asleep. No glasses, mussed hair sticking up in every direction—messy in a way I didn't think short hair was capable of being messy. "I'm okay, really, just really knocked out now, but feeling better. Thanks."

"Good. Sorry to, uh, wake you. I'll let you get back to sleep."

He gave a groggy wave and stumbled back into the dark. I heard the springs of the bed as he hit it.

When I got the door of my room open, I was just relieved to see nothing on fire. It took so little to make me happy these days.

20

Charm Her, for God's Sake

I changed out of my uniform and into my sweats, prepared to begin my drills downstairs earlier than usual. After devouring my apple and cereal (straight from the box, like some kind of caged beast), I gave a quick glance through the book, *that* book, just in case there was some new terrifying bit of knowledge it had to impart to me, but I found no new scribblings inside those pages.

And so down I crept, plank by plank. I could feel my limbs getting stronger, the wooden slats becoming more familiar. I knew where the grooves were, where my fingers could nestle in, and my feet knew how to land as I swooped down or flew up. When I hit bottom, I set my watch and took off at my fastest sprint. My body seemed to be learning the path, committing its curved corners and straightaways to memory. Soon I hoped I would be able to do it without a flashlight if I needed to.

I came to that bend where it opened out into that dilapidated old room and I stopped short, nearly stumbling onto the ground.

Sitting there, propped up on the exposed wall beams beside

that mysterious locked door, was the most effective stop sign I'd ever seen: the photos. I knew it was them without even being able to actually see them, the whole exhibit shrouded beneath a velvet covering. The silhouettes of those twenty-some rectangles, big and small, bulged beneath the swath. One of the framed corners peeked out, teasing and tempting me. I looked over my shoulder—a reflex, as though I expected someone to be there telling me to mind my own business—and I inched toward it. I grabbed hold of the covering and pulled it back in one sharp flourish, unveiling all of them at once.

And as soon as I did, I jumped back, reeling, and gasped.

My eyes skimmed across the surface of these things staring back at me, taking them all in as one cohesive horror show. I wanted to scream but the shock silenced the sound. I had to shake my head and close my eyes to clear my vision. But the sight had been branded into my brain. They had mutated into something terrifying: unraveling, decaying flesh. Photos, it seemed, of a circus freak show, not of the most beautiful people I'd ever met.

I summoned my strength and crept forward, reaching out to paw through them, hoping that some were unharmed. But, no, every one of the pictures of the Outfit had transformed into something grotesque. This was more than vandalism. These looked like portraits taken of monsters. My hands shook; everything trembled. The horror of it all infected every inch of me. These pictures now showed once-perfect people riddled with festering sores, eyes melting down their faces, bloodied and missing features, amputated and jagged limbs that appeared gnawed off by wild dogs. Some looked as if they'd been run through a meat grinder. Their hair was thin and scraggly or entirely gone and replaced with lesions and bulbous purple and green growths.

Their clothing was tattered, and in some cases their entire bodies were ripped open, spilling their internal organs. Lucian's innards were being feasted upon by a rabid vulture.

I had combed through the whole mess, each worse than the one before it, before I found Lance's and Dante's pictures tucked in back. Lance's looked just as I'd last seen it: with that scar beneath his eye, but otherwise just fine. In fact, if anything, it seemed overall more ethereal and powerful than it had the night of the gala. His eyes sparkled, deep and peaceful, sure and firm, holding their ground. His stance, the way he held his arms, the set of his shoulders, all appeared stronger. Dante's photo, on the other hand, seemed just the slightest bit . . . off. His bright smile had faded in wattage. I didn't think I was imagining this, or that I was too influenced by our tiff earlier today. His image was dulled. I studied it for a moment and then I set the other photos back in front of it, looking at each one again—much as it made me cringe to do it. But no, I hadn't missed a thing: mine was not here, and Aurelia's wasn't either. Where were they? Had they been spared? Were they not as warped as the others? Or was it possible they were worse? With fast, jittery fingers, I put the covering over the top of all them again and backed up, scrambling and stumbling, watching the mass of velvet there as though it might come after me.

I turned and sprinted straight back to my ladder, up to civilization. I couldn't be down there with those disfigured images anymore. Up and up I climbed, clawing at the planks with mad, raw hands, until I made it back to my room. I flung the closet door closed and blocked it off, again with that desk chair, then curled up in my bed, hugging my knees to my chest. I closed my eyes, focusing my beating heart, trying to slow it down to a pace that wouldn't give me a heart attack. When I finally succeeded, I reached over, pulling that dreaded book from its home in my night table.

Today's date had been written in on a fresh page with these words:

We mustn't let fear keep us from seeking answers. Go searching. You know where to go. Trust what you see and hear. When something doesn't add up to a sensible answer, it simply means you're missing some key pieces. Be careful, be smart, but be daring.

I shut the book and shoved it back in its place. I could take this riddle to mean only one thing: I had to go looking for those two missing photos and I had to go now. I had to go to the place where my gut told me it didn't want me to be: back up into that passageway that led to Aurelia's office.

With only a bit of a struggle—the crawling made my sore muscles ache and my knees burn until the passage opened enough for me to stand upright—I found my way back to that little peephole. By now it was after eight in the evening, and the room was deserted and dark, save for the dim, buttery glow of the art deco lamp on her desk. It was always locked when she wasn't in there. But I needed to get in, it was just that simple.

I flipped my flashlight back on and shone it all around me, illuminating this musty secret corner of mine. My other hand felt the walls around me, patting at the jagged wooden beams on my sides and the strange rough stones in front. And then I hit an edge with my fingertips—an odd horizontal slice knifed straight through those stones and level with my chin. I had seen something like this before, in my closet, so I looped the flashlight around my wrist and pushed with both hands and all my force. Sure enough, it started to give. I threw my whole body into it, planting my legs firmly on the ground, and pushed harder. It popped, the sound of something springing loose after years of being closed up. Bits of mortar and dust rained onto my fingers in a soft, crumbly spray, and this telephone-book-thick rectangular cutout creaked open. I pushed easily now, and it opened outward, a narrow door hinged on the left side. I craned my neck out as best I could: I was directly above her desk, the flat screen on the back of this doorway. After several failed attempts to pull myself over the ledge into the room, I took a running start.

Clomping against the flimsy floor beneath me, I launched myself at the wall, my foot catching on top of one of the stones, and I pushed off, my hands grabbing at the ledge. Over I went, landing on the carpet of Aurelia's office and thumping my head against the wall. I imagined I had the makings of at least a date-size lump on the back of my head. But I was in.

Now I could get to work. I stood on the desk chair and unhooked my flashlight from where I had stashed it, then scanned the room for plausible hiding spots for a photo the size of Aurelia's. I tried the usual suspects first: inside the coat closet in the corner near the door (nothing, not even a sign of passageways like in my closet); behind the painting over the couch. I examined the floor and the walls themselves for any seams that indicated doorways or secret compartments. I walked around the entire perimeter of the room, running my fingers along the wood paneling, searching for something that didn't quite fit.

I found myself standing before that wall of built-in bookcases. I had read in one of those history books that all manner of sins had been hidden in hollowed-out books or behind façades of book spines during Prohibition. It made perfect sense that this hotel, full of nooks and niches and tunnels, would have something lurking behind a display like this. I started tapping and pushing at some of the books, shaking the shelves to see if anything might open up. It always worked in old movies but it seemed ridiculous and haphazard now. I stepped back and shone my flashlight all around, and then I spotted it: a round quarter-size disk embedded in the wooden border along the far end of the bookcases. When I got closer, I saw the pentagram design, same as I'd seen on that mysterious door downstairs. There could be no clearer sign than the repetition of this symbol that there was evil at work here.

I rummaged through Aurelia's desk and found that key ring buried beneath some papers: a trio of pentagram-shaped cylinders, all different sizes, hanging from it. I tried the medium-size one first—it was the length of a white piano key—pushing it slowly into the disk on the wall and, sure enough, a click sounded, and a pop. Two shelves in the middle of the wall of books opened, jutting out like a loose tooth waiting to be pulled. I tugged on this section expecting the whole column to come open, but this waist-high window was it. I leaned in, shining my flashlight, and found a small room with two velvet-shrouded pictures propped against the wooden beams of a wall.

I slithered over like I was climbing a fence. Once inside, the space enveloped me. It was eerily quiet, like a tomb, and pitch-black except for my flashlight. The darkness was alive and hungry and it magnified the silence, filling the area so completely that you almost believed you could scream and it would be instantly stifled. It was a cell, an isolation chamber. I wanted out as soon as I was finished.

Wasting no time, I threw off the covering and the two photos stared back at me, side by side. My knees weakened the second I caught sight of the horrid changes to Aurelia's photo. The blemishes I'd noticed days ago were nothing—they had bloomed into a whole new breed of all-encompassing, gag-inducing revulsion. Now the woman's luscious long limbs melted like shiny plastic in the sun and seeped onto the ground in the picture. Her bony, yellow-nailed finger chased after an eye that had popped out of its socket on a bungee cord of a vein. Her bird-like neck had been slit and the festering gash oozed shades of red, yellow, and green, which matched the sores and wounds all over her body. Aurelia looked just a few steps removed from Calliope, the once-beautiful girl, who showed up a charred and decaying monster at the gala and in my dreams. I had to look away.

So my eyes fell on my own elusive photo. Why had she pulled mine out from the pack? Why sequester it here with hers?

With the exception of my scars, I had been spared the kind of grisly disfiguration Aurelia's photo had suffered—and since the scars were all mine, they were the ugly truth, so I couldn't be too upset about those. No, something entirely different had happened to my picture. My entire pose had changed; now it looked like I was lying down on my back and there was a smudge of light above my head. I leaned in, training my flashlight upon it and reaching out to touch it. If I wasn't mistaken, it looked like a halo had formed over my head. Could that be right? That didn't make the least bit of sense at all. How had this happened? I was so lost in thought that I must have tuned out the rattling at first. But then my ears seized on it and my whole body froze.

The door. The door to the office shook against its frame, and the soft flutter of voices wafted in. I bolted up.

Of course, of course, of course: the light had been left on, the keys were left out. Aurelia never would have done that if she wasn't planning on returning soon. Something took control of my body and instead of thinking, I took flight. I didn't even cover the photos back up. I just leapt out of that opening, flashlight in hand, waving its light beam around, as I slammed those two bookshelves back into place. I sprinted to the desk so fast I covered the length of the office in only three long galloping strides, threw the keys onto her desk, hopped up onto her chair, flung the flashlight in the opening, and then, springing up on legs I didn't know could jump so high, I hoisted myself through the opening with arms that suddenly felt capable of lifting boulders. I landed with a thump inside, smacking against the hard ground. But the adrenaline coursing through me kept me from feeling the least bit of pain. Instead, it bounced me back up to my feet and infused me with enough force to yank that panel back into place just as the office door burst open.

Aurelia walked in with Lucian trailing her; he swung the door shut behind them. She was talking to him in a harsh tone, one she usually used on me. My sweat-coated head in my hands, I leaned against one of the wall beams, shaking. I closed my eyes, trying to calm myself. *You have to focus, you must listen.* I watched out of that peephole.

"I'm not myself today," Aurelia was saying, as she took her place behind her desk, dangerously close to me. "This . . . *situation* . . . with the gallery and so forth. Oh, here they are." She interrupted herself, waving the key chain in the air. "Beckett will need this later." She held it out with her fingertips for Lucian to take, then she sat in her chair. I hoped I hadn't left a footprint on it. Lucian sat on the couch, looking bored, adjusting the cuffs poking out from his suit jacket sleeves, touching the cuff links to be sure they were secure. "But at any rate, I'm a bit taken aback because I just thought we would have more time to work with. I don't understand how she's gotten so powerful so fast."

"Well, I think early on — " He still wasn't bothering to look at her, as if he just didn't want to give her the satisfaction since she looked to be on the verge of her boiling point. "There are fits and starts with it from what I understand — these jarring shifts and this frightening progress and then nothing for a little while. I suppose that's how it was with us, before, you know . . ." He trailed off.

"Please," she barked, then softened in volume. "I'm not listening to this. If you were doing your job with any competence, we wouldn't have this problem. She would be taken care of. I'm growing tired of this *Haven* and I blame your ineptitude for her having gotten so far."

My heart dropped through the floor, taking my throat, my lungs, my stomach, everything with it.

"Obviously you have some issues you want to address with me, so out with it already," Lucian said in a flat tone, lengthening his leg to look at his shoe now. He couldn't appear less concerned by her mood.

"I see. Aren't you so strong now against me? But I've already spoken of this to the Prince. Just wait until he arrives and you're on your knees begging to be given another chance."

"I don't beg."

"You will. Have you forgotten how this works? I can have you banished any moment I wish. Are you really ready to go back down there? Your role in the recruitment and the revolution can be dramatically downsized to the point of nonexistence."

"I'm starting to understand," he said, perfectly calm and

charming, looking at her now. "This isn't so much about my performance as it is about your jealousy."

She tensed at that, the muscles in her neck straining against the accusation.

How was this possible? Aurelia, jealous of me? Even he started laughing. "That is adorable."

Aurelia seemed to be ignoring him. She rose from her seat and took a spot leaning in front of her desk. She pointed her index finger at the floor, concentrating, and then a small flame sparked up out of nowhere and began to flicker and burn right there in that spot. I felt the shock of that flame burning through me, alighting a new level of fear; the scars on my chest felt it too, tingling and sizzling. I patted at them and then grabbed the pendant of my necklace, nervous, and turned it over and over again in my hand, fidgeting. With her finger still poised, Aurelia drew an imaginary circle and then the flame followed the path until the circle burned low and crackling right on the floor. Finished, she focused on Lucian, glaring. She wound up her arm as though about to throw a pitch and let go, shooting a blazing bolt of fire the size of a baseball at him. He barely flinched and only scooted an inch or two to the side to avoid being hit. He seemed to have witnessed this behavior before. The flame sparked near his feet and he stomped it out.

"Usually you're cute when you're angry," he said coolly. "But this is so unbecoming."

"I won't be spoken to in this manner, certainly not by you. I find this all rather insulting, but I'm only entertaining it because I trust that you'll be put in your place soon."

With that, the flame roared and the Prince materialized out of the darkness, within that fiery circle.

"Did I interrupt something?" he asked, looking from Aurelia to Lucian and back again, his voice calm and honey-like as can be. The flames died down once more and, as soon as he stepped out of the circle, they burned out altogether, leaving not a trace of damage on the floor. He took the seat behind Aurelia's desk, leaving her to sit beside Lucian. She perched herself on the arm of the couch, as far from him as possible, and folded her arms across her chest.

"Lucian was just about to enlighten us as to why he has thus far failed to seize the girl's soul," she said to the Prince. She reached over to the candelabra perched on the credenza behind them, held her finger out, and lit the wicks.

"Oh, good," the man answered, settling back in his chair. He shifted his piercing gaze to Lucian. "Kindly go on, then."

Lucian's entire being changed. He sat up in his seat now, his face set firm. A subtle power shift swept the room. Aurelia stood, arms folded. The Prince rose from his seat and began wandering the room, scanning the book titles and then watching the flat screen. I wondered if he could see me, back behind this wall. Could he know I was here? I had studied this spot from his side and I was undetectable since the peephole peeked out behind the dark frame of the screen. But these people weren't really even people at all, were they? Who knew what they could do, what they could see?

"Yes, I've been making progress—"

"This Haven person, from what I see and hear, has taken to you." The Prince turned around to face him. Lucian sat perfectly upright, stiff, unsure. "And it certainly doesn't seem an unpleasant assignment, yours."

"No, sir. Not at all. She is . . . lovely," he said finally. And at that, even though intellectually I knew that this was someone to fear, not love, I could not help it: my heart purred involuntarily, for the briefest of moments, before sense set in. *Haven, guard your heart. He doesn't really care about you.*

"Indeed, lovely, I'm sure," the Prince said, in an understanding tone. "But there is work to be done, and, as I'm sure you're aware, time is of the essence."

"Yes, I know," he said, defeat edging his voice.

"I trust you've seen the photos?"

"Yes, I have." He hung his head, ashamed.

"Her soul-illuminating powers are more advanced than I expected for this stage." The Prince was pacing now. What did that even mean? "I'm growing . . . concerned . . . with how quickly she's progressing. I know this is never a steady climb and I do expect her to slow down, but this is troubling nonetheless."

I had to keep reminding myself that this character they were speaking of was actually me. It was all coming out too fast for me to even begin to process it. So they thought I had somehow changed these photos? Some power of mine had done this, had illuminated all of the souls of my photography subjects? Is that what they were saying, was I hearing this right? My mind flashed back to the hospital, the photo collage, Jenny, my favorite patient, who used to tell me she only liked the pictures I took of her. Maybe there was something to that after all. But how was it possible they could know all of this about me that I didn't know?

"Yes, troubling," Lucian repeated, with a nervous nod. I had never seen him behave this way, so unsure of himself. I should have been angry, but I felt sorry for him.

Aurelia, in the corner with her arms still folded, seethed quietly until she couldn't help herself. "Charm her, for god's sake!"

she blurted out. Lucian snapped his head toward her. The Prince smiled, the cunning grin of an owner who enjoys watching his pets spar. "What's so difficult?" she snarled at Lucian. "She stares at you with those absurd saucer eyes." Aurelia batted her lashes at him for effect and then rolled her eyes in disgust. Lucian's expression hardened, like his face had been put in a kiln overnight.

"It's not so easy." His voice came out as a stifled roar. He looked down at his hands, opening and closing his fists, trying to cool himself. "She resists me."

"Or maybe you're resisting your assignment," she shot back.

"It's not like it has been with the others."

"Of course not," the Prince said easily, tossing himself in that desk chair again. "There's obviously an extra strength to her, this latent power beginning to engage, that's the *point*. That's why we want her with us and not against us. She would be dangerous against us, a menace." He said it with enough flip confidence that he didn't seem concerned. I turned this over in my mind: me, a menace. It sounded ridiculous.

"I'm not sure it will be possible, she—"

"Enough with your excuses! Just get it done!" Aurelia sniped. She looked away from him, trying to calm down.

"Aurelia!" the Prince censured her.

"I'm sorry, my liege. But," she whispered, "you saw that picture. We are running out of time."

"Lucian." The Prince turned to him. "I'm afraid what Aurelia says is true. If we don't get her soon, then this will end neither well nor cleanly."

"Yes, I know. But I must warn you. This may be . . . unrealistic. She seems to have some sort of . . . will. She's not as prone to being swept up as the others have been."

"I don't understand. You've been feeding her," Aurelia said.

"She's immune to the toxins already. But I'm certainly doing everything in my power. That's all, I'm just trying to . . . manage expectations."

"This is not my problem, yet." The Prince spoke very slowly, to be sure each of his words was heard clearly. "It behooves you to find a solution before it becomes my problem."

"Yes, sir," Lucian whispered, his head bowed.

"Maybe," the Prince addressed Aurelia now, "we should adopt some of the innovations being put to work within the New Orleans outpost."

"You know that's not my style." Aurelia sounded defensive, her posture firmed up. "I find it risky and foolhardy what they do there."

"I think your *style* should be whatever brings results," the Prince chided. He shifted gears: "Where are we with her counterparts?"

"Lance isn't entirely immune yet," Lucian explained with a pained look, like he wanted to be done with this meeting, this business. His heart wasn't in it. "He took ill today, but it's not fully working on him. The toxins just aren't having the effect they should."

I thought of Lance, sick and in bed. So they had been trying to poison us, control us through what we ate and drank here. This was what they did to people. Why hadn't we succumbed to it? At least that would explain my wooziness last night and even, I supposed, my very first night here.

"When we get the girl, we get her associates," Aurelia said. My associates? This was certainly all making me sound much more important than I ever felt, that was for sure. "The kitchen boy is a cakewalk. Etan is working his magic brilliantly on this Dante person. Apparently the toxins have been working, and Etan has already succeeded in coding him—so as soon as the boy is sufficiently wooed and delivers Etan's code back to him, his soul will be ripe for the taking."

"Do we know what the code is?" the Prince asked. "It's such an entertaining parlor game here."

"Allegedly, the boy needs to shave his head, and that will be the sign. Etan thought it would be amusing to make the boy in his own image. He's so playful." She turned to Lucian, a slight smile on her lips. "He's enjoying this process while still getting the job done. You could learn something." Lucian didn't even look at her.

"Excellent," said the Prince. "But the other one?"

"He will be easy enough when we have Haven. In the meantime, Raphaella has been giving him some attention." She stopped for a moment. I could see her thinking, deciding whether she wanted to go on. And she did, tentatively. "He doesn't appear so interested but, again, he will follow when we have Haven. He will do whatever she tells him, I can tell by his eyes."

The Prince nodded at this report. "Keep me abreast of this. Before long we may have to take drastic measures, but for now, please get her of her own volition." Lucian, somber, just bowed his head. The Prince stood, rebuttoned his suit jacket, signaling, it appeared, that he was about to leave. "So, who do we think is expiring tonight?" Now his tone was perfectly light, excited. "I'll be looking forward to having someone returned to me. That is, of course, supposing we don't have another *situation*."

"What happened with Calliope was an anomaly," Aurelia said, in a soft, defensive tone. "It certainly will not happen again, of this I can assure you."

"You can and you will and you must." It was a warning.

With that, he stepped back where the fiery circle had burned and from nowhere the flames flew up once more, the circle re-igniting. Just as fast, he was gone and the embers burned out. My own scars tingled at this. My body felt relieved to have him gone.

Lucian and Aurelia sat in silence, frozen, for several long minutes until finally Aurelia rose from the sofa and reclaimed her seat behind the desk. Glaring at Lucian, she said, "I will see you at half past three. I trust the Vault will be prepared. We have quite a large class to induct, as you know."

"Of course," he said. He got up and walked to the front of the desk, then leaned forward, both hands on the desk, staring her square in the eye. She tried to look away but he grabbed her chin tightly in his hand. "Jealousy doesn't become you."

"And sentimentality doesn't become you," she cooed.

With a little shove, he released her chin and stormed out the door. Aurelia didn't watch him go; instead she focused on some paperwork in front of her, looking like she didn't care. But as soon as the door slammed, she stared off into space, one hand touching her chin. I waited a few minutes but I saw no point in staying forever. I had only a few hours until I would need to make my way down to the Vault for whatever event had been scheduled.

As I tiptoed away from that peephole my body had never felt so weak. I longed to be in my bed—not my bed here, but the one at home, in my room next to Joan's room. I wanted to be nestled in under those covers, free of any worries more grave than tests in school and navigating through that sea of people who were indif-ferent to me. Here, for the first time, I felt the opposite of that. Not only was I not ignored, but I was being watched and monitored; I was important to these people. Important for the wrong reasons, important because they wanted something from me and would harm me to get it if necessary. The weight of responsibility tugged on my shoulders. I wasn't going to be allowed to be left on the sidelines.

～ 21 ～

The Induction

Two-thirty rolled around so much sooner than I had expected. I had tried to nap for a few hours, but never quite achieved sleep—to be honest, I was just too terrified for that—but lying down helped me replenish my waning strength. In my rest, my brain had remained active, searching through the very few possibilities for viewing whatever was to go down in the Vault tonight and deciding on the only viable option: descending to that dark passageway that led behind the cascading wall of fire. I would, hopefully, be able to watch there without being detected.

So, I climbed down, bracing myself at each bend to possibly run into one of the Outfit or worse, Aurelia, Lucian, or the Prince. The Prince made the other two seem almost harmless. Almost. I took soft, slow steps down that pitch-black hallway that led to the Vault, and had to stop myself for a moment. It didn't feel right. What was different this time? And then I realized: the silence. That terrible, deafening silence had inflated to fill this whole space, making even my hushed footsteps echo. I could make out a couple of voices I didn't recognize mumbling to each other, but that was it. The club closed at two o'clock in the morning, so the music had stopped and the people had spilled out. Without the veil of pulsing music, it felt even more like I was just dangling out in the open, begging to be caught. But what could I do?

I tried to creep by as quietly as possible, not daring to turn on my flashlight, instead holding my hand against the rocky, bumpy wall beside me to lead me in until I neared the warm coral glow of the flaming cascade. The voices grew closer, louder too—but perfectly flat and lifeless. I could almost make out the words—it sounded like they were setting something up. "To your right," one would say. Then the other would respond: "It must be perfect." And then the first one: "It will be; there is no other option."

I too would soon be running out of options. That fire wall was now close enough that I could see the figures—two of the bulky, beefed-up Outfit men—arranging some sort of pedestal onto the center of the ring of fire. It was the circumference of the wheel of a tractor and rose up about three or four feet up. One of the men stood on it, testing it out. The other nodded with his arms folded. My steps had slowed—how much farther could I go before I would be visible here in the shadows?

My hand grazed something colder, smoother, raised up from the surface of the wall. I stopped and felt it with both hands now: it was a horizontal metal bar, long and the width of the handle-bars of a bike. I patted at the wall above and found another, and then another below. They were rungs bolted into the wall making a ladder. There wasn't enough light for me to see where this led to. I could either take a chance and go up and risk finding something or someone unsettling waiting for me there or stay where I was and risk being discovered if anyone else decided to use this hallway. Up into the unknown I went.

I climbed slowly, reaching blindly to locate each bar. It helped to not be able to see anything when I looked down, just that dark abyss rather than a cold, hard floor. Even so, my palms began to sweat. Finally, my hands hit a brick ledge and the light from the fire wall lit up what was in the distance: a narrow walkway, the width of a diving board, with a waist-high wall overlooking the entire club. It was a metal catwalk, jutting out from one point of the ledge, and from it hung the colored lights that illuminated this side of the club. I pulled myself up onto the walkway and ducked down on my knees to keep hidden behind the half-wall. I was over the top of that flickering flame now and had a clear sightline.

Down below, Outfit members milled around, gracefully weaving themselves into a circle around the ring of fire, giving the impression that each person had a specific mark. It seemed just dim enough that if I continued to kneel, peeking over this ledge, then I could watch without being spotted. I settled in and prepared for what could be a long night.

At exactly half past three, the lights dimmed to that familiar red glow of a typical Vault club night. The Outfit members stood in their circle all wearing their uniforms—they had been firmly and quietly in place for nearly half an hour, not speaking a word. Soft footsteps shuffled just below me. It was a herd of strangers wearing black dresses and suits and somber expressions. Even from this height far above them, I could tell I didn't know them. An even number of men and women, all slender and stunning. A rough count showed there were twenty in total.

They formed a ring inside the circle made by the Outfit members, filing into place and all staring inward toward the ring of fire. Like me, they all watched motionlessly, waiting for something important to happen. Finally, a spotlight shone on the mouth of the graffiti-emblazoned walkway at the front of the club and Lucian marched in, with Etan right behind him. All bodies pivoted in one motion to watch them cut a path to the ring of fire. Up the spiral staircase they went, taking a place beside the newly installed pedestal, hands clasped behind their backs. They had their backs to me. I wondered what they were looking at. Then the spotlight went out in a flash and lit back up in another instant, illuminating the pedestal. Aside from the cascade of fire, it was the only light. Even the ring of fire itself wasn't burning.

Slowly, the surface of the pedestal opened in two, like a jaw, and that familiar, perfect visage appeared, then her whole body, sheathed in a floor-length gown with a plunging neckline. Aurelia glowed, seizing every scrap of spotlight and reflecting it off her alabaster skin and cornsilk hair. Her rasp amplified through the speakers: "Welcome, my lambs."

A hushed "Hello" murmured back at her from the collective.

"It gives me great pleasure to welcome you tonight as you cross together into the realm of the Metamorfosi. As you know, this is a rare privilege bestowed upon only the most deserving. Congratulations to you for being selected into this esteemed, elite caste. Just as your responsibilities will grow clearer in the days ahead, so too will your rewards. Each of you will have a grand wish granted in exchange for your servitude. Your most lofty desire will be yours for the taking. Prepare for greatness, my pets."

She bowed to them, then rose up again, holding out her hand. A spark ignited along the ring of fire. Hand still outstretched, she slowly pivoted as the flame lit, following the path of her fingers until the ring was fully ablaze. I felt a chill run through me and realized I had broken out into a cold sweat. With slow steps,

Aurelia descended from the pedestal and strolled the perimeter of the ring, her subjects all gazing up at her. The snapping of the flame was the only sound.

Then she continued: "What exactly is the Metamorfosi, you may ask? I tell every new class the same thing: it is where power is born. This is a layer of existence that few get to experience. You may have an idea of inferno—hell, the devil's playground as we like to call it—and then the limbo of purgatorio, where many do their time before advancing to hell or the other way—" She flitted her hand, waving it off. "And then there's dull paradiso—few would aspire to it if they knew how boring it was there." A wave of knowing chuckles swept the Outfit. "Yes, these are well-covered territories. But Metamorfosi is something far greater, a spiritual bridge between reality and the afterlife. This is a realm that has remained secret for ages. This is where the lucky few are granted entrée into a great and powerful army and enlisted to carry out a mission sent to us by our leader, the Prince of Darkness, Satan himself. We are now amassing the best and brightest in an ambitious project, a *revolution,* if you will—" She drew out those words, giving them extra heft. "That will see our numbers grow greatly in coming months. It may take time to come to fruition, but in the end we will be all-powerful, you'll see."

She walked along the ring, looking out at the wide, vacant eyes of her followers. Lucian, meanwhile, stepped back to take a seat on one of the banquettes that ran along the circle. He appeared to be flanked by a handful of velvet-covered cigar boxes and a neat stack of what looked, from here, to be index cards.

"But we're getting ahead of ourselves, aren't we?" She smiled lightly. "Tonight we are here to induct our newest class of Outfit members. And to that new class, I offer these words: remember that you are ascending to a new level of power tonight. There are enclaves like this one across the world but, as I like to say, none so exclusive as ours. When the revolution begins, it is you who will be on the frontlines. And that will be a glorious place to be." With that, she stepped back toward the pedestal, where a silver column rose from below, stopping at a height just between her waist and shoulder, a perfect podium.

"We will begin with our highest honor of the evening. Beckett, please come forward."

From below, the muscular man broke free from his position in the circle and flew up the steps easily. Lucian stepped forward now with one of the velvet boxes. He opened it to display a leather cuff studded with a silver design. I couldn't see from here, but I knew it had to be a skull and crossbones, like the one I'd seen on a few of the Outfit men. Aurelia removed it from the box, placing it around his wrist. Each end had a long, solid silver band where a clasp might have been. But rather than fastening any hooks or fooling with any closure, Aurelia just held her hands around the cuff: it glowed red under her fingers and then the two strips of silver fused together, welded onto his arm.

"Tonight we honor you for your outstanding service, awarding you our highest ranking," she said to Beckett, letting go of his arm. He examined his new accessory and then returned his eyes to Aurelia. "Your meteoric rise has been stunning to watch, and your action in light of recent . . ."—she paused to find the right word—"tragedies has demonstrated both leadership and unwavering devotion to our cause. I thank you and look forward to your continued success in our program." They bowed to each other. "And more immediately, we look forward to your role in the induction of our newest members—a privilege granted to only our most promising disciples." He thanked her and she nodded in response, then he found a place in the background standing beside Lucian. Next, two Outfit girls I recognized were awarded those amethyst necklaces I had often seen—those too were welded on by Aurelia, her fingers joining together two small strips of silver to form a permanent closure. When the girls filed off the stage and back to their positions on the floor, Aurelia stood atop the pedestal to address the group again.

"Well, now it appears we've reached the main event. The moment we have all been waiting for: the induction of our new recruits. There are two distinct milestones to be accomplished in conjunction with this rare honor. First, the signing of the contract. I will award you your contract and tonight Raphaella will administer the incision."

A shudder swept over me. *Incision?* Raphaella made her way up the steps now and took a place at the base of the pedestal. Aurelia continued, instructing the group. I listened closely, mentally taking notes.

"After you have received yours, please proceed to the podium where you will sign it with your index finger. Then hand your contract to Lucian, who will administer your oath while Beckett performs the second phase of the process: the marking ritual. As you know, the ritual will heal your wound and purify all the toxins within. And then, the sale will be complete." She paused to take in the hungry, anxious faces, then stepped down, a stack of sheets of ecru parchment in her hands. "Very well. Let us begin." She called the first name. "Alistair . . ."

An olive-skinned Adonis, positioned nearest to the staircase, made his way up. He reached Aurelia and shook her hand as she gave him a crisp piece of paper. I noticed Raphaella was now wielding a small, ornate golden instrument the size of a pencil. He held out his right hand to her, palm up, and she made a quick slice on his index finger. Even from here I could see a red dot bubble up instantly. They nodded at each other and he climbed the few steps up the pedestal, placed his contract on the podium, and with his bleeding index finger, wrote his name onto the paper, then stepped back down the other side toward Lucian and Beckett as names continued to be called.

I had never been squeamish around blood because I had seen plenty of it at the hospital, but this sent a wave of nausea over me. I found it so terrifyingly unsanitary. How can they do this? But obviously, sterilization was the least of their worries. *These people are selling their souls to the devil. Aurelia, Lucian, they are in league with this prince and he is their leader. He is the devil himself. Haven, you are living among absolute evil.* It all crystallized, but I had to swat it down, stifle this understanding because my breathing was getting too loud. I worried that I wouldn't be able to summon the courage to ever leave this perch. I felt the combined force of all of these people, all of this evil, engulfing me. All of this would be focused against *me.* What had I done to deserve this? Why me? How was I possibly supposed to overcome all of this?

I refocused my attention on Alistair, who was now sitting on the banquette near Beckett. Alistair had taken off his suit jacket, rolled his shirtsleeve up high, nearly to his shoulder. He looked nervous—his face was firm, but his eyes became shifty. Beckett stood over him and pressed one of the black index-card-size papers against the young recruit's bicep, smoothing it out and holding it against his skin. Alistair gritted his teeth as curls of smoke rose off his golden flesh. Slowly, the black paper dissolved and a design began to take shape. Alistair squeezed his eyes shut against the pain as Beckett lifted his hands and this form traced itself, burning into Alistair's skin, glowing in that shape I had seen before: it was the eye with that pentagram-shaped pupil. He clenched and unclenched his fists and finally his whole body eased and he took a deep breath. Beckett put a comforting hand on the young man's back and Alistair looked up at him, nodded, and rose from his seat, jacket in hand, returning back down the staircase to his place in the circle. Those whose names remained to be called stared at him in quiet awe.

It went on this way until all twenty recruits had suffered through this same process. All that changed was how well or poorly each dealt with the pain (a few wept, others cried out in agony) and the location of the marking—some opted for a shoulder blade, a forearm, an ankle. When it was all finished, Aurelia took to the podium again.

"Congratulations to you all. Greatness awaits you."

The outer circle, the original Outfit members, applauded and the new members looked both proud and pained, many still noticeably trying to stifle their wincing from their new markings. Aurelia held up a hand to silence the clapping. Her face grew more stoic than usual.

"This occasion is bittersweet, for, just as we welcome so many new members today, we must say goodbye to someone. This is the natural cycle of our world. As new souls enter Metamorfosi, one must return to the inferno. The day you become one of us, each of you is tagged with a certain expectancy: an amount of time you have here before you're officially turned over to the underworld. This is the exchange you have agreed to. Every deal has its specific terms. None of you knows the amount of time you have, only that it is finite." She paused and looked down at her hands, as though studying them for some guidance on how to continue.

Finally, in a soft voice, she said, "I would be remiss if I didn't address the tragedy of our dear misguided Calliope." I felt the whole room lean collectively toward her, anxious for whatever explanation she might give for exactly what had happened to that beautiful girl. "As you're well aware, she served with great dedication and was one of the finest the Outfit has ever seen. Several of our core members were recruited by her, as a matter of fact." I followed her gaze to Beckett. He hung his head. "Like all of you, Calliope understood what was expected of her and was familiar with the realities of her . . . situation. She gave her soul to us and in return we availed her of the opportunity to be a great artist, renowned and revered. But when her time here was complete, she failed to uphold her end of this commitment. That is to say, she did not go gently. She ran. She turned her back on her one responsibility and went back on her word. And in so doing, she created a situation that put all of us in great danger. Our darling Beckett"—she looked down at him now and he met her eyes—"helped seize her again, but her story ended in a most unfortunate and, regrettably, public manner."

She straightened her posture again, strengthening. "Obviously we cannot have that happening again." Her voice took on a new, stinging quality. The letters of each word were laced with thorns when she said, "Forgive me now, inner circle—" She clasped her hands before her and closed her eyes and the original, most senior members of the Outfit began squirming and writhing. The girls grabbed at their necklaces as though they were being choked, the boys tugged at their wrist cuffs like they were being stabbed. The new inductees gasped as they watched. "Forgive me," Aurelia continued. "But the honor system is suspended indefinitely. This all used to be so civilized, but now we need to ensure that none of you is able to do as Calliope did and run off. Inside this envelope"—she held aloft a creamy envelope, closed with a fat, waxy seal—"bears the name of the one of you who will be ending your tour of duty in Metamorfosi this evening."

She opened it and took a breath, which seemed less genuine regret and more a way to prolong the drama and the pain she was inflicting on her subjects. At last she read "Raphaella." She waved her arm sharply and, at once, everyone stopped tugging on their necklaces and cuffs; everyone except for Raphaella. The gasps rang out as soon as the group could breathe again. Raphaella, her hands still grabbing at her necklace, rose up the spiral staircase, trying her best to choke back tears. But still, she stood tall. Aurelia stepped down from the pedestal to meet her and gave her a kiss on the forehead. "Thank you for your fine service in the realm of the Metamorfosi. Onward to the great below for you."

Touching one hand to her misty eyes to dry her tears as the other hand still pulled at the necklace, Raphaella nodded, accepting her fate. Lucian appeared at her side and Aurelia stood behind her and took hold of that fused strip of silver on the girl's necklace. Instantly, beneath her fiery fingers, steam rose and the silver melted, dripping into her hands and then, just as quickly, turning to dust, which Aurelia shook right off. She handed what was left of the necklace to Lucian, who guided Raphaella up the few steps of the pedestal. Together they stood there as it began to slowly descend, until they were entirely out of sight, swallowed up below. Where were they going? Could this really be a direct pathway to hell?

Aurelia was speaking again and I forced myself to pay attention. "This concludes tonight's ceremony. I urge you all to go convert any and all you can. With any hope, soon we will have these events weekly and preferably with twice as many new faces.

Remember, the fastest way to advance in our organization is by recruiting. Go forth and conquer, my lambs."

She took her place atop the pedestal once more and then she too descended, leaving the group alone. When she was finally out of sight and the spotlight trained on her had snuffed out, the two circles of Outfit members unspooled into a silent single-file line marching out of the main door of the Vault.

I waited until the very last one left and then I waited some more, worried that at any moment someone might return to dismantle that pedestal and extinguish the ring of fire. My watch read just after five. It seemed like the entire world had changed since I'd climbed up there.

As I navigated down the metal bars into the darkness below, I had the sense I was entering some new horror show. I didn't know how I was supposed to stay here after witnessing these rituals. I needed to get back to my room, back to that book. It needed to tell me something, anything, give me a good reason why I couldn't just run outside right now and take a cab home and forget all about this. Or call the cops — although that would be ridiculous, wouldn't it? Who would believe me? What would I say? *I've seen the devil and his followers and they're trying to recruit people and they're buying souls?* I would likely end up being locked away in some kind of institution if I tried explaining that, wouldn't I?

My foot searched for another rung and found the floor instead. I slithered, body against the wall, making my way through the soupy darkness with an outstretched hand until I found the door out into the dim light of the underground maze. I kept a brisk pace until I heard it: the faintest click and rattle of metal on metal and the sound of a door swinging open. It came from the direction of that room where the gruesome photos were kept.

I spun around, searching for any hiding spot. I tried two door-knobs—locked and locked—and then settled for a doorway with no door whatsoever, but in such shadows that would have to do. It was a nook the size of a closet, with nothing but an empty wooden shelving unit, riddled with what appeared to be bullet holes inside and a single neatly empty bottle of some sort of liquor. I heard that voice and flattened myself against the wall.

"You startled me," Lucian said calmly.

"Funny, I didn't think anything was capable of startling you," Aurelia cooed back.

"Can I help you, Aurelia?" His tone became impatient and the metal rattled again.

She didn't answer him; she just started talking. "How did that go? Did she go willingly?"

"She did."

"Always a class act, that Raphaella."

I heard the rattling again and the swinging of a door hinge—it had to be that door I'd seen Beckett open up, the one that was so searing hot to the touch, with that pentagram-shaped key. Was this the path down to the underworld? Was that possible?

I shivered and folded my arms to keep from shaking. Lucian had delivered Raphaella below. This was what he did for a living. He had probably done this countless times before. When he bought souls he did it knowing that one day he would personally have to walk that person down to their ultimate nightmare, to something worse than death, down to this underworld for an eternity filled with torture and who knew what else. How could any part of me ever have longed for him? He was nothing like me. How could my heart have betrayed me like this? Why had I not paid attention when my scars flared up when he was near me? But I knew why—because I didn't want to. I didn't care how wrong he was for me or how unworthy of my blind adoration, I just wanted Lucian in a way I had never wanted anyone else, certainly not any of my crushes at school, which seemed so foolish and laughingly innocent now. I had fallen for this monster. It sounded like he swung closed that final gate, crashing it against its frame.

"Not so fast, darling," Aurelia snapped. "Can you just run this down to our beloved Prince?" I heard the crinkling of paper. And a very long pause. "I believe the answer is yes," she prompted him.

"Yes, certainly," he said, just shy of sarcastic.

"Thank you, my lamb. He needs it now, forgive me." She didn't sound the least bit remorseful.

"Will that be all?"

"Yes." I heard the soft smack of a kiss, and inadvertantly lunged forward, my head peeking out just enough so I could see a sliver of them. Enough to see she kissed him on the lips but he didn't kiss back. He just stood there, perfectly still, uninterested. "Goodbye," she said lingering there, her lips as close as they could be to his without actually touching. She took a step away from him and I lurched back into my hiding place. The footsteps grew closer, that soft click of her knife-like heels against the concrete. I flattened my back against the wall of this nook, hoping the shadows would disguise me enough. She sliced past in sharp strides and then, from the sound of it, seemed to duck back into that hallway to the Vault. When I hadn't heard her footsteps for several long seconds, I crept back out.

Halfway down the corridor toward that room, I got to the point where I could see over the rubble of the waist-high partially busted-through wall clear to the ground.

Lucian was still in there. I froze.

He had his back to me and was crouched near those photos. My reflexes kicked in, and before I could think, my body sent me back to the same spot where I had been able to watch Beckett. I scurried as softly as possible, holding my breath the whole distance. Huddled there, I peeked through between the exposed wooden beams and watched Lucian. He had inched the velvet covering up and kneeled before his own photo. He held a hand out to touch its surface, then recoiled and exhaled deeply and pityingly. With a shake of his head, he stood back up, covered the photos again, and unlocked that grand door.

As soon as he let it swing shut behind him, I took off running. I didn't care who heard me anymore, I just needed to get out of there.

Back upstairs, I found myself pounding on Dante and Lance's door, heedless of the time. The door opened, a frantic Lance behind it, fumbling to get his glasses.

"Am I late? Is it tomorrow? Did I sleep through the whole day? What time is it?"

I could have thrown my arms around him right then — not something I would really do, but I could have — that's how much I appreciated seeing him.

"No, Lance, sorry. It's morning, but really early. You should go back to sleep."

He looked confused. I couldn't blame him. "Then . . . why did you wake me?"

"I know, sorry about that, I—"

"Oh!" He was sleepy but sounded like something just occurred to him. He spoke in a weary near whisper, leaning against the doorframe. "You're nice, but I'm feeling better now. Guess I just needed to sleep it off or something." His eyes were barely open behind those heavy frames, but he kept talking. "Maybe it was one of those twenty-four-hour flus people talk about. Scientifically speaking, I always thought those were something of a myth. You know, I just figured those people actually had food poisoning and didn't realize it, but now I get it. It happens. This was like twenty-four-hour mono. But I'm okay."

"I don't know, I don't think it was," I said. He seemed surprised I would challenge his theory. "Never mind, we'll talk later." I looked over his shoulder and saw that Dante's bunk was still pristinely made: no one had slept there tonight. Lance noticed me looking.

"Haven't seen him. Out all night again." He shrugged.

My heart sunk a bit. I thought of Etan standing by Lucian's side tonight and I wondered and worried what that meant for Dante.

"Thanks," I finally said. I decided that, no, I couldn't tell Lance everything right now. He was still half-asleep, and he would think I was crazy. "I'm glad you're feeling better. Sorry I woke you."

"Thanks for checking on me." He yawned and waved. I was touched that he thought I was that selfless; glad that he could go back to bed not knowing that I had pounded at the door purely out of fear and the selfish need to be comforted by someone. I had completely forgotten that he had been so sick earlier. I couldn't remember anything that had happened before that induction. It all spun and swirled around my head. Why was I here? I didn't belong here. But this wasn't the time to be asking Lance any of this. I looked into his sleepy eyes.

"Sure," I said. "See ya in the morning."

"See ya." Yawning again, he closed the door gently. I stood in that hallway longer than I meant to and then at last went back to my room. I sat on my bed and pulled out that book. I paged through from the beginning, skimming for anything to give me extra strength. But when I got to the most recent entry and turned the page, there was something new there.

Marked with today's date, it read:

What you have heard of Metamorfosi and what you have witnessed is only part of the story. There is much more. What you can count as fact: the realm of the Metamorfosi is where apprentice devils learn their trade, dabbling in death and destruction under the watchful eyes of their Masters. For you though, it is a training ground of a different sort. You can't expect to find all the answers written out for you. But you have been given enough tools to know how to discover things on your own. Continue your search for understanding; continue your physical trials. Be confident in your powers of deduction.

And a final warning: be careful whom you trust.

Be strong. Now more than ever.

22

An Unexpected Visit

This time the thumping down the hall ricocheted from my eardrums through my head and all along my jittery spine. Loud, louder, deafening. And, again, I opened the door, hoping to make it stop. Calliope led them, the whole pack of them, every member of the Outfit and every freshly inducted recruit, marching toward my room, ready to take me. As they inched closer, they aged, getting older by the moment, and then decayed, their skin shriveling like paper charring and curling up in a flame. Their limbs fell to the ground like rotted tree branches, arms and legs scattering in the hallway and crawling toward me on their own, and then heads falling and rolling at me. But I didn't close the door to my room; there was no door. There was just me, left there alone to ward off these advancing creatures. No weapons, no shields, wanting to scream but telling myself not to show them my fear even as my sweat drenched me and my racing nerves made my skin itch with terror . . .

And then my eyes opened. My head flung toward the door—yes, it was there, closed, locked. But the steady drumbeat of that knocking still came at me. *Thump, thump, thump* . . . relentless.

I shook myself awake, trying to snuff it out, but it kept at me, banging at my brain, begging me to face it. I ran my hands over my slick face and damp hair. I held my palms over my ears, but it wouldn't stop.

The door shook in its frame, barely containing the pounding. I took a breath, hand on the knob, and pulled, bracing myself.

And I screamed. I couldn't help it. He was standing right there.

"Whoa, morning," Lance said. He had on his uniform and looked wide awake and ready to start the day.

"Sorry," I panted.

"I was knocking forever. Thought I'd missed you." He looked at me like I was a crazy person. "Expecting someone else?"

"Um, no, sorry. What time is it?"

"It's almost seven. I guess I'm kind of early but I'm feeling way better, and I'm ready to upload those photos anytime you are. I felt bad about leaving you hanging yesterday."

"Photos?" I couldn't even begin to process, I was too wiped out and he was speaking too fast. I was still shocked to discover that I had somehow fallen asleep—it's a testament to how incredibly exhausted I had been that I managed to close my eyes after what I'd seen last night. I shuddered, my whole body shimmied once, fast, as though I were being attacked by ants. It didn't escape his notice.

"Your photos from the Vault? You okay?"

"Oh, yeah. Thanks. I'll just get dressed.

"Sure. Oh, and did you come by earlier or was that a weird dream I had? Not that I have dreams about you, but I have crazy dreams here." He pushed his glasses up on his nose, his eyes darting all around.

"Yeah, no, that was me. I was up late . . . reading, and just thought I'd check on you."

"Thanks, I'm good."

I wanted to say, *I'm not, I'm a mess, I have to tell you what I saw last night, this place is freakish and frightening and I don't know how we ended up here or how we can get out.* But I thought of that book's admonition and I just couldn't decide if I could say something or not, so I didn't.

"That's great," I said instead, with no conviction whatsoever. "Twenty minutes?"

He nodded, looking at me with curious eyes and then backing away to his room.

I showered and got dressed in my uniform in a flash but apparently not fast enough for Lance. When I emerged from my room, I found him pacing outside my door like a guard dog—though not a very good one. He shook, clearly startled, when the door opened. I was just glad I wasn't the only one who was unbelievably jumpy. He played it off though.

"Ready?" He started off down the hall.

"Someone's in a hurry."

"I was cooped up in that room all yesterday. It's just thrilling to be out among the living."

"Right." I shuddered again.

In our gallery office, he uploaded the photos I had selected and settled in to build his slide show: adjusting the order of them, and playing with the options so that certain ones zoomed in and others flickered quickly. When he had it all set, he saved it all and left to load it onto the flat screen at the front desk. I was never so glad to not have that job—a few of the new recruits were stationed there and their eyes somehow already looked more leaden than just last night. I had done a spot check zipping by before and found bits of each of their telltale tattoos peeking out from shirtsleeves. Lance had just left and I had begun searching for the day's press clippings about the hotel—apparently the restaurant had gotten a good review and a trio of stars from something called the *Michelin Guide,* which seemed to be a big deal—when when I heard it. Without the least bit of warning, that rasp stung me: "Haven—"

I gasped and whipped my head to the doorway, a chill spreading across my skin.

"Yes, hello, Aurelia." I did my best not to seem rattled.

"So sorry to startle you," she said, with a mischievous smile. "There's a Joan here for you?"

"Here? Joan?" I couldn't process this. Joan was here? Now? The chill turned instantly into a cold sweat, my stomach dropped. "What's she doing here?" I didn't mean to ask it aloud, but I had lost the ability to filter. *She can't be here, she can't be around these people.*

"It appears she's getting a spa treatment."

"She's at the spa? Now?" Why wouldn't she have told me? This is what I got for not calling home enough.

"We'll be sure to roll out the red carpet and take special care of your guest." This, unfortunately, sounded entirely sincere.

"I'll, um, have to go say hello. I think I'll just, yeah, I'll just run down there now." I was up on my feet now. Aurelia still stood in the doorway. "I'll just be a minute, if you don't mind."

"Not at all," she said. "I'm so glad she's getting to experience all that we have to offer here." I waited for her to clear the doorway and then I bolted out of the gallery, walking to the spa as fast as I could without actually breaking into a jog.

"Joan?" The low hum of a soothing instrumental soundtrack filled the air, along with a sweet, clean scent.

"Surprise, honey!" said the smiling, mummified figure lying on the table. A row of shower heads on a long arm were suspended above, still and dry for the time being but ready to act when called upon.

"Did I miss an e-mail or something?" I was grateful for the cucumber slices over Joan's eyes. If she had been able to see me she would've known something was wrong. But she just launched right in, a mile a minute.

"I don't like to spring things on you, but Michelle thought it would be so cute since I had the day off to come here. She got me this gift certificate. So sweet of her. We had the school bus accident come into the hospital the other day; did you hear about that on the news? It was just horrific, but everyone is okay. She was a superwoman, that Michelle, but I pulled practically a triple shift and so she said she wanted to thank me. I just thought it would be fun to pop by—I read such wonderful things about this spa in the *Trib*, you know. I hope it's okay!"

"Um, yeah, it's great to see you." My mind raced. How fast could I get her out of here?

"I know you're very busy. I asked for you at the front desk and those girls—and they really are all just absolutely gorgeous, and so poised and friendly too—said they would let you know right away, but they had to find you because you're always in meetings and things and they were so sweet and told me to just go and get started here." Joan's demeanor reminded me of that time she got tipsy at the family Christmas party.

"So, what is all of this anyway?" I asked. She looked like a burrito, cocooned in what seemed to be foil, and presumably slathered with some kind of lotion and potion underneath. I couldn't keep my mind from running through all the worst-case scenarios of what could be in there. If only I could've somehow gotten here sooner.

"Why, this would be the milk, honey, and sesame body buff with a seaweed wrap," she said, pleased with herself.

"Wow." I tried to sound easygoing, like myself. "It, um, sounds like a lunch special."

"It is very special, I'll tell you that much. If I got these every day I would be an entirely different person. Ahhh—" I shivered at that, involuntarily. She was blissed out. I was terrified. I wished I could turn the shower heads on, put a stop to this. "—but speaking of lunch, yes, can we have some? I'm almost done here and that restaurant looks just darling—"

"No!" I blurted out, completely rude, but I didn't care. I couldn't have her eating here. I couldn't imagine what damage had already been done. I had to get her out of Lexington, that's all I could think. I wouldn't let anything happen to her. Her lips moved into a frown. "No. I just mean," I said, summoning all my strength to sound normal, "I have a crazy day and all this stuff I've gotta get done. I'm trying to do a good job and all and I feel like they shouldn't see me taking a long break. But maybe another time soon? It's just, you know, one of those days."

"Oh, someone is very busy, indeed, isn't she? I'm so proud of my little worker bee!" She gushed. "This place is just so fancy and incredible, Hav. I suppose I can't blame you for being a worka-holic. I'm so proud of you."

A woman in a white version of the hotel uniform appeared, someone I didn't recognize. I could only hope she wasn't a fully inducted Outfit member. "Time to rinse off, Ms. Terra."

"That's me!" said Joan. "I could just stay in this forever."

"I'll wait for you, Joan. Walk you out and stuff."

I sat in the spa's Japanese garden-like waiting area beside a trickling waterfall and could not have felt less at peace. My leg twitched nervously. I couldn't imagine what might have been in that concoction they had covered Joan with. I was sure there was something to make her feel good, like all was right in this odd world of the hotel. I heard her voice, thanking someone profusely, and she stepped around from behind the waterfall wearing black pants and a sweater. I stood up, on reflex, like someone in a hospital anxious to hear updates about a loved one.

The Outfit member at the spa reception desk, who hadn't so much as looked my way, gave Joan the widest, toothiest grin and gushed, "You look so rejuvenated! Have a nice day and please come again soon!"

"Why thank you, yes, I will certainly be back."

"All set?" I was already walking in the direction of the elevator. "Ready to go?"

Joan stopped. "Hello, gorgeous!" she said, grabbing my hand to stop me and giving me a once-over. "Why, look at you!"

I looked down at myself. "These are our uniforms."

"Lovely, you look just lovely. All grown up!"

"Thanks, Joan." I started walking again. "So, how do you feel?"

"Fantastic. Really fantastic." Her eyes had a mellow glaze. She couldn't stop smiling. "Have you had one of those?"

"Um, no." I hit the elevator up button. *Up, up, up, c'mon.* "They don't really let us. We're mostly just working." The elevator came and I put my hand on her back wanting to push her in, get her moving faster. I hit the button for the lobby and then the one to close the doors, shutting them right in someone else's face, and I didn't care.

"Well you could use one, Haven. You're working too hard, I

can tell." The doors opened again. We were back in the lobby. "But this place is just remarkable!" She looked up at the ceiling, taking everything in. "I cannot believe this is your home."

"This isn't my home," I snapped. She didn't seem to detect the edge in my voice. She was probably still hopped up on unknown toxins from her spa trip.

"You know what I mean, silly. You're a part of this glamorous place. How many high school students could do what you're doing? I'm so proud of you. Now would you just look at that skylight? Magnificent!"

"Thanks, Joan." It came out more defeated than I would've liked. She sat down on the ottoman holding my hand and pulling me to sit beside her. Around us, staffers fluttered by, guests flitted in and out. Two Outfit members watched us from the front desk. "I'm really sorry about lunch."

"Look at that, you're wearing the necklace." She took the pendant in her hand.

"Yeah, I love it. I never take it off, actually."

"You're quite the lady all of a sudden, aren't you?"

"Will you call me when you get home? Did you drive here?"

"No, I took the L this time. I wanted to shop around a little and didn't want to worry about traffic and parking and all. Besides, I wanted to time how fast it was to get to you—pretty fast. I'll have to get back here more often." She winked. "But don't worry, I'll call first next time."

"Great. Yeah." There's no way I would ever let her back in here. Ever. "Call me later? Okay?" I stood up and, luckily, she followed suit. I led us outside. "Next time I'll get an afternoon off and we can go somewhere in the city. I spend enough time here." My voice almost sounded believable. But I could feel my brow furrowing.

"Of course, dear, that would be wonderful!" She pulled me into a tight hug. And I hugged her back, wishing I could go with her and forget entirely about this world I had gotten sucked into. But I knew I couldn't. "I'm so proud of you. You are just doing so well. I can't wait to brag about you to all the ladies back at the hospital!" She let me go, but remembered: "And, oh my goodness, that Aurelia is just beautiful, and she thinks so highly of you!"

"What?"

"I just met her quickly. She said she feels like you two are cut from the same cloth and she's so impressed with your work. Keep it up, honey!" I felt like I'd been stabbed.

"That's great. So you met her." I felt so much like my world had been violated and tampered with. *Please tell me Joan will be okay. I don't care what happens to me, just let her be protected.*

"Okay, well, I have an afternoon of shopping ahead of me!"

With one more hug and a kiss on the cheek, Joan strolled off in the direction of the L. I only noticed now that it was positively freezing outside, but I stood there until she was out of sight.

On my way back into the hotel, my eyes shot to the girls at the front desk. Both seemed consumed with their respective computer screens, but I could feel them glancing back at me after I walked away.

I found Neil Marlinson waiting in front of the gallery. He smiled, big and broad, when he saw me. I collected myself and waved back.

"Hello, Mr. Marlinson."

"Neil, please," he said warmly. "I just had to thank you, Haven, for the copy of that photo you left for me. You can't possibly know how much it means. This . . ." He held up the printout—it was the version that had first been on the wall of the gallery, not as it looked now hidden in Aurelia's office. " . . .

this has made my trip here worthwhile." He held it against his chest.

"I'm glad to help," I said, not sure I really deserved such a fuss.

"You must think I'm incredibly strange, to be so fixated on this." He looked at the picture again. "But it looks so much like her, it's uncanny. It's just, well, you'll understand this someday, but you never forget your first love. You just never do, no matter what happened to take that person out of your life." He sounded wistful and then he caught himself. "I'm sorry. I don't know why I'm bothering you with this." He shook his head. A lightning bolt struck his face, an idea dancing in his eyes now. "I'd like to buy something, anything, as a thank-you."

The gallery was still technically closed to the public, but Aurelia had encouraged me to sell him another piece, so I figured it would be okay to let him in.

"C'mon in," I said as I slashed us in and opened the door. "Have a look and let me know if I can help with anything." I smiled and found a place off to the side, letting him wander through the space on his own.

"Any recommendations?" he called back to me as he stepped farther in, his pace slowing at the wall of photos of the former Lexington Hotel.

"I think those are nice," I said. I walked over to the display where he was and leaned in to the description beside one of them. "These are from not long after the hotel opened, 1908 —" I read on the placard. "Yeah, this place was just in its teens then: sixteen, I guess. It opened in 1892." I was glad for the opportunity to spout some of these facts I'd been accumulating. "Now, it's all redone and modern, but I like how it looked then. There's something romantic about it." I studied the suite of pictures. "That was before it was home to criminals." I laughed. "Capone showed up in '28. So this is how it started before it was infamous, but still really, I don't know, *magical*, I think."

He just nodded, looking at these photos like they were imparting some kind of great wisdom to him. I decided not to get in the way by talking anymore and I let him just watch them for a while.

"They remind me of her: innocent," he said finally, and I couldn't tell if he was talking to himself or if he meant for me to ask him to elaborate. He looked swept up and carried off to some other time. "Maybe this one?" he spoke to a modest, framed five-by-seven black-and-white of the hotel's façade.

"That's a lovely choice," I said. "I'll just have to consult our owner, who's still fine-tuning that price list, but I know she wants to make you a good—"

"I'll give her ten thousand dollars. How's that?"

"Wow, um, okay." I wasn't sure what these things might go for, but it sounded like an awful lot.

"No, really, how is that? Is it enough, do you think, to get the attention of your owner?"

"I think it probably is."

"Good. Then, here—" He pulled out his checkbook and a pen and scribbled the amount in, then ripped out the check along its perforated edge with a swoosh, handing it over. "Take this and let me know what she says."

"Sure," I said, taking the check in firm hands, worried it might dissolve or I might somehow lose it.

"Thank you, Haven. Thank you so much."

"Of course."

"You know where to find me." He gave me a pat on the back

and held my shoulder for a moment, as though he wanted to tell me something else, and then he just patted me once more and let himself out.

I found Lance in the Parlor kitchen, drinking a glass of orange juice.

"Hey I saw that guy again. Did he find you in the gallery?" he asked. The microwave was going. "Have you noticed there are a million new people working here? Where do they all come from?" I took the glass out of his hand, tossing it in the sink.

"Hey!"

"I have to tell you something—"

He cut me off: "Well, then I'm definitely not sharing any of this with you." He read from a piece of paper. "'Hi Haven and Lance, Brie and crab omelettes with carrot muffins, and sausage and bacon. Just microwave for one minute, thirty seconds. Love, Dante.'" I pulled the note from his fingers, but he kept talking, gnawing on a fork now. "You know I didn't think I'd ever get my appetite back, but—" The microwave buzzed. "Yum."

I swooped in front of him, yanking open the microwave door.

"Can I help you?" he asked, taking the fork out of his mouth, like it was a pipe.

"This is going to sound crazy—" In one swift motion, I took the plate out and dumped its contents—which, incidentally, did smell delicious—into the trash.

"Hey!"

"We're going back to cereal. Because of yesterday."

"Seriously?"

I took down a box of Lucky Charms and found two bowls.

"You're breaking my heart," he said to me.

"I know, but yum, look at the delectable cereal waiting for us. You'll thank me later, trust me." Looking pained, he threw himself onto the stool beside me as I poured him a generous bowlful, then one for me. "Here, I'll even give you all of my hearts, since yours is broken over your omelette sacrifice." I fished out a few of the marshmallow hearts from my bowl and plunked them into his.

"That's very thoughtful. I almost forgive you."

I ate three heaping bowls of cereal, matching Lance. I just scarfed them down, fast and furious, as if I hadn't eaten in months. At one point, I even caught him, spoon in the air, just watching me. But the more I ate, the hungrier I felt. I had been running on adrenaline as my fuel last night and then I had crashed and now every cell felt an urgent need to recharge.

"So, I think it's gluttony night at the Vault tonight," he joked.

"Oh?" I wasn't even paying attention, I was too busy polishing off my third bowl.

"Geez, I've never seen a girl pack it away like that," he said in awe. "I mean, except for my Aunt Linda and she outweighs you by about two hundred pounds."

I made no apologies. My mouth was full anyway, so I just tried to smile and then merely said, with a shrug, "I'm hungry."

"So I gather."

We finished up and went our separate ways, Lance disappearing down to the Vault to find Lucian, and me grabbing some of the clips I'd printed out for Aurelia and the Vault photos I'd already had Lance upload. As I walked to her office, I skimmed some of the articles. Dante was mentioned in the big review, lauded as "an able and up-and-coming sous-chef" and "one to watch." And then several of the articles linking to this one and talking up the three-star rating also mentioned him. Overnight, he had become semi-famous. And not only in Chicago; the *New York Times* ran a blurb on the rating and dropped Dante's name, dubbing him Etan's protégé.

My first thought was that I had been too hard on him; he must be exhausted and I ended up getting him more upset. He'd obviously been working even harder than I could fathom—all those late nights, all that prep, to ensure they were ready for a critic like this to come through. And apparently, it had all paid off.

But after last night, my mind had been retrained. Now it went in a direction I never would have imagined. I flashed to all those "new recruits," as they called them, and so many of them were the kitchen staff. Dante had not been among them, but had they gotten to him? He was too smart to fall for all of this, wasn't he?

Then again, I thought I was so smart and look how I had swooned for Lucian. And Lance wasn't exactly entirely immune to Raphaella. *Raphaella.* So she was gone? It seemed unbelievable that a queen bee could be dismissed so easily. This was how these people, these creatures, operated. And I would be an idiot to think that they hadn't been doing their best to sink their claws into Dante. Would he be at the next induction? It made me nauseous to even think about it. My only mild consolation was that little bit I'd heard last night in Aurelia's office: that they're on some sort of schedule with their recruiting, as they call it, and they're not going to seize the others until they get me. It gave me chills.

All I knew for sure was that I had to talk to him. I glanced over at Capone now. The balloons and flowers were all in place and a line of tittering patrons, most in business suits, spilled out. Clearly, I wasn't the only one who had spotted all the good press.

I would catch Dante soon, I would find a way to get through to him.

A urelia called me into her office on the first knock. I took a deep breath and tried to forget that this was the person who had been the ringmaster of last night's horror show. I expected her to be somehow *different*, to strike out at me, to smite me, to steal my soul—however that was done—right then and there and stop this charade of our supposed mentor/mentee relationship. But still, I tried, actively, to not look petrified.

"Have a seat," she said, plenty stern as usual but just a touch brighter, almost in a full-fledged good mood. "As I expect you have read, Capone has received a Michelin three-star rating, the only restaurant in Chicago to receive such an honor this year and one of only a handful in the country. This is a tremendous accomplishment. These are the Oscars of the food and beverage industry. There will be a cavalcade of media clippings to amass on this matter in the coming days, so be prepared." I nodded and held up the stack I'd already printed and was about to tell her but she just kept talking.

"We're not supposed to know who the reviewer is," she said in a tone that suggested that she *did* know and she was rather proud of it. "So we are assembling a gift basket to be sent to the guide's corporate headquarters. Etan will have it for you this morning. It's going to be getting even busier here with this kind of attention. And there will be a special prix-fixe meal the next month in celebration, and a party tonight." She held out a box for me. "Here are the invitations to be hand-delivered to our VIPs today, along with chocolates. Obviously, they need to go out right away."

I took the box and opened the lid to peek at them: there were about twenty ornate, gold-engraved invitations in small folders bearing the hotel logo. It was a feat of origami just to open one. I remembered when Joan was on the planning committee for the hospital's gala opening for the new pediatric cancer wing. They ordered their invitations months in advance. There were more of those, of course, but still. Was it possible that these had just been ordered this morning and were now instantly ready to go?

"Great, thank you. That's very exciting news," I said, starting to stand to leave, but she began talking again, so back down in the chair I went.

"One more bit of business on the subject of social affairs."

"Yes."

"You and the other intern will be coordinating the proms of five area high schools—including yours, as we discussed—to be held here in May and stretching into early June. Lucian will be spearheading this project. He will have point people at the various schools and materials for you to send regarding possible menu selections, décor, music, and so forth. This is important to us—in some ways, even more important than our historic Michelin rating—because it is an opportunity to reach a younger market who can look to us for their event planning in the future, who can become customers of our nightclub and restaurants and future guests here. It's a fine way for us to build an early following and loyalty. This is about the *long term*."

"Got it." I was barely paying attention. I just wanted to get out of there, and the mention of prom planning did nothing to improve my feelings about the place.

"So that's it for now."

"I'll get right on it," I said rising from my chair with the box and all the materials I'd brought in. "These are the Capone reviews." I set them on her desk. "And the Vault photos have been uploaded at the front desk."

"Very well, thank you."

I remembered what was in my pocket. I took out the check and set it on her desk. "And we sold a photo in the gallery. The five-by-seven from 1908? I said I'd have to check on the pricing. He was hoping ten thousand dollars would be adequate."

She leaned forward to look at the check, as I started to walk away. "I would say . . . so." She slowed down to a halt as she studied the name on it. "Why didn't you tell me he came back?" she lashed out, the sound of her raspy anger sending a shiver tingling down my spine. I turned back around to find her staring at me with leaden eyes, the sinewy muscles in her neck tightened into long ropes.

"I . . . I am, I'm telling you right now," I said as calmly and firmly as I possibly could. She seemed to be trying to turn the heat down on her boiling fury.

"All right," she choked out, her face reddened. "Go!" She was so icy, it froze me in place for a second, but I recovered, scurrying to let myself out as she set the check down on her desk and stared at her paperwork with those same dead eyes.

23

Not Human, but Devil

Lance and I worked quietly in our gallery office. He took over the computer, preparing e-mail invitations, and I made a place for myself at the end of the table to hand-address the others. We didn't *hear* her come in so much as *feel* her arrival. At some point we both just registered the shift in the air, a new tension, and we looked up and found her standing in the doorway. She looked at Lance for only a second—long enough to make him nervous, I imagined—and then she just started speaking to me.

"Haven, I would like you to deliver the photo up to Mr. Marlinson's room yourself. I believe it would only be right to thank him for his generous purchase. Bring this note along with the photo and some champagne and chocolate-covered strawberries." Her hand shook for a split second as she held out a sealed note card to me.

"Sure." I stood up from my chair and took the card.

She took two steps out the door and then turned around again: "Sooner rather than later."

As soon as she cleared the doorway, Lance shot me a look that said, *How does she just sneak up like that?* and shook his head.

"Obviously, I'd better do this now."

He nodded, no words necessary.

This assignment required me to drop into the back kitchen of Capone, where the room service orders went out, thereby putting me in close proximity to Dante. I could possibly try to say something now, even though I could hear the bustle in the dining room and knew that a busy breakfast service was in full swing.

I greeted the other sous-chefs warmly even though they all ignored me and just continued chopping and dicing and slicing and preparing. Every burner of every stove was covered with omelettes in various stages of preparation. So much sizzling here, so much toasting there, all sorts of mixing and beating. I didn't need to bother anyone for so simple an order, especially since I was making some adjustments—I wasn't bringing Mr. Marlinson any chocolate-covered strawberries, nothing that anyone in that kitchen could possibly tamper with. A sous-chef pointed me toward an appropriate bottle of champagne (unopened and a brand I'd heard of, nothing suspect). I dunked it into an ice bucket, grabbed a champagne flute, and took one of those domes used to cover plates—I could stick the photo underneath it—and wheeled it all away on a black tablecloth-covered room service cart, like the one Dante had taken down to us so many weeks ago.

As I inched upward in the rickety old freight elevator to his floor, I stared at that sealed note perched against the silver dome. The lights above the door showed that I had five more floors to go. I grabbed that soft cotton-like envelope and even as my fingers began ripping it open, I couldn't believe I was actually doing it. I just knew I had a minute or two at best, and I needed to know what it said. The book had told me weeks ago that I needed to search for the answers that wouldn't be staring me in the face. So

I went searching. I pulled out the crisp card and read these words in Aurelia's handwriting:

You found me.
But I'm no longer who I was.
I did love you then. Forgive me now.

I had to lean against the side of the elevator to keep myself upright. Those words tore at me. I didn't understand. So Aurelia and Neil Marlinson had been together once? She was the first love he spoke of? Could that be right? He was so much older. It didn't make any sense. But I thought of him, this Neil, who seemed so fragile and kind. I realized I didn't know the full story but I couldn't imagine any scenario in which this wouldn't break his heart. I wished I hadn't read it. What was most surprising was how she had ever loved a man like this. Can that brand of evil really love? Did he know what she was? One floor to go. The envelope was mangled beyond hope so I folded it and shoved it in the pocket of my uniform. I set the note underneath the dome on top of the photo. The elevator doors opened and I wheeled out.

He answered the door instantly.

"Haven, hello, come in." He sounded surprised, as he opened the door wide.

"Your photo and some champagne, compliments of the owner. I guess you got her attention." I tried to smile but I felt deceitful.

"That's very nice, thanks," he said. I could see the wheels turning, his mind trying to sort out exactly what this meant.

"Is over here okay?" I wheeled the cart over near the TV and sofa. He had one of the nicer suites, so plush and sprawling with one of those bay windows I loved.

"That's perfect," he said, something tentative in his tone.

"Enjoy." I made my way to the door.

"Thank you," he said, still standing in place, then: "Haven?"

I turned around.

"Did she happen to say anything?" I could see in his eyes that he had so much hope. He was too good for her. I hardly knew a thing about him, but I already was certain of that much.

"She really appreciates your generosity," I offered, but it hurt me. I didn't know if I should tell him there was a note under there. He would find it, and when he did he would just wish he hadn't anyway. Disappointment clouded his eyes. I wasn't sure if I should leave but didn't know how to help him either. I turned again toward the door and he stopped me once more.

"Could I ask you just one more thing?"

"Of course."

"Her name—it isn't really Aurelia Brown, is it?" His eyes implored mine, wanting me to give him the right answer.

"I'm sorry," I said, my most consoling tone. "I don't know. I wish I did. There's a lot I don't know." This was true. And I was truly sorry. I liked this man.

"No, of course." He shook his head, regaining his composure. "I'm sorry, I shouldn't be asking you these silly questions. But that night in the elevator, you were wearing a gold bracelet. I just wondered where you might have gotten that?"

"That was hers," I said. I thought for a moment and couldn't help but add, "And she said it was very special to her."

"Thank you. Thanks for that," he said sincerely.

"I wish I could be more helpful."

"You have, you really have."

"Well, just let me know if there's anything else. You know where to find me." I smiled as I left the room.

As I was getting out of the freight elevator, headed to the gallery, I heard my name in that voice, the voice that still could make my knees buckle if I wasn't careful. I slowed my pace, but then said, *No, what if you just pretend you don't hear it and you keep walking?* But there it was again, calling me softly and then just a touch louder, just enough that I couldn't claim not to have heard it.

"Haaaven."

I braced myself and turned around to face Lucian.

"Haven, did you hear me?" He took my hand in his warm paw and gave me the gentlest of tugs over toward the stairwell where we might be hidden from the guests milling about the lobby.

"Sorry, I zoned out, I guess," I said, hoping this would be explanation enough.

"Where were you last night?" He took a wisp of my hair that had freed itself from its bun, twirled it in his fingers, and tucked it behind my ear. "I thought I was going to see you."

"Oh." I had to try to act normal, like I hadn't witnessed his role in these terrifying scenes last night. "I didn't realize we had actual plans, per se. I thought it was more in the abstract and I knew it was a busy day so I figured you just, you know, got busy." I shrugged. I could have been smoother.

"Well, you figured wrong," he cooed, coming closer. When he was right here, like this, it was still hard to believe he had been assigned to target me, control me, hurt me, defeat me. This, all of this, was an act, a game to him. But I couldn't let him know that I knew this. There was power in letting him think I was still a fool. "I came by and you weren't there."

"I must've been sleeping. I dozed off reading." He touched his warm fingertips lightly to my lips to stop their explanation. Days ago, this sort of thing would have left me pleasantly trembling. Today, though, fear shook me instead. He looked at me with piercing, adoring eyes that said he was prepared to call my bluff and yet he could still reel me in without breaking a sweat. I could see him determining how best to proceed.

"No," he finally said, softly, sweetly. "I don't think you were." He leaned to whisper in my ear in that breathy voice, his arm cradling my back. "I get it, you're playing hard to get. I have a feeling I'm going to win." He stepped away and gave me that smile and that look that could all be taken as heady, dreamy flirtation if only I didn't know better. I wished I didn't know better. I stood there alone, gathering myself for several minutes until I couldn't hear his footsteps anymore.

I needed to talk to Dante. Now. I needed my friend and I needed someone to make sense of all of this with me and I needed to make sure that he was okay. I just needed him. I marched back to the still-bustling Capone, in through that kitchen entrance, and I took the twenty boxes of chocolates we needed, sticking them in one of the larger boxes I found in the walk-in refrigerator. When I stepped out the door, Etan was right there. A jolt stabbed at my heart.

"Why, hello, Ms. Terra. Off to deliver more chocolates, are we?"

My scars flared up. "Yes, with invitations to tonight's party. Congratulations on the three stars. You must be so proud."

"We are. Thank you," he said in a chilly voice. Dante must've told him that I'd been nosing around about him.

"I know I'm supposed to send out a gift basket—"

"Yes, I'll have that for you later today. We've had a bit of an influx this morning thanks to the review." From his tone, you would have thought the review had been horrible. It was clear he didn't like me very much. So I had nothing to lose.

"Hey, I wondered if Dante was around?" I stood on my tiptoes to try to see out to the front of the kitchen, but I didn't spot him. "I really need to see him. It's important."

"I'm sure it can wait until later. He's needed here," he said firmly. I was getting frustrated now, so I decided to push my luck.

"No problem, I know you're busy. Just one more thing though. I wondered if you could tell me what that plant was that you had him give to me. A crazy thing happened to it and I wanted to try to get another one somewhere."

"I'm sorry, I have no idea what you're talking about. I have a breakfast service to tend to." He stalked off, leaving me there with my boxes of chocolates and a growing sickening feeling in the pit of my stomach. I left the chocolates and followed him.

"If I could just see Dante—"

He spun around and stood before me, arms folded: "I told you, he's busy." I noticed some of the other chefs looking on; a few stepped forward, giving the impression they had every intention of keeping me from going any farther.

"Fine then, I'll try later. Please tell him I stopped by." I knew he wouldn't tell him. Who knows what he'd say about me.

I was still fuming when I got to the gift shop—we needed bags for our deliveries—and I couldn't settle down. I wanted to stand in the middle of that lobby and scream, making everyone wake up and listen, forcing it all to make sense somehow. But I couldn't do anything that bold. All I could do was chip away, chip, chip, chip, and needle at these questions staring me in the face.

A new recruit, the one I recognized from last night as Seraphina, was behind the desk.

"Hi there, I don't think we've met. I'm Haven." I held out

my hand to shake hers but she made no motion, so I withdrew it. Angry and feisty, I just wanted to see how she would respond, assess how complete her transformation might have been. I couldn't help asking: "Hey, I had a question for Raphaella. Have you seen her around today?"

She just looked at me vacantly and smiled.

I collected the bags I needed from the supply closet and left without another word.

Lance had long since finished with the electronic invitations by the time I made it back to the office and we set to work assembling the twenty gift bags. We were both sequestered in our own private little internal worlds, when I started to get that feeling like I had when Aurelia appeared at the doorway. I looked up from my bag assembling, trying to gauge if Lance felt this shift too. He seemed content, so I looked back at my work. But then I felt his attention on me again. I looked up once more.

"Did you hear something?" he asked.

"Yeah, I mean, sort of."

"Like maybe a siren or something? I don't know, I'm jumpy today."

"Me too."

We had both gotten up now and left our tucked-away office. As soon as we stepped into the gallery's entrance near that glass wall, we could hear all the voices. We wandered out into the hallway and joined the guests and other assorted uniformed types like us, drifting over toward the main elevator bank. Sirens blared as an ambulance swung up into the front—there was already a fire truck parked out there. Two paramedics ran in the front door. Lance and I just stood there, still, trying to make sense of it all. Two firefighters wheeled a stretcher past the group, speaking into the walkie-talkies attached to their uniforms. A white sheet had been thrown over the body, but the man's head poked out. Lance heard me gasp, and put his hand lightly to my shoulder, as a reflex.

It was Neil Marlinson. His right arm hung down from the stretcher. His pale, dead fingers gripped the corner of a charred piece of paper. I knew, even from so many feet away, that this had to be Aurelia's note. One of the paramedics threw the sheet over his head and stuffed his arm back underneath. I backed away slowly, my hand to my mouth, trying to hold in my cries. Faster and faster I walked until I was running back to the gallery.

I sat in the corner of the office, on the floor, my back against the wall. But I could still hear the sirens. A dread set in, a feeling of failed responsibility I couldn't shake off: *This had been my fault.* He was dead. How could he be dead? I had just seen him. I had just been there with him.

I sat there on that cold floor, my head in my hands, unable to get that image of Neil out of my mind. Calliope and Raphaella had been nothing; this shattered me into a thousand pieces. How had this happened? What was going on here? I heard footsteps, a familiar shuffle, and I knew it was Lance. The feet stepped just inside the door and stopped. But I didn't want to look up yet, not until I could be sure my tears were finished.

"You okay? . . . It's a dumb question I guess, but . . . are you?" he asked, gently.

"I must've been the last person to see him. I was just in there. How did . . . ?" I couldn't finish my thought and couldn't get out anything that made any sense. "I just . . ." I wiped my hands over my face and managed to lift my head back up. I felt like I had to pick up these pieces of myself and rebuild me. Lance stood frozen in the doorway, arms hanging limply at his side, a knocked-out numbness in his expression. He dropped into the chair at the table, listless.

"So, people are saying he had a heart attack or something. Just died on the spot. One of the maids found him. But he seems young, relatively speaking, for that—I don't know, you're the aspiring doctor."

"Yeah. That's not it," I said. I didn't care. I would say it all now, everything I knew.

"And something caught fire in his room—not sure what that was about. The details are all sketchy. We'll find out, I guess."

I stood up in a flash and tossed the remaining boxes of chocolates and notes in the last few bags.

"We have to get out of here. Right now." I picked up as many bags as I could carry. I started walking out of the office and into the main gallery.

"Wait, it's freezing out there!"

"I don't care, I have to get out of here."

"I'm going with you. Let me get our coats though; it won't do any good if we get hypothermia. Gimme your keycard." He held his hand out. I squirmed, trying to redistribute the bags in my full arms so I could free my key from my hip pocket, but I fumbled with everything. He finally reached out and slipped it out of my pocket himself.

"I'll be outside."

"You're crazy," he said as he went back to pick up the bags I'd left. "I'll meet you in five, just wait for me."

I couldn't even think straight—I had been pushed too far and I needed to spill it all out of me, all of this toxic, toxic information bubbling up in me for too long. I just needed to be outside,

I didn't care how cold it was. I went right through the crowd gathered in the lobby and out the front doors, past the ambulance and fire truck and the police car.

In no time, Lance materialized, finding me on the side of the building, still gripping all those bags. He wore his parka now and had mine in his hands. The wind whipped through us as he took my bags from me and handed me my coat and keycard. We divided up the bags and began walking toward the L.

"I was the last one to see him alive. I brought that champagne up to him, that note. Did I do this somehow?" I didn't realize I was speaking out loud until he answered me.

"You're crazy, you couldn't have done this. I don't know what you're talking about . . ." He was talking but I don't know what he was saying. I knew his words were supposed to be comforting, but I was too busy turning everything over in my mind to pay much attention to what he was saying. That book had said to be careful who to trust. I'd have to take the chance that I could trust Lance, because I couldn't be alone in this anymore. I couldn't tell Dante right now, as much as that killed me. "Wait." He stopped, interrupting himself. "What note?"

We reached the L, ascending to the platform, the wind strengthening against us. A train had just pulled up and we raced on. The car was virtually empty, and warm, thankfully. He took a seat right by the door but I kept walking to the very back where there was no one around. He settled in beside me. Our parkas puffed around us like airy floatation devices; the many gift bags littering our laps felt like extra insulation. All of these empty seats and yet we sat right next to each other, with all of our stuff, and it didn't occur to either of us to move. I think we were both too relieved at being away from the Lexington to notice anything else.

For the first time in a while, I felt at ease, even on this noisy, rickety train.

"I have to tell you something—a bunch of things, a whole mess of things—and I need you to listen and not think I'm crazy."

He took a deep breath. "In light of recent events, I'm inclined to believe whatever you tell me—" When he said this, I perked up. "Because you may or may not possibly have saved my life by making me eat Lucky Charms today. So, lay it on me."

That hit me: "First, we're throwing away these chocolates when we get off this train. We'll keep the boxes but we have to find a CVS or something and buy other chocolates to replace these with." He didn't challenge me or ask questions, he just nodded. "And second: We're in trouble. Major life-endangering trouble." I paused to see how he took this. His eyes dove into mine, serious.

"I've been starting to get that idea lately." He pushed his glasses up on his nose, nervously, then took them off altogether and wiped the lenses with his glove, before putting them back on. I sensed a current of understanding pass between us. And I launched in, telling him just about everything: that we were living among devils, that the Prince was Satan himself, and Aurelia, Lucian, and Etan were like his cabinet. I told him that the Outfit were missionaries trying to gain more followers and that they had all sold their souls and were trying to recruit more, that some sort of revolution was in the works. I told him about the induction—"Sounds like honor society," he said, "except not honorable." The only major thing I left out was that I was supposed to have some power to stop it all.

When I finished, we sat in silence for a few long minutes. I could feel him processing all of it, his brain overheating. And then, with that perfectly steady deadpan response I found reassuring: "So, you're basically telling me that Raphaella wasn't after me for my charm and devastating good looks?"

I was glad for a reason to smile. "I didn't say that. I'm just saying that I'm pretty sure Lucian wasn't after *me* for *my* charm and devastating good looks."

"Well, that's his problem." It was very sweet and gentlemanly of him.

"Why do we let people like this have this effect on us?" I asked, somewhat rhetorically, but glad to talk about something that wasn't a matter of life and death even for just a moment. Lance wasn't the type to let any question of psychology go unanswered.

"I guess we often want what we can't have. Isn't that a most basic trait of human nature? Isn't that why, for instance, you girls always go for the bad-boy archetype?"

"Kindly refrain from saddling me with your generalizations, thank you. For the record, I'm never looking for the bad boy. There is no one more shocked than me that someone like that showed an interest in me. And really, I had no clue he was a 'bad boy' until I found out he was trying to steal my soul for Satan."

"Whatever you say."

"Maybe we should discuss why it is you guys always jump at the icy, glamorous girls, the ones descended from lines of giraffes and hourglasses who usually manage to show a lot of skin."

"Point taken. But, much like you, I would argue that this business with Raphaella was an anomaly."

"Speaking of, did you guys talk about anything that could help us figure—"

"We didn't talk about much, I'll tell you that much—" He cut me off.

"Ohhhh."

"No. No, I don't mean it like *that*," he caught himself. "Unfortunately. I just mean there's not much going on there, behind the façade of that giraffe and hourglass hybrid and everything . . ." He trailed off, looking past me out the window now.

I had so much to tell him. But he looked exhausted. I'd had much longer to try to accept it all. He needed to digest this before I threw more at him. I had to be patient.

24

Today Was . . . Unfortunate

Lance and I were all business the rest of the day, trashing those chocolates and replacing each one with far less pretty but far less toxic stand-ins from boxes we bought at a CVS, then scurrying around the city, on and off the L, uptown and downtown, dropping off the gift bags and invitations. I let him drop off the one at the mayor's office—I knew it would make him happy, even though he didn't actually get to meet the man himself. (Not because we were just lowly interns on a messenger run, but because the mayor was at lunch. He probably would have let us in because he was in love with Aurelia, like everyone else in this city, and her name granted us access to places where average folks didn't get to roam.)

We made our last drop-off—to the producer of a local weekly lifestyle TV show—in the Belmont part of town. I hadn't ever been to that neighborhood. At school I always overheard people going to concerts around here, or sneaking into the bars with their fake IDs; it was that kind of place. The streets were littered with music venues and clubs and hole-in-the-wall dives and vintage shops. Everyone looked too cool to hang out with us, but Lance and I were pretty used to that now thanks to so much time spent in such close proximity to the Outfit. Our pace had slowed since delivering the last of the bags, and even with the harsh wind at our backs pushing us ahead, we were at a crawl as we turned a corner, the steps leading up to the L platform now just yards away. Lance stopped first. Just stopped walking, right in the middle of the sidewalk with his hands tucked in his coat pocket. He looked like he wanted to say something but I spoke instead.

"I think we shouldn't go back yet," I said.

"Good. I don't really want to go back there yet." He sighed, relieved. "It's not like they're going to notice. There's a body to remove and a party to throw." He was calm, like me, arriving at this decision coolly even if there was absolute frantic fear behind it.

"And what do we have to do anyway?"

"Plan the friggin' prom?"

"The friggin' prom can wait." I smiled.

He nodded in agreement. "So, what now?"

"I don't know. You hungry?"

He shook his head. "I kinda feel like I might throw up."

"Yeah, I know what you mean."

"How about there?" He gestured with his hand still in his pocket, in the general direction of the thrift stores across the street. We crossed and stepped into the first store, all antique knickknacks, quirky old cuckoo clocks, phones shaped like ducks, and lunchboxes with pictures of TV shows I'd only heard of from the old edition of Trivial Pursuit Joan and I sometimes played. We browsed through the used books, but I could tell he was as distracted as I was. We just scanned the shelves and then walked past, neither of us bothering to pull down any tomes to bury our noses in.

We wandered out and tried the place on the corner, a three-story riot of sights and sounds, music blaring, racks upon racks of vintage clothes, shoes, accessories—everything anyone could ever need to look like they belonged in this neighborhood in any era between 1920 and right now. Lance peeled off toward the men's section, and I roamed over to the vast emporium of worn, beat-up jeans. Dante would've been happy to see me in any of these—I'm sure they all had more personality than what I usually wore. I pawed through them, not really much interested in going to the trouble to try anything on. I stood on tiptoe to see over the racks toward Lance, who looked surprisingly enthralled by a wall full of old T-shirts. It didn't look like he was in any rush, so I figured I might as well make the most of my time.

I walked up and down the aisles of racks, running my fingers over the clothes as the music pounded. I stopped before a wall of unisex accessories—hats and sunglasses and belts and messenger bags—and scanned it all. Maybe I could find something for Dante, anything to jar him into not being angry with me, to remind him that I cared about him and that whatever these other people were telling him, I was there for him. It gave me chills to think of Etan barring the way to him today in the kitchen. I had to get to him before they did. But I couldn't right now. Right now all I could do was try to find something special for the friend I loved—and whom I wished I could tell all the things I'd told Lance. I flipped through the vines of belts, figuring maybe he should have a new one since I was always borrowing his, and I found the perfect choice: black leather with red and orange flames running across it. It was just a little bit over the top, which meant Dante would love it. A fine peace offering. I bought it and found a cozy, decrepit Barcalounger surrounded by stacks of an alternative weekly newspaper near the front door. I curled my feet up and read, waiting for Lance.

Eventually, he bounced down the steps from the store's second level, plastic bag in hand. He plopped down in the weathered floral armchair beside mine.

"Who knew you were a shopper?" I said, pointing to the bag.

"Retail therapy, I guess." He shrugged.

"What'd you get?"

"They had these old tour shirts." He took a gray, worn Nirvana tee from the bag and held it up.

"Very cool," I affirmed.

"And then these, I kind of liked, or whatever." He held his hand up in a fist. On his wrist, he had two thin rawhide strings and a distressed brown leather cuff with two snaps as a closure. He shifted the cuff and something gold glinted. I leaned over to get a closer look and touched my fingers to the cool embedded bit of dulled metal: it was shaped like a wing, just like my necklace.

"Where did you find this?"

"Just in a big bin of stuff, up there." He gestured toward the staircase and shimmied into his coat. "I think I got the only one though. But there was other cool stuff in there, if you want to look."

"Right, no, I was just asking because—" I unzipped the top of my coat and fished around inside the neckline of my uniform, where it had gotten stuck. I pulled out my necklace. "I wear this, like, every day."

"Huh." He studied it.

"I guess guys don't really notice those things." I dropped it back inside my coat.

"No, but maybe it's a subliminal thing and I don't realize

I'm looking at that one all the time," he said. "Funny. Guess we match."

"Well, clearly we both have good taste."

He laughed. "Clearly."

We made our way back to the hotel, walking along the bone-chilling streets and up to the L, onto that rattling train and then back down to the street again. We barely said a word much of the time, but we were enmeshed in our comfortable brand of quiet. It occurred to me that it was possible to gauge how close your friendship is with someone by considering how easy it is to be comfortably silent with them. Those are the moments when you're most yourself.

As we inched along the block toward the Lexington, dusk falling all around us, my pulse began its nervous quiver. I heard Lance breathe out a sigh, unwittingly sharing in my dread. I searched my mind for anything I needed to get out before we were trapped inside again—inside where I didn't feel I could entirely trust the walls.

"Can I ask a funny question?" I said. He looked at me, giving me permission. "Why do you believe me? About all this stuff, you know?"

"Seriously?"

I nodded. I'd been trying to decide whether, if the shoe were on the other foot, I would have been as accepting as he had been today.

"I guess maybe, because, well . . ." He buried his hands back in his pockets and looked down at his feet as we walked. "I know it's not like we're friends like you and Dante or anything, but we're sort of the same—I get you. You're smart, and you're quiet unless you have something important to say. I feel like we kind of see things the same way. We think about things from every angle, maybe even too much. We don't just . . . go along with things. You know what I mean?"

"Yeah, I do."

"I've been wondering what's going on here for a while. They're paying us an awful lot for what we do," he said. "And they're weirdly permissive—letting us into that club, not really caring so much if we drink—they could lose their liquor license for stuff like that. There's always been something off about everyone. I'm kind of relieved that it's not just me who noticed. Maybe that's why I want to believe you. It's usually that everyone else is supposedly normal and I'm the one who's off," he said with a shrug of his shoulders.

"I know what you mean." I couldn't even say anything more; it was just so very true that it blew me away. That was exactly how I felt pretty much all of the time.

"Yeah, part of me knew it couldn't totally make sense," Lance continued. "So basically I'm just grateful someone has come up with some sort of explanation for it all . . . even if this is the explanation. I wish I didn't always overanalyze, but I guess that's just me. Wouldn't life be easier if we were stupid?"

I had to smile at this. "The stupid ones always look like they're having so much fun."

"Tell me about it."

"So you're not wired to just have fun either, huh?"

"I don't know," he said, embarrassed now. "I guess maybe not."

"I don't know what it is with me, but it never occurs to me to just enjoy anything. I'm always thinking days and years in advance. Like I tell myself I'll take it easy and kick back when

I get into college, but I know I won't—then I'll just work harder."

"Yeah, I wish I could flip a switch and turn that off."

"I always feel like the day I let up on myself is the day it all comes crashing down on me. And I guess I'll always feel indebted to Joan because who knows where I'd be or who I'd be . . . so I owe it to her to keep it together. Do you have that feeling?"

"Yeah, it's like the opposite of a sense of entitlement."

We both paused, staring off into space, lost in our own thoughts.

"Wow," I said finally. "We're messed up, aren't we?"

"No, we're just, you know, sixteen. And now we're living in some circle of hell and we're going to become slaves to Satan or just be killed." He said it deadpan, only half kidding.

"Yeah, that's another thing . . ." I couldn't quite let it go. "It's not actually a circle of hell—it's more of another tier of the afterlife that's coexisting with our reality."

"Sorry?"

"Remember when we finished that mural and there was that one panel called *Metamorfosi*?"

"Sure."

"That's like a level of transition for the Outfit."

He was quiet for a moment and then he shook his head. The awning for the hotel was at last in our sights. "This is how it's going to be now, isn't it?" he asked. "We'll be talking and then all of a sudden you'll hit me with something else that'll knock me out and we'll bat some ideas around and then move on to everyday stuff again."

"This is our new normal pretty much."

"Well, at least we're not boring."

*L*ance and I skipped the party that was in full swing in the lobby when we got back to the hotel. It was early, just after seven o'clock, but I felt like I needed to sleep. First, I called Joan to see how she was after her spa trip. She sounded like she was back to herself, but still very much entranced by the Lexington and Aurelia. After we got off the phone, I shut off the light and fell into bed, letting my eyes close. I had just started to drift off, the life slowly seeping out of my weary form, when a buzzer razzed me. My eyes snapped open.

"You're missing a great party!" Lucian's voice filled the room, annunciating each word with milky precision. It could have been a lullaby, if it hadn't startled me so much. I sat straight up in bed and flipped on the light, wondering if my dreams were speaking to me. But, no, it was that box behind the curtain; he was on the intercom. "Haaaaven," he cooed. "I know you're there, I saw you walk in earlier." The voice was sweet and seductive, requiring me to put up greater armor against it. I took a deep breath and tentative steps toward that box. "Haaaven . . ." it came through again. I pressed the button to speak.

"Lucian? Hi, I'm here. Sorry, I was just getting in. What's up?" This was my attempt at sounding easygoing, but I'm sure he could hear that pull of tension beneath my words.

"Good, don't go anywhere. I'm coming down to see you."

I had to pat at the burning scar on my chest; the ones on my back flared too. "Oh, I was just going —"

"Nowhere. Just stay there." The intercom clicked. He had left.

It would only draw ridiculous attention to myself if I tried to run away now, and he would just find me anyway. He would be persistent — he had been ordered to be. I turned hopelessly to the back of that book of mine, but there was no new entry. I was on my own. The knock rattled the door so much sooner than seemed possible. Three hearty knocks on the walls of my heart. I gave my room a once-over, stuffing the book back in the drawer of the night table and moving that chair from its spot barring the closet door. I went to let him in and before I got there, I noticed the door handle shake. It chilled me. But I opened up anyway and steeled myself.

"Hi, I was just about to —"

"I just needed to talk to you for a minute, hope you don't mind."

He came right in, closing the door behind him. There was an extra tremor in his voice, not as smooth as usual. The early sign of a storm rippling the surface of the sea. Casually, I backed up, hitting the desk and then leaning against it like I meant to perch myself there.

"Everything okay?" I asked, though I doubted I was the picture of calm collectedness myself.

"Yes, I just wanted to see if you were all right after the, um, excitement this morning."

"Excitement, right." That seemed to be the favored euphemism for death and general horror in these parts.

"I understand you knew that man."

"Well, he came into the gallery and bought a photo, that's about it. I brought it up to him right before —" I let it hang there, no need to finish.

He moved closer to me, standing right in front of me and staring in my eyes, diving into them, looking for something. But I had closed them off enough — he couldn't plumb their depths and make me lightheaded like he had in the past. Instead I held my gaze strong, giving the impression I wanted to keep him an arm's length away, though secretly every part of me would have loved for it to have been otherwise. But he didn't so much as brush his fingers against my hair.

"I like you, Haven," he said, in a way that looked like it pained him. "Is that so hard to believe?" I didn't answer. I didn't want to. He went on, almost talking to himself. "Maybe it is." He looked away for a second. "But I want to keep seeing you, I need to. I care about you, even if that doesn't make sense to you right now."

A buzz shattered the tension. We both jumped and swiveled our heads toward that box on the wall.

"Haven." Aurelia's rasp hissed out, scaring me enough that it made me lurch toward the intercom. I took a swift step and his hand clamped down on my wrist. He looked at me with a fur-rowed, worried brow. It looked like he didn't want me to answer her, but I was torn between evils. I went to the one I feared the most, pulling away from him. "Yes, hello, Aurelia, I'm here," I spoke into the intercom, still looking toward Lucian. He took a seat on the bed and ran his fingers over that flower on the bedside table: the flower he'd given me, still alive.

"Is Lucian there, by chance?"

Our eyes darted to each other. He had no expression, his face no more than a mask. Since he didn't indicate otherwise, I an-swered honestly. "Yes, he is, he just stopped by."

"Excellent, please send him back up to my office. I have some pressing matters to discuss and some people for him to meet." He hung his head and sighed, looking defeated. An escapee caught just before clearing the gates.

"Of course, Aurelia."

"Quickly please." And she was gone, the static snuffed out.

We looked at each other and he hung his head again. I could tell he didn't want to go.

"I guess you're being summoned," I said softly.

He stood up and ran both hands through his hair, leaving his hands atop his head as he sighed.

"Yeah, I guess I am," he said. "I have so much more to say to you, Haven." There was no flirtation behind the statement, but something else: concern? "But I should go now. I should go." He let himself out.

The minute he did, I thought for a moment and flew to the door to lock it. Still in my uniform, no time to change, I climbed up the ladder in the closet, heels and all, and made my way through that claustrophobic cave of a passageway. I gave up trying not to rip my stockings within the first few feet of crawling. By the time the passageway opened up and I could stand, my knees felt raw and burned. I kept going though, not letting anything slow my pace, and I made it to that peephole into Aurelia's office just as Lucian burst through her door.

"I see we don't knock anymore?" Aurelia said calmly, not looking at him. He marched in and threw himself against the love seat, sprawling out in a way that showed he didn't care anymore about manners or decorum. He didn't speak. "It's impolite to disappear when we're entertaining guests," she continued. "Need I remind you that half of the city—the important half—is at Capone right now, and you should be too?" He studied his tie, not looking at her. "Care to explain yourself at all? Do I need to worry about your loyalty to our organization?"

"You know where I was," he said.

"Yes, this is true. And I hope you were getting somewhere just now." She sounded angry.

"Well, if I was making any progress then you certainly put a stop to it."

"Well, were you?"

"You'll never know now."

"I'll take that as no. Don't play these games with me."

"You're the one who's playing games. After your stunt today I would put our odds very low that there's any chance of getting her. In case you haven't been able to gather, she's sufficiently terrified now and I think she's too suspicious to be wooed."

Aurelia sat back in her chair. And then spoke slowly, choosing her words carefully: "Today was . . . unfortunate . . . in many ways."

"I think that's a safe estimation," he sniped back, bitterly.

"But also . . . necessary." She was quiet for a moment, as though letting herself briefly surrender to thoughts she didn't want to face. "I, perhaps, failed to appreciate how the incident with—" She couldn't say Neil's name, so she backtracked. "—how events such as those of today would reverberate with our sensitive young prize."

"Yes, you did. You acted out of hand, and you know you did. You obviously had something to prove."

"That's quite enough."

"The bottom line is, I think we're scaring her now. I think *I'm* scaring her. She's now at war with herself. I'm certain she's still drawn to me, but she resists with great force. I don't want to say I have lost her, however . . ."

"Is that your official assessment? That she cannot and will not be won over to our side?"

He paused, weighing it. "Yes, I'm afraid it is."

"You do know what that means."

"I do." His words sounded heavy. I could only imagine this meant that things were going to be getting even more dangerous for me.

She sized him up, judging him, with a smirk. I should have been scared, jumping out of my skin at this whole talk about me, this plotting. But something else rose up inside: anger. Fury. It set my blood simmering. What had I done to get myself pitted against this? Why did everyone assume that they could manipulate me so easily? Why should it be a big shock that I'd be strong-willed against them? I could be a warrior too. I had come this far already.

"I'm not fully convinced," Aurelia said finally. "Back off for now. We will reassess as the first day of mass recruitment arrives."

He glared at her, his eyes bullets. "You want me to suffer."

"Maybe." She smiled, straightening the piles on her desk. "But you had an assignment and until it is completed in some acceptable manner, you can't walk away from it." And then, in an icy, accusatory tone: "You like her."

He said nothing.

"That's fine, I don't need to hear you say it to know it's true. It won't surprise you to know that I don't care. We need her soul above all others. We are on the brink here and she will be that one piece we need. Have you looked at your photo again? They are getting worse by the day. She took wretched ones at the Vault too—I had to remove the horrid things from the screen out front. Her soul-illuminating powers are strengthening and there's no telling to what degree her physical prowess is catching up." When she spoke this way, it still sounded like it was about someone other than me. I didn't feel that much stronger. Maybe my arms and legs were getting more used to all the climbing I was doing; my sprinting speed had improved but not to any shocking degree. "It will just be so much easier if we don't have to escalate this to battle. So we will reestablish her trust, and then we will determine our next course of action."

"Fine." He sounded disgusted. "Can I go now?"

She waved him off, calling out as he reached the door: "I'll see you out there. Don't stray too far."

But Lucian had already slipped out, slamming the door shut behind him.

25

We've Got to Do Something About Dante

Some sort of evolution had happened, and my fear and horror of this morning had metastasized into a ferocity that couldn't be reasoned with. It could have been the extreme fatigue that made me feel careless and invincible, but I couldn't stand to hear them talk about how they could so easily play me. I couldn't let them do to me or to Dante or Lance what they had done so swiftly and effortlessly to Neil. So, after climbing back down to my room, I ripped off my destroyed stockings for the sake of appearances, put my scuffed shoes back on, and made one more trip upstairs.

The kitchen of Capone had never been so packed and boisterous—or, at least, not on the rare occasions I'd trespassed back there. I wasn't allowed back here now either, but I shot through it, making a beeline for Dante's station at the front. As I walked, the heads of his fellow sous-chefs whipped to watch me and I heard them call out, "Etan! Etan!" Sure enough, by the time I got close enough to see Dante's dreads tied back in his pink bandana, Etan caught my elbow and yanked me, sharp and rough, back out the way I had come. A scream broke out from my lungs: "Dante!"

I saw him turn around. Everyone around us froze. I felt like the entire dining room heard it and I didn't care. Dante gave me a look of fear—I didn't know if it was for me or for himself. Then everything snapped back into place. He turned back around, the chefs continued cooking, and Etan tightened his grip.

"I'm afraid it's a bad night for catching up with your friend. Try another time," he said firmly, dragging me out with more force than was necessary. He tugged me with one incredibly strong hand and I noticed that in the other hand he brandished a gleaming meat cleaver. I stopped resisting and let him push me, leaving me with an extra shove outside the kitchen's back door.

When I got back to the lobby, I spotted Lance running toward me. He slowed to a walk as he got closer. We met near the front desk.

"Was that you? Is everything okay?"

"Whaddya mean?"

"Yelling?"

"You heard that?"

"I think everyone did."

I was about to open my mouth to respond, but he cut me off. "Look, there's no cereal."

"What?"

"The cereal, it's all gone, every box in the pantry, even the ones they keep in those bulk shipments—"

"Back in that closet off of the walk-in freezer?"

"Yeah."

"How is that possible?"

"I don't know. I just know there's more home-cooked meals left for us in the fridge and I'm not touching that stuff."

"Good, we can't. Who knows what they might be putting in there."

"But I'm ravenous. I mean, brink of starvation."

"I have a couple Power Bars and I have an idea," I said, walking back toward the elevator as he followed me. "Get your coat, we'll make a break for it."

"What's open around here, this time of night, besides the restaurants in the hotel?"

I led us around the deserted, desolate block—the neighborhood really cleared out at night, and I couldn't tell if it felt particularly creepy because of the things we'd started to understand about the Lexington or if it really just was a sketchy area. What little light there was illuminated the cold clouds our breath made. My bare legs went entirely numb. Eventually, after making almost a full loop, I found that dive bar I'd seen from the tunnels below the hotel.

The warm air inside heated our faces instantly as smoke billowed from every corner of the place, from the pool tables in the back to the bar up front. There were baskets of shelled peanuts on every table. I could have eaten thousands of them. But we hadn't even attempted to sit down at one of the sticky, beer-sloshed tables yet when a bald, middle-age bartender with a jiggling beer gut stopped us for ID, holding out his hand and shaking his fingers with an air of impatience.

"Could we just get something to eat?" I asked, trying to channel Aurelia by smiling in a way that might help our cause.

"Not if you're not twenty-one," he said.

"C'mon, we look twenty-one," Lance tried.

"You don't even look eighteen," the man countered.

"We're starving," Lance said.

"And surprisingly well paid," I added.

"Sorry. Move it along. Let's go."

We pleaded a little while longer, unsuccessfully, and finally gave up. I was getting that feeling again, my blood starting to bubble up, until I thought it might burst every capillary; I felt like I just might have the power to punch out a window or something. I was angry now, angry *again,* and I was sick of having to fight for everything: for food that wouldn't potentially poison me; for time with my best friend; for my life. We went back around the corner to the hotel, heads heavy with disappointment, stomachs painfully empty. I dug out a Power Bar for each of us. Lance took a seat on my bed and ripped open the wrapper, devouring the bar.

"You're so smart to have snacks. Why didn't I ever think to have snacks?"

"Probably because you thought we'd have access to food that wasn't going to cause us physical harm."

"Maybe so."

I took a bite of my own Power Bar and kicked off my shoes, tucking them in the closet and then stopped, thinking. "Get out of the uniform—"

"I'm sorry?" he asked, shocked and confused. He seemed to think I was flirting with him.

"No, go change into something comfortable and come back."

"What for?" He got up and went to the door.

"We're going on a snack run."

When he returned—in jeans and a sweatshirt—I had changed into a version of the same thing and I had the flashlight in my hand, my empty backpack on my back, and the panel in the floor of the closet already open. I had folded up the ladder and leaned it against the wall for easier access. Lance had his coat with him. I took it from his hands and tossed it on my bed.

"You don't need this."

"You still have this in here?" He put a hand on the ladder.

"We'll get to that later. Here's something I left out earlier today: remember how all those Chicago books talked about tunnels during Prohibition?"

"Sure." He shrugged. I opened the closet door wide and flicked my head toward it. He walked over and peered down then looked at me and said, "Seriously?" I nodded. He nodded back, impressed.

I warned him to watch his grip and footing, since it was easy to slip, and to take his time and then, together, we made our way down with that lone flashlight guiding us. I would have to get another of those. I led him down my usual path, pointing out the turn that would have led to the Vault.

"I have a secret too," he said then, a little nervous.

"Oh?"

"I know that one—behind the fire wall, right?" he asked. I couldn't disguise my surprise; my feet even stopped walking for a moment to look at him and consider this. "I found it when I was doing some work for Lucian one day, but I didn't get very far and had to go back. We're not the only ones who know about this. You know the Outfit—"

"Yeah, I know."

"We should just watch it, is all." He looked nervous now, recalling whatever had gone on when he was down here last.

"Did they see you then?"

"No, I ran, just booked it. You?"

"I hid."

"Bold choice," he said, with respect.

"Only choice," I said, trying not to let on just how terrified I had been.

"Well, for the record, if it happens tonight, I'm running."

"It was right around here actually." I pointed as we approached that crumbling room.

"Me too. What's the deal in there?" We both looked through the exposed wall beams.

"I'll tell you later, so you don't start running before we feed you."

"Good call."

We walked along together through the warm, musty passages. I could see Lance studying our surroundings, trying to figure out where we were in relation to the buildings on the block. He rolled up his sleeves and then unzipped his hooded sweatshirt and took it off altogether. He had his new cuff on his wrist—it looked nice, like it belonged there, even though I wouldn't have guessed he would have been the kind of guy to wear something so rock 'n' roll.

I shed my sweatshirt too—it was particularly warm down here today. We heard the first strains of very faint music as we reached that doorway into the pantry. We listened first, facing each other with our ears against that rotating panel that would be the way in, just in case we could hear any signs of rustling inside. We exchanged looks that said *It's a go,* and I pushed slowly through the creaky, nearly stuck doorway, Lance following.

Footsteps stomped above and the roar and glass clinking of the bar came to life at the top of that staircase.

Lance pointed. "So that's the place? Where we just were?"

"That's right. Let's make them sorry they didn't let us in. Stock up."

The shelves lining the space were piled high, and since I hadn't fully investigated last time, I was pleasantly surprised—there was more here than I would have guessed. The majority of nourishment did, naturally, come in alcohol form, and the general nutritional value of everything else wasn't much higher than that, but Lance and I moved through, filling up our arms with chips and jars of salsa and packs of pita bread. It wasn't the fanciest place in town and they seemed to have a small menu limited to greasy staples, most of which needed to be microwaved. The freezer was chock-full of bulk quantities of mozzarella sticks, onion rings, fries, but we didn't see any sort of appliance for heating these things. Still, the fridge held a few minor treasures and we took a tub of hummus, a block of cheddar cheese, and some Diet Coke. We would make do. We debated heartily over whether to leave some cash behind in exchange for what we took, and though we were irked at having been denied entry upstairs, we decided we could use the good karma so Lance made a small donation—wedging ten dollars under a bag of chips—just to be nice.

We wanted to head back up with our contraband, but we were too famished. We decided we needed a snack before facing that climb, so we set up a picnic on the outer banks of that dark hallway, in a spot where we could still catch the last of the light from the grand concourse of the tunnel. We ate frantically, silently for several minutes, but once we began to feel sated, we slowed our pace enough to talk again. Now that I had finally started to tell someone what was going on here, I couldn't stop. I wanted to unload more secrets every opportunity I had. It freed me to be able to share all of this with someone. I felt less lonely and less scared. So, I told Lance of the next place he needed to see, the passageway up to Aurelia's office. I told him about the induction I'd witnessed perched up on that catwalk. After I'd been talking for what felt like ages, he had to interrupt me midsentence,

"Before you go on, I'm curious. You asked me earlier why I trust what you're telling me. But why do you trust me?"

I thought back to earlier in the day, to Neil's death, to Dante's distance. But it hadn't been desperation that had gotten me to open up to him; there was more. I tried to put it into words. "I guess because I feel like we're alike."

"You just plagiarized my reason. That's the best you can do?"

"I can't describe it, it's just an instinct. And I generally trust those. When I don't is when I get into trouble." Lucian's face flashed across my mind.

"You just think I'm not smooth enough to be a double agent, right?"

"Not necess—"

"Because you're right, I'd be terrible."

"Smoothness is overrated—even if it takes a little while to fully realize that sometimes." We both laughed.

When we finished eating, we packed our leftovers and our emptied containers and discarded chip bags into my backpack to bring back upstairs—the last thing we needed was someone, or a pack of rats, to find this and make it even less pleasant to come down here. I had promised to show Lance one more thing before we climbed back up and I took him there now.

Together we pulled back the velvet covering over the photos.

"Whoa," he gasped, taking them all in. And that was all he could manage. We pawed through looking for his. When I came across Lucian's, I noticed that he looked slightly less gnarled and decayed than last time. His eyes had been restored to their gray-blue; you could tell it was him and not some horrific anonymous burned corpse. I kept looking through others, until Lance piped up, finding his and kneeling down before it, studying it.

"I held up okay," he said to it.

But I barely heard him. I located Dante's portrait and my heart stopped for just a moment. I leaned in closer to be sure and held out a hand to touch the new impurities that had crept onto his features. It sent a chill running through me. His smile dipped down a bit at the corners now and his eyes had dimmed—you would have to know him as well as I did to detect that. Much more noticeable, however, were those few fiery pockmarks that had surfaced; that was the way it had started with Aurelia's photo when it had turned.

"We've got to do something about Dante," I said, still staring at the picture. My voice came out flat, drained of all life. Lance got up and came over to look, standing just behind me. "They're getting to him. It's starting."

"We will. I promise," he said, his voice heavy, like mine, with concern, processing all of it.

We covered them all again and quietly, slowly made our way back up to my room. We made a plan to meet again tomorrow night like this so that I could acquaint him with the winding passageways up above my closet.

"Night," he said, as he was leaving my room. He rubbed at his eyes, underneath his glasses, weary after our long day. I looked at that scar. We were so much alike—I wondered about that now. "We'll figure all this out." He sighed. I just nodded.

The book was on my pillow when I got into bed, otherwise I wouldn't have bothered reading it at all. My entire body ached for rest. I hadn't even fully understood how I had made it back up that ladder from the tunnels. It had to have been the combined force of having finally eaten something and having Lance there. It was just a relief to not be alone.

I had changed into my scrubs, lain down in bed, and placed it next to me, propping it up with one tired hand. I flipped through and found the page with today's date and new words:

You are to be commended for your fire today, for your aggressiveness, and for your fearlessness in the face of horror. Don't be afraid of your rage. It is a safer feeling than that of fear right now; it is a greater motivator. But you would do even better to convert fear to shrewd, calculated action—that will serve you best of all. To be daring is good, but you need to be stealthy now as well. You need to filter all emotion down to an essence that can be tucked away, undetectable by others.

I got a shiver at that, this power I was supposed to have but just didn't feel. But it went on:

You must maintain the general illusion that you know nothing of what is going on there and that you are oblivious to anything and everything that seems even the least bit out of the ordinary. To those watching you, you should appear to work hard, take orders, and complete assignments with your usual care and quality. Secretly, you will continue your physical training with vigor and your information gathering with a sharp eye. When the time is right, you will assume a role of action, no longer concerned with maintaining appearances. You will know when that time has come and you will rise to battle and aim to conquer.

I turned the page and the writing got larger, displaying a new urgency.

You have reached a turning point in your evolution. You cannot go back, which is to say, most simply, that you cannot escape. Your duties and responsibilities would only follow you now, but along with them comes the opportunity for greatness in your ascension. I tell you this now as I deliver a harsh fact, but one you are entitled to know and must guard with supreme secrecy:

Haven, you will breathe your last mortal breath on May 27.

The book slipped out of my hand for a moment and I bolted up in bed. I had lost the page, but my fast fingers found it again so that I could read that line over and over. I didn't believe it, I couldn't, and I looked at it until the words and the curves of those letters didn't even look like a language I understood. I forced down the swirling nausea in my stomach, the beating of my heart against the cage of my ribs, and my mind racing to calculate the time between now and then: just three months. *Three months.* No.

I was sick of being told in the vaguest of terms that something was going to happen to me—and now *this,* this of all things—and not being told how to prevent it. I was sick of trusting in my supposed strength and I was sick of following these orders as though they would somehow amount to my becoming someone special enough to stave off all that was expected to come barreling my way. Why was this happening to me? When would this awful book give me actual answers? And again, as I read on, it anticipated my anger and arguments, which made me more angry and argumentative.

You are no doubt wondering more than ever who I am and why I am telling you this yet not giving you any tangible help. I won't hide myself forever but I will tell you this much now: I am not present in body there with you. I am not someone you pass in the hallways or spend your days with. I am with you only in spirit and through these words. But you and I will meet at some point, and in many ways, we already have. I will offer you the guidance you need to battle these demons, though I cannot take up arms beside you. But take heart, I know you better than any-one does. And I know you are acquiring the skills you need.

In many ways, we've already met? I thought.

But for the time being, keep your head down, blend in, and give them no reason to question you. Many lives are at stake, with you as their hope. Be strong, winged one.

That was it, the last of this heinous, haunting missive. Involuntarily, my hand pushed the book off the bed, sending it crashing to the floor. That date would not leave my head though. It danced and taunted me. Above my heart, that scar flared to a fiery beast and the two on my back, usually so benign, enflamed like dry kindling.

I curled up in a ball, closing my eyes, trying to make it all disappear, burying my head in my arms. My eyes squeezed so tight I saw bursts of light. My breathing echoed in my head and ricocheted around my body. If my eyes had not been pinched shut so strongly for so long, minutes and hours marching by, I wouldn't possibly have dozed for even a moment. But finally at some point, I felt myself drifting. My body had no choice. My aching bones and muscles and speeding mind had never cried out for rest so desperately.

But there was no peace: as soon as I slept, I dreamt. That same nightmare came to me, the members of the Outfit decaying as they grew nearer to me, trudging down that hallway. But this time, they were led by Lucian, who flickered between the withering subject of the photo and the beautiful creature I had once fallen so instantly in love with.

The next morning, I would have been comforted to have found that Neil Marlinson's death was all over the news, that no one was buying the official statement that it had been a heart attack. But the poor man hardly got a footnote in most of the stories. Everyone was too busy writing volumes on the success of Capone and the celebration over its three-star status. One blog did manage to make greater mention of Neil than the party, and that one—by a writer whose name I recognized from our delivery yesterday—I printed along with the others and placed in the stack for Aurelia, putting it third from the top. I thought little actions like that were a fair way to quench my newfound thirst for acting on what infuriated me while still appearing to be simply doing my job.

It didn't concern any of the hotel's guests either, or at least, not for long. There had been some interest, but Aurelia had been so skilled at expressing regret while diffusing the whole thing in a "these things happen" and "our staff rushed to his aid and did everything right" sort of way that her spin soon made it seem not the least bit newsworthy. Instead, it crossed over into the realm of folklore, entertainment. As I walked through the lobby that morning to Aurelia's office for our usual meeting, I was even stopped by a trio of guests queued up near Capone waiting to get in for breakfast.

"Excuse me, miss?" the woman had called over to me.

"Good morning," I said to the group. "Can I help you?"

"Is it true?" one of her male companions piped up.

"Was it the ghost of Al Capone who killed that guy?" the other man asked, eyes wild with excitement.

"Is this place really haunted?"

It took me a moment to formulate an answer—and stifle the shudder that came as a reflex—but then I smiled. "We should be so lucky," I said, permitting myself that bit of boldness. She just gave me a nervous grin, not understanding in the least. "Have a good day."

As I walked away, I heard the woman say, with glee: "I knew it!"

But I had woken up determined to somehow not look shaken and fragile today, despite what I had read last night. My mind went in directions that made no sense to me now—it had been overloaded with images and information that were all so much out of its realm of understanding that it was short-circuiting and processing things in a way I couldn't have imagined. I found myself thinking again of that painting at the Art Institute. The one that felt so familiar that it was like unlocking a memory of my own. When I had looked at it, I could feel myself as a child lying at the bottom of that hill on the side of the road. It gave me chills thinking that I could end up the same way now, my body and soul discarded, left for dead after facing down the forces at work against me here. But there was something strong, powerful in the girl in that painting. An underlying sense that she hadn't gone gently. Nor would I. This would be a fight.

In Aurelia's office that morning, I didn't have the same dread. As I sat before her, handing her those printed press clippings, she didn't impress me. I had a secret now, a deep one, and at least I knew she couldn't really hurt me today.

As she paged through the printouts, I couldn't stop myself from saying, "Quite a lot of excitement yesterday. Both good and bad."

"Yes, the party was quite a success, though it's a shame about our sweet art enthusiast. These things happen, regrettably," she said coolly and then went about her business dictating what needed to be done. My attention waned a bit as she droned on about the chocolates and notes to be sent out, some new artwork that one of the Outfit members was working on to replace the empty wall so the gallery could eventually reopen, and then the prom planning, which would now be our primary project. I had been preoccupied with all of these other swirling thoughts when something she said jerked me back into the present.

" . . . so yours, Evanston High School, will be held on May 27. It will be the first of the five proms."

I gasped. Hearing that date out loud, knowing its new importance to me, I felt it chiseled into my head, shattering me.

"Oh, I'm sorry, Ms. Terra, do you have a previous engagement? Does that date not work for you?" Aurelia said with pure condescension.

"No, of course not, I just mean . . . that will be here in no time."

"Indeed. So you and the other one—"

"Lance?"

"Lance, yes, will want to get started today, speaking with your classmates who have anointed themselves in charge, getting the planning begun. Decisions need to be made relatively soon to have everything ordered and prepared."

I just nodded, regaining my composure. Before leaving, I tested my nerve once more. There was a question that, if I didn't know all the secrets I did, I would have had to ask. "One last thing," I said, on my way out the door. "Just wanted to let you know I'll continue taking photos of the Vault tonight, since you wanted to keep those current at the front—"

"NO!" she blurted out, before her usual stoicism could take over. It was the reaction I had expected and I got a thrill out of watching the blood rise to her skin. She looked like she wanted to yell and scream but, of course, she couldn't. "I don't think we need you to do that. It was getting too busy on that screen, so we've condensed the slide show."

"Oh, okay, great," I said, so innocently. It would be little skewerings like this that would provide light moments to what were sure to be dark days from now on.

When Lance and I reconvened in our gallery office, I filled him in on my new strategy to try to keep up appearances and he agreed. I didn't breathe a word about that awful date though — my expiration date. Instead, I just hoped he wouldn't notice me cringe or tremble as we began planning the prom festivities. He probably wouldn't since we both had plenty to cringe about on that front. We agreed to each take two of the five schools, and to share the burden of our beloved Evanston High together. Lucian had given him the full packet of all the names and numbers we needed to plan these magical nights. Lance flipped through quickly and groaned.

I looked up from my writing. "What?"

"Guess who's prom chair."

"Please don't make me guess when the payoff is just going to be someone who makes me want to throw up."

"The insipid Courtney Samuels."

"Ugh. It's a good thing we're both handling that one. I couldn't take it alone."

We both shook our heads.

We spent the rest of the day quietly studying those school files and familiarizing ourselves with the vast array of options available for prom night, from mocktails to main courses.

Before packing it in, I went to the cabinet that housed the camera — it was, indeed, gone, and all the uploaded photos had been removed from my desktop too. But most terrifying of all:

back in my room, I discovered that my own camera, that old one I had brought from home, had gone missing from my backpack. I hadn't taken it out since I'd arrived here. Someone had to have swiped it.

Lance and I, being people who appreciated finding order even amid life-threatening chaos, quickly settled into a solid, unassuming routine. Each morning we ate a breakfast of Power Bars and dry cereal stashed in our rooms (along with bottled water and Gatorade). We took our respective meetings with Aurelia and Lucian and then delivered our notes and chocolates, always replacing them with store-bought substitutes first. Before returning to the confines of the hotel, we would treat ourselves to a mammoth lunch fit for a carbo-loading marathoner while we were still out among civilization. We took turns choosing the location, though Lance seemed content to pick Giordano's for stuffed pizza nearly every time. In the afternoon, we made our calls and sent our e-mails to our peers at the five schools whose proms we were planning, presenting them with all the necessary options for DJ's, menus, colors, flowers, favors, and then making note of their decisions.

At night, though, our real work began. Each evening we would go running together through the tunnels below. Back and forth, racing each other and building our speed. Sometimes we would even climb up and down those wooden planks under my closet a couple of times just because we knew it was good for us. It helped that we were so relentlessly competitive with each other, just as we had been with our duels over who knew the most Chicago trivia when we first started at the hotel.

As the weeks went by, I could feel myself getting stronger, my arms and legs firming up; it would take longer for me to feel wiped out. I saw myself improving at a more rapid clip than when I had been doing this alone. Besides, it was nice to hear footsteps other than mine in those quiet corridors. The sound of our breathing and the squeak of our sneakers as we ran side by side became a most peaceful brand of white noise. And then there were the small rewards—we always ended these sessions with a snack pilfered from the pantry of our favorite bar, never taking so much that anyone would notice. We brought backpacks down to carry our savory treats back up above and we would eat quietly, madly, sitting on the floor of my room, exhausted but proud of ourselves.

When Lance and I weren't racing through the hotel's underbelly, we were off climbing through the winding passageways within its walls. Each night, following our tunnel-sprinting workouts, we would find our way up the ladder in search of secrets. Sometimes, there was nothing to see in Aurelia's office. But other times, we would hit it just right, eavesdropping on another tête-à-tête with the Prince or the planning of another induction. Lance crouched on that ledge overlooking the ring of fire, transfixed as he watched one of those rituals for the first time. Afterward, we stayed up until dawn talking about what had gone on—or rather, *he* stayed up talking and I stayed up listening. I got the feeling he just needed to rehash every detail because it had been such a sensory overload: the pomp and circumstance of it all, the slicing of the fingers, the signing of those contracts and the sacrifice of one of their own, escorted back down to the underworld. It was, to be sure, an awful lot to take in. I took solace in knowing that this had all rattled him as much as it had me.

But there was even more to fear as time went on. The Outfit

was expanding like mold. There were so many new souls joining the ranks that we couldn't begin to keep them all straight. One new Outfit member in particular seemed to be recruited as a replacement for Calliope. Her name was Mirabelle and within the first two weeks of being inducted, she produced no fewer than a dozen paintings, Chicago landmarks deserted and cloaked in darkness, gardens in moonlight haunted by shadowy figures, eerily lit boats along the river. The paintings all shared an unsettling air of mystery that fit seamlessly in among the other gallery works. They went up along that wall that had once held my photos and the gallery reopened to plenty of foot traffic and local acclaim. Mirabelle was quickly trumpeted with write-ups in the *Tribune* and the local society magazines and on some well-known art blogs too. As soon as a painting would sell, she would have a new one to replace it the next day. Her productivity was both staggering and, of course, humanly impossible.

Ever since that night in my room, Lucian had kept his distance from me. Occasionally, I would catch him looking over from across the lobby as I passed by, or he might come into the gallery office to give us some bit of prom-related paperwork, but otherwise he kept off my radar. Though I would be lying if I said my ears didn't still hone in on the sound of his voice—a reflex that would take some time to fully fade.

The biggest mystery, though, continued to be Dante. He hadn't yet shown up at the latest induction, which was a relief, nor had he signaled he was ready to take that step by cutting his hair, but it seemed only a matter of time. His only attempt at interaction with me and Lance became the constant stream of food he left for us, three meals a day each, in the fridge in the Parlor kitchen. We would take turns taking out the plates, mashing up the food and making it look like we were eating (putting on a show for any sous-chefs working around us), and then eventually throwing it down the sink or burying it in the trash when they weren't paying attention. We knew that this wasn't our Dante trying to hurt us. It was a poisoned version, but our friend was still in there somewhere—we just had to find a way to pull him out.

I didn't give up trying to talk to him. Once a day I attempted to get to him in the kitchen of Capone, and once a day, I got manhandled by his fellow chefs and thrown out. They never said a word to me. Etan would call over from his station, "He's busy, come back later." And then, with firm faces, the few of them would clutch my arms—which now were permanently bruised—to lift me up, my legs scissoring, and drag me away, so strong and swift that there wasn't even time for me to make a real scene. If Dante had any idea this was going on, he didn't show it. Whether I snuck into the back of the kitchen or brazenly marched in through the dining room and into the front, he never so much as looked in my direction. It was like he was in some sort of invisible sensory deprivation chamber, where all he did was cook brilliantly and perform for the crowd of diners. Lance and I didn't know where he was spending the hours when he wasn't in the kitchen, but we imagined it was with Etan.

So months went by in this fashion, exhausting months of us settling into our strange, eerie new normal. My book gave me nothing new in these months, no guidance, no warnings of what was to come. I called Joan weekly now, and I e-mailed too, trying to give her the impression that everything was fine, but sometimes it made it worse to hear her voice—it made the clock seem to tick louder and faster. I couldn't help it. I lived teetering on a shrinking ledge knowing the date would come when I would be forced to fall.

Part Three

⚮ 26 ⚮

You're a New Woman

It was a Saturday at the end of April, and the icy chill that had frozen the ground and air for months was beginning to thaw, ushering in spring and all the dread it promised, when I stood on the sidewalk outside the hotel waiting for Joan. She had been unbelievably patient since that harrowing surprise visit, and now, after I had put her off as long as I possibly could, I had to gird myself to handle all of her questions, all of those typical parental curiosities, in a manner that would somehow not arouse more suspicion. I had to seem completely at ease.

Lance waited with me outside, making small talk as I kept an eye out for that beloved beat-up Camry. Aurelia had granted me permission to have the afternoon off with a wary look even when I told her I would be spending the day with Joan. Lance, admitting that he didn't like the idea of being trapped in the hotel all alone all day long, asked for the afternoon off to visit his mom too.

"Remind me to show you the latest e-mail from Courtney," he said now, kicking at a rock on the sidewalk. "You won't believe how many different, incorrect ways she spelled *hors d'oeuvres* within the span of a single paragraph."

"She can't spell my name either." It was true. And sometimes she called me Holly. I was suddenly glad not to have been at school these past few months. Although, this was, quite literally, its own form of hell, wasn't it?

"How did she get into honors English?"

"Couldn't tell ya. I'm surprised she can read at all."

"They're just letting anyone in those classes these days."

"There she is," I said, almost to myself as Joan pulled up in front, waving furiously, happily. I waved back.

"So, back around eight, you think?" he asked, taking a few steps away. He adjusted his glasses, a giveaway that he was feeling anxious.

"Probably. You too?"

He nodded.

"Sure we can't give you a ride to the L?"

"No, I'm good," he said waving and then, because he was still polite even in his shyness, he leaned down, just enough to see inside the car when I opened the door, and put his hand up in greeting. "Hi there," he said.

Joan began talking a mile a minute. "Why hello! You must be Lance, so nice to meet you. You're welcome to join us. We're just headed off to the mall." I rolled my eyes: she always was overzealous when it came to me and friends. Lance just said a shy *thank you* and walked on, backwards a few steps and then in the direction of the train.

"See you later," I said as he cast his eyes away, putting his hands in his pockets.

Joan threw her arms around me in a bear hug the second I shut the door.

"Come 'ere, you. Oh, how I've missed you!" She kissed me on

the cheek. "So, Water Tower Place? I think there ought to be a lovely selection there."

"Whatever you say." I tried to sound excited. She had been hounding me for weeks about how we needed to go shopping for a prom dress before all the good ones were gone, and I had finally acquiesced because, well, why not? I might as well at least be wearing something I liked on that day. The questions came fast as we drove through the bustling sun-streaked streets.

"So tell me everything. How's work? Are you eating? Are you sleeping? You look different. Oh, I feel like it's been ages. I've been trying to give you your space, but there were so many times I almost hopped in the car to surprise you again—that spa treatment was just divine. I don't like how you've been sounding, you know. You shouldn't be that tired."

"Oh, wow—" It was a lot to take in at once.

"So, how's Dante?" And now the rush of queries stopped, leaving plenty of airtime for me to answer. Unfortunately.

"Um, he's doing really well, I think. He's getting a lot of attention for his work in the restaurant. He's sort of a big deal," I answered carefully. I didn't want to lie but I couldn't quite tell the truth. "We kind of have different schedules, and he has a bunch of new friends so I don't see him as much these days. He's working a lot."

"Good for him." Joan noticed my gloomy expression and said, "Oh, Haven, c'mon now. I know he loves you. Let him have his fun. Ruthie says he's having such a blast. Be happy for him."

"Oh, you talked to her?"

"Ran into her in the supermarket the other day," she said as she pulled into a parking garage. "I hope we don't have to go too far down like last time. Why are all these people up so early to—"

I cut her off. "What did she say? Ruthie?"

"Oh, yes, just that he was having a great time and meeting some wonderful people. He sounds very happy. Here we go!" She pulled into a spot.

I supposed it was reassuring that Dante was, at least, managing to call his mom, despite whatever was going on. But I still wished he was talking to me. We locked up the car and headed in. Joan threw an arm around me as we walked toward the elevator.

"I know, I know, you aren't the least bit interested in this, but come on, it'll be fun. Macy's, here we come!"

"I really like this one, honey." Joan sat beside the three-way mirror outside my fitting room. I looked at my reflection in the full-length fuchsia number but I just wasn't convinced.

"I don't think it's me."

"None of these are going to be you, dear, because you don't wear dresses."

"I wear a dress every day now, actually."

"Oh, that's right, your uniform! It's just darling. I almost didn't recognize you when I saw you in it that day!"

"It's fine. Can I take this off?"

"It's very va-va-voom," she said as a compliment. "Look at this figure! I do believe you've got some curves." She sounded impressed and squeezed my bicep. "Is there a gym there? Have you been lifting everyone's luggage?"

"No." I tugged at the dress. Every garment so far had been hitting me differently than I expected. I was filling them out in a way I wasn't used to. I guess I hadn't noticed the change so much because it had been so gradual to me. But where I had been soft or scrawny, I was now firm and strong, with taut, rounded little muscles. I almost didn't look like me.

"Okay, okay," Joan gave in. "I can tell you won't be comfortable in it."

She had taken one of everything off the racks—jewel tones, sexy black numbers, long dresses, short dresses—as I trailed her, giving vague, noncommittal answers to her questions about the color and shape of what I wanted. I was at a loss. I waded through the sea of gowns of every hue bursting off hooks in my fitting room. I'd already tried and vetoed nearly half of them.

"There's got to be something you like in there," Joan called in through the door.

I shimmied into another one and took a quick look before I emerged. Well, this wasn't so bad. I opened the door and stepped out toward the big mirror.

"Yes, there's my little angel!" Joan clasped her hands. "Gorgeous, dear, so perfect with your skin tone. I love this!"

I cocked my head to the side, considering it. Not the worst choice, even though I wouldn't have expected to like it. I smoothed it out and discovered hidden pockets on the side. I slipped my hands inside and studied myself. An A-line dress in a shimmering metallic pearl shade, cinched in at the waist and hitting above the knee. Oh, and it was strapless, with a sweetheart neckline. This didn't escape Joan's notice. I could see her debating internally whether to mention it.

"It's neat that it has pockets," I said. "I sort of like this one." Even with that scar in full view, nowhere to hide.

"You should, it's stunning," she said, wheels turning and then, gently: "Does the neckline bother you? I know how you feel about that . . ." She trailed off.

"No, actually." I looked at myself again. For once, it didn't seem to matter quite so much. I had so much worse to consider on May 27. The scar wasn't my favorite thing about myself, and I sure didn't love the two on my back either, but the dress looked pretty, and it was about time I stopped worrying about things that I couldn't change. Let people look away if they're bothered by it. I would never be perfect. I would never be a member of the Outfit. But I looked good. "I like it."

Joan nodded, looking at me with eyes curious for an explanation but not wanting to rock the boat. "Good." She stood up and kissed me on the top of the head. "Then we'll take it."

And we did, along with a pair of strappy, high-heeled Mary Janes, which Joan was impressed I could walk in. "Hav, you're a new woman," she marveled. "You're in heels, you're going to the prom, you're still wearing that necklace I got you." I touched it now. "This all must be the influence of that glamorous boss of yours or something. You'll have to thank her for me."

"Right, I will," I said, barely believable.

We spent the rest of the day catching up over lunch—where Joan filled me in on all the gossip at the hospital—and then strolling Michigan Avenue, browsing and window-shopping until the sun went down and it was finally time for her to take me back to the Lexington. She helped me get my shopping bags from the trunk and gave me a hug, ordering me to take pictures at prom. I didn't mention that I no longer had access to a camera. I said I was sure I'd see her again before then and that we'd talk, and then I gave her another hug, a strong one, not wanting to let go. I felt my eyes well up, but tried to push the tears back.

"You know, it's perfectly okay to be homesick," she said softly. "It doesn't mean there's anything wrong with you. I know you always think everything is a sign that you're not perfect enough.

But it's okay." She put her hands up in surrender. "There, that's all. Gotta let the parent do her parenting sometimes."

"I love you, Joan, thank you so much, for everything," I managed without tears.

"I love you too, sweetie. Fun day. We'll have more of 'em when you aren't working so hard here. Summer is just around the corner. Beach days at the lake, get ready!"

I nodded, smiling and hoping. Hoping so much that I would be there.

I watched her drive away until the last traces of her taillights were out of sight, and stood out there on the sidewalk in the chilly evening air until I had convinced myself that May 27 was going to be okay because it had to be. I would survive it and I would prove that book wrong. I would do whatever I needed to, whoever I needed to fight, no matter what was required of me. This was a game that I was simply going to have to win.

When my hands and feet began to grow numb, I joined the masses pouring into the hotel for their dinners and their drinks and their evening excitement, but that was my prison. As I cut through the bustling lobby with its piped-in jazz music making me wish I could be transplanted to another time and forget all of this, I felt his eyes on me. I permitted myself a quick glance as I passed that hallway behind Capone, the one that I had floated out of after our dinner that one night. And there he was in the shadows, folders of some sort stacked in his hands, looking like he was going somewhere and had momentarily lost his way. He just stood there watching me; I averted my eyes, fast, picking up my pace toward the freight elevator. I missed the good Lucian, the one I went on those few dates with and flirted with, who made me feel special, even though it probably was just an act. The heart doesn't make these distinctions. Mine only knew that it had felt a pull to him and then it had been so disappointed by who he was and by how false his feelings had been. When the elevator doors swallowed me up, I felt relieved.

And lonely.

A look at my watch, however, comforted me: 7:55. Lance ought to be back.

Of all the unexpected and bizarre occurrences I had braved during those past months at the Lexington, I was least prepared for what happened as the prom and that singularly tormenting date on the calendar inched closer. I sensed it the minute I hit the one-week mark. When I woke up that morning, with only seven days separating me from the specter of potential death, I felt a seismic shift in me. My eyes sprung open that morning, wider and more alive, more alert, than they had ever been, taking everything in in a way they hadn't before. Every one of my senses was newly invigorated, intensified, reporting even the most minute bits of data back to me: the scent of whatever delicious buttery, savory poison wafted from Etan's kitchen at Capone as I tried again to talk to Dante; the embellished notes of the trumpet playing its jazzy swing tunes over the lobby's sound system; the caress of the velvet curtain as I brushed past it through the gallery's door; the taste of our pilfered chips and salsa, and our quiet satisfaction, after Lance and I absconded with goods from that bar's pantry following another grueling workout in the tunnels.

It was a strange thing, to be hearty and strong and yet to know that you had so little time left. Instead of being defeated by the weight of that knowledge, something new took over, this desire to outlive everyone each day. Your minutes burst with productivity and perception; everything looks and feels different. I knew something was coming for me, I knew I was as prepared as I could be, as strong as I had ever been in my life, physically and mentally. And I knew that I would just work until that day came to piece together a way to stop it.

Lance and I had done a reconnaissance upstairs looking to see if there was anything on which to eavesdrop, but had found nothing so we ran our laps. We were fast now, neck and neck at breakneck speed. It never ceases to amaze me that when you put time into something, at some point, without fail, you start to see results and reap the rewards. We climbed back up with our snacks and chatted about the latest on the dreary prom planning.

"I still don't understand how Courtney and all of them picked 'Hot for You: The Great Chicago Fire' as the theme," I said.

He shrugged. "It was on the list we gave them."

"Yeah, but we were kidding when we made that one up."

"Well, I guess, joke's on them. Personally, I thought, for sure, they would pick the Roaring Twenties. Three out of five schools prefer Roaring Twenties."

"I know. I mean, hello?" I shook my head. "At least we don't have to get a real cow."

"I believe the theory about the cow starting the fire has been debunked by historians anyway."

"I think it's pretty much just that they want those drinks en flambé, right?"

"Pretty much."

We were quiet for a moment. I imagined he was thinking what I was.

"In all seriousness though," he started, his tone heavier now.

I knew what he meant without even saying it: it was clear, from all of our snooping and poking around, that Aurelia and company intended to buy souls in bulk at these proms, and they would no doubt be pulling out all the stops to do it. There would be plenty of likely contaminated food and drink, and the Outfit would be working the event. It didn't matter what our feelings were toward the people we went to school with, we couldn't just let this happen. I hadn't yet told Lance about the book's warning for me. I don't know what I was waiting for, except maybe I didn't want him to worry or to treat me like I was suddenly fragile. I actually felt less fragile than I ever had in my life. So I would wait until I absolutely had to tell him, if that time came at all.

"I know. We're running out of time. We've got most of the pieces but we just need to know how they fit and how to stop it." I picked up a few crumbs from the carpet and began collecting our empty chip and pita bread bags and jars. We exchanged looks.

"Try again?" he asked, standing up and brushing himself off.
"Yep."

And we ascended the ladder again. This had become a recent addition to our routine—if we didn't find anything on the first go-round, we would take one more look before calling it a night. Sometimes we would even go in shifts. Lance was particularly diligent and could disappear up there for incredibly long stretches of time. It was nice to divide up the work.

This time up there we had more success. Aurelia and Lucian were in her office in their usual places: she at her desk, he on that sofa. But instead of being sprawled out, not caring, as I'd seen many times, this time he sat upright. I found out why a moment later when the Prince came into view. He had been right up against the wall with our peephole and now he stepped away, pacing.

"Yes, so we have a week, but I have to warn you—every day they become harder to control. I . . . I don't know what they may be capable of," she stammered slightly.

"Come, now, my pet, we mustn't get too upset," the Prince soothed.

"I know, my liege, but the photos, they're getting worse by the day. I can't take it." She let the desperation creep into her voice, throwing her hands up, exasperated.

"Then stop looking at them. Or, stop looking at yours, since that's what you really care about," Lucian said, coldly, almost under his breath. She ignored it.

"It's a sign. Her powers, her soul-illumination skills are getting stronger."

"You could always destroy your photo. Of course, that would be suicide."

"Lucian." The Prince faced him, his name snapping out like a serpent's tongue. "I'm not sure what has come over you, but it's time you remembered your place." Lucian averted his eyes from this wrath as the Prince looked to Aurelia again. "You're well aware of the soul illuminator's unique trap. She holds the key. You cannot destroy those marred photos yourselves, as the subjects, or it would be death for you. If you want to erase these photos, we have to destroy her, or win her soul."

Aurelia gathered herself, upright and professional. "Lucian has proven unsuccessful. I propose we remove him from this assignment," she said.

"I'm just not sure she can be swayed," Lucian said slowly, weighing his words.

"Very well, then that is it for her," the Prince said easily. My hand shot to my mouth to stifle a gasp. Lance looked at me with wide, worried eyes. "She either joins us or we kill her. It's that simple."

"My liege," Aurelia started. "She's too valuable to us. I think she may not yet know what she is. We may have to be more direct with her, present her with her options, *sell* this life to her. I will try once more and then, if necessary, we pounce. We can make a decision on the other two when we've chosen our path with her."

"All right, try then," he agreed. "But Lucian, if you are forfeiting her, then we will need to see better numbers from your recruiting among the masses."

"Yes," Aurelia concurred, with a smirk. "I'm afraid you're actually not accomplishing much at all these days. Why, our overall numbers are increasing exponentially but Etan and Beckett and Mirabelle are doing the heavy lifting."

"I assure you I will redouble my efforts," he said, his voice hissing but dulling to a pained whisper.

"Yes, you will," the Prince said, with ease. And then with a nod of the head toward both of them, he disappeared, a fiery ring flaming around him on the floor and then extinguishing itself just as fast. Before Aurelia could say a word, Lucian burst up from his seat and stomped out, slamming the door with such strength that even Lance and I felt it, jumping at it in unison. We crept back out. That had been plenty for today.

That book began speaking to me again later that night. For the first time in weeks, I looked in those pages and found today's date written in. I didn't know whether to be relieved that I had a guide again or worried—if it had wisdom to impart, it meant I must need it. I curled up to read:

Prepare to be bold and fearless. You have nothing to lose now and it is time to begin asserting your strength. Let your adversary know that you are something to be reckoned with. Stand tall, be firm, be forceful, and trust yourself. It's time.

The funny thing about that book, even when it wasn't speaking to me in specifics, even though I wished it could just spell everything out for me instead of forcing me to figure so much out on my own, it was still oddly comforting. Sometimes it just helped to be reminded that there was some force in the universe that seemed to have my back and seemed to think that I could make it through. I needed all the support I could get, wherever it was coming from.

27

I Need to Talk to You

After what we had glimpsed in Aurelia's office the night before, I shouldn't have been surprised that she answered the door the next morning when I arrived and said, "Come, it's time for your performance review." She pulled the door shut behind her and marched in sharp, scissoring strides to the Parlor. A manila folder was clutched to her chest—I wondered what could be in there. I scurried along behind her and then caught up, matching her stride for stride. I stood tall.

A table—the same one where we had sat together that one morning when I first started—had been set for us. We both took the same seats we had taken before. The kitchen door burst open and out came one of the girls who had received a necklace at the first induction ceremony I had witnessed and . . . Dante. He carried a tray with two small teapots and two teacups. The girl had two multitiered trays stocked with all manner of sweets and baked goods. While Aurelia was busy giving the girl marching orders for the rest of the day, Dante served me. When he placed the teacup in front of me, his eyes looked in mine. They were the eyes I remembered and had missed, vibrant and dancing.

"I hope everything will be to your liking," the girl said to both of us. Dante stood quietly beside her then they both disappeared behind the kitchen door. Aurelia began pouring her tea and as I grabbed mine, I spotted something inside my cup. Written in honey but with such precision and delicate lines he seemed to have used a quill, Dante had left me a message: *Library Tomorrow 10 p.m.* My eyes shot back in the direction of the kitchen, but he was long gone. I tried to conceal my joy. I don't know what had happened, but I was getting my friend back. I poured tea into the cup, dissolving the message, but simply knowing it had been there warmed me and gave me an extra push to power through this meeting. Whatever would come my way.

Aurelia took a sip of her tea, steam rising from her cup. At least this time around I had a better understanding of why she liked things so hot. "Before we begin, I wanted to show you this." She pulled a magazine out of the folder and handed it to me. On the cover of *Chicago* magazine, next month's issue, Aurelia stood, arms crossed, eyes gazing out. Beside her was a silhouette of the hotel, except it was made up of dozens of smaller photos, put together in the shape of the Lexington. I looked at these pictures and saw so many familiar faces: Dante, Lance, Etan, and lots of members of the Outfit. Sprinkled in were a few candid shots of guests at the Vault. Near the top, featured prominently, was a photo of Lucian, but above him, at the very top . . . was me. Me in my uniform walking down the lobby. I couldn't even imagine when it had been taken. From time to time through these months, we had had various professionals on hand snapping pictures for one reason or another—more since the opening (and since I was taken off of photography duties). This one of me, surprisingly, looked pretty good. Across the bottom of the cover it read: "Rebuilding a Landmark."

"Wow!" I couldn't help it, it just slipped out. I flipped inside to the story and found more pictures: some that I had taken of revelers at the Vault; a shot of me with Lucian; me with Aurelia on the night of the opening; and even Lance and me on our matching ladders painting that mural. "This is . . . nice," I said, trying not to sound too effusive. Aurelia looked pleased with herself though. My scars were as hot as that teacup.

"You'll find we say some very nice things about you in there. Go ahead, you can keep that copy." She gave me the broadest and warmest of smiles.

"Thank you." I set it beside me on the table. "I look forward to reading it." I was jumping out of my skin.

"Good. Now, I'm sure you're aware that this prom season marks the beginning of the end for us."

"Yes." My mind parsed that sentence for its full meaning. Did she know that that particular date was one I feared? *Calm down,* I scolded myself. *You have to maintain an air of serenity, like she does; it shows power.* "Time flies when you're having fun," I added, a little too dull in delivery to be believed, but with a renewed strength behind it. Not wishy-washy, no girlish smile. Progress.

"Yes, so I thought it only right that we have our performance review today, since there's so little time left."

"All right," I said. My whole body braced for what might come at me.

"First I want to say, you have done a fine job here. I think you already know that."

"Thank you."

"Truly extraordinary work in the gallery. Your photography is"—she corrected herself—"was beautiful before, you know . . ." She seemed sorry to have gone down this path. "You've done excellent work in handling our customers and media clients and in keeping me informed of what is being written about us and so forth. And I understand you're doing exceptional work planning these prom events for the schools."

"Thank you."

I could tell from the tensing muscles in her delicate neck that this was not going as she had hoped. She seemed to have expected to find me more eager and striving, the way I was the last time we sat in these seats. But she carried on.

"I have said this before and you'll see I say it in that article: I see you as my protégée and I see you playing a major role in our organization here."

I said nothing. I just stared at her with a serious expression. She studied me for what felt like a very long time and finally I saw something change in her eyes. She leaned in, her shoulders less rigid now, easing.

"You may not feel that you entirely understand what goes on here. You may not feel you entirely understand . . . me." Her voice came softly, slowly, a shift I had trouble processing. "But I understand you, Haven." She paused as though deliberating how much to share. "I was you. In every sense I was you once." She had said something like this when we had first met at this table, but then it was full of bravado. Now there was a wistfulness, a vulnerability, behind it. I didn't want to believe it, or to take it in and let it rattle inside my brain or heart, but it caught me so much off-guard, this side of her.

"I was like you: focused and thoughtful and serious and unsure. I had my goals and feared being overlooked as I pursued them, as I'd been overlooked in other aspects of my life." She sat back in her seat, looking somewhere over my shoulder, thinking. I just sat trying to gauge how to read this—as truth or some sort of act?—trying to reconcile this conflicted figure with the woman I'd watched command such dangerous men in her office. My mind was jumbled. I didn't know this Aurelia and I wasn't prepared for her.

"I wanted power, influence, and a home, a place that was all mine that others wished to be on the inside of. People like us never have a true home," she said, and I couldn't quite be sure what she meant, but could only guess that she never had a Joan in her life. "I was tired of feeling my nose always pressed up against the glass looking at these perfect lives of those around me. I wanted others to be looking at me this way instead. I didn't want to be invisible, as I imagine you don't either." I gave no reaction.

Undeterred, she continued. "I didn't fit in either. For one reason or another we all get sized up and sorted out and some of us get left behind. So I retreated into my world of art and music and history, my escapes. I dreamed that one day, rather than being mocked for my interests, I would be celebrated for my taste, my world would be the one everyone would wish to be part of. Boys can be heartless, yes, but girls can be truly cruel—when they either feel you are not like them or, worse, if they sense you're actually somehow better than them. I suspect I don't have to tell you that." I looked away for just a moment. "And when presented with options by a tall, dark stranger, I decided I didn't have it in me to take the time to reinvent myself—to go to college and hope things would turn out differently, hope to find people like me. I wanted change now. I haven't looked back since . . ." She paused, then added, "Hardly at all. There are, of course, bumps in any road—" She took a breath, then began once more, slowly. "—and choices that require certain . . . people . . . to fade into the distance. But this is what life is." Neil, that was it. So she was thinking about Neil.

She leaned forward now, lowering her voice in a way that couldn't help but get my attention. "But I was also . . . *marked,* if you understand what I mean." I shuddered at this, even though her tone was more gentle than she'd ever been with me. "There is no easy path for us—*that* you need to know. There is no purely easy, clean, good path, none without casualties. So we just have to choose the one that will allow us to reach our full potential. There are pros and cons to everything."

I couldn't remain silent any longer. "Some are greater than others though," I said quietly, though just as gently. She looked away.

"Of course. And my path was not perfect. But when you are someone who strives for everything, to have everything, you make sacrifices. In turn though, you reap such rewards. And we deserve these things." She tapped the magazine. "You must know that."

"I suppose I can imagine." I was completely thrown off. She had never been more compelling. It was impossible not to be affected by her letting down her walls, this rare glimpse into her past.

"That said, I would like to extend an invitation to you to join the Outfit, Haven. And it is my great hope that you will accept."

I had no words. I could feel the troubled crinkle forming between my eyebrows. Finally she continued in the same sincere, softened tone, speaking to me like an equal. "You would be our youngest member, and in time, very little time, you will be our most powerful member. It is that simple."

Before I could attempt to speak, she rose quietly from her seat.

"I won't ask you to answer now. You may tell me the day before your prom. Kindly think it over." She rose from her seat, smoothing her dress. She took a few steps to leave, but stopped just behind where I sat so still and puzzled. She leaned down to me, her hands on those precise spots where the scars burned on my back. "And, Haven," she whispered, "please think very, *very* carefully."

As soon as she left, I shot up from the table and ran all the way to the gallery to find Lance in our little office. I told him every word.

Every night I had begun diligently rereading the entries in the book in the time between finishing up our work and before beginning our nighttime adventures in the tunnels and the hotel walls. At our appointed time of ten o'clock, without fail, Lance would knock on the door. I would let him in, we would each have a Power Bar from our oft-replenished stash, and then we would start climbing either up or down.

But the knock came so early tonight—it wasn't yet nine—that it startled me enough that I looked out the peephole before answering. I was glad I did. It wasn't Lance at all; it was Lucian. My whole body went numb. Standing there in his perfect suit, he looked back over his shoulder as though worried that someone might come up behind him. He tapped his foot and fidgeted with his hands. I held my breath, wondering if I could simply not answer, pretend I wasn't there, have him go away. My morning with Aurelia played in my mind. Why was he here? Had he been sent to take care of me? I heard my name through the door, not in that usual seductive tone, but softer this time, almost a whisper: "Haven." I said nothing. I just backed up slowly, trying not to make even the slightest sound. The door handle began to jiggle. That was all it took: my legs sped off, to the closet, flinging open the door and diving down into the passageway in the floor, climbing down into those depths so fast that I could hear my heart beating. But loud as that was echoing in my ears, it still wasn't enough to drown out the lock clicking and the door creaking open upstairs and the unmistakable shuffle of foreign feet invading my room and then that voice softly calling my name again:

"Haaaven?" It stopped me in my tracks, halfway down that ladder. A fever rose over me and I was paralyzed against it all. I couldn't move. "If you're in here, please don't be scared. I'm not going to hurt you. I just need to talk to you."

My mind flashed to the scene I'd left above. I remembered pulling the closet door behind me, but I hadn't shut that door to the passageway. I tended to leave it open in general, out of fear that its tight hinges would stick and leave me trapped below every time I went exploring. Do I climb back up and try to shut it now? It seemed too risky. I couldn't get myself to move up, but I slowly forced my legs to creep farther down, as quietly as possible.

I could still hear his footsteps. I hoped he would give up and leave, but then they stopped. A streak of light sliced through the opaque passage. I gasped. "Haven, I know you're down there. Will you listen to me for a minute?" In a flutter, my legs scrambled down farther, my footing sloppy, my fingers snagging at the boards. A crack and whoosh filled the air above me. I slowed enough to look up and Lucian was descending so fast, so agile, he seemed to barely be touching the boards at all. He was gaining on me. My feet hit the ground too hard, stumbling, and a stinging grip grabbed my upper arm like an iron shackle. My stomach dropped. *Trapped.* Another arm looped around my body and held me, my back to him, his hot breath in my ear.

"I'm not going to hurt you. Will you please trust me? I know you have no reason to, I know this. But please, please don't run away." I nodded, a nervous nod, and he loosened his grip. With that tiniest release, I wound up my right arm just enough and jabbed my elbow quickly into his chest.

"OW!" he barked, hurling forward and letting me go in the process. I was free. I ran just a few steps, enough to make it to that open doorway, through which scraps of light from the few bare bulbs of the tunnel had penetrated enough to catch us in a murky glow. And I stopped. Because he had. I backed up against the crumbling brick wall beside the doorway and let my guard down just the slightest. Hands on his knees, he stood hunched over, wincing, and looked up at me. "Nice shot," he said.

"Thanks."

He straightened up, slowly, stretching. "And I deserved that."

"What do you want?" I asked, anxious to get on with it, even though I was terrified of the answer.

"I just need to talk to you. I'm sorry for letting myself in . . ." He reached into his breast pocket and pulled out a card that must've been the master key, then returned it to its place. "But I just didn't think you'd let me in otherwise, and it's vital that I get to see you tonight." He squinted, it seemed, with concern. Eyes locked on mine, he took a few steps forward.

"Why?" My words stopped him in his tracks. "What do you need to tell me that's so important?"

"I know about your talk with Aurelia today—" he started. "I know she wants you to join and I also know that you're probably not going to."

"You're not going to change my mind."

"I've known that for a while. That's why I've been giving you . . . space." He faded to a whisper. I could hear the catch in his voice, the sorrow. I could hear it, but I couldn't believe it.

406

"Then what do you want?" I almost hissed it. I wanted him to go away. I wanted to go back up to my room, alone. I didn't like being trapped down here with him. And he made me angry now; all I could see before me was this beautiful thing that I had fallen for and that had manipulated me. The past couple of months I had tried to avoid him as best I could, pretending he didn't exist, though that's not the easiest thing to do. Even in a hotel this big, you're bound to run into the person you least want to on a daily basis. It hurt me to look at him now because my heart still remembered every second of that kiss the night of the opening. That kiss had still been the most remarkable couple of minutes in my entire time here. It made me ill that it had been with him.

"You have to listen to me," he said slowly. "Believe me when I say this. They are going to try to kill you, Haven. As soon as you formally turn them down, they're going to just come after you. Stall as long as you can. I don't know exactly when, I just know they will kill you and you have to be careful," he pleaded, his tone dripping with fear.

"I know," I said with as much fortitude as I could, wanting those two words to carry enough weight to prove I could handle whatever was going to be unleashed upon me.

He looked at me, confused. Then his eyes scanned our mysterious surroundings, this dingy entry point to the underground labyrinth.

"Yeah," he said finally, hanging his head with guilt and shame. "I guess you've figured out a few things, haven't you?" I nodded, coldly. "I have so much to tell you, Haven, so much."

"Why should I trust you?"

"That's a fair question. I don't know that I have any answer that will convince you."

"If you're the one who's been sent to kill me then I'll fight you. Don't think I won't. And if you win then it'll be on your conscience." I stopped for a minute. "I guess you don't really have a conscience, do you?" I almost found that funny, almost. "Well, I feel sorry for you then."

"You're right to be angry."

"Yeah, thanks. I am."

"I owe you an apology and a lot more." He stepped forward again, farther into that dull glow, and stared off into the darkness, as though figuring out where to begin.

I decided to put it all out there. I had nothing to lose. "Just in case it changes your mind about killing me—"

"I'm not here to kill you." His face scrunched up at this, truly hurt by it.

"Well, I might as well tell you. I really fell for you." I tried to say it as matter-of-factly and as emotionlessly as possible. I noticed my fingers starting to fidget. I picked at my cuticles with nervous energy, but couldn't stop. His eyes found mine, but my eyes darted away, fixating to the side of him. It was just easier. "And it's pretty embarrassing that I was just some sort of assignment to you."

"That's not true."

"Whatever," I snapped. "I don't feel like listening to you lie to me some more."

"Okay, you may have been . . . at first . . . before you came here. That was the plan. I go after you. Etan, Raphaella, they had their targets. But whether you believe me or not, this is true: you . . . charmed me," he spoke slowly now, struggling to find the right words. "I was—I *am*—enchanted by you." He let it hang there in the stagnant air for a moment before going on.

"I find that hard to believe. Considering what you're surrounded with here."

"No, it's true. You should see the way your eyes watch the world and everything around you, like it all has something it's telling just you. There's a spark there; when you look at any of us it makes us feel like there's so much we don't know and we want to know, like you're taking us in and we're the only one in the room. I'm not used to that, to someone being engaged like that. I mean, you've seen the Outfit. They may be beautiful but they're essentially robots, most of them, drained of life. But you're real, and I promise you that my feelings, no matter how this started, were real. You surprised me, Haven Terra." Now his voice fell to a whisper, and his gray eyes got far away. "You made me regret everything, made me second-guess what I'm doing, what I've been doing. And that's something I didn't know I was capable of feeling anymore." He shook his head. "But this is where we are now. And this is why you will trust me: since I can't be with you, since you won't have me, I will do everything I can to help you beat them, even if it kills me in the process."

28

I Want You to Win

Lucian paused for a moment, probably to let that sink in with me. I turned it over in my mind: he knew that I couldn't be swayed to join the Outfit and that it was possibly a suicidal decision I had to make, so now he was sacrificing himself to me. "This is how I will make it up to you, this is my gift to you, and please accept it with my gravest apology. Tell me you forgive me or I won't let you go." He had said that line to me before. Back then, he had said it almost flippantly. Nothing was really at stake. But now, lead laced his words giving them an ominous weight, and a thin, teary mist clouded his eyes, sinking my weary heart.

"I forgive you. I do," I said softly, but firmly.

He breathed out a deep sigh of relief. "Can we start over?" He held out his hand for me to shake. I realized I'd had my arms folded, and I gave him one last is-this-a-trick? look. But he looked sincere. It occurred to me that my scars were silent. I placed my hand in his, giving him my strongest grip. "Thank you," he said. I nodded. "So, if you want, if this is where you're comfortable, in these glamorous surroundings you've led me to

. . ." He checked my expression to see how his attempt at humor had gone over, but I held steady. "We'll do this right here. Actually, this is probably a pretty good place to chat." And with that, he began unbuttoning his suit jacket. "Aurelia hates it down here—and if she had known that your room connected to all this, she never would've put you in there, by the way." He slipped off his jacket and spread it out on the ground beside where I stood. "And the others are only permitted down here on special assignments, so we ought to have it to ourselves." He took a seat on the concrete floor, gesturing for me to sit on this makeshift lily pad he'd made for me. "Please." Reluctantly, I took my place on his jacket on the hard floor, and there we sat, watching each other like we were strategizing in a presidential war room. "How should we do this?" he asked. "You probably have a lot of questions. I'll tell you what little I know of the immediate danger and then you can fire away. Good?"

"Okay." I studied him, prepared to take in absolutely every word he said, to burn it into memory and extract from it every bit of knowledge that could possibly aid me.

"It's probably going to happen around your prom, even though you would think she would wait until all the proms are over because there's much for her, for us, to gain from these events. But she's impatient and sometimes she makes a decision based on emotion rather than strategy. That's a great weakness. She'll be offended and furious when you officially tell her you won't join. She's delusional and used to getting her way so she's still holding out the hope that today might have swayed you. So she'll act fast even if it isn't smart for her. I believe you know about the photos, don't you?"

I nodded.

"They changed because your powers are just beginning to form. It's impossible for anyone other than you to know what your powers will be, but based on this, you're already what we call a 'soul illuminator.' You can expose anyone's true nature. What that means right now is, always trust your instincts because they're right."

Something occurred to me and I cut in: "Did you take my camera? The one I brought with me?"

He looked away, all the answer I needed. "I'm sorry. Aurelia ordered one of the Outfit to do it, but I thought at least if I did it then it would somehow be less intrusive."

"Right, a kinder, gentler theft," I said mostly to myself. "How'd she even know—"

"Aurelia had your things searched the day you got here—"

"Of course she did." I sighed.

"But that was even before she knew about your powers and all, so she didn't know what she was looking for then. Well, she knew that you had extraordinary powers, but she didn't know you're a soul illuminator." He looked pained. "But maybe I can make it up to you with more secrets?" he offered.

"Sure." I gave in. "Here's a question: so, my picture is changing too. What's the deal?"

"It must be telling you something about yourself, about who you are."

"And your picture? I saw it and—"

"It started to change back a little, right?"

"Yes." I didn't understand.

"I saw that too. I didn't think it was possible. That's your influence on me, if you can believe that. I haven't taken a soul in weeks. You make me want to be better than I am. All of my regret shows in that picture now . . ." He sounded appreciative, as though I had done something. "The photos show the subjects' true souls, that's why they're so disfigured. If you destroy their souls, you send them back to hell. So you need to slash those or burn them or do anything that will harm the photo itself and in turn harm the person pictured."

"I'll go right now then. What am I waiting for?" I burst out. But I was scared.

"You can't. Here's the problem: there's a small window when you're able to do this. You can't go after them until they come after you first."

"Who made up that rule?" I shot back, angry.

"No one made it up, it's just how it works. It's like the sky being blue. You could go right now and stick a knife in the hearts of every one of those photos and nothing would happen."

"Okay, so after I get attacked or whatever, then I slice these photos, but what about mine or Lance's or Dante's? What if someone does the same thing to ours?"

"Unless they've sold their souls to us, they—and you—can still only be killed the old-fashioned way."

"Well, that's reassuring."

"All three of you will get tougher to kill as your powers set in, but we don't really know how strong you are yet. Do you?"

I didn't want to give anything away, so I simply said, noncommittally, "I'm not sure," which was true.

"Well, you'll find out soon enough, I'm afraid," he said, sincerely sorry.

"So then all these people die?" I didn't want this on me. I didn't want to be responsible for the deaths of anyone, no matter what monsters they were.

"They were dead the minute they sold their souls. When you kill members of the Outfit or one of . . . us." He stumbled on the *us*. "We don't die, per se, we just get turned over to the underworld. Everyone here is part of the upper class of the underworld—that's why we're allowed to be here at all, in this transition realm of Metamorfosi. It's a privilege. But if we fail here and are 'killed' then we get banished to the underworld and must do our time moving through the circles of punishment below. Then the Prince—you know the Prince? He *is* who you think he is—"

"I know."

"He determines whether we get another chance to continue our work up here."

He stopped for a moment. I had thought I heard my name being called out, but figured I had to be imagining things. But then the scratch of sneakers against the boards of the passageway made us both jump, and I couldn't ignore the sound of someone else breathing the same stale air.

"What time is it?" I asked.

He glanced at his watch: "Five after ten, why?"

I rose to my feet. "Lance," I whispered.

"Will he just go away?" Lucian asked.

"No, and I won't let him," I whispered back. "Give me a minute."

I crept back through the darkness to where the ladder emptied out.

"Lance? It's me," I called out. In what little light filtered all the way down from my room, I could see his form getting nearer. And then it halted.

"Haven?" The beam of a flashlight zapped in my direction.

"Hi," I said, squinting into the musty air.

"Are you okay?"

"Yeah, I—"

He started moving again, flashlight still on, dangling from

his wrist now. "I knocked and there was no answer, so I—" He reached the last plank and I gave him space. "I thought I'd better come looking. You know your door was unlocked?"

"Sorry!" Lucian called out from the opposite end of our room in near darkness. "My fault."

The flashlight shined at me again, like an interrogation lamp.

"Are you okay?" Lance mouthed the words this time, whispering with practically no sound at all, his eyes registering the shock.

"I'm fine," I whispered back calmly.

"Should I ask you hostage questions?"

"No, I'm good. Promise. But maybe a rain check for tonight?" I kept my voice as soft as possible. "I'm doing recon."

He looked skeptical, straightening his glasses. "Is that what they're calling it these days?"

"I'm serious," I said, a little bit miffed. He eased up.

"You're sure everything's okay?"

"I swear."

"Come by afterward, just so I know, okay? I don't care how late it is. Not like I'm sleeping much these days anyway, you know?"

"I will, promise. See you later?"

He nodded back and with one last look in Lucian's direction, began his ascent.

Lucian was on his feet, pulling something from his jacket pocket when I got back. He looked up and tossed his jacket back on the ground, holding the small item toward me.

"Sorry, I forgot I wanted to get rid of this. I took it back when I was upstairs." In his hand was that single black flower that had never shown any sign of withering since he gave it to me in February. "It's poison," he said sheepishly, tossing it in one easy motion out into the tunnel.

"I know."

"You never got rid of it though?"

"I figured whatever it was, it wasn't working."

"Yeah, your immunity set in earlier than anyone expected." He gestured back toward where Lance and I had been talking. "He's a good guy, a lot like you."

"I know." And I did. He felt like a part of me.

"I asked him today, you know, about joining the Outfit." He settled back down, lounging on the floor now. I returned to my spot on his jacket.

"What did he say?" I asked, though I didn't need to.

"What do you think? He thanked me and said he would think about it and get back to me, but he didn't really mean it. He's smart; he's trying to buy himself time."

Lucian and I sat there talking until nearly dawn, barely noticing as the quiet hours passed. It was as if the clock had stopped and the night had gone elastic, stretching to accommodate however much time we needed for me to learn everything I possibly could.

True to his word, Lucian answered all my questions. And I had many. *How had we ended up here in the first place?* One of them, a representative of the underworld, sat on the state's Board of Education. Each county had a program like this, and we had been recruited first because we had something that they wanted, that could be used for their purposes—all three of us had powers on the verge of taking shape. *What's this revolution that they're recruiting for?* It's a movement underground to gain a foothold here. They wanted to take over, be free to create chaos—that's when they're at their most joyous and exalted. Death, destruction, war, madness, they thirsted for it, that's all they wanted. "Now that I'm starting to feel again," he said, "I can see how this must sound, but you get rewired when you become part of the underworld, and the things that make you happy aren't things you would ever have expected. You crave these things, you need them."

He was impressed that I had witnessed an induction. He did explain a few mysteries: the tattoo was infused with the blood of the Prince, and it corrupted the bodies of the Outfit and changed them to devils from within. The necklaces and cuffs were given later after members had established themselves and signified greater responsibility while also giving Aurelia and the Prince greater control over the wearers, the ability to track them wherever they roamed and also maim them when necessary. "These precautions are necessary when our members are in the realm of Metamorfosi but not when they're returned to us below."

"Then what happened with Calliope?"

"She escaped at exactly the moment when her necklace lost its hold over her, when she was supposed to return to the underworld. But she ran. That had never happened, hard as it is to believe. The necklace generally keeps a balance regulating the flow of the devil's blood from her tattoo, keeping it from destroying her instantly. But when Beckett cut that off, then she withered fast. And she knew that would happen—she must have planned to die on the front steps of the hotel like that. To send a message." He shook his head, like he really did mourn her loss. "Beware of Beckett. He's gunning for my job now and I suspect it will be his . . ." He trailed off.

I didn't need him to finish that sentence. I understood that with each word he was sealing his own fate more securely. My greatest confusion was how a soul was actually bought and sold. He chuckled when I asked, which I took to mean he was making fun of my naiveté—it must be some highly sordid or prurient act, things I knew precious little about.

"I don't really appreciate the laughter," I said, scowling.

"No, it's only because it's so much easier than anyone would ever imagine. No two are acquired the same way, but it can honestly be set in motion simply with a verbal agreement."

"Oh," I said, embarrassed now.

"Yeah, so you're the one who needs to get their mind out of the gutter," he joked. "It just requires the expression of a deep wish, whatever it is, and then the willingness to give up everything in order to have it. It's that simple. We can't seize a soul by force. A person has to give it willingly. You must go of your own volition to the dark side. And once you do, once you say you would do anything, give anything for something to come true, it's mostly done. There's a process called coding that proves to us the soul is ready to be taken over and then it's all sealed with the blood and the tattoo. Then you're fully controlled.

"No two are seized the same way, each is a new deal. Now, there are ways that we entice. As you found, judging from your supplies upstairs," he said, his voice heavy with regret, "all the food and drink is infused with certain enhancers to impair judgment. Even the flowers in the lobby have powers to help influence and break down defenses. And"—he looked away now—"I would be lying if I said there wasn't, at times, some sort of show of . . . affection that went along with these proceedings. But that's not all the time and when it is, it's more just added color, not any requirement necessary for the transaction of the sale."

"So I wasn't so off base after all," I said coldly.

"But nothing is final until they sign their contracts. That seals their fate."

"Well, isn't that just so . . . civilized."

He could sense my patience waning again and the anger creeping back in, I could just tell. And it's true, I felt stuck in this cycle, wanting to hear all of this and yet unable to listen to it without these emotions flaring up, much as I tried to bat them down.

"I have a question for you," he said soothingly, breaking me out of my simmering fury. "Do you know what you are?"

"I think I might. But it seems too unbelievable."

"It's true, Haven." He leaned in, watching my eyes, in the hazy light. "You are still learning, but you are an angel, in every sense of the word." He was quiet for a moment. When spoken out loud, those words had such certainty to them. In my head, they made no sense at all, but to have this said to me now, I could accept it. I could take it in as the truth, as the missing piece that would unite all the disparate bits of my life that hadn't made sense. "That's what those markings mean on your back. And then the one above your heart too."

"How do you know about those?" I knew that one had been visible in that photo of me, but I thought the ones on my back had been covered the whole time I'd been here.

"I know, because I had them too." It would've been enough to just hear that we shared this, but his use of past tense struck me and he must've read it on my face. "A few years ago, I was just like you. I was marked for good, and I could have gone that way but I wasn't strong enough. Aurelia got me. So here I am. When you make the choices I've made, those markings go away. Everything that's the least bit imperfect on the outside goes away, but inside, you just rot, you begin to resemble those photos. Aurelia had the markings too, you know."

"She told me that." So it had been true.

"That's why we rose through the ranks. When you have those you are marked for power, to lead. You're far beyond the level of the Outfit. But *you* determine whether you become angel or devil. The Prince got to Aurelia years and years ago. And then she came for me. Two years ago, I was graduating high school in Des Moines," he said, clearly amazed at all that had gone on since that time.

"So what happened?"

"I just fell into this. I was kind of a prodigy, I guess. I graduated early and by the time I did, I was already taking a bunch of classes at the university. With AP credits and stuff, I entered college with the status of a midyear junior."

"Whoa."

"It's not as great as it sounds. In high school people didn't really get me. I kept to myself. In college it was already starting out to be the same. Just me in the library. Speaking of the library, most of those books in the one here are mine." My eyes bulged at this; he kept going. "So, Aurelia showed up and—" He stopped. "You sure you want to hear this?"

"Yeah, I think it's good for me to hear." I needed the whole story, no matter how much I would hate hearing it.

"So she, of course, was assigned to target me. I met her at a party, one of the very few I attended. I had been there twenty minutes, talking to no one and—"

"How does that happen?" I had to interrupt; he had lost me. "How does someone like you walk into a party and not have anyone to talk to?"

"That's the whole thing. It wasn't this version of me. It was me without the fancy clothes and the confidence and the reputation. All of that stripped away."

"Go on." It was still a stretch to imagine, but I tried.

"So, she went after me, and that was certainly something new for me, and I got swept up. She seemed to have this inside track on how I could be this awesome and powerful person and build this whole scene here. There was just, you know, this little catch. But by that time, it was too late—I had already tasted enough of this exciting new life to get addicted to the power and the instant gratification of it all. I had felt invisible before. If you go the dark way as Aurelia and I did, you quickly fade away from your former life. You get a new name, a new identity."

"But don't people wonder where you are? Don't they try to find you?"

"The groundwork is set long before the induction happens, the gradual pulling away from family. When possible, they prefer to recruit those who might be going off to college or are already on their own. The ultimate goal is to get the city's richest and most powerful sucked in, but for now, they're just building numbers any way they can. Often, those remaining behind are led to believe that their loved ones died. But the 'inductees' never know any of that—by then they're too wrapped up in their new lives."

"So they're brainwashed."

"I suppose."

"Like in a cult."

"More or less. That's how it is for the masses—and over time they just disappear into this new life and are never found. For those of us who are marked—Aurelia, me, Etan—we're stronger and we aren't, of course, brainwashed; we don't turn into drones. We remember where we came from, but for the most part, we didn't necessarily have much that we were leaving behind."

"But that man, Neil, found Aurelia?"

"He spent decades looking. We still don't know how he tracked her down."

"Decades?"

"They were together when they were sixteen, seventeen, around there. Some small town, middle of nowhere out west. Aurelia should be in her late forties now," he explained. I permitted myself a tiny smile that he noticed. "What?"

"Well, I mean, so she's like a cougar going after you, sort of."

He grinned back at me. "I suppose you're right; never thought of it that way."

For a few silent seconds, I ran through everything he had told me, turning it over and over but still drowning in it. "So what am I supposed to do? Isn't it kind of impossible for me, just me, to just—" I couldn't quite say "kill them all" but he knew.

"You know, you're stronger than any of them, and stronger than we were. And I can tell you the night we knew: it was the opening, when the lights went out."

"What do you mean?"

"That moment was a clash of good and evil. That was when your powers first began to take shape and that was like an involuntary warning sign going out. Whenever someone like you comes up against someone like us, there can be cataclysmic effects."

"Well, that's good to know. Why are you telling me all of this, really?" I had to ask again. I had begun our night like this and now I imagined the sun was coming up. We were both lounging, reclining on the floor—which I was too bone-tired to find uncomfortable at this point—as though lying on the grass under a starry sky. It shouldn't have seemed so peaceful here, but it did. It felt oddly, refreshingly safe. Lucian had long since shed his tie, unbuttoned his shirt, and rolled up his sleeves. My eyes had grown weary and I propped my head up on my arm.

"I want you to win," he said as he had before. Then he added, with finality, "It's too late to save myself."

This time though, I wasn't letting him off so easily. "Maybe it's not. Why can't you just break free or something?" I grabbed his hand, pushing up his sleeve. "You don't have one of those cuffs. It's not like Calliope. You could go."

"It's much more complicated. I don't have a cuff because I'm bound by more than that. For now, all I can do is help you."

"But what will happen to you?"

He breathed a long sigh. "When the time comes, you'll have to banish me, Haven. There's a chance I'll come back here at some point, but I don't want this kind of life anymore."

"There must be a way to run away, reject it all, to repent."

"It would require me fighting against them both, Aurelia and the Prince, and who knows how many others. I don't think I can survive it. When you're of the ruling class like me and you try to get out, it's a whole other level of battle. I don't think I could do it right now."

"I'll help you. You can. We can get you out."

"That's what I love about you," he said sweetly, sincerely, but in a flat tone to end this debate. "You think any of this is possible. You can't worry about me. Save yourself. That's what's most important. I just wish I'd met you before I was so . . . so chained to all of this."

I didn't say anything. I didn't know what else I could say. We were silent for quite some time. I lay on my back, staring up at the crumbling brick ceiling, sorting through all of what he had told me, letting it settle. Finally he spoke again: "Do you think you could ever truly forgive me? Could you ever look at me again the way you did before you knew all of what I've done? All the souls I've condemned to the underworld?"

"Each of us has heaven and hell in him — I read that once."

"Maybe. But your proportion is probably ninety-nine percent

heaven and one percent hell. And I'm likely more the opposite."
He smiled, shaking his head. And I had to smile too. He looked
at his watch and pulled himself up, dusting himself off. "Wow, I
guess I should go."

"Me too," I said, even though I could have been content to stay
there indefinitely, letting time slip away. It felt as if we had been
talking about other people all night, not the horrors I would now
be left to face. I rose to my feet, shaking out his rumpled suit
jacket, which I would have secretly liked to keep as a memento of
our night. But instead I handed it back with a thank-you.

"Are you okay climbing back on your own? I'm going to head
to the Vault I think . . ." He trailed off and made no motion to
leave. I just nodded. He turned to go but then spun back to face
me again, his hand holding my arm for a moment. "You have to
make it through this so that you can undo the damage I've done."

"I will."

"I know you will."

His eyes searched mine once more and then he planted a kiss
on my forehead, letting his lips linger there. He combed one
hand through my hair and then let me go.

He walked down the hall toward the Vault, so slowly, as though
he didn't want to ever arrive where he was going. I watched, unable to completely turn away until he was swallowed up in that
winding path to the club. I could still feel the twisting sting from
that dagger of heartbreak even when I knew the boy I sent away
wasn't really right for me.

29

Rendezvous at the Library

Lance and I spent the entire morning talking, before heading to our office where we vowed to keep our conversations strictly business, just in case. He sat rapt as I recited it all from beginning to end, every bizarre fact Lucian had told me.

After bombarding me with questions, he said, "It's just mind-boggling, right?"

"Yeah." I had to agree. It was a lot.

"And you're sure this all checks out?"

"I guess so."

I couldn't blame him for asking. I would have questioned it all too, but I had the advantage of that book of mine. I had peeked at it after climbing back up to my room and it had confirmed what Lucian had said.

What you have heard is correct. You are an angel in training. It's a position of strength and power and should be treated as such. You are here now because you are being tested. The only way to test good is to immerse it in evil and force it to find its way to the top. Trust the knowledge you have been given and continue seeking further enlightenment.

I didn't tell Lance any of this angel business—I was still trying to digest it all myself. But I wondered. I mean, he had some sort of powers too, whatever they were. With our scars, our childhoods, of course, I had to wonder. I just let it float around my mind for the time being. For now, I needed him to flex his equally impressive, though much less mystical, powers.

"Hey, by the way, I have kind of a project for you. I don't know if it's possible, but if anyone can figure it out it would be you."

"I'm intrigued," he said. "Try me."

Just as dusk was setting in, I was at the front desk picking up the stacks of menus for the prom when I saw her. She was walking up from the Vault elevator at the back of the lobby. I thought I was imagining it at first, but no, it really was Dr. Michelle, here in the Lexington Hotel. Relief swept over me, the way it always does when you spot a friend unexpectedly just when you need her. Maybe I could get her to duck out with me for dinner or something. I really just needed to spend some time with someone from my old world. And I certainly didn't want her dining here. What was she doing here anyway? It was too early to be hitting the Vault. I noticed now that she was walking beside Mirabelle and wore a black cocktail dress. I called out before thinking, walking toward them:

"Michelle! Dr. Michelle!" She didn't seem to hear me but Mirabelle did and our paths met under the chandelier. "Hi!" I gave her a hug and noticed she didn't quite hug me back. I was gushier than usual but I didn't care. "What are you doing here? Another wild girls' night at the club? Wow, you look amazing, this is so pretty!" She wore sky-high heels and her hair, usually in a ponytail, now fell across her shoulders in soft waves. "How's everything? Joan came by recently and said you were the hero of that school bus crash." I was talking so fast, I couldn't help it, but as soon as I stopped, I saw it: that look. She just stared at me with those empty eyes that everyone here seemed to have. I looked straight into them, through them, searching for life. My stomach lurched and my blood ran cold. "Michelle?"

She smiled, a hollow smile. "I'm sorry," she said in a perfectly sweet, dull tone. "You must've mistaken me for someone else."

I opened my mouth to speak but had no words. Mirabelle draped her hands on Michelle's shoulders like a shrug. "Come, Evangeline," she said to her.

I could only stand there, frozen, as they walked away.

Rattled as I was, I tried, with Lance's help, to spend the rest of the day focusing on what good I had to look forward to: the rendezvous with Dante. We were ready and waiting for him a good half hour before our appointed time. There had been only one guest browsing the library when we arrived and soon we were left entirely alone. At five minutes after ten we heard the squeak of sneakers slapping at the part of the lobby floor not covered by carpeting. I looked out the door to see Dante running, as fast as I'd ever seen him run, in his chef's uniform, straight for us. His expression, the pain of his eyes and grimace that overtook him, told me he was running away from something, someone. He glanced quickly back over his shoulder as he crossed the lobby.

Just a few paces from the door . . . he dropped. Fast and hard against the ground making a dull smack. Every part of him seemed to give out simultaneously. I hit the ground with him, leaning over him, and I heard myself shouting his name, shouting for someone to call an ambulance. I checked his pulse and felt it there, fast.

His eyes fluttered and just before passing out he gasped:

"Under the floorboards, my bed, a box . . . find . . . Please. So much to tell you." And then he was out.

Two paramedics slid him onto a stretcher and wheeled him out the front doors, causing something of a scene. Lance and I followed; I held Dante's limp hand as we rushed to the awaiting ambulance. After they loaded him in, the brusque male paramedic barked at Lance and me, "No room in here, gotta go."

"Please. I can't leave him."

"It's okay," said his female partner. "One of you can come."

"You go," Lance said kindly. "Call me with updates, okay?"

I nodded. I couldn't speak.

I climbed in to join the EMTs in back. As soon as the siren came on, rousing me, I piped up: "How is he?"

The man took a blood sample while the woman hooked up an IV.

"Stable," she said. "We'll get some fluids into him. They'll run some tests."

"Do you think he would last okay if, I mean, I know it's out of the way but could you possibly take us to Evanston General?" I pleaded with them. "I know it's a longer way but my mom is there . . . she's a nurse, please, can you, please?" I felt the tears welling up.

"I don't think it's prudent," the man said.

"Oh, I don't know about that," said the woman. She yelled to the driver, "Hey, Lou, any chance we can hit Evanston GH?"

I looked to the front and saw the man's eyes in the rearview mirror; he must've caught my tears.

"Sure, if you say it's okay!"

"Thank you so much, thank you!" I called out to him.

I had the attendants at the ER front desk page Joan the minute we got there. I was seated at Dante's bedside—he was still out cold—when Joan came in.

"Honey, what happened? What's going on?" She was frantic. She's never like that at work. I stood up and she grabbed me into a hug, but kept her eyes on Dante.

"It's hopefully nothing. Dr. Joe said he's stable, but I just wanted you to check him out, make sure he's okay." What could I tell her? I couldn't tell her what I wanted to.

"But, Haven, what *happened?*"

"I don't know." It was the truth at least. "He's just . . . he's been working hard and I think it's just exhaustion. He passed out."

She gave me a skeptical look but she nodded anyway and kissed me on the forehead.

"I'll check everything out."

"I'll wait out here." I squeezed Dante's hand as I left. And then I had to ask, fear rising anew: "Hey, is Michelle working tonight? Thought I might say hi."

Joan was looking over Dante's chart, barely paying attention. "Oh honey, I thought I told you—she just got a position with a hospital in Oregon. She's got family out there or something and had been waiting for it to come through. Happened so fast. She said she'd e-mail you to say goodbye. Poor thing was so overworked at the end, she was like a zombie or something."

"Thanks." That was all I could muster. As I walked away, Joan was speaking to Dante, as if he were awake.

"Now, Mr. Dennis, I just saw your mother the other day. She's not going to like this at all." She whipped the curtain closed around them.

I had a few minutes and went up to pediatrics. There, I scanned that bulletin board and found it easily. It had been layered underneath so many other faces. She was just on the edge of the picture of Jenny. Michelle's arm was around her, a hint of her face in the frame, but I could see it had indeed started to change. Her skin had grown scaly and taken on a greenish tint, her features all tugged downward as though in a few days' time they would slip off her face. I snapped it off the wall where it had been pinned, folded it, and tucked it in my dress pocket.

"So he's going to be okay?" It was now after three in the morning and Dante had been given the green light to go home as soon as he woke up from his deep slumber. Ruthie had arrived to sit with him. Joan sat beside me in the waiting area—coffee in her hands, cocoa in mine.

"He'll be fine, honey. I'm so glad you came here, that was good thinking." I leaned my head on her shoulder and yawned. "He's very weak. He really hasn't been sick or anything that you've noticed? His levels are just all out of whack."

I wanted to tell her everything but I couldn't. It would probably just put her in danger too, and I couldn't do that. I couldn't live with myself if any harm came to her.

"Not that I know of, but you know, Dante's tough and doesn't like to complain so maybe he just didn't say anything." That, at least, sounded plausible.

"Honey, are you okay? Are you working too hard? I know how you can get about things. Even though it's such an exciting place, and I do love it there, I have to ask."

"No, I'm fine, I'm great." I nodded and smiled. "It's really . . . great. I'm just worn out from today, that's all."

She kissed my forehead. "Of course, dear."

I dozed off in the lounge with Joan and when Dante finally awoke, around seven in the morning, I went in to say hello
and goodbye before heading back to the Lexington. The minute
Dante saw me, his heavy eyes did their best to light up, but he was
still groggy: "Happy birthday, Haven," he said, smiling. I looked
at Ruthie, confused.

"He doesn't seem to remember that he's spent the past several months interning," she said shaking her head. "They say it's
temporary, I just don't know. We'll get him home. You'll visit,
Haven? Maybe that'll help?"

"I'll come by tomorrow. Promise."

She gave me a hug.

Joan drove me all the way back to the Lexington. When I arrived, I asked around and found "Evangeline" in the spa folding towels. It was still early enough that there wasn't anyone in the
waiting area yet, but I wouldn't have cared if there had been.

"Hey," I called out as I neared. She looked up, blankly. "If you
did ANYTHING to Joan or any of those kids at the hospital—or
if you ever do—" I couldn't quite finish. "Stay away from my
friends and stay away from my family." I couldn't control myself.
I swung my arm out and knocked over the stack of towels she'd
just folded and stomped away. She didn't say a word.

I headed for Lance's room next. He answered the door, it
seemed, even before I knocked. He had followed Dante's directions and pried open the floorboards beneath their bunk beds.
Nestled in among the wood beams, he'd found one of the chocolate boxes we always delivered and opened the lid. Inside it was
empty except for a handful of brittle crimson quarter-size stars
that had the texture of cinnamon, a handful of dried black bell-
shaped flowers, and turquoise pods resembling vanilla beans. A

recipe printed in Dante's script on a sheet of Lexington Hotel stationery urged "In case of emergency, take one of each of these herbs, crush to fine powder, dissolve in water, and drink."

The next day, Lance and I smuggled Dante's box out of the hotel on our usual chocolate delivery run. After making our rounds, we took the L all the way out to the end of the line, Evanston, to pay Dante a visit. He smiled warmly at us and was his typical friendly self, but he was far from recovered.

"How are you feeling?" I had nestled myself onto the bed next to him. Lance sat nearby at his desk chair.

He shook his head. "I feel like I've been run over. I mean, I've never actually been run over but I imagine this is how it would feel. Just like all achy and I'm beat."

I felt his forehead with the back of my hand. "You're still feverish, Dan. I don't like that."

"Yeah, neither do I. And I'm exhausted, like, all the time. I've just been sitting here and watching reruns of the trashiest TV I can find."

"Well at least you're back to normal in that respect." I smiled and he elbowed me in the arm. But I could see him thinking.

"So, tell me again," he tried. "I was a chef at the Lexington Hotel?" He still didn't remember anything that had happened since the morning of my birthday.

We tried to tell him again all that we had witnessed and come to learn about the hotel, hoping it would jog his memory, but it was too much—he couldn't even remember who Etan was. And really, it was so wild, who could blame him? Finally Lance pulled the chocolate box from his bag. "You probably don't remember, but you told us to find this." Lance held it out to him and Dante took it in unsteady hands. He opened the lid and touched each of those odd items as though it was the first time he'd seen them, holding them up and studying them. Lance and I traded concerned glances. I'm sure he wondered, like me, whether our friend would ever be returned to us.

I pulled out the sheet of paper inside the box.

"Dan, do you remember writing this recipe out?" He took it from my hands and read it, shaking his head. He looked defeated.

"This sucks, guys. It feels like this stuff belongs to someone else. I know that's my handwriting, but I'm just drawing a giant blank."

Lance fidgeted with the mousepad on Dante's desk. "Well, it says 'In case of emergency,'" he proceeded gingerly. "I'm not an advocate of totally blind trial and error with these strange herbs or whatever, but it kinda seems like this might qualify as an emergency. What do you guys think?"

"Gotta say, I think you just might be right," Dante agreed.

"Really, D?" I wasn't sure I was entirely onboard.

"The man's got a point, Hav. I mean, I have no memories of months of my life. I still don't have any idea what they gave to me that knocked me out. There isn't much I trust anymore, but I do trust myself. And if I wrote this out and collected these things, then maybe it was for a reason like this."

"I'll grab some water," Lance said, already up from his seat.

"Are you sure?" I asked after he'd left the room.

"I promise, Hav, I am. I'm just sick of feeling this way. I know there's stuff locked up in my mind somewhere that can help us. I just have to get to it."

Lance returned and Dante followed his own instructions, taking each of the odd ingredients, crushing them to dust between his hands, and sprinkling the powdery remains into his glass of water. "Cheers!" He hoisted the glass in the air and downed it in one long gulp. Seconds later, we watched silently as his eyes registered confusion. "Whoa," he said finally, slowly. "Okay, so I'm gonna sleep now, but it's fine, it's all good. I'll be back. I bet I will. We'll see . . ." He trailed off as sleep overtook him. I checked his pulse and found it perfectly normal. We stayed with him until Ruthie came home and then asked her to please call us as soon as he woke up.

On our way to the L, we noticed a stunning creature—a young man with a model's bone structure and an athlete's physique—following us those few blocks, boarding our train and then trailing us back to the hotel. We kept our conversation dull and we overexaggerated certain points—"What a shame he has no memory at all," "doesn't even know who we are"—but despite our fairly smooth performance, we were chilled to the bone. Our stalker was in the Outfit, and he was obviously there to remind us there really was no escape.

30

You're Next

Back at the hotel, Lance was eager to show me the work he'd done on that assignment I'd given him. Just as I suspected, he not only had a far nicer cell phone than I did—very slim and full of tricks—but he also happened to know a thing or two about how to take it apart and put it back together again. First, he had me change into the cowl-neck short-sleeved sweater (which I had never liked anyway, but Joan had forced on me) and jeans I had sacrificed for our experiment. He had made a few key alterations to both. For one, he had anchored his cell phone on the inside of the extra material at the sweater's neckline, sewing a little flap made from one of his old T-shirts as a pocket for it.

"See, so the phone is in place here." All business, he dug his hand into the neck of my sweater. "And the camera's eye is lined up through this tiny hole I cut in your sweater—sorry."

"No, please. This is the most I've ever worn this sweater."

"And so the wire runs from the inside of the sweater down to your jeans and inside your right jean pocket. If you'll kindly feel inside there—"

I did as I was told: "Wow!" Inside my fingers found a remote control the size of a stick of gum with a doorbell-size pushbutton.

"That's your remote control."

"But how—"

"They took the camera away from our office but they left the accessories," he explained. "So from there, all you have to do is start snapping."

"Really?" I hit the button a couple times. "That's so cool."

"Yeah. And then I'll e-mail them to myself, print them out, and scrub them off the hard drive of the gallery computer."

"That's totally amazing, Lance. Seriously, you're some kind of genius."

"Thanks," he said, proudly. "I try."

"So, should we test it out?"

In less than half an hour skulking around the Vault, looking like we were just there to hang out, I managed to snap group shots of a slew of the newer Outfit members. We finished up with a stroll through the lobby so I could get a couple of the new girls at the front desk. We would amass a collection of these photos and then, when the time came, I would destroy them.

The next two days we checked in with Ruthie so often, we succeeded in making her more worried than she had already been about Dante. The first two times we called, he was still asleep. It was going on sixteen hours now. The third time we called he showed signs of stirring—a relief. And the fourth time we had her ask him what day it was: "Is it Haven's birthday?" we heard on the other end of the phone. Our hearts sank. The following day brought no better news: "He still doesn't seem to have any idea what the Lexington Hotel is," she said. "And he's sleeping all the time. It's just not normal at all. I don't know what to do." We didn't either. Lance and I debated endlessly at what point Dante should be taken back to the hospital, not that we imagined there was much they could do for him there.

Prom was now only two days away, but we had seen shockingly little of Lucian and Aurelia, besides our nighttime spying rituals. But when we keyed into our gallery office, we found a note waiting on our desk in Aurelia's delicate hand. Just seeing it sent a chill.

Haven and Lance,
Kindly report to the ballroom to decorate for Saturday's festivities.
Yours, Aurelia.

When we did, we found at least two dozen members of the Outfit already at work moving and setting tables, arranging the lights and DJ booth, setting up a lighted cityscape meant to be the Chicago of 1871. They had even brought in the life-size replica of a cow we had ordered. My mind flashed to all of the ridiculous photos that would be snapped around it on Saturday night. I felt bad for the thing.

Beckett strutted around with a clipboard in hand, barking orders at his minions, and made his way over to us.

"You can do tables"—he pointed to me—"and you can hang lights," he ordered Lance, before walking away. It was the most he'd ever said to either of us. I guessed that Lance was thinking the same thing I was: we were severely outnumbered in this room. The place was teeming with Outfit members and yet it was virtually silent. There were none of those little conversations that made the day pass. They all shot us glares out of the corners of their eyes.

Lance and I headed in our opposite directions and set to work. I unfolded a flame-colored tablecloth, while across the room he climbed to the top of a towering ladder, which either of us might once have balked at, but after all of those nighttime drills seemed so much less intimidating. So much had changed in these last few months.

I had just placed the last favor at its setting and heard the crash—the explosive fireworks pop of shattering glass.

My head whipped in Lance's direction, just as he wailed. The ladder was empty; he was lying on the ground. I ran to him; no one else moved an inch. Every member of the Outfit continued doing whatever mundane task they were engrossed with, not saying a word, not even so much as looking at him.

When I got to him, he was picking shards of broken glass off the arm of his uniform. A few smashed torches lay scattered around him.

"Careful, it's easy to lose your footing up there," Beckett said as he passed by us. Lance wouldn't have made a misstep. We climbed steeper slopes than this in the dark every night. He hadn't fallen on his own. Lance shot me a look that confirmed this.

"Are you okay?" I whispered. "Can you stand up, do you think?"

"Fine, I'm fine," he said, slowly raising himself, bits of glass and the crushed wood of the torches raining down from his body. He had twisted when he fell, landing on his stomach, and some of the sharper pieces had sliced straight through his vest and shirt in clean swipes across his torso and chest. I wondered how deep they went.

"You're pretty cut up, aren't you?"

"A little," he said, wincing but trying to cover it up.

"Can you make it downstairs? If they're not too bad, I can take care of it."

"Yeah, thanks." I could see the sting in his eyes.

We got to my room and I made a beeline for that first-aid kit and all those extra bandages. "Does it feel like you'll need stitches?" I asked as I pulled out my supplies and set them on the desk.

"I don't know," he groaned. "I'd rather not, I mean, if you don't have to."

"I'm flattered that you think I could do stitches on you. We would have to take you in for that."

"Oh. No, I don't think I need them."

"Come 'ere, let me see. And take that off already." I waved toward his shirt and vest. I removed the cap from the bottle of antiseptic and laid out a buffet of bandages, all different sizes, and gauze. Then I wet a clean washcloth and applied some antibacterial soap.

"You have to be careful," he called out to me, his voice pained. "First Dante, now me. You're next, Haven."

"I know," I said. I finished up and returned to the main room to find him still unbuttoning his shirt. "Do you need help? Are you not able to move your fingers?" I grabbed his hand, wondering if he might have some nerve damage even though his hands were only slightly nicked from the glass. Nothing too catastrophic-looking. "Squeeze my hand." He did without a problem.

"I'm fine." He resumed unbuttoning slowly.

"Then what's wrong? Let's bandage you. You must be covered in glass." He shed his vest and shirt and still had on a white T-shirt underneath. He stopped again. I got the picture and softened my tone. "I know this is weird, but seriously, I practically grew up in a hospital, remember? I've seen it all, so no need for modesty. This is just like another day at the office for me."

He looked like he wanted to say something but then he gave up and shook his head. He lifted his shirt up and off. Because of those years at the hospital, my trained eyes went to the wound first: a sharp, ragged slice, bloody and oozing across his abdomen. Then, professionalism fading, I absorbed the rest of him: strong arms with muscles bulging beneath the skin and broad shoulders, tapering down to a rippled torso that looked as if stones had been skipped across its surface and had frozen that way.

"It, um, looks like all of that running and climbing and all is paying off, I guess," I stammered.

"Thanks," he said, so shy it was barely audible.

I suddenly understood the concept of someone looking vastly better out of their clothes than in them. For an instant, I couldn't help but wonder how I would stack up to that comparison. I had never really encountered any sort of bare flesh in such close proximity to me, ever. I had pretty much exaggerated about my experience at the hospital: the parade of wounded and aching there was much different than this, and, truthfully, I saw mostly arms and legs and glimpses here and there, and a lot of old people or kids. Not friends of mine, not . . . *this.* This fell into another category entirely.

Quietly and quickly, I cleaned the gash and applied antiseptic and bandages. Then I tended to his forearms and hands, making sure no slivers of glass had been left behind. He wore that cuff on his wrist every day, and now I pulled a shard of glass from near that single wing. We didn't speak. For the first time since we'd met, the silence between us felt . . . off. I was eager to fill it but at a loss as to what to say. I didn't want to feel this way with Lance.

"You're all set here," I said finally. "Was that it? Any other scrapes or anything?"

"No, thanks though." He had already grabbed for his undershirt.

"I'll leave out a couple of these," I said as I reassembled all of my first-aid supplies. "We'll, or you'll, want to change that dressing—" My fumbling hands knocked the capped bottle of antiseptic off the desk onto the floor and he lunged for it on reflex. When he bent forward, I looked and couldn't stifle a gasp.

Lance's bare shoulder blades bore the same scars I had on mine.

He heard my reaction and froze, then rose slowly, so slowly now, until he was facing me. He handed me the bottle and I set it down on the desk, eyes still locked on him. *That* was what he hadn't wanted me to see. And that glimpse had been enough to know: he was like me. He had to be. Do I tell him? We both tried to speak at the same time. I let him go first.

"There's some stuff I guess you don't know about me"—he shrugged, searching for the words—"that I don't even completely know about myself."

"I've seen those before." I had my uniform on, which I generally appreciated for its ability to cover up the multitude of sins on my skin, but if I could have easily shown him my matching scars at that moment, I would have.

"You have?" He looked puzzled; I could see him trying to figure out when he might have possibly exposed those.

"On me."

His eyes bulged. His jaw dropped just enough to register shock. "Do you . . . do you know what they mean?" he stammered, his eyes darting around, as though someone had been listening in.

I nodded. "Yeah. You?"

He nodded too. "A very recent development."

We both sighed.

"Yeah, I guess we've gotta be better about pooling our information," I said.

"I know, kind of a flaw in our study group here."

"Well, any other secrets I should know about?"

He didn't answer very quickly, which indicated the affirmative. His shoulders fell and I could see him decide to give in. He headed for the door, waving for me to follow.

When we got to his room, Lance opened the desk drawer and produced a small stack of postcards, handing them to me. I pawed through—each had a different picture of Chicago and its landmarks, and all were vintage shots from years past—I flipped them over, but there was no writing whatsoever.

"I know, so it seems nuts, but when no one is in here and it's just me, these have messages on them. They just appear. But they're never signed."

"What do they say?"

"You know, the usual: *wish you were here; you're in danger; you're not just a run-of-the-mill outcast, you're some kind of freakish angel.* And then they mostly say to make sure you don't get into too much trouble and to take my cues from you. You're, like, the ringleader, I guess."

"Seriously?"

"Yeah. And, weirdly, they say this thing found me, I didn't find *it.*" He held up his cuff.

"I heard that too, with this." I pulled out the necklace.

"I guess it's like our membership card in a club."

"Where'd you find these?" I held up the stack of postcards.

"They were with that book I found for you. These were there marked for me in the same box."

"Yeah, the book . . ." I thought about it. "Now's probably a good time to mention: I sort of get messages in there like your postcards."

"I'm sorry?"

"Yeah. I thought you'd think I was crazy, so I didn't say anything before."

"I know how that goes," he said, letting it roll off him. "Anything interesting in there?"

I couldn't have asked for a better time to bring it up: "Well, the major bullet point seems to be that . . ." I just blurted it out. "It's prom day—they're going to kill me then. I don't know how. It just gave that date, May 27. I didn't want to say anything." Saying it out loud, it sounded as absurd and bone-chilling as it had that first time I'd read it. But now that the date was so close, its finality made my head spin.

"You didn't want to say anything?" He spat out the words.

"I figured, what was the point?"

He shook his head, took his glasses off, and furiously polished them against his shirt. "I don't even know where to start."

"I mean, I'm not going to let it happen so easily, but I figured, why get everyone upset?"

"You're completely ridiculous. But I'll let that go." He breathed a stressed sigh and leaned against his desk, arms folded. "Like we needed another reason to hate the prom?"

"I know."

And then he caught himself. "I'm sorry, that's not funny."

"No, it is, actually."

"No, it's not, but . . . I'm just kind of freaking out, in general. I know that's not cool to admit but . . . I am."

"Yeah, it's okay, you're in good company."

"Why though?" he said finally, softly. "Why us? Why is all this happening to us?" That word—*us*—reached out now and grabbed my heart, holding it tight, holding it together. Warm and comforting.

"Well, I guess maybe—" I started, not entirely sure what I would say, but he jumped in pointing his finger in that professorial way.

"I know. It's because we can handle it. This stuff is coming at us because we're capable of handling it."

"Wow," I breathed. "Good answer."

We didn't bother going back to set up the ballroom that afternoon. What did it really matter at this point? Instead we called Dante, who had some good news.

He launched right in: "Omigod, I have GOT to talk to you guys!"

"Dante?" A smile rose to my lips, a reflex. It sounded like him, finally.

"How soon can you get here?" He was manic, in a good way. "I've got so much to tell you, it's, like, some crazy shit!" Lance watched, trying to gauge what I was hearing. I gave him a thumbs-up.

"That's amazing, D, we'll hop on the train right now."

"Can you do me a favor?"

"Anything," I said.

"I will love you forever if you bring me some pizza! I'm dying to eat something that isn't contaminated or some kind of poison or, you know, my mom's boring healthy stuff."

I had to laugh. "You got it. See you soon."

Before long, Dante was not only telling us what we already knew—his name, his address, his job at the hotel—but things we didn't know at all. We sat in a circle on the floor of his room, the pizza box in the center.

"There's a whole dark room full of these strange plants down by Alcatraz. They use that stuff in everything. Most are aphrodisiacs, uppers, mind control, brainwashing kinda stuff. But some are deadly," Dante said between mouthfuls of pizza. "God, this is good. I feel like I woke up from a coma."

"They gave you something that night," I prompted. "They knew you were going to meet me. What made you arrange that meeting, anyway?"

"I don't know, they must've changed the concentration of something they were giving me and all of a sudden, I was, like, awake again. I saw you coming into Capone and saw them not let you talk to me. I didn't understand and I asked Etan. And, now I remember this, he got furious at me. So then I just stopped asking questions. I tried to go back to however I'd been before so that I could just, like, pay attention to everything and figure stuff out. And that's when I slipped you that message in your teacup. But they must've known."

"What did you take the other day? Before you went to sleep?"

"Etan had said when I first started working with him that that's the trifecta, those three spices. They're not anything I'd ever seen before, and he goes somewhere to get them. Not the garden."

"I bet we know where," Lance interjected.

Dante looked confused.

"We've got some things to tell you too. Later though." I wanted him to keep going, now that his memory was working again.

"So, anyway," he continued. "That's the trifecta for balance, if you serve someone something that's too strong for them, which occasionally happens. It's a sort of antidote. I started skimming some in the last few days, before I got knocked out."

"But where have you been when you haven't been working?" I asked, impatient now, wanting to know everything, wanting my friend fully returned to me.

"I don't know. I'm sorry," he said blankly. "I wish I knew. I know I was at Capone a lot. I think we worked through the nights a lot. And I have flashes of other places, but I can't recognize them or make sense of them."

"I bet it'll come back. It's probably like a posttraumatic stress thing," Lance said in a soothing tone.

"Maybe you're right," Dante said. "So what've I missed? What've you guys been up to?"

Lance and I looked at each other, now wearing matching expressions, no clue where to begin. Everything we'd said the past couple days had gone in one ear and out the other, but this time, we knew he would understand. We both shook our heads and had to smile at how grand the task would be to fill him in.

"Us? Not much," I joked.

"Yeah," Lance seconded. "Pretty boring stuff."

Since Dante seemed up to it, we told him everything. Everything. The three of us stayed there until Ruthie came home and dusk fell. Lance and I took turns relating this shared history of ours, each of us filling in the gaps in the other's tales, jumping in with forgotten details. It's a funny thing—the more time you spend with someone, the more they can change in your eyes. You find yourself studying everything about them, the shape of their face and the way their lips curl when they say certain words, their tics. The smallest things like that can become fascinating. And then it can catch you off-guard when you realize how much you've learned from the countless hours with this person—hours that ticked by without your even noticing—and all of a sudden you know them as well as your closest friends. You know when he's going to adjust his glasses and when he's going to put his hands in his pockets or when he's going to still be watching you when you've looked away.

When Lance and I got back to the hotel that night we had to keep up the illusion that Dante was still ailing, even though he hated sending us back. "I feel like I should be with you guys! I can't let you sit there with these targets on your back. I need to help you," he had pleaded.

It all fell on deaf ears. "No, Dan," I'd told him. "It's just not safe for you." So Lance and I returned and ran our drills like usual, but with an extra spring in our step thanks to our afternoon with Dante.

By the time I got into bed, I was both bone-tired and emotionally spent. I snuggled into the covers but before I could let sleep take me, I pulled out that book. It had this to tell me:

Fear nothing. And, above all else, never fear failure. Don't let that feeling hold you back from anything. Attack the possibility of it head-on so that you know you have done everything in your power to stave it off. Proceed as though it is not an option, trust in yourself no matter the odds. Trust in those dearest to you. Trust in your instincts and don't second-guess yourself. Be comforted by the knowledge that you have come a long way and if you keep looking ahead, you will keep moving ahead, no matter what stands in your way.

I didn't appreciate reading that f-word, *failure,* when the day I'd been bracing for was so close at hand, but I tried to extract what I could from the entry. No sooner had I tucked it back in my night table, than I felt myself begin to drift, at last, to sleep.

It was so real. So achingly, bloodcurdlingly real. As always, I had opened the door to the thump and shush of it and found them all there, marching down that hallway, coming for me, the entire Outfit, new recruits and old. All decaying as they went, like dead animals in the desert sun awaiting vultures. Limbs, heads, all dropping to the ground, littering their path. This time though, Aurelia led them all, reaching out with brittle hands, those chalky tentacles, specifically for me. "Why won't you join us?" she wooed me, so sweetly as she made her way down the hallway.

This time, the dream didn't stop outside my door. I ran to my bed and they followed, hovering around it as this grotesque Aurelia leaned toward me, her eye now running down her cheek watching me on its tether cord. "If you don't join us, we will fight you," that sweet voice said. "And you will perish. Make no mistake. You will perish." She reached out, yanking at my arms with those spindly fingers like fiery spikes against my skin. As the others cheered, I thrashed harder against her grip.

Aurelia's scorching claw reached down, clutching my necklace, pulling my whole body up with it. Though she tugged and tugged, the chain refused to be snapped off. It felt like a noose wearing away at my neck. She held up one hand, pointed her index finger straight up, and a flame appeared above it, like it was a candle. The fire danced and focused into a sharp thin line. With that narrow beam, she held my necklace away from my body and sliced straight through it. It radiated such fierce heat I thought she had slit my throat in the process.

"I'm clipping your wings," she hissed, handing the necklace to Etan beside her. "Among other things." Then she grabbed a clump of my long hair with such force I thought the hair would rip right out of my head, and she sliced with that fiery beam as I thrashed against her, screaming at the top of my lungs. She took one more fistful and did it again and then let me go with an extra shove, so I landed in a heap on my bed.

Then it was over. The nightmare was over. Everyone in the Outfit was gone; she was gone. And I was panting, sweating. I flipped the light on in my room, and my eyes then adjusted to it. I caught my breath, slowing it as best I could and when I finally had it in control, I wiped the sweat from my face and ran my fingers through my hair.

It was gone.

I grabbed at it with both hands but all that was left of my hair were jagged chunks. A shriek, long and piercing, tore from my chest. I couldn't make it stop. I flew up from my bed, tossed the chair from the closet door, and opened up to the mirror. My hair had been hacked to uneven bits. My door burst open and Lance ran in ready to pounce but stopped short when he saw my reflection. He didn't say a word. I turned slowly. My face was sweaty and hot, my eyes teary.

"I thought it was a dream," I said, still dazed. "But it wasn't. All this time. That wasn't a nightmare. It was real."

He stepped slowly toward me and put his hand in my hair, inspecting the mangled layers then looking me in the eyes.

"We'll be okay," he said. "We'll be okay." And after a pause, trying to lighten his voice, he said, "You know who'll fix this?" He held up a piece of my hair. "Dante. This strikes me as just the sort of thing he could do in his sleep." I tried to smile, but couldn't quite. Even Dante wouldn't be able to fix what worried me the most: this had just been the warning, the flare that went up announcing something was coming for me.

"She got my necklace too," I said flatly. "Cut it right off." I looked at his cuff; he did too. He folded his arms across his chest, thinking, thinking.

"Stay here. They won't come back," he said, determined. "There's a chance they're in Aurelia's office now. Maybe I can find something out." He was already climbing up the ladder.

"Wait," I said. He stopped. "You know what—that's a good idea. I'm coming with you." It was the last thing I wanted to do, to be honest. I didn't want to be anywhere near any of them. I had only just stopped shaking.

Lance looked me up and down. "No!" he said, with surprising force. "I mean, I don't think you should."

"I'm going with you," I said again, this time right behind him, one foot on the bottom rung of the ladder.

He let out a sigh. "I'm guessing there'll be no convincing you otherwise?"

"Good guess."

He gave in. "Let's go."

I followed Lance up, crawling single file through the narrow passage until we were able to stand. We crept along through the darkness until we found our usual lookout perch. No one was in Aurelia's office, but the light was on, and a lit candle flickered. I noticed the bookcases against the back wall—that sliver had been left open.

"She's in there," I mouthed to him. "We just have to wait."

And we did, standing there for minutes upon minutes. It had to have been at least half an hour when the office door opened and Lucian walked in, closing it with a bang behind him. He wandered over to her desk and scanned it side to side, touching some of the piles, peeking at the papers. His eyes brushed across the wall behind which we stood and I wondered if there was any chance he knew we were watching. At last he spoke up.

"Your vanity has become a problem," he projected out, in his bored tone, in the direction of the bookcase. "We don't have time for this, Aurelia."

At that, she slithered out so gracefully from that slim opening. She was again the beautiful Aurelia, not the one who had attacked me. With a turn of the pentagram key in that panel along the wall, she sealed up the space.

"I'm not sure I care for how you're speaking to me," she said, settling into her desk chair. "But I know how you'll make it up to me." She stopped for a moment. "But then, you called this meeting, didn't you? So perhaps you should go first."

Lucian seemed uninterested in spending any more time there than he needed to. He cut right to the chase. "You may want to rethink launching the plan this weekend. Perhaps wait until the last of the five dances to seize your target. It would make more sense. That way we will have already done so much recruiting. If we do this now, and something does not go according to plan, then we'll jeopardize the entire project."

"Too bad. Is that all?"

He sighed. "Yes, that's all, Aurelia."

"Now have a seat, you make me nervous," she barked. "Obviously this will have to be done quietly, preferably toward the end of the evening so we've had ample opportunity to recruit. The kitchen staff will be concocting particularly potent formulas to assist with our efforts and we'll have the old guard, our finest of the Outfit, there at the dance. Dispatch the new members to the Vault instead. We don't want any amateurs."

He nodded.

"I hear that there's a chance we may still be able to convert Etan's boy," she continued. "My spies tell me his memory is still failing but if Etan's toxin worked properly then he should be returning for the prom, with the coding in effect. And I'm still of the belief that Haven and Lance will come to their senses when they see the clock ticking and accept our generous offer."

I felt Lance's posture become more rigid. Still plenty rattled from what had just happened in my room, I involuntarily grabbed his firm upper arm at this news, gripping him so tight, he turned to me and mouthed, "Ow." I mouthed back. "Sorry," and let go.

"But now for my brilliant idea," Aurelia said to Lucian, looking pleased with herself. "Our dear, foolish Haven. If she doesn't join, she's going to be so sorry that she's made things so difficult for herself. Since you have failed stunningly in your mission, it falls to you to correct the situation."

"What are you saying, Aurelia?" he asked her, his face marble.

"You will destroy her," she said slowly and simply, with that smirk. She picked up a letter opener and caressed its sharp edge as she paced. "And you will be monitored. If you fail, someone else will be waiting in the wings and you will be made to watch as one of our more blithely heartless henchmen takes care of her, and you will be left to the Prince himself."

His face fell. My hands rose to my mouth to stifle a gasp, but I was too loud. Lance put his hand over my mouth too and we froze.

Aurelia's head snapped in our direction. I said a silent prayer hoping she thought that sound had simply come from Lucian.

Lucian piped up now. "I thought the plan was for me to oversee, to help pair up the others for recruiting purposes, and to take care of Lance," he said in a hostile tone he seemed unable to fully control.

She held up her index finger and closed her eyes, like a beast sniffing out prey. She opened them, staring at him now, and said very calmly, "Plans change. I strongly advise you to adapt." In one swift motion she flung the letter opener at her flat screen monitor—essentially at us and just to the side of Lucian's head. It sparked and smoked like it might explode, and we took off through the passageway. When we got to the point where we had to crawl, we moved so fast I could feel my palms tearing from the coarse floorboards. We were panting by the time we made it down the ladder and hit the floor of my room.

So it would be Lucian, then. My mind raced trying to process this new twist. Could he really kill me? But he would have no choice; if it wasn't him it would be someone else.

"We'll figure this out," Lance said finally. We were seated on my bed, trying to sort out what we'd heard. "We have all day." It was just after six in the morning. We had heard all the plotting we could hope to hear. Now the onus was on us to determine how to use all of this to our advantage, to save our lives. It was a tall order. "Supposing," he started, "that we did bring Dante back. How could we get him in safely?"

"Are you serious? I don't want him here. I'm scared of what they'll do to him."

"I know, but hypothetically. Are there ways we could get him in here to help us without getting him . . ."—he was searching for the right word, anything other than *killed*—" . . . caught, as soon as he sets foot back here?"

"Well, I mean, we can't walk him in past the front desk Outfit girls. He's obviously a major target, and short of putting him in a Trojan horse, like something out of AP English, I don't really know what can be done."

"Trojan horse. Greek mythology, gift left for the people of Troy after battle but filled with Greek warriors ready to jump out and destroy the city," he said, thinking aloud. "You might be on to something."

31

Time for a Change

About an hour later, I had just finished getting into my uniform, and was shaking a towel through my wet—and horrible—hair, when a knock came at the door. It was Lance, already in his uniform and bearing a bag of chocolate boxes and a list of those few places to hit. "They left us this list in the gallery, only a couple places. I'm sure we'll be tailed," he said, walking right into my room. "I talked to Dante. I'll do the deliveries, you're going there. He'll fix that hair. And give him this." He handed me another bag with a chocolate box. "Everything he needs is in there. I'll fill you in on Operation Trojan Horse. Or, rather, Cow."

Dante was waiting for me, scissors out and ready to go the minute I arrived at his place. I had tied and pinned back my choppy mess of a hairstyle and stuck it all under a hat, and as I let it loose now, he did his best to hide his shock. "This is going to be just fine," he said, touching my head delicately, as he ushered me into the desk chair he'd positioned before the mirror in his room. "We'll get her for doing this. Taking souls is one thing, but botching up a haircut is inexcusable." He tried to be light, but I could hear the quake in his voice. Raking his fingers through, he shook out the hacked-up layers. "I can totally do something with this," he said. "I promise you."

"I owe you one." I was starting to feel better already.

"Um, you kind of helped save my life, so I think we're good, honey." He took a comb out of his back pocket and pulled it through my locks. We were silent for a few long minutes as he studied me before he began clipping.

When I couldn't hold it in anymore, I spoke tentatively. "Dan, I feel like I failed you as a friend. I did, didn't I? I'm so sorry." I had wanted to say this for a while now but needed to wait until he was feeling better. But now that he was, I wasn't sure I was up to hearing the answer. He stopped cutting for a moment and his face turned serious. He spoke to my reflection in the mirror.

"It wasn't you, Hav." He shook his head. "I got swept up, you know? He understood me, Etan did."

"I understand you," I offered.

"No, sweetie, you're nice, but do you understand what it's like to be sixteen and gay and out, like, way out, not figuring it out like most everyone else at school? I mean, are you a gay guy who likes to cook?"

"I guess not," I said, disappointed in myself.

"This is stupid," he said, smiling to himself now. "But I just really want to be in love, you know what I mean?" He had a vibrant spark in his eyes that I had missed these past months.

"You've always been a romantic. You like chick flicks more than I do." He gave me a playful smack on the shoulder, then started cutting again.

"There's just never anyone to be in love *with*. I feel like it's just me on this island, waiting for hot guys to join me, but no one knows who they are yet or how to get there yet."

"They will though, and they won't be like Etan."

"Yeah, I mean, I know he played me."

"It's okay, we all got played."

"But he had this whole spiritual thing too, saying I could be young and beautiful and successful instantly and, like, forever. It seemed like he, and everyone there, had everything figured out, you know? Like they were leading these perfect lives."

"I know, believe me. Hey," I said, ready to move on to more important business, "Aurelia seems to think you might still be able to be converted to their side."

"Oh, they're not taking me without a fight. I've got plans for them. You can't keep me away." He stopped cutting. "Don't you have something for me? From Lance? I was told there would be a top-secret file for me. I'm ready to go!"

"Are you sure though, about coming back? Because I really don't want you to feel like you have to. It's totally okay; you've been through enough already—"

He cut me off. "Hand it over." I hopped off the chair, rifled through my things, and dug out the chocolate box Lance had sent along, which I knew would be completely devoid of any candy. Dante tossed the lid on the floor and found inside a slip of paper with an address, where he was to meet Lance at six o'clock that evening, and his chef's coat.

"Excellent." He left the box and its contents on his bed and snapped his fingers, motioning for me to get back in the chair. "I'm going shopping later."

"I'm sorry?"

"I've got a little list of all the plants and spices and things I'm going to take from that garden. I'm going to mess with their recipes at prom tomorrow night."

"So you're officially coming back?"

He plugged in the hair dryer. "If for no other reason than to avenge the slaughter of your hair."

I had to smile, worried as I was. "That's very chivalrous," I said. "But we've still got some matters to discuss: do you know about this business of 'coding'?"

"Hold that thought," he said, firing up the dryer. He pulled the brush out of his back pocket and went to work styling. When he was finished, he leaned down next to me, put his arm around my shoulders, and admired us both in the mirror. He had turned my ravaged hair into a sleek bob falling just below my chin.

"I love it," he said, giving me a sloppy kiss on the cheek. "You're lucky your face can pull this off; not everyone can."

I had never considered cutting my hair this short, but I looked at it now — so drastic and defiant — and it wasn't bad at all. I looked like a very different me. Maybe this was the warrior version of me, the persona that would be able to face this most daunting day and the battle that awaited me. Dante had managed, like he always did, to make it all better, and I felt good.

"Thank you, Dan, really." I turned to him. "I don't know what I'd do without you."

"Dante is back!" he announced, proud of himself. I was so grateful.

After the haircut, we parked ourselves in the kitchen, snacking on the cookies Dante had baked the day before (he was back, indeed), and discussed strategy for the evening to come.

The plan would be for Ruthie to drive Dante into the city this afternoon to the warehouse of a theater prop rental company, where he'd meet Lance under the guise of choosing a new cow for the prom. They had a ton of fake cows from a citywide art project several years back in which the life-size things were stationed on street corners and outside landmarks. While he was browsing, Dante would climb into the underbelly—they had access panels and were hollow inside—and he would be delivered later that evening to the hotel and swapped for the other cow. There, he would wait until the time came for him to sneak out of the cow, into the kitchen, and disperse his antidotes into the food that had already been prepared for the prom festivities. It was a fine enough plan, but there was one last necessary step.

We were back in Dante's room, but this time he was the one in the chair and I was wielding the scissors. I cut off the first dreadlock and paused to let him take it in.

"You know you secretly wanted to copy me and get a new look," I teased, but very gently.

"It'll grow back," he said solemnly, like a soldier going into battle. "Time for a change." I continued on, clipping until they were gone.

"You're sure you're okay with this? You know you're going to be like bait, right?" I asked, before I finished him off with the electric razor. We had decided this might be a way to throw them off his scent, in case someone were to spot him tampering with the food in the kitchen. They would just think he was one of them and declare him nonthreatening. Anyone looking on would simply believe that it was a signal he was ready to sell his soul and had come back to do it.

"It's okay, it's for a good cause," he said, but his skittish eyes told me he was nervous. We were silent for several minutes until, finally, perhaps looking for something to take his mind off it, he blindsided me. "So what's up with you and Lance?"

"I don't know." I tried not to sound surprised, but it came out defensive. "You were like a zombie. I had to hang out with someone."

"Just wondering."

"Don't give me that look," I scolded.

"I'm just saying, he's a total Clark Kent," he whispered. This was our universal name for stealthy cute guys, who didn't realize they were cute—which is really the best thing.

"I know, I've sort of been thinking that lately."

I brushed the clippings off Dante's face and shoulders and looked at him in the mirror. Not bad. I had returned the favor after his coifing handiwork.

The time came too soon to say goodbye and I hugged him, told him to be careful, and tried not to think about what lay ahead for him.

I found Lance in our office, sending e-mails to his mom. I owed Joan a call but I hated the idea of it; I wasn't sure I'd hold it together. He looked up when he heard me walk in.

"Hey," he said, then pointed. "Dante did that?"

"Yeah, crazy, right?" I felt a little exposed—it was strange not having my hair to hide behind.

"The man is skilled. It looks nice." He pushed his glasses up.

"Thanks. What's going on here?"

"Nothing." He closed out of his screen. "Killing time until we meet with Courtney."

"Ugh, that's right." In all the excitement I had forgotten she was supposed to come with a few other prom committee stalwarts to okay the look of the ballroom.

"You're not bailing on me."

"No. I just don't know which is worse—having to show them around today or figuring out how to cheat death tomorrow."

When Courtney and two of her identical cohorts arrived that afternoon, we greeted them formally, with handshakes, as though establishing ourselves as more powerful than we had been at school. She looked me up and down in a strange way, as if she couldn't quite place me. I just smiled. We showed them up to the ballroom, pointing out all the details. A handful of Outfit members were still in there, tending to the lights and making sure everything was in place. They acted like we weren't there, even when Courtney said, perhaps too loudly, "Wow, everyone is like so superhot here."

The three girls walked around the entire perimeter slowly, whispering, like people in a museum. After all this time around the Outfit and braving the likes of Aurelia, people who truly meant us harm, I was so much less impressed with Courtney and her ilk. They really weren't so powerful at all, were they? There was no reason for them to have any hold over us. I had seen true terror now and she wasn't it at all. She was nothing. We stood back and let them be alone and after some time they wandered back over to us.

"It'll all do just fine," Courtney said.

Lance and I had rehearsed this. "We're so glad. You know, it's really important to us to have everything perfect and it occurred to us just today that this is not the kind of cow you had in mind," I said, as we all gazed at the beige beast.

"Huh?"

"We realized," Lance explained, "what would really 'pop'—to use one of the words from your many e-mails to us—would be . . . a spotted cow."

The trio looked at the cow again, with serious faces. Courtney whispered urgently to her minions as if they we were discussing the threat of nuclear war. And finally, they turned back toward us.

"Yeah, spotted cows are hot," Courtney said. "Thank god it's not too late."

"I know. Phew," I said. "So, anyway, that will be delivered tonight and all in place for tomorrow."

"Good," she said. She dug into her purse and produced a check from Evanston High School. And with that they were gone.

As Lance and I passed the front desk headed back to the gallery, an Outfit member called out, "Ms. Terra?" I stopped, surprised by the formality. Lance gave me a look too.

"Yes, hi."

"Ms. Brown would like to see you." I forgot to breathe for a moment. Lance and I traded worried glances.

"Of course," I said to the girl.

"I'll catch up with you later," Lance said, trying, I could tell, to sound as normal as possible. "Hey, can I borrow your key? I have to grab my book from your room." I knew what he was doing: he was going to keep an eye on me from our hiding place within the walls. I handed him the keycard.

Aurelia didn't say a word about my hair. She simply let her eyes linger on it and didn't bother suppressing a smirk. She was an entirely different person from the one who had sat across from me at the Parlor, telling me about her life choices. I sat in that familiar chair, my stomach tying itself in knots, wondering if this was going to be it. The real beginning of the end for me. I felt naked somehow, facing her for the first time without my necklace. The only mild comfort was looking to that wall behind her and knowing Lance would be there watching, at the ready if I needed him. That gave me strength.

"Just a little business to tend to," she started, frosty, as she shuffled papers on her desk. "As we discussed the other day, I am certain that there are tremendous things in your future. I just need something from you—" She reached from her desk drawer to pull something out, but she stopped when I piped up again, for the sake of stalling.

Summoning all my courage, I said, "Yes, but what exactly do you see? In my future?" I wanted to add, *Because if I went along with this it would have to end with me in the fiery pit of hell and that's not a future I'm interested in,* but I showed some careful restraint.

"Well, I'm glad you asked that. What would *you* like to see in your future? Because whatever it is, it can be yours."

"Just like that?"

"Just like that," she affirmed.

"Well, the thing is, I always have dreamed of becoming a doctor," I said. She nodded like this would be easy, no problem. "And their oath is 'First do no harm.' I, um, don't think that's the oath here."

She glared at me, but kept her tone bright. "Perhaps you have questions. Maybe that's the issue." In her pursed lips and strained neck, I could see her mounting frustration. I sat up more rigid, and didn't say a word.

She continued, "To be honest, Haven, I've grown tired of this. I won't beg you. There might have been a time when the idea of becoming the ideal you, that perfect version of you, would thrill you. Silly me, I thought you would warm to the idea of being comfortable in your skin, being happy and successful, enjoying the attention and adoration that could come with something like this rather than spending your life worried about what everyone thinks of you. The taste you've gotten of this life should be more than enough to convince you."

"Well—" I started, but she put up her hand.

"However, if all of that hasn't cinched it for you, then this should: what happened last night, that was just the mildest glimpse of what lies ahead for you if you don't join us. This will not end well for you."

"But I've seen what happens to these people, the Outfit," I spoke up now, firm as I could. "Why would I want to become a perfect shell, this zombie-like creature who seems dead inside? Who seems to have everything anyone would want, but has no desires or feelings or passions or anything?"

"But don't you see? You wouldn't be that. Those people only wanted something shallow and that's what happens." They meant nothing to her, I could tell. "Their souls are ripe for the taking because there is little they truly care about." She leaned in, her voice getting hypnotic, wooing. "You're *marked* for greater things, Haven. You're a greater prize, and you would reap a greater reward. You would achieve all you wanted and fast. You would be more beautiful than you would ever imagine, more confident, the kind of person women want to be and men want to be with. And you would have success, instant success, without breaking your back to achieve it, without having to compete and worry if you'll end up on top—"

"See, I'm sort of used to working for things and I like the way it feels."

"That's a problem that is easily overcome, I assure you."

"And what are the terms specifically?"

"Well, you get everything you wish, in record time. For you, perhaps, that means flying through undergrad at the top of your class, going to a fine medical school, getting placed at the most prestigious hospital, and then of course emotional and physical matters involved with looking and feeling like your ideal. We would draw up a contract with the particulars—"

"And then at some point I start taking lives and souls," I said, cutting her off.

"We call it recruiting. And in return for what we've given you, you provide us with new recruits."

"So I could, for instance, cure cancer but then I would take more lives than I would save. That's how this general equation is always going to come out, right?"

"I don't know why you're focusing on the negative."

"I don't understand what's in it for me."

"You would command such power. You've never felt true power before. You would find this intoxicating. Because of your pedigree you would be so much *more* than the rest of the Outfit."

"Thank you, but—"

She put up her hand, stopping me. "When you say no, I don't know that you fully understand. You will either join me or we will be at cross-purposes with each other—which is something I cannot tolerate." A look blazed in her eyes, a flash that made me shudder. She rose up from her chair gracefully, and yet kicking it back several feet with her sharp heel. I jumped and scrambled to my feet. She walked to the front of the desk to face me. Her voice dropped a register and was so deliberate and smooth I felt ill.

"I'm going to do you a favor," she said finally. "I'm going to not accept an answer right now. I'm going to give you twenty-four hours to come to your senses. Tell me yes then or you won't live to tell anything ever again."

I said nothing. I just left, as fast as I could.

~ 32 ~

We'll Always Have Metamorfosi

That evening when Lance went to the prop house, I stayed behind anxiously awaiting his return. When he finally showed
up outside the gallery door, reporting that all had gone well, together we went to the ballroom at the scheduled time to monitor
the great switching of the cows. The hubbub didn't escape the
notice of Beckett and a few of the Outfit, who happened to be
lingering in the room, finishing up their work.

"What's this about?" he barked at us as two burly men wheeled
one cow in and the other away.

"A last-minute change," Lance said.

"The prom committee decided they wanted a spotted cow," I
added. "One became available, so we wanted to give them exactly
what they requested."

"Just do it fast."

Lance and I nodded to him as he and the others left the room.
I looked at the spotted cow being set into place and tried to imagine how Dante had curled himself up to fit in there. It hurt me
just to look at it, but it was necessary.

Alone in the ballroom at last, Lance and I shut off all the

lights, opened the panel, and helped a crumpled Dante as he crept out.

"I'm like a friggin' contortionist after that!" he sighed in a whisper.

We wished him good luck and closed the doors behind him.

At 3:30 in the morning, as the hotel slept, we crossed our fingers and enacted the final step in our plan. I waited behind in my room as Lance went to the ballroom to retrieve the room service cart from the back prep kitchen. With any luck Dante would be tucked under the tablecloth on the cart's bottom shelf. Lance would wheel him down the elevator, past the front desk, to the deserted kitchen of Capone. There Dante would have twenty minutes to complete his work before finding his way back into the cart, where I would be ready to wheel him downstairs.

I checked my watch and put the gourmet sandwiches I'd found in the Capone fridge onto the cart—if anyone asked, Lance and I were simply enjoying a late-night snack. Dante came running from the direction of Alcatraz, carrying a canvas tote bag full of supplies, and dove under the tablecloth. I pushed with all my strength and wheeled him to his old room.

Once safely inside, Dante climbed out.

"Mission accomplished," he said. I gave him a hug and Lance patted him on the shoulder.

"Did you see anyone?" I asked. "Etan? Or anyone in the kitchen?"

"Negative," Dante said, proud of himself. "I timed it totally right. That's when Etan takes whatever meetings he goes to and does his daily harvests."

"Scavenging for ingredients in hell and whatnot," Lance added.

"Exactly. So, it was all clear. The other folks won't roll back in until maybe five. I replaced all the jars of their poison mixture—which is like salt and pepper to them; it goes on everything—with the antidote. Then I sprinkled it into everything that was already made—all sorts of dough, drink mixers, you name it."

"Nice work, man," Lance said.

"Thanks." His eyes canvassed the old room. "But it's pretty friggin' weird to be back here. And let me tell you, that cow was not comfy. My back is, like, killing me." He started unbuttoning his chef's coat.

"Well, you were cooped up for an awfully long time," I soothed.

He stretched and squirmed while Lance set out a little feast of the food I'd pilfered from the bar's pantry in the tunnels earlier in the night.

"You're probably starving," Lance said, gnawing at a piece of pita bread and handing another to Dante.

"Thanks. Hey, Hav, I have kind of a medical question."

"The doctor is in."

"Do scars, like, get worse ever?"

"Whaddya mean?"

"Like, remember all those ones I've had forever from falling when I was a kid?"

"Sure."

He turned around and flipped up his T-shirt, exposing his bare back. "It's totally nuts, but they, like, disappeared, almost all of them, except for that one on my arm and these two." Sure enough, his back, which had once been riddled with shallow scars from crashing down on rocks and branches when he tumbled out of that tree so long ago, was nearly smooth. This was a kid who used to wear T-shirts when we went to the beach at Lake

Michigan. Now he just had a pair of deep marks on his shoulder blades, identical to Lance's and mine. He was one of us. I looked at Lance now. He stopped chewing.

"Wow, I guess there's some more stuff you might need to know."

I t was impossible to preserve any sense of normal after the day we had had, but it almost felt that way as we sat on the floor, snacking on our stolen goods and filling Dante in on any of those pertinent bits of information we might have left out the first time around. And then we plotted, each of us bringing something to the table. The goal was to prevent the sale of as many souls as possible, off the Outfit, and, of course, remain alive ourselves. Dante had already gotten his antidote into the kitchen and he had more at the ready to administer at the event itself, if necessary. Lance, the budding architect, had his maps, painstakingly detailed, of our passageways and tunnels and the quickest routes for each of us to take from one location to the next throughout the course of the night. He had contingency plans and a host of exit strategies for each possible room and situation, along with a detailed outline of what needed to be accomplished tomorrow night and in what order. I had blind faith and a couple of sharp knives.

And so we sat, planning as the early morning hours wore on, creating an interlocking harmony out of our three trajectories. It struck me that, subject matter aside, this is what it might have been like these past several months if this internship had turned out to be the experience we had expected: Dante, Lance, and me sitting around on a Friday night, sharing some snacks and talking. That would have been really nice.

When we finally felt as prepared as any of us could, we adjourned our meeting. It was after five in the morning and we all knew that we had to sleep. But none of us quite welcomed the thought of having to close our eyes and potentially invite in the demons that had attacked me the night before. So we took turns. Two of us at a time drifted off while one stayed up on guard. We stayed in Lance and Dante's room, as I had no interest in being alone in mine. The hours passed without interruption.

Saturday was eerily quiet in that calm-before-the-storm sort of way. We saw no traces of Aurelia or Lucian but spotted some familiar faces from school checking into the hotel in the afternoon. Lance's mom swung by dropping off his rental tux, and Dante's tux too, all crammed in the same garment bag (we didn't want Ruthie stopping by the hotel, just in case anyone happened to be watching). I wished I had had a legitimate reason to see Joan. I called her but feared I couldn't stay on very long without her wondering what was with me. I stood outside on the sidewalk with my cell phone pressed to my ear. I remembered the day she dropped me off at this very spot. I had had no idea what I was in for back then and yet I had still been nervous. I could laugh at that now.

"Are you getting excited? You'll be beautiful in that dress. Take pictures!" Joan urged.

"Thanks, yeah, I will."

"Just a few weeks and you'll be back here for the summer, can you believe it?"

"I know." But I couldn't believe it. I could hope, but I couldn't quite believe.

"The girls at the hospital are so excited. It's just not the same without you. We need you there to keep us young!"

"I try."

"Well, honey, have a wonderful time tonight and I want to hear all about it tomorrow, okay?"

"Sure."

"Say hi to Dante. I'm so glad he's better, and that Lance."

"I will . . . I love you, Joan. Thank you for, you know, for everything, all the time." It sounded so feeble, but what more could I say without getting her nervous? I could feel the beads of sweat springing up along my forehead. It had to be in the eighties.

"Haven, honey, don't be worried about this silly dance. I know it's not your thing, but you're going to have fun. Maybe it'll surprise you."

"Thanks."

"I love you, dear."

"Love you too."

"Talk tomorrow."

I hoped so.

Lance and Dante were picking me up at seven. Two pseudo-semi dates to the prom? Add that to the ever-expanding list of things I never would have thought might have happened back when I moved into this hotel. At five minutes to seven, I sat on my bed in that dress, my heels on, my new hair and makeup—minimal, but still—done, and I stared down that book. I had managed to put off looking at it all day, as though remaining in a state of blissful ignorance could save my life. But I had a responsibility to myself to read it now. I had reached the end, just a page or two left to be written upon. It couldn't have much still to tell me. Sure enough, today's date was marked, and this:

Forget about dates and times and whatever you have been told may happen today and begin acting in a manner commen-

surate with who you are and who you want to be. You have all the tools to make it through today. Just be smart, be strong, and don't lose faith in yourself.

You are more equal in strength to these creatures than you have realized. Own that feeling. Command it. Command them. You will need every ounce of your power to attempt to defeat them. Regardless of the final outcome, I can guarantee that the bloodshed and destruction will be far greater if you don't fight to your full capacity. Rise up, winged one—it's time.

It continued to give me mixed messages, this thing. It must just be a nice way of not wanting to tell me I'm definitely going to die today. Or else it was a not-so-nice way of telling me I have nothing to lose, so live the day with that in mind.

Three quick knocks rattled the door, just in time to save me from thinking too much.

I opened up and Dante stood there, a black fedora atop his freshly shorn head.

"Happy Prom," he said, pretending to be excited.

"Here's hoping it is," I said kissing him on the cheek.

He held out a piece of hotel stationery he had origami'd into a flower. "And you don't even have to water it," he added with a smirk. I had to chuckle.

"Thank you, you're too kind." I set it down on the night table, in the spot once occupied by Lucian's flower that had refused to die. "This reminds me. I have something for you too."

"You do? Aw shucks." Dante tossed himself onto the bed.

I dug into my dresser and took out the small plastic bag from the vintage store in Belmont. "Is Lance standing us up?"

"That guy is *still* getting ready."

"Really?"

"In his defense, I kind of hogged the mirror."

"Not surprised. Well, in the meantime." I handed the bag to him. "This is the finishing touch for your ensemble."

He pulled out the belt with the flames. He laughed.

"I love it! I'm putting it on right now!" He stood up.

"Just a little something to remember our time here. We'll always have Metamorfosi."

"You said it, sister." He unlooped his belt, the one with his name in sparkles that I wore our first night there. "By the way, um, hello, you look totally gorgeous, Hav. Spin around or something." I did, very embarrassed. His got serious for a moment. "A daring choice," he said, noting the significance of my wearing this particular style. "I'm proud of you."

"Thanks. If ever there was a time to be daring, this is it, right?"

He smiled and finished looping his belt. Another knock came at the door.

"Come in," Dante said in a high-pitched voice.

Lance peeked in: "Hi." He stood in the open doorway. He simultaneously looked perfect and yet bewildered that he was in a tuxedo.

"You look . . . really pretty," he said to me, stumbling. "You too, Dante," he added.

"Thanks, you too—handsome, I mean," I said, just as smoothly.

"Thanks. Check this out." Dante held his jacket open to show off the belt.

"Very nice," Lance said.

"So, whaddya say? Should we get this party started?" Dante asked, a touch of nervousness slipping out through his pep.

I grabbed my purse from the bed and its lightness reminded me of the weightiness of tonight.

All I had in there was a Swiss army knife. Of all things. Dante was already out the door.

"Hey, just one thing before we go." They both turned around to face me. "I, um, I don't really know how this is all going to go tonight. And I just wanted to thank you both for everything and tell you that—"

"Nope," Dante blurted out. We looked at him. "Save it. Tell us tomorrow," he said.

"But—"

"Tell us tomorrow," he said again, annunciating each word so I understood perfectly. "Okay?"

"Okay." I nodded with as much confidence as I could muster.

"You know what?" Lance stepped forward, pushing up his sleeve and unsnapping his cuff. "I think you should have this tonight." He took my hand and fastened the cuff on my wrist, a corsage.

"But . . ."

"No. Please. There are no clipped wings tonight," he said, holding my newly cuffed wrist.

"Well, if you're sure—"

"I am."

"Thank you." I touched the delicate golden wing embedded in it, a mirror image of the pendant I had had. "Well, I promise to give it back as soon as I retrieve mine."

"I'll hold you to that," he said.

As soon as we reached the lobby, we had to slow our pace to begin processing it all. Limos pulled up outside, and classmates of ours, whom we hadn't seen in so long, milled around, greeting each other and climbing the grand staircase in packs. To see them rush in, all bubbly excitement and wide eyes, was to see ourselves on that first day in the hotel. Girls hugged, boys gave each other fist bumps, and all—even the ones who considered themselves too cool to care—took in the hotel's grandeur. They gazed up at the chandelier, sparkling more than ever, a few of them even pointing. They craned their necks to see what lay around every corner and motioned back to the elevator that could take them down to the Vault—a place that, judging from the snippets of conversation we caught passing by, everyone seemed curious to check out. And their dreams would be coming true; tonight the under-twenty-one crowd was allowed in, provided they wore the fluorescent bracelets that would be slapped on their wrists at the door. It was a funny feeling, being reminded that these places that we had had the run of for several months held such intense allure for others.

"Does anyone else feel as weirdly nervous about seeing all these people as they do about facing mortal danger tonight?" Dante asked, as the three of us ascended the staircase amid the masses flowing in.

"I'm glad it's not just me," I admitted. It was a little over-whelming, a shock to the system to suddenly be surrounded by people our age, these people who never paid us much attention but who, at least to their credit, weren't devils meaning us harm. They had no idea how very different the three of us were from them. It was like observing another species, to see them entirely consumed by things like getting the perfect group shot in front of the spotted cow, where a group of girls, all cheerleaders in well-coifed updos with not a hair out of place, struck a pose as one of their dates snapped away.

The party was in full swing: music blaring; lights blinking; our fellow classmates squealing gleefully, sipping their flaming, supposedly virgin drinks and chomping on precious canapés served by the Outfit's most elite members. We stood in a corner, surveying the scene within earshot of a posse of seniors—the most well-known clique in the school. The boys tossed back their drinks, slouching coolly with hands in their pockets. The girls hung all over them; they all looked like naturals at this place. But a pair of blondes nearest us, both in sequined gowns and precisely stenciled makeup, had their eyes set on the drink station across the room, where two magazine-ad-perfect Outfit men doled out glass after glass to smiling girls and their intimidated dates.

"We've totally gotta just camp out over there, he's so hot. And the other one too. I could go for either one," one of them said.

"I bet they're models," said the other.

"Like, underwear models."

"They must go on break sometime."

"But, oh my god, they're probably hooking up with, like, ALL these totally hot bitches. I hate them." Both scanned the room, letting their ire skip from Outfit girl to Outfit girl. I had to smile at this. I followed their line of vision, out of the corner of my eye, and saw them watching Mirabelle. A glance at Lance and Dante, and an exchange of smirks and shakes of the head, told me they had been listening in too. Like me, they were probably thinking, *Oh, what those girls don't know.*

"So I hear everyone's hitting the club later," one of the girls' dates, whom I recognized as the football team's quarterback, announced to their little group. "You guys in?"

"Totally!" said the first blonde.

"Dying to see that place!" said the other. "But we need more drinks, right back. C'mon Stace." Arm in arm, the girls beelined for the bar across the room. I had never spoken to any of them in my life, but I knew who they all were and, for the first time ever, found it oddly comforting being near them: they were a brief escape. They had no idea what was going on tonight. If only I could have come here tonight feeling that same way.

I was used to feeling removed from these people, feeling like I hovered on their periphery, but now, I felt that way for an entirely new reason. I knew things that they didn't—I knew they were at risk here and I knew that Lance, Dante, and I, of all people, were the ones expected to keep them safe. This knowledge pushed down into my skin; it made my now-so-exposed scars flare in protest and fear. How was I supposed to not fear failure? That didn't make any sense at all. I wondered if Dante and Lance felt this now too.

Dante's eyes followed each server, just as they seemed to take note of his presence. He whipped his head around keeping them in his sights. I could feel his anxiety radiating from him.

"I'm gonna start my laps. That okay?" he asked Lance.

Lance was in charge of our schedule. He had said to us last night, "If you'll be the talent, I'd like to be the 'architect' of the plan." He had even made little quote marks around *architect* with his fingers. "What's with the quotes?" I had asked. He looked embarrassed. "That's what the postcard said—I'm the 'Architect.'" To which Dante had declared: "Well, then build it, baby!" So we were in agreement, and Dante and I were plenty relieved since neither of us knew where to begin coordinating everything.

Dante would be stationed in the ballroom, on the front lines of the battleground for the buying and selling of souls. He would monitor the party guests, look for signs that any of the poisons had managed to seep into the food and drink and if so, he would administer the necessary antidotes, spiking drinks with any of the loads of potions and spices he had tucked into every pocket of his tux. Unfortunately for him, he was also a target—Etan could easily hunt him down any minute and decide to try to take his soul on the spot. There was no way around it.

I had to destroy the photo of Aurelia, which meant destroying her in the process. While I snuck off to Aurelia's office, Lance would keep an eye on Lucian to check that he didn't follow me. Then he would make his way downstairs where all the other Outfit photos were stashed, including the ones snapped with Lance's cell phone. They were ready to go. We'd even removed the glass from the framed ones (all but Aurelia's in her lair) for easy access. He would guard them until I came and then I'd slash them all, since only I could do this, and we'd all, presumably, be safe and they would return to hell. When I thought about all that needed to happen tonight, I had to actively work to fend off my nausea.

Lance nodded at Dante, giving him the go-ahead.

"And then there were two," I said to Lance.

"Yep." He looked nervous. I wished he didn't look exactly how I felt. He seemed to know this and his face firmed up. "Do you see how many of the Outfit are here? Heavy hitters. So we'll hang out a few minutes and then do some recon."

I nodded. "I feel like we should be holding drinks."

"Good idea: a prop. Don't go anywhere." He went off in search of our props. People were dancing; I was counting the minutes until I would have to go. The next part of the schedule would be far more terrifying than this. An Outfit girl buzzed by with a tray, and a whole swarm of guys stopped her, swooping in to grab what looked like pigs in a blanket. One, with shaggy hair and a crooked smile, attempted to chat her up: "So, do you, like, work here? Or are you in school?" I tried to shuffle out of the way. I was so engrossed in this mating dance, I almost didn't realize another one of the guys in the group was actually speaking to me.

"Hey! Hey," he said again, getting my attention. "Do you go here? Evanston?" It was a kid on the basketball team.

"Yeah," I said coolly.

"I told you," another voice said, moving forward from behind the pack. He licked his fingers, speaking with his mouth full. Jason Abington.

"Hi. I was in your English class," I said to him, simply. "You have, like, twenty-five of my pens. The blue ones . . . they're translucent?"

"Ohhhh . . . yeah, you." He snapped his fingers, suddenly placing me. "You look different."

"I cut my hair."

He sized me up. "Cool. Looks good."

Courtney swooped in, looping her arms around Jason's shoulders and neck, attaching herself in barnacle fashion and recapturing his gaze for the moment, though he looked a little bored by it all, if you asked me. The shaggy-haired guy and the basketball star each got claimed by Courtney's fellow prom committee members. Everyone pairing off so predictably, so easily. How nice for them.

"Come, Jas, you've got to see the cow I picked out, he's the cutest!" Courtney cooed at him, shooting me a look.

"Enjoy," I said to Jason, not feeling that pang I might've once felt. I wasn't interested. After all I'd seen and the people I'd met, this crowd just seemed so lightweight. Even their romances, which had been so fascinating at school, looked dull up close now. "Go have fun. She really knows her bovines."

Lance appeared with our drinks. "Let me guess, they were trying to draft you for mathletes."

"How'd you know?" I took the flaming glass. "Thanks. Yikes, this thing again." Despite Dante's precautions, I wasn't going to drink it. It was a prop only.

"I know." He shook his head. He moved in front of me. "So I know it's earlier than we planned, but Lucian is over there, over my left shoulder, straight back." He said it calmly but with an edge that implied the Grim Reaper had arrived and it was show-time. I looked quickly and then back into Lance's eyes.

"So I should go now, shouldn't I?"

"Yes," he said. "You okay?"

I nodded. "I'll meet you downstairs. . . . after . . ." I didn't have to finish.

"If I don't see you in ten minutes, I'm coming after you. In the meantime, I'll keep him away," he said. "You're sure you want to do this part alone?"

"Yeah, just keep an eye on him."

"Good luck, Haven. You can do this." I took one last look and thought Lucian might have spotted me. And I took off, walking fast, abandoning my drink on the table where a pair of junior-year girls from the dance squad were taking tickets outside the ballroom doors.

"Hey!" they shouted at me in unison.

I scurried down that grand staircase, slaloming around the glowing couples strolling up to the ballroom hand in hand, ready to have the night of their lives. I didn't know any of them all that well, but I still hoped, as I ran by, that the night would end with-out them being drafted into this legion of enemies. I hoped, now that I thought about it, that I would see them again. That this night wouldn't be it for me. But I had to banish thoughts like that as I continued on, marching in long, sure strides through the bustling lobby to Aurelia's office.

"Might as well start at the top," Lance had advised. "Remember, you're going to have to bait her, let her come after you. But when, *when,* you finish her off, the window will be open for you to be able to destroy the rest of the Outfit, hopefully before they get to you." There was a lot of hope involved here—and hope can be a pretty powerful thing.

33

You Have to Do This for Me

Lance had been confident during our planning session that Aurelia would be in that lair of hers tonight because he figured she wouldn't want to stray far from her portrait. That would serve as her gauge as to the success of the night: as soon as that photo changed back to its beautiful former state, she would know that I was dead. I took the Swiss army knife from my purse and tucked it into the slim pocket of my dress—it felt heavy there, laden with significance. As I breezed past the front desk and into that hallway, I braced myself and found my head filled with only one thought, one image: that painting, *La Jeune Martyre.* The girl in that painting had to have been brave and heroic and strong, despite the outcome. She had done something worthy of being immortalized. I had once been a kid on the verge of death left lying in a ditch somewhere but had survived that. Tonight I might end the night discarded and left for dead again, but I wasn't going to let that happen without trying to do something gutsy and noble first.

But I had to slow down. Even in the dim light, I could make out that imposing figure. Lance had anticipated something like this, and he had been right. Arms crossed, strong as stone, Beckett stood guarding the door to Aurelia's office. His eyes zapped toward me. He didn't say a word. I stopped in my tracks ten feet in front of him.

"I've come to give Aurelia my answer," I said to him, almost sweetly, trying to steady the tremor in my voice. "But I'm going to say no. And she won't like that very much." Beckett's eyes narrowed. "You know, if you killed me before Lucian did, just think what it would do for your reputation." I could see him weighing it; for several seconds he didn't budge an inch. Then slowly he rocked side to side on his feet. "Catch me if you can." I took a slow step backwards.

In a flash, he pounced.

I hurled my purse at him and ran, faster than I ever would've imagined I could in heels. Out the hallway, past the front desk, with him trailing me closer than I would've liked. I flew down the stairwell to the Vault, blasting past the duo guarding the door before they knew what hit them, right through the mouth of the club. Inside, it was already bustling and positively teeming with Outfit members. I sped straight through, weaving around the lively weekend crowd. I looked back a split second and seemed to have lost Beckett, but gained new pursuers. As I ran, the new recruits of the Outfit honed in on me, practically lighting up as I passed. One by one they began trailing me, a pack forming, winding and pushing through the crowd. I forced my legs faster, knocking over anyone in my way. I stumbled and tripped through that dark hallway behind the fire wall and spilled out into the tunnel. As soon as I neared that half-gutted room where I knew Lance would be waiting, I started yelling.

"They're all right behind me!" I turned the corner and, sure enough, there was Lance. He stood beside the photos, including the new ones we'd printed out and taped to sheets of poster board propped against the others, and held a gleaming switchblade for me to take. My entire body was slick with sweat.

"Go time," Lance declared.

I lunged for the knife, prepared to start slashing, just as the angry herd set in. They were upon us now, sweeping into this room, possibly thirty of them hurtling toward us.

Gripping the knife handle as firmly as possible in my sweaty palms, I began slicing in wide swaths. I did one of the group photos first, striking with sharp, long strokes and then smaller hatches, trying to cover everyone. Those people dropped to the ground, crackling and kindling. The rest swarmed us, Lance swinging at them, throwing punches and blocking them from me as best he could, trying to hold them off while I cut their photos to ribbons. There were more than I expected; some had been up manning the prom—Beckett must have rounded them up when I thought I'd lost him chasing me. Lance grabbed one of the rotting wooden boards he'd set aside in advance, swinging wildly at our attackers, trying to mow them all down. He smacked them so hard, a sharp crack snapped the air and the wood, and they went flying.

Then, like a bull loose from his pen, Beckett came charging from the back of the group. He pummeled Lance, taking him down with a thud that echoed in my chest. He was stronger than the rest of the Outfit combined, teeth gritted, eyes burning with rage. The stakes were higher for him: he fought for status, for the chance to become the new Lucian. I lost focus for a millisecond and an Outfit woman—Michelle, it was Dr. Michelle—knocked me to the ground. "What happened to First do no harm?" I shouted at her, battling back. But she had backup; so many others tugging at my hair and clawing at my dress and arms, I flailed wildly to shake them off.

Kicking, crawling, I sliced and sliced, stabbing at the photos as fast as I could, even as these men and women, the ones I'd so admired at one time, tried to rip me apart. They came at me from every side, such an onslaught that I couldn't get off the ground and was left hacking away madly at the photos, throwing my arm out like a pickax, stabbing and then using the leverage to drag myself along the floor toward my next target. Every time Beckett got ahold of me—yanking my leg so hard I thought he might pull it out of its socket, twisting my arm behind my back so that I was in danger of slicing myself with the knife—Lance was on him in the blink of an eye, throwing himself at Beckett or peeling the brute off me with such force I wouldn't have believed he had it in him if I hadn't seen it.

And slowly, through it all, the numbers diminished. One by one, the Outfit members dropped around us both, morphing into their ugly images from the photos and then charring and turning to ash, until it was just Beckett. His photo required so much more than the others. I had already delivered a couple sharp slashes to the heart but had to keep at it, again and again and again, until finally he doubled over and fell to the ground.

Catching our breath, Lance and I lay beat up and bruised, our faces flat against the warm, grimy floor. Beckett slowly deteriorated in the space between us until, with no warning, his body sparked and flared into a crackling fireball. Lance and I, still on the ground, jerked, the flame sizzling and licking at us as we tried to scramble away, singeing us both on the leg. Even as his decaying figure burned, he spoke to us. "Don't be too impressed with yourselves," he struggled, in a gravelly tone. "You won't last the night." Then the charring began, taking over every inch of his skin, slow as could be. It seemed that the higher their station within the hierarchy of the underworld, the longer they burned. Lance and I didn't speak; we just lay there, as Beckett flamed out. I imagined Lance felt as achy and bruised as I did. I couldn't begin to find it in me to lift myself up.

But I felt it, even as Beckett's corpse sparked in death and defeat—I felt the change in the air, a tingle at the back of my neck that told me I had to move. I could feel him there. I wondered if Lance could feel him too. I wondered if Lance had more strength than I did right now. Because I really couldn't imagine having to take on another murderous soul and one that would be even more deadly. That I was still alive felt unbelievable to me, something that deserved a few minutes of celebration, and of healing, before I had to be thrust back into this battle. But his footsteps grew closer. *Get up, Haven, you have to get up,* I told myself. I saw those shoes first. One of them kicked, hard and sharp, against Beckett's burning form, not even flinching when the flame caught onto his sole, just stomping it out and kicking again, turning the hissing Beckett over.

"You . . ." Beckett's wheezing voice stung the air.

"Me," the voice replied, reaching down to the sizzling figure to extract a jingling key ring from what remained of Beckett's jacket. I knew those keys, I knew where at least one of them led: that door. I had to move. Now. I had to move. Slowly, I pulled myself up on my hands and knees, head still bowed. I was too late.

Lucian's hand grabbed my upper arm, fast and firm, yanking me to my feet. I screamed. "Where's my photo?" he asked, emotionless, cold. "I know you didn't destroy it."

I couldn't find my voice. From the corner of my eye I saw Lance roll onto his side. He was trying to get up, trying to help me.

Lucian shook my arm. "Why?!" he yelled at me. "Don't you know how much easier that would've been?"

"It's over there," I choked out, winded, jerking my head to the back corner of the room. I had asked Lance to pull it out from the rest, keeping it separate, just in case. He stomped over there now, yanking me along with him. On the way, he bent down to swipe something gleaming from the ground—the knife. He grabbed the photo in its frame and with me in one hand, and the picture, keys, and knife clutched in the other, he trudged over in the direction I had feared: back toward that dreaded door that felt like fire and dropped into the underworld. As we inched closer to that entryway, my legs scrambled to slow our pace, but were too weak to do much good.

"Answer me!" he barked at me again, dragging me along as I stumbled. "Why didn't you do away with me like the others?"

"I just . . . I couldn't. I didn't want to. I hoped—"

"I don't know where you get this hope, with all that's gone on here," he spat, stopping before the door. I could feel the heat emanating from behind it. He dropped the photo on the ground and fumbled with the keys, almost dropping them too, which showed me that he was nervous at least. "You have one last chance," he said, key engaging in the lock, clicking. With one hand, he flung open the guard bar and tugged open that mammoth metal door. A rush of heat flew out, blowing us back. It felt as if it took all my skin with it, and I had to close my eyes. When I opened them again, all I could see below was a great black abyss, with wild, hungry flames churning at the very bottom. We both stood only inches from the drop-off. I felt woozy, like I might just keel over into it and be done with. I tried to steady my feet, rooting them, and pushed back, leaning away from it. I would save my energy and try to spring it all on him at once, lunging away from this. I couldn't go down there.

He jammed the cool handle of the knife into my palm and dropped to his knees, taking me with him, so we were level with his photo. It was dangerously close to falling in, the frame edging out an inch or two into the open doorway. "Will you just do it?" he shouted over the roar, shaking me. I couldn't even look at him. I focused instead on his picture. Up until right now, as I kneeled at the gateway to hell, I had still held out hope that Lucian would defy Aurelia. His picture had been changing back on its own. It was nearly perfect now, a sure sign that his soul was healing. But if he was capable of throwing me into this hellfire, then my instincts clearly hadn't been anywhere near as solid as I'd thought. He barked at me again: "Will you just drive that knife into my picture? . . . Please? Will you?"

And this time, I could feel the glimmer of desperation behind his words and that's why I said, softly, fighting back tears: "No."

His grip loosened. He bowed his head. Somewhere behind us, I heard Lance grunt as he made it onto his feet.

Lucian rose too, but on heavy legs. It seemed that he was crumbling from within. "Then that's it," he said, his tone suddenly wistful, fragile even. "That's it. You have to throw me in."

Lance charged, a rush of footsteps, but then stopped dead in his tracks, his shoes squeaking to a halt, as though wondering if he'd heard right. I wondered myself. My eyes flicked up at Lucian's and I stood up, letting the knife drop.

"What?" I managed.

"You have to do this for me." He turned toward Lance, still at a distance, and tossed the key ring to him. "One will lock this place up but the other one gets you into Alcatraz. Etan's circling Dante in the ballroom," he explained. "I know he's going to pounce. He'll probably take him down there and then there won't be much time."

Lance nodded at this, thinking, then asked, "But Haven got Etan's photo; it's over here." He pointed toward the shredded pieces, scattered all around.

"It's going to take a while to go into effect since he wasn't physically down here. It's the same way with the others who are still upstairs. So, unfortunately, he'll have time to do whatever he's planning to do to Dante. But you can slow him down."

"Got it," Lance said in a serious tone, letting his next challenge sink in.

After a pause, Lucian spoke to me again, delicately, "And so I need you to do this for me now." I searched his eyes. He went on. "As soon as Aurelia finds out I went against her orders, she'll destroy me herself. I can't let that happen. I have to go back by your hand. If one of them gets to me then there will be no hope of my coming back. I need to make it look like we fought, like I tried . . ."

I looked at Lance, hoping he might have a better idea, but he shook his head in sincere apology. We had been over this. I was the only one with the full power to banish any of them.

"This is what you want?" I asked, unsteady.

"She'll be out for my blood and if she takes me it's a far greater offense. It means she had to because I betrayed her, I betrayed them all. Then I'm banished to the underworld for eternity. But if it's you then it's different—then I do my time down there, my punishment for failing in this assignment, but there's always a chance I can return here to recruit again, where there's more freedom and it's possible to one day . . . escape." He looked like he wasn't sure he even believed this could happen but was trying to convince us both. "It's not easy but it's possible. If I ever do get back here and I find the courage to run away from this darkness, will you help me, Haven? Will you help me fight them all then? Will you help me try to change then and be like you? To be good instead?"

I felt tears rising again but I battled them back. I couldn't afford to break down now, I still had too much ahead of me tonight. "Anytime." It came out as a whisper. But I meant it. If I ever had the power to assist in that fight, I would do it. He wasn't like the others.

"Always be careful, Haven. Be strong . . . and be you."

I nodded.

"Take care of her," Lucian called over to Lance, who I could tell wasn't going to leave until Lucian was gone.

Lance looked at me and then said to him, "To know her is to know she can take care of herself."

Lucian smiled. "That's true."

"But she and I will look out for each other," Lance amended.

"Fair enough," Lucian agreed. He inched closer to the edge and looked at me expectantly. "Please, Haven. Now."

I opened my mouth to speak but realized I had no words. There was too much I wanted to say. And none of it that I could get out free of tears. "Goodbye," I offered, in a broken voice. " . . . for now." I placed my trembling hand on his heart and held it there, unable to push even the slightest bit into the roaring fire beneath. He grabbed my wrist, just below that cuff, and raised my hand up to his lips, kissing my palm, then set it back against his chest. With no warning, and little if any strength from me, he dove into the pit.

A split second before his descent, his foot kicked out in one quick motion, snagging the edge of that photo and catching it just enough to send it into the flames with him. As I watched his free fall, it seemed as though it happened in slow motion, the way a feather takes forever to finally reach the ground. He kept his eyes locked on me until, at last, in a flash, he disappeared into the fire so far below.

I felt the tears start to well up again. I didn't know if that had been the right thing; I didn't know what was right anymore. But if he ever did come back, in search of an escape from that afterlife, I would help him. I had wanted to help him now, but he just wasn't ready for me.

Lance grabbed my arm, squeezing it, like he was pumping the life back into me, reminding me I couldn't allow myself to mourn any of this right now. He pulled me back from that precipice and swung the door shut, securing the bar and locking it tight. All the while, I just stood there so very still.

"I know it doesn't feel like it right now," he said gently, "but you did good." I nodded. "There's more to do though. You still have your knife?" he asked, attempting to nudge us back to the pressing business at hand. I couldn't speak. I could only nod again. Slowly, I felt inside the pocket of my dress—it was still there. He folded his knife up. "Good luck, Haven. You can do this."

We went our separate ways; we weren't finished yet. I looked at that great door once more before leaving, and then, shaking out my head, my arms and legs, shaking it all off, I did my very best to push Lucian to the back of my mind.

~ 34 ~

A Decline, Without Regrets

Beckett, I was glad to discover, hadn't even entertained the possibility that I would have survived his attack. As I neared Aurelia's office door, not only was there no one guarding it in his place, there wasn't even anyone manning the front desk. That gave me the slightest thrill—being underestimated could end up working to my advantage. I tried to summon every bit of strength, pushing aside the ache, the fatigue, and all the fear. *Think of what you've just done. You took them all on, you can do this,* I tried to tell myself.

I lifted my fist, knocked—for old times' sake—and then just pushed open the unlocked door. Aurelia was seated at her desk, her back to the door as she watched the flat screen on the wall, which had apparently been repaired. She looked over her shoulder at me. For a fleeting moment, surprise swept her face but she worked to extinguish it.

"Haven?" She sounded only a touch startled, but recovered. "I had hoped you wouldn't be dropping by, but here you are. Perhaps you'd like to watch with me."

I held my face steady but my eyes fell on what she had been

watching—instead of running through press clippings and the looped reel that usually played at the front desk, the screen now displayed security footage. The real problem was the top half of the screen devoted to the ballroom. I took a few steps forward, to be sure, but there was no mistake: it was Dante being dragged out of the dance by Etan and another of his cronies, a new recruit. My heart stopped.

"Oh, you'll like this show. Have a seat and watch with me," Aurelia said. "This will be fun. Let me get you caught up. They just escorted him out. Caused quite a stir but everyone just assumed it was underage drinking, you know how it goes."

"What are they doing? What are they going to do to him?" The questions came out involuntarily. I didn't expect any answers.

She leaned back, still glued to the screen. "He's about to become one of us. Unfortunately, Dante had some blood taken after his little bout with, shall we say, food poisoning, the other day. I might as well tell you, one of the paramedics was one of ours." My mind raced linking up all these bits and pieces. "So it will take very little now for him to enlist with us: he gave his consent weeks ago and now that he's given blood, it appears the coding has gone into effect." She was looking at me now, with those flinty sapphire eyes. She clicked her mouse and the bottom of the screen flashed to Alcatraz, where Dante kicked and writhed as Etan and his henchman dragged him along the walkway to that cage in the middle.

"He'll never sign." From the corner of my eye, I saw Lance trailing them.

"We have methods of coercion, trust me," she assured. She hit a key and the image blew up to fill the screen: Dante was now locked in that central cell, with Etan seated across from him.

"Yes, see." She pointed, excited. "That's a vial of your little friend's blood and we have a lovely antique quill there for him to sign with. I suppose it won't be so easy with his hands restrained like that—" They were somehow chained to the tabletop. Lance skulked along the periphery, in the shadows, undetected so far, but I didn't like the equal ratio of devils to angels-in-training. I couldn't quiet the fear that our side wouldn't come out on top. "But he'll make do, and in a timely manner, or else we'll just call the whole thing off, if you know what I mean." She clicked again and half of the screen returned to the prom.

I struggled to clear my head: I had to trust that Lance could do this, that he could help Dante; I couldn't lose sight of what I had to accomplish here. Aurelia would love for me to be distracted, I thought. *Focus, Haven, focus. Get this back on track.*

"I don't want to watch TV anymore," I said, trying to sound strong. "It doesn't matter anyway. Even with Dante, your numbers are still really falling."

"Oh, is that right? I hope you realize the only reason I'm letting you live right now is because I fully expect that the others will be here soon. I'm not sure how you got past Beckett but he's a master in the art of rounding up his troops quickly and silently." Aurelia must have been so focused on the action in the ballroom that she didn't bother checking the Vault's surveillance cameras. She didn't know. I squared my shoulders.

"That's true, he is. But I'm afraid he already did that once tonight and now he and a whole mess of them are . . . gone." I saw a wave of panic set in, softening her features, much as she tried to still it.

"I can't imagine what you mean." She inched her chair back.

"You know, gone."

"Ah, so your precious Lucian fought for your honor. Well, I'm sorry to report that he will be paying for that."

"No, Lucian"—it stung to say his name—"is gone too."

Now terror flashed within her. "Oh," was all she said.

"So it's pretty much just you and me now."

I paced slowly in front of her then, steadying my stance, determining how and when to strike. I wandered around toward the other side of her desk, scanning it so she would assume I was looking for that particular key that would let me back into the hidden space with her photo. It was nowhere to be seen, which Lance and I had both feared and anticipated. I hadn't spotted that key on its usual ring with the one Lucian had just used and now it just seemed to have vanished compltely. So, the contingency plan then.

"Well, you're still welcome to follow him. You do know, I'm still waiting for your final answer on my very generous offer to join the Outfit in a leadership role."

As I stepped closer toward the bookcase, she swiveled her chair to keep an eye on me.

"Consider this my decline, without regrets."

"I thought that I had sent a clear message with our talk and my visit the other night. Tell me, how *are* you enjoying your new look? I hope the change has been as traumatic as it is dramatic. Do we need to have our talk again about beauty being the most powerful commodity?"

"Funny," I said, chilling my voice. "I always thought it was brains." Watching her, I ran my hand along that part of the wall of bookcases, behind which the photo lay. I had gotten too close. She stood up slowly and then in a flash, it came at me: a crystal paperweight. I ducked and it shattered all around me. My heart thumped and shards of crystal flaked onto my sparkling dress, but I popped right back up to see her wild eyes getting closer. This was good. I picked away again. "No wonder Lucian liked me so much. I don't have such a fiery temper."

That did it. She waved her arm as though throwing a pitch and launched a flaming ball of fire at me. I lunged fast, like a soccer goalie wanting the other team to score. Sure enough it hit the bookcase and started burning instantly. The heat flew off of it in stinging rays and my skin felt like it was crisping up just being that close to it. And yet, I didn't move out of the way. I needed her to try to hit me again.

"You didn't really expect him to kill me, did you?" I asked. "The funny thing is, I don't need his charity or his attention or any of it. For all your power, you're the one who really needs him. You need him hanging on you, don't you? You need to know that you're everything to him. And I thought you were such a strong woman. I guess I was wrong."

Her eyes burned now; she threw another blazing comet at me and then another, and I dove and lunged trying to stay in roughly the same spot, even with the flames licking so close to me. The wall burned fast now, a hole forming that I would soon be able to run through. So I kept it up. "Maybe he didn't like it that secretly you look like that photo I took, that that's the real you. No matter how you dress it up, that's still what you are."

She charged at me, throwing rapid fire. To escape the flames, I had to jump and dive from my spot, hitting the ground hard, my knees and palms sliced from the crystal as I crawled away.

"You know, I have almost envied you these past few months," she said, shooting at me. "Your wide-eyed innocence, your virtue. But don't pretend you haven't learned from me. You do realize that even if you somehow win here, which I highly doubt, you will still lose, don't you? There will always be more battles for you to fight." I scrambled on all fours, tripping and slipping to escape the fire raining down around me, so fast, unable to get my footing. And I knew that there was a kernel of truth in there, but I knew what she was doing too. She wanted to tear me down to rubble so I wouldn't be able to do what I had to do. I yelled back up from the ground.

"Too late with the speech. I'm already a different girl than the one I was when I started here. The damage has been done."

"Very well then," she said slowly. She threw one more fiery burst at me; this one sprayed and flared into a wall of fire then she leapt into the air at me. The room began to cloud from the flames crackling and raging. My skin burned from the heat radiating on all sides and a new layer of smoky mist emanated from the fire. I crawled back toward the bookcase that had burned straight through now, offering entrée if I could get over there. But the haze wrapped itself around me, drowning me, slowing me down. Before I could fight back, Aurelia was upon me, choking and engulfing me. I struggled against her, crawling closer to that cell-like room, fighting her off and coughing through the poisonous cloud squeezing the air from my chest. I didn't know if I could make it there before the smoke overtook me. Her hands on my neck felt like they were sizzling right through my skin. But still, I crawled on my torn elbows and knees, inch by inch, and as I got closer, something else took over: it was in my sights now, if I could just keep going. And I did, faster and faster. Still trying to shake her off me, I crossed through that burning opening, the flames trying to taste my skin. There sat the two photos.

The smoke tightened around me as Aurelia grabbed me again,

strangling me, her hold so strong, I couldn't get out from under her grip no matter what I did. I looked and understood why—she was hovering above me, off the ground. I gasped and refocused, reaching back into my pocket for that knife. But it was gone. My head flung in the direction I had come from. It must've fallen out. I couldn't make it back to get it.

I gathered my strength and rose up from the ground, through her oppressive hold and the intoxicating smoke. I steadied myself and reeled back, then charged. With all my force, I dug my sharp heel into Aurelia's heart in the picture, shattering the glass and puncturing the photo. The grip around me loosened and new-found passion flooded my veins and infused every muscle, every part of me. I kicked my heel into it again and dragged my foot down, from top to bottom, again and again. Something leaden dropped to the center of the floor, crashing down. My head swiveled to see her, looking first as she might if she were her proper forty-something age, and then morphing into that monstrosity as she had appeared in the picture. She lay on the ground, withering as the whole room burned around her. She pointed a spindly finger at me.

"This isn't the last time we'll meet, my lamb. And until then, there are so many like me out there. Someone will rise to fill my role and you will find yourself besieged all over again. This will not end well for you. There will always be someone coming for your soul. You are too powerful not to be destroyed."

With that, the decrepit, crumpled figure began to spark and burn. I stood paralyzed by the act I had committed, even against someone this vile. But I woke myself up—I had to get out of there. The photo itself, I noticed, was oozing now. I crouched down, and something glinted at me. My necklace was looped on the corner of my own photo. I grabbed it—the chain was intact, some-how, as though it had regenerated itself after being cut—simply holding it in my hand made me feel stronger. I twisted it around my wrist; no time to mess with the clasp. But I was distracted by something even more perplexing. My photo didn't look at all like it had before. I shrieked when I saw it: it looked like a version of *La Jeune Martyre* except with *me* lying on the ground, halo over my head.

A chunk of the wall near the front of the room collapsed in a fiery crash. I ran past the heap that had been Aurelia to her desk, tugging on that flat screen to try to open the passageway door, the safest exit it seemed. As I did, I couldn't help but watch what was on the screen. The top half still showed Alcatraz. At just that moment in one smooth, lightning-fast motion, Lance crept up from the moat—he must've swam to avoid being seen—stealthily unlocked the cell, when Etan and his associate had their backs turned, and rushed in. By the time the Outfit guy knew what hit him, Lance had him in a chokehold and had snatched anoth-er set of keys from him. Lance threw him to the ground then ducked, bobbed, and weaved to escape Etan's pummeling fist, and knocked over the vial of blood, shattering it onto the floor, every last drop spilled. Etan scrambled for the pieces, looking for any remnant.

Meanwhile, Dante jumped in his seat, like he was yell-ing something. Lance, who seemed to be following his orders, reached into Dante's jacket pocket and produced a sharp leaf of some sort. In one swift motion, he jammed it into the neck of Etan's guy. He was just unlocking one of Dante's chains when Etan connected a punch to Lance's jaw that knocked him down and left a red burn smoking from his skin. Dante reached into his breast pocket for another leaf and stuck Etan in the heart and he slumped instantly. I had to look away, as a reflex. My eyes fixed instead on the bottom of the screen. Even in the scorching heat of this room, it sent a chill through me: it looked like it was set on an image of Aurelia's office, until I noticed all the people. Running.

The ballroom was ablaze!

Half of it was already burning, and a chain reaction set off around the rest of it: each flower arrangement and centerpiece exploded one by one into flames. Still, the room remained half full with people who appeared in no rush to leave despite the chaos around them; even the DJ continued spinning. It took only a moment to realize why: he was one of the Outfit. The remaining Outfit members continued serving drinks and canapés and danced as though nothing was wrong, and because they did, at least a few dozen of our classmates stayed behind as the rest ran for the doorways. They clustered in the center of the dance floor, the safest spot, as the flames burned along the periphery. It was as if they thought this pyrotechnics display was just some very elaborate part of the decoration. A new fire ignited, and my eyes darted toward it. No, it couldn't be—but it looked like Mirabelle. On fire. And then the same thing happened to the Outfit guy who had followed us to Dante's house. One by one, the Outfit members were bursting into flames. No warning, they just began sizzling up.

A chunk of the ceiling crumbling from flames tumbled down to my feet, making me jump. I gave the TV one last tug—hopeless—as I noticed my more successful counterparts, Lance and Dante, fleeing Alcatraz, leaving Etan and his friend sparking and beginning to ignite back in the cell. The heat and smoke rose, as the entire room crackled and spit around me, the fire spreading so haphazardly now, out of control. My heart sank: I had to give up on this passageway; it wasn't opening. Maybe Aurelia had discovered it and had it sealed when she replaced the TV. It didn't matter—I had to get out before I burned to ash. Aurelia, whose own flames were burning brighter, her form creating a blockade at least three feet high and growing near the front door, was slithering toward me, slowly, slowly. The conflagration had nearly reached the front door of the office now too, but it was the only way out. I would be boxed in within minutes. That was it: I'd have to jump over Aurelia to get to the door.

Sweat dripping off of me, I gathered everything I had in me and ran the few steps I had room to run, then launched myself up, springing on legs that had never been asked to take such a leap. I tucked my legs up to clear her as she clawed at me, trying to grab hold and singeing the soles of my shoes to the point it felt like she burned right through them. I landed on the other side and wound up my leg, kicking and kicking at what little of the door hadn't been burned up. At last it crumbled and I fled the inferno, racing out into the relative safety of the hallway, coughing and panting.

35

Be Strong . . . and Be You

I could hear the screams before I even reached the lobby—the shrieks and clomping of shoes that tend to accompany a mass exodus. A sea of our classmates fleeing the ballroom, and other hotel guests, who must've smelled the rising smoke, vacating their rooms and spilling out of the stairwells.

Looking straight up to the skylight, I could see people scurrying on every floor, knocking on doors, alerting each other since, mysteriously, not a single fire alarm had sounded. But down in the lobby now, it was just too many people, everyone pooled by the front entrance waiting to trickle out into the street. Everyone had a sense of frenzy, yet it didn't translate into any rapid motion because the crowd was too enormous for the space, so they sifted one by one by one through the front doors, barely moving. The backup was so great that there was virtually no movement on the packed grand staircase either, everyone inching along, anxious to leave.

At the top of the mezzanine, leaning over the railing, I caught sight of a jumping, waving figure. Dante. He placed his hands around his mouth and shouted over and over to be heard above the clamor: "HAVEN! HAVEN! UP HERE!" I waved both arms in the air. I had never been so relieved to see him. I pushed through the crowd to get to that ottoman and once there I climbed up to the top of its raised center, elbowing anyone in the way, anything to be closer to Dante and get a better vantage point above the masses. "You get her?" he shouted down.

"Got her!" I yelled back up, raising my arm in a thumbs-up. My voice, despite a smoky rasp, had never felt stronger or more proud. My heart was still beating so fast from all I'd accomplished against Aurelia, a sense of supreme invincibility washed over me. Even as these frantic bodies surged around me, I allowed myself just a second to savor the stunning truth: I had somehow come through that battle with Aurelia and won. I felt so powerful thinking about it, it almost made me forget my aching muscles, my scraped and scratched and torn flesh. It seemed like that had been accomplished by someone else but, no, *I* had done that.

Dante put both arms in the air in a victory cheer. "Yeah!" But the celebration had to be brief.

"Do you need me up there or the Vault?"

"All set here. Try the Vault. With Lance. Use this to get people out!" He held his hand up, about to throw something. I steadied myself on the top of the ottoman, praying to make the catch. He lobbed something the size of a grenade over the balcony to me. It was a good throw, right on target. I saw it coming at me and needed it to not explode in my face. I held up both hands making a landing cushion and caught it firm and tight in my palms, breathing a sigh of relief. Green and riddled with bumps, it looked like some type of exotic fruit but was actually from that mysterious garden. Dante had said last night that he had stolen as many of the rare plants as he could find: all you had to do was smash them into the floor, shattering them, and they would release a sort of tear gas that could not only get people to disperse, but also neutralize any poisons in the air.

"Be careful!" he yelled back.

"You too!" I called out, just as a huge crash erupted in the ballroom. It sounded as if some part of it had caved in. The crowd yelped, pushing forward, a stampede overtaking the stairs.

I leapt off the top of the ottoman, twisting my ankle as I landed on the ground and feeling the slightest crunch—my high heel—but remaining on my feet. I felt a superhuman energy. I reached down and pulled that broken heel clean off and then with all my force yanked off the other one too. Now I had flats. Thank goodness I'd gone with Mary Janes; that ankle strap was handy.

I had to wrap my head around this one final task—the only thing that stood in the way of us getting out of here alive. It needed to be done, that's all there was to it. I took off, back through the lobby to the stairwell down to the Vault. I had it to myself, which was a bad sign: no one was clearing out of the club yet.

I ran through that light-splashed tubular entranceway and couldn't help but slow to a halt when I reached the club. The place was packed, the DJ still spinning, music thumping. Everyone still drinking and dancing. No one here seemed to have any idea the hotel was on fire. I wondered where Lance might be and, as if answering my thoughts, an explosion sounded in the far back corner of the room and a cloud of smoke engulfed the area. As Dante had promised, the haze sent revelers scrambling for the exit and covering their faces, leaving those standing near me wondering aloud to each other, "What was that?" "What's going on?"

"Fire," I told the group nearest me, prom-goers who had

filtered down to this underbelly. "You've gotta get out. Over there, go!" As they headed for the exit, I slipped through the crowd, to the opposite side of the back area, over by that blazing wall of fire.

I was about to throw down that sphere Dante had given me when I heard my name from the space behind me.

"So, it's Haven, right?"

I turned around to find Jason Abington standing there, hands in his pockets, looking oddly shy. This obviously could not have been a worse time. I just stared for a moment.

"Can I get you, like, a drink or something?" he went on.

"Jason, hi, wow, really? Now, of all times?" I shook my head. "I'm kinda busy, but thanks. And don't take this the wrong way, but you've gotta get outta here. Like, now. Trust me, you'll thank me. Go." And with that I slammed Dante's plant into the floor and a puff of stinging smoke exploded out of it. The people standing around me began flowing toward the front exit, a relief. Another tear-gas bomb went off in the distance, echoing mine. Then I felt a tug on the skirt of my dress. Maybe he thought I was playing hard to get?

"Jason, you have to—" I started as I spun around. But it wasn't him. A hot poker wrapped itself around my calf and another clamped onto my thigh, melting my skin and forcing me to the sticky, drink-splattered ground as I let out a scream. Crumpled on the floor, gripping me, was the charred, twisting mass of what was left of Aurelia, embers still glowing. Amid the chaos, she had slithered down here, following me, not ready to let me get away with what I had done. I kicked and crawled, trying to wriggle out from her grasp as she tried to drag me closer to that wall of fire. I had no doubt that if she got me near enough, she would find the strength to throw me into it. My beat-up palms, ravaged from this night of horrors, clung and dug into the floor as my legs scissored trying to buck her off me. A scream rose to my lips again but was instantly drowned out by an explosion shattering the air, like the crackle of a firecracker. I knew that sound by now.

I looked up to discover a body of one of the few remaining Outfit members combusting above in the ring of fire. A collective, primal scream broke out and then another body exploded into flames, then the DJ. The dozen people still on the platform flew down the spiral staircase and pushed their way into the crowd leaving the club, pushing, pushing, making the whole mess of them spill out faster and with far greater urgency than they had upstairs. The entire space was consumed by a thick, suffocating cloud now. Hard to see. No one to help.

All I could do was keep fighting for my life. Punching and kicking, I knocked Aurelia off me for a split second and tried to get to my feet. But she launched herself at me once more, pulling me down again, clutching my aching leg in her searing grip. I flailed messily to break free, and just when I thought I couldn't hold her off any longer, I felt it—the slightest loosening of her grasp. She was weakening, her charred, disfigured body growing more brittle. I delivered a final swift kick, sending her sliding across the floor and turning her to sizzling, simmering ash.

A strong hand grabbed my arm, pulling me away and lifting me to my feet.

"Nice job," Lance said. His tuxedo jacket and bow tie were long gone, his shirt was untucked, torn and dirty. He had mostly dried from his dip in the Alcatraz moat, but he looked just as weathered as I did.

"Thanks," I panted, steadying myself on bleeding legs. Even in this smokiness, I could feel that we were alone now.

"Ready to get the hell out of here?" he asked. In the space behind him, the flames of the Outfit members had spread, joining the ring of fire's perimeter. The whole platform looked like a blazing cauldron. I froze.

"Only if we can run and not walk to the nearest exit." Lance followed my line of vision.

The entire platform, a ball of fire, crashed to the floor.

Lance and I looked at each other with knowing eyes. And we took off speeding, out the back exit, into the tunnels. We bound down those corridors just like we had all those nights blowing off steam and making ourselves strong. Behind us, the fire rolled and rumbled, spitting at our backs, the thick smoke hanging in the air like a net trying to stop us. Blood raged in my veins, and I felt a superhuman surge. Though I had been beat up, battered, and bruised, I felt stronger than I ever had before. We sprinted at a speed that I didn't even know we were capable of, generating so much wind it felt like we were riding in a convertible.

The fire was catching up with us, threatening to overtake us, sweep us into its blazing maw. Through that tunnel we soared, until we reached that hidden door into the pantry of the bar we had pillaged nightly, and raced up the steps, taking them two at a time until we emerged directly behind the bar, knocking into the bartender who had once kicked us out and toppling over a whole shelf of bottles that crashed and shattered in our wake.

"Fire! Fire! Get out!" we yelled as we rammed straight through the dense crowd of drunk patrons looking for their Saturday night fix. They all scowled at us like we were playing a prank and they didn't move an inch.

But by the time we had cleared their front door and thrown ourselves into the warm night air, we heard the manic rush of the herd storming out.

We kept running down the narrow alley between the worn brick buildings, running and running as shrieking sirens pierced the night.

It took several minutes before it occurred to us that we had made it. Lance and I didn't even slow to a walk until we had run almost to the other side of the block, back to the hotel. Then we let our bones and muscles cry out; we let our feet drag so it was almost as if we weren't moving forward at all. I had the sense that I could drop right there, just collapse in the alley and sleep for days and days. The volume turned back up on the rest of the world, reminding us that we were still a part of it: the murmur of a thousand nervous strangers asking one another what happened and that befuddled shuffle of all these confused bodies standing around getting in the way. An ambulance whirred and whistled, shaking us both awake, and came screaming down the alley. Lance took me by the wrist, yanking my whole body over to the side of one building, sending himself stumbling too, to let the noisy, bleating monster pass without hitting us.

We smashed against the wall, tripping messily, practically drunk with exhaustion. And as we recovered our footing, he grabbed me to steady me against the brick wall of the building. Before I could even process it, his lips were on mine as he pressed against me, stealing my breaths and making me dreamily dizzy. Like vines, his arms wound around me, pulling me close, his hands webbed in my hair. I didn't even feel the bricks against my back. I didn't feel anything but him.

Slowly, he inched back, loosening his hold on me. As soon as our lips parted, in awe, I couldn't keep it in: "It was you . . ."

He pushed his glasses up on his nose, that nervous tic telling me I was right.

"It was you in the Vault. The night of the gala. Not Lucian."

I noticed for the first time that we were probably standing too close to the hotel. Smoke billowed all around. We could feel the heat emanating from the building and the soft misty spray of so much water pressure ricocheting off the ages-old façade from the fire trucks' serpent-like hoses. Flames danced in the sky. He gazed up silently watching, then looked at me. He rested his shoulder and head wearily against the wall, still so close I could stop his words with another kiss without even having to move, but I let him talk first.

"Yeah, I followed you guys. I never trusted him—never thought he was right for you—even before we knew what he really was. So I followed you when you left the gallery. Then when the power went out, he disappeared and . . . I took a chance."

"Yeah, well, I'm really glad you did."

"I'm glad you're glad." He meant it too.

We both stared off for a moment, retracing the whole whirlwind from the past few months to the past few minutes.

"So, I guess this is why they say you remember prom forever," I said finally.

"No kidding," he said. "So, not to jinx anything, but I can't help but notice that it's after midnight and you're still alive." He shrugged, like it was just another casual observance.

My body received the news like an electric jolt.

"You're right. How 'bout that?" I let it sink in. "But, I mean, I still feel kinda, I don't know, *mortal.* Are we angels now? Am I an angel? Do you have any thoughts on this matter? I hope?"

"Well, you know, I got one more postcard message today . . ."

"Oh yeah? What did it say? Illuminate me." I brushed off my dress. It had gotten beyond dirty, torn at the hem. I looked like I had been through a war zone—which was about right.

"Well, actually, it said to tell you—and I'm paraphrasing here—at the end of the night, if we were both still here that we've passed the first test toward full-fledged angelhood."

"Okay . . ."

"And that apparently we'll be notified when it's time for the next test."

My heart fell. "Oh . . . great. There's another test."

"Yeah. And also, I'm supposed to let you know that your 'mystical powers'"—he made quotes around the words—"are becoming stronger, but to be patient with your physical powers because they'll take longer to start up."

"I'm sorry?"

"Yeah, I don't know EXACTLY what that means—"

"Um, I just destroyed a pack of devils and outran a ball of fire."

"Yeah, I'm guessing you did that all on your own."

"Whoa." I had to pause to recall exactly how I had done this. Confidence can do a lot for a girl, even misplaced confidence.

"Not sure if you noticed but we don't have wings yet."

"I'll have to remember that."

"Thanks, because if we've got another 'test' like this ahead of us, then I'm gonna need you there and all in one piece."

I liked how he said that; I liked us as a team. "It's a date."

I looked out into the end of the alley, where it met the street. People were cordoned off from the building and I could see the edge of an ambulance, and the back of an EMT bandaging up someone sitting in back. He moved out of the way and Dante came into view. He caught me looking and smiled and waved, then pointed to a square of gauze being secured on his forehead. I frowned and he shooed his hand at me like he was fine. He pointed at the EMT, who was young, cute, and not facing Dante at the moment, and he nodded his head in approval. I nodded back. Lance tugged my wrist and pulled me back, kissing me again. As he did, rock-size pieces of the building crumbled down around us. Without unlocking ourselves, we slid over a few steps to avoid being pelted. But I pulled back just long enough to reach my arm up and catch one of the gold disks of the façade that had been hurtling right for us.

"Ow," I said, shaking it now.

"Wow." He looked up. "Good save."

"Thanks." I turned it over in my hands and held it out. "A souvenir."

He took it and studied it. The disk was nicked, chipped, weatherworn, but the LH insignia was clear. "I think this is us. You know, I think I'm the *L*. You think?" He held it out, pointing to it.

I looked and nodded. I liked that. And he was; all along it had been him. "L, yes." I smiled. He kissed me again, scooping me against him with one arm. The sirens and the fire and the people all around, none of it mattered right now.

Not all the remaining questions would be so easy to answer though. In the days that followed, Aurelia, Lucian, and all the very public and known members of the Outfit would be assumed burned to nothing in the fire and the people who had adored them and admired them from afar would accept this as fact because it was as mythic and mysterious as they had been themselves. But I still had so many mysteries left to be solved, and I couldn't settle for such simple explanations. How many souls had been lost tonight? How many had we saved? Somewhere, there were more like Aurelia and I had that burning sense that they would find me or that I would need to find them. What more would I be called upon to do? And when would I finally learn about my past? But I would have to wait to discover these things. I would have to wait to make sense of so much. Right now, I took a deep, smoky breath as the sirens roared around us, Lance's heart beating against mine, and I reveled in being alive.

Acknowledgments

Wow, I've been so lucky to have so many phenomenal people helping me grow my wings with this book. A few extra-special thank-yous:

To my amazing agent, Stéphanie Abou, for years—and years and years—of encouragement and friendship. I can't thank you enough for always being there to listen, to read and offer advice, and to field my millions of questions. What can I say? You're the best. And to the lovely Hannah Gordon and my friends at Foundry Literary + Media.

To my incredible editor, Julie Tibbott, for your laser-sharp eye and tremendous guidance. I've learned so much from you and I'm so grateful to have had you shining your light on *Illuminate!* And to the whole team at Houghton Mifflin Harcourt for your support and hard work shepherding this book.

To the fantastic Stephen Moore, for your great enthusiasm and for helping the book reach an even larger audience.

To the brilliant and inspiring Richard Ford, for always having the perfect words of wisdom and for telling me to keep writing no matter what.

To my family for being the best cheering section a girl can ask for: my loving parents, Bill and Risa (who introduced me to all the great books as a kid); my fabulous sis (and trusted first reader!) Karen, for looking over those early drafts; and my wonderful in-laws Steve, Ilene, Lauren, Dave, Jill, and Josh.

To my unbelievably supportive friends for letting me talk your ears off about this book, with an extra shout-out to Sasha Issenberg, Jenny Laws, Ryan Lynch, Jessica Mehalic, Poornima Ravishankar, Anna Siri, Kate Stroup, Jennie Teitelbaum, Kate Zeller; and Eric Andersson, Albert Lee, Kevin O'Leary, Jennifer O'Neill, and all my pals at *Us Weekly*.

To Brian, of course, for, well, *everything*: for your endless patience and love and for keeping me going through the marathon of writing this book.

And, finally, to you, the reader: Thank you so much for picking up this book and devoting some of your time to living in Haven Terra's world. I so hope you've enjoyed reading these pages as much as I've enjoyed writing them!

Whitelaw — Pray and

PRAY AND DIE

PRAY AND DIE

Stella Whitelaw

This first world edition published in Great Britain 2000 by
SEVERN HOUSE PUBLISHERS LTD of
9–15 High Street, Sutton, Surrey SM1 1DF.
This first world edition published in the USA 2000 by
SEVERN HOUSE PUBLISHERS INC of
595 Madison Avenue, New York, N.Y. 10022.

British Library Cataloguing in Publication Data

Whitelaw, Stella, 1941-
    Pray and die
    1.   Private investigators - Fiction
    2.   Women detectives - Fiction
    3.   Detective and mystery stories
    I.   Title
    823.9'14 [F]

    ISBN 0-7278-5592-1

Typeset by Hewer Text Ltd.,
Edinburgh, Scotland.
Printed and bound in Great Britain by
MPG Books Ltd., Bodmin, Cornwall.

One

"Look, is this really necessary? You know who I am."

"Jordan, you can't go breaking and entering premises and pretending it didn't happen each time you're caught."

"But I used to work here."

"As far as the law is concerned you are one of the peasants now," said Sergeant Rawlings, slamming the Custody Record shut. "You were found straddling the windowsill of the offices of Hemsworth & Co, Solicitors, Dayton Road, Latching. Don't tell me you were comforting a seagull with vertigo."

"I hadn't broken into anywhere and I hadn't entered," I protested, filtering my gaze on the familiar bleak walls of the station.

"Do you want a cup of tea?"

I nodded, wondering how I was going to get out of this one. It was humiliating. My first day working on my first case and I get arrested by a fresh-faced puppy probationer who should have been patrolling the streets looking for the real villains.

"Thank you," I said. It was canteen brew in the same thick cups which the Admin Officer thought appropriate for both law keepers and breakers. It wasn't my high-profile Earl Grey but I needed the liquid and the caffeine. "Can I have a biscuit?" I added.

"Still not eating, Jordan?"

"Not the point. Show me food which isn't murdered, poisoned with chemicals or stuffed with additives and I'll eat it. I might eat fish from the sea but at least it has a chance of getting away."

Sergeant Rawlings produced some ancient digestive biscuits rimmed with fluff from the depths of his desk, then showed me the way to the cells. I knew the way. He didn't have to show me.

1

"You'll have to wait in here, Jordan, until someone comes downstairs to interview you. It's hardly the Hilton, sorry."

The cells hadn't improved. Still narrow, rectangular cubicles with half-tiled walls, scuffed lino on the floor and a bunk bed with a thin plastic-covered foam mattress. The blue plastic had unmentionable stains. I didn't want to sit on it. I was pretty fastidious.

"I'd like some paper and a pen," I asked, knowing my rights.

"Want to write a letter?"

"No, my memoirs."

My name is Jordan Lacey and I live in a bedsit in Latching, West Sussex. No, that's not exactly accurate. I live in two bedsits, a side-by-side arrangement, like Siamese twins. It means I have two kitchens, two keys, two numbers and two doorbells. It can be confusing. On the other hand, not many people know and it could be handy in an emergency.

Sometimes I think I'll knock a hole through the joint wall to save me putting on a robe every time I have to go out on to the landing to get to the next room. And since I only have one kettle, that means a lot of commuting between rooms. I'm saving up for a second kettle.

Latching is a faded seaside town, its glory lost in the past. It became fashionable to take the waters at Latching about 1798 when Princess Amelia, long-forgotten sister of the infamous Prince Regent, came for a holiday visit. The building of the railway brought more visitors, but a cholera outbreak and then a typhoid epidemic sent the visitors scuttling back again.

It's a mixture of soaring Regency terraces, charming crescents with elegant Georgian houses, boat-porched fishermen's cottages, ghastly thirties semis and even more horrendous sixties-to-eighties concrete developments. The powers that be even demolished a gracious Edwardian mansion and garden to put up a deformed multi-storey car park. Right on the front, overlooking the sea, blocking the view. Brother, have they got tunnel vision.

Although solvent, I'm not exactly rolling in the stuff. I had a good job with the West Sussex police, working in the Criminal Justice Department. CJ deals with the prosecution process, conviction service, court liaison, the tape library, warrants, licensing, the Coroner's office and the Police Service solicitors. I had originally worked with Crime Management which does all the interesting things: drugs, special investigations, special branch, fraud. But when I developed asthma, they swiftly moved me off the polluted streets to paperwork.

After shuffling documents for a few months, I began reading them. Unfortunately I found it necessary to tell a certain Detective Inspector what a prat he was (not the exact word I used, but near enough). He was not amused although the vicious rapist who'd just walked free due to the same DI's incompetence was laughing fit to split his black leathers.

Since I would not retract my statement – in fact I broadcast it around the station with maximum impact – I was suspended and then asked to leave.

It was while suspended on full pay that I got this idea of starting out on my own. OK, Latching is not exactly a hive of criminal activity but it has its statistical share of adultery, fraud, insurance claims and contested wills. I would become a private investigator.

And up the road is walled Chichester. Now Chichester has been there since Roman times and you can't tell me it hasn't got a backlog of missing people/money/dogs/cars/antiques. I was prepared to tackle anything.

It was not easy to find the right accommodation for an office. I did not want to work from my bedsits. They were my bolthole. But I needed a place with class and style, a cross between a lighthouse and a theatre. It had to have space. No poky and damp basement dump with areas curtained off for privacy for me. My clients would have the full treatment. Armchair, coffee, carpet, desk. The client in the armchair; me at the desk – coffee percolating seductively on the carpet, wafting out the aroma of exotic Brazilian plantations.

The retail trade in Latching is gradually being eroded by the big boys; the supermarkets on the outskirts of the town eat trade and the huge DIY stores sell everything from raw-plugs to complete kitchens. Shop after shop has closed, been boarded up and hung with estate agent's signs.

3

Stella Whitelaw

The corner shop on the junction of Rex Street with the old High Street had been empty for over a year. I'd walked past it a hundred times, taking the short cut down Rex Street to the seafront. Suddenly I saw it with different eyes. I liked the rich maroon paint and the step up to a corner entrance with carved overhang. It was at the end of its lease and they were glad to let me have it at a rent I could afford. It was the perfect front. I would operate as a shop. Clients could browse without attracting attention then gravitate to the back office for the business.

It had once been an upmarket opticians so the two windows were small and bowed. Spectacles don't need acres of plate glass and I didn't want a big display window to fill. But what was I going to fill it with anyway?

The first thing I did for my shop was to make three smart signs with black plastic stick-on letters. OUT TO LUNCH. BACK SOON. CLOSED FOR REDECORATION. They would cover any length of absence.

The shop was at the oldest end of the original High Street where commerce petered out into a residential area. Opposite stood solid, three-storied semi-detached Victorian houses with pillared porches and tall windows which cost a fortune to curtain. Few were left to single occupancy. The rows of tenant bells indicated the number of flats these once sturdy and spacious family residences had been carved into.

Next to my shop was a drab hairdressers with plastic flowers in front of net curtains; then a Mexican restaurant that did not open until the evening. A peculiar youth cult place occupied the other corner site, selling huge posters of unshaven pop stars, second-hand videos and tapes. It belted music all day long. There was a general store that stocked a bit of everything from postage stamps to a dusty tray of rose quartz. The two other shops were boarded up and empty which I viewed with interest as useful extensions to my activities.

I was weighing a chunk of heat-generating rose quartz in my hand when the idea for a shop came into mind. I would sell junk. Not a lot of junk, only high-class pieces. I had no money for stock and I did

4

not want to be bothered with suppliers, deliveries, VAT and all the other time-consuming rigmarole of genuine shop-keeping. A few really nice pieces of junk could stand in my discreet windows; a couple of shelves of jumble sale books for browsing and some cheap Monet reproduction prints on the walls. It would look . . . intriguing.

"Do you want that rose quartz?" The shop assistant was a frowsy blonde with ragged hair, long red fingernails and a wrap-over pinny protecting her short skirt and blouse. "They have healing properties, y'know."

"And boy, do I need healing," I said, putting the quartz back on the tray. "But I've only come in for Ajax, Flash, J-cloths and a good scrubbing brush."

"Planning a spring clean?"

"Moving into the corner shop."

"Welcome to Skid Row."

I cleaned the place as if it had an infectious diseases court order slapped on it. There were just the two rooms, the front shop and a back room and an outside loo. Eventually it was whistle clean but empty, big enough for a new political party. Where was I going to get my high-class junk? And office furniture? I needed decent furniture. What about advertising? I had to advertise but discreetly. The problems of being self-employed sent me back to the store for a wrapped tuna sandwich and a carton of soya milk.

"My name's Doris," said the blonde, offering me a squeeze out of a tube of hand cream which she kept under the counter. "The local paper gives readers one free advert. You ought to advertise your shop. Make 'em curious. Otherwise nobody'll come. This end of town's dying anyway."

I grinned, handing back the cream. "Thanks for the tip, Doris. What the hell, I'll have a bar of walnut chocolate too. They say we eat 350 lbs of chocolate in a lifetime and I'm way behind."

I sat on the floor of my shop, composing my advert. Doris had given me a back copy so that I could use the form. By the time I'd finished my tuna sandwich, it was ready to post.

Stella Whitelaw

HIGH-CLASS JUNK – INVESTIGATE THE POSSIBILITIES BUT DISCREETLY – HIDE AND SEEK ME – I'M THE BEST PI IN THE BUSINESS

Those who needed a private investigator would understand.

My first client was a woman called Ursula Carling. She'd seen my advertisement and I was just what she wanted. She said she thought her husband had been playing around. Although they had talked about divorce, Ursula was convinced the other woman was sending her hate mail and making nuisance phone calls.

"It sounds distressing. Please tell me about the mail."

"It's such awful stuff," Ursula said, pacing my empty shop like a grieving panther. "Enquiries from undertakers about the measurements of the coffin required for my funeral. She's put my name on a mailing list for sex aids. I even got a call from an Escort Agency, wanting to know what kind of boy I wanted. This woman hates me so much, it's unbelievable."

She tipped out a carrier bag full of junk mail and crudely printed hate messages. Paper spilled everywhere. "Look at all this. Disgusting, absolutely disgusting stuff and it's driving me mad."

"How unpleasant," I said, turning over a few of the messages. They were repulsive. Nasty stuff. "What did you ask for? A six-foot Swede or a small Italian number?"

Ursula looked at me blankly.

"Why haven't you been to the police?" I asked quickly.

"I didn't think they would be interested. All I know about this woman is that her name is Cleo and she works for a firm of solicitors locally somewhere. I want this persecution to stop and this woman warned off."

"Have you made any enquiries yourself?"

"No, of course not." Mrs Carling looked round the sparse room. "I don't want her to think this rubbish upsets me. That's what she wants, isn't it? She's a nasty, vicious piece of work."

"Do you know who she is?"

"I've just told you. Her name is Cleo and she's a secretary with a

6

firm of solicitors. That's all I know. I want you to find her. Give her a scare, a warning. Then all this would stop."

"I'm sure I can find her. It can't be too difficult. There are not that many firms of solicitors in Latching. It won't take long."

"But don't let her know what you're doing. Not at first. Just find out where she is and let me know."

I nodded sympathetically. I'm good on sympathy. Junk mail is bad enough but hate mail is enough to give anyone a nervous breakdown. Ursula looked near to it. She was tall, thin and myopic, her glasses like milk-bottle bottoms. But her eyes were cold behind the thick lenses. Her hair was a tinted grey and set to last. She wore a pale lilac suit, broach and scarf, very tasteful.

"But surely if you are discussing divorce with your husband, it doesn't really matter what he does," I added, without thinking.

"We're not divorced yet," she said indignantly. "So it's still cheating."

I was not so sure but she was paying and I'd take the money and find this Cleo, point out to her that it's an offence to send offensive literature through Her Majesty's mailing system. Her Majesty was not amused. Though if they privatise the mail service, it might not be so. "Ten pounds an hour, plus expenses."

She seemed taken aback. She was probably used to paying cleaner's rates. I thought she was wasting her money.

"Or, if you prefer. Fifty pounds a day plus expenses."

"I'll pay the day rate," she said quickly, probably thinking it would work out cheaper. I knew it didn't. A day was a day, an hour was an hour. I could probably find this Cleo person in five minutes flat if I put my mind to it. I'd put a stop to the whole thing.

"Next time you come I'll have a chair and some coffee," I said, feeling sorry for her. It was no fun being asked for the size of your coffin.

I needed surveillance gear. My wardrobe could fit into a plastic bag. I began to comb the charity shops and there were dozens of them in Latching – Barnado's, Cancer Research, a saintly local hospice, Madame Curie, British Heart Foundation, Cats Protection League with photos of lost cats, Oxfam, Sue Ryder, the lot. I bought a few felt hats, Crimplene suits and crumpled raincoats. Yuk. Then I spotted abandoned junk. The heavens opened, revealing the glory.

When I opened my shop, the north facing window displayed a china chamber pot covered in flowers and over-printed in gold letters that said "God Save the King". The east facing window had an Indian shawl and a faded hand-painted fan so old and fragile, I didn't even dare breathe on it. I had found an unending source of supply. It just needed a discerning eye.

The bolt slid back and I jolted awake. The door opened and Sergeant Rawlings grinned, noting that I was sitting on the writing paper.

"Come on, Jordan. Someone'll see you now."

"Who?" I stuffed the pen in the pocket of my jeans hoping he wouldn't notice. Hoping it wouldn't be the DI who had got me sacked.

"Detective Inspector James. You don't know him. After your time. He's new, transferred from London, East End."

I followed Sergeant Rawlings to the interview room, wondering if I'd get another cup of tea, though he could keep the mouldy biscuits. My neck hurt from dozing off in a cramped position. I sat down on the chair indicated, planting my elbows on the table. Something had to hold up my head.

DI James came into the interview room and sat down, stretching his neck. Perhaps he'd been trying to sleep too. He was tall, craggy, with dark hair, crew cut and piercing blue eyes, ocean eyes, granite-jawed, hunched shoulders and a chest bursting his shirt like the Incredible Hulk. I bet he worked out. He switched on the tape, hardly looking at me. There was something about him but I did not know what it was.

He went through the usual procedure. Full name, date of birth, home address. I yawned. All of the usual police caution, verbally.

"Do you understand?" he asked laconically.

"Yeah, yeah," I said. "When's the tea coming? I've got a throat like the bottom of a pond."

"I must inform you that the right to legal advice includes the right to speak to an independent solicitor on the telephone. Do you wish to speak to a solicitor on the telephone?"

"No, I don't, thank you," I said. "I don't have a solicitor and if I had one I wouldn't want to speak to him. This is all a mistake and I just want to go home."

He looked at me as if I was something from outer space. I knew my uncombed hair needed washing and my clothes were creased and my stomach rumbling. The rumbling was their fault. They are supposed to feed prisoners.

"I'm making enquiries into the alleged break-in at Hemsworth & Co, Solicitors, Dayton Road, Latching. I now propose to question you about the matter. Do you understand?"

I liked his brilliant blue eyes. They were clear, but fathomless. I have a thing about blue eyes, although none of the men in my life have had blue eyes. It must be this sea addiction. The sea has me hooked. I walk the pier every day of my life. It takes exactly eight minutes to the far end and back. Sometimes the pier's legs straddle the sea and the waves send spray into my face. Sometimes it is stranded on the sand and I can peer down into the strange life scuttling about on the bed.

"Do you always talk in that funny way?" I asked, conversationally. "It's not natural, you know. Perhaps you should see a psychiatrist. They can help you to relax. After all, if you were in bed with the love of your life, would you say: 'I now propose to question you about whether you love me. I'm making enquiries into our alleged relationship. Will you be giving me the glass-eye in the morning?'"

DI James flinched. Perhaps I had touched on a raw spot. He was new. I should have been gentler. I leaned over and tapped his hand with the borrowed biro. It was leaking. It left a blue streak.

"Only joking," I said.

He choked back a remark and spoke into the tape. "On being cautioned, Miss Lacey leaned over and marked my hand with a pen."

Excuse me? Did he have an undetected sense of humour?

"Where's the tea?" I went on. "I shall feel faint any moment now. It's hours since I had anything to eat."

9

"It's coming," he said, recovering. "Can we get on with this interview? I've never known anyone waffle on with such a load of rubbish."

"Fun though, isn't it?" I gave him a sweet smile. I can also do a sweet smile when necessary. I practise several times a day.

He looked down at his notes for support. "You were found breaking and entering the premises of Hemsworth & Co, Solicitors, Dayton Road, Latching at seventeen fourteen hours. When apprehended, you said: 'Get lost, buster.'"

"Did I really? I don't remember. I was too upset at the time. It was terrible, Inspector. I'd never been arrested before." I put on my frail and hurt, little-woman look which is difficult at a looming five foot nine. It was acting. I didn't get the part of the courtesan in *The Comedy of Errors* at school for nothing.

"So would you like to say what you were doing there?"

"Of course."

The tea arrived. I stirred in two packets of sugar though I prefer Sussex honey. DI James was cool, professional, a dish. He had a bold face, a cleft chin and stubble shadow, like it had been a hard night. And a deep voice with undetected accents. East End? Oxford? Where?

"You see, Detective Inspector James." I gave him his full rank and leaned forward. They like their full name. "It's all been a mistake. I wasn't breaking and entering the premises of Hemsworth & Co. Oh no, never. I was actually trying to get out. They'd locked me in. They didn't know I was still in the loo. Don't people check these days? After all, it could have been a little old lady with her knickers in a twist."

"I beg your pardon?" He looked distant and bored.

I sighed. I thought I had made myself clear.

"I wasn't trying to get in, DI James. But I was trying to get out. Not entering into . . . but emerging . . . out of. Get it?"

Two

T he usual brrm-brrm of the *Jaws* signature tune followed me
out of the police station. Jordan is a river in Palestine not an
ocean off the coast of Australia. Their juvenile humour has not
improved since my previous forced departure.

I told DI James that I'd been at Hemsworth's to make a will. They
employed three secretaries and I'd really called in to see if one of
them was Cleo or knew of a Cleo. But I wasn't telling him that. I'd
spent all day cruising solicitor's offices and one clerk had a vague
notion that there was a Cleo who worked in Chichester. It was a
start. The five-minute boast stuck in my throat.

DI James looked incredulous as well he might. What had I got to
leave to a cat charity? A collection of Simply Red tapes, some decent
reproductions and books, a clapped-out mountain bike.

"I had to go to the Ladies, couldn't unlock the door and the staff
apparently forgot about me and went home."

I could see he didn't believe it. "So how did you get out?" he
asked with a pained expression. "Pick the lock with a hairpin?"

"Not exactly. I had to unscrew the lock fixture off the door."

"Had a screwdriver with you, did you?"

"I used a metal nail file. The rounded end. Then I opened a window
and was climbing out when your intrepid officer arrested me." I did
not mention my handy pocket kit – torch, miniature screwdriver,
plastic specimen bags, various keys and hairpins and bits of wire.

It was such a ridiculous story, they had to let me go. I didn't say
that I'd slipped into the Ladies in the hope that I could have a
sneaky look round when they were otherwise occupied. I hadn't
reckoned on getting locked in the loo.

11

On the way back to my bedsits, I called in at Rick Weston's second-hand store. He was unloading a big lorry in the forecourt. He had obviously finished a house clearance. Furniture, pots and pans, chipped china, lampshades, books, blankets, towels and tableclothes littered the pavement. It was the sad debris from the end of a life.

"Death, eviction or mortgage repayments?" I asked, wandering round the various piles of goods, my eyes sorting like laser beams.

"She's gone into a nursing home," said Rick with no expression.

I spotted the fringe of a rug rolled up like a giant brandy snap. The reverse was all muted blues and reds of old Persia.

"How much for that tatty old rug?" I said.

"Twenty pounds." He didn't even look at it.

"Ten," I said.

He nodded, throwing a torn orange satin bedspread on the linen mountain. I stuffed the ends of the rolled rug into carrier bags before Rick could change his mind. He unloaded a small button-back Victorian nursing chair on to the pavement. It was upholstered in deep rose velvet, worn and shabby from years of burping babies.

"Twenty pounds," I said, choking back my desire.

"Don't be silly," said Rick, still without looking. "Genuine Victorian button-back. A hundred and twenty."

Rick was a solitary young man. He never said much. His mother, Betty Weston, had met his father on a package tour to Tunisia. She got more than a wonderful tan. She tried to claim on her holiday insurance but the company read her the small print. She became a single mother long before it was the norm or fashionable to be a one-parent family.

I knew all this because his mother lived in a new bungalow on the Fareham Estate. I was sent there once when a prowler was spotted on the estate. My enquiries were side-tracked by her obvious pride in Rick's achievements.

"Rick's turned out a really good boy, he has," she told me. "Started the business himself. Works hard."

Rick liked hauling furniture around, driving his old van with one hand, constantly switching stations on his radio till he found

12

something to suit his mood. Sometimes he wore a big stetson, pulled down low, which he'd found at some house sale. I don't think it had occurred to him that his surname suited the headgear. He used it as a kind of screen.

The "really good boy" knew how to drive a hard bargain. We eventually settled on eighty pounds for the chair, to be paid by installments. He agreed to deliver to the shop for free and threw in a yard of paperbacks he didn't want anyway.

"How about that two-drawer filing cabinet," I mumbled, mouth dry as a stale Weetabix. I wanted that too. Then my office would be almost furnished, except for a desk and that could wait. "Oh dear, the lock doesn't work."

He turned the key with one hand while writing out my bill with the other. "Works. Do you want it?"

"Yes, but I've no more money. You've skinned me."

"Pay next month. On tick."

"I'll give you a free investigation if you ever need it, although I'm sure you'll never be that desperate. Or your mother, if there's another prowler." I knew I was gabbling but his kindness had thrown me.

He smiled, his white teeth as dazzling as no doubt his father's had been many sunny years ago. I nodded. Call me kind-hearted, call me stupid.

I couldn't wait to unroll the rug in my office the next morning. Fortunately Rick Weston was in a hurry. He dumped the stuff and drove off at a rate to some auction. I didn't want him to see it in all its glory. The rug was beautiful, a bit worn and threadbare, but the colours still glowed richly. It would last me out. My magic carpet, dream weaver, weave me.

The chair stood on the rug as if they were made for each other. Perhaps they had been companions in some turn-of-the-century nursery. I brushed the fabric lovingly and then dusted the yard of books and put them on the optician's display shelves. I left the filing cabinet till last but I didn't even get a chance to turn the lock. Someone was knocking urgently on the door of the shop.

Ursula Carling was standing on the doorstep, trembling, her

careful grey hair all awry. She was carrying a Marks & Spencer green carrier bag well in front of her as if it was about to blow up.

"Look at this! Look at this! She's gone too far this time. I'm going to the police," she shrieked, hyperventilating. "I can't stand it. This is driving me . . . insane."

I took her by the arm and led her to the Victorian button-back and sat her down with a comforting pat. She couldn't go to the police. I needed her fifty pounds a day.

"There, there, Mrs Carling," I said, plugging in the coffee percolator with one hand and taking the carrier from her with the other. It felt moderately heavy but not particularly angular. Not a bomb, I decided hopefully. "Come and tell me about it. I'll make some coffee."

"It's quite dreadful . . ." She covered her face with her hands and shook. I needed a supply of tissues, aspirin, brandy. I made a mental shopping list. "This . . . thing was on my doorstep. I found it this morning when I went to get the milk in. That woman is horrible, a devil."

"How can you be sure it was her?"

"She shops at M&S."

"So does half the population of Great Britain."

"No one else would do such a dreadful thing to me . . ."

I let her cry, her blue eye shadow streaking like frayed sky, and made some coffee. Fortunately I'd brought some bone china mugs from one of my kitchens. I didn't tell her it was soya milk. Some people have a problem with soya. She stirred in a lot of sugar which disguised the taste.

I took the carrier bag out the back and opened it. I reeled against a wall. Inside was a cat, a very dead cat. Stiff as a board, eyes glassy, a nasty congealed head wound. A hit-and-run case. My heart thumped wildly. I liked cats, even dead ones. One day I would have one of my own.

I put the poor moggie in the shade and went back indoors. I needed a coffee now. Ursula had recovered.

"Have you found that woman yet?" she glared at me.

"I'm tracking her down. At least I have eliminated certain firms where she is not working. You didn't give me much to go on. Are you sure you don't know her surname?"

"The letters were just signed Cleo."

"What letters? You didn't tell me about any letters."

"You didn't ask me."

I stared at the rug hoping the intricate colours would give me patience. "Perhaps you'd like to bring the letters in. They could be helpful to me in my enquiries."

"I don't want anyone else to read them."

"My only interest in them would be to see if they hold any clues. You do want this investigation to be concluded quickly, don't you?"

Her eyes registered cash signs and she nodded. "I'll bring them in. What about the, er . . . ?"

"I'll see to everything. There's some very worried owner in Latching, wondering why her cat hasn't come in for breakfast."

"Thank you. You're very professional."

It was the first time that a softer expression had touched Ursula's face and I glimpsed the conventional prettiness that had once been there, long before this Cleo arrived on the scene to breed bitterness. I meant to ask where the husband was now. I didn't even know his name.

"You didn't tell me your husband's name."

"Oh, didn't I? Arthur. Arthur Carling. I've a photo here."

The photo was of the two of them, arms entwined, standing at the end of Latching pier. They were both much younger, much happier, windblown. Arthur was a tall, handsome man with twinkling eyes. They looked a good match.

"Arthur looks very nice."

"A charmer," said his wife drily, tucking the photo back in her wallet. "And don't I know it. A real ladies' man."

She went then and I locked up, putting BACK SOON in the window. I took the moggie round to the police station. DI James passed me in the entrance hall. He had his dead-tired, haunted, up-all-night face on.

"Has anyone reported a lost cat? Black, one white ear."

"Why?" He hardly had the energy to say that one word.

15

"I've got him here. Hit and run."

"Put it in the bin."

He was elsewhere. A man on a different planet. I had to bring him back.

So I rounded on him. "How can you say such a thing? This cat was special to some family. The owners are worried stiff right now, calling, searching and when they know the cat is dead, they are going to be overcome with grief. Don't you know that a cat that's loved is part of a family? How can you be so callous and insensitive? Where are your feelings? I suppose they've been destroyed by years of inhuman police work."

"I'm too tired for a lecture, Jaws."

"Jordan, please!" I practically yelled the word at him. I was sounding more like Ursula by the minute. It wouldn't do. I calmed down with effort. "May I report one feline corpse in a procedural manner? Name unknown. Breed indeterminate."

I went round to Doris and bought tissues and aspirin. She couldn't oblige with the brandy. She suggested apple cider.

"Not quite the same alcoholic impact but I'll take a bottle. I might need it for myself."

I sat on the button-back and unlocked the filing cabinet. The top drawer had green metal-slung files marked Gas, Electricity, etc. I looked through them. They were of little interest but I learned that the house was called The Beeches, Lansfold Avenue, Latching, and the owner was a Mrs Ellen Swantry. She was now encased in a three foot by six single bed with a flowered duvet in a nursing home, and no hope of escaping except inside a coffin. I hoped that I wouldn't end up that way. Take me out quick. I don't care about the pain, God, but make it quick.

The lower drawer was stuffed with old brown files stacked on top of each other. The papers were curled and stained; coffee, tea, mud. They looked as if they went back to the Crimea.

I bundled the gas and electricity correspondence into a neat pile for the recycling bin in the car park. I caught sight of a letter from a solicitor's firm in Chichester, Messrs Rogers & Whitworth. It had

16

been typed for a Mr Rogers by a secretary who referenced herself at the top as CC and was about some boundary dispute with a neighbour. There were few details and Mrs Swantry seemed disinclined to discuss the matter.

That solicitor's clerk had said something about Chichester. His memory bank had been hovering vaguely but it was worth a chance. I dialled the Chichester number, prepared for zero response. "Do you have a secretary called Cleo?"

"Oh yes, Cleo. Just a moment. I'll put you through."

I waited, amazed, searching for a pen, a pencil. Born lucky, that's me. By the time they put me through I had pen and paper ready.

"Hello, Cleo Carling speaking."

It took me three seconds to take in the name. I repeated it like an idiot. "Carling? Cleo Carling did you say? Are you related to Arthur and Ursula Carling?" I got their names out with difficulty.

"Yes, I'm their daughter."

"Are you sure?" At times the truth can throw you.

"Of course. Who is this, please?"

She sounded pleasant, normal, not the kind of person to leave dead cats on doorsteps. What was going on? Was Ursula completely round the bend? This was her daughter.

"My name is Jordan Lacey and I'm a private investigator. I'm doing some work for your mother, Ursula Carling."

"Good heavens. What sort of work? I don't understand."

"I'm afraid I can't explain over the telephone. Can I come and see you? When would a meeting be convenient?"

"I don't want to sound unhelpful, but is this really necessary? Surely I'm not involved?"

"In a funny sort of way, you are. I'm not really sure of anything at the moment and I would be grateful for some clarification. I'd like to talk to you. Can we meet?"

"Well . . . I suppose so. Would this evening suit you? I finish work at five. You could meet me outside the front entrance of the cathedral."

I liked that. It had style, like a medieval pilgrimage.

17

"Thank you, Miss Carling. That would be fine. Five o'clock then. It won't take long."

I needed a breath of fresh air, something to wash away the smell of the police cell and my depleted sleep. I took the short cut down Rex Street and braved the cruising cars that were searching for parking spaces along the front and crossed the sea road to the shore. There were steps up on to the promenade but I climbed the grass bank in silent protest. I hated all the poured concrete that was gradually suffocating the spirit of sea-lashed Latching.

The sea was far out, a distant greeny-blue mirror of the sun. It was calm today, a clear line on the horizon between green sea and the blue of the sky. Sometimes it's churned up like espresso coffee, waves exploding on top with lashings of creamy froth. It's the sand beneath that changes its colour. But today the sea was washing serenely in rhythmic waves, the pebbles moving and shuffling with barely a sigh.

A great expanse of wet sand beckoned my bare feet. I pulled off my socks and trainers and stumbled over the grey and fawn pebbles until I reached the pools and eddies of water. The sun drenched my face and I stood, open-mouthed, to absorb its healing rays. How I love the sea. This is where I want to die. On the beach. In the sea. I don't care how. It's my natural habitat. I'm a sea person.

I walked the beach, singing Gershwin. "The Man I Love." I didn't know all the words. Crabs scurried away in horror. Small fish darted back to deeper water. A dog stopped to listen and howled tenor in unison.

"Watch the traffic now," I said to the dog as it raced back to a distant owner.

When I reached the yacht club where rainbow-sailed surfers skimmed the waves, it was time to turn round and walk back to the pier which stalked the sea like some giant hump-backed centipede. I tried to make this a daily walk but sometimes there wasn't time. Or I walked eastwards towards Shoreham past the weathered boats drawn up on the shingle and chalked FISH FOR SALE signs – crab, mullet, huss, and plaice at special prices.

Somewhere near the pier I climbed to the upper level, mingling with the chip-eaters and burger-biters, roller-skaters and pushchair-pushers. I knew where I was going. I was going to look at Trenchers. It was another of my daily walks, a nostalgia fix. Trenchers had such a history. I loved the place. No one even looked at it these days. One day the council would tear it down and build another multi-storey eyesore.

Trenchers was a huge, terraced, boarded-up Edwardian hotel, slate roofed and imperial. It broke my heart to see it in its present state. It was right on the front, so elegant in design that nothing could destroy its looks. Once crowned heads had stayed there, heads of state, film stars of the thirties. I could imagine them on the first-floor wrought-iron balconies drinking champagne, walking the promenade with parasols, their limousines parked in the spacious grounds behind the hotel, playing croquet on the manicured lawns.

Now every window and doorway was planked with boards and nailed up, painted cream, the garden a derelict dump for rubbish. The council said it was going to be developed but they never said how. Didn't they know the place was reeking of history, that ghosts walked the empty corridors and the soaring staircase? They could pull it down and put up retirement flats but the ghosts would still be there, walking their night-long vigils, rustling, tiptoeing.

I soaked up the ambience of the hotel, wishing I had a couple of million to buy the place, restore it, return the building to its former glory.

One of the basement doors had been forced off its hinges, despite the sturdy bars. Weekend hooligans. I dreaded to think of what they had done inside. On the other hand, I had never seen inside the hotel, only looked with longing at faded photographs in Latching Town Museum.

No one was taking any notice of me as I climbed over the low wall and slid down the steps to the gaping door. In the cavernous gloom I saw stainless-steel kitchen tables and a long range of cooking equipment. The floor was littered with bits of ceiling plaster and take-away cartons, beer cans and crisp bags.

The interior was a gloomy mess. To the left were more corridors and passages to something that looked like a wine cellar. At the far end were narrow stairs leading up to the floor above. Everything had been destroyed, wrecked by vandals, fitments pulled off the walls, counters desecrated, a cold cabinet smashed. Wrinkled condoms . . . what a grim place in which to discover the joy of love-making. I hoped their passion had been so urgent, it transcended the surroundings.

Several billion dust mites started me coughing. I didn't have my Ventolin inhaler with me.

Empty houses can be alarming, especially large empty vaults like Trenchers. Sounds echoe, exaggerating the size; shadows loom, taking on weird shapes, a man, a beast, nightmarish distortions. The air in Trenchers was stale, breathed-over a hundred times, smelling of dust and dirt and mould and vermin and decay. Yet all the lost living survived somewhere . . . the loving, the longing, the bitterness, the quarrels. Chefs still bustled over the steaming pots, the waiters scurried with trays, the dumb waiter clanked its dishes upstairs to the grand silver-service dining-room.

I was aware of the atmosphere. When on the force, I could tell instantly whether a house was happy or hiding something. Trenchers was harder to define. It didn't yield its secrets easily.

I looked up at the hole in the ceiling, hoping to glimpse the vestibule or the famous grand staircase, sweeping upwards.

Instead I saw a grey-stockinged leg wearing a sensible laced-up shoe. It was slowly swinging around. I moved closer to the hole, taking care where I trod, till I was right underneath.

It was a dead nun. She was wearing one of those modern habits, grey skirt, blouse, and grey cardigan, her hair covered with a grey fabric kerchief. I could see her outline clearly because light was washing down from the glass dome in the roof above the vestibule. She was hanging from a meat hook.

I swallowed hard.

She was on the edge of my vision. I was seeing, but not seeing. Her face was hidden by the flowing folds of the kerchief though I was not sure if I wanted to see her properly. If death had come violently, her staring eyes would reflect the horror and pain. Her skin would have changed colour; her flesh was already decaying. I did not know how long she had been there, nor did I want to know. No one can escape death but this wasn't my job any more. None of my business. I looked no further. It's what the police are paid for.

Trenchers was completely still. Nothing moved. There was only my breathing.

I'd seen quite enough. She had been dead a while, perhaps a few days. There was congealed blood. I re-tracked fast but carefully, my heart pounding. This was no time for a sprained ankle. A can skittered over the floor and the noise was like clashing cymbals, echoing everywhere. I clambered up the steps and over the wall and I didn't care who saw me.

My route to the police station was on auto-pilot. I was hardly aware of anyone or anything. The nun hung in my mind, and that's not a joke. It was a wonder I didn't get run over. I ignored the red pedestrian lights, didn't wait for the little green men, darted across roads against the traffic.

The forecourt of the police station was a reassuring collection of panda cars, motorbikes and bicycles. I rushed up to the desk. Sergeant Rawlings looked at me over his spectacles. They needed cleaning.

"Another dead cat, Jordan?"

"No, a dead nun."

"A what?"

"A dead nun. Very dead."

"Now that's different."

I planted my elbows on the counter top. "Why is it that no one ever takes me seriously? I tell you, she's dead and she's a nun. I found her."

"What did she die of? Overdose of communion wine?"

"Tacky, sergeant, tacky. No wonder the force gets a bad name. She's slung up on a meat hook in Trenchers Hotel. Now it's over to you and your band of valiant sleuths. And no, she's not one of my clients."

I turned on my heel and marched out, still unnerved. I needed coffee and a hot shower. The sky was torn with pewter clouds now; rain heading from the east. If I didn't hurry, I was going to get wet and I had to be in Chichester by five o'clock to meet Cleo Carling. Just time for a quick call at the shop. My priorities surfaced.

There was still some coffee in the percolator and I heated it up. Hot mug in hand, I hurried round, tidying and putting things straight. My office had to be pin-tidy, even if my bedsits were days past their weekly onslaught. I was still shaking.

It was starting to rain, pattering on the windows and streaking the glass. The door flung open and a young man almost fell into the shop, bringing a gust of rain with him.

"I must have it!" he gasped. "It's wonderful; it's marvellous. I've only twenty pounds. OK, it's worth double but I've no more money."

I put down my mug without breathing. He was in his twenties, hair spiky blond and wild eyes glazed, jacket flapping. Yet he did not look really dangerous. He was waving a twenty pound note which was hardly life-threatening.

"Can I help you, sir?" I said in my best shop voice.

"That chamber pot. It's divine. God Save the King. I must have it. It is for sale, isn't it?" His eyes were suddenly flooded with despair.

"Of course," I said, taking it out of the window and scraping off the six pound price label which I had stuck on its bottom.

"How much?" His lower lip was trembling.

"Twenty pounds."

He nearly collapsed with relief. Clearly off his rocker.

"I'll take it. I'll take it."

He staggered out of the shop, the precious chamber pot in a second-hand carrier bag. I didn't know selling things was so easy. I dug through my cardboard box of trove from the charity shops and picked out a delicate blue milk jug. It said DELFT underneath which I knew was somewhere in Holland. I stuck the same six-pound price label on it and put it in the window. It looked lonely so I added some blue glass necklace beads in a careless swirl.

The young man put his head round the door again. "If you ever find another one . . . ?" he said hopefully.

"I'll keep it under the bed for you," I promised.

Three

C leo Carling occupied my mind on the short train journey to Chichester. I tried to put the nun firmly out of brain activity. What was this family up to? I should have learned by now that nothing is straightforward. It's like the men in my life. They are complicated. I'd rather live with a cat.

As the flat fields, dunes, swamps and housing estates flashed by, I thought about Ursula Carling. She was warped, bitter, revengeful, distraught, hysterical – a fifty-year-old woman standing on the edge of undeniable middle-age and not liking what she saw ahead. She wanted Arthur to reassure her that she was still pretty, still desirable, still capable of holding on to one man's devotion.

I remembered the photograph that Ursula had shown me. Arthur looked pleasant, dependable and fun to be with. He had the kind of face that would look good in sleep. He would be considerate and not snore or sleep with his mouth open. Amalgam fillings should be kept to oneself. Only your dentist should know.

Chichester was a friendly sort of town, geared with plenty of pedestrian walkways for strollers and shoppers. Sections of the ancient town walls were wide enough to walk on, giving uninterrupted views of other people's back gardens. I like back gardens. They give away so many secrets. Front gardens are on view, designed to be seen, but back gardens bear the true nature of the occupants.

I wandered by the Market Cross, a splendid octagonal open-sided shelter built by some far-seeing bishop in 1501, all gargoyles and carved symbols intended to scare the serfs. The cathedral was open on one side to the city, a patchwork of medieval stone with bits and pieces of masonry built on over the centuries, its spire soaring above the Sussex plains. The site had once been fields; now it was in the centre of town.

Cleo was easy to recognise. She was a neat young woman in her early thirties, dark hair bobbed, a smile ready on her face. She was wearing the kind of grey tailored business suit I could never wear, ten denier stockings, court shoes. I shifted uneasily in my jeans and sneakers. Perhaps I should have dressed up. A jacket at least. But she had spotted me and was coming across.

"Hello, I'm Cleo Carling. And you are Jordan Lacey?"

"How did you recognise me?"

"You've got that intense look of concentration. It's your job, always being alert, I suppose, looking out for things."

I grinned. "You're being flattering about a job which can be terminally tedious and boring. Thank you for agreeing to meet me."

"I hope you're going to tell me what this is all about. My mother is employing you, you say? Well, I guess I shouldn't be surprised. She does do some strange things."

"Is there somewhere we can go and talk?"

"Across the road there's a converted church. The café stays open late and we could get a cup of tea."

"Good idea." I knew the place. It was an innovative use of an unwanted red-brick Victorian church. Inside there were craft shops, stamp dealers, antique stalls, a café. Better than pulling down a solid building and putting up another tatty discount outlet.

We settled ourselves at a table in the aisle, ordered a pot of tea and I asked for two slices of carrot cake. Ursula was paying.

I told Cleo about her mother's accusation, watching her face for any reaction. She was either a very good actress or her astonishment was genuine. At one point she seemed quite distressed and it was fortunate then that the tea arrived and she could busy herself pouring it out.

"I don't believe all this rubbish," she said, stirring her tea vigorously. "I don't get on with my mother, haven't for years but that doesn't mean I'd do this. It's too weird for words. You do believe me, don't you?"

"I've seen the stuff that's being sent to her and it's pretty nasty. She is genuinely upset by it."

"OK, so she's upset. I'm sorry. But I'm not sending it."

"The letters are signed Cleo."

Cleo nearly spilt her tea. "That means nothing! So someone is using my name. She could be sending the letters to herself. I don't like being accused of something I'm not doing."

"She told me that you were having an affair with Arthur, her husband, but didn't say that you were her daughter. She implied that you were some unknown third person. Unless, of course, there's another Cleo in existence and she doesn't mean you at all."

"No, she means me. She's unstable, vindictive," said Cleo. "Not a happy woman. Arthur wasn't my natural father. She married him when I was nine years old. He was fun, like a big older brother. She was always jealous of how well we got on. My father was Ursula's first husband, Ted Burrows. I was only three when he died and she rarely mentioned him."

"I see . . . but no one would send themselves a dead cat."

"Perhaps she just picked it up in the street and brought it along to you for dramatic effect. I wouldn't put it past her."

I shook my head. I remembered Ursula's hysteria and the blanched colour of her face. You can't act the colour of your face. "She was nearly out of her mind. She wasn't putting it on. So you and your mother don't get on particularly well?"

Cleo sighed deeply. She was reliving a disturbing past.

"She's a very difficult person to live with. I left home to go to business college which was good for me. I had such fun. I came home and got a job but she was so awful, I walked out. That was about three years ago. It seemed sensible to have my own place in Chichester. Time to flap my wings."

"And you keep in touch?"

Cleo looked somewhat ashamed. "No. We don't even meet. I occasionally phone, send her a birthday card or something but she doesn't respond. My fault, I suppose. She's not interested in what I do. My stepfather, Arthur that is, was quite different. He often came into Chichester for lunch. I didn't want to cut myself off from him. He was like a rock to me."

"That's understandable. He looks a nice person."

"Great. He was a wonderful father."

Cleo wasn't helping me much. If it wasn't Cleo then it must be someone else sending all the hate mail. I was going to have to search much further afield.

"I wonder if you could give me a list of your parents' friends? Or anyone you might think would have a reason to persecute Ursula," I said, chasing round the last crumbs of carrot cake with a damp finger.

"There's lots. My mother has a way of alienating people. They've had to move twice because of neighbour trouble."

"That sounds more like it. Can you jot down a few names and addresses – if you can remember them."

"Of course." She took a leather-bound notebook from her handbag, being that kind of well-prepared person. Her pen was an initialled gilt biro. Not a cheapo from a jumbo pack sold by Woolworths. She began writing in neat script, nothing like the angry capitals of the hate mail.

"Thanks. I suppose I ought to speak to your stepfather next. He might be able to shed some light."

She looked up quickly, her pen stabbing the page. Her eyes were suddenly clouded with grief. The lowering sun rays through the stained glass windows sent streaks of ruby and emerald light across her hair, changing her into a rainbowed junkie.

"But you can't," she said in a low voice.

"Why not?"

"Because he's dead. He died January. Didn't Ursula tell you?"

"Dead? Oh, Lord, Cleo, I'm so sorry. She never said."

The anguish was written all over Cleo's face, unanchored pain.

"I think Ursula Carling owes me an explanation," I said, all the facts changing places in my head. Perhaps she was round the bend, in which case I was unlikely to get paid. "She's been very economical with basic truths. What on earth is she playing at? Tell me what happened."

27

"He had a heart attack in hospital. It was all very sudden. I didn't even know he was ill or I would never have gone away on a skiing holiday. When I got back from Austria, it was all over, funeral and everything. She hadn't bothered to contact me."

"Well, that's enough to make anyone deliver a dead cat."

Cleo was clearly upset. I thought I ought to let her go home to what was probably a neat, well-kept flat in a nice part of Chichester.

"I didn't do it," she said, blowing her nose on a clean white hankie. "It wasn't me. The cat or anything." I believed her.

My two bedsits welcomed me. They always did. There was something about their comfortable size, the old-fashioned sash windows, the funny sloping ceilings, and my collected treasures that say hello every time I walk in and ease out of my shoes. I switched on the kettle and took out a flowered bone china mug. It was one of my favourites. I wondered how much it was worth. I'd paid fifty pence for it at a car boot sale.

The table by the window was covered with Ursula's hate mail, the threats, the abuse, the sinister accusations. I shuffled through them with new eyes before piling them on the floor, out of sight. No, this surely wasn't Cleo's work. She couldn't be that crude or vitriolic. I'd have to start looking elsewhere.

I only had one chair. It was a narrow two-seater, high-backed settee with hard arms covered in pussy-willow plush velvet. I always sat on it sideways, my feet draped over the other end. There were four cushions for comfort. I wasn't mean with cushions.

Even the pictures on the walls soothed me. Monet, Matisse (in his red mood), Vuillard – whom no one has ever heard of – and Manet. I love the Vuillards; he was a French painter, late nineteenth century, who painted homely pictures, a man reading a newspaper, a woman feeding a baby, a woman sewing. He was mad about walls and his paintings feature acres of wallpaper roses, bookshelves and laden mantlepieces.

The two kitchens are fairly obsolete. Number One kitchen is used only for early morning tea and late night chocolate. I wash my smalls in the sink, also face, hands, hair and other parts. I don't have a wardrobe so the kitchen unit houses my few clothes and shoes. There's a short hanging rail for shirts and jeans. Coats hang behind the door.

Kitchen Number Two is used for making tea, coffee, chocolate, pouring juice, heating soup and burning toast.

It was while I was slaving over a hot chicken curry a few weeks earlier, adding all the right ingredients – sun-dried tomatoes, basil, coriander – that I decided I was never, never going to cook again. From now on it was going to be the three S's – sandwiches, salads and soups. I might occasionally add extra nourishment to a soup by way of diced vegetables, lentils, pearl barley, chopped parsley, egg, cheese, sherry, croutons. If you could eat it, you could soup it.

As I made this momentous decision, my old friend Joshua had his feet up on my settee, drinking a cold beer, doing my crossword. I let him eat the curry, sample all the side dishes, finish up the raspberry pavlova and then I told him it was The Last Supper.

Joshua was really upset and borrowed a fiver from me for a taxi to the station. His hooded eyes were full of despair.

"You can't mean it," he said on the doorstep, distraught. "All those gorgeous dinners. I love them. And you such a good cook."

"The only thing in my fridge from now on is going to be ice," I said.

There are quite a few men in my life. I collect them like homeless strays. Unkind people might say they were misfits. They drift in and out at inappropriate moments. I am fond of them in different ways, wish I could take what I like best in each, put these qualities together and there'd be my fantasy prince on a white charger coming to claim me. I've been celibate for six years which says a lot. My hormones do have a problem.

Joshua is a gentle giant, sad-faced, hesitant, a widower. He has asked me to marry him many times, and in the same breath checked if I could cook. Since he's seriously short of money, I think he's really looking for a meal ticket and a warm back in bed.

I like him because he makes me laugh. A man who can make you laugh is a treasure.

Derek is an upright citizen of the realm, a fresh-faced bachelor, an accountant, but so mean, I once watched him counting the contents of a packet of frozen broad beans. He doesn't tip or give me presents. He also has a short fuse. I can imagine him stamping his feet as a little boy. He always wants his own way. But there are many things I like about him, too. His serious manner on subjects that interest him, old concrete pillboxes and wars, his clean nails, his cut profile, his rampant kisses. I make fun of his meanness, pull his leg. He gets worried if he thinks he's going to have to pay out for anything. I don't want him to worry. Life is too short for such pettiness. So I put the money in the charity box.

But the musician is someone special and plays the trumpet like a man possessed. He is my angel man, the Harry James of Latching, the Maynard Ferguson of Great Britain. My flesh goes weak with longing.

I've loved him and his music for many years. I once followed the big bands round the south coast. Sometimes I did not know which I loved the most, the man or his music. He was music. He lived for it. The pure high trumpet notes made my stomach clench. They were a moment to die for.

I was seventeen when I first met him. He spoke to me after a jazz concert. It was like the back door to heaven. I bought his tapes, listened to them incessantly. Then I heard he'd married a singer and was happy. The dream fell away, dissolved into a pool of teenage tears. By then I had joined the force and his music became a rare treat to savour when I was exhausted and my soul needed repairs.

I still like him but he loves his wife so it's a no-go situation from the start. It doesn't stop me dreaming, though, and I'd go a long way to hear him play.

I remember hearing him play "Tin Roof Blues" and I nearly died with suppressed desire. The slow rhythmic beat of the drums, the mellow string bass and the soaring liquid notes of the trumpet sent chills down my spine and prickles along the base of my neck. How that man could make a piece of metal sing. What he could do to my back.

He seemed to live in a different world. His eyes were so dark, I

30

could never determine their colour however much I looked. The floppy hair, the stooped shoulders, kindly eyes narrowed behind glasses. His mouth was strongly curved, a shape that could coax such sounds from an instrument, long musician's fingers.

I brought myself down to earth. I could never walk back to my barren life without taking something of him with me. The moony days were over. It would be emotional suicide. But I'd had to speak to him, on that first meeting. Just a few words would do.

"Doesn't it hurt, all that blowing?" I asked, pushing to the front of the crowd of fans. He was signing autographs but he looked right at me. It was so strange, that look. Something happened between us straight away.

"It only hurts when I get it wrong," he'd said. "It doesn't hurt when I'm getting it right. Don't go, young lady. Stay and have some coffee. I need to unwind."

But I have had to let him go, every time, because of the wife. And I won't say his name, because of her. God, this sisterhood thing. It strangles me.

And there's also Eddie, the Cary Grant of West Sussex. He's six feet tall, darkly handsome, also wears glasses, long ago divorced, that kind of velvety liquorice voice. He's a romancer, dancer, charmer, drinks vodka and smokes like Southampton Docks. I can be hanging on to his arm and he's bending to light another cigarette, apparently oblivious that I'm coughing, choking and wheezing for breath.

"There, there, Jordan," he'll say, making ineffectual hand fanning movements which only distribute the smoke more evenly around me. "Got your inhaler?"

He'll have to go. He's going.

So don't come to me for advice about men. I'm a loser. Leave them alone if you can. If you can't, pick a good 'un. If there aren't any around, then get a cat and a library ticket.

Sometimes I sit in the middle of my circular rug and chant: "Magic carpet, magic carpet, grant my wish, fly me to Arabia," but nothing happens. Perhaps I should ask Rick for my money back.

* * *

I started reading the brown files from the bottom drawer of the filing cabinet. They didn't make any sense. Local names were listed and some of them I recognised. It seemed to be about some classified organisation. I couldn't concentrate properly because it was a long time since I had eaten and I was tiring. A slice of carrot cake is no substitute for a meal.

I saw Trenchers Hotel mentioned and that really grabbed my attention. Some meeting was being held there. They were hiring a private room for their meeting and an agenda had been circulated. The agenda was graded Highly Confidential and was simply initials and numbers. Heavens, why was I wasting my time looking through this stuff? I should be following up Ursula's friends and neighbours. But something was nagging at me and I couldn't work out what it was. What had Trenchers to do with this? The place where I had seen the hanging nun. Even back then it had been drenched in mystery.

It was dark now so I went for a walk to clear my head. I love the beach at night. I walked along the promenade, all alone except for the gulls, runaway dogs and the incoming tide. A Safeway shopping trolley, solid with rust, was being washed ashore. It looked like something from an alien ship. Any moment now a simian finger would reach out and claw its way up the shingle.

The gulls were still active. Don't they ever go to sleep? They were swooping about, dropping shellfish on to the rocks to break the shells. There was a lot of squabbling and fighting, much like people.

And there were shadows shacking up for the night in the shelters with mountains of sleeping bags and stacks of newspaper for warmth, empty beer bottles rolling about under their feet. Latching has its share of the homeless but a shelter on the beach is better than a shop doorway. I felt thankful for my two bedsits. I was lucky to be able to afford them, but not for long if I didn't make a go of this investigating business. I needed another client.

She arrived the next morning, thin and anxious, skirts flapping. Her tortoise had gone missing. She thought someone had stolen it.

"Well, they are quite valuable these days, aren't they? And Joey is over twenty years old."

"Why don't you go to the police?"

"They'd think I was a nutcase."

I tried to look serious and concerned. "Can you give me a description?" I couldn't help liking her. Anyone who really cared about a tortoise has to be nice. She didn't quibble about my rates.

"Cheap at the price if you find Joey," she said.

That's the kind of client I like but I didn't hold out much hope of finding Joey. He was probably on the beach trying to chat up some rock, searching for his lost youth.

Four

O ne thing for sure, I was going to have to speak to Ursula
Carling pretty quick. That lady had not been straight with
me. She had a lot of explaining to do. Yet I was convinced the hate
mail was genuine. Just call it a gut reaction.

Her consent form was on file. I had cobbled together an official-
looking document on my portable typewriter, added a professional
style FIRST CLASS logo culled from a colour Sunday magazine,
edged it with a heavy in-set black line so it implied legal and had
the whole thing photocopied at the Photo Shop on top quality
parchment paper. It looked good so I took a dozen copies for
future use. I had started a file marked Ursula Carling though there
was little in it.

The consent form was for clients to sign, agreeing to my terms of
payment. I didn't want any arguments later with clients saying:
"Oh, I didn't know you meant every day," or "What's this about
expenses?" The form also contained full name, address, phone
number and brief details of the investigation for the time ahead
when I had so many clients on my books, I got confused. The age
of client, I filled in myself. It was an impertinence these days the
way every form asked for your age. I always put "over twenty-
one" and let them hyperventilate. For Ursula, I put "preserved
fifty-ish".

I jotted down her address in my notebook, admired the window
displays, put the BACK SOON sign on the door, locked up and
went out.

Soon I would have to get myself some wheels. Turning up at an
investigation on a bicycle, even a racing model, was not image

34

making. But Latching is so flat, it's ideal for cycling. I put on my helmet, unchained my bike from the parking meter (I love that), and turned it in the direction of Ursula Carling's home.

Lansfold Avenue was quite a way out beyond the terraces of Georgian and Victorian houses, or the wide roads flanked with sprawling Edwardian villas, many of them now converted into nursing homes for the elderly or bed-and-breakfast hotels.

It was a tree-lined road with detached houses built between the wars in solid and varying styles. Ursula's house was a mock Tudor number with a neat garden, trimmed shrubs and a lilac tree. The house next door was older with a lot of mature beech trees which overshadowed Ursula's front bay window.

It rang a bell. My filing cabinet had come from that house, The Beeches. I knew its electricity bills intimately. I looked at its shuttered windows and imagined the cobwebs.

I rang another bell. Ursula came to the door in a pink candlewick dressing gown holding a pastel tissue to her nose. Her hair was crumpled flat on one side as if she had just got out of bed.

"Oh dear," I said. "You've got a dreadful cold. I won't stay long. Just a few questions. Do you mind?"

"No, come in. I want to hear how far you've got with your investigations. As long as you don't mind a few germs."

Ursula wasn't going to be pleased at what I had to say, but I went in just the same. The hall was decorated in pale colours with even paler prints fading to nothingness on the walls. I couldn't imagine the masculine Arthur living in such a pristine environment. Perhaps she'd had it all redecorated since his death.

"I've had a flu jab," I said confidentally. "My asthma makes me an 'at risk' person. They work very well. Haven't had a cold the entire year."

She went into the kitchen – tiled white and pale grey – and put the kettle on. This was the kind of instant hospitality that I liked. Perhaps I had misjudged the woman.

"So have you found this ghastly woman, this bitch who is making my life a misery?" She spoke so vehemently that it started her off coughing. I waited till her breathing had calmed down.

She was laying out a tray with a pretty lace cloth and small bone china cups and saucers decorated with tiny primroses. She added a matching milk jug and a sugar bowl and tea strainer on a dish. It was like something out of a thirties film. I looked around for a maid in starched cap and apron.

"How charming," I said, knowing I could drink three of those midget cups at one go. "Lovely china."

I carried the tray through to the sitting room as she was coughing again. The sitting room was . . . guess what? White and pale mauve; an even whiter carpet. I was glad the soles of my shoes were clean. Cycling does reduce the dirt.

"Lovely," I said again, balancing the cup and saucer and trying not to drink quickly. "Tell me what you know about Cleo." I wanted to dangle her on a line before reeling her in.

"Tell you more? What do you need to know about that wretched woman? She's a menace to society. Ought to be put away."

"Have you ever met her?"

"Er . . . yes, I may have."

"Don't you know for sure?"

"I'm sorry. All this has really upset me and my memory is affected."

"What does she look like? Can you describe her?"

"Look like? I don't know . . . she's small, dark . . . maybe she's changed the colour of her hair. There's no saying what she might have done to her appearance."

I put down my cup and saucer carefully. "I should have thought you would know what your own daughter looks like."

Ursula gasped on a sip of tea, spraying her dressing gown down the front. I took the cup from her before she spilt any more.

"You know? How did you find out?" she asked hoarsely.

"There's no point in pretending to be surprised, Mrs Carling. Cleo told me. Once I had found her, of course. It seems odd that you didn't mention that she's your daughter."

"You've . . . seen her?"

"Yes. We met yesterday. I had a long talk with her. I don't think she's your unpleasant persecutor, the sender of hate mail."

36

"But she is, she is. Cleo and Arthur are having an affair. I know it."

"How do you know? What proof have you?"

"They meet in secret. There are letters . . . dozens of them."

"Have you got the letters?" It was difficult to keep the incredulity out of my voice.

"No, I destroyed them."

"Then what makes you think they are having an affair? Isn't it a little unusual between father and daughter? Surely you are not implying incest?"

She didn't like that word, you could see it. She fussed around as if trying to wipe it out of the air, make it disappear.

"It's not like that . . . that word," she began. "It's different . . . Arthur is my second husband. He's not Cleo's natural father. She was nine years old when I married Arthur."

"Thank you for telling me that," I said sarcastically. "I could have wasted half a day down at the Records Office looking for Cleo's birth certificate or your marriage lines." I emphasised the half a day wasted and watched the mathematical blink of her eyes. "Perhaps you'd like to save my time and your money by telling me when Arthur died."

She went white and started to cough so much, I had to get her a glass of water from the kitchen. I have a lot a sympathy for coughers, being one myself when the asthma is bad.

"Cleo . . . ?"

"She told me. Of course, she did. How could you expect to keep something like that quiet? Mrs Carling, I'm a detective. I'm paid to find out things. Why didn't you tell me the truth?"

She blew her nose, clasping the sodden tissue in her hands. "It was last January, the second weekend in January. He died in Latching Hospital after a massive heart attack. It was all very sudden. I didn't expect him to die. He only went in for tests after getting some chest pains, angina we thought. Then on the Monday morning, they phoned up and said he'd died in the night, been found dead in bed."

She squeezed a few tears out but I was not impressed. I think she was glad to have Arthur and his muddy boots off her white carpet.

A man would have cluttered up her pale house with his grubby things, underpants on the floor and wet towels.

"So if Arthur has been dead for nearly nine months, why do you think Cleo is sending you all this hate mail? There's really no point, is there? After all, their affair, if it ever was one, is quite definitely over."

"Because she hates me; because she can't forgive me for having kept Arthur. Because Arthur would never leave me. She wants to make me suffer, to hurt me. She's cruel and vindictive. There's nothing she wouldn't do to get even with me."

"Mrs Carling, this doesn't ring true as a motive. We have to think of something else, perhaps someone else. Let's go back to square one."

I couldn't move her from this conviction that it was Cleo. I thought she was wrong. If this wasn't a play for attention there must be someone else in the picture. Some other person who hated her.

I went to Latching Hospital in the afternoon. I had a friend in admissions. She had been mugged one evening, walking home from work, and I'd been on duty at the station. Apparently I must have been extra kind and understanding and she's never forgotten.

"Hi, Gale," I said, breezing into her office, by-passing the patient counter. "How's tricks?"

"Great," she said. Gale Rogers was a bright, bubbly young woman. I noticed there were beads decoratively braiding her fair hair. "I've had a wonderful holiday in Barbados with my new boyfriend. The weather was heavenly."

"Your hair looks good. Did it take long?"

I let her tell me the lengthy administrations of the beach hair-dresser. My hair is coarse, tawny-red stuff, frizzy when it rains. I pull it back in a scrunchie band or plait it thickly into a rope. It could never look as elegant as Gale's. Eventually we got round to the purpose of my visit.

"Arthur Carling? With a C? OK, I'll look up his admission date. It won't have been wiped off the records yet. We keep everything for ages these days. The memory byte on these machines is amazing. All on a chip, too."

I don't understand computers but I agreed that it was amazing. Gale tapped on the keyboard and in moments, Arthur Carling's record came up on screen. She didn't mind that I leaned over and read the details for myself. He'd been admitted on the Wednesday, been seen by two different doctors, had a chest x-ray and electrocardiograph. There was a list of medication prescribed. A third doctor – on the weekend shift – had pronounced death from heart failure on the Sunday at three thirty a.m. and the body had been removed by a firm of Latching undertakers on the Monday. Ursula had moved fast.

"There was no need for a post mortem because he'd been receiving medical treatment at the hospital. That's the law."

"Thanks, Gale. You've been a great help. I wanted to make sure that his death was completely natural."

I don't know why I said that but I suppose some suspicion had been lurking at the back of my mind. I'd been told so many half-truths, I needed to know that Arthur had died normally.

There was only time for some quick food shopping before racing back to my shop. I'd just remembered that BT were coming to install a telephone and answering machine, two essential components if I was going to function efficiently. I was tired of using the draughty call box at the end of the road and waiting in it for return calls.

The telephone engineer was propping up his equipment on the pavement outside. He tapped the BACK SOON sign.

"Been here half an hour," he grumbled.

"Sorry, I got held up."

The frost thawed with cups of tea and the packet of chocolate Hobnobs I'd just bought. I watched them disappear like Smarties. Oh well, I'd only have got fat.

I updated Ursula Carling's file. I knew from experience that one should make notes as soon as possible after an interview. The human memory is never reliable. A seemingly unimportant detail could be forgotten or only half remembered.

It was glooming over with herring-bone clouds when I shut shop for the night. No more customers but the new telephone and answering machine looked good. I hadn't sold anything. Tomorrow I would change the window display.

My sitting room welcomed me with open arms as if it had been waiting for me all day. The room was clean and cream and uncluttered by furniture. There was my corner desk with a chair, the aforementioned moral settee in another corner, a second-hand television set and the rest of the room was open space. I could breathe in it. I ate at one end of the desk, laying it in a civilised way with a woven mat, cutlery, napkin and flowers in a vase. I could be as fastidious as Ursula in my own way.

I viewed with pleasure the prints by my favourite painters, splashing colour on the walls like a child let loose with a paintbox. The only untidiness was books. They had to be piled on the floor as there were no shelves or a bookcase. Cuttings and magazines, leaflets and brochures were filed on the floor. It was handy to be able to look up almost anything without having to trundle off to the public library or WHSmith. WHSmith is a really useful shop. I use all its facilities.

The kettle jug went on and I shed my clothes on the way to the bathroom. A drink in the bath is one of my regular vices, be it coffee, tea, wine or a gin and tonic, ice and lemon. On a really bad day, it could be a large brandy. This evening it was decaf, black, sweetened with honey. I ran the bath water hot, threw in a handful of Radox Herbal and allowed myself to sink and soak. Funny how I didn't think of Ursula, Cleo or Arthur and their triangular problems, or the ardent young man who spent his last twenty pounds on a regally inscribed chamber pot. It was that hooked-up nun who worried me. What had she done to deserve such a gruesome end?

What had that poor woman discovered that merited a fast removal to a more heavenly place? Was Trenchers the headquarters for some dope gang or customs rip-off? Was the spacious ballroom stacked with contrabrand brandy and cheap cigarettes? Had she been left as a tacky warning to some other gang who were trying to rustle in on the Latching territory? It worried me.

The warm water and the honey were inducing drowsiness. I

drifted on to some dream raft, only half awake, my thoughts pool-hopping like an errant dragonfly.

My two doorbells rang. At least you can hear them. I wrapped myself in a jumbo bath towel and trailed downstairs to see who was at the door. I opened it half an inch and saw the expectant face of Derek. He had a paper bag in his hand. Surely not a present? He had never brought me anything, except sample sachets that come free with magazines. Once he brought me a single camomile tea-bag. Wow, was that a red-letter day. I was speechless.

"This was stuck in your letterbox," he said hopefully, obviously waiting to be asked in. I suppose I was drawn to him because he was so insecure. I knew how he felt. There had been a time when I'd rather sit in a corner and read a book at a party. Fortunately my years in the force had cured me of that crippling shyness, but there were still moments when I could find nothing to say.

Like when I met DI James. Or crossed his path. Nothing to say.

"Isn't this a bit late for a social call?" I said, tucking the towel more firmly across my bosom. His lusty eyes were focused on my wet shoulders. He had an insatiable sexual appetite, probably because he didn't get many opportunities and his hormones were rampant with desire.

"Thought there might be a cup of coffee going," he said casually. "Haven't seen you for ages."

I sighed. That was the end of my quiet evening. "OK, come in. But it'll have to be brief. I'm on my way to bed."

I took the paper bag from him and led the way back upstairs. Now I would have to get dressed again. With any of my other men, I could have stayed in a robe and been unmolested. But Derek would see it as an unconditional invitation. He was running his fingers up and down my bare back as we climbed the stairs. I didn't dare flinch an inch in case the towel slipped.

He was a dapper-looking young man. I'm not sure who ironed his shirts, but someone did. He always wore a tie. His shoes were polished to military precision.

As I made another cup of coffee, I opened the bag. Inside was a slice of carrot cake. The bag was over-printed Church Café. I digested this information and it gave me a cold shiver. Cleo and I had obviously been watched. But by whom? Not Ursula: she hadn't known that I'd tracked Cleo to Chichester and met her in the café.

A new, unknown person had entered the scenario and I didn't like it. Someone had been watching us. I'm the one who's supposed to do the surveillance.

"I'd better put some clothes on," I said, hurrying into the other room to recover. I didn't like the implications. Cleo wouldn't have sent the cake. There'd be no point. Yet she was the only one . . . perhaps I had got too near the truth. I went over the conversation in my mind. What had I said or she said, that had precipitated such weird behaviour?

"Must you?" I heard Derek say as I left. Such wit.

It needed a couple of sweaters, jeans and big socks before I felt safe from his hands. I came back, ready to be pleasant to Derek. He'd switched on the television and was sitting sideways on my settee with his feet propped on the arm. It was the floor again for me.

"Got any cake?" he asked.

He knew perfectly well that I had, but still I put the slice of carrot cake on a plate for him. As I chased a dampened finger round the crumbs in the bag, I was reminded that I had not eaten and the telephone engineer had devoured my biscuits.

Now I have a good sense of smell. My finger stopped in mid-air. It was pungent.

Suddenly I flung myself at Derek. I suppose he hoped it was unbridled passion.

"Don't eat it," I said, knocking the plate off his lap. He looked at me, astonished. "That cake. I think it's poisoned."

I didn't just think. I knew. That smell was bleach or sodium chlorate.

"Are you sure? Have you got an aspirin?" Derek asked weakly.

Five

I t was a different sergeant on the desk the next morning but he'd
obviously heard of my previous visits. The tired old grapevine. I
anticipated the wind-up.

"Hello Miss Lacey, what is it this morning? A dead cat? Or is it
another dead nun?"

"This is a slice of poisoned carrot cake," I said, offering the item
in its paper bag.

"How do you know it's carrot cake?" He was a great comedian.
Ought to be on the *Jerry Springer Show*.

"Because I had some the day before. Could you please arrange to
have it tested in the path lab?"

"You say you ate a piece of the poisoned cake the day before?"
Thick as well. It almost hurt.

I took a deep breath. "If I had, I don't think I would be standing
here in Latching police station. I would probably be in an IC unit or
iced in a local mortuary. The slice I ate yesterday at the Church
Café, Chichester, was fine. Delicious, actually. Then some person
bought another slice, tampered with it and delivered it to my home,
obviously hoping I would eat that too. I think the poison is sodium
chlorate, or bleach as it's better known. I'd like that confirmed, and
to know if the dose was lethal."

"We'd better take a statement from you," he said, holding the
paper bag gingerly. "Would you like to come through, miss."

Thank goodness he was taking me seriously at last. I gave him a
brief smile and followed him inside, ignoring the concealed snig-
gers. Wooden-tops. The tests would take twenty-four hours plus. I
gave them my new telephone number which I had managed to

43

memorise overnight with various visual aid tricks. It made me feel established.

Later I let myself into my shop. It still smelt musty despite all my cleaning so I opened both doors for a through-draught. It brought in a whiff of brine and gutted fish straight from the beach. I longed for a look at the sea.

I rummaged round in the charity shop box and found a man's straw panama hat, banded with leopard skin. I really wanted to wear it myself as hats are a good disguise for my hair but this hat would have stood out in a crowd. Disguises are for merging. I put it in the side window. Perhaps it wouldn't sell. In the front window, I laid out a drawn thread-work traycloth, creamy with age, trying not to think of the Edwardian wife who worked it long ago, and stood an egg-shell-thin bone china cup and saucer on it. The prices were sheer guesswork.

A stud bought the hat in twenty minutes flat. He did not quibble at the ten-pound ticket but peeled the note off a wad, already strutting at a disco in the hat, cutting a Travolta. I replaced it with a framed collection of dried flowers like old tea leaves and some dusty books. They could both gather another layer. I was getting bored with window dressing.

Ursula's hate mail was in a large brown manila envelope and I tipped it all out on the floor, trying to look at it with an indifferent eye. The content of threats and vile accusations were not my present concern. There must be a common denominator, something that linked them, apart from the one fact that they were sent to Ursula.

They were written with a black marker pen. The sender did not have time for cutting words out of newspapers and sticking lines together. No newspaper . . . perhaps, and this was a thought, money was tight. Newspapers are expensive despite the price war. I read most of mine in the public library which stays open till seven thirty p.m. or WHSmith which doesn't.

There were some ill-formed letters with pot-hooks and hangers but the capital S had a distinctive swirl and the crossbar of the T was never completely straight. The scrivener had not consciously tried to alter their style, confident of being undetected. Nothing else struck me.

I turned the lot over and a thunderbolt thundered in. The taunts were all on the backsides of junk mail. Adverts for double-glazing, insurance, mobile phones, cut-price holidays. But three were identical. That was a pointer. They were handouts for the amusement arcade at the end of Latching pier. I often go in when I walk the pier especially if its raining and the narrow wet decking is slippery. It's always warm, noisy and it's fun to watch people losing their money.

I put them in my pocket, locked up the shop after hanging GONE TO LUNCH on the door even though it was only eleven o'clock. The promenade was busy with holiday-makers enjoying the weak autumnal sunshine. Their collective age was depressing . . . frizzled grey hair, walking sticks, bent backs. Electric wheelcarts glided noiselessly, their occupants as intent on steering as if it was Brands Hatch. Schools had gone back so retired people were taking advantage of special rates. Fortunately Latching's reasonable house prices also attract a younger element and the mums were out pushing buggies or steering new and gaudy plastic three-wheeled pedal bikes.

The pier is free. I'd be broke if it wasn't. I like all its moods. Crowded, deserted, lashed with waves, buffeted by the wind, stranded over wet sand when the tide's receeded halfway to France. Last winter it was closed on several occasions when gusts of fifty miles an hour made the whole structure dangerous to walk on. I'd have risked it simply for the exhilaration of battling the elements.

The noise from the arcade assaulted my ears long before I reached it. I wandered in, relaxing into the warm fug, a grin on my face. The same thin grey woman in a navy raincoat was feeding two-pence pieces into the Roll-a-Penny machine, waiting for the cascade of coins that was mounting up on the edge of the shifting shelf. She was always there, totally addicted.

Half a dozen race track screens exploded with crashes and penalties and acceleration; monsters fought each other on battlements; knights in armour plunged swords into adversaries; bombs exploded; aircraft blew up in mid-air. Every machine was an orgy of destruction.

The manager hung out in a sort of armoured booth. A lot of money was generated in a day. I thought the glass panels were probably bullet-proof and he had certainly locked himself in. Taking no chances these days.

He was a heavily built young man, barrel chested with distressed stubble and tight blue jeans. He looked at me without interest. I suppose people were always peering at him. I knocked on the door and showed him the handouts.

"Wotcha want?" he said, opening the door an inch.

"Can I speak to you? About these handouts."

"S'legal. Nothing wrong with them."

"I never said that. Can I come in?"

I held up my hands to show I wasn't carrying a gun. It was a ridiculous pantomine but the man was obviously nervy. He decided that such an idiot couldn't possibly be a threat.

"Two minutes," he said, like someone in a film.

I stood in the small space with him, surrounded by a bank of money, breathing his Brut deodorant. No wonder he was nervous. There was a fortune stacked in coin bags and plastic wallets. At least one business in Latching was making a profit.

"Can you tell me when these leaflets were distributed?" I asked.

"Are you from the council?" The man was still suspicious.

"No. Nothing's the matter, I assure you. I just want to know when and where these went out and who did it."

He appeared to relax a degree but he was really watching the punters. "We did it in the summer. A promotion." He seemed pleased with the word. "People don't know we're here at the end of the pier so we got these printed and handed them out along the front."

"Looks as if it paid off." I nodded towards the crowded arcade.

"Nairh. This is quiet."

"Who handed them out?"

"Casuals. Blokes who wanted a day's work."

"Have you got a record of their names?"

"Nairh. Are you sure you ain't from the council?"

I shook my head. "Thank you very much, Mr . . . ?"

"Jack. Just call me Jack."

"Thank you, Jack. Do you ever play these games yourself?"

"Nairh, you can't win. Mug's game. Sometimes I race a few cars."
He smirked sideways. "I'm a brilliant driver. Hundred and fifty's
nothing. One handed."

I made to leave. Suddenly he seemed sorry for being so abrupt
and ducked down under a shelf. " 'Ere, want a teddy? On the 'ouse."

He was offering me a small burnt-sugar brown teddy with a
forlorn button face. It was one of the tumbled teddy mountain in the
crane machine. I could not resist it.

"Thank you," I said, tucking the teddy inside my anorak. Poor
teddy, he deserved a better home than this madhouse. He could sit
on my windowsill and watch the world go by. Write his memoirs.

I spent the afternoon at the Social Security department poring
through the names of the unemployed registered in the area. They
owed me a favour. A year back I'd put them on the track of a family
living off a web of benefit frauds and they got the credit.

OK, Cleo might have been handed a leaflet and kept it, but not
three. It didn't seem likely nor would she have kept them. Besides, I
got the feeling that she did not come to Latching by choice in case
she bumped into Ursula. Chichester was her town now.

It had to be someone else. I had established that much. Who else
hated Ursula so much? Cleo said something about their having to
move twice because of neighbour trouble. Perhaps I should follow
that up. It might have been serious trouble but I could hardly go
back to the police station and enquire about possible resting charges
relating to Ursula. They would be sick of the sight of me and could
refuse to give me the information. I was not on the force now.

The staff were very helpful at the local newspaper. They even had
a cuttings library of sorts but there was nothing filed under Carling.
I thumbed through a pile of back numbers until my arms seized up.
There was one mention of Arthur Carling and I thought I had
struck gold. But it was nothing really. He'd won a minor chess
tournament in the sticks. I made a few notes.

It had been an exhausting day but I had nothing to show for my labours. My head ached with all the close work. Perhaps I ought to have my eyes tested.

The shops were closed as I walked along the pedestrian-only streets. It was creepy with so many boarded-up shops and derelict sites. Latching was dying. It would be a nebulous resort by the turn of the next decade, housing the homeless, the deranged and the terminally ill.

Although the police had boarded up the basement door at Trenchers after removing the body, it looked to me as if the hooligans had been back already. The door was swinging open as the evening wind gusted off the coast, creaking and protesting at its loss of status as Latching's premier hotel.

I went into my Girl Guide mode and climbed over the wall, going down the steps, intending to shut the door. There was a lot more rubbish in the front yard, turned over by the police in their search for a weapon. I peered into the depths of the kitchen for no good reason. I knew what it looked like. Why should I want to go into it again? It was a stupid move.

As soon as I was inside the gloomy old place, I changed my mind and turned to leave. Something felt wrong. I shivered. But at that same moment, the door closed with a sonorous clang.

"Hey!" I shouted. "Don't close the door. I'm in here."

I expected to hear size ten boots crunching over the debris but whoever shut the door did not answer. I banged on the door panels.

"Let me out. Don't play around. Open the door."

Then came the sound of hammering. Someone was nailing planks across the door. I yelled out, thumping and kicking at the door. It must be the police making the place secure.

"Help! Officer! I'm inside. Let me out. OK, I know you're only doing your duty but get me out first."

It was no joke. He must be totally deaf. Don't they have medicals these days? I got out my pocket torch and flashed it around hoping to find a crack in some window where the light would show. I continued yelling, my language deteriorating. "Let me out, you moron. I'm getting sick of this and when I get very sick, I also get very mad. Hey, cloth ears, this is no joke. Hell, you bastard. Open the bloody door."

Suddenly I was very frightened. The hammering had stopped. I didn't like what I wasn't hearing. There was no human sound at all, only the reptile hissing of wind through the cracks. I listened intently. The derelict hotel was empty yet it breathed. I could hear something or was it my own heartbeat? My pulse rate soared. I had to get out before uncontrolled panic set in.

I remembered that there was a flight of stairs at the back of the kitchen. I swept the beam from the torch across the floor, taking care where I stepped. As soon as I found the stairs, I made sure there were no gaps or broken treads, then switched off the torch to conserve the battery.

Keeping one hand on the wall, I climbed carefully, testing each step before putting my weight on it. I kept thinking how the nun had been found upstairs and that's where I was going. I knew the elaborately pillared main entrance was securely boarded but I was hoping that some shoddy workman had cut corners on a back window or better still, overlooked one. The stairs led to a labyrinth of passages. Those long-ago waiters and waitresses must have cursed the miles they totted up in the course of their work. The passages led to some kind of servery before a wide archway opened out into the main dining room.

Through the gloom I could just make out a platform where an eight-piece orchestra had played light classical music for the diners; wrecked tables were piled up in a corner like a funeral of animal bones; the carpet under my feet was torn and damp, riddled with silverfish. The rain had got in and it smelled like a rotting cabbage forgotten at the bottom of a fridge.

I stood listening again. So far so good, but was I alone? My senses were beginning to play tricks. I could hear scuttling on the boards . . . rats. Oh my God, I hated rats. I switched on my torch and flashed it around the room. The shadows darkened and grew in size as the light picked out the ornate ceiling, the ruined drapes, the tipped-up chairs.

The tall windows of the dining room were securely boarded. It was beginning to get chilly, windows rattling and curtains blowing. There must be gaps somewhere if the wind could get in. I found my way to the ballroom. It was even more depressing though I could see it had once been a large, beautiful room. The proportions were still elegant under all the grime and squalor, but there were no stocks of smuggled alcohol or cigarettes, racks of pirated designer clothes or stolen leather jackets. One theory out of the window.

I felt around to find where the draught was coming from. It must be somewhere. Then I froze. I definitely heard a movement. A footstep . . . nothing like a rat scuttling about. I shrank back against the wall, dousing my torch, trying to control my breathing. I didn't know how long I waited. Someone had to move but it wasn't going to be me. I'd stay there till dawn if necessary. Very carefully I eased down and picked up a broken chair leg. I couldn't see how I was going to get out of this without a weapon.

My eyes were becoming accustomed to the dark. I could pick out shapes and none of them were moving. I was starting to shake and there was little I could do about that.

This was all my own damned fault. I should have left the basement door open, let the police do their own dirty work. Why should I bother to check on their procedure? Now I was incarcerated in a derelict hotel and no one knew I was there. Unless there was someone else in the building . . . and it might be the murderer.

My held-back breath escaped in a long gasp and a flashlight blinded me in the face. I squinted into the beam, mouth gaping, waiting for one petrified second for a knife to plunge into my chest.

Then I moved. I was like lightning but someone else moved faster, pinning me against the wall with his weight, knocking the breath out of me. I gasped loudly.

"Jesus! Jordan Lacey. It's you. What the hell are you doing here?" The flashlight wavered and I caught sight of a tall figure and dark face looming over me. I knew that stooped look, the shape of the head. He lived in my dreams.

"Oh, God, it's you. Detective Inspector James . . ." I said weakly.

"I saw a light and thought there was an intruder."

"I thought you were the murderer . . . that poor n-nun."

I felt like throwing myself into his arms with the sheer relief of being alive but he was not the sort of man to throw yourself at. I needed his arms around me. For a second it almost felt as if his arms were around me. They should have been holding me closely. But I could hear the disapproval grating in his voice as if I was an irresponsible schoolgirl.

"Didn't you hear me yelling and banging on the door?" I said, turning to the attack instead. I was getting mad. It was perverse. I should have been overflowing with gratitude. "You locked me in, you fool."

"I did not lock you in," he said coldly. "I've only just arrived."

"Go and look," I said. "Someone has hammered planks across the basement door. It could be the murderer. How are we going to get out?"

He looked at me with pained resignation. "Grow up. I've got a key," he said.

Six

The first thing I did when I got home was to make myself a strong tea and slurp in a generous tot of twelve-year-old malt whisky. The warmth went straight into my veins. Then I threw together a tuna, cheese, lettuce, tomato and chutney sandwich, about an inch thick, and ate it like a starving Balkan refugee. It took me ten minutes to calm down.

DI James and I had had a flaming row on the pavement outside Trenchers, buffeted by the bitter wind, lit by headlights and the yellow sodium street lamps overhead, wind lashed, wave lashed. You'd have thought I would have been grateful, being rescued from a night in that damp rabbit warren of a mausoleum – I was fast going off the place – but, oh no, I was furious that he'd scared me rigid, that he'd discovered me in such humiliating circumstances.

He, quite rightly, decided that I didn't deserve rescuing and strode off without offering me a lift home.

"Find your own way home," he yelled at me, pointing rudely with the key. His eyes were blazing.

I stomped away in any direction, completely disorientated by the experience. I found myself walking the wrong way towards Shoreham which added ten minutes to the normal journey home. I would have to apologise if I ever saw him again. He'd probably make sure he kept out of my way in future.

I took another tea, laced with whisky, to the bathroom and soaked the damp out of my bones in piping hot water. By the time I rolled into bed, I was relaxed enough to read a few pages of Victor Hugo. I was reading *The Hunchback of Notre Dame*. With 280 close-print pages, it was taking me a long time. I don't remember putting the light out or closing a marker into the book. The next moment it was morning and the gulls were kicking up a racket for their breakfast on the roof outside my window, a thin sun peeking round the cracks. I leaned over and pulled back one curtain. The sky was cloudless, azure blue, washed over and fresh for a new day. How I loved early morning. It wasn't going to rain for a few hours.

The cocoon of warmth in the bed was for reflections with no man within reach. What I wanted was one normal, red-blooded man who would love me deeply and tenderly, make me laugh, try to understand me and my needs. I wanted to love someone. To make him the joy of my life. Was this asking too much?

I dismissed these futile thoughts. What was I to do next? Perhaps the neighbours would throw some light on the situation. I'd phone Cleo to confirm Ursula's previous addresses and go visiting. Ursula might consider it snooping but private investigating was a stylised form of snooping.

Cleo was helpful again, took my new telephone number in case she thought of anything. I didn't tell her about the doctored carrot cake.

"By the way," she added. "I did think of one thing that might be useful."

"Shoot," I said, the phone piece tucked between chin and shoulder. I was thumbing through the street map of Latching, looking up the two addresses I'd written down this time. It seemed the Carlings had lived around Latching all their married life.

"My Dad, my real father. Ted Burrows, that is. He died in suspicious circumstances. It was never really sorted out and my mother would never talk about it. I was quite small when it happened. It's probably got nothing to do with this but . . . well, I thought I'd better mention it."

"She gets more interesting by the minute," I said, making another note. "When did he die? What were the funny circumstances?"

"Some time in the early seventies. I was only a little girl. I hardly remember him. Something to do with a river and a car. Sorry, I haven't any more details. Perhaps you could ask her."

"I doubt if she'd tell me. Ursula has a handy knack of developing amnesia when she doesn't want to talk."

Probably a red herring. I couldn't be sidetracked by every aspect of Ursula Carling's life. It was much too far back to be of any consequence today. Only if it was pouring with rain and I was within a stone's throw of a Births and Deaths Registry would I do anything about Ted Burrows. Then I would look up his death certificate.

The first address Cleo had given me proved a complete dead end. I was not surprised. There had been so many changes in the developers' pull-'em-down happy hour. I hoped those bureaucrats who'd been in the planning department were turning in their graves. They'd given permission for the most beautiful house in Latching, right on the seafront, to be pulled down . . . for what? A multi-story car park and a bowling alley. There were dreamy sepias of the house, all creamy and gracious, photographed at the turn of the century. The planners should have been strung up.

The Edwardian house, at the back of town, where Ursula and Arthur started married life in a ground-floor flat, had disappeared too, making way for an ugly purpose-built red-brick block. The house next door had been demolished for the same commercial reason. So there were no neighbours to ask.

Address number three was more fruitful. A semi-detached in a leafy grove, outrageously bijou once, twee now. Ursula's half was in good condition with mature shrubs and, yes, a mature lilac tree. Perhaps lilac trees were her trade mark wherever she lived.

I went to the house next door. Before the door even opened, I knew it was a time-warped sort of place. The net curtains were of the faded forties, green painted tubs sat with sad geraniums, flaking and blistered magnolia paint clung to the window frames. The sparrow-like woman who opened the door was clearly in a time warp with her cross-over floral pinny, her tired fawn hair in a blonde net, the blank expression of one whose life had ended in a different era. When I explained who I was and that my investigations were connected with Mrs Ursula Carling, her face came alive.

"Good heavens. Ursula Carling? Is that woman in trouble? I

wouldn't be at all surprised. She was trouble. The best day of my life was when she moved out."

"Really . . . Mrs . . . er? I suppose you wouldn't have time to tell me a little about when she lived next door," I began.

She couldn't invite me in fast enough. "Of course. Come in." She spoke in jerks. "I'm Mrs Yarpole. I was just making my elevenses. Would you like a coffee? Instant, I'm afraid. Nothing fancy here."

"Instant will be fine, Mrs Yarpole."

She showed me inside and we passed a closed door to the front parlour, one of those hibernating rooms used only on special occasions. I glimpsed a back sitting room still strewn with the debris of the evening before, needles stuck in rolled-up knitting, magazines, newspapers, a pipe in an ashtray, two Horlicks mugs. So there was still a Mr Yarpole about and I was glad.

Mrs Yarpole made coffee in two sturdy mugs with heated milk and set them down on the green-topped kitchen table. The whole kitchen was painted that intense wartime green. No fancy tray-cloths in this house. She took the lid off a tin of malted biscuits and pushed it towards me.

"Now what do you want to know?" She took a biscuit, broke it in two and began some expert dunking. "My, I could tell you some stories."

"What can you remember about her? What was she like to live next to?" My dunking was not so successful. Half a biscuit broke off and sank soggily to the bottom of the mug. I fished the goo out with a spoon. Why do we do this to perfectly good biscuits?

"Well, now. She was a very smart-looking woman, nicely dressed, regular at the local hairdressers. So pernickety though. That poor husband of hers daren't put a foot wrong. I used to hear her, many a time, reminding him to take his shoes off as he came into the house. She always did her washing on a Monday, regular as clockwork. Got quite sharp with me if I hung out washing later in the week and if it was a Sunday! Well, bless me, you'd think I'd broken all God's laws."

I gave up dunking and drank some coffee. "Did you ever have a row? Did anything really get up your nose?"

"I'm not easily upset. She was just a pain in the arse, 'scuse my language, Miss Lacey. It was the television on too loud, my son's pals staying late and leaving on noisy bikes, the weeds blowing over the fence. Could you believe it? As if I'd do it on purpose . . . I'm not a gardener but she said the weeds were blowing over. She was never happy unless she was complaining about something. I was glad when they moved."

She chattered on for another ten minutes, getting into the swing of talking but there was nothing definite. I suppose she didn't have many visitors. Nor did I think Mrs Yarpole was sending Ursula hate mail or dead cats. She did not seem to know where the Carlings had moved to, nor did she care. I finished my coffee and rinsed the mug out in the sink.

"Thank you, Mrs Yarpole. You've been very kind and helpful. Not quite what I'm looking for but it all builds up an interesting picture of Mrs Carling."

"Come back any time," she said, nodding from the door, her hair escaping from the careful net. "I expect you really ought to talk to the Adels; they live the other side. She set fire to their house."

I was back in an instant but the door had closed. "Mrs Yarpole, please. What do you mean?" I shouted through the letterbox.

"You'd better ask them," she said and switched on the vacuum cleaner to end the conversation.

I went straight round to the Adels'. It was a tidy house, neat and precise. I introduced myself and Mrs Adel told me the whole story on the doorstep, her gaze not moving. Ursula had complained about her dog, Rusty.

"Always on about Rusty, she was. Bee in her bonnet."

"He seems a lovely dog," I said, stroking his head.

"Yes, he is lovely, isn't he, but this is my second Rusty. The first Rusty didn't bark. He was very well trained. But Ursula insisted he was leaving his you-know-whats all over her garden. It wasn't true, though. I'm very particular. My dogs don't run around loose. Anyway, one night, I smelled this awful burning and Rusty was barking this time and there was good cause. Someone had pushed burning rags through the letterbox. But I had time to call the fire brigade and we got out the back way."

56

"And you thought it was Ursula Carling?"

"She was the only one who ever complained about Rusty. But it could have been any of the slobs let out from the pub up the road. I'm not saying it was her. There was no proof. But she moved soon after."

I thanked her and patted Rusty's golden labrador head. I walked away thoughtfully. Ursula Carling was not exactly an ideal neighbour to have. I was glad she didn't live next door to me. But Mrs Adel was not the person writing vile messages on the back of junk mail and posting them to Ursula. Of that I was sure. Rusty wore the fluorescent yellow harness of a guide dog.

The tide was on the turn when I reached the beach. I sat on a stump of timber that held up part of a wooden groyne and watched the waves sending up feathery spumes of water. The next wave slapped hard against the wood and tossed a mountain of water, splashing the shining brown shingle into submission.

Last night's rough weather had piled up a mountain of seaweed on the beach and the mobile caterpillar-wheeled fork lift was already out, raking over the shingle and taking the strong-smelling glutinous stuff back out to sea.

When did I last eat properly? Did I have any breakfast? It had been a rush that morning. I couldn't remember.

Maeve's Café on the front did a good plaice and chips. You could taste the salt of the sea. She bought the fish straight from the fishermen on the beach. I think she fancied one of them, his face burnt brown, thigh-high rubber waders, yellow oilskins and all. Very fetching. Each morning they pulled up their boats and set out makeshift counters alongside their lockers. They had their regular customers and would be sold out by midday unless it was raining. If it was raining, they packed up and went home.

Maeve's Café was not exactly a salubrious place – apart from her name. I think that she'd changed it from the more urbane Mavis. The café was always steamy and overheated from the open chip fryers. The tables were covered in worn marigold patterned oilcloth and the china was heavy white earthenware. Like as not, you'd get a bent fork.

"Plaice and chips, Maeve. Cup of tea, weak."

"Honey, no sugar," she added, nodding.

"I'm over at the corner table."

I had a lot of reading to catch up on. I opened a heavy law book on the table and started at page one. Defamation. I ought to know something about defamation. There was sure to be some client being libelled or slandered and I should have the know-how at my fingers. If I got any more clients, that was. I had that failure feeling looming.

A man at the next table glanced at me so I turned sideways from him. Drat him. I wanted peace to work, not a pick-up. I tried to freeze him out.

"Jordan . . . not reading?"

I didn't stir though I knew the voice. "No, I'm standing on my head."

Funny, how you don't recognise people out of context. He was wearing a blue check workshirt and jeans; a dark grey anorak hung over the back of his chair. He was eating a mountain of greasy sausages, beans and chips, sloshed with tomato sauce. He registered my look of disgust.

"I ordered a double helping," he explained.

"Don't they feed you at the station?"

"Don't you remember the cooking?"

It was DI James, last night's James Bond, my *bête noire*. I closed the book. I had to apologise to him. It might as well be now.

"I owe you an apology," I said slowly. "I was very rude to you last night when you got me out of Trenchers."

"You were upset. PMT. Female hormones up the creek."

I tried not to kick him. "There's nothing wrong with my hormones," I said. "I was very frightened and your sudden appearance alarmed me even more."

"Understandable. I do have an alarming appearance."

I had to laugh but turned it into a small apologetic cough. DI James had the most unalarming type of male face, a bold ruggedness that invited confidence and trust. But I liked that throw-away humour. It scored points with me instantly. I wondered if we could get on to a less competitive level.

"So, DI James, am I going to have to address you formally all the time? What's your christian name?"

He didn't answer but peered out of the steamy window as if the outside world was more fascinating. Perhaps he'd forgotten his first name. "James," he said.

"I know that. Your first name, birth name, christian, whatever you get called at home. Don't you have one?"

"It is James. My name is James James. No jokes please. And I don't have a home. Nothing special."

His eyes held mine and his face had a steely look as if daring me to laugh again. "My parents were probably drunk at the christening," he added.

I hoped I looked as appalled as I felt. "They need shooting," I said. "Fancy landing you with that handle for the rest of your life."

"As a youngster, people called me Jimmy. The lads at the station call me Jim. I loathe Jim." He looked quite depressed as if a lifetime of explaining his name was a burden he'd like to get rid of.

"Parents can be idiots. My mother had been on a holiday to Palestine, fell in love with this river that flows down to the Dead Sea. I suppose it's not too bad, being called after a river."

"A bit wet," he said, sloshing on some more tomato sauce.

Mavis arrived with my plaice and chips. The fish was golden and succulent. James offered me the sauce bottle but I shook my head.

"I have no intention of spoiling the taste of fresh fish with sugar and modified starch." I had a sudden inspiration. "I won't call you Jim or James off duty. If it's all right with you, how about Jay? The initial J? It sounds classy. Jay's what I'll call you."

A fleeting distaste touched his cold, dour face. It was a face now without expression; a craggy plane of skin and muscle with features of stone that barely moved. Essential for a good policeman.

I tried to see his eyes without staring and without warning my stomach contracted. It was a gut feeling. His eyes were a brilliant blue and masked with secrets. They reminded me of my bone-melting trumpeter. I gave him an undeserved smile because of this coincidence.

"Not Jay," he said about fifteen minutes later. "My ex-wife called me Jay. She was classy. I should prefer not to be reminded."

"Sorry. OK, James then, every time," I conceded quickly. I didn't want to compete with an ex-wife. I hadn't known he had an ex-wife. Even exes could hang up a new relationship. They had a funny way of intruding. "No problem."

"I know about grief," he went on. "The other day, you were at me, because I didn't understand grief. But I do. I still have feelings."

"Sorry," I said again. "I didn't know."

I was making my meal last, savouring the taste of chip by crinkly chip. James was now on to his second helping of apple pie with ice cream, the fat-filled pastry an inch thick. Where did all the calories go? He was racehorse lean, though good shoulders bulged through his workshirt.

"Look, I know I'm not in the force any more, but what about my poor nun? What do you know about her? Surely it's fair to tell me something. Do you know who she is or was?"

He gave me a condescending look. I could have killed him. But the eyes held me.

"I guess it won't hurt if I tell you what we know. Her name was Ellen Swantry and she'd been working with a group of nursing nuns who run a local hospice called St Helios. She was in her sixties and tired of living alone in her big house. I suppose she thought that turning to religion would salve her conscience. St Helios was the answer."

His words washed over me. Ellen Swantry. I had her filing cabinet. I had read her electricity bills. Dear heavens, I felt I almost knew her although our only meeting had been through a hole in the floorboards at Trenchers. I swallowed hard. My enjoyment of chips vanished. I pushed the plate away.

"Greek word for the sun. I know their charity shop well. How did she die?" I could have added that I shopped at their shop for my stock but stopped myself. It was irrelevant.

"We are not quite sure . . . we don't have the pathologist's final report yet. We believe she was put on the meat hook after death. Placement of blood. You know that it drains after death. She'd been laying on her side for a time, then hooked up. Mrs Swantry had also been strangled with a length of nylon twine, the kind fishermen use.

The beach is littered with bits of it. Though oddly, she'd been suffocated before that. Someone was making very sure she was dead."

I was glad I'd finished my plaice and I was equally glad she didn't die on the hook. James was looking twitchy as if he had to leave soon. "Poor lady. What else have you found out?"

"Is she one of your clients?" he came back quickly.

"Of course not, it's my natural curiosity. Wouldn't you be curious if you'd found a dead nun in a derelict hotel?"

He was shrugging himself into his anorak. "She'd been dead for about twenty-four hours. No relatives have come forward as yet. No one is claiming her. Dead end really. Sorry, Jordan, not supposed to be a joke. The nuns have got a small plot of land next to a chapel and she's going to be buried there."

"I'm glad someone is going to give her some peace. I'm sure she deserved it."

He was getting up to go. I did not know how to detain him. I've no skill with men. That's for certain.

"I suppose you haven't found a tortoise, have you? Weighs about two kilos, mottled brown and black shell, a bit chipped. Very friendly," I added desperately.

He looked at me in disbelief. "There's a chipped tortoise in the station yard, chomping its way through canteen salad. It was found by a panda on beat patrol in the middle of the A27, heading towards Southampton."

"That's Joey," I said, glowing.

Later I found that he had paid my bill at the counter. He'd said he didn't have a home and that worried me. Nowhere special. That was sad.

Seven

After returning Joey to his owner, I took part of the afternoon off, scouring the charity shops for more display goods. Trade had been brisk. The cheque was in my pocket, ink hardly dry, so it was spend, spend, spend. She had insisted on paying me for two full days, though I explained that I had done nothing.

"You could've gone to the police station yourself," I said.

"But I didn't and you did," she said, her delight brimming over at having Joey back in the fold. She was tickling him under his leathery chin. He seemed to like it. "And that's what I'm paying you for. Thank you, Miss Lacey. I shall recommend you to my friends."

If only all my clients would be as grateful.

I called at Rick Weston's office, ignoring the bargains on display in the forecourt and paid for the filing cabinet and another installment on the Victorian button-back. He tried to sell me an ugly wardrobe with knuckled knobs but I wasn't into big furniture.

The tide was out now in early evening, one of my favourite times. The tide at Latching goes out for miles. You can hardly see the sea from the shore, only a hazy knit of water and sky. Acres and acres of flat, wetly wrinkled sand stretches towards the horizon with small smatterings of rocks which catch the unwary swimmer underfoot. Swarms of black-winged gulls search the newly turned rivulets of sand for stranded fish and minnows, baby crabs. People walk their dogs, looking like Lowry people from a distance.

I'd been home and got my wellington boots and an extra jersey. I'd ruined enough trainers wading through puddles and the small streams that pour off the shingle as the sea recedes. I trudged, head

62

against the wind, breathing in the clean cold air, taking it deep into my lungs, the twitchy airways at ease for once.

It was back to square one with this case but where on earth was square two? Where should I go now? Scrutinise the letters, Cleo, the dead cat or Ursula herself? There had to be an alien item I'd overlooked. Someone along the line wasn't being straight with me. Perhaps it was time I did a little surveillance. But who? Cleo? Ursula? Mrs Yarpole? Mr Yarpole? How about their nameless son with the noisy friends and obstructive motorbikes? My head was spinning uselessly as I came off the beach.

As well as a selection of display goods from the charity shops, I'd been collecting a box of personal props. I blame my drama teacher at school. As well as the courtesan, one year she made me play Hamlet just because I was the tallest girl in the class. It gave me an aversion to learning words but a penchant for dressing up.

In the force I'd been involved in a couple of great undercover jobs, once as a tarty street walker which was a failure as no one gave me even a second glance. The next patch was as a refugee beggar sitting on a pavement and I earned seven pounds thirty-seven pence in half a day. The charmers at the station made me spend it on drinks all round in the pub. I went mad and had two orange juices.

The next morning I didn't even open up the shop. I went into my office and got out of my jeans and sweatshirt, changed into a fawn skirt which had seen better days, baggy cardigan and a man's rumpled raincoat. The clothes had been washed but not pressed. My trainers were scruffy enough and wouldn't show much under the dragging skirt. I tucked every scrap of hair under a mud-coloured knitted tea-cosy and rubbed cold black coffee into my skin for a weatherbeaten look.

Mirror. I needed a long mirror to judge the effect. I put it on the shopping list for my next trawl. The Mexican restaurant was not open as usual but the windows gave an approximate reflection. I shuffled into the general store next door. Doris was stacking shelves with a special-offer brand of baked beans.

"Got any stale bread?" I croaked. "Not eaten for days."

Doris sighed with exasperation, inspecting her blood-tinged nails. "You people . . . always after something, something for nothing."

63

I put on a crestfallen look and began to shuffle back out of the shop, unironed shoulders hunched, sucking in my starving cheeks.

"Here you are," said Doris quickly, putting a currant bun and an apple in a bag. "But I don't want to see you again."

I clutched the goodies to my chest, mumbled my thanks and got out of the shop fast. So far, so good. But I needed a bag lady's bags. I snatched a couple of evil smelling, tied plastic refuse sacks from the back of the restaurant. Then I took the bus to the end of Lansfold Avenue. Too far for the elderly to walk.

"Ain't you got a bus pass?" said the driver as I got on. I shook my head. "You ought to apply to the council for one. You're entitled, y'know."

I nodded and sat as far away from the other passengers as possible. The bags were emitting a strong spicy odour from some chillies. Everyone was glad when I got off. I found a low garden wall where I could sit and bask my old bones in the late autumn sun. A straggly hydrangea bush half hid me from view but I could see Ursula's house clearly. I tried not to look at The Beeches next door, where the nun had lived.

Definitely currant bun time. As I bit into the white dough, expecting a soft pulp of sweetness, disappointment hit me. It was stale. Oh well, it was a hand-out. The currants fed my craving for sweetness and I sucked on them till they shredded themselves in my mouth and their skin got stuck between my teeth.

I began to shift uneasily. The bricks were hard under my bottom and turning as cold as a bite of winter. What was it I could get down under? Piles? I scrunched up a few folds of surplus raincoat for padding. Come on, Ursula, do something before I die of boredom. I fished a stained menu out of a refuse sack just for something to read: red snapper in cilantro, fresh tortillas and burritos, plantains with ground beef, black beans and rice. The prices made me gasp. No wonder they were closed so often.

A creaking gate made me look up. Ursula was walking along the pavement, dressed entirely in black like an elongated spider. Long black coat nearly to her ankles. Black velvet hat. Small black bag clutched in gloved hands against her stomach. She had recovered from her cold. She was going the other way which was just as well as I didn't have time to compose my face.

I shuffled after her keeping a decent distance. Her nose would soon pick up chillies. She glanced at me once as she checked traffic before crossing a road. I scratched my nose in a thoroughly disgusting way. She walked quite fast despite the heeled court shoes, and my shuffling gait collected a few skips and jumps so that I could keep her in sight. Some kids jeered at me and I put out my tongue. I hadn't done that for years. It was quite liberating.

She turned off at a small chapel, a plain brick-built place, half cemented over and covered in Sussex pebbles. The garden was well kept, lawn mowed, a few weeping trees hoovering the air. Then I saw a small crowd at the far end of the garden . . . several middle-aged women in grey skirts and cardigans and jackets, grey kerchiefs over their heads, people in wheelchairs wrapped in rugs, several leaning on sticks, a man of the cloth with the Bible in hand. One of the nuns was tall and elegant. She seemed to lean into the wind.

It was a funeral and suddenly I knew whose funeral and a cold shiver ran along my spine.

My poor nun . . . and Ursula was there, being stately and commiserate. Neighbourly. My head was humming with thoughts. I'd heard this hum before but dismissed it. Flotsam was floating around like bits of planetary garbage, refusing to lock themselves and make sense.

Something was there, staring me in the face but what was there? I couldn't grasp it. I swore at myself, calling myself the dimmest of the dim. First Class Investigations (FCI) was going to fail from the start if I didn't resolve this case. I huddled under a canopy of whispering branches and watched the ceremony, the murdered nun put to rest in a plain coffin. Ashes to ashes, dust to more dust.

DI James was standing at the back of the mourners, looking detached. I thought that it was nice of him to turn up, wearing a dark suit, white shirt, mournful tie. But I guess he was watching too, as I was.

"Ellen Frances Swantry, at peace at last, with her loving Father . . ." the cleric's voice rang out across the sward. It was starting to rain, that needle-fine rain that drifts off the sea. Ursula put up a small, telescopic umbrella to shield her hair. I wondered if my coffee stains would run.

As the coffin disappeared from sight into the earth, people began to talk and break up. They were coming my way. I fell on to my knees beside a flattened overgrown grave. The name on the gravestone was unreadable . . . but the dates 1769–1798 were . . . They died so long ago when Latching was nothing more than a sprawling fishing village with sea-bathing for the reasonably rich.

"Bless you, my dear," said one of the nuns, touching the shoulder of my dirty raincoat. She didn't mind the chilli. I sniffed. I was horribly moved and tears sprang to my eyes for no good reason at all. How could some people be so good and so kind? DI James strode past, glancing at Ursula.

There were cars waiting for the disabled to take them back to St Helios. Perhaps they would have tea and special cakes now, something to warm them up and remind them that it was not their turn yet. Ursula was shaking hands and leaving, obviously not invited back to the hospice. I was tired of following her but the day wasn't over. She didn't go home but headed towards the centre of town. Where was the dratted woman going now?

She steered a course straight for Trimpers. I should have known. The hairdressers. The rain had rearranged her careful styling and she was going to have it fixed.

I sat outside on a refuse bin, eating the apple. There was only one bruised bit of skin which I spat out into the gutter. It's not difficult to deteriorate.

An hour later, she emerged, not looking much different. She then began an afternoon of serious shopping. I was bored rigid, trundling after her from one fashion store to another. Latching was well served with dress shops. I collected disgusted looks and turned up noses.

Enough was enough. The smell of synthetic shop perfume clogged my nostrils. I tossed the refuse sacks into a bin and headed for the pier. I needed some fresh air. Once on the pier I pulled off the hat and scratched my hair into its usual tangle. The wind immediately tangled it some more and I began to feel like my old self, shedding the raincoat and straightening my back. Now I looked like everyday teenage grunge. I was so lucky. I was doing what I wanted to do and today, somehow, I had made progress. Nothing connected yet but it was all there. Oh yes, it was there. I only had to put it together.

An angler pulled in an elongated, slithery silvery fish with lethally pointed sharp-toothed jaws. "What's that?" I asked.

"Garfish or garpike."

"Surely you're not going to eat it?"

"My cat likes it."

"But all those bones."

"One long bone down the back. You can soon rip it out."

I shuddered and moved on. As much as I love cats, they are voracious animals with their consumption of meat, fish and anything that moves. First I had to rid myself of the taste of funerals and the smell of chillies. I leaned over the rail at the end of the pier, drinking the ozone from the churning sea. Sometimes you could see the hump of the Isle of Wight on the horizon but not today with the low rain clouds pulverising the sky. The Channel was rushing in, slapping at the structure, plumes of spray drenching the lower levels and a cluster of dedicated anglers. The remains of the day drifted like departing guests over the horizon.

"Jordan?"

It was my trumpeter's voice. His brown-sugared voice. I dissolved into a pool of female confusion. He'd found me with my face stained with coffee dregs, hair like a bird's nest, and I was wearing charity throw-outs. His dark eyes smiled, dark and mysterious as the deep sea beneath the pier.

"Hello sweetheart," he said, wrapping his arm round my waist. We leaned out to sea together in a timeless moment and I could feel his heart beating against my side. He was my height, warm, solid, rounded, a real person. I closed my eyes and arranged myself against him, savouring the closeness, drinking in his gorgeous smell.

"This is coffee on my face," I explained. "It's a disguise. I've been on surveillance."

"You look wonderful. I've always wanted to go out with an

undercover Indian woman. They have such beautiful manners. Have you got a diamond in your nose?"

"No. Why are you here in Latching?"

"We're doing a concert tonight at the Pier Theatre. Didn't you catch the posters? Are you coming?"

How could I have not seen the advertisements? The near-miss gave me the shudders. He might have been – played his magic and gone, and I would never have known.

"Try stopping me."

"Join us for supper afterwards. A few of the boys."

"But don't you have to go home?"

"I am allowed to eat."

A slight emphasis was on the word eat. I understood. That was as much as he allowed himself to stray. To eat with me, a meal in a public place with some of the band.

"I'd like a tuna and anchovy pizza with warm red house wine and salad piled high in a bowl," I said, suggesting a cheap meal. Musicians did not earn much.

"So would I. Bet I can pile my salad higher than yours."

"I'm an expert. Years of practise." We looked at each other without words. It was a hopeless situation and always had been, and we both knew it. A half-forgotten longing from long ago that we could do nothing about. "I've been following a client today, to see what she gets up to. And she went to the funeral of a nun who was horribly murdered."

He was a man of music and melodies and soaring sound. This cushioned him in a different world and he wasn't exactly listening. I don't believe he knew I'd left the police force. "Poor little girl," he said vaguely to all five foot nine of me. "How awful for you. Try not to think of the nun."

"I found her body," I added, glad to unburden the guilt and tell someone.

He groaned and moved a tendril of my hair with the tip of his nose. "You're much too young and sweet for such sordid experiences. We're having an early rehearsal, Jordan darling, and I have to go. I'll leave a ticket for you at the box office and see you after the show."

He planted a kiss somewhere behind my ear and was gone. I stood quite still so I could pretend he was standing beside me, so I could feel the person he saw in me, young and sweet and vulnerable.

I wandered back to my shop and opened it up belatedly. I washed off most of the coffee out the back and changed into my jeans and sweatshirt. A woman came in, interested in the framed picture of pressed flowers. All my price tags were now six pounds. It simplified life. But she did not look as if she had any money to spare.

"My mother used to press flowers," she mused nostalgically, her mind wandering back to running as a child across a sunlit lawn with daisies threaded in her hair. "We used to do it together on a big table with sheets of blotting paper. Do you know, you can't get blotting paper now."

"This has just been reduced," I said, rather enjoying the power. "Sale price of three pounds."

"I'll have it," she said.

I replaced it in the window with an amber goblet, big enough for a pint of brandy. What did people use these things for? It was too big for anything sensible. Just a dust collector.

The general store was near to closing so I whipped round to get some food. Another forgotten meal day. I went along the shelves at the speed of light and took the last loaf of granary bread, some creamy goat's cheese, a bag of tomatoes and a jar of green olives.

"Looks like you're making another pizza," said Doris, totting up my bill on a calculator. "Did you enjoy the currant bun?" she added without a bat of her false lashes.

"It was stale," I said.

"What did you expect? An Oscar nomination?"

Eight

I put away the food I wasn't going to eat and got ready to go to the jazz concert. While I scrubbed off the remains of the bag lady, I mentally surveyed my wardrobe. This didn't take long. At least everything was clean. I never put away anything that needs a wash. A good massage of medicinal shampoo got the itch out of my hair. That knitted hat was suspect. I took more care than usual which showed how seriously I was taking this date.

I put on clean jeans and a blue denim shirt that has pale blue flowers embroidered on the yoke, cowboy-style. It had been a bargain in a sale and bought for its hard-wearing qualities not the fancy yoke. I staggered about in leather boots for a few minutes, then remembering he was the same height as me, changed into my best trainers. My hair was tamed into a tawny rope. I poked at my lashes with black mascara which was a token beauty routine on special occasions.

Just as I was thinking of leaving, the doorbells rang. It was Derek. His eyes widened with approval. "Hey gorgeous," he said, moving in fast. "This is my lucky day."

"No, it isn't," I said. "I'm just going out."

"Anywhere interesting? I could come along."

My reply needed careful wording. I didn't want him tagging along to the jazz concert with me, a possibility if he knew I had a free ticket and he'd only have to pay for himself.

"It's the Mayor's Charity Gala at the Cumberland Hotel to-night," I said smoothly. True, it was, but I didn't say that was where I was going. "The tickets are twenty-five pounds at the door. Bound to be plenty of room. They won't turn anyone away."

His face hardened as it did when confronted with the thought of actually spending money. "A bit pricey," he said eventually. "Twenty-five pounds is a lot."

"It's all for charity."

"Charity begins at home," he trotted out predictably.

His indecision hung in the air. I gave him a cup of tea and a couple of Grandma Wild's home-made cookies to calm his nerves while I did some fast tidying-up. Perhaps I was half hoping to bring a special visitor back with me after the show . . . just for a coffee.

It was difficult to remember what the attraction had once been with Derek. I suppose I had been lonely, feeling vulnerable. He had an immaculate clean-cut English look, the result, I knew now, of hours of self-preening and primping and steaming at a ironing board. His profile was good with a classical nose. But a nose is an accident of birth and not the result of character building.

He tried to finger my waistband as I put the biscuits on a plate. I side-stepped the embrace.

"Don't you like me any more?" he asked plaintively.

"Of course I like you."

"You don't go out with me any more."

"You don't ask me."

He'd liked it fine when I cooked supper, rustled up a picnic for the beach, paid for my own ticket to a show. I couldn't forget that tea-bag, gift of the century. It made me curl with laughter. Had he ever bought me flowers? No. Chocolates? Not even a Mars bar. Perfume? Not a whiff. OK, I'm not a chocolate person and rarely wear perfume. But I love flowers. I even have a vase. There are always flowers and plants in my two rooms in various stages of mortality. It's hard to throw away flowers before the sap has finally dried up. I've kept two cyclamen corms in the dark from last year to plant again this winter. That's a flower person.

For years I've nursed this longing to fall deeply in love and to be loved in the same wonderful way, to cherish and be cherished. I wanted to be courted by a man with a warm and generous heart who'd spend his last pound without saying it was his last, who didn't count his change in front of me, who left tips that reflected how much he enjoyed my company.

The atmosphere cooled. Derek didn't know how to handle it. I put on my black leather jacket, a twentieth birthday present from my parents. It still looked good. The pockets were silk lined and I remembered finding inside their loving card. "To our dearest daughter. Love Mum and Dad." I tried not to think about them. Their last present to me.

"Time to go," I said. "Coming?"

He pretended to think about it but he'd made up his mind a long time back. "No, Jordan, I don't think so. I'll see who's down at the pub. Might be someone I know in the Bull."

He tried to kiss me outside on the pavement but I wasn't having it. I was saving my love. A fast manoeuvre made it look as if I was heading for the Cumberland Hotel, but then I back-tracked down Field Alley, a narrow eighteenth-century path between high brick walls, and cut along the seafront to the Pier Theatre. It was a narrow escape. Field Alley was supposed to be haunted. Tonight there was only me slipping through the shadows.

The ticket was waiting for me in the box office. It was in an envelope with my name in his bold handwriting. I kept the envelope. It was a good aisle seat, about halfway back, with an excellent view of the stage. I settled myself into the plush warmth, savouring the pleasure ahead of listening to great jazz, feasting my eyes on him.

It was an old theatre, recently refurbished with comfortable dark red Dralon seats, modern lighting and sound equipment. The bar and café were really part of the pier complex and had not received the same face-lift. The dome above the auditorium let in an eerie green light. I could see the shapes of seagulls sitting on the structure. Just before the show started, the shutters would clatter over the dome giving the birds heart attacks but the light would still filter through the cracks. I don't know why they bothered.

The Carling case was a long way from being solved but I'd made a deal of progress since Ursula's first tearful arrival at my office. Perhaps I'd spend some of the Joey cheque on a decent print for the office wall. If I was going to stick to the name First Class Investigations (FCI – close to FBI) then the image had to improve.

But this was time off and I could relax. The music would refresh my soul, wash out the stale rubbish. Finding the nun and being imprisoned in Trenchers had put the taste of fear in my mouth and that had to go too.

It was nearly a full house. People of all ages were still coming in; some were those that remembered the BB Brown Band at its height in the seventies and others, younger fans who were just discovering its music. A few instrumentalists had grown old with the band; others were recent transplants like my trumpeter.

As I gazed round the auditorium, I caught sight of a small, oval face peering over the edge of the balcony front row. Her cap of polished dark hair shone like a conker in the artifical light. It was Cleo Carling. It gave me a start. She was the last person I was expecting to see. But why shouldn't she like jazz? BB was internationally famous and people travelled miles to hear him. Why not come along the A27 from Chichester? But she said she rarely came to Latching . . . so what? This was one of those rare occasions.

Cleo was doing what I'd been doing, looking around the theatre and drinking in the atmosphere and excitement. But I shrank back in my seat so she wouldn't see me. I did not want her to think I was following her. It was essential to maintain her confidence in me.

The balcony at the Pier Theatre was a narrow affair reached by two staircases from either side of the auditorium. It went back six rows. Cleo had an end seat in the front row and was leaning over like a child on an outing.

My attention was instantly hooked by the band ambling on stage, carrying their instruments. They arrived in the casual, relaxed way that jazzmen do, chatting, eight of them; four went to the standing microphones at the front of the stage, the string bass and drummer to the back, two electric guitarists to chairs at the side.

The trumpeter stood left front of stage. Although he was not that tall, he had immense stage presence. His evening suit was perfectly tailored, sat easily on his shoulders, a sharp crease in his trousers, his dark hair flopping over his brow, boyish and unruly. They always teased him about his immaculate appearance during the show, calling him unflattering names. It was part of the camaraderie of the band. Everyone got ripped off about something, even the legendary jazzman BB himself.

There was a high buzz everywhere like champagne bubbles. I could not stop the bubbles fizzing through my veins.

BB was getting old now, slightly stooping, a mane of silvery hair down to his hunched shoulders; but he still played with all the old magic.

As the clapping died down, I glanced across and up to the balcony. Cleo was sitting back now. At the rear of the balcony hung heavy red velvet curtains. One of them stirred as if a window had been left open. I was distracted by the curtain and missed the first announcement by BB.

"A-one, a-two, a-three," he said, foot tapping, forefinger beating. He brought his trombone up to his lips and they swung into "Sweet Georgia Brown". I was carried away by the haunting sound and great beat.

The trumpet soared with a voice of its own. I hoped his wife knew how lucky she was. I hoped she treated him well. She didn't go to jazz concerts. "She has enough of it at home," he'd told me once. I would have followed him to Tibet and back.

A movement at the side of the auditorium caught my eye. Someone was hovering in the dark, moving silently and slowly, pausing every now and again, to peer. It was a tall, thin figure, trying not to draw attention to himself. It was not a member of staff. The theatre attendants wore black and red jackets. I timed the pauses. He stood still just long enough to look along the row of faces. He was searching for someone. I felt a flutter of disquiet.

I've been in the business long enough to have a sixth sense about such things. And I knew he wasn't looking for me. My ticket was a last-minute gift, lodged in the box office just before the show started. No one knew I was coming.

He had to be looking for someone else. My skin crept and it wasn't from the magic of the music. Something was wrong. An uneasy feeling stirred my stomach like migrating spiders.

Then I lost sight of the figure. He was behind me now and I could hardly swivel round to watch. They were playing "Tin Roof Blues", one of my favourite tunes and the plaintive sounds from the four soloists found chords within my body. Usually this piece would carry me away on clouds of sound but tonight I was distracted.

The figure appeared again on my left. He was still moving slowly, inspecting each row, still searching. His clothing was dark, face and hair in the shadows. But my whole body was alert and it wasn't because of the blues. Something weird was going on and I didn't like the smell of it.

I froze in my seat. A quiver of fear gripped me. He was easing up the stairs, towards the balcony, not making a sound. No one else seemed to have noticed. I decided to speak to one of the attendants. I got up during a wave of applause, not wanting to cause a disturbance, and moved silently to the back of the auditorium. They began playing "Down By the Riverside", a perennial favourite of every foot-tapping jazz fan.

But before I could speak to anyone, I suddenly saw that the figure was right behind Cleo. The curtain was moving round him like a cloak. I saw a tiny flash of steel – it might have been a knife, mirror, screwdriver, anything. I sprang into action, my heart pounding, and raced up the stairs two at a time towards the balcony. One of the attendants spoke to me sharply; someone in the audience hissed; others glared. It was pure reflex.

By the time I got to the back, the figure had gone and a window was banging. I whipped the curtain aside and saw that it led out on to a narrow, railed ledge. It had begun to rain and the wind blew a fine spray into my face, blinding me for an instant. Down below, I saw a dark figure running along the pier towards the deep sea.

I checked quickly on Cleo. She was looking around, disturbed, either aware that something was going on behind her or chilled by the sudden draught from the open window.

If he'd climbed down, then so could I. Without thinking, I legged it out on to the ledge and saw that there was a fire escape ladder pinned to the wall. How handy. I shinned down the metal rungs, relieved that I did not have to do anything heroic.

Stella Whitelaw

The figure had a start on me but I could run faster. My leg muscles responded and I surged forward with all my old power. The figure was darting between the glass partitions that stood centrally along the length of the pier.

He plunged into the amusement arcade. Would I recognise him among that crowd of punters? He merged immediately into the throng of fruit machine, slot machine and race track addicts. He could be any of those feeding coins into machines.

But he would be breathing as heavily as me and I reckoned I was in better condition. He couldn't normalise it in the few seconds he had ahead of me. I scanned the arcade quickly, moving down the aisles, the racket of coins and pop music and exploding missiles loud in my ears.

I couldn't see him. Had he gone straight through the players and out the far exit? That's what he must have done. A commotion started right behind me and I swung round. A youth in jeans and dark bomber jacket was whacking the glass sides of a roll-a-coin machine with a length of wood and a cascade of silvery ten-pence pieces was shooting down into the metal scoop. For a second, I was distracted.

His pals whooped with joy and began shovelling up the money. People fled as the youth began hitting the glass windows along the row of machines. Glass splintered and money flew in all directions. People screamed. The manager strode over, muscles bulging and buttons bursting, shouting at the youths.

The thug wasn't my fleeing dark figure, I was sure of that. This youth was shorter, puny in every way except in violence and greed. I reacted automatically. I still remembered how to do a flying tackle and we both went down on the floor, knocking the breath out of us.

Jack added his considerable weight. I felt like the filling in a sandwich. We rolled over, panting. Some orgy. All heaving and pushing and no passion. A couple of bouncers arrived and added their twenty-four stone's worth. The youth didn't have a chance of escaping though his pals had scarpered with pockets bulging with cash.

76

"Cor," said Jack, eyeing me with admiration. "That was some tackle. Ain't you the girl who was here the other day, asking questions?"

"That's right, Jack," I said, getting up and dusting down my clothes. I was starting to look a mess and there was a rent on the shoulder of my best shirt. "Look, I can't stop. You can deal with this moron now. Call the police. You may catch the others. There were plenty of witnesses."

"Thanks a lot. I owe you."

I grinned. "No need. You gave me a teddy, remember?"

A couple of bright-eyed old ladies started to clap as I went out. That gave me quite a thrill. The rain was coming down steadily, blown by a north-easterly that chilled the marrow. I trudged back to the Pier Theatre, hearing echos of jazz music on the night air. I had lost the man altogether. He had vanished.

I slipped back into the theatre by the legitimate entrance, showing my ticket again. They looked curiously at my dishevelled appearance.

"Just went out to get a breath of air," I said. "The music, you know. Too much."

At first I couldn't see in the dark and stood at the back to accustom my eyes. They were playing "Mile End Stomp". BB was marvellous for his age. In fact his trombone had a mellowness now that was pure angel music. My trumpeter had loosened his bow tie and unfastened the top button of his shirt. Sweat shone on his face. He did not look at the audience. He played from somewhere within himself.

Cleo was not in her seat.

I started at the empty place at the end of the front row. I realised now that the man had not run towards the amusement arcade. He had back-tracked round the side in the other direction and come into the theatre again through the front entrance. I had been following the wrong figure.

Then I heard a cry, a small sound from somewhere below. A cry tinged with panic.

The only places situated below in the theatre were the staff rooms and the two cloakrooms and toilets. I flung open the door of the Ladies and ran along the narrow corridor which led to stairs down to the basement.

Cleo was on the floor at the bottom of the steep stairs. She was sprawled in an unnatural position, arms across her face as if she had been protecting herself. One of her shoes lay about halfway down, a dainty black patent leather pump with gold stripes across the front.

I felt for a pulse. It was faint but there, and she was still breathing. I didn't dare move her in case there was any injury to her back. Her legs looked all right. No bones sticking out at funny angles.

"Cleo, Cleo," I whispered close to her ear. "Can you hear me?" There was no response. She was out cold. "We'd better get you to hospital. And fast."

He was waiting outside the theatre, pacing the top step. It had closed and most of their equipment had been loaded on to the coach and was ready to leave. The band were either going out to eat or had started their journeys home. He was wearing jeans and a denim shirt. Our clothes were physically mirrored, only his shirt was minus the embroidery. He had my leather jacket over his arm.

"Jordan, I was worried," he said, not a word of reproach. "They found your jacket on your seat. I knew something had happened."

"I'm so terribly sorry," I said, getting my breath back. "I saw someone in the auditorium and thought they were stalking my client, or rather the daughter of my client. I chased them out on to the pier but caught somebody else instead trying to steal cash from the arcade. Then I came back to the theatre and found that Cleo had fallen down the stairs to the ladies' cloakroom and knocked herself out, so I went to hospital in the ambulance with her . . ."

"Hey, hey, slow down, sweetheart," he said, taking my arm. "I can't take all that in. Could you explain it again in words of one syllable for a simple musician?"

I did explain again but, although he nodded occasionally, I'm sure he didn't really understand what had happened. He only knew that I had gone hare-brained around the pier in the dark and missed half the concert.

"So you missed most of the second half," he said.

"Yes . . ." My voice was almost inaudible.

"And I have to go home now. It's too late for supper."

"I know . . ."

"But I'll walk you home. You've got mud on your face." He wiped it off with the corner of a handkerchief, carefully and gently. He knew all about true love.

The rain clouds had scudded away and left a perfect night sky studded with stars but I couldn't enjoy it, knowing I had ruined my evening with him. He talked about the show, winding down, and I tried to make intelligent remarks but I was shattered and my shoulder was beginning to hurt.

"And you've torn your pretty shirt," he said, stopping under the yellow glow of a street lamp outside my home.

"I fell on the pier, in the arcade. The floor was slippery. There must have been some nasty jagged bit lurking." A nasty jagged bit like broken glass.

"It's not bleeding," he said inspecting the rent. Then he kissed the bare skin of my shoulder beneath and I nearly forgot to breathe. "I'll see you again sometime, Jordan. The next time we play in Latching."

This was goodbye then. The moment had arrived. The tears welled up and threatened to choke me. I began to shake.

"There, there, baby," he said, folding me into his arms. He rocked me gently. "It couldn't be helped. These things happen."

"But . . . I wanted . . . everything to be . . . perfect," I wept.

"I know. I know . . ." he soothed.

Then he took a flat plastic box out of his pocket. "This is the band's latest CD. I want you to have it. When you listen to it, Jordan, remember that every time I play the trumpet, I'm playing for you."

He kissed me briefly and then he was gone, striding off into the night. I stood holding the cold CD disc, dying by inches, the door of my mind closing on the pain. He had no way of knowing that I didn't have a CD player.

Nine

T hey kept Cleo in hospital overnight as she had a slight concussion. I went to see her and she was sitting up in bed looking small and frail, her cheek discoloured, stained mauve and yellow. She said she had slipped and fallen down the stairs to the toilets.

"I don't really remember much," she said. "There seems to be a blank area in my memory. I think I fell, caught my shoe on something. They were new and the soles slippery."

I didn't say what I thought. There was no point in frightening her. The hospital smell was overpowering, a mixture of antiseptic, body odours, urine and boiled greens.

"How are the bruises?" I asked.

She grimaced. "A bit tender. But they'll fade."

"Do you want me to tell Ursula where you are?"

"No, thank you. I doubt if she'd be interested."

"But your own mother . . . ?"

"She doesn't care about me."

"I don't understand her . . ."

"She wouldn't bother to send me a get well card."

"Can I get you a magazine or a book from the kiosk downstairs?" I was starting to feel I ought to make tracks. I'm not good at this sick-bed thing.

Cleo began to shake her head then stopped abruptly as if it hurt. "Don't think I could read a word," she said. "A bit of a headache."

"How are you getting home?" I wished that I had four wheels so I could offer her a lift. I went to the window. This wing of the hospital was one of the few tall buildings in Latching and the rooftops spread below like an tumble of fallen Lego. The sea glinted in the distance in a low line of shallow waves. A gang of gulls wheeled and dealed, fighting over the tide's incoming flotsam of dead fish.

"They're laying on a hospital car. There's a rota of voluntary drivers who ferry patients home. Everyone is being very kind. And thank you for coming in the ambulance with me. They told me that it was you who found me. So we both missed the second half of the concert. What a shame, Jordan. It's such a good band."

She looked too tired to talk any more so I said goodbye, said that I'd be in touch. I had a word with the young ward sister on my way out. She was a prim miss with rigid brass hair who looked too young for all the responsibility.

"Is Miss Carling going to be all right?" I asked. "She looks very poorly."

"Are you a relation?"

"Her sister." I didn't actually say yes.

"Miss Carling has concussion but the X-rays show no fracture. We're letting her go home tomorrow on the understanding that if she feels sick or the headache gets worse, she's to contact her own doctor immediately."

"Cleo's very sensible. I'll keep an eye on her," I said, all sisterly.

"You were very lucky to find her awake. She was fast asleep just now when her other visitor came."

I stopped in my tracks. "You say another visitor? Who was that?"

"I don't know. He slipped in when I was busy with a patient. He only stayed a few moments. Stood at the end of her bed and stared at her."

"I wonder who it was. Can you describe the man?" I asked, overly casual to cover my apprehension. 'I'd like to thank him for making the visit."

"I hardly saw him. Only a glimpse through a gap in the curtains. Tall, middle-aged, dark clothes."

"Thanks," I said brightly, nodding. 'I think I know who it was."

I no more knew who he was than she did, but there was a good chance it might have been the dark figure stalking Cleo at the jazz concert. The thought was chilling. Whoever it was, I wanted to know how he knew that Cleo had been taken to hospital. The only way he could have known was if he was at the Pier Theatre last night too; perhaps he had pushed her down the stairs.

I shivered, pushing the creepy thought away. I had to stop thinking like this.

Back at the shop, I opened up, dusted my display windows and did some paperwork. I made a mug of black coffee and unlocked the filing cabinet. The lower drawer needed turning out. It was full of dog-eared and stained beige files and paper going brown with age. There might be something I could sell to a dealer. People bought old letters and documents. There was a tiny shop down a side street in Latching that was stacked to the ceiling with boxes and albums of Victorian and Edwardian postcards and letters. Enthusiastic collectors climbed over each other and the resident guard dog to comb through the stock of goodies in the cramped space.

At first I couldn't make head nor tail of the correspondence and papers. There were a lot of minutes of meetings covering the years from 1941 to 1948. At first it looked like some sort of club or association, then I noticed a badly duplicated and smudged official-looking logo at the head of each sheet of paper. Photocopiers had not yet been invented. The paper was poor quality stuff.

The minutes had been meticulously kept; littered with obscure references, initials, oblique cross-references. One word leapt out in flashing lights. Trenchers.

```
4.5 The management at Trenchers are not happy
    with the situation.
4.6 JD to contact.
```

Not happy about what situation? My senses were suddenly alert. During the Second World War, several Heads of State sought asylum in Great Britain and were given plush accommodation at Trenchers. It was supposed to be a military secret but everyone knew.

I sorted the minutes into date order and began to read them more carefully. It dawned on me that the official logo was that of some kind of Government department. The Civil Service jargon was like a

82

foreign language. My eyes felt they were crossed with the strain. The lines of feint, stencilled typing began to blur.

The upper drawer of domestic trivia seemed to have nothing to do with all these papers from the war. Yet there must have been some reason for keeping them.

```
3.1 The BMA has affirmed the necessity of
    this action.
3.2 The Western Desert, Tripoli, Libya and
    Greece will be the main areas of
    distribution.
3.3 This is regarded as a matter of supreme
    urgency by FC. (Note: section 4.12b)
3.4 Minimum run 100,000,000. Suggested
    maximum 259,600,000. Confirm.
```

I blinked. Two hundred and fifty million what? Helmets, packets of chewing gum, condoms? There was nothing to give me a clue.

There was another mention of Trenchers.

```
11.1 The management of Trenchers refuse to
     have military camouflage painted on
     exterior walls.
11.2 This could draw unwanted attention to
     its use.
11.3 Latching is not of strategical
     importance and sources confirm that it
     is not a bombing priority. (Note:
     section 17.1a)
```

Well, they were wrong there. Latching did get bombed during the war. Incendiaries, high explosives and the odd stray doodlebug. The Germans had been targeting the railway line and the gasometer but missed.

My coffee had grown cold. I was mystified. How was Trenchers linked with Ellen Swantry, apart from the fact that these files came from The Beeches? And how come she was murdered in the same hotel so many years after these incomprehensible minutes were taken, typed on a stencil skin and copies roneod off on a cranky machine? Why were they stored at The Beeches anyway? Surely they should be in some dusty Whitehall basement?

I picked an answer out of the air. Supposing Ellen had been present at these meetings? Supposing she had been the young shorthand-typist patiently plying her Pitmans, then typing and duplicating the lot afterwards for distribution? The list of people present at the meetings was signified by initials only. OS could stand for Oswald Swantry or Oscar Swantry. Or Oliver.

Supposing our Ellen had fallen for Oswald/Oscar/Oliver and eventually married her boss? She could have taken an extra copy of the minutes for her own keeping or as some kind of insurance for her husband's future. Maybe he instructed her to make copies as a precaution.

Maths are not my strong point but I could work out ages. That would make Ellen Swantry over eighty now and the nun on the hook had been in her sixties. No, Ellen hadn't been a lovesick shorthand-typist who married her boss. She had come along much later and married Mr Swantry, a much older man, long after the war.

The solicitor's letter which had led me to Cleo was in the Carling file now. I reread it again for any light.

Dear Madam,
Having perused the Land Registry's Records,
we are of the opinion that this dispute has no
founding in law being a purely non-verbal
agreement. It might, of course, be possible
to pursue a by-law but we would advise you
that this procedure would be costly and with
no guarantee of success.

The letter was addressed to Mrs Ellen Swantry, The Beeches, Lansfold Avenue, Latching.

Ursula Carling also lived in Lansfold Avenue and the house next door to Ursula's tidy Tudor box was shrouded with beech trees. This was a dispute between Ursula and Ellen Swantry. No disguise necessary this time. I was going to check on Ellen Swantry/Beeches/ boundaries – in that order – and Ursula Carling's involvement. But surely no one would kill a neighbour over a domestic dispute? A boundary was no motive for murder.

So how did Ursula come into all this? Or perhaps she didn't. Buying the filing cabinet along with my other furniture had been a fluke. Perhaps the only connection was that Ellen, widowed and vulnerable, simply couldn't wait to get away from her difficult neighbour and into the peace of the nursing order.

Quickly I tidied the files and stacked them away in a big manila envelope. It was none of my business but I knew I ought to mention them to DI James, in a roundabout way. I could hardly go into the station with the files and say: 'Look, sir, something weird was going on at Trenchers during the war and Ellen Swantry, the murdered nun, had copies of wartime files connecting Trenchers and a Government department." He'd laugh me off the premises. Usual irritating chorus of *Jaws* from the wooden-tops.

The house next door to Ursula's in Lansfold Avenue was indeed The Beeches. The great trees blocked all the light from the double-fronted bay windows and a heavy branch looped over the wall and shadowed Ursula's front room. She'd probably complained about that too.

There was a forest of FOR SALE signs on posts. Rick had said the owner of my purchases had gone into a hospice, not realising that Ellen had taken vows and gone into the hospice to nurse the terminally ill. I'd bought Ellen Swantry's button-back chair, her Persian rug and had her filing cabinet in my office all the time and not known it, at least at first.

Empty houses fascinate me. They still hold so much of past owners, echoes and feelings and dislocated thoughts. The over-grown trees completely hid my casual peering into the dark lifeless windows.

I tried to act like a prospective buyer, making little squiggly notes on a scrap of paper. It looked as if the rooms had been stripped of furniture and carpets. There was little left of Ellen Swantry's occupation, only discoloured patches on the walls where her pictures had once hung.

A larder window around the back was very slightly open. It was only a crack but a little patient jiggling loosened the faulty catch. I found some bricks to stand on and pushed up the lower half of the window, then eased my leg over the sill and ducked my head down and under. The marble shelf immediately under the window took my weight and I was able to shift my knee on to it and swing my other leg up and in.

When I was a WPC I arrested some kids for doing exactly this, breaking and entering an empty house. They got supervision orders.

The house had that damp, stale smell of creeping desolation. The red-tiled larder floor was cracked and grimed, littered with dead flies and mildewed food particles. The kitchen was painted a ferocious dark green with more grimy tiles on the floor. It was desperately in need of modernisation unless a time freak wanted to preserve an enamelled gas stove from the forties and a brown earthenware sink for a museum.

I wandered about downstairs, depressed by the dismal surroundings and lost family feeling, half expecting the shadows to shift of their own accord. The bay-windowed front rooms had ugly cast iron fireplaces filled with dead leaves, soot and bird droppings. There was little sign of recent use. The back sitting room was cosier and the fireplace had been boarded up and replaced with an imitation gas log fire. Ellen had spent more time in here. A pile of recent magazines lay curled on the floor and a number six knitting needle had escaped being packed.

Upstairs were four good-sized bedrooms. Three were bleak and musty as if they had been unoccupied for years. Only the big front bedroom held any signs of habitation. I imagined my Victorian chair and Persian rug in this room, in front of the fire, not used but there to fill a space. And there was a lot of space to fill. The ornate marble fireplace held the ashes of a recent fire. Where the carpet had once lain were bare wooden boards, the worn pink lino surround scattered with small odds and ends.

It seemed that in the last few years, Ellen Swantry had lived mainly in these two rooms, shutting off the rest of the house.

I sifted the ashes carefully. Had she been burning old love letters from her husband or some younger lover from the past? A fragment had escaped the flames and using the corner of a magazine, I lifted it on to the palm of my hand. It had a lion's head imprinted on it with a thin metallic strip about an inch from the edge. It looked vaguely familiar yet vaguely foreign. Half a printed word had survived – "ence". I ran through the words ending in "ence". It didn't take long. The only one that made sense was "pence". I grinned at my own joke and put the fragment in a plastic specimen envelope. I would show it to the clever man in the postcard shop. He might be able to identify it.

Dark narrow stairs led to an attic. The window in the roof was shrouded with cobwebs; the area cluttered with towering and cumbersome chests of drawers, bulbous double wardrobes and tatty bamboo tables that even Rick had declined to sell. They were destined for jumble sales, scout huts and bonfire night. I tried to open a couple of drawers but they were stuck and the smell of rotting linen put me off any further investigations. I'd had enough of groping round this sad old house. I needed light and air and a walk by the sea.

There were facts I could check: their marriage licence would give me the husband's name and occupation. He could have been a Civil Servant during the war. But why should I? It wasn't my case. But I was curious, one of my catlike tendencies. And there would be immense satisfaction in solving this murder for the West Sussex police. They might regret giving me the push. I saw myself sauntering into the station, leaning on the counter and saying casually: "Oh, by the way, Skip, I know who put the nun on a meat hook."

I legged it out of the larder window and slid the window down behind me. The garden was overgrown and I thought I could see the reason for Ursula's discontent. A concrete air-raid shelter, left over

87

Stella Whitelaw

from the Second World War, straddled the boundary, probably shared by both houseowners during the raids.

The squat concrete building was covered in weeds and brambles, the steel door hinges rusted solid. It must have offended Ursula's fastidious eye for years. No wonder she was fighting to get rid of it. But its demolition would need the consent of both parties if the cost of it was initially met by both neighbours. I understood the dispute. It was a monstrous eyesore.

I brushed off leaves and cobwebs and fetched my bicycle from where I'd hidden it in the bushes. What a strange morning. I felt I had stepped back in time . . . that war, long before I was born, still shaping people's lives.

Back at the shop, I washed up, made more coffee and sank on to the Victorian button-back. I needed more clients or First Class Investigations would wind down faster than I had started it up. The rhyming of FCI with FBI was no coincidence. Say it quickly and someone might be fooled.

"I need to advertise," I said aloud, startled by my own voice. It was the first time I'd spoken aloud that day. I picked up the phone, needing human contact. I checked with Rick that the filing cabinet, chair and rug had all come from The Beeches. He was usually open on a Sunday.

"Why do you want to know?" he asked in his Sussex accent. "Cleared the whole house. Not a lot there. Some of the rooms were empty. She'd been selling off the best pieces. Made a few bucks."

"The chair and the rug were good."

"Old lady's favourites. They hang on to those bits, however hard up they get."

"And can you remember where you found the filing cabinet?"

"In the attic. Forgotten stuff. I didn't touch the furniture. Not worth my time. Any complaints?"

"None at all," I said. "Have you got a long mirror? Sort-of nearly full length so I can see half of me?"

"I've a twelve by thirty-six inch. Eight pounds."

"Good condition?"

88

"Mirror is OK. Just a lick of paint. I'll put it aside."

I had a sudden craving for oranges, juicy plums and a sweet Galia melon. The house had dried me up, sucked the moisture from my pores. I was dehydrated with thinking and tired of looking. I trawled the High Street for fruit. Doris wasn't open and didn't sell much fruit anyway. She only stocked potatoes, onions, carrots and rock-hard swede. Fruit was exotic.

"We don't do exotics," she told me when I first shopped there. "Only apples."

I went to the huge supermarket at the back of town. It sold everything, in and out of season. It stayed open ridiculous hours and was teeming with itinerant families trundling trollies up and down the aisles, talking on mobiles.

I took my bag of plums down to the beach, wiping them on a tissue, eating them as I walked, spitting the stones back into the bag. Grazing is a bad habit but my body overrode my disapproval. I settled for a perch by the fishing boats. The tide was coming in, sweeping over the scattering of rocks and filling the gullies. Waves splattered the groyne with feathery plumes, speckled detergent foam encroached the sand. A low mist hung on the horizon, obscuring the sun's rays. A few seagulls gathered hopefully at a distance then squawked off in disgust when they discovered the bits were orange peel.

A frayed length of thin blue nylon twine lay nearby and I swallowed an orange pip. Ellen Swantry had been strangled with blue nylon twine. Some sort of motive was slowly coming to the surface. The files from her house . . . they were evidence that she was no ordinary nun.

I'd have to tell DI James. It wouldn't be fair to keep the Superstars in the dark if they were at a dead end.

"Perhaps they'll take me on as a consultant," I said to a black-headed gull who was eyeing my snack. I threw him an orange segment and he flew off with it in his beak, thinking it was a superior kind of prawn.

Perhaps they'd let me use the police computers in exchange. Now that would be a fair bargain. My fingers itched to get on a keyboard and search for the information I needed.

As I sat watching the waves, a familiar twinge cramped my abdomen. My time had come as they used to say in Victorian novels. I knew there was no way round the oncoming pain and nausea. The only panacea was a hot water bottle clutched to my stomach, a couple of paracetamol and the hope of sleep.

Not surprisingly I overslept.

The sergeant on desk duty looked up as I went in the next morning. "Common or garden bleach," he said before I could say a word. "Near lethal dosage. You'd have had a nasty spell in hospital if you'd eaten that lot. Do you want to press charges?"

"I've no idea who sent it," I said, chilled. I'd forgotten the poisoned cake. "But I've gone right off carrots."

"Not surprised. Prefer chocolate cake myself."

"Have they seen the report upstairs?"

"They know all about it."

"Aren't they interested that someone tried to poison me?"

"Lot of serious crime about just now. A near-miss doesn't rate much police time. A near-miss . . ." He started chuckling. This was the resident comedian.

"Can I see DI James?"

"He's out on a ram-raiders job. Some kids last night drove a car into the window of an off-licence. They smashed most of the stock. Only got away with the canned lager."

"Ram-raiders in Latching? What is the world coming to."

"But I expect he'll see you when he comes in. He may want to shake you by the hand."

"Me?" I looked mystified. We were hardly on hand-shaking terms. Suddenly I really wanted to see him. A few minutes would do, even if he was offhand, remote, controlled. I was in a bad way. It was rampant hormones.

"Our home-grown heroine," the sergeant said, whipping out a local evening tabloid paper from under the counter. He smoothed out a page.

There was a photo of the amusement arcade on Latching pier with the manager, Jack, standing outside, arms akimbo, looking fierce.

The headline was "WOMAN'S FLYING TACKLE TACKLES THIEVES". I didn't read any more.

"You're famous," he smirked, tapping the paper. "Can I have your autograph?"

Ten

Publicity. That's what I needed for FCI and now I had got it. The newspaper story had most of the facts right. What they didn't know, they made up in their usual random fashion. They said I was twenty-four, had flaming red hair and was a regular arcade player. Ten per cent right. I did have reddish hair. I tried to hide my elation.

"Wow!" I said, hitting the air.

"Careful now. Don't let it go to your head."

"Free cuppas from now on, eh, Sarge?"

"Don't go twisting my arm, Jordan. I'm very sensitive to extortion."

I wished I had someone to whom I could send copies of the newspaper. There was no way I could send a copy to my dreamy musician. Maybe I'd carry a cutting around and show it to him one day. My mind shifted into fantasy gear and his arm was close against me, his sugar-brown voice admiring my courage, my fearlessness, my trigger-fast reaction.

"Miss Lacey? Jordan."

A man's voice broke into my dreams and I must have given him the smile that is reserved for another. He looked startled, flinty. He also looked tired, dead beat, undernourished, his face drawn, blank eyes. His usual look.

"Been up all night?" I understood.

"Ram-raiders," said DI James. "Gutters running with whisky and gin. Tipsy dogs staggering home or sleeping it off in doorways." He tapped the newspaper. "Who's a clever girl?"

"Training," I said smugly.

92

"Do you want a medal?"

"No, I want five minutes of your time. I'm serious. OK, you know that someone has tried to poison me with carrot cake laced with bleach. Then someone tries to kill Cleo Carling by pushing her down the stairs to the toilets at the Pier Theatre. And there's still the dead nun. I take it you haven't found out anything about her death yet?"

"And you have, I suppose?"

"Yes."

I wasn't going to say any more until he invited me in and took me upstairs to his office. This had to be official.

"Two minutes in my office," he said, inviting me round his side of the counter. "Not a second more."

"I don't know why I'm doing this," I said, following him.

"Public duty."

"Public joke. And the joke's on me. I'm trying to track down the writer of hate mail sent to an upright female citizen of Latching and I'm half poisoned, stalked, imprisoned, and nearly a witness to a gruesome murder."

"Jordan, you do exaggerate." He went straight to a drinks machine and got two polystyrene mugs of instant coffee. It was mud coloured and tasted the same. He took his black.

"You drink too much coffee," I said. "And eat too much junk food. It's not good for you."

"Don't try to change the habits of a lifetime."

"I make excellent coffee," I hesitated. "One day . . . perhaps . . . you might like to try it."

He nodded, too tired to be more than distantly polite.

"Look, I know Ellen Swantry is nothing to do with my case but in a way she is. She lives, or rather lived, next door to my hate mail client, Ursula Carling. They were embroiled in a legal hassle about an air-raid shelter that was built on both their gardens. But that's by the way. I also bought some of Ellen Swantry's house clearance furniture for my office . . ." James's eyes were glazing over, darkly, ocean floor eyes. "Again, nothing to do with either case," I added hurriedly, "but the point is that in the bottom drawer of a filing cabinet I found documents which must have been classed as A1

Secret and Confidential during the Second World War. Something to do with the War Office."

"Is all this relevant?" he asked, clamping on a yawn.

"Yes, definitely. Wake up, buster, we're coming to the best part. These documents refer not once, but several times to Trenchers Hotel. Now that can't be a coincidence. Ellen Swantry was found murdered in Trenchers. Don't tell me that there isn't some connection."

He was dragging himself back from the brink of sleep. "Where are these documents? And what are they?"

"They're minutes of meetings. I've got them in my office. All dated during the Second World War. There's a kind of code."

"I'd like to look at them."

"I hope you can make more sense of them than I have." For some reason I didn't mention the scrap of burnt paper with the lion's head that I'd found in the fireplace of her bedroom. That seemed private to Ellen and I had a feeling for her. "Come round for them anytime." He had a car. I was tired too.

I was nearly out of the door when I remembered the other purpose of my visit.

"Can I use the PNC – only occasionally I hasten to add. It takes a million years to find facts outside and it's all on your database."

"No, you can't."

"You could leave me, just accidentally, and look the other way."

"No."

"I am a heroine. I deserve better treatment than this. And think of it as police cooperation. You don't get that from your normal run-of-the-mill private investigator. I'm useful to you lot."

He was too tired to argue. "Two minutes," he said again, his brain stagnating to a halt. "And don't spread it about." He waved me away. I didn't argue. I ran downstairs to the computer room.

"Hi. I'd like to do a quick search," I said to the startled WPC on duty. "It won't take a second."

The national computerised database was always being expanded, thank goodness. It began as a record of stolen vehicles, then included details of criminal records. The national fingerprint collection can also be reached through the PNC.

I flicked through, trying to find Births, Deaths and Marriages, but I was out of luck. I searched for Marriages and Deaths, hoping to pin some names and dates to the Swantry household. Some hiccup or perhaps I wasn't using the system properly. And when did her husband die? Judging by the state of the house, she'd been a widow for a long time. Perhaps he had been a much older man.

I tracked the Civil Service file, using Swantry and Trenchers and the Second World War. But I kept coming up against classified or user code for entry. Fat chance. I ran in some of the coded references used in the minutes and the computer hated them. Not listed . . . not listed, it displayed with monotonous dismay.

"Thank you so much," I said to the WPC. "Just what I wanted. A few things to check. Such fun, aren't they?"

"Depends what you mean by fun," she scowled.

"Better than the telly. All those confidential files. I bet you have a great time checking up on your neighbours." I bit on my tongue. She looked offended. "But, of course, I know you wouldn't do anything like that. Professional integrity and all that."

I fled before I could make an enemy. It doesn't take much to antagonise people. There are a lot of short fuses about.

Back at the office I phoned the new Family Record Centre at Myddleton Street, EC1. I knew they didn't do phone enquiries but the Press Office might come up with something if I put on a WPC voice and made it sound an official enquiry.

They were so helpful. Everything was on microfilm and it took hardly any time at all to zip through it. Oliver Swantry, forty-two, Civil Servant, and Ellen Robinson, twenty-two, shorthand-typist, married at Marylebone Registry Office on 3 June 1954.

"Do you want a copy?" the nice Press Officer asked.

"Not necessary," I said. "You've been wonderful. But could I ask you to look up when Oliver Swantry died?"

This took a bit longer. There was no record of his death. I was confused. This would make him about 102 years old now. *Guinness Book of Records* stuff.

Ursula Carling was outside the shop waiting for me to open up. She was whacking a folded newspaper against the side of her fawn

pleated skirt and making little, short, angry noises. She caught sight
of me and hurried in.

"So this is what you're doing instead of getting on with my case,"
she snapped. "Chasing around the pier half the night after thieves. I
hope it wasn't in my time. I'm not getting it on my bill."

Another short fuse.

"Of course not," I said smoothly. "You'd better come inside, Mrs
Carling. I've got a lot to tell you. Not exactly about your case but in
many ways, it's relevant."

I took the woman through to my inner sanctum. "Let's have some
decent coffee. They serve hot mud at the factory."

"Factory?"

"The police station. I've just been there. I had quite a few things
to check."

"About me?" she sniffed.

"No, Mrs Carling. Your case is confidential. No, it was in
connection with your neighbour, Mrs Swantry. Did you know
she recently joined a religious order at the St Helios Hospice,
nursing terminally ill patients?"

"So what? The Beeches is a dreadful house and she's let it go to
pieces. That ramshackle garden. It's a disgrace. Weeds everywhere,
blowing over into my garden and I wouldn't be surprised if there's
vermin. That's what breeds rats, you know, dirt and neglect."

"She was an older lady on her own and she couldn't cope. It was
getting beyond her. It happens to all of us unless we are lucky
enough to be within a loving family unit." I let that item sink in. "I
suppose you realised that she had been gradually shutting up the
house and living in two rooms?"

"No, I didn't. None of my business and I'm not interested. I
have no communication with her except through my solicitors."
The look on her face changed gear. "Are you telling me that Mrs
Swantry's been sending those vile things? I wouldn't put it past
her."

It was not hard to imagine anyone sending Ursula hate mail. I felt
like sending her a few home truths myself. But women like her are
blind and deaf. They cannot see their own flaws and they will never

learn. They are so self-centred that nothing can shake the core of their total belief in themselves.

Perhaps that was the motive of the sender. To shake Ursula Carling's cement-hard complacency and belief in her own right-eousness. The messages had certainly shaken her, but not in that way. She was even more certain of her reserved place on the martyrs' cloud. Something pale or pastel, of course.

"It could be a possibility . . ." I began carefully. "Why do you think Mrs Swantry might have been sending your hate mail?"

"How should I know? I don't get on with the woman. So pious, so good, always going to church. Of course, even religious people can have twisted minds. And she's absolutely adamant about not having the air-raid shelter demolished. Says it's there in case there's another war. What rubbish. If there's another war, it'll be nuclear and we'll all be blown to pieces in the first half an hour."

She searched in her handbag and brought out a handful of envelopes. "I've brought you the latest batch, envelopes and all, just as you said I should."

That blew away the Ellen Swantry theory. I looked at the post-marks. All posted after her death, and from different parts of Sussex, but mostly from Chichester. I couldn't see Ellen as an active ghost. Ordinary brown envelopes, the kind that Woolworths sell in bulk packets and there were a couple of pre-paid envelopes that come with junk mail. The sender had crossed out the printed address and written Ursula's with the same black marker pen.

"Have you read them?"

"No, I remembered that you said not to. You can have the pleasure."

"There might be fingerprints." How was I going to get them fingerprinted? I had no idea. James might let me look at the Police National Computer once in a while but the entire fingerprint system and the Criminal Records Office of the force were not at my disposal. Unless I could get the dabs past him on some other pretext. It was a pity I'd told him about the poison pen letters. I would have to come up with a different story.

"Are you feeling better now that you are now longer reading the letters?" I put the bundle away in the filing cabinet, out of sight. They felt contaminated. "You could just forget all about them. Why not go away for a holiday or something?"

"No, I can't just forget all about it. I want Cleo caught. I want to see her punished."

"But there's no proof it's Cleo. You are only surmising that it's your daughter and there isn't a scrap of proof. It could be someone else." I had to be tactful here. "It could be someone from your past."

She stiffened, her cultured hair flying out in steel darts, eyes defused behind her thick glasses like a lighthouse beam in a fog. "I don't have a past, young woman."

"I didn't mean that kind of past," I said hastily. Wrong word. "I mean someone you used to know or had dealings with."

"My life has been full and fruitful," she bristled, still uptight. "I couldn't possibly remember every person I've ever met. Are you telling me you can't solve this case?"

"I am eliminating certain people. The letters you've brought me today will be really helpful. Not long now and it'll be wrapped up and you can go on that holiday."

"I don't go on holidays."

What a woman. I couldn't make first base with her. One last question, the loaded one. "Mrs Carling, how is it that you have been speaking about your neighbour in the present tense when you know she's dead? And you went to Mrs Swantry's funeral even though you disliked the woman."

Ursula was thrown by the abrupt question. For a second her body collapsed and then straightened itself again through sheer will-power. Her face blanched under her Yardley make-up, leaving rouge like a clown's splodges of crimson.

"I thought it was a neighbourly thing to do," she said, recovering quickly. "I wondered if the estate agent offering her house might attend, or perhaps a prospective buyer so I could introduce myself. It never hurts to make the right contacts."

Pathetic. Weak as last month's dish water but I pretended to accept it. "Ah, I see. Being sensible . . . er . . . yes."

Ursula Carling finished her coffee and made an excuse to go. I was glad. Her emotional swings were exhausting. A marshy-faced woman came in and bought the huge amber goblet. She said she was going to put pot-pourri in it and stand it on the stairs. Some people have nothing better to do.

I made a quick tour of the charity shops, found a few bargains. I was running short of stock. It was a confusing day. My notes covered several pages.

I caught the leaking warmth of the afternoon sun on the beach. The mini-train driver was making the last trip of the day. What a soul-destroying job, trundling three-quarters of a mile up and down the front with three wagon-loads of screaming kids dropping ice-cream everywhere or a party of merry ladies from London on a day trip to the coast and a liquid lunch. He wore a uniform of sorts with bits of braid. He gave me a weary wave.

I sat on my rock and watched the sun flushing the clouds strawberry pink and molten gold. Feathery clouds forked the sky like royal icing. A long way out, the black speck of a windsurfer was heading back to land before it grew dark. Black crows perched on the timbers of the groynes, watching my half-eaten apple with greedy eyes. The wind swept chilling fingers from the sea and shadows grew in the nebulous gloom, slowly cooling the sand and the pebbles. Autumn was sinking into an early winter.

That house, The Beeches, haunted me even when I was away from it. The emptiness of the rooms and Ellen Swantry's solitary existence gave me the creeps. Had I missed anything? I didn't fancy going back unless I wore a decent brimmed hat and passed as a prospective buyer.

The sea has such healing qualities. The soft swish-swash of the waves was an endless massage, relaxing muscles and nerves and spirit. Seaweed wafted its pungent vapour into my twitchy tubes; the gulls provided raucous music, their acrobatics a ballet for the eyes. And the deep blue and green of the sea . . . the colours of peace and quietness and calm.

So far neither of my careers had been an outstanding success. I wasn't cut out for the police force, not even the brains department, despite my years in it; too much of a free spirit. I said what I thought and that wasn't always appreciated. FCI had hardly got off the ground; in fact it was bogged down. Finding Joey couldn't be classed as an investigative wonder. More a lucky chance that he had survived being flattened by a forty-four-ton container lorry.

Twilight washed ashen and sent me back to the shop to open Ursula's latest mail. I'd been putting it off. I felt dirtied by the stuff, the way porno films and magazines are a mental health risk. The damage was insiduous.

In the office, I tidied, swept, dusted, and made strong black coffee. I rearranged the window displays and put a chipped shepherdess in the space left by the departure of the amber goblet to its fragrant future.

Wearing surgical gloves (nicked from the hospital on my visit to see Cleo . . . I thought this was permissible since I was working in her interests.) I cut the envelopes open with a knife. They could determine DNA from saliva though I wasn't sure about dried saliva mixed with cheap glue.

It was the usual mixture of abuse though I detected a slight shift in emphasis as though the sender was growing weary of the game and wanted it brought to a head. And I thought the messages had begun to take on a personal vibe as if the sender knew I was reading them.

This change was disturbing. Perhaps I should warn Ursula to take more care than usual. I rang her number but there was no answer. The phone rang and rang. It seemed ominous. Didn't she say something about playing bridge in the evening? Or was it the kind of thing she might say and not do?

The phone rang and I picked it up, hoping that thought trans-ference had reached Ursula. But it was Joshua and I certainly hadn't been thinking about him.

"Hello heroine," he said. He was a sweetie. I'd always liked Joshua and had known him for years. He was some sort of inventor for a tool firm, working from home. I never quite understood what he did. He ambled through life, always desperately short of money, somehow surviving but slowly going downhill like some exhausted hairy mammoth.

"What a brave girl, getting herself in the newspapers," he went on. "I knew it was you straight away. If you feel like any more flying tackles, you could always practise on me."

I laughed. He could always make me laugh.

"I wasn't really brave. I just happened to be there at the right time. Anyone would have done it."

"Not me," said Joshua, who despite his size hated violence of any kind. "I'd have merged with the background. Jordan darling, you need a break after all these heroics. Do you fancy a couple of days at my place? No strings, your own room. We could walk a few lanes, talk, watch a few videos."

It sounded idyllic. Joshua lived in a rambling, run-down sort of cottage in a village the other side of the Downs that was unspoilt, with genuine sheep-spotted fields and twittering birds.

"Sounds a wonderful idea. I need to get away from the case I'm on at the moment. It's bogging me down. I might come back with some decent ideas. Will you meet me at the station?"

"Sorry, Jordan. You'll have to get a taxi. I've been in bed all week with a viral infection and I don't think it would be wise to drive yet. Antibiotics, y'know. They make you drowsy. And could you bring in the odd shopping? I'm running short of a few things. Write this down, will you?"

He was running short of a lot of things. The list grew. As I wrote down cheese and butter, bread and tea and eggs, my brain stopped being compliant, easy-going and amiable. It went razor-sharp and suspicious. I was being used. Joshua didn't want my delightful company. He wanted a nursemaid. He wanted someone to cook, clean up and do a week's laundry. I wasn't going for a nice, relaxing weekend; it would be a sink-and-stove slog from beginning to end.

"Viral infection?" I repeated, trying to get the right tone of regret into my voice. "Oh dear, I can't come then. Remember my asthma? I might get really bad if it went on my chest. Sorry, Josh, not this time. I'll phone your local grocer and get them to deliver the goods. Perhaps we ought to add a few tins of nourishing vegetable soup."

I could feel his disappointment coming in waves over the phone. He'd planned the manoeuvre with all the cunning of a general at war. I said lots of encouraging things about looking after himself and taking care, put the phone down with a pang of sadness. Poor Joshua. Why did I get landed with these low-grade men? Was it something in my nature that attracted them? The weak to my strength; the indecisive to my determination; the wimpish to my resolution? I had my faults and plenty of them but I needed a man who would be caring of me, not the other way round. Someone like my trumpeter who belonged to someone else.

I opened the last of the letters. It was longer than the rest. Same black marker pen and written on the back of an offer for cut-price double glazing.

> **YOU EVIL BITCH. LEAVE CLEO ALONE. I KNOW WHAT YOU ARE TRYING TO DO. IF YOU HARM HER AGAIN, I'LL KILL YOU. AND I MEAN IT. I'LL TORCH YOU.**

The words chilled me with their intensity. I could feel the venom pouring out of them like a river of prurience. The writer really hated Ursula. If you harm her again . . . had Ursula something to do with Cleo's fall?

But the writer had given himself away. He knew that Cleo was in hospital, that she had been injured. This could only mean one thing. He was the man who had stood at the end of the bed and stared at her.

There was no way he could have known that I'd also visit Cleo in hospital that morning, or that the ward sister would tell me about his odd visit.

He did exist. He was real. And he was becoming dangerous. Someone was going to get killed.

Ursula? Cleo? Hell . . . was it going to be me?

Eleven

U rsula's phone kept ringing. My imagination saw burning rags and petrol bombs pushed through the door. The hate mail had changed gear, gone up a notch in hatred. These were death threats now.

But I couldn't go to DI James again. He'd think I was paranoid, show me the door. And I didn't feel like sleeping outside her house. I wasn't hired to protect the woman. All I could do was make sure she was warned.

I got on my bicycle and sped to Lansfold Avenue. Wheels, wheels, where art thou? I was sick of cycling everywhere. Perhaps my handy friend Rick, could put a vehicle my way. I wasn't proud. A vintage 1920 Dodge would suit me, black upholstery and hood, yellow bodywork.

Ursula's house was in darkness, so was The Beeches. I pushed my hastily written note through the letter slot and it dropped into one of those little wire boxes. Saved wear on the carpet. The note warned her to be very, very careful, to stay in and not to take unnecessary risks. Without frightening her, I tried to say that the writer might be changing his tactics.

The glass porch was one of Ursula's additions and totally out of keeping with the mock Tudor frontage. It was filled with plants and knee-high stone ornaments. Both doors were of patterned glass etched with some kind of drooping lily. I suppose she wanted more light in the hall.

Ursula was still hiding something from me. She'd been secretive about Cleo and again about Ellen Swantry. What else wasn't the lady telling me? How could I sort this out for her if she blocked my way by not giving me all the facts?

The house was shrouded in darkness. Didn't she leave a light on anywhere? What I really needed was a look round her house, to ferret out her secrets. I was shocked at myself. Jordan Lacey, tut-tut, not breaking and entering again? An empty house is one thing but someone's home is definitely not kosher.

Still I tried a few windows round the back, mostly out of habit. She had burglar locks on them. None of them would move and I was not prepared to break a window. There were limits. Outside was a Victorian-style conservatory tacked on to the side of the house, very ornate, another of Ursula's illuminating ideas. I dragged an oak garden seat close to the house, stood on it and then, balancing on its sturdy back, heaved myself up on to the ironwork construction which seamed the roof of the conservatory to the wall. My trainers gave me a good grip and I shuffled along the top edge, holding on to the ledges of the bedroom windowsills.

She had not drawn the curtains but it was too gloomy to see inside. The bathroom window had frosted glass but something else drew me to look at it again. The glass was steamed up. I put my hand against it. The glass was warm. Then I saw an eddy of steam filter out of the air vent. Now I knew what it was that I could hear. It was running water. The hot water was running amok.

What should I do? Ursula might be lurking behind the curtains in the darkness, not wanting to be seen. Perhaps she always took a bath in the dark due to excessive modesty. That would follow. But the bath could be overflowing, soaking the pale carpet on the stairs, flooding the pastel hallway, leaving a nasty tidemark. One thing for sure, if she had an immersion heater switched on, she was running herself up a hefty heating bill.

It was not easy to decide what to do. My WPC training took over. Gingerly I climbed down from the conservatory roof on to the garden chair, picked out a fair-sized stone from the rockery and smashed a glass pane in the kitchen door. I covered my hand with a handkerchief, reached through the jagged hole, found a bolt and pulled it back, then turned the door handle.

I held my breath, waiting for the burglar alarm to go off but there was nothing. Not exactly silence for I could hear the sound of rushing water. Perhaps Ursula had forgotten to set the alarm when she went out. But that was not like her.

If she had gone out . . . I raced up the stairs, my feet sinking into the sodden stair carpet. The landing was thick with steam, swirling round like a Scottish mist. I began to feel dizzy and caught hold of the wall to steady myself. It was making me cough too. I pushed my way through the steam, wafting it around to clear my view.

Ursula was sprawled on the bathroom floor, almost naked, all arms and legs, half in and half out of a damp satin floral robe. The bath was full, water slopping over the rim, the overflow unable to cope.

I turned off the taps, plunged my hand into very hot water, pulled out the plug and turned back to Ursula. She was quite still but I found a pulse.

"Ursula? Ursula, can you hear me?"

The door to the front bedroom was open. Through the hot mist, I saw an orange glow. It was a wall-panelled gas fire and instead of a healthy blue-based flame, they were a burnt orange colour; a sure sign that the flue was blocked and the house was filling with carbon monoxide. Snatching a towel to cover my mouth, I crawled in and switched off the fire.

I staggered to the front windows but the damned things were double-glazed and I couldn't see how to unfasten the locks. I was starting to feel really giddy and sick. I stumbled downstairs, hanging on to the banisters, gasping for breath, retching, and managed to wrench open the front door. Seconds later I flung open the porch door into the front garden to find the remains of the day.

A blessed blast of cold night air blew in and I gulped at the oxygen, drawing in great lungfuls. I shambled upstairs and hauled Ursula along under the armpits, then bumped her inert body inelegantly down the stairs, the best that I could without hurting her. I dragged her into the porch. Her face was very pink and her lips bright red. She was unconscious but still breathing and there was a faint pulse. I made sure the airway was free and rolled her over into the recovery position.

I rang 999 for an ambulance, then crawled upstairs again for a blanket off her bed to cover her modesty and a towel to dry off some of the wetness. By the time the ambulance crew arrived, I was absolutely worn out, slumped against a stone dwarf. And was I glad to see them.

"Gas fire blocked," I croaked. "Carbon monoxide poisoning. It must have knocked her out just as she was getting into the bath. The water was overflowing everywhere."

"Well done, miss. You did very well. We'll take over now," said the ambulance man, going down on his knees beside Ursula and opening his medical bag. "Twenty-four hours in hospital and she'll be as right as rain."

"That's good," I said weakly.

"What's her name?"

"Ursula Carling."

"You'd better come along too, miss. You don't look too good. Your arm looks a bit red. Better let the doctors have a look at you. What's your name?"

I got to my feet. "All right. I'll just go and lock the back door. Back in a sec."

I made my way to the kitchen, went out of the back door, and using the same oak bench, climbed over the fence into The Beeches, eased towards the front of the empty house and along the pavement to where I'd left my bike. The ambulance was parked outside, lights flashing. They were carrying Ursula out on a stretcher, wrapped and strapped, busy negotiating the gate. I got on my bike and wobbled slowly to the other end of Lansfold Avenue. No thank you, I didn't want to see any doctor, however dishy. My arm was hurting but I'd rather look after myself.

I made straight for the coast. I still felt nauseous and dizzy but it was wearing off and ten minutes walking the beach would put me right. I had no idea how long the effects might last. Twenty-four hours in bed the ambulance man said. There wasn't time for that sort of indulgence. Besides, I'd just had an extra stretch of bed.

The shingle crunched and slid about as I stumbled around in the dark. The multi-coloured lights strung along the promenade did not reach far enough to illuminate my path down to the sand. Luminescence from the waves torched a pattern of light on the water. The pier looked like some long-legged prehistoric monster striding out into the Channel. I half expected it to roar.

The tide was still going out, leaving wide stretches of flat wet sand. I splashed through a tiny rivulet running down and water seeped over and into my trainers. I squelched on for a few yards, enduring the discomfort of wet feet; then I took them off and walked barefooted, dangling the trainers by their wet laces.

My clothes were damp and clammy and I began to shiver in the chilled wind. This was not sensible. The sand was cold and wet to my feet and my toes curled in protest but they got used to it by the time I reached the sea. I rolled my jeans up to the knees and waded through the shallows, gulping in ice cubes of air from Siberia, ridding my lungs of the poisonous fumes. I splashed cold sea on my arm and hand until the pain receded.

By the time I wheeled my bike home, I was feeling pretty knackered. I needed a bath and my bed. A long, dreamless sleep would put me right if my brain would only settle.

When I got in, I drank three glasses of water to calm my stomach, threw my damp clothes on the floor and filled the bath with tepid water. I was too cold to go straight into anything hot and I had to keep my arm out of the water. I smoothed aloe vera gel on the tender skin. Poor Ursula, what a mess for her to clear up. She was going to have a shock when she got home from hospital. I hoped she was insured.

Someone had to call the Gas Board to report the blocked flue. Me, I suppose.

Wrapped in my duvet, I made a quick call to the twenty-four hour gas service hotline. I gave the girl Ursula's address and explained about the fire.

I could hardly think straight.

"And who are you, miss?"

"A neighbour," I said. "Mrs Carling has just been carted off to hospital, unconscious. Blocked flue. Her house could blow up at any moment. Perhaps someone ought to pay a call."

I began to dress, slowly and painfully. Then I remembered that I had intended to go to bed. My brain was not working. I rolled into bed in my T-shirt and was asleep in moments.

Not a dream around.

Detective Inspector James stood on my doorstep, suit crumpled, tie askew. It was morning. He'd obviously had another heavy night, face saturnine and withdrawn, but I was glad to see him. I couldn't say the same for him. Didn't the man ever sleep? He greeted me with a scowl.

"Morning, Jordan. Y'know, you cause me more trouble and strife than half the villans in West Sussex," he said. "Why don't you stay at home and take up knitting?"

"I can't knit," I said.

"What were you doing in Ursula Carling's house when someone attempted to kill her by carbon monoxide poisoning?"

"What, me? In her house?" I blustered.

"Dear girl, you left a note in her letterbox, warning her to be extra careful. Then the ambulance crew reported an unsung heroine who rode off into the night on her bicycle. Who else could it be? Jordan, this is becoming a habit. Have you got a fixation about getting your name in the papers?"

"You didn't tell them who I was, did you?" I panicked. "I don't want whoever it is to come after me too."

"No, I didn't tell them," he said with resignation as if I was a difficult witness. He looked at my arm. "What's the matter with your arm?"

"Oh . . . the bath water was too hot."

"Do you always get in arm first? Most people use their feet. Have you got anything you want to tell me? Are you going to ask me in or is this going to be a doorstep interrogation?"

"Come in, James," I said, just as wearily. "I'll make some coffee. It's the one thing I can do well."

"I'll believe it when I taste it," he said ungraciously. "And what do you mean, I don't want them after me, too? Do you think you're in some sort of danger?"

"Yes. Yes, I do."

He followed me upstairs. It seemed strange to have him so close behind me. I could feel him staring at my back as if I had forgotten to dress properly. I made a quick check.

He looked drained. He sat down heavily and for a moment I thought he had fallen asleep. I could have nosed the bristly hair in the nape of his neck and he would never have noticed.

I poured out orange juice, opened a packet of deluxe muesli, made toast and lashings of coffee. He had that up-all-night, unbreakfasted look. He couldn't be civil when his stomach was hollering for food. The colour came back into his face and he gave me what passed for a smile.

"The coffee is excellent," he said a little later, downing a second cup. "Thank you, Jordan. Now I want to know everything. Start at the beginning and don't leave anything out."

"Is this a statement?" I didn't want to be had on a charge of breaking and entering, as well as several other dubious practices.

He held up his hands in surrender. "Look, no pen, no tape. Don't be so suspicious, lady. This is on the QT."

"How's Ursula?"

"Recovering. Driving the nurses up the wall with her orders. Desperate for her glasses but wouldn't wear a temporary pair. Then she wanted the pillows changed; said they were full of dust mites."

"They probably are."

"Don't change the subject. Start talking."

So I began at the beginning, trying to remember everything. It was a long story and it had grown in all directions in a few days. So much had happened. James listened intently, occasionally asking for a point to be clarified. His face changed, intensified.

"I think you've trodden on a hornet's nest," he said, helping himself to more coffee without asking. He rasped butter across a slice of golden toast. "Although you may not have achieved much."

"Thank you for the vote of confidence."

"I'll remember not to hire you if I want anything investigated. I'm not saying that your hate mail case and my murder investigation are

109

connected in any way, but it is interesting that so many strands cross."

"I'm glad you think so. At least you know now why I'm sure you need certain information and why I keep trying to see you. You had to know everything."

"And I thought you had a crush on one of my officers. A bit OTT."

"I want to see that pathology report. And I want a DNA test on some envelope glue." I ignored the insinuation. He couldn't really mean it. It must be James's idea of a joke. He had lost the knack of being normal in the company of a woman, that was for sure. I started to clear the breakfast things; a big hint. There was the shop to open and a customer might be outside, panting for the porcelain shepherdess.

"I'll see what I can do. But no promises."

"How did you know where I lived?" I asked as I showed him out.

"I'm a real detective. You made a statement, remember? I looked up the files."

"And I'll want to know what caused the blockage in the chimney to Ursula's bedroom."

He glanced at his watch. "Eight fifty-five. End of interview."

He strode down the street without a backward glance. Ungrateful bastard. And he'd finished up the last of my expensive home-made Seville marmalade.

There was an elderly man peering into the shop window but not at the chipped shepherdess. It was the old books he was interested in. I let him come in and browse. He wandered round and picked up four slim hardbacks which I had tied into a bundle with string.

"How much?"

"Six pounds."

"Young lady, these books are worth at least six pounds each. Don't you have any idea of the value? Look, this is a first edition of the poet, Raff Edoney."

"Heavens . . ." I put on an intelligent look but I'd never heard of the poet, despite all my reading. "What a find . . . never had the time to look through the books properly."

110

"You're the lady detective, aren't you? The one who was in the papers and caught those thieves in the amusement arcade on the pier? You were very brave."

"Er . . ."

"I have a proposition to make."

I looked at him: not at his age, surely? Then I realised I'd misinterpreted his remark. He was thin and seedy and his clothes, though once respectable and good, were so old and worn that I doubt if Oxfam would have taken them. The frayed cuffs of his shirt brushed against his wrists like a fringe of lace.

"I would like to employ your services but I cannot pay anything except a modest sum. However, I can be of use to you. I am more than willing, and would enjoy valuing your collection of books and putting realistic prices on them. Perhaps we could calculate time for time? My time for your time."

"You could have bought those four books for six pounds, then sold them elsewhere and kept the profit," I said, amazed at his honesty.

"So I could. It never occurred to me, nor is it my way. Well, what you do think of my suggestion?"

"Done," I said. "Come into my office. Would you like some tea or coffee?"

"Tea, please. Milk, no sugar."

He told me that his name was George Frazer. He'd married late in life and his wife and he had had one son, Ben. His wife had died from cancer and the two of them had lived, not always amicably, in a small basement flat in Latching, part of an old terraced house that had been divided.

"A year ago, Ben walked out. He was sixteen," said George Frazer. "I haven't seen him since."

"A year . . . ?" I knew already that the search would be useless. Track gone cold. I'd never find the boy.

"No, I realise that you might never find him. I don't even want you to tell him that I'm looking for him. Nor do I want to make him come home. I just want to know that he's alive and where he is and what he's doing." Mr Frazer stared into his tea, his face working with emotion.

"But don't you want him to come home?" I said gently. "Seventeen is very young to be out in the world, coping alone."

"No, I don't want to ask or demand anything. It's his life. He's better off without an old man around but it's the not knowing that's getting me. I want to know what's been happening to him, that's all. A couple of lines; a couple of pages, just some sort of report from you would put my mind at rest."

Dear God, I could make it all up and this trusting old man would believe me. How did these evil thoughts leap straight into my head? I must have bad genes.

"I'll do my very best to find Ben," I said, pushing the cop-out firmly to the back of my mind. "I hope I'll soon have some good news for you."

Mr Frazer had brought some snapshots of his son, a long, lean gangling sort of youth with a toothy smile. I chose the best for photocopying. I took notes about his friends, his hobbies, his ambitions but Ben didn't seem to have much of anything in his life. He had no friends, did nothing, had no plans for his life. He just walked out one morning, after breakfast, his usual grubby rucksack hanging from his shoulder. Nothing to cause any suspicion about his intentions.

I hoped I wasn't going to find a record of him being in the county morgue with a John Doe label tied on his big toe.

Twelve

A missing person made a change from hate mail and awkward clients. By now Ursula would have recovered and be wearing a "I told you so" look on her po-face and insisting that Cleo had stuffed tights down the flue despite the fact that Cleo was not physically or mentally the roof-climbing type. Nor could she have got into the house undetected. It was burglar-proofed like Fort Knox.

I wanted to find young Ben Frazer. A man as honest as his father deserved to sleep at nights. Even now he was on his knees, sorting through my boxes of books and putting prices on them.

I went down to the print shop to design a handbill. Geoff, the owner, was always helpful and had lots of ready-made printed headings which he let me use. He'd printed my FCI business cards, small, discreet, on best board. He looked through his folder of samples.

"Have you seen this person?" he said. "That'll do for the top heading over the photograph." He jiggled about with scissors and paste. A real make-up man.

"It's essential that people don't go rushing up to him and scare him off," I said, not sure about the rest of the wording. "We only want to know where he is . . . and if he's been seen."

"How about this one? All information in strictest confidence? Or – information only required? Then your phone number."

"That'll have to do. If we put don't approach him, it makes it sound as if he's a dangerous criminal and I don't think he is."

Geoff ran off a hundred copies and kept the original in case I needed any more. The modern photocopier reproduced well, not too grainy or fuzzy. I paid him and kept the receipt. I might be able to claim legitimate expenses but since Mr Fraser wasn't paying a fee, it was academic.

I toured Latching on my bike, putting up handbills outside the library, town hall, department store, post office. I even put one on the wall outside the police station which was a bit cheeky. Then I got the train to Chichester and did the same there, though I was sure Ben had gone to London. Didn't all youngsters go to London? The bright lights, the teaming streets of Soho, the excitement and energy drew them like a Pied Piper; they thought a fortune was waiting to be swept off the grubby pavements. Perhaps I could combine both cases. I might trawl Whitehall, see what I could pick up about Oliver Swantry. Except he wasn't my case.

Cleo gave me another lead, bless her. She phoned later that day to thank me for visiting her in hospital and again for being with her in the ambulance. I told her about Ursula's brush with death, unconsciously gauging the tone of her response. She was genuinely alarmed, upset even. If it wasn't genuine, then she should be taking leading roles at the Chichester Festival Theatre.

"It could have been an accident, couldn't it? A bird's nest or something fallen down the chimney?"

"The Gas Board will investigate and I'll let you know what they come up with. Don't worry, I'm sure there's a very simple answer."

Something simple like a couple of bricks or a lump of fast-drying cement.

"What did you find out about her neighbours?"

I could hardly say that one of them had been horribly murdered and slung on a meat hook in an empty hotel.

"Her neighbours are a real mixed bunch and there's motivation like an epidemic but none of them seem the types. You know the business with the air-raid shelter? Your firm of solicitors were in correspondence with both parties."

"That's been going on for years, before I joined the firm. The Swantrys have been clients since they moved into The Beeches, sometime in the late fifties."

"Any chance of looking at their file?" I never missed an opportunity.

"They're supposed to be confidential," Cleo said dubiously. She was obviously thinking I had scored a lot of Brownie points recently. I deserved something.

"But it's not like a doctor," I put in quickly. "It would be helpful and I wouldn't get you into trouble. You could just leave the file on the desk and go outside for a moment. There's probably nothing in it, a bit of conveyancing, wills . . ."

"Perhaps, I don't know . . ."

"Think it over, Cleo. No hassle. A few minutes, not a second more."

She was thinking it over but not saying, wondering if she dare risk her job but wanting Ursula off her back too.

"By the way, I bet my mother hasn't mentioned her sister, Rosie Broadwater. She's got an elder sister. They haven't spoken for years."

"A sister? No. Rosie? Does she live in London?" I had that feeling. I knew the answer. The vibes were in the air. I was already buying my ticket.

"How did you guess? She lives near Clapham Common, that's south London. I've got her address. I always send her a Christmas card."

"Why aren't they on speaking terms?"

"Ursula would never say, always clammed up. A taboo subject. Here's her address: 104, Park Side South, Clapham Common. Mrs Rosie Broadwater. She's a widow."

Mr Frazer was making good progress with the books but I made him go home. I wanted to shut shop and spend the evening planning my route for the morrow. A day wasn't long in London when you had a lot to do.

"I sold the china shepherdess to a man while you were out," he said, handing over six pounds. "He pointed out the chip and I pointed out the 1906 date on the pedestal. I said he'd be lucky if he was only chipped after ninety-odd years of handling. He was convinced."

I had to laugh. "You did well. Thank you." I gave him the first edition of the obscure poet. "Call it commission," I said, when he hesitated about taking the slim book.

"Well, thank you very much," he said, clearly chuffed.

I took an early train to London the next morning, squashed between commuters doing the crossword, reading newspapers, chatting on mobiles or catching up on their sleep. It was a good opportunity to write up my notes and check my route. I never wasted time asking permission but, armed with sellotape and tacks, put handbills in good strategic spots . . . underground exits, shop entrances, along escalators, by lift bells. If they lasted a few days, that would be good enough. Most posters get defaced or torn down by then if not protected by glass. But the graffiti mob had even started scratching glass.

The terminal stations were the centre of all movement so I concentrated on them, even took some copies into the office of the transport police. They were helpful even though Mr Frazer hadn't officially reported Ben as missing.

"A very delicate domestic situation," I explained, not explaining. "Too complicated to go into. It would take me half an hour."

They hadn't got half an hour, nor had I, but they kept a handful of leaflets which they said they would distribute among their officers.

I also went round some of the homeless hostels which was depressing. They shook their heads. No one recognised Ben. One homeless young man was much the same as any other. I even put some posters up outside Harrods. I wasn't fussy.

After a tuna and salad sandwich at a café, I took the Northern line to Clapham Common, strap-hanging with the commuters, still scanning faces for that open toothy smile. There were plenty of aimless youths drifting the underground, undernourished, roughly dressed, nowhere to go, no jobs in view. But none of them were Ben.

Rosie lived in a stone-faced Victorian terrace house, a solid two-up-two-down, in a long string of houses that backed on to the railway line. Rosie had geraniums in pots and the doorstep looked as if she scrubbed and whitened it daily. Perhaps this house-proud gene ran in the family. Didn't run in mine.

I rang the polished doorbell and heard footsteps coming to answer. The woman was tall with a mop of wiry grey hair like

Ursula, but there the resemblance ended. She carried more weight, had a pleasant, homely face with eyes that were bright and keen. Not the kind to waste her time sending hate mail to a sister, even if they were estranged. I knew that straight away.

I introduced myself, giving her a card. "I'm investigating a case of hate mail which is being received by your sister, Ursula Carling, and I'm wondering if you'd mind answering a few brief questions."

"Hate mail? I'm not surprised. Ursula is not the world's most popular person. But you don't think I'm sending it, do you?" she asked briskly. "I wouldn't waste a stamp on her."

"No, no . . ." I said hastily. "The mail is all posted in Latching or Chichester. You'd hardly keep making that journey just to post a letter."

"I could have an accomplice," she suggested. "Send the stuff to a friend in a jiffy bag. Get them to post it at intervals. There's always a way round these things. I read a lot of books, you know, mostly detective."

"But you're not a suspect," I assured her. But the thought took root. She could be sending it to Cleo. "I just need you to fill in a few gaps in Ursula's life. I don't think she has been exactly upfront about telling me everything."

"I bet she hasn't. She wouldn't be upfront about the day of the month. Come in, whatever you said your name was."

"Jordan Lacey."

"Come in off the doorstep, Miss Lacey. I was just making a pot of tea. I expect you'd like some. What a wind. North-easterly they said on the weather forecast, enough to bite the bone."

She showed me into a back sitting room. It was a comfortable room with a couple of deep but well-worn armchairs, several bookcases crammed with books, a corner television, small tables and a forest of house plants and dried flower arrangements. The room had a genuine lived-in look, so different from Ursula's antiseptic, don't you dare breathe on anything, germ-free environment.

Two large tabby cats were curled round each other on one of the armchairs, tail over tail, paws crossed.

"I'll sit there," said Rosie, giving the cats a friendly push to one side. "They're moulting. You don't want hairs all over the seat of your trousers."

I went down on my haunches to stroke their bony heads. They were big cats, ink-striped fur, pampered and well fed. They broke into throbbing motorbike purrs, nudging my hands for more, competing for attention.

"They're lovely. What do you call them?"

"Bill and Ben. Oh, I know it's hardly original but they're brothers. How do you like your tea?"

"As it comes. Hot and wet."

Rosie brought through a tray with two unmatched cups and saucers, a plate of tumbled chocolate digestive biscuits and a solid brown earthenware teapot straining in its knitted cosy, spout steaming.

"Do you live alone?" I asked.

"Yes, except for these two monsters. They've taken over the entire house." The cats had spread again so she pushed them aside. One climbed on to her lap, taking possession. The other squeezed himself into the space down the side of the chair. Rosie was completely hemmed in. "My husband died a long time ago. We didn't have any children. I worked in the post office but I'm retired now. Would you mind pouring, dear? I can't reach the pot."

I poured the tea and put the cup on a convenient table. I crunched a chocolate biscuit and the sweetness immediately raised my energy levels. Post office? Could be convenient.

"Now the garden takes up all my time and I've a nice little greenhouse. I grow most things from seed," she added proudly.

"Would you mind telling me why you and your sister are estranged?" I didn't like asking but it was what I'd come to find out. The tea was hot and strong. I started to feel at home. Bill – or was it Ben? – got tired of being squashed and overheated, jumped down and hauled himself up on to my lap, digging his claws into my leg as if it was a tree. I swallowed the needle-sharp pain. He did a few circuits before rolling up and going back to sleep.

"Ben likes you," said Rosie with satisfaction. "He doesn't go to many people."

I like to think it was Ben's approval that launched Rosie into her story, though hesitantly at first. She peered into her tea as if looking into the future – or was it the past?

"I'm six years older than Ursula so we were never really close. And she was such a goody-goody even as a little girl. I missed my dear husband and grieved for him when he died. You see, we hadn't been married long. I never thought I would meet anyone else. Didn't want to really, never looked around. But working in the post office, you get to know lots of people by sight, the regulars you know. One of the gentlemen was always very pleasant, tall and good looking with lovely manners. I liked him."

She paused as if reliving her memories. I didn't dare speak in case she changed her mind. It was causing her some distress and she seemed too nice a lady to suffer. The room was filled with a milky stillness.

"Well, we met by accident in the library. I was changing my books. I didn't recognise him at first, not being over a counter you see, but he knew me. He was one of my regulars. We seemed to have a lot to talk about and it was very enjoyable."

Her voice dropped and I could see that the memories were painful. But she had to go on. I had to make her talk. I wanted to know everything. "Yes . . . ?" I prompted gently. "Then . . ."

"I suppose you could say he began courting me, gave me a little pot of African violets, so pretty it was, then my favourite Turkish Delight; several times he treated me to tea and scones at a Lyons Tea Shop. I was very happy – for a while. Then Ursula came to stay with me. She'd got fed up being in service and found herself a job in London and it seemed sensible that she should lodge with me, cheaper and more convenient. But that was the end of my gentleman friend. From the moment she set her eyes on him, she was after him. He didn't stand a chance, poor lamb. They were married within a year."

"You mean, he was Cleo's father?"

"Yes, he was Cleo's father. Ted Burrows, my gentleman friend.

She stole him from me. I saw Cleo a couple of times when she was little. He brought her to see me. Nice little girl. She has his dark looks and gentle ways. But I've never spoken to Ursula since. She knows what I think of her."

"What a sad story," I said.

"I've got over my anger and hurt now. But she's not my sister any more and I won't have anything to do with her. And if someone is sending her nasty letters, then good luck to them."

"What happened to Ted Burrows? She married Arthur Carling at some point, didn't she?"

"Oh, Ted died. Some accident at work. Yes, Arthur Carling was her second husband. I never really heard what happened to Ted. I'm sure Cleo missed him a lot. She was only a little girl when he died and he was a good father to her. I think Ursula was jealous. We lost touch for a time. But Cleo sends me a Christmas card now. Never any address. I don't know where she lives."

"I suppose you know that Ursula has been widowed again? Arthur Carling died in January. A heart attack. And for the last few months she's been getting all this hate mail, really nasty stuff."

"No, I didn't know Arthur had died. I'm sorry about that. Another nice man, I believe. She seems to attract the good ones, can't think why. But I won't say I'm sorry about the hate mail. She deserves all she gets."

"She thinks Cleo is sending it to her." I didn't mention the dead cat and the carbon monoxide poisoning.

"Stuff and nonsense. All her imagination. Probably sending it to herself to get attention and sympathy."

"But that hardly makes it worth employing me at my daily rates."

"No, that's true. And Ursula's always been tight with money. Can't bear parting with it. You make sure she pays you regularly."

I thought I ought to go. I'd upset her enough. Rosie insisted on giving me a couple of busy Lizzie plants for my flat and a bag of cherry tomatoes from her greenhouse. I stroked Bill and Ben and was reminded of the other Ben, showed her his photo.

"Never seen him," she said. "Good-looking lad. Pity, isn't it, these days, the way they go off."

"Shall I tell Ursula that I've seen you?"

"Heavens no. But you can tell Cleo, if you see her. I expect she has grown up into a nice young woman."

"Yes, she has," I said warmly. "You'd like her."

It was a quiet journey home to Latching although the train was making its usual racket over the rails, people were talking and idiots were making mobile phone calls, broadcasting their extremely boring personal business to all and announcing their whereabouts as if being on the train was next door to the moon. I watched the quiet, dark countryside flashing by, my thoughts in a turmoil. My client was not a very nice person. I was beginning to think I might leave her to wallow in her hate mail but I needed the fifty pounds a day and trying to asphyxiate her was a crime.

I couldn't find a single suspect. It all pointed back to Cleo but I felt it couldn't be her. My senses were against it. Everything told me that she was innocent even though she had a strong motivation and Ursula had been unkind to her for years.

As for Ursula sending the stuff to herself . . . it was difficult to believe that she would commute to Chichester for months just to use the postal service.

Latching station was deserted at that time of night. There weren't even any yobbos about. They were still in the pubs, drinking themselves legless. I hurried down the side streets and alleyways, my hand tight on the biro in my pocket. Stick it up someone's nose and the pain would make them think twice about attacking you.

A Panda car cruised alongside me and slowed down. "Are you kerb crawling?" I said coldly. "Don't you know that's an offence?"

DI James put his head out of the open window, face half shadowed. "Do you want a lift, Jordan? The pubs will be out soon. We've had word there's a mob war on tonight."

"Oh dear. Am I going to need my biro?"

"Don't joke. Get in the car and I'll give you a lift home. Be sensible for once. Hanging about the streets tonight is asking for trouble."

I got in the back of the Panda. He had another officer in the front

Stella Whitelaw

passenger seat who grinned over his shoulder at me. I didn't know
him. "Hello, Jaws."

"Evening all," I said in my best Jack Warner voice. I'd seen the
film on Saturday afternoon television.

"Been sleuthing?"

"I have had a very successful day."

"Found a dog-end with tell-tale lipstick?"

I ignored him. I was too tired for juvenile jokes. The back seat was
dark and smelly with all the stench from the half-washed, the
petrified, the drunk. The sooner I got out for a lungful of fresh
air, the better.

"I live here," I said, as we reached the corner of my road. "This'll
do." The back of James's head was unnerving. I was worried I might
reach up and touch it, knowing the shorn hair would feel like velvet.
He affected me as if the full moon held magic. My unattended body
shrank a whole size.

"Go straight in, Jordan," said James abruptly.

"Yeah, yeah," I said. "And just as I was planning a midnight
walk along the beach. Wanna come?"

"I'll take a rain check on that one," he said, looking straight
ahead as I slammed the door shut. He still didn't look at me. Some
blank walls were more inviting.

"Don't reckon on it," I said to the night air. "You may not get
asked again."

The moon was an orange globe, solitary in the darkness, hung
and glowing.

Damn the man.

Thirteen

A cloud bank lingered off the coast, holding down the fog with its wet tentacles. It was inexpressibly melancholy with the debris of the night's yob fighting littering the seafront, broken bottles, crushed Coke cans, sprayed paint, splashes of blood, broken panes of glass in the beach shelters.

I needed an early morning walk to clear my head. I'd wrapped up in thick fleecy sweater, tracksuit bottoms, scarf and trainers but still I was cold. It came from not eating properly and drinking too much tea and coffee. Yesterday had been a biscuit day, all day, not exactly nutritious but indulgent and now I felt carbohydrated and fat. It was time I had a decent breakfast.

My hair was wet from the damp air by the time I'd run-walked to Flood Point and back. A heavy storm in the thirties had flooded the seafront and people had needed rowing boats to negotiate the area. It was difficult to imagine the scene though there were faded brown photographs in the public museum that showed the level of the severe flooding. This morning there were just a few puddles.

Maeve's Café was on the point of opening. Mavis was pulling up the blinds, taking chairs off the tables and standing them on the floor. She unlocked the door and beckoned me in, already in a gaudy plastic apron.

"Breakfast, Jordan? I've put the kettle on. How about orange juice, scrambled eggs, toast, honey, coming up on the double? Anything else? I don't suppose you've eaten for days. I could eat with you if there aren't any customers. Or do you want to be left alone?"

"No, I'd like some company, Mavis. My mind's buzzing. It might settle down if I had some civilised conversation."

"Got a tricky case?" She didn't comment on my use of her real name.

Tricky case? What was she on about? I'd never told her about my work. The Latching grapevine was at work here and Mavis had receptive ears. She picked up a lot while waiting at tables, standing behind the counter serving drinks and sandwiches. People didn't watch what they said. They thought she was a plastic dummy and no one was listening. But Mavis was.

Mavis brought over cutlery and paper napkins and laid the table at speed. She put a glass of orange juice in front of me and then disappeared into the kitchen. I could hear her banging saucepans around, the electric egg whisk buzzing, plates clattering.

"Tricky case? I don't know what you're talking about."

"Come off it, Jordan. I know you're working as a private investigator, a private eye, like on the telly." She planted a big teapot on the table and shuffled cups and saucers about, throwing on spoons with deadly accuracy. "And you were the one who tackled that thug on the pier, weren't you? Saw it in the paper. Pity there aren't more of you about. Back bone of Olde Englande."

"You're simply guessing."

"My friend, Doris, told me. You know Doris, she works in the little grocery store near your second-hand shop."

"Oh, Doris," I murmured. Doris had been talking. "Not merely second-hand . . . some of it is good stuff."

"We go dancing together every Wednesday afternoon, to the tea dances at the Pavilion."

"Tea dances? Do they still exist? I thought they went out with the thirties."

"You're not living, girl. They're thriving. Two pounds at the door and a cup of tea and cake thrown in. Mind you, their cakes aren't up to much but the dance music is strict tempo and there's plenty of partners."

"I didn't know that men could still dance," I said. "I thought it was a forgotten social grace."

"It's mostly retired gentlemen with good memories and strong legs," said Mavis with a frustrated sigh. I remembered the way she had looked at James. "Nothing much else works. Their equipment is in retirement. But they're nice movers."

"Arthur Carling used to go to the tea dances regularly," she went on, spreading butter liberally on a slice of toast. The golden globules fell through the aereated holes and spread on the plate like drops of molten sun. "He met a young woman there. Always the same woman. They pretended that they hadn't arranged to meet, but they had. They didn't dance much. They sat in a corner and talked."

"How did you know it was Arthur Carling?" I asked.

"From his picture in the papers. He won some chess competition. Arthur Carling went to the weekly tea dances while his wife was at the hairdressers. After the dance, at five on the dot, he would go and pick up his wife in the car and take her home. My sister works in the hairdressers."

I groaned. Mavis, Doris and her sister were better sleuths than I was. So Arthur had been seeing someone, sitting in corners, eating stale cake. "What did this young woman look like?"

I didn't really want to know. I thought I knew already.

"Small, dark, slim, late twenties. Hair straight and bobbed. Pretty smile."

Cleo . . . my appetite fled. It couldn't be a coincidence. Cleo had been meeting her stepfather on the quiet – she had said as much. Now it was confirmed. She had been meeting him on a regular basis and in Latching. But she said she never came to Latching. Or had she said she never came to Latching now . . . I couldn't remember her exact words.

I had been dismissing Cleo from my enquiries but she kept coming back like a bad penny. How much had they liked each other? Cleo had been nine years old when Ursula married Arthur. He'd looked a few years younger than Ursula in that photograph on the pier. The age gap between Cleo and Arthur might be only twenty years, making her twenty-nine to his forty-nine in that last year. Not too much of a problem.

"So . . ." I said casually, licking crumbs off my lips. "Why are you telling me all this?"

"Well, Ursula Carling is one of your clients, isn't she? Doris has

seen her coming to your shop. And there was that awful business of
the poisonous fumes in her house, knocking her out. Someone is out
to get her, mark my word."

"Mavis, is there anything you don't know? Are you working for
MI5? How did you know about the carbon monoxide?"

"First thing she did when she came out of hospital yesterday was
to phone for a hair appointment. Besides, I keep my ears open in the
café. You'd be surprised what people talk about. Perhaps Mrs
Carling ought to have police protection."

"The police would want danger money."

Mavis nodded. "She's an awkward lady. The girls in the hairdressers hate doing her hair. She's so fussy and it's never right.
They're always having to give her free sets because of her complaints."

"But none of this merits trying to kill her."

"Perhaps it was meant to scare her."

Like being trapped in a derelict hotel all night was meant to scare
me. Someone knew we were after them; someone thought we were
getting closer. I couldn't see it myself but the signs were there.

"Your policeman friend comes in here regularly. The one you
fancy."

"I don't fancy him," I said flatly.

"He drinks an awful lot of black coffee. It's not good for him, all
that caffeine. You should tell him."

"None of my business," I said. I knew he ate too much junk food.
I knew his system was overdosing on caffeine. I wanted to make him
a salad, feed him strawberries from my mouth.

I went to pay for my breakfast but Mavis wouldn't take any
money. She told me to have this one on her.

"I'll call in a favour sometime," she winked. "Might want somebody following."

I nodded but hoped that she wouldn't. I didn't want to destroy
her faith in me.

The murder of Ellen Swantry was still on my mind. Something was
eluding me like a bird singing a flat note. I felt sure I had missed a

vital clue at The Beeches. Not surprising since I had been on tenderhooks, expecting to be caught by the Old Bill at any moment. I would not have minded being caught by James, although it would not have improved his unfairly low opinion of me.

It was important that I trawled round the house again; this time with permission. I called the estate agents and made an appointment for later that morning. They jumped at it; not many people were interested in the big old house. Then I went through my props box and kitted myself out as a respectable middle-aged matron, complete with plum-coloured felt hat.

"Cor, you look as if you're going to the Tory Women's Annual Conference at Brighton," grinned Doris, putting down her duster.

"How did you know it was me?" I said crossly, tugging down the hat brim. I thought the sober tweed suit, buttoned-to-the-neck crepe blouse, pearl earrings, and excruciatingly uncomfortable court shoes clamped on my toes had completely obliterated the casual laid-back Jordan Lacey.

"Is this a disguise?"

"Of course it's a disguise. You don't think I would actually want to wear these clothes. They're disgusting."

"You can't disguise your eyes," said Doris tactfully. "The eyes are the mirror of the soul. Here, try my glasses on."

The counter went out of focus, blurred, zapped the beginning of a headache. I took them off quickly.

"Wow, that's some prescription," I said blinking. "Too strong for me, Doris. But I get the idea. Tinted glasses would be useful."

"I've got a stigmatism," she said.

"As long as it doesn't stop you tea dancing," I threw in to confuse her. It did. She gave me a weird look. A point to me, I thought.

The estate agent's representative was a youth in his late teens; first job, first suit, first client perhaps. He was very nervous, sweat beading his pale brow unless he was in for a dose of flu.

"Good morning, Mrs . . ." he consulted his notebook. "Jones."

"Good morning," I said pleasantly, using a deeper voice. "I'm sure this won't take long. I like the look of this house."

"Great." He unlocked the front door and we stepped over piles of junk mail on the floor. "This is the hall," he said unnecessarily. He knew all the patter. It could do with modernisation, could be very comfortable, needed doing up, good solid condition, possibilities. I went into raptures over the ornate cornice moulding, the carved oak banisters, the hideous fireplaces. He began to relax, thinking he had a sale, planning how to spend the commission on his new girlfriend.

He took me upstairs. "This is upstairs."

He'd go far, this boy.

The front bedroom grate still had the charred remains of whatever Ellen had been burning the day before she moved, but more leaves and soot had fallen down the chimney, adding to the mess.

I noticed a litter of feminine bits and pieces swept into a corner where Rick had probably tipped out a bedside drawer before loading the cabinet on to his lorry. I longed to turn them over.

"What a wonderful view," I enthused from the window.

"And this is the bathroom," said my helpful guide.

I clucked over the stained claw-footed bath, the prehistoric lavatory and rusted pipe work. The other bedrooms were empty as I knew but we had to look at them. We were downstairs and about to leave when I said: "Oh dear, I'm sorry, I've left my gloves upstairs. I'll just pop up and get them."

I raced upstairs before the boy wonder could follow me. I went straight into the front bedroom and down on to my knees, scooping a handful of the charred matter from the fireplace into a clear specimen envelope I had carried in Mrs Jones' large leather handbag. I also shovelled all the stuff from the bedside table into a supermarket plastic bag and hoped he wouldn't register its sudden appearance on my arm. He didn't, being much too busy pointing out the garage, the shed, the amazing rose-bushes. All this gushing was wearing me out. I was getting verbal fatigue.

"Thank you so very much," I said. "I'll let you know. I really, really love the place."

"I don't think we have your phone number," he said, consulting his notebook again.

"It's ex-directory," I said, hinting mysterious and famous and being plagued by fan calls. They didn't have my address either which showed how efficient their office was.

I couldn't get back to the shop fast enough, stripping off the hat as I went through the door, kicking off the shoes. I bet I had got corns. The surgical gloves, compliments of Latching Hospital, were in the filing cabinet. The charred bits had to be handled like gold dust. I shook them gently on to a sheet of white blotting paper, separated them carefully with tweezers and removed the leaves and other debris.

I still had the original fragment and put it on the edge of the sheet. Although I couldn't fit them together, it was clear now that they were scraps of banknotes. But I didn't recognise them and couldn't make out the denominations.

James had to see these. I put a sheet of cling-film over the bits to stop them blowing about and rang his direct line. He answered first time.

"Detective Inspector James."

"It's Jordan. I need you. I mean, I've found something interesting at The Beeches," I said. "I think you ought to come and see them."

"Did you break in?" he asked suspiciously.

"Of course not, don't be silly. As if I would."

"I'll be round right away."

Afterwards I wondered how he knew where my shop was. He'd been to my bedsit but not to the shop.

The coffee-pot was filtering out its perfume of love very nicely by the time James arrived. Two mugs were set on the tray and I had loosened my hair. I knew he wouldn't notice but a girl had to try. He was wearing a dark polo-necked jersey and casual belted trousers. Where was the tie? Where was the suit?

"This is my day off," he said.

"Sorry. I won't keep you long."

"Long enough for a cup of coffee, I hope," he sniffed, flicking through the old books on display. "So what have you got to show me?"

I sighed. Work came first. I took him through to the back room and he went straight over to my desk. He bent over intently, moving a few pieces with a tip of a lead pencil. He'd forgotten all about coffee.

"Where did you get this stuff?"

"At The Beeches. They were in the grate of the upstairs front bedroom, Ellen Swantry's bedroom. I think your people missed them when they went through there, thought they were bits that had fallen down the chimney. I don't blame them. It's easy to miss some things."

"Will you stop talking, Jordan. I can't concentrate. They're banknotes but the like of which I've never seen before. British, I think. I hope forensic can determine what they are and when they were burnt. The Bank of England ought to be able to identify them, even bits as small as these."

"Ellen Swantry burnt them. I'm sure she did. I've got that feeling. Who else would be in her bedroom? She was hiding something and this might be what she was hiding. These banknotes could be why she was murdered."

"Dear God, preserve us. You're turning into another Miss Marple. Nuns don't get brutally murdered for a handful of banknotes."

"I don't think they're forgeries but they might be. Although there's a metallic strip."

"I've no idea if they are forgeries. I had noticed the strip. I'll make a call."

He took out his mobile and phoned the station. He asked for a car to bring over exhibit trays and other equipment that he would need to transport the fragile pieces to forensic. I tried not to listen or look pleased. Then he sat down on my Victorian button-back and glanced at the coffee pot.

"You may have found something useful," he said grudgingly. "We've never discovered anything remotely like a motive. We were at a dead end. Sorry, still not a joke."

"I know. You don't joke," I said, pouring out two mugs of coffee and opening a packet of honeyed oat crunch biscuits. He took one and bit into it. Thank goodness, he was normal with biscuits. It was strange, a kind of intimacy, having him there, sitting on my antique chair. His long legs asked to be tripped over. I moved very carefully.

I hoped the police car would arrive discreetly. I didn't want their flashing lights to scare away any prospective clients. James read my mind.

"Don't worry, Jordan. I asked for an unmarked car, knowing you are a sensitive soul."

His sergeant was in plain clothes too. I smiled my appreciation and found a third mug. They packed the scraps with infinite care. I was impressed.

"Will you let me know? I mean, if you find out anything . . . I am an interested party after all."

"I'll tell you exactly what any member of the public is entitled to know. Nothing more, nothing less."

"That's not fair," I said, instantly regretting the expensive biscuits. "I'm being helpful. At least you could tell me what you find out."

"There's no question of you getting any priority information," he said as his sergeant carried out the boxes to the waiting car. "I'm grateful that you took civic responsibility by informing me of your find. I won't ask how you got into The Beeches, but you look cute in that suit. Are tweed and crêpe de Chine coming back into fashion?"

Fourteen

The plastic bag of flotsam from Ellen Swantry's bedside drawer stood unopened in my office for a whole day. I couldn't bring myself to check it out, busied myself with other work. It seemed an invasion of privacy, like going through her laundry basket. I had begun to like the woman and she had died publicly enough.

She had rattled around in that big old house, living in a degree of genteel poverty, only able to afford to heat two rooms, selling off the furniture and pictures, yet continuing to fight for what she thought were her rights in regard to the boundary dispute with Ursula Carling.

It must have been a wrench to leave her home and devote her few remaining years to the terminally ill; then to die herself in mean and despicable circumstances. She didn't deserve such an end. Or did she? No one knew much about her.

People's bedside drawers hold secrets. They fold their daytime selves away into them before they sleep. Mine has no secrets because it isn't a drawer. I have a long two-shelved coffee table for my books, clock, night cream from The Body Shop, inhaler and a little teddy-bear who looked so sad on a charity stall at a summer fête that I just had to give a home. I carried him hidden inside my T-shirt all day like a third bosom. His ears have perked up a bit and he's not so lonely now with the arcade bear Jack gave me beside him.

Finally I could put it off no longer. I tipped out Ellen Swantry's secret self. She flooded the floor. Hair grips that had lost their grip sprinkled in patterns, hairnets floated like grey cobwebs, bills, receipts, a half-used tube of intensive hand cream; a crumpled horoscope cut from a newspaper that told Ellen this was going to be a wonderful month. Perhaps heaven was wonderful. She knew now, one way or another.

A half-eaten tube of Rolos, damp and mildewy; a packet of Welldorma sleeping tablets with several empty bubbles; letters. I thumbed through the letters. Several were from the Order of St Helios saying how delighted they were with her decision to join them and detailing the necessary arrangements. I'm not surprised they were delighted. Ellen Swantry had apparently offered them the proceeds from the sale of The Beeches. It made sense. She was going to leave her home to make a new home with them.

I wondered if the offer still stood now that she was dead. Would an intention in a letter be legally binding? Or was there some nephew lurking in the background who would want his due inheritance? Did James know about this? The thought of his brilliant eyes blinded me for a moment. I sucked in on my breath.

I tried to remember who had been at her funeral. No one had caught my eye as a possible relative, but then I hadn't been looking for one.

The last envelope held a photograph. I turned it over eagerly. It was photograph of the old air-raid shelter that straddled the two gardens. Perhaps Ursula had sent it to Messrs Rogers & Whitworth as proof of its eyesore rating. I looked at the photograph closely with a magnifying glass but it was nothing more than an ugly concrete block half hidden in a bank of earth, covered in weeds and brambles, its steel door rusted solid.

There was a booklet of matches, the kind hotels give away. The Hilton, London, was stamped on it in gold. What could a nun possibly be doing at the Hilton? Rattling a collection box in the foyer?

I needed a place to think. I took my disappointment down to the beach. An early winter fog had crawled in and there was no seam between the sand and the sea. It was all one bleak grey panorama and yet magical in its strangeness. The edge of the sea was a killing field, carcasses of fish shrewn upon the wet cement-like sand with flocks of seagulls going crazy over the fresh flesh. There were more severed heads than fish; grinning cat-faces with eyeless sockets. The heads were a delicacy and birds went for them first. I started to feel sickened by the slaughter.

The mist was so thick that the seafront hotels and boarding houses slowly disappeared from view. Even the long-legged pier was swallowed from sight and I was all alone. My only point of reference was the sea. If it was coming towards me then I should back off, fast. The tide could race in over the endless sand.

A solitary reduced figure was coming out of the mist like in Lawrence of Arabia, emerging from a desert mirage. The thin black shape was moving quickly. It was not Omar Sharif perched on a camel. It was a boy on a bicycle.

He went by swiftly and I was left with the quarrelsome gulls and the dainty little ringed plovers running swiftly in unswerving lines across the sand on their tiny feet.

Ellen's bedside drawer had held no surprises. No secret documents, no incriminating telegrams or stock-piled junk mail to send to Ursula. No black marker pen. The photograph and the matches were only marginally interesting. She had been using the matches to burn the currency. I remembered a scattering of thin, designer sticks in the grate. Had she met someone at the Hilton, someone who prompted her into that insane burnt offering? Had that someone been so incensed by her action that he had strangled her and then hung her on a hook like a side of beef?

The mist was so damp that my hair was beginning to curl into dew drops, then trickle down my neck with icy fingers. I stood very still as the mist rolled off the sea. I couldn't even see the waves, only hear them crashing some distance away. The tide was still going out and retreating fast over the flatness in a last desperate escape from the bondage of the land. I had no idea which way to go. My sense of direction was nil and the gulls were no help.

"James . . ." I called hopefully. My voice sounded feeble and pathetic. Did I really expect a Panda car to loom out of the mist to rescue me, lights flashing, siren wailing?

There must be fingerprints on the photo or the matches. But would they tell us anything? Despondancy leadened my boots. I wasn't getting anywhere with anything. I had no hope of finding Ben Frazer; Ursula's persecutor had covered his tracks; the tortoise had been a fluke.

Epitaph: She was a lousy detective but brilliant with animals.

I stood in the cold, chilling fast. I was lost. This was not the time to panic. There were sounds but nothing was real.

I thought I could hear something, like footsteps squelching in the wet sand. I swung round but saw no one. The footsteps had stopped. But I could still hear a sea-less sound. It was breathing, slightly out of breath breathing. Someone who was older, not used to chasing over the beach in the dark.

I waited. "Hello," I said but my voice was thin and reedy.

There was no answer.

I froze. Someone was there. I knew it. There was nothing in my pockets except a biro pen. My screwdriver was at home. I was halfway across the Channel, well, almost, and defenceless. I did not know which way to run. My legs had lost their running tone even if I knew which way to go.

A wet spaniel came charging out of the mist and greeted me like a long-lost friend. He scampered round, barking and panting, his brown coat flattened into wet curls, his brown eyes glowing with fun.

"Hello, boy! Hello, boy! Are you lost too?"

Whatever he was, he'd decided that my company was better than none. Cheered by his enthusiasm for me, I set off with a more determined walk but the dog did not seem too keen on following. He crouched down, tail wagging. Then I realised this area of sand was becoming wetter and rivulets were washing over the toes of my boots.

"Oh dear, wrong way," I said, making a half-turn.

I thought I recognised several dead fish and grinning skulls as we walked back. The dog sniffed at them but wasn't into fish. It was growing dark, much earlier now that we had lost the extra hour of British Summer Time and I sharpened my step. This was ridiculous. I'd never been lost on the beach before and I'd walked its four-mile length a hundred times.

"Come on, dog," I said. "It can't be far now . . ."

Unless I was walking parallel to the sea and not back to the shore at all. At this rate I would end up in Bognor Regis.

Then I saw a thin, looped string of tiny lights, far distant in the mist winking like a half-imagined fairy ring. The promenade lights had come on and the sulphur street lamps were throwing banners of orange down on to the wet sand. I could have kissed the entire town council for their prudence.

The dog sensed my joy and leaped around, leaving sandy paw marks on my jeans. We set out briskly towards the lights, over drier sand, stepping over a scattering of rocks, then white and ghostly buildings loomed ahead and we were clambering up the steep and slippery pebble shelf on to the promenade. People, cars, traffic lights . . . suddenly they all seemed wonderful.

"We've done it," I said, fondling the dog's head.

"Where the hell have you been?" said a man in a waterproof Barbour jacket and holding a lead. "I've been looking everywhere for you, damned dog."

The spaniel trotted obediently over to his master without a backward glance. Some friend. My role was over.

Derek was waiting on my doorstep, the collar of his raincoat turned up like Humphrey Bogart. The garment was too big for him and flapped around his ankles. He probably bought it in a sale. His face lit up as I arrived.

"Hello, stranger," he said.

"I'm sorry, Derek," I said wearily. "You can't come in. I'm cold and I'm tired and I'm very wet. And I have a lot of work to do."

"I'll make you a cup of tea," he offered.

Yeah, yeah . . . my tea, my biscuits, my time, probably my supper later as well. I knew him of old. He could make a five-minute visit last five hours. And I didn't want him kissing me. No, sir. I needed my mind on my work.

"No, thank you. I've got masses to do."

"You can't mean it?" He looked hurt, then huffed.

"Yes, I do. Don't you ever listen to what I say? You can't just call

on me and expect me to be available, whatever. I'm a working girl. I
have a business to run."

"Oh yes, I know, you and your modern independence." He spat
the statement out as if it was dirty. "You certainly know how to hurt
a person."

"Don't be an idiot," I called after him as he walked away. "I only
said you couldn't come in. Make a proper date if you want to see
me. Invite me out to something." As if he would; he'd have to pay. A
no-go area.

I went indoors quickly. I didn't like the grievance etched on his
face. He looked vicious and it wasn't nice. He needn't make me feel
guilty. I'd only said no for once. Still, I locked both my doors
because, God knows why, that look frightened me.

The two doorbells started ringing, shrill and imperative. I ignored them, getting out of my damp coat, drying my hair with a
towel, filling the kettle with water, trying to stop my hands from
shaking.

Still the bells rang, rang, rang. I threw up the window and leaned
out. "Go away," I shrieked down. "I said no and I mean no. Go
away."

A figure was below on the doorstep, shoulders hunched in a bulky
grey anorak. I wasn't seeing straight. I ought to have recognised that
crew cut.

"Jordan," he called up. "Don't be daft. It's me, James. Let me
come in. I've got some information for you. Am I welcome?"

"Yes." I didn't say how much.

"You look about as welcoming as a crocodile." He did not dare
mention the word Jaws.

"It was someone else," I explained. "A pain, a pest. I thought it
was him, pestering me."

"You look frightened."

I slumped, elbows on the sill. "Sorry, James. I'll come down and
let you in." Relief rolled off me. Derek was an unknown quantity.
But James was here and I was safe.

James shot me a bemused look from the doorstep. I went down
and unlocked the front door. "What's all this about? Why have you

turned yourself into a fortress? I heard all those bolts going back. Why are you looking down the road? Shall I dig a moat?"

I shook my head. "Just making sure." I had to stop myself burrowing into his arms. He looked big and tough and safe. "How about a bowl of soup? Would you like some soup? Lentils, barley, chickpeas and onions, green peppers. Touch of garlic. It's all ready. Made it myself." I was gabbling.

"Magic."

I have really old-fashioned gold-edged china soup bowls and two long-handled silver soup spoons, relics from the tableware of some big Edwardian house. It was pleasant to share the opulence with someone who appreciated their solidity. James weighed the spoon in his hand without comment. I served the soup with bacon-and-cheese-flavoured croutons. The combination was gastronomic.

He sat on the floor with his back against the radiator. He looked very much at home. I clouded my eyes so that he would not know what I was thinking. I wondered what he had come to tell me.

"This is good," he said. He didn't ask for more but I gave him a second helping anyway. I remembered how he had paid for my fish-and-chip lunch without asking.

"Those fragments of currency you found," he began at last but cautiously. "Very interesting."

"Oh?"

"An expert from the Bank of England has had a look at them. He got pretty excited. He said he'd never seen anything like them before. Hardly anyone has but there was enough data to confirm several important facts. Firstly, they were genuine British currency. The bits of metallic thread still visible on some pieces proved that. They were something new that the Bank were experimenting with around that time. But the notes were not easy to identify or date. In fact, he seemed to think there was something extremely rare about them."

I was nearly hyperventilating. "For heaven's sake! He's the expert. Does he or doesn't he know?" I hardly knew what I was doing, slopped soup over the rim of the shallow bowl.

"Don't be so impatient, Jordan. Interrupt me again and I'll go.

We're talking about a major discovery and one which might provide a motive for Ellen Swantry's murder. And I'm only telling you this because you found the pieces in the first place."

"It's called cooperation," I murmured, calming down.

"Apparently, during the Second World War, the War Office, in conjunction with the Bank of England and the Treasury, produced banknotes to be used by the armed forces in the event of a possible coin shortage or breakdown of Royal Mint production. In 1941 the Bank of England prepared eight million five-shilling and eight million half-crown notes. This move was also to conserve silver which had to be imported from the US and repaid after the war. However, they were never used and destroyed after the war."

"Destroyed—!"

"Heavens girl, I said don't interrupt. In the same year the Bank made two hundred and fifty-nine million notes for use by the armed forces in the Western Desert and other battle zones. They were known as BMAs, British Military Authority notes."

"Two hundred and fifty-nine million? What denominations?"

"One pound, ten shillings, five shillings, half a crown and even a one-shilling note. There was a lion and a crown in the design. They were due to be pulped in 1948 or 1959 but—" He hesitated.

"Well . . . ?"

"No one is sure if they were destroyed. Some were. The rest completely disappeared, vanished off the face of the earth, millions of pounds worth. Think of their rarity value now. Every one a collector's item. A fortune in printed paper."

"And Ellen Swantry was burning them in her fireplace. The first piece I found had 'ence' on it – two shillings and sixpence." My voice nearly cracked.

James leaned foward, his unfathomable eyes brilliant. I was transfixed. "And I bet she knew where the rest were, where they were hidden. That's why she was murdered, because she wouldn't say."

"Trenchers Hotel," I said on a long breath. "The hoard is hidden somewhere in Trenchers. It follows. Heads of State stayed there during the war. Security was strong. Secret meetings of the War Office were held there and Oliver Swantry was part of that set-up, I'm sure." I couldn't stop the excitement rising in my voice.

"Slow down," said James calmly. "You may well be right."

"Let's go to Trenchers right away. Now."

"Hold your horses, Jordan. You're not going anywhere. And we're not starting any search in the dark. Tomorrow morning is soon enough. My men will move into Trenchers and take the place apart, brick by brick."

My heart missed a beat for two reasons. "But you can't," I said, stabbing out the words. "You can't demolish that beautiful old hotel. It's history, it's a landmark, part of West Sussex's heritage. You can't touch it."

"Claptrap. We want to get to the truth."

"But you can't stop me being there."

"Oh yes, I can. I'm grateful for your help in my investigations but I have to remind you that from now on it's official. I have a warrant. You are an informant, a valuable one but that's all."

"But you can't tear down that beautiful staircase, that elegant ballroom—"

James said a rude word about the elegant ballroom and beautiful staircase. I was beginning to regret my openness.

"I shall picket the hotel, get the Conservation Society on my side," I said, outraged. "You wait and see."

"Oh grow up, Jordan. You know you won't do anything of the kind. You are just as keen as me to find out who killed Ellen Swantry and why. You may not be a good detective but deduction and investigation is in your blood."

I swallowed any further retorts. Everything was in balance. He was right. I was going off like a loose cannon (current phrase in the tabloids), but Trenchers meant a lot to me and I had no idea why.

"There's something else," I said, the words coming out against my will. I didn't have the resources and needed his help. "I've a few other bits and pieces from The Beeches which might be of interest to your investigation."

"Jordan? Bits and pieces? What do you mean?" His voice dropped an octave. The chill crept back into his voice which no amount of home-made soup could warm up. The first frost of winter. Isobars from Siberia. I was never going to find anyone to warm me. My slender hopes were sliding away on the ice. I felt as if the ceiling was lowering on my head. I could hardly stand his face being there, so close, yet so far away.

"Her bedside cabinet. Er . . . I've got some stuff from it."

This was one very angry Detective Inspector. He heaved himself up from the floor and suddenly the room was crowded.

"Would you please explain what you were doing, removing evidence from The Beeches? I can't believe this. Haven't you got any sense? I'm conducting a murder investigation and you walk off with some of the victim's possessions. I could book you for this." He turned on his heel, practically grinding up the carpet pile. I saw little tufts sprout, rescued the soup bowl.

I didn't like the way he was treating my carpet. "Don't shout at me. Your people had already been through The Beeches. This stuff was left there. They missed it. They ignored the contents of her bedside cabinet which was strewn on the floor. It's not my fault if they are thick and incompetent. What was I supposed to do? Call you up at the station and get you to send some jerk over? I'm sure that would have gone down really well."

"Where are they now?" He was grinding his beautiful white teeth.

"In my office at the shop. And keep your hair on, what little you've got. There's nothing mega. No keys to the safe, no plan of Trenchers with X marks the spot. I am capable of evaluating what I found."

"I don't think you're capable of evaluating a snow-plough in a snow-storm," he glared.

Derek seemed almost a sweet-mouthed saint by comparison.

James was shrugging himself back into his anorak with minimum effort. He would never visit me again. This was back to square one minus in the white charger stakes. My knight. I'd be on HRT before I found anyone half as attractive. Call him attractive? I must be out of my tiny mind. He was eyeing me like an enraged bull.

141

"I'll let myself out," he said. He did. I listened to his footsteps going down the stairs. I washed up the bowls and spoons with hot water, apple-scented detergent and a few tears. The tears made them really sparkle. It was very dark now and time to draw the curtains and shut out the night.

My doorbells rang again and I flew downstairs. James had come back. He wanted to talk, perhaps apologise, and I flung open the door, my face glowing.

"And who the hell was that?" Derek grabbed my wrist in a vice-grip, almost jerking me off my feet. His eyes were narrowed, his mouth working in a baby's gummy machinations. I'd never noticed how thin his mouth was before. The look on his face sent fear racing through me.

"As soon as my back's turned, I see my girl making up to another man."

This was not the time to point out the physical impossibility of that statement.

"Don't be stupid," I snapped, straightening my spine. I would not be frightened by this jerk. "That was not another man. I was not making up to him and I am most certainly not your girl."

"I thought we had something going," he snarled.

Well, we certainly don't now, buster, I nearly said aloud, even if there had been one or two moonlight moments when I had been off guard. They'd been nothing more than moments because despite Derek's soaring testosterone levels, he was a drag. He was all promise, bluster and no go.

I tried twisting out of his grip but he flung his other arm across me, pinning me to the wall. I gasped at the suddenness.

"Don't think you can treat me like this," he went on, tightening his grip and pushing hard on my wrist. I froze, waiting for the bone to snap. It didn't – but my patience did.

"Let me go at once, you idiot. You're hurting me," I said furiously, wrenching myself free. "And stop acting like a fool. This is so stupid."

"You'll be sorry," he ranted, hurrying down the street. He was a coward. I just had to stand up to him and he was off. "You wait and see. Mark my words." He flapped away like an outsized bat.

I slammed the door on him and leaned against it weakly, rubbing my sore wrist. I'd had enough of men for one night. No wonder Ellen Swantry became a nun.

Fifteen

P olice-speak is a conveniently condensed code to bemuse both villains and citizens of the realm, but I had got the message. Detective Inspector James was giving me the push. My pride dissolved into a puddle. There was a longing inside me so achingly strong, so desperate to be recognised yet it was still being denied existence. I must hold some kind of world record for non-consummation.

Another six years of celibacy stretched directionless. It was enough to send anyone heading for the Prozac. I looked at my hands, searching for liver spots.

All my instincts said make for the beach, the sea, talk to the gulls, listen to the waves. But Derek was prowling outside somewhere and I didn't trust him. It was time I stopped thinking about myself. Ursula Carling was home from hospital now. Tomorrow I should go and see her. After all, she was still my client. My bread and soya spread. It was time for hard speaking.

I put on some music. Simply Red washed the walls pink.

Ursula's face was pale with nothing much written on it. Something had happened to her metabolism. I recognised the state. She was in shock. The carbon monoxide poisoning had rocked her suburban complacency. The hair was in reverse spin, all tangles; her pale skin looked dry and flaking. It hadn't seen a moisturiser for days.

"Come in, Jordan," she said with unusual civility. She was wearing a pink jumper with pleated grey skirt, pearl necklace. "The ambulance men told me that you saved my life. I owe you my thanks. I could have been in my grave by now if it hadn't been for you." Tears shot into her eyes. "Do you believe me now? That someone really hates me enough to kill me?"

"It could have been an accident," I said gently. "A bird's nest or something."

"The Gas Board said the flue was blocked with rubble. Don't tell me that the gulls dropped a couple of buckets of rubble."

"Funny things, birds. I've seen seagulls throwing shells on to rocks but, of course, never down chimneys."

"I tell you, someone is after me. At first it was the junk mail, then the hate messages and the dead cat. Now they really want to kill me. I'm too scared to even go out. I may even have to cancel my appointment at the hairdressers."

She was in no state to even pour boiling water, so I made instant coffee, being careful how I handled the delicate china. Crunch time for effort. This was not good enough.

"Drink this," I said. "You'll feel all right in a few days. It's just that you're still in shock. After all, it was traumatic for the system. Is there anyone who could come and stay with you? How about your sister, Rosie?"

Ursula's look sharpened for one instant. It heartened me. She would recover, in time. She was one tough cookie, underneath. "Rosie? How do you know about Rosie?"

"I'm a detective, remember? I'm supposed to find out about things. I've been to see Rosie. She's a very nice woman."

Her brain was fast-forwarding over this information. She stirred the coffee till I was sure the pale rose pattern would come off the cup.

"If you say so . . . I wouldn't know. I haven't seen her for years. We . . . er . . . had a few words."

"I should think you had more than a few words. You went off and married her gentleman friend. Why don't you tell me what happened."

I got up and looked out of the window. A burly man was standing outside The Beeches, legs planted like a prospective buyer. He had a developer's demolishing look. Surely not another block of undistinguished flats?

145

Ursula was obviously embarrassed. It might help if she wasn't being watched by me so I kept looking outside. I only hoped she was going to tell me the truth this time and not a pack of lies. I was sick of her lies.

"Rosie . . ." I prompted.

"She's my elder sister but we never really got on. I don't know why. Perhaps I was a difficult young woman. I had a lot of bright ideas for getting on and Rosie didn't. She was happy with her library books and her job at the post office. I wanted to improve myself." She seemed disconcerted. Memories bugging her.

"Nothing wrong with that."

"I went to stay with her. I'd got a nice job in a big department store in London. It was a really posh, upmarket store. I was in millinery. Women wore hats then. Everything was so smart, it felt really weird going back to her little terraced house in Clapham every evening. I didn't belong."

She sounded lonely and tired and lacking in hope. Was she remembering those heady days of falling in love, when suddenly it was spring in winter? I waited, letting her remember. I knew all about seasonal longings. It was always spring in my winter.

"Of course, I fell for Ted Burrows. He had such wonderful manners. And he was quiet and handsome looking, lovely thick dark hair. He was too good for Rosie and anyway she didn't need him. She'd already had one husband. Wasn't that enough for her?"

Her words chilled me. I could well imagine that Ursula made a dead set for him. She'd been pretty, younger. Rosie didn't stand a chance. Nor would she have put up a fight. She wouldn't have known how. I wondered how many books Rosie had read in the intervening years. Thank goodness she had Bill and Ben now. God bless therapeutic cats.

"It was true love and a happy marriage," Ursula was saying but she didn't sound convincing. Her voice was measured and precise. "Cleo arrived very quickly. She was a gorgeous baby, all her daddy's dark hair."

"And what happened to Daddy and all his lovely dark hair?"

Was she going to tell me the truth? She seemed to say whatever suited her. She was smoothing the arm of her chair like an iron.

"He died. It was an accident at work, a shocking accident. I was very upset. Then I met and married Arthur Carling. He really loved me until Cleo grew up and stole him from me."

I wasn't going to go into that. "What sort of accident?" I asked more sympathetically. "Can you tell me?"

"It was a car accident. His car skidded and went into a river. The car wasn't found for nineteen hours . . ."

"I thought you said it was an accident at work?"

"He was on his way to work." She could twist anything. It was a skill. Was someone with him? Was that the unacceptable truth?

"I know it must be painful for you, reliving all these memories. By the way, who collects you from the hairdressers now that Arthur has . . . er . . . passed on?"

"I can't see what that's got to do with anything but I get a taxi. Tell me, Jordan," she went on, straightening her pearls, her confidence returning by the minute. "Are you any nearer to solving this case? Every day is costing me a fortune."

I didn't point out that she hadn't paid me a penny yet. Perhaps I ought to send weekly invoices. At this rate I'd need a secretary.

"No, I haven't solved it. Everything points to Cleo, I must admit, but none of the facts fit. It's purely a personal instinct but I don't think she's capable of such idiotic behaviour."

"Rubbish. You're just being sentimental. Taken in by her naïve charm as everyone is. Miss Lacey, if you don't get a move on, I shall go to the police station and put the facts before them, including the blocking up of the chimney with the intention of killing me."

"I do agree," I said. "I think you should go to the police. I'll give you all the information I've gathered and you can take it with you. But think first, remember the facts could then become public . . . reporters hang around police stations like fleas . . . it could be in all the newspapers."

Bold words. I wish I felt that confident. I was eyewashing myself. I didn't have a clue. Every avenue had come to a dead end. I was left with no one but Cleo. But I liked her. How could it possibly be Cleo?

"Take care. Look after yourself," I said, rising to go. There was something about Ursula. I could only stand so much of her even when she was on the floor, unconscious.

I took Ben Frazer's photo out of my pocket. I didn't know why I did it. "Do you know him?" I asked.

She took the photo from me. "Oh yes. That's Ben. He used to do some gardening for me after Arthur died. Then he stopped coming. Didn't say anything or let me know, not a word, no apology. These young men, easy come, easy go. Nothing matters to them, no loyalty to an employer. And I paid him well."

"He's missing."

"I'm not surprised. He didn't like gardening."

Two hours of searching at the Family Record Office and my arms were fit to break. Those record books weighed a ton and I'd been heaving the quarterly tomes, four to each year, from shelf to desktop and back again all afternoon. Even the pages were heavy, burdened with the deaths of so many millions of people. More recent years were computer recorded.

I paid for a copy of Ted Burrows' death certificate. He died from drowning. Nothing much to go on. Yet Cleo had said something about mysterious circumstances. It didn't seem particularly mysterious to me.

Oliver Swantry was less straightforward. I'd gone backwards and forwards in time searching for possible dates but there was no record of Oliver Swantry's death. I'd covered twenty years but found nothing. I came out into the street, confused, deafened by the noise of traffic, coughing in the dust and fumes. My Ventolin wasn't in my bag. I'd left it in a different jacket pocket. Fool.

I ducked into a sandwich bar in a local market street and ordered a goat's cheese and sliced tomato sandwich on brown granary, had it made up for me at the counter. The coffee was good and strong and I thanked the boy in a white overall and cap. He gave me a toothy grin. I took my sandwich to a high stool and hoisted myself up to think.

Was Oliver Swantry still alive? If so, then he was breaking

records. My maths would put him at knocking a hundred plus. He'd been a middle-aged Civil Servant when he'd married young Ellen, perhaps his secretary. This afternoon I'd checked their marriage entry at a Marylebone Registry Office. Maybe they had a London honeymoon. It was all so vague.

Was he even important? I felt sure that his War Office activities and the printing of millions of notes had something to do with the death of his wife, a kind and harmless nun, planning to spend her last years helping others.

The hospice ought to be visited. That generous offer to sell The Beeches and give the money to the hospice might be relevant. Supposing someone didn't want her to do that? Supposing The Beeches was stacked to the rafters with these collectable notes and she had to be stopped. Did killing her stop the sale? There were a lot of imponderables. No wonder I was confused. Perhaps I should stick to lost tortoises.

The train journey home was slow and agonising. I hit the rush hour, had to stand till Gatwick where backpacked air travellers disgorged themselves for a warmer climate. I could never commute, become a rail prisoner. And people paid for the privilege. I was sick of luggage in my face, people barging through compartments, tinny Walkmans thumping discord through my ears, and having to listen to other people's conversations. I was developing phone rage . . . call me anti-social but I spent the journey trying to think up something really nasty to say to people who use their mobile phones constantly on the train. Leave the office at the office.

Even though it was late and black aired, I heard a seagull screeching as I came out of Latching station. It welcomed me back.

Once I had loved London; now I never wanted to see the place again. The history was great but I couldn't breathe there and the crowds were horrendous. Perhaps it had always been so. William Hogarth painted the teeming hordes, brawling, drinking, uncouth. Nothing had really changed, only cars for carts, bikes for horses, take-away cartons for sewage, noise and fumes.

I wasn't thinking straight as I walked home. This was Latching, a time-warped seaside resort trying to catch up with the present.

Nothing could harm me here. The fresh night air opened my airways. I could breathe again. But suddenly I was spun off my feet, a hand hard across my throat, a sweetly pungent pad pressed against my nose. My nostrils gasped.

It was all so sudden. I was completely off guard, focused on getting home and pulling myself together. A radius bone pressed rigidly on my windpipe, half throttling me. I thought my neck was going to break, windpipe snap. There was too little flesh on my neck to cushion the pressure.

Was this how Ellen Swantry died? Chloroform, strangulation and then the meat hook? I could smell death in the air.

My senses reeled, my head caved from inhaling the volatile liquid. But self-preservation galvanised me into action and my body bent forward, twisted sideways sharply and a knee came up in one co-ordinated movement. He doubled up in pain, groaned from the pit of his stomach. The odour fell from my nose. It was a pad of chloroform. Panic surged through my veins. Another smell wafted from his clothes . . . tobacco.

I tried to see who it was but the man was staggering, turning away, out of my grasp. I tried to grab at his covered face. He looked like nobody, nobody I knew. But then how could I tell in the dark, winded, terrified and damaged by pain?

My WPC training took over. I tried to register height, build, clothes. One half of my brain programmed to make a sober analysis while the other half concentrated on fight and flight. The tobacco smell clung to him. He had strength, muscles. This was no wimp. This was fit.

He straightened up and made a futile grab for my wrist, catching my sleeve. I thought better about hanging about and began to run. I knew more short cuts and side streets and alleyways than a whole shade of eighteenth-century ghosts.

Down Holbert Street, through Field Alley, on to the seafront promenade, sprayed by the waves from a high tide. I crouched among upturned fishing boats drawn up on the shore, my footsteps drowned by the crashing of the waves. Then I lost him in the darkness even though he knew his Latching too. A tall, crowlike figure, fit, lean, muscled. It wasn't Derek, who was my height and paunchy. He couldn't run, not even after a take-away vindaloo.

I was nearer my shop than anywhere else. The Mexican restaurant was open and I made for its bright lights, flinging open the door to the welcoming waft of chillies and tacos and the sound of South American salsa music. I bee-lined to a table in a far corner, sat facing the door, held the leather-covered menu in front of my face. The restaurant was busy for once. I always thought it was on the point of closing. The waiter was small, brown skinned, wearing a green waistcoat and tight boots.

"I'll start with corn chowder soup," I said hurriedly, hardly reading. "And a cold beer. I'll order the rest later." This meant I could still hide behind the menu. The waiter brought the cold beer straight away as I knew he would. I don't like beer but this was medicinal for my bruised throat. I drank slowly, to make it last, hid my torn sleeve. Another torn sleeve. My hallmark.

There was someone outside on the pavement but I couldn't be sure who it was. It was an odd thing to do anyway, stand outside a restaurant. The figure did not consult his watch or scan the street for a late date. The glass of beer was slippery in my hand. I couldn't control it.

The waiter brought a steaming bowl of corn chowder and it was a meal in itself. I was not hungry. I had to force down each spoonful. Soup and beer, what would my stomach think of that mixture churned up? Serve me right if I was up all night, hung over a basin.

I put money on the table and slipped into the ladies' room, then, when the staff were otherwise occupied rushing in and out of the kitchen, sidled out by their back door. There was no problem in hoisting myself over the fence into the next-door back yard. It was one of the empty shops. I'd been there a couple of times before, just to look. I knew there was a window which didn't fasten properly, opened it and climbed inside.

The empty shop was creepy and musty; heaven only knew what it had once sold. I hoped it wasn't an undertakers. I kicked over an empty coffee jar and a pile of telephone directories. A narrow passage led to the front of the shop. My eyes were becoming accustomed to the gloom. The street lights threw some illumination into the shop and I ducked down behind the counter, crawling along until I had some sort of diagonal view of the street.

The man was still outside the Mexican restaurant, peering inside now, no doubt wondering how he had missed me. He went inside. Perhaps he had got hungry. Then he came out in a great hurry and began peering into parked cars.

Fear dried my body. I climbed under the counter and made myself as invisible as possible. My hand closed over something small and furry and dead. I nearly screamed, then I realised it was a ball of wool, petrified with age. It was a wool shop, one of those old-fashioned shops that sold knitting patterns and knitting needles and had skeins of wool stacked on shelves on the wall. Not many people knitted these days when a sweater was cheaper to buy ready-made.

I was inhaling dust, drawing shallow breaths, trying not to cough. This had not been a good day for my asthma. There was no way I could stay under the counter. I hunted around for some kind of weapon and found what I wanted – a steel knitting pin, the kind you need four of to knit socks. It was buried in the lower groove of a sliding cabinet door.

I was only half breathing. This was not the real world. Time was something I had forgotten. The beer was having an argument with the corn chowder in my stomach. It was not a happy situation.

There was no one outside now. Suddenly I didn't care if he was in wait for me. I wanted to be somewhere familiar and safe. My shop. I went out the same way I came in and shadow-shimmied into the tiny parking space behind my shop which I never used. I held the knitting pin point forward. The feel of my key going into the lock of the back door was beautiful. I slipped into my own place like a glove. There was no need to put a light on. I knew every inch of the way. I checked that both front and back doors were locked and bolted.

My other Ventolin was in the filing cabinet. A few pungent puffs settled my breathing. I switched on the percolator to heat coffee and sat in the Victorian button-back in the dark, stretching and rubbing my aching legs. It looked as if I would have to spend the night here. I put on an extra jersey, composed a new shopping list: spare blanket, sleeping bag, spare toothbrush.

I felt transparent. I forgot whether I wanted James or not. I was just a shade of blind.

Sixteen

T he wind went wild in the night. Barking mad. Loose windows rattled, doors shook, cans rolled about in the gutters. I slept fitfully, thinking every sudden noise was someone trying the door. Twice I got up to check on the street outside, seeing alien shadows hovering by every tree, imagining a figure catching sight of me and moving in for the kill.

But no one in their senses would hang about on a night like this. It wasn't fit for a lugworm to put its head above the sand. The rain slashed at the last lingering leaves, tossing them to the wind, trees groaning in despair, hammering at window panes, each heavy drop a measure of chilled cloud.

I was getting cold, wrapped myself in some old man's charity overcoat which smelled of fusty wardrobes. My distaste for the garment was overcome by the fear of frostbite. Charity clothes for surveillance were one thing; to wear them by choice was another. Could I also sense evil outside? Suddenly I realised the whole game was evil. This was no genteel Latching charade; I'd been locked in Trenchers, attacked on the street; Ursula had been half gassed in her home, Ellen Sawtry had been murdered. Not exactly Monopoly.

Any sympathy for Ursula's persecutor had gone. It had been an emotion chosen to justify my own dislike of Ursula. Cleo was a delightful young woman but she might easily have a new man friend, unmentioned as yet, unnamed for good reason, someone unscrupulous. Nice women often fall for thugs, philanderers, rakes, blackguards. She was still the number one suspect. But how could she have done all these things? And to her own mother? Hardly dutiful daughter syndrome.

In the dim light of a creeping dawn, I boiled some water and woke myself up with a hot wash, soaking my hands up to the elbows in the bowl to bring them back to life. Then I switched on the light in the back room and got out all the junk mail that Ursula had given me and spread it out on the floor. I emptied the bag from Ellen's bedside cabinet and lined up the items alongside the junk mail. I had no idea why. The only reason seemed to be that the two women had lived next door to each other.

Perhaps there was a link, a common fingerprint of some kind.

I sat cross-legged on the Persian rug, a mug of three-mg caffeine black coffee at my side, staring at the evidence. Somewhere amongst all that lot was a scrap of information that I had missed. My head began to ache through lack of food and sleep and too much coffee.

There was nothing, nothing at all in the junk mail that I had not scrutinised a dozen times before. Black marker pen on the back of unsolicited mail. Hairnets, grips, old receipts . . . mostly faded and unreadable. The lid of the booklet of matches flipped open.

Something was written inside. Oh God, how could I have missed it? There was a phone number scribbled inside the lid in biro pen. A local number – 596836 – with the Latching code. I swallowed hard. This was the key. This must be the link. It was too early to dial the number but my fingers were twitching.

I picked up the photograph of the garden of The Beeches. I had thought it was a photograph of the air-raid shelter. Look at it in a different way, I told myself. This is simply a photo of a garden – forget the shelter. Anyway, why would anyone take a photo of a mouldering dump of concrete?

Fence, shrubs, untended flower beds, a rustic seat, a few pots of wilting geraniums. I peered closely at the rustic seat. Something had been carved on to the back of the seat, two words . . . a name? I got my magnifying glass out of the filing cabinet and squinted at the letters . . . an L, a V, and was that squiggle at the end an R? Definitely an S, a T, and a Y. The vowels I took a guess at.

It flew together . . . OLIVER SWANTRY. It was so macabre . . . putting a seat with your husband's name in your own garden. How could Ellen have ever sat on it? Yet, according to the Family

Records Office, Oliver wasn't officially dead. But Ellen thought he was dead enough to have bought a memorial seat and an inscription. There were no dates.

Time blurred. I fancied a rustic bench in my memory, somewhere along the coastal path, high on the chalky Seven Sisters, where I could watch the rush and suck of the sea for ever.

The thought of mortality shook me. My trumpeter, James, me . . . all on the downward slide. Who would go first? Tears prickled at the back of my eyes. I didn't want either of them to die. I sat back, staring at the photograph in my hand, trying to ground these torments. It was telling me something but the message wasn't getting through. Was taking that photograph Ellen's way of leaving a message to the world? What the hell was it?

I had to know more about how she died. I had to have the autopsy report. DI James, you have got to come clean. Forget it, forget it, I flailed at myself. This isn't your case. Ursula Carling is your meal ticket. Let the efficient West Sussex police force work out the nun; you've already given them enough help.

But I wanted justice for Ellen Swantry. She deserved it. I wanted to know who killed her and why.

Six twenty a.m. I could hardly start making phone calls at dawn. Detective Inspector James came into my mind strongly, tall bodied and cool of eye, and I lost all concentration. Damn the man. Get out of my life, get out of my mind. I needed warming up and cleansing. The health club would be open soon for the morning. I could do with a sauna and steam bath and half an hour in the hot jacuzzi.

I was out just before eight. I had the steel knitting pin in my pocket and I wasn't about to cast on a sock.

The health club was in an old converted schoolhouse, pebble-dashed, gabled, cobbled yard. There was a faded sepia photograph in the reception area of the school taken in 1860 with rows of obedient children in pinafores sitting on benches in the dusty sunshine.

I took off my clothes in the locker room and stuffed them in an empty locker. I didn't have twenty pence for the lock. A warm shower ran off my body in a gentle caress. I had the place to myself so I didn't even bother with a towel as a sarong.

Billows of searing steam blew into my face as I opened the patterned glass door to the steam room. Thick eddies rose from the vents, white and pure vapour. God, it was hot. Gingerly I sat on the wet plastic bench, drawing my knees up to my chest in case someone else was there. By the time my eyes became used to the hot fog, I realised I was alone.

My twitchy airways drank in the steam, became soothed and lubricated by the damp heat. They relaxed and almost immediately my breathing was infinitely easier. Next to the sea, this was the best place in the world for me. I imagined James with me, stretched out on the other bench, his skin glistening with sweat, tendrils of hair on his body dripping with moisture. I knew there would be dark hair on his arms from glimpses of his wrists. Once I'd seen him in his shirt-sleeves with the cuffs pushed up. I shuddered with desire. It was time to close my eyes and surrender to dreams.

There came a point when I could stand the heat no longer. I made myself stand under the shock of a cold shower, then went into the decadently warm and bubbling jacuzzi, sinking down to my neck, feeling the jets of pummelling water massage the ache out of my body.

One day, when I was very rich, when I had both time and money, I would have a jacuzzi in my own home to soak in every day. I would offer calling friends a casual twenty minutes in the jacuzzi and we would stand our mugs of tea on the floral tiled edge and poke each other with inquisitive toes. The room would be white marble walled with Grecian columns in each corner and loops of green garlands strung round the plinths. Very tasteful. There would be a concealed hi-fi system with button controls at hand and I would play Grover Washington Jnr and Spiro Giro, George Michael and Simply Red, till my more classical friends screamed for mercy.

I thought I heard someone go into the sauna but I did not open my eyes. After another cold shower, I went back into the steam room. I would finish off with ten minutes in the sauna, then be ready for the day. My breathing was near normal by now. The steam was growing thick and undisturbed. I stretched out, accustomed to the heat now.

157

I don't think I fell asleep but I certainly dozed off for a few moments. There hadn't been much sleep during the cold night. Some sound woke me up. I half expected to find a pink and naked woman peering around the glass door and coming in to join me. The sauna suite had designated male and female times. No mixed bathing in Latching.

Clouds of fresh steam billowed out of the vents. It worked on a thermostat system. Suddenly it was far too hot for me. I might faint if I stayed in any longer.

I peered towards the door, looking for the push bar and leaned on it. It didn't move. I pushed harder. It was a heavy glass door, self-closing. What was happening? It was impossible to move. A new wave of hot steam seared my back. The system was going berserk.

"Take it easy . . ." I murmured grimly. I didn't panic, not yet. It was only a technical hiccup. The door was stuck, suction or something. One extra push would break the air lock. I gave it a sharp, hard shove.

But nothing happened. I sank down on to the floor where it was a few degrees cooler. I was starting to wilt, struggling for breath. This was ridiculous. A tremor of fear began to grip me. The steam was as thick as broth now.

I was becoming afraid, very afraid; cold fear and panic to my bones released adrenalin. Without it, I would die. There must be a panic button somewhere. Wasn't it a Health and Safety regulation?

My eyes were smarting but I made myself crawl up on to the benches, to feel around, search the streaming walls for some indentation. They were running with water, slippery and silky. I was never going to come here again. I was finished with steam rooms. This was a nightmare.

I was beginning to shake, gasp. My skin was on fire. I couldn't touch it. I ached with terror. Scalding was a terrible injury. I'd seen children scalded by kettles of boiling water, or saucepans of soup stock tipped sideways, their skin peeling off like tissue paper.

It was becoming more difficult to breathe. I was taking in rapid, shallow mouthings. I dropped to my knees as the heat was a few degrees less intense nearer the floor. My lungs were grateful for the more acceptable air but the relief did not last long. The vents were blasting out hot steam as if in a frenzy that an Ice Age had descended on Sussex, freezing Latching in its grip.

I felt around the streaming walls again for the panic button. Where the hell was it? Surely there was one though I had never noticed it during my many visits to the health club. I was groping about in low-lying cloud, like a primeval monster in a disaster movie.

"Help! Help!" I started to shout although I knew the room was sealed. I banged on the door frantically. I was beginning to feel like a shrimp cooking. Any minute now I would shed my skin.

"Please . . . someone, help me . . ."

There was nothing, absolutely nothing with which to break the door. The steam room was empty of anything but plastic benches. If I'd been locked in the sauna, I could have swung the bucket, the ladle, ripped up the wooden racks to use as missiles. But the steam room was completely bare. My nails sought cracks in the tiled floor in case one of them was loose. How about the ceiling? I couldn't even see it.

The heat higher up was unbearable. I held my breath for a count of ten as I stood up. My lungs couldn't manage any longer. Sweat was pouring off me. But my fingers had found a round shape at the top of the wall. I had to drop down for a moment, gasping and coughing, then with a last effort stood upright again. It was a button, recessed into the wall. I thumped it hard, again and again. A tiny, red winking light came on, barely discernable through the blanket of steam.

The staff kept me immersed in a bath of cooling lukewarm water till my fingers were wrinkled like prunes and I was definitely beginning to sprout a tiny fish tail. I obediently drank pints of water, swallowed salt tablets. The management were hopelessly apologetic; they'd discovered the thermostat was on the blink. They couldn't explain the faulty door but maintenance were looking at it. An ambulance arrived. They wanted to cart me away still naked because of the reddened and tender skin. Riding naked in an ambulance was not my idea of a scenic tour of Latching.

"Look, the skin isn't actually swollen or broken," I protested, still shaking. "Wrap me in a bag or something."

They settled for cling film and then a supported light cotton sheet. They put me in a side room off ward three at Latching Hospital. Coming to this hospital was getting monotonous. They'd be naming a bed after me soon. A young doctor thought I was light relief at the end of his night shift and began to laugh.

"Locked in a steam room?" he grinned.

"Not funny," I said as he fixed a saline drip in my arm.

"Sorry. It just seems funny. It's been a long night of hernias, gall stones, perforated ulcers. You're the first pretty girl with nothing on."

"OK, I understand. Ouch."

"Does that hurt?"

I nodded. "First degree burns usually do."

"I'll get the nurse to put on a paraffin gauze dressing. At least it's all very clean. Anywhere else that needs wrapping up?"

"Er . . . the soles of my feet. Palm of my hands. My nose . . ."

When DI James arrived in the doorway, I looked like someone practising to be an Egyptian mummy. Some bits of me were still visible. I was only wearing a thin hospital robe. He spotted the bruise on my throat.

"Who did that?" he asked, reaching the bed in three strides.

"Some joker with a problem and a pad of chloroform. It was last night." I didn't know what else to say. I was surprised to see him. I had never thought to see him again, not after our last meeting.

"You didn't report it. What's going on? This is an official visit. The hospital called us. They were not happy with the circumstances of your injuries."

"That makes several of us," I said. "I am certainly not happy with the circumstances. The thermostat was tampered with and somehow the mechanism of the door fouled up."

DI James was being official. I was glad about that but I couldn't help wishing for some glimmer of anxiety.

"I'll get it checked out. Do you think someone was trying to kill you?"

"Do I heck . . . ! All I know is, it gave me one big fright. Perhaps they were trying to scare me off. Look, James, I'm getting really close to knowing more about Ellen Swantry's murder. And I want to ask you about the autopsy. I need the details, to know exactly how she died. Were there any traces of chloroform?"

He touched the bruises on my throat very gently, looking at them this way and that. I almost stopped breathing. He was so close, I could see a sprinkling of grey hairs touching his temples. He was beginning to go grey. It seemed so infinitely sad that he was ageing, I quite forgot what we were talking about.

His face was very near. The air was perfumed with his male smell. I tried to breathe the air that he exhaled.

"Jordan? Who did this to you?"

"I don't know. Some man followed me from the station, caught hold of me round the neck, put this pad on my mouth . . ." I wouldn't let myself get upset, but I was close, inching towards female collapse. I started at the window blinds, hoping they'd calm me.

"Look, Jordan. This is no joke. They are trying to frighten you off, that's for sure. Maybe something about Ursula Carling is getting tricky. You haven't solved that one yet."

"Don't rub it in . . . it's like trying to find an invisible man – or woman. I don't know what to do next or where to look. It's all dead ends. Everything that I follow up leads to nowhere. James, I need your help."

"No, nothing doing, Jordan. You know I can't. And keep out of my case before you get really hurt. Doesn't all this tell you something, you idiot? Someone out there thinks you know something and they are determined to shut you up, any way that works. Next time you might not be able to find a panic button."

It was like diving into a dream. I had such a feeling of attachment to this man but it was obvious that he did not feel the same. I was just a nuisance. I wanted to ask him out, to suggest a concert or a walk on the wetly bleached beach, knowing that I would regret it for the rest of my life if I didn't even try. A moment only happens once and I let the moment pass.

"I suppose you're right," I said meekly.

He left soon after, the nurses fluttering around him like antiseptic moths in the doorway, being small and feminine beside him.

They let me go home three days later. Funnily enough it was the insides of my elbows and behind my knees that hurt the most. The skin there is especially thin. It felt odd going back to my bedsits, as if I had been away years. They didn't seem mine. The rooms smelt stale and stuffy and I threw open all the windows and then had to sit down to catch my breath.

While I was sitting down, I opened the mail. The usual bills, circulars, junk. But one piece of junk was junkier than the rest. On the back were the words: MIND YOUR OWN BUSINESS. YOU'LL GET MORE THAN YOUR NOSE BURNT NEXT TIME.

This was Ursula's mad junk mail writer. But was it? My stomach contracted with fear. How did he know? Had he shut me in the steam room, fiddled with the thermostat? I thought of the man who had attacked me three nights ago – or was it four? – was he something to do with the lost fortune in currency? Or Ursula? I scrutinised the writing with a magnifying glass. It seemed different.

But he knew who I was, what I was doing and where I lived. That gave me a bad feeling. But which one was he? Ursula's persecutor or Ellen's killer? It would help to know which man was which. If only I could find out, I might be able to untangle this mess.

Then came a chilling thought. Maybe they were the same person. I picked up the phone and dialled the Latching number that had been on the Hilton Hotel booklet of matches that I found in Ellen's bedroom. It rang a few times and then someone picked up the receiver. The voice was West Sussex, casual.

"Weston Second-hand Furniture."

"What?"

"Rick Weston. Did you like the desk?"

"The desk?" It all seemed like long ago that an office desk had turned up on my shop doorstep unannounced. "Oh, yes, Rick, thank you. It's great. Nice wood. I haven't paid you yet."

"Four hundred pounds."

"What?"

"Forty pounds."

"I'll come round soon."

I put the phone down. Rick Weston. It followed. Mrs Swantry had sold pieces of furniture to Rick several times in the past and then asked him to empty her house when she left it. Of course she would have written his telephone number down somewhere.

I turned the hate message over. It was printed on a winter advertisement for the amusement arcade on the pier, giving revised hours of opening. A new advertisement, one I had not seen before. I was back to square one again and I couldn't think straight. My skin hurt everywhere. It was time for a painkiller.

Seventeen

T he sea had been refrigerated by a sudden deterioration in the
climate from hostile isobars. In the days I had been in hospital,
winter had crept swiftly along the coast; no one sat on my rock now.
The last of the small birds had emigrated. Only the hardy gulls
stayed to squawk from the rooftops and skim the icy seas. Even the
fishermen only took their boats out on calmer days. I wondered
what Mavis was doing for fresh fish. Perhaps she had frozen the
excess summer catches and was entertaining her bold, dark-skinned
man in the back parlour.

The *Thelma Rose* and *Shirley Dean* were pulled high on the shore,
their dan flags fluttering like black mourning, nets piled under bits
of sodden carpet. Customers arrived by car to buy fresh fish for their
freezers but had to go to the Iceland supermarket instead.

I wore layers of loose, floppy clothes because my skin was tender
to the touch. The dressings were still on the insides of my elbows and
behind my knees. And, to my acute embarrassment, on my cheeks
and nose. I had burned my cheeks. Looking in a mirror was a
meeting of monsters.

The pier was empty except for a few intrepid anglers and boys
fishing from the lower level. They huddled into their anoraks and
woolly hats, munching beefburgers and chips, clutching thermos
flasks of strong hot tea, watching their rods and lines.

Tears of Allah swept in from the sea. The tide was high and the
sea was choppy, brown and cream, churning up sand from the bed,
swirling mud and pebbles.

Despite my medical disguise, Jack, the manager of the amusement
arcade, recognised me as his heroine and slapped me heartily on the

back. I flinched. He was wearing his usual assortment of sweaters and T-shirts.

"Hello there, ducks," he said heartily. "If it isn't my Saint Joan, my shining Lady of the Lamp." He'd been watching too many late-night films on TV. "Come and have some coffee. You look a bit flushed. What have you done to your face? Been overdoing the sunbed?"

"Someone tried to cook me," I said, following him into his little office. It was still a chaos of paper and rubbish and take-away dishes. He found an electric kettle and two mugs and a dribbling jar of instant coffee. I doubted if he could find anything else.

"Tell me who it was and I'll bash 'em in," he said, scowling.

"I wish I knew," I said, trying to find room to perch my bottom. "Tell me, Jack, when did you put out these advertisements? The ones about the pier in the winter?"

"Oh, those are new," he grinned. "Do you like them? Got to bring the business in. People think that when the winter comes the pier closes down. We've got to tell them we're still open." He flicked through a pile of freshly printed leaflets with pride. "Pretty good, aren't they?"

"Are your staff putting them out?"

"I hope so. I haven't paid good money to have them sitting in my office." He stirred the coffee with a stained spoon and added a sprinkling of powdered milk substitute. Not exactly wonderful, but I drank it. He was a kind man despite the rough exterior. I actually trusted him. "The deckchair men are glad of a bit of cash off season and there's Alf. They push them around the town."

"Who's Alf?"

"You must know Alf. The train driver. He takes the mini-train up and down the promenade in the summer. He can always do with a bit extra in the winter."

"Where can I find Alf?"

"I've no idea. Nobody has addresses. They appear and disappear. I don't ask questions. Look, miss, I'm sure you know what you're doing but it seems to me whatever you're involved in is getting nasty. Why don't you pack it in? I'd give you a job any day. You

165

could be my part-time manager, then I'd take the odd day off at the races. I like the horses and cars. Y'know, Goodwood."

He was looking at me with a sort of anxious beached-whale look. I saw the gleam in his gooseberry eyes and was sorry. I finished the coffee and put down the brown-stained mug.

"Thank you, Jack. I'll remember that. I might give it a try. Like the new wall notices."

Jack grinned. Round the walls were notices: "Don't Spend More Than You Can Afford. We'd Rather 100 People Spent One Penny Than One Person Spent A Pound."

I went out on the pier and wondered why I always attracted men that I didn't want, even when they were nice. The day was fading fast, the lurid promenade lights coming on in strings, headlamps flashing along the coast road, wing-tips winking green and red making for Gatwick Airport in a slice of dark sky.

I walked easily, gaining strength from the clean sea air and the bracing wind. Some stranglehold was breaking up inside me, senses lately blunted were suddenly sharpened. I was no longer trapped. I tried to wash myself empty of all the excess information I had been carrying around. Trenchers, The Beeches, Ursula, Cleo . . . they were only accidentally caught up in the same web of intrigue because they were neighbours. Whispers echoed in the vaulting halls of my head even if I could make no sense of them yet.

In the town it was late-night shopping. People were getting ready for Christmas already. They shopped in preparation for the coming siege. I only needed an extra carton of soya milk, some luxury bread . . . garlic or sun-baked tomato or granary special crusted with cheese.

A man thrust a leaflet into my hand. "Come to the pier," it read. "Forget WINTER. Have FUN in the amusement arcade. Open daily till 9 p.m."

I looked up at him. He was tall and stooping, a weather-beaten face lined and weary, wearing a navy woolly hat pulled low on his forehead.

"Hello," I said. "Don't I know you? You drive the mini-train along the front in the summer, don't you? Sometimes you wave at me."

"I wave at a lot of people," he said with resignation. "It's part of the job."

"Can we talk?"

"Sorry," he said, turning away. "I've got work to do."

"You can do that tomorrow," I said, catching his arm firmly. "I know a decent café near here. We'll have a cup of tea. Just a cup of tea and a chat. Surely you're not afraid of me?"

"No, of course not, miss." He seemed thrown, on edge, looking along the pedestrian shopping street as if wondering whether he could make a run for it. He was reluctant to stay. He shifted his weight from one foot to another. "I got things to do."

"They'll wait."

I marched him into Maeve's Café and sat him at a table in a far corner, putting him in the seat against the wall so he would have difficulty getting out. I nodded at Mavis behind the counter and she knew exactly what I wanted. She held up two forefingers in the shape of the letter T.

He was sweating. Funny that, because it was not especially warm in the café. The door kept opening, letting in a draught of cold air. He was ill at ease and longing to escape.

"I've seen you lots of times, driving the mini-train," I said. "All those kids . . . and the drunks. They seem to have a great time on the ride."

"Don't talk to me about the drunks," he said, moistening his chapped lips. "The women are the worst. A day out at the seaside for them is a boozy pub lunch and a noisy ride along the promenade. I don't think they even look at the sea."

"Have you been driving the train for long?" I asked. Mavis appeared with a big pot of tea and a plate of toasted teacakes, dripping with melting butter, which I hadn't ordered. She winked at me and I let it go. I poured out the tea and let the man help himself to sugar. He was into the teacakes without any prompting. Dear God, he was hungry. My smile folded itself away in pain.

"Only this summer," he said, his mouth full of teacake. "I had another job once, office job, before that. This suits me. The freedom, you know. Nobody bothers who you are."

"But it's getting cold now. It's going to be a bitter winter. Not much fun in the winter, is it? Not having a proper home."

"You're right there," he said, spooning in more sugar and stirring energetically. "The winter is going to be hard. Still, I'm fit. I'll survive. There are a lot worse off than me."

There was something about him that was gentle and mannerly. He had a pleasant voice. His chin was coarse with grey stubble and he needed a shave; his clothes were shabby and ill-fitting. The grey pallor of his face spelt cold and hunger. No way was I going to offer him a roof for the night but I felt like it. I couldn't house all the homeless of Latching. It was his decision. I wasn't cut out for St Jordan of the Homeless.

He had once been good looking. I could see a different man behind the poor feeding and despair. His voice had roughened from the company he kept but there were still the roots of a suburban upbringing in the vowels. He had learned to speak in the days when families spoke proper English, when it was necessary if you were to get a decent job. Nairadyes henyfink goes. And I don't mean regional accents. The rich variations of the British accent is part of our culture.

He was pretty nervous. His hand shook lifting the big white cup, slopping the tea. Homeless men seem to lose their confidence in being able to talk to women. I suppose it shatters them, wondering if they smell, need a bath, knowing where they slept the night before and the night before that. It might be oozing out of their skin.

There was something about his face that nagged me. I didn't know him just from driving the mini-train. From the beach, the driver had been faceless; I waved to the peaked cap and the gold-braided uniform. The man himself was blurred.

"What did you say your name was?"

"I didn't, but it's Alf."

"Alf?"

"That's what I said."

He looked uncomfortable. If he hadn't been hemmed in by all the chairs, he would have got up and gone. The last teacake was temptingly sweet in front of him and he wanted it. It confused

168

him. If he could have sprouted wings, he would have flown.

Suddenly his shoulders slumped. It was as if he was tired of the deception, drained by the hard life of living rough.

The mask fell away. I knew exactly who he was.

Eighteen

"Arthur Carling," I said.

He did not need to reply. Relief and panic swept over his face in waves of contradiction. His blank, mourning eyes lit up for a second then sank back into his own personal pit, his suit of sorrow.

"Not dead then?" I went on.

He put down the cup and lifted his hands from the table in surrender. He tried a smile, fleeting, but it was a nice smile. "Only half dead," he said, drily. "How did you know?"

"Ursula gave me a photograph. You've changed a bit."

"Yes, of course I've changed. But there's still something left of the man I once was, is that it?"

"Did you send me this?" I asked, taking the Mind Your Own Business threat message out of my pocket. He nodded and looked away, burrowing down some dark corridor. "And how did you know about my nose?"

"Sorry, it was a mistake," he mumbled. "I've been following you. I thought you were going to ruin everything. I was desperate to make you back off. But I didn't have anything to do with what happened to you in that health place."

Ruin everything? I could see I had to tread carefully with this wounded man. Chloroform, carbon monoxide poisoning, all the hate mail, a dead cat . . . he might be a very dangerous person under that numb exterior. Somebody tampered with the steam room door.

"I don't want to talk about that or Ursula," I said, trying to gain firmer ground. "Let's forget her for the moment. But I'd really like to know how you did it, you know, disappeared? After all, you've had a proper funeral and been cremated. You're supposed to be

170

dead. Quite an achievement." I tried to infuse some lightness into the conversation. "Ursula thinks she's a widow and Cleo grieves for you."

It was the wrong thing to say. He groaned like a tortured animal, pushed at the air as if warding off a knife in the ribs. I knew straight away that he cared about Cleo, that she was the one bright light in his life and that Ursula had been right about his feelings. It was too late to retrieve the words.

"But Cleo's all right, really, I promise. You were a patient in Latching Hospital, weren't you?" I probed quickly. "A heart attack or something, wasn't it?"

Arthur Carling dragged his mind back from wherever it had slipped. He impaled me with a look that was pure pain. He stirred more sugar into his syrupy tea. Then he started drawing circles on the oilcloth with the base of his spoon. He had no idea what he was doing. Mavis would go ballistic if he ripped it.

"Yes, I was in hospital in Latching. But it wasn't as serious as a heart attack. More a warning. Angina, they said, that's chest pains. I had tests and a chest X-ray. I have to take medication to prevent any further attacks. I get a doctor in Shoreham to prescribe them."

"So how come the hospital authorities thought you had died?"

Arthur Carling shrugged at the memory. "It was too easy. I was in a two-bedded side ward with this other chap. He was a vagrant who had collapsed on the street and been brought in. He was in a bad way. On the Sunday night, he had a massive heart attack. I tried to find someone to come and help, but no one ever came. God knows where everyone was. Perhaps there was an emergency elsewhere. It was while I was wandering round the hospital, trying to find a nurse or a doctor, that I realised just how easy it would be to walk right out. No one would ever know."

"But the vagrant had died . . . ?"

"Oh yes, he was a goner. No chance." He hesitated. "You've met my wife, Ursula. You know what she's like . . . it was a heaven-sent opportunity I'd never get again. I had to get away from her."

"Ah, opportunity makes the thief. How can we resist?" I said.

"I lifted him over and put him in my bed. He wasn't stiff or anything. We were both wearing hospital-issue pyjamas. I put my watch and hospital name tag on his wrist. The stud fastening on mine was faulty and it was a simple matter to remove it and fasten the strap on him. His name tag, I just cut off and threw away outside. They're only thin plastic. We were near enough the same height so I put his outdoor clothes on over my pyjamas and walked out. They smelt disgusting. They'd thrown away his boots so I went bare-footed. Ursula had taken home my shoes. They were brown, well polished, I remember. Nice pair."

"But what about identification . . . er . . . afterwards?"

"I knew Ursula would never agree to identifying a corpse. Far too squeamish a procedure for her. Cleo was on holiday. And faces change when they're dead, don't they? They drop or something. Ursula would identify the watch and that would be enough with their documentation. The chart was there, and their hospital records. No autopsy was needed because I'd seen three different doctors earlier in the day. None of them would remember my face. I was just another grey-haired, middle-aged man."

"What did you do?"

"I walked out, in the middle of the night, into the street. Walked anywhere. I don't know where I went. Down to Shoreham, perhaps. The sea was always to my right. I could hear it pounding the shore. It was a strange walk. I was hoping they'd think that the vagrant had scarpered through fright. No one would bother to look for him. He wasn't important. Just another bed they could use after it had been fumigated."

"But why did you do it? You weren't only getting rid of a difficult wife, you had also cut yourself off from Cleo."

"I know, I know." He buried his face in his hands. "That was a big mistake. Somehow I had a wild idea I'd be able make things right, see Cleo and reassure her, somehow let her know that I was still alive. But it didn't work out like that. For a start, I had no money, no job. You can't do anything without money. I became a has-been, a drop-out. What would she want with a deadbeat like me anyway? Sleeping rough . . . well, you've lost everything when you get that low. No, she should be finding herself a nice young man who'll look after her. With me out of the way, they'd soon be queueing at her door, I thought."

"That was months ago now. Where have you been, Arthur? And it is you, isn't it, who's been sending Ursula all this unpleasant hate mail?"

"Yes, it's me." He nodded, his face working. It looked like remorse. "What a fool. I don't know why I did it. I wanted to scare her, to make her pay for the way she treated Cleo. Make her suffer. You don't know how unkind she's been to that girl, over the years, always putting her down, always on at her, making life unbearable as if it was Cleo's fault that she was born. It's no wonder Cleo left home."

"And the letters from Cleo?"

"I don't know anything about any letters. If Ursula said there'd been letters, then it wasn't true."

"But she brought some to me. They were typed. Do you think Ursula might have sent those herself, just to frame Cleo, to implicate her? She does seem to have a kind of vendetta against her daughter."

"She's a lonely and bitter woman. I always thought she hated Cleo because in some way the pregnancy spoilt things between her and Ted. Then having such a pretty little daughter . . ."

I didn't pursue it. He was confused enough.

"Were you having an affair with Cleo?"

"An affair?" Arthur looked shocked. "Heavens, no."

"You're not her natural father."

"Sometimes she seems like a real daughter to me and I really love her." He seemed more relaxed now, ready to talk. "Ted didn't last long. Ursula drove him round the bend. Well, she would, wouldn't she? Not happy unless she's making someone's life a misery. Cleo couldn't stand it. She left home. But I had to know how she was getting on. We used to have lunch together in Chichester."

"And meet for tea and cake in Latching?"

Another fleeting smile crossed his face. "My word, you're a good detective," he said. I accepted the compliment. No point in denting the image.

"So you found out about the tea dances, did you? While Ursula was having her hair done, as usual, regular appointment. I just wanted to see Cleo and talk to her and make sure she was all right. You see, I love her. I don't think she knows how much."

He savoured the words. I had to tread carefully.

"So after you disappeared, you started bombarding Ursula with all these nasty messages. Is that right?"

"I thought they might frighten her, make life as scary and uncomfortable for her as she had made it for others. Ted, me, Cleo. We all had to put up with her. I wasn't actually going to do anything."

"And a dead cat? Hardly an empty word."

"Oh yes, that poor moggie. I found it in the road. A spur of the moment thing. Poor taste, I agree. It didn't mean anything. What happens now? Will they send me to prison?"

I wasn't going to tell Arthur that he could be charged on several counts. It was an offence to send threatening letters through the post; the swap with a corpse was also an offence.

"And how about the carrot cake?" I asked, ticking another off my list.

"Yes. I was watching you and Cleo having tea together in that converted church café in Chichester. Neither of you saw me. I was behind a pillar. It alarmed me a lot and I got very jealous of you. You sitting there with my Cleo. You looked as if you were getting on well together. I didn't like the idea of Ursula hiring a private detective. Having my revenge was one thing; getting caught was another."

"So the poisoned cake was a warning?"

"Something like that. I spiked a slice with bleach from the bathroom. We use a lot of bleach, having to share. I didn't actually want to hurt you. I wanted you to clear off, leave us alone. It was none of your business. Sorry."

"But it was. Ursula employed me. It was my job to find out who was persecuting her. It is against the law, you know. And against the law to send someone poisoned cake."

"Well, I know nothing about the law. Life's dismal enough. All I had was catching sight of Cleo occasionally from a distance and the summer job driving the mini-train. I'd managed to rent a really grotty room but it was cheap; no bed, just a mattress on the floor. I buy clothes from the charity shops, live on junk food and bread and jam. The only consolation is not being nagged by Ursula day and night: take your shoes off, put your laundry in the basket, wash up, dry up, go shopping, fix the car. You've seen the house. It's a sin to even breathe on anything."

"So it was you watching Cleo at the jazz concert, was it? Creeping about in the dark, making her fall down the stairs?" I tried not to sound accusing, but facts were facts.

Arthur shook his head. "No, Miss Lacey, believe me, I didn't make her fall. That must have been an accident. Her high heels, I expect, caught in something. Yes, I thought I could stand in the theatre somewhere and just watch her for a while and listen to the music and pretend to be civilised for a short time. It all went wrong when you spotted me."

"But I lost you and went after a different villain."

"I slipped over the side of the pier and climbed down a girder, hung on underneath. The tide was coming in and it was raining. I got wet."

"But you dried off in time to go and see Cleo in hospital."

"Yes. I was sorry then that I had sent you the cake. You looked after my Cleo really well, getting the ambulance and going with her to the hospital."

I noticed the pronoun "my". "I like Cleo. She's a very nice young woman. Yet, all along, she's been my chief suspect. But somehow I couldn't believe it."

"Cleo? A suspect? You were way out there, miss. Cleo wouldn't hurt a fly. She couldn't. She's far too gentle."

"Everything pointed to her. She had the motive and the opportunity. You see, Ursula had you nailed down in your coffin and cremated before she even told Cleo that you had died. Cleo was devastated, shredded. It makes a good motive for revenge, especially when it's obvious that Cleo cared for you . . . cares for you," I corrected. Tenses were not my strong point.

Arthur Carling seemed to be faltering. His thoughts were more than he could bear. He slumped over the table, his head in work-scarred hands. His emotions had wrestled him into the ropes. Did he have a labouring job now, the demolition of an old house? Moving rubble? I didn't ask him. "No more, Miss Lacey. I can't tell you anything else. There is nothing more to say."

He pulled off his woolly hat; his grey hair was stamped flat as if it had been painted on his head. He looked worn out. But I wasn't finished yet.

"Would you like some more tea?" I asked politely, like Eliza Doolittle.

"I couldn't swallow another drop. I'm drowned in the stuff. Let me go. I've got to get out of here."

His skin seemed to hang in folds as if his pretence had been glued on and it had slewed off. But I had to know more. He'd disappeared once; he could disappear again. Slope off to Shoreham. I might not get another chance to talk to him.

"Arthur, please, sit down. I believe you and I will try to help you if I can. Things are not as black as they seem. Perhaps you can get your life back together. I know Cleo would understand why you did what you've done and she would be so happy to have you alive again. Believe me. But I need to know a few more things. About the carbon monoxide poisoning . . . you must have known that what you were doing could have had a lethal effect. All that rubble down the chimney." Suddenly I couldn't imagine Arthur perched on a ladder. No way.

"Carbon what? I don't know what you're talking about. Look, I've got nothing more to tell you—"

"And did you follow me from the station at Latching the other night? Someone followed me and tried to throttle me, put a pad of chloroform over my face—"

He groaned aloud. "No, no, it wasn't me. That's ridiculous. You've got to believe me, miss. Where would I get chloroform from? I'd never have done such a thing, never . . . look, I've had enough of this. I don't understand. I have to go." He stumbled to his feet, nearly pushing the table over. "I gotta find a Gents."

He nearly sent the china clattering to the floor as he elbowed his way past me and out of the café and into the cold day. I hurried after

him, miming to Mavis that I'd pay her later. He went into a public
lavatory on the seafront. That had been true.

My head was spinning with all that Arthur Carling had told me. I
believed him. It was the kind of stupid thing that a man at the end of
his tether might do, without thinking of the consequences. I knew
what it was like to be rocked. Not by living with a woman like
Ursula for years, but there are certain emotional events, like loving
people who don't love you back, that put you through a spin-dryer
till you don't know which way you're facing.

I stumbled on a pavement crack, my thoughts in tatters. If it wasn't
Arthur Carling stuffing rubble down his wife's chimney; cooking me
in the steam room; fixing me with the chloroform – then who was it?
Fear chilled to the roots of my hair. Someone else wanted me out of
the way, thought I was getting too close to the truth. Perhaps I ought
to put another quick ad in the local paper: HAVEN'T A CLUE. PI
RETIRES THROUGH LACK OF LEADS. TAKING UP CRO-
CHET. Then they might leave me alone.

Arthur didn't seem to be coming out of the Gents. I could hardly
go storming in, waving my licence. Supposing he'd forgotten to take
his angina medication that morning? Suppose the stress of the
interview had taken its toll and he'd done an Elvis? I went up to
a total stranger about to relieve himself in the Gents and asked him
to check for Arthur.

The young man was highly amused, cocked an eyebrow. "Anything else you want me to do in there, miss?"

"No thank you," I said primly. "Just see that my friend is all
right. Tall, middle-aged, greyish."

The young man took a long time. Probably sharing the joke with
all the other occupants. I was starting to think I'd missed him when
he came out, zipping up, still grinning.

"No one in there called Arthur."

"Are you sure? Tall, fifties, grey-haired, shabby."

"Nope. Hey, I'm Joe. Would a Joe do? I could dye my hair."

I left the ebullient Joe to go fill up with beer again at the pub on
the front, no doubt repeating the story a dozen times that day till the
novelty wore off.

How could I have missed Arthur, unless there was another way out? He hardly looked fit enough or skinny enough to have climbed out of a window. There must be another exit.

And what was I going to tell Ursula? I had solved her case. I said this to myself twice for confirmation. I'd done it. Arthur wouldn't be sending any more missives, I felt sure of that. I could present my bill – minus days in hospital – and pay a few outstanding accounts with the money. And was I going to tell Cleo the truth? Or would it hurt more to know that Arthur was around, alive, and had purposely cut himself out of her life?

Not my problem. I would write a straight report for Ursula. Typed. Professional. Call him an unnamed assailant. Get it down now. Never did like the clerical side of police work.

I went back to my shop. Mr Frazer was working inside, kneeling on the floor. He had finished pricing the books and was stringing up cheap paperbacks into bargain bundles.

"People will buy the duds if there's one decent book in the middle that they really want to read. Five books for a pound. What a bargain. Have you any news of my son yet? I saw the posters around the town. Very nice. Thank you."

I hit my head. I'd forgotten about Ben. "Not yet. It's early days. Don't worry, we'll find him."

If only I could. That would really make my day. He must be somewhere. I would concentrate on Ben now.

A woman came in and tried to haggle for the old fan. What did she think I was? A street Arab? I knew she really wanted it. Her greedy eyes were devouring the fragile silk, the threadbare embroidery. I didn't want to sell it to her. She was the wrong person.

I stuck to my six pounds, felt like upping it to twelve. She was about to flounce out, feathers all huffed like an indignant hen, when she produced a charge card.

"Cash," I said.

"Really, you're impossible. Everyone takes plastic these days. It's a normal trading practice. You'll soon go out of business, young woman, if you don't move with the times."

I was putting the fan back in the window, carefully splaying it out, when the woman opened a leather wallet stuffed with notes and laid out a reluctant fiver.

"Six," I repeated.

She threw a pound coin on the counter. The coin rolled, teetering, as if practising for a casino career. I was sorry she was buying it now and was half inclined to say it was not for sale. But six pounds was six pounds and I hadn't sold anything for days.

"Please cherish this fan," I said as I carefully wrapped it in ironed, second-hand tissue paper. "It once belonged to a very beautiful, titled woman. A lady in every sense of the word." I stressed lady.

All rubbish, of course, but I had to say something. Anyway, it might be true.

She pursed her lips and left without even a thank you. I fancied that her eyes glittered with triumph. Dammit.

"Probably worth sixty," said Mr Frazer, putting a hardback copy of *Gone with the Wind* with battered paperbacks entitled *Love Me Bandit, Dangerous Vices, Lasso Larry* and *Cooking with One Egg*.

"I'll never make a fortune."

"Is that what you really want, Jordan? To make a fortune?"

I didn't know what I wanted. I couldn't find a glib phrase. My mind was a cage. I wanted to right wrongs, make people happy, spook villains, keep my shell-like to the ground. See the musician. Oh yes, I wanted to see him, touch his sleeve. I was hollowed out with wanting him. The stars were shedding ashes on my longing.

And JJ. I needed to strike up some sort of rapport with DI James. There was something going there. A cosmic dating. The computer in the sky.

I wanted the kind of mortar that doesn't wash away. Work that one out, buster, I told myself, hammering in the nails.

The door swung open and an Arab walked in, red check headscarf flung over one shoulder like Yasser Arafat on television. He walked right up to the counter, tapped it, arrogantly.

"I've come for the dough," he said.

I thought it was a hold-up. Something snapped. I went bananas. My voice rang out like a steel hawser. "Get lost, mister! You've come to the wrong place, mate. All you're going to get is six pounds and some loose change, so piss off."

His jaw dropped like a sledge-hammer. He was poleaxed.

"Jordan! Miss Lacey! It's me, Rick. Remember, you owe me."

Nineteen

He took a small black cigar out of his top pocket, flipped open a booklet of matches and struck a light. He bent over the flame but my eyes were fixed on the matches. It was a Hilton Hotel booklet, the same as I had found in Ellen Swantry's bedroom.

"Where did you get those matches?"

Rick Weston glanced at the booklet. "These? Oh yeah, they fell off a lorry. Do you want some?" He delved into his pocket and brought out a handful, tossed them on to the counter. "I give them to all my customers. The feel-good factor."

He gave them to all his customers. Mrs Swantry had been a customer. He flicked the headscarf, a token sign of where he was conceived. Mr Frazer nodded to me as he slipped out into the street. I took a deep breath to straighten out on a wild line of thought.

"About the desk, Rick. Thank you for getting it. I think it's great. I know you prefer cash but I only have six pounds odd. Will you take a cheque for the rest?"

"Don't leave yourself short. You gotta eat." His eyes swept round the empty shop.

I made out a cheque for thirty-five pounds and gave him the fiver from the fan. It felt contaminated but I guessed he fiddled his taxes. That left me a pound plus to live on. I could do it. No gourmet caviare today. It was macaroni again. The feast with a hole in it.

Rick took the money and blew out a haze of smoke. I tried not to cough. He hadn't heard of asthma or pollution. The pungent smell clung to his clothes. "This place is a bit bare. You need some glass-fronted cabinets."

"No glass-fronted cabinets, thank you."

"How about a couple of gilt half-circle wall tables to stand things on?"

"Sorry, I've enough furniture for the present."

"They're out in the van. Wanna look? Classy. Look a real treat." He cupped my elbow with stiff fingers and steered me on to the pavement where his grubby white van was parked. He had ignored the meter. He flung open the back doors and presented the tables like a magician. "Waddiya think?"

I tried not to stare into the van. The tables were stacked to make room for a couple of mattresses propped on their sides. Both the mattresses were stained, smelled dampish, had beech leaves sticking to the blue ticking. On the floor of the van was an extending ladder. At the back I caught sight of a shovel and a sandy-rimmed bucket.

"You'll never sell those," I said lightly, putting my hand on a stain. It was still damp. Mattresses take a long time to dry out. I remembered the smell of boarding school dormitories.

Rick rubbed his chin. "Gonna burn 'em. Like the tables?"

"Lovely."

"Do you want 'em?"

"I'll think about it." I was acting weak.

"Gotta go."

He drove off, sure he'd made a sale. I watched the van till it was out of sight, trying to make sense of what I had seen. What did a second-hand furniture dealer want with an extending ladder and a shovel? Then there were the two mattresses. Surgical thoughts sliced like cold steel. Had he put them on the ground as insurance in case he fell? But why? What had he against Ursula, if Ursula had been his victim?

Or had he made a mistake and put the rubble down the wrong chimney? There might be some point to torching The Beeches. Light a fire in the grate, fill the rooms with black smoke, set the chimney on fire. Difficult to sell a house blackened with smoke. That kind of thing could put a purchaser off.

But there was no way anyone could mistake a house, especially a client's house, even in the dark. It was a theory without a motive.

I wheeled my bike on to the road and fastened my helmet. I could cycle to Lansfold Avenue on auto-pilot these days. It didn't take long to find a neighbour who remembered seeing a white van parked in the road late at night on the Sunday. The woman at number thirty-eight was observant.

"I thought it was funny. But I was watching the *South Bank Show* at the time and forgot all about it. Was he up to something?"

"I'm not sure. But thank you for your help."

"Any time, miss."

That put the time after eleven p.m.; hardly a good time to be buying furniture or delivering a sale. Why did I feel so sure that Rick was involved? It was all circumstantial. Had he come across Ellen burning currency in the grate and got greedy? Had he found a bundle of banknotes tucked away in some old chest of drawers from The Beeches? But Rick was not particularly bright and might not know their value. And why Ursula? She had no connection with The Beeches. She only went to Ellen's funeral. That was hardly a threat.

My blood ran thinner. There was someone else behind all this. A drenching silence invaded my head. My nose remembered being crushed against a jacket that reeked of tobacco. No ordinary cigarette smoke. Cigar smoke.

I was annoyed with myself because I could not think properly. A chorus of voices was clamouring in my head, fragments of information floating in a vortex of muddy water. DI James had to be told. It wasn't just urgent. This was my life. He had to know all these new facts – but my skin remembered his fingers lightly touching my bruises and I slipped, unresisting, into a golden dream while I waited for some personal word that did not come. How could I face him again with these rampant thoughts surely visible in wanton neon across my brow? I breathed his name into the air, momentarily forgetting the smoke.

I would have to follow Rick Weston myself, keep tabs on him. What a surveillance, from one dreary house clearance to another. He might spot me. He was used to bag ladies, knew most of them around Latching. What line of business would be legitimate on the streets, in daytime, that no one took much notice of? And I wasn't going to fool around in a mini-skirt with black fishnet stockings as I had in my beat days.

A contact lent me her second-best uniform. It didn't really fit but we did a bit of safety-pinning. The hat looked quite fetching.

"Just keep walking about, peering at cars. People don't look at you, hoping you'll go away, take off. We're bogy-men. You don't actually have to give anyone a ticket."

"This is absolutely perfect," I said, grinning. "I'll wear thick glasses, do something to my face. Freckles perhaps."

"Spots. Spots are easy. Give yourself acne. Try to make yourself look infectious."

"How can I repay you?"

"I'll think of something."

I spent the next day following Rick round the streets of Latching, getting on and off my bike, strolling streets and checking parked cars. It did not seem to click with anyone that most of these roads did not have parking meters and a traffic warden was totally out of place. I spotted several out-of-date licence discs. This is what our police force should be doing; out on the patch, checking on Joe Public.

He did nothing out of the ordinary. It was a very dull day. He moved a lot of junk. He was going to get lung cancer, all that smoking. There was no eye contact. You need the patience of a saint for survellience . . . the boredom, the bum-ache, the sweat, the creeping lethargy. I couldn't stop yawning. Then I saw Sergeant Rawlings walking home in civvies. He barely glanced at me. I caught him up and adjusted my pace to his steady stride.

"Don't look surprised. Just keep walking," I said out of the side of my mouth. "I want you to give a message to DI James."

"Jaws, when are you going to grow up? You look ridiculous. What's the matter with your face?"

To his credit, he kept looking ahead and walking at the same even pace. His voice was low and conversational.

"I'm tailing Rick Weston. I'm pretty sure he put the rubble down Ursula's chimney and that it was he who attacked me that evening. He smokes and he's got a ladder in his van."

"Clear as mud."

"Tell DI James. please." I sounded desperate and I was. "Remember the nun who was murdered in Trenchers? Somehow it's all connected and I'm mixed up in it. Please, Sarge, just this once. Take me seriously."

"Seeing I've always fancied you, I'll tell him tomorrow."

"No, tomorrow might be too late. Haven't you got his mobile number? Can't you ring him today?"

"You owe me."

"I'll buy you digestive biscuits, milk chocolate, a jumbo packet. Two packets."

"You certainly know how to tempt a man."

I stopped to examine a blue Ford Escort. The disc was three months out of date. "Look at this, disgusting."

"Careful. That's my son-in-law's car."

I pretended mock horror and peeled off in a different direction. Rick was humping a wardrobe out of house. He was impressively strong. I hadn't noticed the hard muscles before. I remembered those muscles and cringed. I knew, instinctively, that they had pinned me against a wall, crushing the breath out of me.

Now I was free of Ursula Carling and her nasty squabbles and turbulent marriages. If I wanted a few days off, I could have them. I'd earned the time. If I wanted to follow up any Ellen Swantry leads, there was nothing to stop me. The death of the nun had quilted me but the attempts on Ursula's life and mine . . . trying to scare me off had only made me more determined.

One way of dealing with unpleasant things was to pretend that they were not so, as the heroine did, so sensibly, in *Cold Comfort Farm*.

It had taken three attempts to alert me to the danger I was in. I'd been lulled into thinking it was coincidental or accidental because I'd connected them all to the Carling case. Now, having met Arthur Carling and heard his story, I knew he had nothing to do with them.

God would not mind if I arrived at the St Helios Hospice on my bike. He couldn't possibly be a snob. It was two large double-fronted, four-storied Victorian houses joined together by a glassed-in covered walkway. The in and out drive was wide enough for ambulances and hearses and there was a parking space for visitors' cars. There were pots of winter pansies flanking the shallow steps to the entrance door and a wheelchair ramp alongside.

I parked my bike beside a Daimler. All men are equal. I pressed the entryphone button and announced my name and business.

A peachy-cheeked young nun unlocked the door mechanism, took my card and glided away on saintly feet to the Mother Superior. I waited in the hall, inspecting the cheerful, spiritual pictures – no naked martyrs riveted with arrows and bleeding here. A lot of people passed through the hall like it was Clapham Junction to eternity. It was a busy and bustling place.

The nun reappeared, just as silently. "Sister Lucinda will be pleased to see you," she said. "Please follow me."

I'd expected Sister Lucinda to be a round jolly person, not the professional-looking nun who rose from her desk to greet me. Her robes were immaculate, the white bits pristine, her beautiful face and porcelain complexion the envy of any woman and vaguely familiar.

"Come in and sit down, Miss Lacey. How can I help you? I'm afraid I don't have very long." Her voice was low and modulated.

Sister Lucinda looked as if she worked out. Perhaps she lifted weights in the privacy of her cell, or sneaked out to the gym in trainers and tracksuit.

"Thank you," I said, glad I was modestly dressed and my wild hair tamed into a plait. "I won't take up too much of your time."

"Poor Sister Ellen. We were all so distressed by the manner of her death and that she had so little time here, doing the work she loved," said Sister Lucinda calmly.

"Can you tell me something about her background and how long she had worked here?"

"If I can. Sister Ellen had been doing voluntary work here for several years. She was a widow, lonely, and felt the need to commit her remaining time to our cause. She had some secretarial skills, rusty of course, but everything is useful in a place like this. She came

186

to me, explaining that she could no longer cope with her big house and would like to become a nun. I explained that it was not as simple as that; that she had to receive religious instruction from Father Raymond, but she was happy to begin at once."

"And in return she would give you the proceeds of her house sale?"

Sister Lucinda's smile stiffened. "Not exactly in return, Miss Lacey. It was what Sister Ellen wanted to do. There was no coercion. How did you know about this?"

"I have some of her papers. I was wondering if this commitment still held now that she has died. She might have previously left the house to a relation in a will."

"I understand that there are no relations. Our solicitors are looking into the validity of her letters of intent, to see if they constitute a will in our favour. They seem to think there will be a favourable decision."

I nodded. "I'm sure it's what she would have wanted. I'm trying to get a clearer picture of Sister Ellen. Weren't you worried when she went missing? She had been dead twenty-four hours when she was found."

"Yes, we were concerned when she didn't return. She had been away on retreat for religious instruction. We thought she had stayed on. Some people do."

"Can you tell me what she might have been doing at Trenchers?"

"The hotel? I have no idea. She hated the place and often said it should be pulled down."

"Why should she say that?"

"I believe she had some kind of phobia about empty places."

It didn't ring true but you couldn't argue with a nun.

"You've been very kind," I said, rising. "By the way, what has happened to Sister Ellen's personal effects? Are they still here?"

"On joining the order, we give up all worldly possessions. Of course, we are permitted one or two small items," she added graciously. I noticed she was wearing a good, modern watch – one of her small items. "I cannot think Sister Ellen's few belongings are of any interest. In fact, I was about to dispose of them."

Sister Lucinda delved into the lowest drawer of her desk and brought out a plastic bag tied with a label marked Ellen Swantry. It was a pathetic collection: a fountain pen, a small cheap silver-metal crucifix, her glasses in a spectacle case, a pair of good leather gloves, a heavy brass key, packets of hairpins, brush and comb, tatty toothbrush.

"Not much," I said, making to hand back the bag. "Do you think I could borrow the key for a day or two? Just an idea."

"Sorry, that must be a mistake. I don't believe the key should be among Sister Ellen's effects. I'm sure it belongs to the hospice. I'll remove it."

"I should still like to borrow it." I could be stubborn.

"I'm sure the key is ours."

"Just a silly idea," I tried smiling. "Humour me."

"I don't understand why, but if you insist."

"Thank you. I will return it."

I knew where it fitted. I'd already seen a similar one in DI James' hand on a rain-lashed, windswept evening that had taken my breath away. I was ninety per cent sure it was a key to Trenchers. Ellen Swantry might have hated the place but it hadn't stopped her keeping a key. I wondered how long she had had it. How many years? It followed that she hadn't had the key on her when she was murdered or the key would have been in police possession, not with her personal effects at the hospice.

Someone else also had a key or had broken into Trenchers. I'd found the basement door open. Perhaps the murderer had forced her into the hotel, waylaying her as she returned from the retreat – or even before she went to it. That fortune in notes was a strong motive. Perhaps it had all gone terribly wrong. Maybe the chloroform had been merely to keep her quiet while she was held prisoner. Maybe the strangulation had been a threat that went too far. And the meat hook? A macabre way of throwing the police off scent? But somebody had done it. Impaled her.

I needed air, and the air outside was fresh and living despite the cold wind. Although I approved of everything the hospice was doing and the way they maintained a happy, cheerful atmosphere, the place still had that underlying promise of death. Sister Lucinda was like an angel of mercy – a merciful angel of release – with her face of flawless perfection and calm unhurried manner. No one was in a hurry to get to Heaven.

A name popped into my head. Lucy Grey, luminous and dewy eyed. That's who she was. Sister Lucinda had once been on the cover of every glossy magazine, one of London's top photographic models. I remembered newspaper stories of her high-living social life. What had made her give up such a glamorous and lucrative career?

The key fitted the back entrance of Trenchers, turning stiffly. I didn't bother to cover the entry. I had a key; it spelled entitlement. My flashlight lit up the interior of the hotel and there was plenty of daylight creeping in through cracks. The police might have missed something because they didn't know what they were looking for. I was looking for signs of enforced habitation.

There might be something left behind, something overlooked when the murderer fled, leaving Ellen Swantry to prematurely meet her Maker.

The police had swept out the ground floor and filled bags full of debris for forensic. They had not touched the grand staircase and elegant, high-ceilinged bedrooms. I crept up, slowly and carefully, my eyes crossing with extensive scrutiny. In the far corner of a front bedroom were signs of occupancy. A squashed pillow, a dingy orange satin bedspread, a pail, empty cartons of milk, crisp bags and sandwich containers. The officers probably thought some vagrant had been dossing down for the night. I searched around the sorry litter and found what I was looking for, a single hairgrip still gripping a strand of grey hair. I put it in a plastic specimen bag. Ellen Swantry must have shed hairgrips all over Latching. She kept the industry going single-handed. Fine hair does that.

"I've got to speak to you," I said at the station desk. He'd come down from his office. He glowered at me, twitching a pen in ink-stained fingers.

"Speak then. I haven't much time."

"About Ellen Swantry—" I began.

"Jordan, for heaven's sake, leave it alone. Not the nun again. Get on with your own case and leave the police to the serious work."

"I've solved the Ursula Carling case. Job done. Report filed, case closed. And I'm not far off solving your case too."

DI James slapped the counter in exasperation. "Success has obviously shifted your brain off its axis. I'm glad you've resolved your hate mail case. We can now all sleep more safely in our beds. Who was it?"

"Arthur Carling. Her dead husband."

"The phantom poster."

"Not dead. Faked it. Been driving the mini-train all summer along the front. And he didn't put the rubble down Ursula's chimney, shut me in Trenchers, try to chloroform me on the street or lock me in the steam room at the health club. No sir, not guilty, not the type. Whoever murdered Ellen Swantry kept her prisoner in Trenchers for at least thirty-six hours, maybe longer. I haven't touched the evidence. It's still there for your boys. But I have brought one item of interest which I found on a bedroom floor. A room with a view." I produced the grey hair and grip in the bag. "Get a DNA fix on that."

He looked at me with a brief glance of admiration. "I'm glad you haven't forgotten everything the force taught you." A thought struck him. "How did you get in?"

"I used Ellen Swantry's own key. That speaks for itself. She must have had a connection with Trenchers."

"Let's go," he said, pulling on a coat and turning up the collar. Energy surged into him. My heart volunteered an extra beat.

"Am I coming, too?" I couldn't keep the amazement and hope out of my voice.

"I'm not letting you out of my sight, but don't read anything into it."

The words were like kisses on my ears. We went out to his car. It was tidy inside, no litter or crisp bags. Immaculate man, wash me. I told him the rest of my theory about Ellen's death. He seemed to agree with me, if silence and grunts meant a degree of agreement. He parked at a distance to Trenchers, no need to draw attention. We went in the back way, using my key. The sprawling cream building was eyeless like a mausoleum; the colonial influence more apparent by day in the Indian-style ironwork. I still loved the old place but now my affection was tempered with fear.

James was angry that his officers had missed the pillow and pail. Their search had concentrated on the ground floor where the body was found.

"Bloody fools," he growled.

"They probably thought it was some dosser," I said, excusing the button mob. "Like trying to find a needle in a council tip, especially if you don't know what you are looking for. Sister Lucinda from the hospice told me that Ellen Swantry, or rather Sister Ellen, could have been missing for thirty-six hours. They thought she had gone on a retreat but it was only when she didn't return that they became alarmed. The key was among her personal possessions." It all came out in a rush.

"Do slow down, Jordan. It makes me tired just listening to you."

"And among the bits and pieces I found from her bedside cabinet at The Beeches—"

"The what? There was no bedside cabinet."

"Sure, there was no cabinet – it had been cleared with the rest of the house contents. But the drawer had been tipped out on the floor. You, as a man, would not have recognised what a woman thinks is essential to keep close at hand at night. You know, survival kit . . . Rick Weston is the second-hand dealer who cleared the house. He could have come across some of the currency in an old piece of furniture. He might have seen her trying to burn the stuff in the grate. There was a Hilton Hotel book of matches on the floor and then I saw Rick using a similar freebie. But he has dozens of them. He gives them away."

"Slow down. I'm still not following you."

"Then there's Ted Burrows, Ursula Carling's first husband and Cleo's real father. He disappeared in suspicious circumstances. And

Oliver Swantry – Ellen's husband – has no death certificate. He would be over a hundred now if he's still alive."

"Not exactly robust enough to strangle his wife and string her up. Or pour rubble down Mrs Carling's chimney."

"Unless he's into aerobics."

"I'll send forensic round to collect this stuff. They might get something off the pillow and the bedspread." I noticed he didn't touch anything. "It does look as if they were trying to get information out of Ellen. I wonder if any of those Bank of England notes are circulating; the ones which should have been pulped in 1948."

"There's that collector's shop on the corner of Stone Yard; the one that's always closed," I began, but he was ahead of me, striding out of the hotel.

For once the shop was open. It was packed from floor to ceiling with shelves and boxes of postcards, cigarette cards, comics, magazines, old and yellowing and collectable; stacked boxes of coins and medals and war memorabilia, old ration books, petrol coupons, clothing coupons, identity cards.

A large Labrador heaved himself off the floor and inspected our ankles. Mr Arkbright was small enough to fit into his shop, alert enough to have a mental record of every transaction.

"DI James, West Sussex police," said James, showing his identification. "This is Miss Lacey, an associate." I put on my associate face. "I'm hoping you can help with my enquiries." He produced a clear plastic wallet in which was one of the burnt fragments from Ellen's grate.

Mr Arkbright's face lit up as he took the wallet from James. "Another one! Excellent. But what a pity it's nearly destroyed." He put a jeweller's glass in his right eye and peered at it.

"You know what this is?"

"Currency of the realm. Printed by the Bank of England in the last war as a wartime measure. Never issued."

"You've seen another? Recently, you said?"

"A few weeks ago. A half-crown note. I gave the young man ten pounds for it."

"Ten pounds for one note?" I said numbly.

"If you brought in a thousand-pound note issued in 1928, it would be worth twenty-eight thousand pounds now. Work it out for yourself. The currency note I bought is coming up for auction next week. It'll probably fetch ten times what I paid for it. Just tell me where I can get some more."

"Do you know this young man? Did you get a name? Would you recognise him?"

"No, sorry. Never seen him before. Not one of my regulars."

"Can you describe him?" I asked impatiently.

"He looked like any other young man of today that you might see around Latching. I was far too interested in the note to look at him."

"Unshaven, beard, glasses, tattoos? Clothes?"

"They all wear the same clothes these days. It's a uniform. Jeans, T-shirt, trainers."

"Did he say anything about where he got the note? Or whether he had any more?"

"No. I asked him the same questions. But he wouldn't say for definite. He seemed pleased with the cash. I had a feeling he would be coming back."

"And has he?"

"Not yet."

James handed him a card. "If he does come back, please give me a ring. Nice shop you've got."

"Anything you want to sell, someone else will buy."

I pulled James out of the shop and a few yards along the pavement. He glared down at me. My breath caught on a sharp easterly wind and made me cough.

"Dust?"

"A hundred years of it," I gasped.

"Is that why you dragged me out in that ridiculous manner?"

I shook my head. "No . . . it's the orange satin bedspread at the hotel. I've just remembered where I'd seen it before. Ages ago, on the pavement in front of his shop. He was unloading his van."

"Rick Weston?"

"And the description. Jeans, T-shirt. Fits him to a T. I'll go and see him."

"You won't go anywhere near him. Do you hear me? That's an order."

When did I ever obey orders?

Twenty

J ames took me home, declined a coffee, drove off without a
backward glance. I consoled myself that he had taken me along
as his associate. It could be called a statutory kind of progress.

I could not remember when I had last eaten so I pulled out all the
stops and made a fast cheese omelette with three eggs, puffy, golden
and ripping with melted mature Cheddar; ate it with a hunk of
buttered granary bread. My stomach received the offering with
gratitude; my salivary glands rejoiced that all was not lost; my taste
buds celebrated with hysterical fervour.

The two doorbells rang. I peered from behind the curtains like a
neighbour. I was not risking another confrontation with the pos-
sessive Derek.

It was Rick Weston, standing on the pavement with a large
rectangular painting, his cowboy hat tipped back. The nerves round
my spine chilled; my goose-pimples pimpled. I was not sure about
Rick any more. Yet he was so solitary. One of the jeans and T-shirt
brigade; only those hooded eyes betrayed something different. I
flung up the window and put my head out.

"Hello," I said. "Can't come down. Running a bath."

"Do you want this picture? Can't sell it. You could put it in your
shop or on the wall of your flat."

He held it up. It was a hack painting of a Scottish loch in a
traditional whisky mist. "How much?" I asked. I didn't want it. But
I was ready to pay out good money to get rid of him.

"Two pounds. A bargain. You'll make double."

"All right." I was so pathetic. "Can you deliver it to the shop? It's
too big for me to carry."

"Are you going to the airshow at Shoreham?" he asked.

"I didn't know there was one."

"On Sunday. I'm saving up for a plane. I'm having flying lessons. I'm not always going to be a second-hand dealer. Pleasure trips, that's what I'm going to run for the trippers. Sussex Sunspots, I'll call my plane."

It was the longest speech I'd ever heard from him. The ambition in his voice was unmistakable. Rick did not want to spend his life heaving crates of battered saucepans out of damp and derelict houses. The sky beckoned.

"Do ya want to come with me?"

I wondered if I had heard properly. Had I suddenly developed glue ear? I tried not to feel snobbish. My social status was nil.

"The airshow," he repeated. "Do you want to come with me? Aerobatic stunts, First World War aircraft, Spitfires, jet Harriers. Great day, crowds of people, stands, stalls."

I hovered on the thought. "Well . . ."

"You deserve a day off. All the hours you put in."

How did he know what hours I worked? Was he just guessing or had he followed me home, late one night?

"OK." I was sorry I did not sound more enthusiastic but I was up to here, somewhere vaguely mid-chest, with men. There was only one man I had ever wanted and he was making music for his wife. And DI James didn't know I existed.

"I'll pick you up at nine thirty, Sunday morning."

"No need. I'll go in my own car. Simpler." I thought of the buckets and shovels and ladders in the back of his van and cringed. We didn't know the truth but I knew why I was going. It was to see if I could learn something, snooping, spying, asking a few artless questions. Also it provided a lesson in humility. The hospice had rubbed off.

DI James phoned later in the week, left a terse message on my new answerphone. I couldn't phone back because I was coping with Ursula. I'd sent Ursula her account and she promptly had hysterics on my doorstep. It was *Brookside* and *EastEnders* rolled into one. The language was hardly the millinery department of a Knightsbridge store, more a coster barrow out Mile End way.

When I told her that Arthur was still alive, she went pale and nearly fainted into my arms – an awesome experience. I had to revive her with a glass of my expensive Napoleon brandy but since her account was a hefty one and I had charged every genuine expense, I would look upon the brandy as client discount.

"Alive? Alive? But he can't be! I buried him in a graveyard. I witnessed the coffin. Get him dug up – the dental records will prove that he's dead enough." She had spun way out of control.

I ignored the agricultural suggestion. No point in digging up that poor vagrant. "No, the dental records, if he ever had any, belong to a homeless man. I've seen Arthur Carling in the flesh, spoken to him, given him cups of tea and buns and he's very much alive, Mrs Carling."

"I hope you didn't put the tea and cakes on my bill," she wept. "I'm not paying a penny for him or anything."

I hadn't. "Surely the important fact is that the hate mail will now stop? I've discovered that Arthur has been sending it and it's finished. He's promised to stop. Aren't you pleased? Does it matter whether he's alive or dead? You don't love him. And he's not coming back to you. He could be stone dead as far as you are concerned."

"I'll lose my widow's pension," she wailed, screwing up a damp handkerchief. It smelt faintly of lavender. Perhaps she wept lavender tears.

"You'll have to sort that out yourself," I said, not offering any help. Her cheque was safely locked away in my filing cabinet. "I could recommend a good solicitor to help you." In Chichester, I nearly added.

She was still not grateful, her face closed with disapproval, and I wondered if she had any idea of the effort that had gone into solving her case. I knew that my investigative talent needed honing but I had certainly used up a lot of energy on her behalf. It took more time to calm her down and it was when she had gone that DI James phoned again.

"I have several new facts you should know," he said in a voice like ice.

"Shoot." Mentally I was sending Ursula's cheque to deserving causes – the rent, electricity, insurance, phone bill. "What have I done to merit these confidences?"

"Kept out of my way for three days. It's been like a Bermudian holiday."

"Watch your tan, buster," I said, slamming the phone down. He phoned right back.

"Hey, Jordan, what have I done to make you mad at me?"

It was what he hadn't done. Like taste my lips, stroke my wrist, ease the worry lines from my brow with his warm breath. Enough to make any woman tear up her Wonderbra and send him the bits in the post.

"Not a good day," I sighed into the marshy air. "Ursula Carling has just bitten my head off for solving her case, like I'd resurrected husband Arthur on purpose."

"She doesn't like the result?"

"No way. Not what she wanted at all. She'll probably sue me for loss of her widow's pension."

I thought I heard a chuckle. "This'll take your mind off such trivialities," James went on. "Remember the sandwich carton and crisp bags found in the front bedroom at Trenchers? A couple of decent dabs. One set belonged to the deceased lady. And minute fibres found on her clothes matched the orange bedspread. Hairs on the pillow also belonged to her. Your theory was right. Ellen Swantry was kept prisoner there. Fragments of floor debris found near the hair roots matched a sample taken from Weston's white van during a routine brake test recently carried out by my officers."

"Oh dear," I said on a long breath. I was shaken. "So she was taken in the van." I thought of the looming airshow.

"And we have evidence of when his white van was parked only a road away from Trenchers."

"Latching is a small place. It could have been there for any reason." I tried to erase the catch in my voice.

"On the same night that someone shut you into Trenchers and hoped you'd break your neck falling through a gaping hole in the floorboards?"

"How do you know?"

198

"Because Weston was careless enough to get a parking ticket. Left the van on a double yellow from four thirty p.m. till whenever he drove off after hammering those planks across the basement door. There was an RTA early that evening in the same road and the van was reported still there and unattended."

"I'm going out with him on Sunday," I said in a voice I did not recognise. "To the Shoreham Airshow."

"Cancel it." He used the kind of barking command that made criminals shake. "Don't go."

"That'll only make him suspicious. I might find out something."

"You might find yourself strung up in a hangar. Be sensible. Wait till I tell you that he's in the clear before you go gallivanting round the countryside with him."

"Since when have you had the right to tell me what to do?" I wanted to slam the phone down again but I didn't. There were things I wanted to know. Teeth-gritting time. "So what else do you know, DI James?"

"Nothing I'm going to tell you. Just keep away from the Westons. Let the professionals do their job. You chase up lost tortoises and roll-a-penny thieves."

"That's not very nice."

"I'm not a very nice person."

How could I tell him he was wonderful, that I adored every short hair on his head, that his voice sent shivers? No, I couldn't. I had that certain thing called pride. A useless commodity, especially to a woman who needed the man who didn't need her.

I also needed a sauna, a steam and a swim like I was dehydrating. My fear of the health club had receded in direct relation to the need. I wasn't going to let some fool murderer stop me from soothing my twitchy airways with steam. There was a clean towel in my sports bag, swimsuit, shower gel, body lotion, talc, money. What more could a girl want?

"Thank you for telling me what you have."

"That sounds ominous. You're not usually so polite."

"I'm developing politeness."

* * *

199

As the reception clerk at the health club checked my name on screen and got me to sign the attendance book, I had an idea.

"Do you mind?" I asked, leaning over the counter with a winsome smile. "I want to check if a friend of mine has been in recently."

I flicked the pages back to the day of the steam room trauma and ran my fingers down the list of names.

It was a horrible, spidery feeling; ice chilling my spine. About halfway down was something I did not want to see. It was part of a name, "Bet" . . . which was crossed out. Then she'd written in Elizabeth West. Was this Betty Weston, Rick's adoring single mother? She'd checked in at eight thirty and left again at eight fifty-five. It fitted.

"Do you check everyone who checks in?" I couldn't think of alternative words. "I mean, do you know everyone?"

"No way. How could we?" said the receptionist. "We have a membership of over five hundred. It's impossible to know everyone. We can't remember everyone's names."

"But you remembered that I'm Betty Weston just now."

"Oh yes, you're a regular member. We know you."

Full marks for memory and observation.

The Sunday of the Shoreham Airshow was cool and treacherous. Rain clouds gathered in the sky, planning their own show. The field next to the airfield was full of parked cars churning up the earth in furrows, disgorging aircraft fans with rugs, themoses and folding chairs. I wore my best jeans, high-necked sweater, boots and my good leather jacket. It was supposed to be a date.

Rick was waiting for me. He wore jeans, a cream polo-necked jersey and a flying jacket. It was obviously a date. We nearly matched. I wondered if he had a white silk scarf tucked in a pocket.

"Jordan," he said, dispensing with the Miss Lacey bit. No more the customer. "Let me show you around."

He was a good guide, brimming with near adoration of winged machines. He knew a lot about aeroplanes and their flying performance. We watched the Diamond Nine vintage biplane team take to the air in perfect formation. They were stunning.

"These planes have no wheel brakes. I'll fly 'em one day."

We inspected the giant Catalina on the ground. "This baby saw reconnaissance, bomber and anti-submarine service, air-sea rescue, won two VCs in the war," he said admiringly. "And she's still airborne. You'll see her take off later. She's the largest aircraft to use this short runway."

Into the air sailed a frail First World War triplane, then an old green-camouflaged Spitfire spluttered overhead; the Team 50 flying YAK 50s began synchronised aerobatics. I nearly broke my neck watching their aerial choreography, gasped at the timed cut-offs, spins and dynamic dives. It was meat and veg to Rick. He'd withdrawn. He hardly knew I was there.

"Wait till you see the RAF jet Harriers! Got your ear-plugs? They take right off here on the runway . . . Straight up! These are the Crazy Stunt planes. Wing-walking. Need their heads tested." But he wasn't talking to me. I was blotting paper.

The girls waved and gave away free chocolate bars as we walked past the parked yellow-painted stunt planes. The wing-walking biplanes were covered in gaudy adverts for a brand of chocolate. "I don't know how they do it," I shuddered. "I'd die of fright."

"Takes nerve."

We watched the Pegasus team drop six parachutists with high performance chutes. The free-fall manoeuvres used smoke generators to create sky trails. It was like a silent fairyland.

Rick obviously lived for flying. Strange how I had known him and his shop for years, seen him driving around Latching unloading junk from his van, never realising that this secret longing was breeding under his T-shirt slogan. In a way I approved but also I was afraid. I did not know him at all.

"These are the planes that I fly," he said showing me round a group of Tiger Moths and Piper Cubs. They looked like toy planes. I'd seen them buzzing over Latching a hundred times, totally unaware that Rick might have been at the controls of one of them, dreaming his dislocated dreams.

I tripped over my own feet. I was becoming uncoordinated. It was all that craning skywards. My neck felt funny.

"Wanna look at the stands?" He was trying to put me at ease, steering me jauntily through the crowds. It was hard to cope with this change of relationship. I wasn't his girlfriend but I had to pretend. "There's books, memorabilia, flying clubs, joy rides, uniforms. Wanna go up in a helicopter? I'll see what the queue is like. Not feeling cold, are you?"

"No." I thought the weather was just right for a crowded show. Too hot and the St John's Ambulance tent would be packed with heat exhaustion cases; any cooler and everyone would have stayed at home and watched a video.

He'd disappeared into the crowd before I could say no to the helicopter. He was getting tense but it was not with passion for me. The object of his infatuation didn't have legs, skin or use blusher, only wings and props and landing gear.

The first drops of rain sent the crowds scurrying into a big refreshments marquee. I bought two beakers of tea and balanced them awkwardly, looking around for Rick, but he did not seem to be anywhere. I stood, sipping my drink, wondering how much longer he would be. If this was as far as the date went, another two minutes of hanging around and would be off.

The marquee was packed with people escaping the rain. The smell of wet clothes, alien deodorants and pungent hair lacquer irritated my airways. I felt a familiar clamp across my chest. I had to get out. I was gasping for air, groping for my Ventolin. My arm jerked like a puppet and I spilt the tea, down my front and drenching a woman pressed against me.

"Sorry, sorry," I tried to say, mopping her coat with my scarf. "My fault . . ."

She glared at me and muttered to her companion about some women having no co-ordination. I had to agree with her. I needed new lungs and three arms for co-ordination. And some women had no sympathy when it was obvious I could hardly breathe. We were packed so tight, yet my knees were buckling.

An arm pulled me through the crowd, pushing people aside, half lifting me off my feet. I fell into the fresh air, rain spattering my face. I hung on to his arm, coughing. He took the slopping tea out of my hands.

"Use your inhaler," said DI James, tossing the tea away with scant regard for the litter notices. "Then get the hell out of here. I told you not to come."

I exhaled, inhaled the steroid, held for a count of eight. My breathing calmed. The rain was sticking to his cropped hair like a film of dew.

"The hell I will," I said, once I had enough breath to speak. "He's just beginning to trust me. I'm getting somewhere."

"I'm in no mood to pick up pieces of you scattered all over the airfield. Go home and dust your shop or something."

I started wiping rain off my face with angry swipes. There were so many things I wanted to say but couldn't; so many things I would like to do with him . . . bones melted. I was impatient with the frustration of only being on the fringe of his life. It was no good. I needed a vaccination to cure me of the pox. I had to find some stability; this emotional seesaw was playing havoc with my hormone level. My endocrine glands were in a twist, turned in on themselves, poleaxed with rejection. It would be his fault if I had to have a hysterectomy.

"Go play cops and robbers," I said, stalking off. "That woman put a teaspoon in her pocket. Go read her her rights."

"Don't say I didn't warn you," said DI James, going in the opposite direction.

I could have hit him for what he wasn't saying.

But he'd gone. The rain eased and a great Flying Fortress took the air with magnificent dignity, engines roaring. I shook rain-washed tea off my jacket and as I did, Rick appeared out of the crowd, thumbs in his belt.

"Wanna see inside the Catalina? She's a beaut. Lands on water, y'know."

"Sure," I said, strolling after him. We went between stalls and tents, taking care not to trip over the wet guy-lines. The spiky grass glistened with rain, pathways turning muddy. I must have missed a low-slung rope, for suddenly I found myself falling, arms flung out, unable to save my dignity.

I wasn't sure if I hit my head.

*   *   *

When I came round, something was happening to the ground. It seemed to be moving with a jerking, rumbling, stomach-shaking regularity underneath me. It couldn't be an earthquake, I thought, shaking my head – but I had trouble moving it. And it hurt.

I tried to put out a hand to steady myself but found both wrists were in cuffs behind my back. A tight harness banded my chest like a straitjacket, fixed at the back, keeping me upright. It was made of wide straps of grey fabric; another strap was bolted across my waist like an airline safety belt.

I couldn't move. Yet I was being jolted bodily over the ground. My feet were leaden. I managed to tuck in my chin and look down. The tops of my boots were encased inside steel shoes and these contraptions were bolted to a sheet of metal, painted a gaudy yellow. Glimpses of grass and spinning trees and tops of tents came in and out of a blurred vision.

Under my feet there was a sudden roar and shuddering vibration and terror flashed to the roots of my hair. It was the roar of a propeller turning. I screamed and screamed but nobody heard. I knew where I was now. I was standing on the top wing of a plane, strapped and bolted on and the earth was moving because the plane was slowing taxiing towards the tarmac runway for take-off.

I was wing-walking.

Twenty-one

S omething hard was suctioned across my eyes, blurring my vision, the rim biting into my eyebrows and cheekbones. I fumbled with the cuffs, recognised that they were soft-metal toy calibre from the joke shop on the seafront and soon found the catch to get them off. My hands flew to my face and fingered the heavy rubber goggles. I prised them off and twisted my head round as far as I could go.

I was standing on the top of the wing of a yellow-painted Tiger Moth single-engined biplane, strapped into a harness which was attached to a two-legged metal support with back rest and arm bars and bolted to the wing. Behind me and below the top wing I could see the fuselage, painted with advertisements for chocolate, the cockpit and the pilot's head and shoulders. He was wearing a flying helmet and goggles. I yelled at him, waving my arms. He waved back cheerily, gave me the thumbs-up sign. He obviously thought I was all right.

What I could see of his face was weathered, forties, dark moustache. I didn't know him. It wasn't Rick.

His hands went to the controls and he turned the rumbling plane, skittering at the end of the runway. I shouted until I was hoarse, waving my arms to attract attention. The crowds thought it was for dramatic effect and waved back, clapping the desperate Pearl Buck performance.

He opened out the throttle, engine snarling, and the plane began to gather speed along the runway. The wind blinded me. I hastily put the goggles back on. If I was going to get out of this alive, I had at least to see what was coming.

The pilot pulled up the nose of the plane and we were airborne, gaining height, skimming over the tops of show tents and nearby houses. The South Downs loomed ahead like ridged green pancakes; Chanctonbury Hill a sparse crown of stunted trees. The River Adur was a smear of silver to my right. My stomach went sick with terror.

Part of my brain was registering that the pilot, whoever he was, knew what he was doing with my added weight on top. This was not someone still taking lessons. He had minimised the back-shattering take-off with skill and got the plane smoothly into the air as quickly and deftly as possible. But it was terrifying. I shut my eyes to the roads and cars and streets below. I clung on to the side bars, my knuckles going bone white, aware that only the shoulder harness and metal shoes were keeping me safe aloft.

The plane banked slowly and circled back over the crowded airfield. I hardly dared look down, but I had to. Rows of toy planes were parked in a far corner; the beer tents fluttered like crumpled rags; a fuzzy hedge of people lined the runway paths behind the security fences. Sand and sea stretched beyond. My hair loosened and began to stream in the slipstream. The pilot wheeled over the shore and I caught a glimpse of white horses riding the dazzling waves and tiny sailing boats, their coloured sails like scraps of tissue paper.

This pilot, whoever he was, was not out to kill me. It was the one reassuring thought. The only reassuring thought. He was flying with great care. But Rick – for I was sure that it was he who had trussed me up on to the wing – either meant to scare me to death or warn me off the case once and for all.

I closed my eyes and prayed to Someone or Something Up There for the flight to end. It was no joy ride. I knew nothing about heights, guessed at a low 200 feet, to give the paying customers a thrill and video view. Some thrill; I was trembling so much, I could feel my knees knocking. The wind was cold against my face, drying the clammy beads of perspiration on my brow. My mouth was like the inside of a sack. I was beyond wailing or screaming. The pilot took an occasional glance upwards, craning over the cockpit edge. He probably thought he had his regular girl wing-walker.

We were flying at about 100 mph, a trail of coloured smoke like a bridal veil belching from the exhaust. I tried to judge the speed against a Panda chase on a motorway.

Suddenly the plane began to climb, the horizon dropped away and I hung on to the bars for dear life through a shiver of turbulence. I nearly passed out with fright but the harness held me firmly in place although all I could see was a changing canopy of blue ahead and scurrying clouds laden with rain. A few spots hit my face, stinging. My swollen tongue tried to lick them in. I opened my mouth and a scattering hit the palate like a spray of soda.

The pilot shut off the engine. I screamed at the empty nothingness, the silence, the limbo. Panic rose in my throat in a wave of bile.

The little plane slowly rolled over. The engine burst into life again and we went into a sequence of loops, spins, tipped into dives, stalled turns, rolled off the top . . . it was aerobatics plus wing-walking. This was taking personal ambition too far. Was he insured? I screwed my eyes shut and concentrated on surviving. The wind screamed in my ears like banshees, a pervasive white noise.

I knew I was going to die as the world turned upside down and the ground came rushing up to meet me. I'd never been one for funfairs. My head was spinning, bursting with pressure, body sweating out life's moisture, sweat trickling down my body. Excruciating pins and needles were attacking my legs. Hang on in there, girl, I told myself desperately. This can't last for ever, though it seemed like for ever. The pilot would want a cup of coffee soon. I tried weakly to transfer the aroma and taste of fresh coffee into his thoughts. It didn't work.

He pulled back hard, blasting away on full power, and a minute jerk alerted my traumatised body to some new experience. The harness felt fractionally looser across my chest. My stiff fingers explored the fabric straps. The tips found a disturbance on the edge of the smooth webbing. It was a cut, a tiny straight cut. Someone had tampered with the harness.

For a moment I felt amazingly calm. I knew the worst now. There was nothing more to scare me. At some precise moment in the near future, the harness was going to rip apart and I was going to fall.

Funnily enough, I wondered who would look after my shop and I was glad I didn't have a cat who would pine.

I closed my eyes, waiting for each jerk, waiting for the end. The engine of the Tiger Moth roared in my ears. I'd go deaf if this went on much longer.

Then I became aware of a much louder phut-phutting noise and squinted vaguely in the direction of the new sound. It was a helicopter flying alongside, its rotor blades chopping and batting the air. I recognised the military markings and a wave of relief engulfed me. DI James must have found the real wing-walker tied up somewhere and commandeered the helicopter. They were flash signalling to the pilot to land. They must be in radio contact too. It wasn't the Middle Ages.

Another millimeter of strap gave way. I knew I didn't have that much time, might not be able to stand the impact of landing and braking. I began an elaborate pantomime, worthy of my many school performances, pointing to the harness and then miming a violent ripping apart. My drama teacher would have been proud of me. I hoped that someone on the helicopter was watching and understood.

We were losing altitude, turning again. A blast of torrential rain hit my face, blinding the goggles like a carwash. The plane was circling the airfield, losing speed, everything was a blur of colours and shapes. I was getting very tired. Another plane roared past and straight up into the sky. It was a giant Blenheim Bomber like a throbbing airship out of *Star Wars*.

The right shoulder strap snapped and the end flew up and caught me sharply across the face. I gripped the armbars, desperate that what was left of the harness and the lap belt would hold till we landed. The wind was strengthening and I was nearly bent in half against it. Some seagulls fluttered past, unconcerned, wheeling seawards. I couldn't hold on much longer.

The helicopter was rising, moving sideways, positioning itself above the Tiger Moth. The noise was puncturing my eardrums and I was pummelled by the down draught. A man was being winched out over the side and lowered, helmet and goggles obscuring his face. He was like an angel in green combat fatigues descending from Heaven. It seemed like hours, but could only have been seconds before he was swinging level and was standing on the wing beside me.

The little plane began to labour under the extra weight. The commando strapped a light harness under my armpits which was attached to his heavier contraption; he leaned down and wrenched my feet out of my best boots. I stood barefooted on the cold, wet wing, shivering, buffeted, feeling I was going to be swept off at any moment.

He put his mouth close to my ear.

"Hold on to me," he yelled. I didn't need telling twice.

Then he slashed the two remaining straps of the wing-walker's harness with a knife and we swung into the air, sailing upwards like puppets on a string. I pressed my face against the rough cloth of his fatigues and emptied my mind.

DI James hauled me into the helicopter cabin.

"How come you're always soaking wet?" he growled. A witty retort was out of the question. I couldn't say a word. I was glazed dumb with shock.

Rick Weston and his mother, Betty, were taken to Latching police station and charged with the murder of Ellen Swantry and attempted murder of Jordan Lacey. The charge sheet read like the plot of a novel.

At Mrs Weston's bungalow on the Fareham Estate they found traces of Trenchers debris on both mother and son's shoes. The police also found a container of chloroform solvent which Rick used to clean second-hand refrigerators. It could be bought at any chemist's shop if its proposed use was accepted as genuine.

Also in his storeroom, they discovered an old chipped bone-china Derby teapot in which he'd hidden nineteen half-crown Bank of England notes destined for the armed forces in the Second World War. The serial numbers followed that of the note which Mr

Arkbright reluctantly had to withdraw from the London coin auction. He was understandably upset.

The police wouldn't even let him keep the note as a souvenir. No heart.

Rick and his mother vehemently denied killing Ellen Swantry. They admitted taking her against her will and keeping her prisoner in the hotel . . . but killing her, no.

"I gave her a whiff of chloroform to keep her quiet, that's all," Rick protested. "I didn't kill her. No way. She was no use to us dead."

"We went out to get some fish and chips and when we got back we found her strung up and very dead. We panicked," said Betty Weston. "It was awful but it wasn't us that done it. I swear. We were only after the notes. It was money, for Rick's future."

It was all about greed and money and ambition. I was fed the fitted pieces like a toddler at a picnic.

"Mrs Weston was ambitious for her son. She was the brains behind their scheming. Rick's ambition was for himself and his simple dream of a flying operation. He thought his dream was close when he found a small cache of the notes stuffed in the back of a desk he'd bought from Mrs Swantry's house. He knew it wasn't Monopoly money." DI James felt he owed me some explanation.

"It was as if he sniffed a possible fortune within his reach. He did not know what the notes were or their true worth, but he could not rest until he found out. Ellen Swantry had to be persuaded to tell him if there were more notes and if so, where the rest of the hoard was hidden."

"So overnight they became villains," I said to James. "Do we know why Ellen Swantry was burning notes?"

"No idea. Conscience perhaps, before she became a full-time nun."

"A tricky career move."

"The cut on your cheek is healing," he replied with what almost passed as tenderness. He'd come to see me after his shift. My asthma had not enjoyed the trauma of wing-walking and the doctor in A&E had insisted on a few days at home.

"They had not intended to murder Ellen Swantry, only to frighten her into telling them where the rest of the notes were." I was staying cool, despite the heady intoxication of being visited. The nurse in casualty had closed the face wound with a butterfly strip of adhesive. She said there shouldn't be a scar.

"They're being charged with manslaughter. I think it was an accident. Maybe Rick pulled just too hard on the twine in a sudden fit of anger and frustration. The pair panicked when they realised the woman was dead and they tried to make it look like a crime of violence."

"With a meat hook they found in the hotel kitchen?"

"Right. But which they deny."

"And why did they take her to Trenchers?"

James looked at me darkly as if he'd just signed the Official Secrets Act. "The War Office meetings were held at Trenchers Hotel. You were right there and she told them that much. Latching was considered safe from the bombing. And the banknotes were stored in a reinforced area off the genuine wine cellars, but she didn't tell them that. There were only two keys to this underground vault. Oliver Swantry held one of them."

"Who held the other one?"

"A Bank of England official. He hasn't been traced."

"Have you broken into the wine cellars yet?"

"We're waiting for permission. I had to fill in a dozen forms. And guess what else we found at the Westons' bungalow?"

"A signed photo of King Kong?"

"Close. It was a photograph . . . a wedding photograph of Ursula Carling and her first husband, the accident-prone Ted Burrows. And guess the name of the cute bridesmaid?"

Suddenly I knew. "Betty Weston?"

DI James nodded. "Apparently Ted Burrows was her stepbrother. Their mother married twice, hence different surnames. But she always thought there was something fishy about Ted's death, and that Ursula had driven him to it somehow."

"So the rubble down Ursula's chimney was another ill-conceived plan? Long-delayed sibling revenge. Did you check on the mattresses?"

"Right again, Holmes. We found enough left of the mattresses in burned debris in Weston's yard. Flecks of the same cheap flock stuffing were found in Ursula's back garden."

The police dropped the charges relating to me for lack of evidence. I didn't go to the Westons' trial. I was too busy on another case.

The Beeches was sold for development as a rest home for retired gentlefolk and Ursula also sold up and bought a tasteful flat in Norfolk which I guess she immediately repainted in her favourite sugary pastels. The young couple who bought her confection in Lansfold Avenue liked primary colours, red and indigo, which didn't show sticky little fingers.

Both new owners agreed that the air-raid shelter was an eyesore and should be demolished. On their first day, the workmen made a gruesome discovery. Inside the shelter, near the heavy steel door, was the mummified body of a man.

The dental records confirmed that the body was that of Oliver Swantry of The Beeches, Lansfold Avenue. The body, although shrivelled, was well preserved because of the vaultlike, airless atmosphere of the shelter, and a PM indicated that he had probably died of natural causes – either a heart attack or suffocation from lack of air or both.

Whether Oliver had been shut in the air-raid shelter on purpose or accidentally, only Ellen would have known. Maybe she had not discovered that her husband was accidentally shut in until it was too late. She must have been in a torment of indecision about whether to call for assistance or not. By the time she decided, if she ever did, it was probably too late anyway. Oliver Swantry had died surrounded by security boxes stuffed full of Bank of England army issue banknotes. The locked wine cellar at Trenchers was empty.

The garden seat outside became Oliver's memorial gravestone. A nice touch.

I felt I had to make sure Oliver's death was properly registered. It was the least I could do for him. I checked at the Family Record Office in London. The staff were beginning to recognise me.

212

Afterwards I called in at the same street market café, remembering the good coffee. I ordered a prawn and salad sandwich. It was freshly made by the same blond boy who had served me before. He gave me the same smile but this time it clicked.

"Ben? It is Ben Frazer, isn't it?"

He jerked back, scattering prawns all over the counter. His face went pinched. He looked ready to run.

"Hold on. Don't be alarmed. Hear what I've got to say, Ben. Your dad only wants a phone call from you, to know that you are all right. There's a special line you can use. You won't even have to speak to him. I think it's called Phone Home and you can leave a message."

"You've made a mistake, miss. My name's Joe."

"He just wants a call. Will you do it? Please?"

"No, I won't. He doesn't understand. I've got a life of my own. I'm not going back to that dump."

"All he wants is to hear from you," I pleaded. "Just to know that you are all right. Nothing else."

He paused, then shovelled a generous scoop of prawns into my sandwich. "You've got it all wrong. Some other guy, sorry. He just looks like me."

"Great coffee," I said with a bright smile. "Here's the phone number of Phone Home."

Cleo Carling set up house with her stepfather and whatever their relationship might become was nobody's business. They bought a terraced cottage in a back lane close to the city wall. Arthur smartened up and got a part-time job as a guide in Chichester cathedral.

I was invited to their house-warming party.

"And bring a friend," said Cleo over the phone. "We both can't thank you enough. Arthur's getting well again and he loves his job at the cathedral. I'm looking after him and he's looking after me."

"Sounds great. Of course I'll come to your party . . . and bring a friend."

I took James to the party. He had been fractionally more civil to me since my apprentice wing-walking. Rosie, Ursula's sister, was also invited to the party and it was obvious that a family of sorts was bonding. It was all very satisfactory.

There was music coming form the stone-faced cottage and welcoming lights in the windows. I tripped in my new boots as we walked up the paving stones to the front door. James gripped my arm to steady me and a surge of wildness also threatened my stability. God, how I loved this man. But of course I didn't say it aloud. He was already striding ahead to open the door.

So I am still one of the talking wounded. But perhaps it isn't the end. Perhaps one day he will look at me and see the real Jordan Lacey.

Something still irks me about the Sister Ellen murder and I am afraid to follow my thoughts. Why didn't she take her spectacles with her on the retreat? She was going to read the Bible, wasn't she?

Ah, perhaps she forgot them in her haste. Maybe they were her spare pair. That was the answer. But I couldn't get that pathetic plastic bag of belongings out of my head.

I stood in a corner at the party letting the laughter and chatter float over my head. James was standing across the room, head and shoulders above everyone else. I watched him. A pen, a small cheap silver-metal crucifix, her glasses in a spectacle case, a pair of good leather gloves, a heavy brass key, packets of hairpins, brush and comb, toothbrush.

"Sorry, that must be a mistake. I don't believe the key should be among Sister Ellen's effects. I'm sure it belongs to the hospice," I heard Sister Lucinda saying in her smooth voice. "I'll remove it."

I remembered the hospice with its modern security locks and entryphone system. Sister Lucinda had been lying. The key fitted Trenchers and I knew that because I used it to open the back entrance. She might have witnessed the abduction, followed the Westons, guessed Sister Ellen was being held prisoner in Trenchers, used the key to open the door and found her conveniently unconscious. It would have been only too easy to kill her, especially if you were fit and strong.

And especially if the motive was The Beeches, spacious and

substantial. Especially if the house sale would raise a staggering six-figure sum and the hospice wanted that money now. Needed it. Even a saint might not be prepared to wait too long.

Then I remembered why Lucy Grey had given up her modelling career. There had been a nasty fraud case, a lot of money being embezzled. Not exactly good publicity.

"Excuse me, James," I said tentatively, touching his sleeve. "There's something I want to tell you."

He gave me one of his tired looks. "Not again . . ."